"Poul Anderson, always a master of science fiction, here delivers the best of his many novels. A true masterpiece, *HARVEST OF STARS* is an important work not just of science fiction but of contemporary literature. Visionary and beautifully written, elegiac and transcendent, *HARVEST OF STARS* is the brightest star in Poul Anderson's constellation."
—Keith Ferrell, editor, OMNI magazine

"A VIVID, FAST-PACED NOVEL ON A GRAND SCALE. Anderson's mix of action, colorful characters and fascinating concepts make *HARVEST OF STARS* a great read."
—Larry Bond, author of *VORTEX* and *RED PHOENIX*

TOR BOOKS BY POUL ANDERSON

*forthcoming

HARVEST OF STARS

POUL ANDERSON

A TOM DOHERTY ASSOCIATES BOOK
NEW YORK

HARVEST OF STARS

Copyright © 1993 by Trigonier Trust

Cover art by Vincent Di Fate

A Tor Book
Published by Tom Doherty Associates, LLC
175 Fifth Avenue
New York, NY 10010

www.tor.com

Tor® is a registered trademark of Tom Doherty Associates, LLC.

ISBN: 0-812-51946-9
Library of Congress Catalog Card Number: 93-15627

First edition: August 1993
First mass market printing: July 1994

Printed in the United States of America

0 9 8 7 6 5

To Frank and Laura Kelly Freas

ACKNOWLEDGMENTS

For information, advice, and other helpfulness I thank Karen Anderson, John G. Cramer, Víctor Fernández-Dávila, Robert Gleason, A. T. Lawton, Bing F. Quock, and P. Wright. They are not responsible for whatever mistakes, misinterpretations, and inelegances remain here, but they saved me from quite a few.

Thanks are also due Frank J. Tipler for good-naturedly letting me show some ideas of his misused in the future as, alas, many an idea has been misused in the past or is being in the present.

DRAMATIS PERSONAE

(Some minor figures are omitted)

Dolores Almeida Candamo: General director of Earthside operations for Fireball Enterprises.
Arren: Lunarian, an agent of Rinndalir.
Pierre Aulard: An engineer and a director of Fireball.
Jack Bannon: An officer of the (Chaotic) Liberation Army.
Gabriel Berecz: The download of an ecologist.
Esther Blum: Regent of the Homesteaders.
Jerry Bowen: Designer of the laser launch system.
Charissa: A settler's daughter, later wife to Hugh Davis.
Charlie: A male of the Keiki Moana.
Cua: Lunarian, a space pilot.
Erling Davis: A descendant of Hugh Davis.
Hugh Davis: A ranger on Demeter.
Kyra Davis: A space pilot and consorte of Fireball; her download.
Demeter Daughter.
Demeter Mother.
Rory Donovan: A bartender in Tychopolis.
Manuel Escobedo Corrigan: President of the North American Union.
Anne Farnum: A Chaotic.
Jim Farnum: A Chaotic.
Hans Gieseler: An employee of Fireball.
Anson Guthrie: Co-founder and master of Fireball Enterprises; his downloads; his reincarnation.

Juliana Trevorrow Guthrie: Wife to Anson Guthrie and co-founder of Fireball Enterprises.

—*Helledahl:* Captain of the Fireball spaceship *Bruin.*

Felix Holden: A colonel in the North American Security Police.

Isabu: Lunarian, an agent of Rinndalir.

Robert E. Lee: An intuitionist and consorte of Fireball.

—*Leggatt:* A magnate within Quark Fair.

Lin Mei-Ling: Wife of Wang Zu and consorte of Fireball.

Luis Moreno Quiroga: A friend of Anson Guthrie in his youth.

Sitabhai Lal Mukerji: President of the World Federation.

Boris Ivanovich Nikitin: A friend of Kyra Davis in her girlhood.

Niolente: Lunarian, ally of Rinndalir.

Noboru: Child of Demeter Daughter.

Christian Packer: A descendant of Jeff Packer.

Jeff Packer: A son of Washington Packer.

Washington Packer: Director of Kamehameha Spaceport and consorte of Fireball.

—*Pedraza:* An officer of the North American Security Police.

Consuelo Ponce: A scientist and consorte of Fireball.

Rinndalir: Lunarian, a Selenarch.

Basil Rudbeck: Director of research at Lifthrasir Tor.

Rusaleth: Lunarian, Lady Commander in Phyle Ithar.

Juan Santander Conde: A director of Fireball, eventually emeritus.

Enrique Sayre: Head of the North American Security Police.

Ivar Stranding: A former lover of Kyra Davis.

—*Stuart:* Captain of the Fireball spaceship *Jacobite.*

Zeyd Abdullah Aziz Tahir: A sheikh of the Muslim community in Northwest Integrate.

Eiko Tamura: A technician in L-5 and employee of Fireball.

Noboru Tamura: Father of Eiko Tamura, chief of space operations in L-5 and consorte of Fireball.

Nero Valencia: A gunjin of the Sally Severins.

Wang Zu: A dispatcher in L-5 and consorte of Fireball.

Xuan Zhing: Visionary on whose theories the Avantist movement was founded.

Clarice Yoshikawa: A technician in the North American Security Police.

EPILOGUE

EVEN LAST NIGHT, death was no more than the brightest of the stars. The suns have drawn close together in the sky, as if to hide themselves from that which nears, and Phaethon was lord of the dark. Outshining Sol, its whiteness stood like a light kindled in a prayer for peace, a beauty almost too great to bear. Strengthening hour by hour, it was still clear to unaided sight when it set at midmorning.

We will not shelter our awareness on dayside. There is no shelter. We will be here, beholding. I will do whatever I can to calm the terror of my poor beasts, who must see and not understand.

The weather has been calm. Snow decked the hills, their glens were full of blue shadow, trees gone leafless bore icicles that shivered light into a thousand colored brilliances. But some clouds came to veil the west, and our last sunset flamed. Now a wind has sprung up, shrill and keen. A dust of ice grains drifts across the land. Through roots and rock I feel how monstrously the seas rage afar.

Phaethon's radiance goes before it, a pallor that mounts from the southeast until it touches the zenith. Birds rouse at this strange dawn, I hear them calling their wonderment; a stag bugles, wolves howl.

I must help my creatures. Abide me. I love you.

—And I love you. I'll wait.

The planet starts to rise. So huge has it grown that more than an hour passes before it is aloft. Meanwhile it swells further. Gibbous, it is wanly aglow on its night part, where starlight falls on its own troubled weather; but in the eyes that are left among us, it has drowned every star. The day part dazzles, a writhing of storms between which I glimpse mountain ranges, glaciers, and frozen oceans melting. Our snow glisters begemmed. Eastward, thunderheads rear. Phaethon makes phosphorescent their battlements. Lightning plays in their depths. Unnatural at the heart of winter—no, this too is nature, is the reality to which we belong.

The ground shudders. Wind shrieks. I bring what comfort I may to hawk and hare, fox and crow, vole and sparrow. They will not have long to be afraid, but I will spare them as much as I can.

Black spots appear on Phaethon: smoke, ash. Volcanoes have awakened in hordes. A line races across the disc, jagged, a crack open on molten depths. A quake billows beneath us. Hillsides crash down, louder than the oncoming hurricane.

I return. Our spirits embrace.

Phaethon begins to sunder. It will strike before it breaks fully apart, but an incandescent tide spills forth. This world shakes and roars.

Farewell, beloved.

The first meteors blaze.

—Thank you for all you gave and all you were. I love you.

PART ONE

kyra

1

HER CHANCE WAS one in seven, unless the ghost lay at none of his old lairs. Then it would be zero, and finding him become a race against his enemies. Kyra more than half hoped that she, at least, would draw blank. Beyond Earth she dealt with vastness, vacuum, sometimes violence, but she had never been quarry. Por favor, let her simply and honestly report that Guthrie wasn't here, and return to space.

Nerve stiffened. She had given troth.

Besides, if the task did fall on her, with any luck it shouldn't prove dangerous. She'd merely be a rider on crowded public carriers. Nobody ought to suspect that she bore Fireball's lord. If somehow the hunters learned she had visited Erie-Ontario Integrate, there were ready answers to whatever questions they might ask. The first several years of her life had passed in Toronto. How natural that she spend a short groundside leave taking a look at childhood scenes. Nor would she have to respond personally. By that time, supposing the occasion arose at all, she and Guthrie would be on the far side of the sky.

It tingled in her. She, his rescuer!

Maybe. Whatever happened, she'd better keep a cool head and a casual bearing. First concentrate on traffic. Scores of little three-wheeled cycles like hers wove and muttered their way among hundreds of pedestrians. On most the canopies were deployed, nearly invisible, shields against the weather. She had left her bubble folded, in an irrational wish to be free, today, of even such slight confinement. Nothing larger was allowed on this street, but vans threw their noise and shadows down off the monorail overhead. Now and then a flitter went whistling above them. No matter how hard the times, here the megalopolis churned.

Turbulence eddied from each of the bodies and bodies and bodies that hurried, dodged, dawdled, gestured, swerved, lingered. Colors and faces lost meaning in their swarm. The air was thick with their breath, harsh with their footfalls and voices. Wind drove clouds like smoke across the strips of sky between walls. It struck through Kyra's hapi coat. Her blood welcomed the sharpness, which cut away part of the stench and claustrophobia.

Had this sector gone hellward in the past couple of decades, or was memory just softening itself? She wasn't sure. Her parents had seldom brought her east of the lakes. Whatever the truth, she ought not to feel threatened. These were human beings, and better off than many. Yes, look, that dark woman in her sari, that caballero with bells on his wide-brimmed hat, that hombre whose brotherhood emblem and big scarred hands declared him a manual worker, that couple who by their green garments defiantly proclaimed themselves believers in the Renewal as their grandparents had been, what harm could they do? The menace was High World, the wielders of forefront technology, money, influence—more exactly, those of the High World who in this country were the government. It sprang from a mathematical theory.

Nevertheless grimy cliffs, murky doorways, guards in shops where the windows once held more and better goods, the crowd above all, took on a nightmarishness. Was she following an asymptote, struggling closer and closer to the Blue Theta but never quite to reach it?

Abruptly she did.

Gigantic though it was, the complex had been hidden from her by the surrounding masses. Nor could she now see it as a whole. A kilometer away and well aloft, vision would have swept up walls, piers, arches, roofs, towers, a-soar in azures and whites, to the Greek letter crowning the central spire. Here she made out only height and a broad gate standing open.

It was enough. Gladness leaped.

For a moment Kyra frowned. Why these mood swings? She'd been at risk before and stayed zen. Exhaustion? It hadn't been a long drive from the tricycle rental to here. Of course, earlier she'd cabbed from Kamehameha to Honolulu, ridden the suborbital to Northwest Central, and changed maglevs twice on her way to Buffalo Station; but that was scarcely an ordeal.

Bueno, no doubt the knowledge of what was at stake had gnawed at her more than she knew. Silently reciting a peace mantra, she sought a place to park.

There. She stopped her motor, dismounted, wheeled the machine over to the rack, inserted a coin, and keyed the lock to her thumbprint. Fifty centos paid for an hour, which should be plenty. If not, she had cash to release it. Because rain appeared possible, she sprang the canopy loose. No sense in risking wet saddles, control board, and luggage box, when she might depart with such a cargo—and maybe a passenger—that discomfort would distract her attention from danger.

No time to gas off, either, though she'd better not make herself conspicuous by haste. She passed through the crowd and the gate into the court.

Tumult faded away. Again she felt naked. The area wasn't deserted. People went to and fro, tenants, personnel, shoppers, visitors. Traffic seemed so sparse, though, so subdued. Maybe, Kyra thought, it was the contrast with the scene outside, not only thronged but alien—poor, primitive, powerless, the Low World that everywhere on Earth underlay the high technology yet had no real part in it.

Or maybe the magnificence here simply overwhelmed its occupants. Mosaic pavements surrounded fountains, gardens whose flowers and shrubs were the work of genetic artists, an outsize holo presenting a ballet recorded on a low-weight level of L-5. Against the curtain wall, ten stories of arcades lifted to a transparent roof. Sunbeams lanced past clouds. Beyond them stood the wan daylight Moon, like a homeland glimpsed in dream. Yes, she thought, right now the very Lunarians were in her mind more akin to her than these fellow citizens.

She bit her lip and strode on to the keep. The foyer at this entrance was almost empty. A maintainor rolled by on an errand, but a metal zodiac in the ceiling had gone dull for lack of polishing. Two men sat in loungers. One, sepia-hued, wore a drab coverall and smoked a cigarette. Kyra caught a whiff of cheap tobacco-marijuana blend and reflected with a moment's wryness that however well or ill the Avantists had succeeded in controlling the ideas of North Americans, the vices had usually eluded them. The other man, robed, was totally hairless, his skin deep gold, his features . . . peculiar? A metamorph, his heritage left over from days when in certain jurisdictions on Earth experimentation with DNA was almost unfettered? They didn't speak, probably they weren't acquainted, nor did they watch the multiceiver. It showed a woman exhorting a youth group to learn and live by correct principles and report anyone who deviated to the authorities so they could enlighten that person.

Kyra shivered a bit. She had mostly dwelt apart from such things. Snatches came to her on newscasts, in written accounts, from the lips of witnesses. Sometimes they struck hard. (A child taken from his parents and they charged with abuse because they had repeatedly told him not to believe what he heard in school about Xuan's great insights. An importer, who made her objections to various regulations conspicuous in foreign media, harassed to bankruptcy by the tax examiners and then convicted of tax evasion. A documentary on a rehabilitation center, the blank smiles of the inmates and the bland denial that they were there for political reasons: "This nation is in the process of transcending all politics.") Always, though, she told herself that it was unfortunate but it couldn't spread farther nor last much longer. Today she had seen, felt, smelled a piece of the reality.

At the directory board she keyboarded "Robert E. Lee" instead of speaking the name. Ridiculous; did she think yonder men were secret agents listening? Bueno, she wasn't used to this game. The screen displayed "D-1567," which she already knew, and directions for getting there. Her memory being excellent, she didn't pay for a printout, but went straight to the fahrweg and signalled. The door retracted. She entered. Having no need of a cuddler to help her absorb the slight shock of acceleration, she stepped immediately from strip to strip until she was on the fastest.

The ride took a bad ten minutes, with three changes, including the vertical. To keep tension from ratcheting within her, she observed other folk as they got on or off or traveled along. They were less varied than what she had seen in cities elsewhere on Earth or on the streets here. Their garb ran to the same kinds of coat and trousers, tunics and tights, or unisuits, conservatively colored. Even fancy clothes, a man's ruffled blouse, a woman's iridon dress, had little of the flamboyant about them. Men were beardless and the haircuts of either sex seldom reached below the earlobes. For twenty-three years, now, among High Worlders and many Low Worlders of the North American Union, conformity had been a requirement of success. More and more, it was becoming a requirement of survival.

She noticed exceptions. Three boys flaunted scalplocks, feathers, and fringed garments. Several bearded men in headcloths accompanied women in veils and muffling ankle-length gowns. Also bearded were a pair of obvious Chasidim and a man displaying a pectoral cross whom she guessed was an Orthodox priest. That one talked with a burly fellow in blue, who wore a cap badged by a silver two-headed eagle and a truncheon at his belt. Most likely he was a constable of a tenants' association. In a complex this size, whole blocks of units could be the sites of special communities, internally autonomous—not unlike Fireball, Kyra thought, except that in North America the present government tolerated their existence only reluctantly, because it wasn't feasible to abolish them, and tried to keep a close eye on their doings.

Nevertheless it was a shock when another large man boarded. His outfit was tan, crisply form-fitting, a sidearm at the hip. An armband bore the infinity symbol of Avantism. Silence spread around him like waves when a stone falls into a pool. Officers of the Security Police seldom came here in uniform.

Did his glower single Kyra out? Her pulse quickened. Dryness prickled her tongue. What a stupid oversight it had been, hopping to the mainland in bright tropical jacket, shorts, sandals. Even in Hawaii, she remembered, such were frowned on nowadays. She'd paid little attention, for Earthside she mainly associated with company people on company property.

She braced herself. She wasn't doing anything illegal, yet. Her identicard showed she was a citizen, nominally.

Scant comfort. A foreigner, arrested, would have more rights, more help to appeal for, than she would.

The Sepo got off. Kyra let out a breath. For an instant, she leaned on the cuddler beside her. Nonconformers looked at each other and, bit by bit, resumed their conversations.

The telltale flashed that she was approaching her destination. She crossed the strips, signalled jerkily, went through the door while it was still withdrawing, and caught the safety rail lest she stumble.

Anger flared. This was nonsense! She was a spacecraft pilot, able to handle herself at anything from zero g to ten. She wasn't aged or sick, she was twenty-eight years old and her genome promised her another century or so of robust health if she heeded her medical program. All right, she was on a job new to her, possibly hazardous, but that was no excuse for blinkiness. Get on with it, girl.

Nobody else was in the corridor. She jogged through its pastels to the door marked 1567. The exercise warmed blood and spirit. Odds were that nothing waited for her, and that she'd return directly to the spaceport. She grinned. After this much fidgeting, what a letdown. She touched the bell plate.

At the station she had used her informant to make a quick, anonymous audio call, verifying that Lee was at home. He ought to be; these rooms were his main work-place as well as his quarters. When she now got no response, misgiving wakened again. Had he gone out? She dismissed the emotion. Doubtless he wanted to scan her first. It was a natural precaution under the circumstances. She straightened, shaped a smile, and hoped he enjoyed the view.

Men had told her she was handsome. She agreed, without letting it go to her head. Tall, broad-shouldered for a woman, otherwise slender but well outfitted fore and aft, she cut her sandy hair in a Dutch bob to frame hazel eyes, prominent cheekbones, straight nose, full mouth. When she spoke, her voice was a bit husky. "Saludos, consorte. I'm Fireball too, my name is Kyra Davis, and I've got urgent company business."

The door slid aside. "Come in," Lee said. He saw the surprise she failed to hide, and the strained tone yielded to a chuckle. "I reckon you haven't seen a picture of me. With a name like mine—and as a matter of fact, my folks live in Roanoke, where I was born. But Lee is a good old Chinese name."

He was short, slim, clad with the carelessness of a bachelor who need not keep up appearances at work. His features were boyish, though Kyra didn't believe a profes-sional intuitionist could be much younger than she. As she entered, nervousness resurged and made him talk on, pointlessly: "The family's been over here for a couple of hundred years, genes were getting pretty diluted, but when the refugees arrived in Jihad times, some were ethnic Chinese from Southeast Asia and three or four of them married into my lineage. Since then, bueno, you know how people tend to stick close to those they know and can trust—endogamy's gotten common—"

He stopped and swallowed. Kyra sympathized. "'Fraid you might have said too much?" she answered. "Don't worry, I'm not a psychomonitor, not any kind of police. I'm Fireball, I told you. Here, let me prove it." From a coat pocket she drew her card case, to offer him the company ident that stood for so much more than any government issue.

"Yes, gracias," he mumbled. "Excuse me. I've got to— Excuse me. No offense meant, but . . . if you'd follow me, por favor?" He led her toward an inner door.

On the way she observed her surroundings. This living room was unpretentiously furnished, cluttered with souvenirs, keepsakes, a chessboard, a bookcase holding codices that could well be heirlooms. Pictures on the walls, not activated at the moment, were probably of kinfolk and the hills of his homeland. A large viewscreen gave an outlook from the topmost spire, just below the theta. That scene was heartcatching. The integrate became a geometrical wilderness of pinnacles and green biospaces, glimmering away on every hand till it lost itself in the hazy air, as fantastic as anything at Luna or L-5. Westward she spied the giant leap of waters in Niagara Park and, dim beyond them, certain towers she remembered. North and south she made out the lakes, dull silvery sheenings in the mist. She decided she liked Robert E. Lee.

The next room was cramful of equipment. It included three big multiceivers, as many different computer terminals, and a vivifer that must be for full-sensory input, not entertainment. A molecular scanner quickly verified that her ident was genuine and had not been tampered with. The informant on his wrist was a fancy one indeed; maybe the company had supplied it, considering what it must have cost. It checked not only her thumbs but her retinae, and confirmed that the patterns matched those in the card.

Lee smiled apologetically. "This was required, you understand," he said. "We scarcely need to take a DNA sample! Now, uh, consorte Davis, what can I do for you?"

Kyra's heart lurched. She must gulp before she could utter the question. "Do you have Guthrie?"

He stared. "Huh?"

"Anson Guthrie. The jefe. Are you hiding him?"

"Why—uh—"

"Listen. I've proven myself to you, but if I have to go further, muy bien." The story tumbled from her. "Washington Packer sent me. You know who he is? Director of Kamehameha Spaceport. He called several of us into his office earlier today. He told us Guthrie's been in the Union since shortly after the government occupied Fireball's North American headquarters. He was smuggled in and squirreled away so he could be on hand to mastermind our strategy on the spot. It wasn't really a gyroceph thing to do, Packer said. We needed to react fast and decisively. International communications are too likely tapped, but we have secure lines inside the country.

"Packer had just gotten word. He didn't say where from, but prob'ly it was a mole in the Security Police. Whether a Chaotic or an agent of ours, I don't know. The government's planning a second stage of crackdown on us. Within the next two or three days, they'll take over everything. And it seems they've learned the jefe is on hand. They have a list of half a dozen places where he may very well be.

"Packer was able to retrieve that list from our cryptofile. Of course, he'd been careful not to know, himself, where Guthrie was hiding. His information didn't include how to access safe lines to those places, so he dared not phone them. The best he could do was send one of us to each.

"Us—I mean, we were that number of persons out of those who happened to be on hand. I'm a pilot myself. We were also ones he figured he could rely on, and who could leave the port without it seeming particularly suspicious to the watchers outside, and soon return looking just as natural. Whoever finds Guthrie is to carry him back, so he can be put in a spacecraft and sent out of reach before the Avantists are there to stop it.

"Bueno, is he here?"

Kyra stopped, out of breath, faintly dizzy. Had she really needed to go on at such length?

Lee's gaze stabbed at her. "God damn," he murmured, "you *are* genuine." And: "Yes. This way."

The words hit like a thunderclap. Then suddenly she was altogether alert and cool. It felt as if a singing went through her bones, but every sense was opened full, the universe grew supernaturally vivid, while her mind sprang. Thus had she felt before when her life came to depend on nothing but herself, once in a boat wreck on a surf-swept Pacific reef, more than once in space.

Lee brought her to another room, where he had his bed, a closet and dresser, a desk and some hobby material. He played with model aircraft, she saw. A half-finished historical piece, skeletal biplane, wistful centuries-old memory of days when humans flew in machines they could build with their hands, effused a tang of glue. A viewscreen was tuned to a nature reserve—the North Woods, Kyra guessed fleetingly, for the well-ordered, well-tended trees were conifers, and canoes glided over the water behind them. Only a few people were in sight, but background noise indicated a campsite was close by. Not that a campsite was ever far away, in any such area.

The irrelevancy evaporated. Lee was saying: "He stays out of the circuits except when he's in contact with his officers. Those lines are tap-proof, we hope, but why take unnecessary chances? Otherwise he's in a hidden, shielded safe. He had it installed by the first agent of his who rented this apartment, which was decades ago, I reckon. He can look out, listen, call me by voice, and of course I can provide him with whatever material he wants for information or pasatiempo."

Curiosity flickered in Kyra. What did Guthrie enjoy hearing, reading, watching, vivifying, after more than a hundred years as a wraith in a box? His personal style kept the earthiness recorded during his mortal existence, but maybe that was a fake, a public relations ploy. . . .

Lee halted before a flatscreen. Like those in the living room, the image it projected was not in motion. Full face, a man's head and shoulders—that haircut and high-collared tunic went out of style generations ago, the subject must be somebody Guthrie had liked or admired or— Wait! She'd seen him in a history show, hadn't she? Mamoru Tamura, the mayor who guided L-5 through its first great crisis—

Lee saluted. "Emergency, sir." Now that action was upon him, he had lost his own hesitancies. "Pilot Kyra Davis brings news from Director Packer. The government's preparing a raid. We'd better get you out of here."

"Judas priest!" exploded a rough basso. "Move!"

Lee touched the ornate frame at certain points. The

entire unit swung aside. Was it a dummy? Had Guthrie watched through the portrait's eyes, heard with its ears, as he almost seemed to speak with its lips? The space behind held an object. Lee reached in, detached it from a portable terminal, and brought it forth.

"You take him, consorte," he said. "Explain the situation while I get a bag or something to carry him in."

Kyra held out her hands. The weight that descended into them was oddly little, two or three kilos. Shouldn't the founder and captain of Fireball mass more? His undertakings ranged from end to end of the Solar System and on toward the stars. The person, the mind that had been copied into this program, it had itself—no, he had himself—fared the whole way to Alpha of the Centaur and back. Surely there must be more to him than this.

But no. A human brain held less material.

And ghost-Guthrie required no complete brain. A neural network equivalent to a cerebral cortex. Sensory centers capable of handling electronic, magnetic, photonic inputs. Motor centers capable of outputs into control devices. A memory unit. Software encoding what he was. Maybe a bit more than that. Kyra didn't know; psychonetics wasn't her field. But not much more, surely. Otherwise, the rest of what she held was instrumentation, minimal auxiliary apparatus, a battery, a case.

The whole of what she held was her liege lord. They had never before met, but he it was to whom she had ultimately given her troth, and who had given her Fireball's.

"Sir," she whispered. "Sir."

She had seen the case depicted and described, and others like it. (How very few like it.) Yet to confront, to grasp the presence was as overwhelming as had been her first encounters with love and death.

The sheer simplicity became incomprehensible. This was just a box of dark blue organometal, hard, glassy smooth, edges rounded off, seams nearly invisible. Its flat bottom was about twenty by thirty centimeters, with five-millimeter discs set flush to protect several connectors. It rose about another twenty centimeters to a curved top. Two more discs on either side marked additional

connectors. Between each pair a larger circle, four centimeters across, covered the diaphragm that served as an
ear. A similar one on the front surface was for the speaker.
On that same face—so must she think of it—were two
hemispheres, the diameter of the audio caps.

The volume was approximately the same as for a large
human head. Anson Guthrie's? He had been a big man.

The hemispherical shells split and drew back, like
eyelids. Two flexible stalks, five or six millimeters thick,
emerged. Their ends bulged out in knobs about three
centimeters wide. With snakish deliberation they extruded themselves to their full fifteen centimeters and
twisted in her direction. From within the knobs, lenses
gleamed at her.

"Hey, don't drop me, girl," boomed the voice. "Put me
down and pick your jaw up off the floor."

Could a man make jokes after he was dead? Bueno,
Guthrie often did, unless that was a calculated pretense.
But now, with the hunt on his track? Most carefully, Kyra
lowered him to the desk beside the model airplane.

"Okay, brief me," Guthrie ordered. The synthesized
sounds, which could have come from a living throat, bore
an accent. She had heard that it was American English as
spoken in his youth, and knew he was apt to use expressions from that era.

She rallied her wits and repeated what she had told Lee.

Guthrie shaped a whistle. "Sanamabiche! How the
devil—? Yes, we'd better up anchor right away. Good
man, Wash. Good lass, you. I won't forget."

Lee brought in a daypack. "Will this do?" he asked.
Kyra frowned, uncertain. "It won't draw attention," he
said. "You see them everywhere these days. They leave
both hands free."

She nodded. "Muy bien."

"You mean you didn't have something of your own,
Davis?" Guthrie growled. "No forethought?"

"I'm sorry, sir," she replied, stung while acknowledging
that the criticism was fair. "We were terribly rushed."

"And you and Wash and the rest aren't schooled in

skullduggery. Sure, I understand. Take me and stuff me," which sounded obscurely like another jape, "and we'll be off." The lenses swung toward Lee. "You sit tight. When the cops bust in, be surprised. You don't know nothin'. Nobody been here but us chickens. Can you do that? They'll interrogate you, which'll be no fun, but I don't expect they'll deep-quiz, if you give them no cause to suspect you. Are you game?"

Lee stood straight. "Yes, sir."

"You can run and try to hide if you'd rather. I don't think it's a good idea, though. That'll show them you probably are involved, and they'll be on your trail with every high-tech sort of bloodhound they've got. Chances are they'll catch you pretty quick. You're marked, known, registered, identified, forty ways from Sunday, you being a resident citizen of this great free republic. As a member of Fireball, you must have a lot of extra data in your dossier, too. When they've run you down, they will squeeze your information out of you, and worry about Fireball's wrath later. That won't be nice at all."

Indeed it wouldn't be, Kyra thought. Not torture; that could bring trouble with the World Federation, and wasn't guaranteed effective anyway. Rehabilitative medical care. Chemicals and phased electropulses opened up a mind as a man peels an orange. They often left it in a very similar condition.

"I truly believe your best bet is to stay put and play dumb," Guthrie finished.

Lee nodded, a spastic jerk. "Yes, sir."

Guthrie's tone gentled. "I'm sorry, Bob. Sorrier than I can say. The one solitary excuse I've got for skiting off and leaving you is that a lot of people are at hazard."

And a lot of hopes, Kyra thought.

"I understand," Lee said, thinly but steadily. "If anybody can balance this skewed-up equation, it's you. Go."

The phone chimed. He turned toward the room's outlet.

"Hold," Guthrie rapped.

"What?" Lee asked. The phone chimed again.

"Don't answer." A lens cocked itself at Kyra. "Davis,

how did you know Bob was at home? You wouldn't have wanted to hang around waiting for him and getting noticed."

"I, I called," Kyra said. "Public booth. When he responded, I broke off."

"I supposed it was a miscall," Lee added. The phone chimed. "They happen. I didn't think any more about it." The phone chimed.

"That could be a Sepo scout," Guthrie declared starkly. "They're mighty quick off the mark when they want to be."

"Packer said—the mole said—in two or three days," Kyra stammered.

"That's what the mole said, whoever he is. How long did it take him to get to someplace where he could halfway safely pass on what he'd learned? How precise was it? Did the main office meanwhile decide to advance the schedule?"

Kyra recalled the officer who boarded the fahrweg. As far as she knew, even nowadays uniformed Security Police weren't too common a sight anywhere. (Plainclothesmen might be something else.) Had he been on a different assignment, or was he a forerunner?

"They like to case the territory and stake it out good before they make a pinch," Guthrie went on. "Let's have a quick reconnaissance of our own. Bob, your big screen can sweep the area."

The phone fell silent. Lee moved to play whatever message was perhaps being recorded. "Halt!" Guthrie commanded. "They'll have meters to show you're doing that, if it is them."

Lee yanked his hand back. "Right," he gasped. "I forgot. Yes, you are the jefe." A world of meaning pulsed in that informal word. He took the case and bore it into the living room. Kyra followed.

They stared at the sky view from the spire. Something glinted high overhead. Lee set Guthrie on a table and operated the controls. Vision sprang upward, magnified, amplified. A lean teardrop poised, black and white, on its jets. Kyra estimated its altitude as three kilometers. From that distance, with optics less capable than what she routinely used in her spacecraft, you could count ants on the pavement below. She sensed her sweat, acrid and chill.

"Yeah, Sepo," Guthrie said. "You didn't get here any too soon, Davis."

"What can we do?" she heard herself ask.

"Let me think. I've studied those cochinos over the years, and I remember others like them in the past, around the globe. Maybe you could still walk out with me and ride off, unmolested. I wouldn't bet on it, though. Chances are, they've already got the gateways watched. By men in civilian dress, naturally."

Kyra wondered if that had been so when she arrived. Probably. Maybe not. It made no difference, she supposed. They wouldn't stop every person who went in or out. It would be too laborious. Worse, it could alarm their prey, who might then wipe incriminating data or otherwise inconvenience them. But anybody who emerged looking the least bit suspicious—as it might be, with a bulging sack between her shoulders—would get an instrumental scan. If anything the least bit unusual registered—as it might be, a neural network—that would be that.

Acid burned her gullet.

"Since you haven't touched the phone, Bob, they'll assume you've stepped out," Guthrie continued. "They'll try again in a while. Eventually, of course, whether you answer or not, they'll come in. Two-three hours from now, maybe. Let's see what your pals in B-24 will do for us."

"That may be nothing, you know," Lee said harshly. "At best, it can't be much."

"Beats sitting still, doesn't it? Come on. Bag me and hit the road. The sooner we leave, the less likely we are to encounter a Sepo along the way."

"Where to?" asked Kyra. This fragment of hope calmed her belly and turned her heartbeat high.

Lee went to shut the safe and fetch the daypack. "I've kept tabs on the occupants of my safe houses," Guthrie explained meanwhile. "Not to meddle in their private lives, nor in any great detail. Christ knows I've had plenty else to keep me busy. But I'd gathered enough that when

Wash Packer's man left me in my temporary lodgings, it was Bob Lee I signalled, by an innocent-looking message on a computer bulletin board, to come get me. You see, he'd cultivated some folks in this complex who don't like the Avantists either. That was smart of him, though I suspect he did it mainly because he's a friendly, outgoing, curious type. Anyway, it decided me on the Blue Theta. Every fox wants two holes to his burrow."

2

THEY DARED NOT talk on the fahrweg. As they left it, Lee thrust himself past Kyra, who carried Guthrie, muttering, "Let me go first everywhere. Don't speak unless you're spoken to."

Arabesques swirled multicolored on corridor walls and Arabic script above doorways. Many entrances stood open. Behind some were shelves bearing wares for sale, food, clothing, utensils, flowers, gewgaws. In front a man would sit cross-legged on a cushion, smoking or crying out enticements or seemingly lost in meditation. Occasional rooms had been converted to serve coffee or simple meals exotic to her. Odors enriched the air, cooking, smoke, perfume, scents wholly strange. Noise did too, voices, soft-shod feet, now and then a plangent flute and a thuttering little drum. Ordinary North American outfits were less in evidence than loose, flowing garments, whether robes or gowns or blouse and trousers, usually white. Those who wore them and filled these spaces with commotion were dark caucasoids, men bearded and often sporting headcloths, women veiled. Yes, she'd spied a few of them earlier. Here they were in their own domain.

Arabian Nights! She had seen the Near East on multiceiver news, documentaries, and dramas. Sand, dust, dried wells, salt rivers, desolation. Machines and nanotechnic arrays, hectare by hectare reclaiming the land. Ordered, carefully designed life advancing in their wake, green fields, sparkling buildings, modern industries, new societies. Reservations for those few remnants who had hung on in starveling fashion after the ecology crumbled, ample provision, excellent medical care, rehabilitative education for their children. Oh, the World Federation had a right to be proud of what it was doing there. Why would anybody want to inhabit a fantasy, a past that never was?

Lee threaded his way through the crowd. At his heels, Kyra observed closer. No, she decided, whatever this might be, it wasn't an act, it wasn't a pseudo-culture to fill the void in people who had nothing real to belong to, like the Na-Dene or the Amazons or the Manors. She glimpsed a coppersmith in his shop, but he used a power tool and his neighbor was repairing an electrical appliance. The technology was as good as anything that Low Worlders could afford or handle. When a wide sleeve happened to pull back, she saw an informant like hers on the wrist beneath; obviously the owner needed to know more than the time; he wanted quick access to calculation, databanks, and communications. Another man's insigne declared his employer to be Global Chemistry, which meant that he was concerned with building structures atom by atom. Two small boys in djellabahs passed, their heads shaven except for topknots, but the books under their arms were science texts.

And yet, Kyra thought, this was all just about as contrary to Avantism as she could imagine. Surely no one here seriously believed that Xuan had quantified the forces of history to the point where it could be managed, nor shared the ideal of a world thus brought ever closer to total rationality. Surely the government, from its Advisory Synod on down to the average local administrator, itched to break up every such old maverick community, scatter its elders and take over entirely the schooling of its children. In theory that was possible, of course: an internal matter over which the Federation had no authority. In practice, traffic and communications wove Earth too closely together; too little could be covered up; too many High Worlders of all nationalities were in constant touch and shared too many opinions; they, or the general public itself, might well force other governments, at least those that were democratic, to apply pressures still more severe than Fireball had lately been doing—Her mind was adrift. She hauled it back into real time.

Twice Lee paused to exchange brief greetings with a man. Kyra grew aware of disapproving glances. She must seem luridly immodest. She told herself this wasn't a sealed-off enclave. They'd get a lot of outsiders, some on business, some curiosity seekers. Doubtless a certain part of their economy depended on it. Still, she felt vastly relieved when Lee stopped at a door and it retracted for them.

They entered a room of opulent carpeting, low furniture, gilt and silver tracery. The young man who admitted them signed the door to close. He bowed deeply as another, gray-bearded and strong-featured, attired in caftan and keffiyeh, came in through an arch at the rear. To that one Lee made respectful salutation, saying, *"Salaam aleyk."* Kyra stood miserably self-conscious.

"Aleykom es-salaam," replied the older man. His gravity surrendered to a smile. "To what do I owe this pleasure?" he asked in English with slight accent. As he looked closer, the smile faded. "Do you have trouble, my friend?"

"Ana nuzîlak," Lee said awkwardly.

"A-a-ah. Come, then." The man issued a sharp order. The servant hastened off. The host led the new arrivals onward. In a chamber behung with white perlux, suggestive of a pavilion, he gestured them to sit on the floor at a table of genuine wood. Joining them, he nodded at Kyra. "Remove your burden if you wish, señorita."

"Gracias, sir, but—" Catching a glance from Lee, Kyra said hurriedly, "Gracias," and slipped the pack off.

Lee spoke with full formality. "Sheikh Tahir, may I present Kyra Davis, a consorte of mine in Fireball Enterprises? Pilot Davis, por favor, meet Zeyd Abdullah Aziz Tahir, Sheikh of the Beny Muklib. He is among the leaders of . . . his nation."

Tahir regarded the woman narrowly, yet somehow

courteously. "Bienvenida, Pilot Davis," he said. "A space pilot, I presume?"

"Y-yes, sir," she answered. "Uh, por favor, excuse how I'm dressed. There wasn't time and I didn't know—"

He nodded. "Of course. Robert Lee would not appear this suddenly were it not an emergency situation. Nor would you, I am sure."

"I'm a, a total stranger . . . to your customs, sir."

Tahir smiled again, crinkling his craggy face. *"Wellah,* but it shall be forgiven you. I hope you will find time to tell me something of your work and yourself. If you fare among God's stars, you are fortunate."

Lee shifted where he sat. "Neither of us is right now, I'm afraid," he ventured. "In fact, we're desperate."

"You made that plain." A tap sounded on the door. At Tahir's bidding, it opened. A boy brought in a tray with coffee service and a bowl of date cakes. He set the refreshments on the table, bowed, and left. When the door had shut behind him, Tahir invited: "Partake. *Kheyr Ullah."*

Lee blinked. "Beg pardon?"

"You do not know? Since you said you had alighted at my tent, thus claiming my protection, I thought you understood what follows. Bueno, this is the Lord's bounty. Eat, drink, be my guests."

"You're too kind." Lee cleared his throat. "We'll be honest with you. I'm not of your tribe or faith or anything. Not much more than an acquaintance, really, who's picked up a few tag-ends of information about your people. I've no claim on you."

"You have shown friendship and more than friendship. I rejoice if we can respond."

"The Security Police are after us."

Tahir threw back his head and laughed aloud. *"Bismillah!* Why, that makes it all the better!" Immediately he harshened. "Are they close behind?"

"No, I hope not. I think we have a few hours before they decide I've flown the coop. But then they'll ransack the Theta."

"That will take time and much manpower, as large and varied as it is. Will they have reason to guess you are here?"

"I, I don't believe so. That is, they've kept somewhat of a watch on me, I being Fireball, but I'm nobody important and there are hundreds like me. Many of them are getting raided too. And it was ordered only a couple of days ago."

Why was it? Kyra sought comfort in her tiny cup of coffee, hot, thick, and supersweet.

Tahir stroked his beard. *"Wah.* Then they will not search this quarter early, unless they know you have been in the habit of visiting us."

"I visited plenty of other places, in this complex and elsewhere. I don't remember ever mentioning to—my neighbors, my casual associates—that I went here for anything except a café with good food and entertainment."

But Guthrie got wind of that, had an inquiry made, and found out that more was involved, Kyra thought. An old fox, all right. Through the fabric of the pack, the case nudged hard against her thigh.

"You were seen in the corridors today," Tahir pointed out.

"Excuse me," Kyra blurted. "I wonder if I wasn't noticed harder than he was."

The sheikh chuckled. "I am certain of that. It is helpful."

"I met two men I know," Lee admitted.

"Give me their names later. I will speak to them, and perhaps find them errands in distant parts. As for anyone else, you know we are not friends of the Avantists. If the Sepo ask questions among us, they will probably have to do it at random, and they will get very few frank answers." Tahir took a cake and munched it as if this were a social call.

"You can't keep us long," Lee said.

"True. Word would leak out like . . . like electrons quantum-tunneling through any potential barrier I can raise. But *insh'llah,* I can shelter you until tomorrow, and then help you proceed. You wish to leave soon in any case, do you not?"

"Crack, yes! We—that is—" Lee's gaze dropped to his lap.

Tahir considered his guests. "What do you feel free to tell me? Bear in mind, what I do not know, I cannot reveal, should worst come to worst and I go under deep-quiz."

Kyra shuddered. Tahir noticed. "That will scarcely happen, señorita," he assured her. "Likelier would I die first, resisting arrest, in such wise that not enough brain is left for them to probe. But let us be cautious."

She ran tongue over parched lips. "You have a, a right to know—something," she stammered. "We, Lee and I, we aren't simply escaping to save ourselves. If we could explain—" If Guthrie would speak—

Lee raised a hand. "We can't go into detail," he said fast. "That would be really dangerous. But, bueno, you know how friction's grown between Fireball and the government, till it suddenly claimed to have found evidence that agents of ours were behind the supposed accident that had scrambled the database in the Midwestern Security Center. You may remember how the company offered to cooperate in an investigation, and you certainly know how, regardless, the government occupied our North American headquarters to—probe this and related matters in depth, it announced. The Sepo have been burrowing and snooping since then. Bueno, I can tell you, it'll be in the news, now they're going to take over everything of ours in this country."

Tahir shaped a soundless whistle. *"Hayâtak!* Will you not then shut down all your operations dealing with the Union? A catastrophe for it, surely. Its economy is in a poor enough state already."

Lee sighed. "I don't understand their logic either. They're doing it, however. I'd better not say how I learned, but never mind, the whole Solar System will soon hear. Davis and I have, uh, extremely important information to convey. Uh, we can't trust any communication lines any longer, you realize. We've got to go in person."

Tahir's glance drifted across the table and downward. Kyra thought uneasily that he wasn't admiring her legs. He looked back at Lee. "I am glad to pay some of the debt I have owed you," he said, "and by your trust you honor my people and me. Gracias. We will try to be worthy of it."

A memory flitted through Kyra, someone historical whom she'd once read about. Yes, Saladin.

"You've done Señor—Sheikh Tahir a favor, consorte?" she asked. Too late she recalled Lee's warning, that she should play passive.

Their host took no umbrage. He must be used to dealing with outsiders. "Indeed he did," he told her. "Two years ago, a nephew of mine fell into trouble. He is a proud young man, fire is in him. All of us know that Avantism will bring our way of life to oblivion if it goes on. Most of us bide our time, believing that God will not let this happen. Hamid studied biotic engineering. The blasphemies he was required to study also, Xuanist doctrine, and that he met even in the scientific programs, at last enraged him beyond endurance. He began to speak out openly, in public, until he was arrested. When Robert Lee heard, he got Hamid released, and then enrolled in a company school safely off in Ecuador."

"Aw, it wasn't much," the other man mumbled. "Fairly minor charge, first offense, and he was still classed as 'developmentally disadvantaged,' which meant he might not have known any better. All I had to do was speak to my coordinator, who influenced the right person in the government. Fireball and the Synod were at odds, yes, had been for a long time, but no open break had come yet, and plenty of people on both sides were anxious to avoid one. Of course, with the charges dropped, Hamid would've been marked ever after, and probably soon come to real grief. But he's bright, and the company likes to acquire new blood when it can, you know. Actually, I got some boost out of the affair myself."

Alarm prickled in Kyra. "But that shows you have connections here!" she exclaimed.

"No, no. I told you I went through Fernando Pardo, my superior. He passed it on to somebody else, who 'took an interest in the case' and did the negotiating. No records were kept where they could be traced. Fireball's been heedful of such things in North America since before I went to work for it."

Guthrie taught it how, Kyra thought.

"I hope your nephew is happy now," she said to Tahir.

Did pain flit across his countenance? "Yes," he answered slowly. "We hear from him. Of course, he is becoming . . . a full dweller in the High World . . . the secular world. But that was . . . inevitable. And he is free. They will never take him and remake his mind."

Best shift the subject. "You must have been well acquainted here already, to learn about the matter," Kyra remarked to Lee.

"Only a bit," he said. "Sheikh Tahir and I happened to fall into talk in a coffeeshop one evening. We repeated that a few times, he invited me to dinner in his home, I showed him through local company workplaces. Don't worry, that was on multiceiver, not in person. Nobody there knows about the relationship. But it was just mutual curiosity and, uh, friendliness, nothing more. I was surprised when he told me about his nephew."

"I was full of rage and grief," Tahir said. "Sr. Lee struck me as a compassionate man. He might have influence. What could I lose? God provides."

"Gracias," Lee said ruefully. "You flatter me. To tell the truth, I never read you even that well. This culture is too foreign to me. No offense. I didn't grow up dealing with a lot of different kinds of people, the way you did. But today, my turn to be desperate, I guessed you might be willing to help us."

More than a guess, Kyra reflected, and mainly Guthrie's idea. Having gotten word of Lee's connections among these folk— How? The Hamid incident? Would news of that have circulated through the company clear to its master?

Not directly, she supposed. Still, virtually all that happened could go into hypertext, stored in a secret database that was probably located off Earth. From time to time Guthrie could plug into the main computer.

During that while, he would *be* it, with all its capacity to store and search and correlate. When something seemed especially interesting, he would put it in his personal memory before he disengaged, and investigate further.

Having, then, gotten word of Lee's connections among these folk, Guthrie must have sent an agent or two to go quietly among them and write him a report. When he needed a base in North America, his knowledge of this possible escape route decided him on Lee's dwelling.

Yes, a quasi-immortal could think that widely, that far ahead.

Regardless, he had barely gotten away, and the hunters might well bring him down.

Kyra realized that a silence had fallen while she sat alone with herself. Tahir stirred. "Let us go to business," he said. "I do not see how the police can blockade the Blue Theta for long, if at all. Too many people go in and out, often on necessary errands. For example, this community gets most of its food from a nanofac it owns in the Syracuse district. Similarly for others, such as the Crusoes. The gates will be closely watched for some time to come, of course. Disguise—but will you be carrying anything that might betray you to eyes or instruments?"

"I'm afraid so," Lee admitted. "A special computer."

Tahir nodded. "I thought as much." He pursued that no further. Instead: "Bueno, perhaps I can arrange for something plausible that will screen it. Meanwhile, you two must plan. We brothers cannot do more than convey you to someplace nearby. Consider what your moves after that shall be."

"We will," Kyra breathed. "Oh, yes."

"It is wise that you wait secluded," Tahir counselled. "I regret that this establishment has but a single guest room, with just one bed. If you wish, Pilot Davis, we can put you in the *harim.*"

Kyra started. He grinned. "That means my wife's domain," he said. "My only wife."

"But how can we talk then?" She met Lee's eyes. He half shrugged. "No, gracias, sir, but better we share that room." Recollection stirred. "Uh, if you don't mind too much."

Tahir's amusement continued. "We are no Wahhabis. It is reasonable that a young couple who have been separated should desire a night's privacy."

He'd better give his household more of a story than that, Kyra thought. Unless he simply told them this was none of their business, and they accepted and kept their mouths shut.

Lee flushed to the tips of his ears. "I can behave myself, consorte," he promised her.

Comic relief. Laughter whooped from Kyra. "I'll try!" she answered. Did Guthrie guffaw to himself?

Tahir rose. The fugitives followed suit, Kyra picking up the bag. "A boy will shortly bring you a meal," the sheikh said. "He will knock and wait until you admit him. If you want anything else, press zero-three on the telephone. That will activate my informant. Otherwise you will be strictly isolated. May I someday be able to offer you better hospitality."

"You c-couldn't better this, sir," Kyra vowed.

The room was down a short hall. Tahir stood aside and beckoned his guests in. *"Yerhamak Allah,"* he said low. Kyra guessed that was a blessing. The door shut on him.

She looked about her. The chamber was of modest size but decently equipped. Behind panels, a minibath adjoined a closet with drawers. A multi stood beside a table which accommodated a basic computer terminal. Two Western-style chairs suggested that others from her milieu stayed here occasionally. The floor was luxuriously carpeted. Although the walls were plain white, a viewscreen beneath the ventilator showed palms and jasmine around a pool. She couldn't tell whether the scene was real or synthesized. It seemed too pretty to be true, but tightly managed nature tracts did exist. The bed—the bed was wide enough that two could lie well apart.

Not that she expected anything carnal, under these circumstances. Certainly she felt no such urge. As tension ebbed, weariness flooded up through her marrow.

Lee saw. "Me too," he said, "and I didn't travel through six time zones before this chase began."

"Should we take Sr. Guthrie out?"

"You bloody well better," rasped from the pack.

Lee drew the case forth and placed it on the table. The eyestalks emerged and swung to position. Kyra thought of aimed guns. Warmth took her by surprise: "You done fine, you two. Now relax, why don't you? No booze handy, I guess, but a hot shower could work wonders."

A tingle ran the length of Kyra's spine. She groped for something commonplace to say. "Aren't you pretty high-wired too, sir?" After lying helpless in the blackness of a sack while his fate played itself out.

A wolf might have laughed. "What's a spook got to be scared with? No glands, remember?" Softly: "Do slack off, lass. You're bushed, as well you might be. We'll talk later."

"I—" A sense of how thirsty she was overran everything else. "Bueno, gracias, sir."

In the bath cubicle she swallowed three tumblers of deliciously cold water and splashed more on her face. Besides towels, she noticed, toothbrushes were provided, manual but new in their plastic cases. Yes, and a comb, a shaver, mouthwash, mild stimulants and painkillers. She'd found a good dock. Refreshed by the knowledge, she postponed showering and returned to perch on a chair. Lee followed her example.

"We've lucked out, haven't we?" Kyra said. "For the time being, anyhow."

"Luck's not a function just of chance," Guthrie replied.

"I'm sorry. I didn't mean there hadn't been intelligence." Kyra straightened where she sat. By all accounts, the jefe máximo despised sycophants. "But we are lucky in having Tahir on our side. He's quite a man, isn't he?"

"A leo," Guthrie agreed. "I've considered Islam to be one of the human race's bigger mistakes, but he might change my mind for me."

"He doesn't seem like a, a Low World leader."

"He isn't, really," Lee said. "Besides being a councillor and judge in this community, he's the purchasing agent for whatever supplies that its industries need from outside sources. That involves him with high as well as low tech, and everything it implies."

Kyra hesitated. "I don't rightly understand," she confessed. "That is, I know a little about the economics. People, the majority on Earth, those who haven't the skills or abilities that the forefront of the world wants—of course most of them don't struggle along in some kind of primitive self-sufficiency. It isn't that simple. But I'm not sure how it does work."

"No reason why you should be," Guthrie said. "If you're a space pilot, you've had plenty else to occupy you. And you spend your Earthside time in High World enclaves, don't you?"

"Bueno, I—"

"Judas priest, woman, don't feel guilty about doing what's sensible!"

Lee brought Kyra back to her question. "It doesn't work in any single fashion," he said. "It's as varied and variable as the groups involved. In fact, 'High World' and 'Low World' are a false dichotomy. They not only interact in countless ways, they shade into each other."

She frowned. "Can't you give me some specific data, though? For instance, Tahir's society. If it needs something more than basic citizens' allowance, it has to pay. That means it has to produce and sell something for which there's a demand. What, in this case?"

"No one specialty. Assorted goods and services. A little tourism and entertainment, though mostly these people are too proud and clannish for that. Handmade items—mainly curio value, because North Africa floods the market with the same kind of art." (Yes, Kyra thought, each piece unique, individually machine-made according to a self-diversifying program.) "But most of the men here have outside jobs, some fairly high-tech, some not. Gunjins, for instance. This culture has a martial tradition."

"Where did it come from?"

"Part old American. There was a wave of conversions to Islam in, uh, the twentieth century. Especially among afros, I believe. But the ancestors of these folks were mainly Near Easterners, refugees from the Holy League, after the *Befehl* broke down and the Europeans pulled out. Muslims were already unpopular in the West, often discriminated against. This immigration made matters worse. Things got really horrible during the Grand Jihad —segregation, restriction, outright persecution. They were driven in on themselves, their own resources. Naturally, they reacted by emphasizing their cultural identity; you may think they've exaggerated it. By the time they could mingle freely, many didn't want to. Also, by then the tech development curve was rising too fast for a lot of them to catch up. The end result was communities like this."

"You do like to hear yourself talk, don't you?" remarked Guthrie.

"I'm sorry, sir." Kyra heard the hurt in Lee's voice and felt a twinge of resentment on his behalf.

"Oops," said Guthrie. *"I'm* sorry. No insult meant. When I haven't got any effectors, just this damn box, it's hard to make plain I'm twitting you. You're a scholar by temperament, you want to explain things in full, sure, fine. I'm an occasional motormouth myself, they tell me."

Kyra straightened on her chair. "Maybe we should concentrate less on the past and more on the future," she snapped. "Our future."

"If we aren't too nervous to make sense," Lee said unevenly.

"I don't think you are," Guthrie told them. "You're both first-chop people, with more reserves than you know. Anyway, thinking about things before going to sleep, you're apt to wake up with a few solutions to your problems."

Even he, Kyra thought, required a strange kind of slumber. Certain lines rose through memory to chill her.

For in that sleep of death what dreams may come
When we have shuffled off this mortal coil—

The prosaic voice hauled her back: "Assume Tahir can get us smuggled out. He warned us that's about all he can do. We've got to plan beyond then. First we'd better review the situation as she is. What should we warn Tahir about? What spoor are we leaving for the cops, and how might we cover it?" The eyes swiveled toward Lee. "Bob, they'll soon pull your lock code from the file and let themselves into your place. I'm sure you weren't so stupid as to have an unregistered code."

"N-no, sir, of course not," Lee said. "I'd have been in trouble in case of a spot check or, or anything unusual."

"Once upon a time in this country, some men composed a fairy tale and called it the Bill of Rights. It said something quaint about the right of the people to be secure against that kind of thing."

"I know. I was educated in a company compound."

"Me too," Kyra murmured.

"Yeah," Guthrie said. "One point of friction between Fireball and the government. We resisted having our kids dragooned into the public school system. Well, never mind now. I get grumpy, that's all.

"The point is, the Sepo will make a fine-filament sweep of your quarters. Have you left anything to indicate I may have stayed there? Be honest, and don't be bashful. I won't think the less of you because you aren't a cloak-and-dagger pro."

Lee frowned, stared into space for a few seconds, then shook his head. "I don't believe I did. They may find the safe, though it's pretty well screened, but in that case they'll see it was installed long before my time. I recorded nothing germane to you. The communication lines you used also go back to well before I moved in. You know better than I how safe they are."

"Quite safe, as far as detectors and taps are concerned. When they're not in service, they cut themselves off without trace from the rest of our net. Okay. You'll need an explanation of why you were absent, one they'll accept without much inquiry. That wants corroboration. Think. What might you have been doing? Having a fling in a Low World den of iniquity? I've got the connections to arrange for witnesses to that on fairly short notice, if you're willing."

Lee's scowl darkened. "I don't know, sir. I mean, I don't care if they snicker. But if they ask around, they'll learn that sort of thing isn't in character for me. That could be hard on . . . your friends too."

"Any better ideas, then?"

"No, I'm afraid not. At first, you said I should simply play ignorant. It doesn't look so straightforward now. Let me think more."

"Do." The lenses focused on Kyra. "Your turn, Pilot Davis. Any reason for them to suspect you've had a hand in this?"

"No," she said. "I'm just a spacer who chanced to be at Kamehameha when Dr. Packer needed couriers."

"Anything in your background that might single you out?"

"Bueno—bueno, I'm third-generation Fireball, but that's common enough, isn't it?" Kyra paused. She must force herself a little. "My parents are North American born, but they've lived in Russia the past, m-m, fourteen years. They didn't want to move, but the company transferred them, actually to better positions—for their safety, I suspect. You see, Dad's fierily anti-Avantist. He grew more outspoken for every new law and regulation the Synod got passed." A smile twitched. "Mother's a cooler head."

"I see. Yours isn't the only family we've had to move. What do they do?"

"Dad's an analytical physicist." She heard the pride rising. "These days he works on antimatter, designs for improving the large-scale production of heavy nuclei. Mother's a biotics programmer. I have a younger brother in the Academy."

"Wait. *Those* Davises?" Guthrie was still for a moment. "Damn, I know I've met their names before, but most of my memories are banked elsewhere. I'm sorry."

It was decent of him to apologize, Kyra thought. "Not your fault, jefe. You can't store everything in . . . your personal database."

If he were hooked to his main hypercomputer, she

thought, he could summon anything in Fireball's files, including detailed recollections of his direct experiences. He'd need less computer capability than that to project a face of his own into a multi, a human play of expressions, instead of having to speak from within a blank box.

"Thanks," he said. After another silence: "Close-knit family, eh? I daresay you've spent a lot of your Earthside time in Russia with them."

"Yes. And otherwise, oh, sightseeing, vacationing around the globe. Hardly ever in the Union, except Hawaii." Mountain, forest, strand, surf, reef, ocean, remnants of a past that had been wonderfully alive; a hula, a luau, done for the tourists but still remnants of a past that had been wonderfully human; the Keiki Moana, graceful, wistful, remnants of a future that had failed. "Otherwise this country is depressing." How sour that word tasted. "Not that I've been much on Earth at all since getting my captain's rating. I've had some long hauls."

"Really? Where?"

"Asteroid and cometary prospecting tours, as far as the Kuiper Belt. Outer planets, ferrying for the scientific stations. Once on Taurid work, emergency call."

Muy bien, she was bragging, and quite aware of Lee's awed stare. But the idea was less to impress Guthrie than to give him an estimate of her potentials.

"Whew!" exclaimed the artificial voice. "You've put yourself in my everyday memory for certain, Pilot Davis, and when I consult your file, that'll also go permanently into this can. God damn, in the old days I'd've met you personally and congratulated you. In my flesh days I'd've given you a big wet kiss as well. Fireball's gotten too mucking huge."

Virtually a nation in its own right, Kyra's mother had remarked once. It *is* a nation, her father replied, more so than most that bear the name nowadays.

Oh, yes, he added for the benefit of the child who was listening (as she understood later), legally it's nothing but a privately held corporation, chartered in Ecuador, carrying on a variety of enterprises across Earth and throughout the Solar System. Their importance gives it nothing but enormous wealth and influence—legally. In fact, though, it provides most of its people with most of what they need, from homes and schools and medical care to help against the governments that claim them. If we choose to swear full fidelity to it, Fireball will pledge us the same; and then we are no longer just employees, we are consortes. That's no mere contract, that's a constitution. And think about our customs, generations-old traditions, everything we share, far over and beyond any material treasures— A nation, I tell you.

That wasn't quite correct, Dad, Kyra now thought. The nation, that's us, and our sovereign territory is all of space.

Yet through his computers and his communication lines, a single ghost was still able to rule it, keep it together, stave off its foes, set it reaching for the stars. How much longer could he? Already his grip was loose— No, wrong. He had always left the members as independent as possible. That was the real wellspring of Fireball's strength.

Guthrie recalled her mind to him. "Okay," he asked, "what brought you to Earth this time? Vacation?"

"Not really," Kyra said. "I was in L-5 while my ship got a routine overhaul. A special cargo was going to North America, organic cryocells. That meant regulations called for a human pilot. The usual man had taken an accidental radiation dose and was in DNA therapy. I offered to substitute and they agreed." Why not, given a person of her qualifications, humdrum though the flight was? "Turnaround time would be about three days, because unloading that stuff is finicky. It'd allow me to visit my parents or maybe get in some surfing."

"In short, you arrived by pure happenstance, and if the cops play back the log, that's what they'll confirm. Your family's dossier might raise eyebrows, but I doubt they'll check that. When you don't report back for liftoff, they may wonder. On the other hand, they'll have a lot else on their minds. Besides, once the clampdown on the company has been announced, it'll seem perfectly natural for you to sit tight wherever you are."

"I'm safely anonymous?" Excitement fluttered. "I can walk right out of this place?"

"Um-m, maybe not that easy. Let's double check. How'd you travel here?"

Led by sharp questions, Kyra described her itinerary. With dismay she remembered the bubbletrike, locked in a time-expired rack and traceable through her thumbprint.

"What about the rental period?" Guthrie demanded.

"I entered that I might return today or it might be tomorrow. I didn't know which, you see."

"Smart girl. Well, if you can't spring the vehicle tomorrow, I don't suppose anybody will notice the unpaid meter right away, and then the matter will be for city maintenance, not the cops—at first, anyhow."

"You can do better than that," Lee proposed. "Call on a public line once you're outside, tell the agency you had to go elsewhere because of an emergency and they should send somebody to pick up the trike. It'll carry their code, which the lock will open for. Charge the extra expense to your credit. I daresay that sort of thing happens every once in a while, and they'll think little or nothing of it."

"Hey, Bob, you have the makings of a pretty slick desperado," Guthrie said.

"Bueno, then," Kyra said gladly, "I can leave you in a safe place, sir, and convey in person whatever message you want to send Dr. Packer. Or someone else?"

She heard grimness revive. No, she realized, it had been there all the while, under the surface.

"Unfortunately, we can't lay that straight a course. For openers, I wonder if I have any safe place left me, anywhere in this country. The more I think about it, the more I suspect who's behind the whole halloo. The worst enemy I could have."

The breath hissed between Lee's teeth. Had he guessed? Kyra could merely whisper, in sudden cold, "Who?"

"Myself."

"What?"

"My duplicate. My *Doppelgänger*. The copy of me that went to Alpha Centauri."

Memory stormed back. How old was she when the *Juliana Guthrie* came home? Seven, eight? Yes, seven. The event was not a triumphal entry. After all, the data had been beamcast ahead, received long in advance. The samples being brought were necessarily few and small, their molecular structures already analyzed, mere trophies. Nevertheless, that arrival was oddly muted, and everything about it dropped out of the news, out of public attention, with a speed that in retrospect seemed equally peculiar. She had half forgotten it.

Guthrie went on. His matter-of-factness was more frightening than any dramatics. "We downloaded into each other, he and I. I had more experience to enter, of course. He was inoperative for a lot of years in empty space, outbound and returning. Else he'd've gone bananas from boredom. But the idea had been that *I* would be on the trip, and yet not miss out on everything that happened to *me* at home. While he was gone, things changed in the Solar System. I never wanted to stay in charge forever, but I decided that under present conditions Fireball had better have a backup. So I arranged to keep his return as inconspicuous as possible. By agreement, after he was brought up to date we deactivated him and I had him tucked away against a day of need."

And when that second Guthrie was awakened again, Kyra thought, it would be as if no time whatsoever had passed for him.

Momentarily she wondered which of the two she confronted physically, the original or the double. Then she saw that it made no difference.

"In North America," she foreknew.

"Yeah. A silly choice, with the Avantists in power? Shouldn't we have stashed him someplace really secure? Well, a judgment call. When Fireball built new headquarters for this country, I had secret crypts and capabilities put in. I'd seen the Renewal and the Jihad and a slew of lesser disasters, and Avantism was then on the horizon. Be prepared. It seemed to me he could be as safely hidden there as anywhere on Earth, more safely than in most locations. Off Earth, this one of me ought to have ample protection.

"The Synod was making the Union government heavier-handed every day, and our conflicts with it were getting worse, but I never expected it'd dare violate our contractual rights the way it's done. I smelled too many weaknesses under the preaching and the swaggering. I knew the Kayos in embryo, as an organized resistance, already then. Nothing that happened since, till very lately, caused me to change my opinion. Someday in the not too distant future, all hell was going to let out for noon in North America. At that time, it might well be important to have another me on the spot, taking charge locally. That might save quite a lot of lives and property."

The part of Kyra that stood aside wondered whether this was conceit bordering on megalomania. No, she decided. Guthrie had proved himself too often, and he was too realistic to be modest. The plain truth was that he, hooked into a net, could steer Fireball, or a cut-off section of Fireball, through a crisis better than any junta of humans or any purely artificial intelligence. The power sprang from more than experience, knowledge, innate generalship. It was authority. Divine right, almost; something that could call on men to die, and be heeded, because it spoke for that which gave meaning to their lives. He was the founder, the master, the presence. He was Fireball.

But leaders could fail and their causes perish.

Kyra heard a sigh. Wryness recognized that Guthrie had shaped it without lungs, as he shaped every word he uttered. "When the troops occupied that building, I was caught flat-footed," he said. "Suddenly there was no way to reach my double, let alone brief him. The best thing I could think of to do was have myself sneaked to Earth and into the Union."

A bold move, Kyra thought, but it had worked well until now. Instead of being paralyzed, dependent on communication with a center which the Sepo now oversaw, the company's North American subdivisions acted shrewdly, on their own, in the Fireball tradition. Their directors protested and negotiated. Meanwhile a shipment of isotopically pure titanium ordered by a government plant in the Union somehow went to Québec, which somehow chose to keep this treasure despite the indignation of its powerful neighbor. Meanwhile the company's Southwestern energy receiver central regretted that for technical reasons it could no longer feed surplus megawatts into the national grid. Meanwhile guardsats reported mysterious small objects arcing over the ocean between California and Hawaii, and a Guatemalan delegate to the World Federation Assembly called for the Peace Authority to investigate what might be a North American violation—

"I hoped we could force a settlement that'd give us back our status and leave the Synod weakened," Guthrie continued. "Again I've been surprised. The big crackdown's begun, and we three are on the lam." (Kyra guessed that that meant they'd perforce gone hyperbolic.) "Why? Are they so hard up they'll court a retaliation that could ruin them? None of the intelligence I've collected suggests that. They're in a bad enough way that they're willing to take risks, but they aren't kamikaze yet. They must think they have a pretty fair chance of coming out ahead of the game.

"How? Each minute of the past few hours, I've gotten more convinced that they've clapped hands on my other self."

Concentrating on the background of events, Kyra had not seen what that implied. Awareness came like a blow to the belly.

"But they didn't know where he was," Lee protested, as if trying to fend off the fact.

"Somehow the Sepo learned," Guthrie replied. "With hindsight, I can make a guess. Three persons besides me knew. I won't name names, even to you, but they were close associates of mine. Two still are, off Earth. One, a North American, was visiting here several months ago when he was killed in an accident. Or so the world was informed, in the usual way, with the usual material, including the body. I was sorry, but I've said goodbye to many friends. . . . Now I recall how such things can be faked, if you have very good technicians and a very well-organized operation. Including a synthesized corpse. It wouldn't need to pass close inspection, only to fool his relatives. It was cremated according to his wishes.

"I suspect he was kidnapped and deep-quizzed. Probably with no specific object in mind, just to get a lead on anything that might be helpful against us. Sayre is capable of arranging any outrage. He's also a bright son of a bitch, who must know that if his government doesn't soon do something drastic, it's doomed. If I'm right, he learned about my twin."

"What really became of your friend?" Lee asked low.

"Dead, after they finished with him," Guthrie answered flatly. "I hope. For his sake."

Kyra shuddered.

"If the Synod knew my double was hidden in our HQ, it could invent a pretext and seize the building," Guthrie proceeded. "Then the government would stall, make a fuss, claim it wanted to compromise, but drag matters out, while it—" the machine voice barely stumbled— "reprogrammed its prize. Now it has me on its side, knowing most of what I know."

"Surely not!" Kyra cried.

"Not everything, but enough," said remorselessness. "Everything that was in his personal memory, which means more or less everything a human would retain, including the locations of my old-established hideaways. News of the last two decades, easily downloaded into him. Ample information about the company, from the discs they've seized—nothing top secret, of course, but Fireball doesn't have many top secrets.

"Mainly, he knows how I think. He knows I've entered the country, because he'd've done the same, because he is me. He'll make some almighty shrewd estimates of what I'll do next."

Kyra kicked out against the nightmare, like Lee. "Are you sure of this? It sounds awfully far-fetched."

"If you can suggest a hypothesis that fits the facts better, I'd be delighted to hear it."

"But could they really . . . change him . . . and not destroy him, make him useless? How?"

"They could," Lee told her. "The theory of it touches my field, so I can imagine the methods." Briefly, his hand touched hers. "I would rather not describe them."

3

Database

THE CONTROL PROVIDED by the World Federation Meteorological Service was limited, and over weather, not climate. Northwest Integrate would always have more rain and clouds than clear skies, until Earth as a whole had profoundly changed. However, the previous week a lengthy wet spell had yielded for a while to dazzling sunshine. On the first day of this, Enrique Sayre took a moment to admire it.

The local Security Police building was broad and deep rather than high, a fortress. Still, the view from the roof bore comparison with what he saw from his flitter before he landed; and after he stepped out, a boisterous cool wind laved his face and yodeled in his ears. It smelled of salt water, with the slight tang of chemicals and ozone that bespoke energies at work. Traffic sounds rose through it, an oceanic murmur, up toward soaring gulls and glinting aircraft. The city climbed likewise, from streets, bridgeways, monorails, dymaxions and other lesser edifices, to prideful tower heights. Biospaces glowed intensely green; although they were negligently maintained of late, nature was moving in, grass, weeds, saplings. Some distance off, Elliott Bay shone argent, less troubled than formerly by shipping and sailboats. Beyond the structures on the farther side, Cascade snowpeaks raised white against blue.

Sayre could understand why Anson Guthrie located his North American headquarters here. The man had been born and raised in Port Angeles, on the Strait and not far from the Olympic Peninsula's mountains and forests. The disembodied program must have yearned back. Sayre threw a glance at the Fireball building. It reared on Queen Anne Hill, its lines suggestive of a spacecraft at launch, arrogantly higher than his. But now the infinity flag flew on its pole too.

Guards saluted as Sayre walked from his flitter. He returned the gestures. The men were mainly ceremonial, an adjunct to robotic monitors and guns, but ceremony was important. Xuan himself had admitted that humankind remained largely a creature of instinct and emotion. Taming the brain stem and limbic system to the service of the cerebrum would be the work of lifetimes.

Sayre had progressed sufficiently in the disciplines to recognize, and not to care, that he was physically unimpressive—a short, slight man, sharp-featured but with a receding chin and blond hair plastered in thin strands to a round head. He had refrained from getting any makeover except correction of myopia and of a liability to stomach ulcers. His uniform was plain, hardly distinguishable from a common officer's. It was what he did that rated salutes.

Entering a fahrweg turret, he descended to the office he had commandeered. Personnel sprang to their feet with more salutes. Impatient, he brushed past them and sequestered himself in the room beyond. From his desk he phoned the laboratory. The line switched him immediately to Clarice Yoshikawa.

"Sir!"

"Is the new program ready?" Sayre asked.

"Yes, sir," replied the chief of the technicians whom he had summoned from Central Command back east in Futuro. "We were testing all night." More than that showed in her haggardness. Stim and supp would keep a person going only up to a point, and Sayre had driven the team pitilessly since they arrived.

"Have you gotten it right at last?"

Exasperation, close to anger, spoke, however levelly: "Sir, you know we have just the single piece of Guthrie hardware. All we can do is make copies of the software, revise them, and check them out in limited ways, till we put them in that one computer and they become conscious."

"While you're at it," Sayre replied, "tell me what month this is."

Fear stirred behind the firm visage. "I'm . . . very sorry, sir. Wasn't thinking. Dead tired."

Sayre smiled. "I know. You people have worked like engines. Never fear, the files will record your loyalty. I may be overstrained myself. This is so important, so urgent."

He heard the quiver of relief. "Gracias, sir. I hope this time we've succeeded, not produced something that raves or gibbers."

"We'll find out."

Yoshikawa ran tongue over dry lips. "You realize, sir, even if it seems right, we won't know for sure. Excuse me for repeating what's elementary, but psychomedicine isn't an exact science yet. A live person given ideational reconditioning can still surprise us occasionally. Here we're trying it for a download. There's scarcely any experience with them."

Sayre clicked his own tongue. "You *are* exhausted, aren't you? Talking like that. However things develop today, you and your team shall have, m-m, twenty-four hours of deep sleep and twenty-four of recuperative treatment. Keep going for another two or three hours first. Can you do that?"

"Of course, sir," Yoshikawa said, instantly livening. "We're anxious to know the results too. It's for the Transfiguration."

Sayre's finger drew the infinity sign. "It is." He leaned forward. "As for the uncertainty, yes, I'm well aware of it, not merely because you warned me at the outset. If the new Guthrie appears satisfactory, the government will go ahead with him. My duty will be to keep close watch, as one does over any important person whose loyalty isn't unquestionable. If he seems to deviate, we have punishments to bring him back in line, and rewards to offer for good behavior. With luck, given computer speed, we'll soon condition any remaining intransigence out of him."

His statement was so obvious that he wasn't revealing any secrets, although Yoshikawa and her people had not been told explicitly what the authorities planned. To give a self-aware program a virtual hell or a virtual heaven should be technically simpler than to do it for flesh and blood. The trick was to discover what were horror and ecstasy in this particular case. Sayre's career had made him skilled in finding such things out.

"Eventually," he added, "we'll have to let him go forth on his own, but by then we ought to be sure of him."

"Muy bien, sir," Yoshikawa said. "Shall we make the change immediately?"

"Stand by," Sayre ordered. "I want a preliminary private session with him as he is. I'll call you when I'm ready."

He left the office and proceeded to the laboratory level. At first, as he strode down those corridors, activity buzzed and clicked. For the most part it was machines at work. Reports flowed in, this suspicious activity, that incorrect idea expressed, such and such a citizen who had dropped out of registry, now and then an outright crime that the civil police thought might be politically motivated, inquiries from other command posts throughout the Union, intelligence from abroad that had relevance to the tasks of Security. The computers assimilated, scanned, retrieved, made correlations, determined who should have what information. Nevertheless plenty of personnel sat at the consoles or went from room to room, carrying materials. Humans still had to make the final judgments.

Soon that should not be the case. Sayre often regretted that none of the current progress in artificial intelligence was North American. But when government insisted that the mind was algorithmic, because this was what Xuan had said, and scientists who suggested otherwise got into trouble—

Sayre had argued on their behalf. In his position he could dare do so. The quantum-mechanical, nonalgorithmic approach was not necessarily subversive, he maintained whenever circumstances allowed. It simply required careful handling. Were it true, Xuan's great insights would stand basically unchallenged.

Within his own mind, Sayre shrugged. The work going on in Europe and on the Moon was bearing him out. Doctrine would have to adapt itself to reality. And consider what power would soon be available, to revitalize Xuanism by striding light-years toward the Transfiguration. Not the obsolescence and extinction of humankind, but its apotheosis in union with the thinking machine—for thought had proved to be of a subtler nature than cyberneticists foresaw, yet it *was* a set of physical processes.

As witness Anson Guthrie. Sayre quickened his steps.

Halfway down a certain hall, two guards ported their shock guns when he appeared. Pistols were holstered at their sides. Beyond them reached empty rooms and quietness. His team had taken over the psych lab. That handicapped the Northwest cadre, but they could refer any problems elsewhere. As imperative as secrecy was, Sayre had instructed that Guthrie be moved no farther than from the Fireball building to here. A closed door showed where Yoshikawa and her subordinates waited. Sayre went on. Near the end of the passage, he signalled another door to retract and entered a small, viewless, sparsely furnished chamber.

The box on the table turned its eyestalks to look at him. "Alpha," Sayre greeted with Avantist formality.

Predictably, Guthrie did not respond, "Omega," but formed a grunt.

Sayre kept his tone mild. "Surliness is stupid, you know. I hoped that sheer boredom, if nothing else, would have made you ready to communicate."

"I've got my thoughts and memories for company," said the download. "When I'm not subactive."

"That state interests me," Sayre remarked. "Equivalent of sleep, but none of your kind has ever made quite clear what it . . . feels like."

"I couldn't make clear what any part of being a download feels like," Guthrie answered. "Not that I'd try for you."

"Do you enjoy your condition, or dislike it?"

Guthrie sat mute. For a moment, irrationally, chill went along Sayre's backbone as he wondered what this truly was before him. Humans and their machines had made it. Did they afterward understand it? Would they, ever?

The whole thing had seemed so cleanly scientific. Given the theoretical knowledge and the technological capability, you could download a personality, map it into the software of a neural network which itself mapped the unique brain that bore the personality. True, the process was slow, complex, expensive, imperfect. It performed no clean, swift scan, but instead a pervasion, the special molecules in their legions, brought by bloodstream and cerebrospinal fluid to conduct their cell-by-cell examinations while the subject lay half-conscious under electrophasing. Then came resonances with external fields, to recover the data. Then a battery of hypercomputers to interpret and order the findings. Meanwhile, treatment to rid the subject of his tiny inquisitors and bring him back to normal. Design, test, redesign, retest. Eventually, the program, the download—approximation, sketch, ghost of his mind. It had his memories, with the inclinations, beliefs, prejudices, hopes, outlook, style of thinking, entire awareness. But it was not the flesh-and-blood person. It ought to be as comprehensible as any other artifact. It ought to be as controllable.

The stories of all downloads declared that it wasn't.

How controllable, ultimately, was anything?

Sayre quelled a shudder. He told himself he was overtired, overwrought. Discipline returned, and he spoke levelly. "See here, I'm making one final effort to be friendly. Have you enough knowledge to appreciate that? You were oblivious a long time, and the updates you have since received were audiovisual only. I wonder if you realize what a concession this visit of mine is."

"I know you're the head of the Security Police, and therefore *ex officio* a member of the Advisory Synod, which quietly tells the legislature what laws to pass, the judiciary what decisions to reach, and the executive what to do." Guthrie sounded unimpressed. "I also know you're nothing special in history. It's had your sort again and again, like outbreaks of acne."

Sayre couldn't hold down a flick of anger. He flushed. "You betray your ignorance," he snapped. "Unique, decisive, irreversible events do happen. Fire. Agriculture. The scientific method. Xuan Zhing and his system."

"I've heard that one before, too."

"You have not! Who else properly analyzed the dynamics of social action? Science, not witch doctors or folk remedies, science put an end to smallpox, AIDS, heart disease, cancer. Do you imagine anything but science can put an end to injustice, wastefulness, alienation, violence, all the horrors humans make for themselves? If you had troubled to study Xuan's mathematics—"

Sayre broke off. It was ridiculous, preaching like this at a program in a box. Yes, he certainly needed some rest and recreation.

Yet the concept caught him as often before, uplifted him, refreshed and recharged his spirit. Not that he claimed personally to have seen or grasped every facet of the vast achievement. Few intellects reached that high. Even Xuan, throughout the decades of his labors, had drawn heavily on the computer resources of the Academic Internet, as well as acknowledging his debt to earlier thinkers. The likes of Sayre must depend on what they were taught in school, with lectures and semipopular writings to deepen it somewhat afterward. Nevertheless he could appreciate the *fittingness* of it all—the same processes shown to have been at work in Han Dynasty China and Imperial Rome, in Islam and Cao-Dai, in chronometry and calculus. He could be convinced by its arguments that, given modern information processing, the market economy was obsolete, with its inefficiencies and inequities. He could be inspired by the prospect of establishing and maintaining conditions so well planned that society must evolve toward a sane order of things, as a spacecraft launched on the right trajectory must pass among the multitudinously changeable forces upon it to the desired destination.

Fleetingly, not for the first time, he knew that what made and kept him a dedicated Avantist was none of these proven propositions, not really. It was a logical *non sequitur*—a vision, if you will—and therefore nonrational. But Xuan's scheme allowed for nonrationality, irrationality, and the chaos of nonlinear systems. They were powerful elements in the course of events; his reasoning took them fully into account. What had captured Sayre's imagination was Xuan's afterword. The thinker was at last simply speculating, the prophet was no longer prophesying but imagining. He agreed that nobody alive in an imperfect and limited present can foresee what will happen in a future that has approached perfection and abolished limitations. Still, one dared look ahead, and in fact there had been those already in the nineteenth and twentieth centuries who did. They saw dimly, Xuan more clearly, the Transfiguration—a thousand years hence, a million?—and it in its turn might be only a beginning—the whole cosmos evolving from blind matter to pure intelligence—

A surprise jolted Sayre back into Guthrie's hereness. "I did study the math," he heard the download reply. That had not been said earlier, no matter how intensive the interrogation. "After all, as a doctrine it was acquiring more true believers every day. Your Avantist Association was becoming a political force to reckon with, uh-huh. Though mainly because of the half-believers, the hordes who supposed the scheme must have something going for it because everybody said it was objective and scientific, didn't they? I'd better check it out for myself. So I got a logician to help me, and we waded through the psychotensor matrices, the *lao-hu* operator, the quantitative studies, enough of the whole schmeer to give me a pretty fair notion, before I decided my time was worth more than this."

"Which proves you learned nothing," Sayre retorted. "Did you never ask yourself why those ideas appealed to so many?"

"Sure I did, and came up with the usual reasons. Oh, yes, the world was in a bad way, in the wake of the Renewal and the Jihad and the other hydrophobias it'd been through. This country wasn't the worst off, but it had better days to remember than most did, which made its people feel like they'd fallen further and harder. Xuan had made some predictions that were more or less right and issued some prescriptions that weren't totally absurd. North Americans always have been suckers for salvationism. Enough of them swallowed Xuanism—or, I should say, its sound-bite slogans—that your gang got itself elected, never mind how. The last halfway free election the country had."

"Nonsense. The public saw what was being accomplished."

"Some positive things, yeah. Mostly of the flashy sort, tenements, reclamation, universal genetic counseling, et cetera, et cetera. Nothing I couldn't have thought of myself, with common sense and experience of people."

"Untrue. You might as well claim that Einstein thought of nothing you could not have yourself."

"Different case entirely. General relativity was new. It explained a good-sized chunk of reality. At bottom, under the fancy language and equations, Xuanism is the same collectivist quackery that's been peddled these past two or three thousand years, over and over and over. Longer than that, I'll bet."

"No. For the first time, we have a theory that explains the facts of history."

"Some of the facts. Astrology or a flat Earth explain some of the facts too. The rest of Xuanism is just about as useful as they are. Or as disastrous, rather. Exactly how well has the Union done under its Avantist government? Where have all your restructurings and redistributions and reorientations brought you, except deeper into the swamp? Somebody said once that a fanatic is a man who, when he's lost sight of his purpose, redoubles his efforts.

And your purpose was never scientific anyway. It was religious. Crank religious. Why, your power elite don't call themselves a board or a council but a synod. Interesting connotations, hey? As for your pipe dream of a world-intelligence that'll eventually embrace the whole universe—"

"Bastante!" Sayre exclaimed. "I didn't come here to listen to your nescient ranting."

"No, you're an intellectual," Guthrie gibed. "You believe in the free exchange of ideas."

"Among minds capable of it, minds that have learned sanity."

"Yeah, I reckon I am an anti-intellectual. Always have been. Listen. I was born in 1970, when the young intellectuals were rampaging over the college campuses. They admired Mao and Castro, the way the earlier generation of them had admired Stalin. They went on to become tenured faculty, and I was glad to drop out of school. Their successors bred the Renewal and cheered it into power, because it was going to save the environment and purify society. But *you* are *different*. Sure."

Sayre took three long breaths. Slowly, his hands stopped trembling. "Are you absolutely sealed in the past? I came to give you one last opportunity. Don't make it impossible for me."

"Why, what'd you like to do?"

"Preserve you. We need your hardware, custom-made as it is, but in due course we can have another unit made for you. I have thought we might then talk. Not necessarily dispute; converse. You have been through so much, you are such a large part of history yourself. My colleagues and I—scholars, scientists—would be very interested." Sayre paused. "You might also be. So I've hoped."

"When my past self was young," Guthrie replied, "he'd argue with true believers in assorted glorious causes. Gradually he found out that at the core, fanatics are all alike. Sayre, you're a bore. You're a busybody too, and more than a bit of a sadist, but mainly you're a bore. Spare me."

The man struggled with indignation and managed to

keep his voice steady. "Have you given the slightest consideration to what will happen to you if you continue in this attitude? First, disconnection."

"What, again?" asked sarcasm.

"Bueno, of course we have to do that in any case. We need your hardware for the newest replacement we've developed. If it works properly, and my techs think that this time it will, then it will continue in your network. But as I said, eventually we can make a new one for you, and you'll waken again. That's if you'll give me reason to expect at least a minimum of cooperativeness from you. Otherwise, I'm afraid you'll be too great a potential danger. With regret, I'll have to order your discs wiped."

Guthrie was silent.

"Oblivion," Sayre told him. "Nonexistence. As if you never had been."

"No different from what's always waited for everybody." Guthrie sounded cool. Had he been linked to an imaging computer, the picture would likely have shrugged. "Unless there is something after death. I doubt that very much, but if there is, I suppose I'll get a share of it."

It really would be too bad, having to destroy this fascinating relic. Maybe he could be frightened into reasonableness. "Or we can use you as experimental material," Sayre warned.

"You've been doing that to a succession of copies you've made of me." Did this Guthrie feel pity and terror on their behalf? If so, he concealed it well. "I don't see any point for you in torturing one more. Except revenge. Or plain old fun. Aren't Xuan's apostles above such emotions?"

The damned, perverse diehard was right. The work already done would be amply difficult to keep secret, involving as it did a number of specialists. Unless the need for secrecy came someday to an end, anything else that was unnecessary multiplied the risk. If word got out, not only would an operation of turning-point possibilities be compromised, the Chaotics would make it part of their propaganda. ("See, the government isn't content with what it does to ordinary human detainees in the correction centers—")

Sayre sighed. "Termination, then. We'll keep you until we are sure of the new model, but I do not think you will ever rouse from this switchoff. I'm sorry."

That was no longer quite true.

"My last words," Guthrie said, "are, up yours."

Sayre blinked. What did that mean? No, he would not give his prisoner the satisfaction of asking.

Eyestalks retreated. Guthrie had withdrawn.

Sayre resisted the temptation to scream him back to attention. Instead, the man went to the phone. "You will make the conversion, Yoshikawa," he directed.

The team appeared within two minutes, bearing their apparatus. Sayre stood aside and watched. The task was simple, this part of it.

Yoshikawa unscrewed a covering disc and touched the switch beneath. Noiselessly, Guthrie ceased to function. Deft hands opened the case, removed the discs, and set them aside.

Sayre regarded them pensively. The flickering, flowing web of exchanges—electrons, holes, photons, fields—that was thought had died away. Frozen within the configurations of atoms were those patterns which recorded memories, habits, inclinations, instincts, reflexes, everything that had operated in the forebrain of living Anson Guthrie, together with some indeterminate fraction of its ancient nonhuman inheritance; and everything that ghost-Guthrie underwent after the transfer until the making of this copy; and everything that afterward passed through the copy's own sensors and cerebrations.

Such were the program and database, those several thick discs which had been placed in a rack on the table. The hardware was an analogue of the long-disintegrated brain itself, the inborn potentialities, the capabilities it had gained and the losses it had suffered through a turbulent lifetime. No other software was compatible with this. Every download, of the few that ever existed, had been as unique in every way as its mortal prototype.

But organisms could be modified. So, by different methods, direct rewriting and superimposed sequences, could programs be.

Yoshikawa inserted the new discs. For a while she and her team worked with instruments they connected to the case. Sayre shivered, waiting. Finally they conferred, removed the meters and scopes, closed the box. Yoshikawa switched the circuits back on.

Eyestalks extruded. Sayre summoned total self-mastery. He trod forward to meet that gaze. Looming above, he said, "Guthrie."

"Y-yes." The reply lagged. The lenses roved about before they steadied on him.

Sayre smiled and spoke with great gentleness, as one did to correctees at certain stages of their re-education. "Bienvenido, Anson Guthrie. Do you know what you are?"

"Yes, I . . . do." The words stumbled. "I'm not, not used to it—yet—"

"That's all right. To be expected. Take your time. Familiarize yourself. You'll have all the help you want. Ask any questions you wish. Your memory will show that we are completely honest with you."

In the silence that followed, the ventilator seemed to whisper unnaturally loudly. "You seem to have been," said the object at length. "I feel sort of confused, but I think it'll straighten out."

"It will, I'm sure. Let's make a little test. What are you?"

"I'm a copy—of a copy—of a copy made from a live man— But you've given me new information!" Sudden strength rang forth. "I was wrong. I didn't understand the situation, nor what Xuan was getting at, not really. I'll have to think more about that, but—" The voice trailed off. After a minute: "Well, Sayre, my mind is changed. We're allies. Thanks. I guess."

4

A KNOCK SOUNDED. Lee and Kyra tucked Guthrie in the closet before they admitted the servant. He wheeled in a dinner cart, set the meal forth, salaamed, and left them. They brought their lord out and settled down to eat.

Kyra discovered she was ravenous. Seasoned lamb, pilaf, eggplant, pita, cucumber salad dressed with yogurt, sweet side dishes, soured milk, fruit sherbet, coffee, all were prepared in ways strange to her but tasted supreme. Lee said it was traditional fare. These folk must have gone to considerable trouble and expense getting their nanotanks programmed for the ingredients. Maybe they bought some from an actual farm.

Nourishment restored hopefulness and, for a while, kept exhaustion at bay. After the servant, summoned by a buzzer, had removed the debris, talk began to range freely, beyond matters of escape and comeback.

Lee seemed to gain less animation than Kyra. When she remarked on it, he explained wryly, "This isn't my kind of escapade. I've led a pretty quiet life."

"Oh, I don't know," she said. "You've knocked around with lots of odd people, haven't you? And gotten familiar with 'em, too, which is more than I probably could."

"Bueno, my work demands that."

Yes, she thought, an intuitionist had to be a peculiar combination of intellect and sensitivity. S/he must possess a basic grasp not just of modern science and technology but of society; not just history, diagrammed structures, analyzed dynamics, but individual human beings; not just the High World but enough of the relatively backward cultures and subcultures that s/he could see—no, feel— something of their interactions with it. On that basis s/he was supposed to develop models and write programs, to generate ideas and make proposals that had a fair likelihood of being partially right. S/he might thus anticipate the results of some change, especially on the human level, and indicate ways to forestall or mitigate those that were undesirable.

Guthrie had created the profession, Kyra remembered. He set in motion the first studies and experiments, then the first recruitments. Fireball gained so much thereby, even at that early stage, that other companies were quick to imitate, and finally governments did. She harked back to a lesson in school. As part of her education, she was to know about this, whether or not it ever impinged directly on her. Guthrie himself had recorded the lecture. He didn't appear in the multi. A faceless box wouldn't appeal to youngsters, and he reserved re-creations of his mortal image for occasions more special. Artfully prepared scenes accompanied the homely voice.

"The classic example from the past is the automobile. You've seen it in historicals, a live-piloted ground vehicle fuelled by hydrocarbons. It became practical and started taking over from the horse in a single generation. Well, any fool in those days could've seen that happening. A smart fellow could've predicted that this'd lead to a major industry. The subsidiary industries, like oil and highway work, would join in to make a combination that'd dominate the economies of whole nations. But I don't believe anybody planned for oil reserves gaining vital strategic importance, till possession of them was suddenly one of the considerations that wars were being fought over. The explosion of suburbs and the dry rotting of inner cities, strangulated traffic, air not fit to breathe, all these caught people more or less by surprise. I'll barely mention a revolution in sexual styles, to titillate you and make you want to study further on your own.

"I don't say the auto was the exclusive cause of all this, but it sure had a lot to do with it. Nor do I say the auto should've been suppressed, or kept for an elite while *hoi polloi* crammed into public transit. But with foresight, assorted entrepreneurs could've done plenty of good and, not so incidentally, made plenty of money.

"For instance, the internal combustion engine was a ghastly mistake. With a proper flash boiler, which wouldn't have been hard to engineer, steam could've edged it out, burning a great deal cleaner. Autos could've been banned in city centers early on. The public would've gone along with that if small, nimble runabouts like our bubbletrikes had been available. This would have helped keep the cities pleasant to live in, and they might have sprawled less.

"I repeat, there wouldn't have been any final answers. No doubt the solutions would've generated problems of their own. Brains by themselves aren't enough. That they are, that's the grand perennial delusion of the intellectuals. But damn it, our brains were meant to be used!

"Now think about your world today. Look around you and think. Tech innovations; changing relationships between institutions; as simple-seeming a question as where to locate a new facility; a human race as fragmented and tumbled-about as pieces in a kaleidoscope." The multi showed that forgotten toy in action. It carried more impact than conventional pictures of fractals and chaotic systems. "Don't you agree we need people who consider these matters, not just in words and numbers and equations and charts, but with their guts?" His metaphor for the entire organism was equally striking. "They can't hand us a planned optimum course, and what they do offer is often wrong and always incomplete. But they make one Jupiter of a difference. Believe me, they do."

Kyra glanced at Lee. He looked too young to be that important. Of course, he was merely one among many. Like the rest, he concentrated on knowledge of a given area, which was why he lived where he did. Most of his overt work he performed at home, on the computer or in his head. But it required more than quantitative data. He must get out, make a point of meeting a variety of folk, cultivate them, develop a sense of their thoughts and feelings, the unspoken as well as what they could express in words.

He needed to be simpático and observant, she thought. Which he pretty clearly was.

Recollection and reflection had shot past while he was saying: "You've had the real adventures."

"Not when I could help it," she laughed.

"An explorer in old days on Earth, Amundsen, claimed that adventure is what happens to the incompetent," Guthrie added.

"You know what I mean," Lee argued in his earnest fashion. "Tahir said it. You, Pilot Davis, you've walked on Mars,"—

(Halfway up Olympus Mons, vision swept across rocky vastness to a subtlety of desert hues, rolling away beneath rose-petal heaven. Hazed by a dust storm that glinted in sharp daylight, a crater reared like a castle guarding the edge of creation.)

—"asteroids, comets,"—

(A stride set her afloat. The worldlet was little more than a darkness, faintly a-sheen where a crest jutted out of shadow, a piece torn from the sky that otherwise encompassed her. Stars filled that night, their multitudes overwhelmed it, unwinking brilliances, colors clear, steel-blue Vega, amber Arcturus, smoldering coal that was Betelgeuse. The Milky Way torrented in frost and silence. Then as she flew, the shrunken sun hove in sight, and her helmet stopped radiance down to save her eyes. She barely descried the outermost flight feathers of its zodiacal wings, and a spark that was a planet.)

—"and beyond."

(The ice of Enceladus glittered as if stars had been strewn over it, from a scarp at the left rim of vision to the near horizon on the right. Few shone overhead. Saturn drowned them, topplingly huge, tawny-bright, emblazoned with cloud-bands and with swirls that were cyclopean storms. Almost edge on, the rings were not the jewel-work she beheld elsewhere but an unfading meteor-streak across her whole viewfield. Two sister moons gleamed, drawn scimitars. Through silence she heard her pulse beating. Tears stung. When she blinked, they caught in her lashes and Saturn made rainbows of them.)

"I've been a tourist twice on Luna, once in L-5," Lee said. "Otherwise the universe outside Earth exists for me only in books, the multiceiver, and the vivifer."

"I was lucky in that regard," Guthrie reminisced. "In my salad days there were still places on Earth where the nights were decently black. Sometimes in the mountains, especially, looking up from my sleeping bag, I'd *feel* how this globe was a tiny dancer amongst a billion billion campfires."

Kyra wondered if that was what had first turned his dreams spaceward. She thought of herself groundside, straining to make out a few wan pinpoints. Too damn many lights, wherever you went. Even in midocean, they fogged the dark and glared down from orbit. Too many people.

"Not that I'm sorry for myself," Lee said hastily. "I know how fortunate I am, to do interesting work well rewarded."

Fortunate indeed, Kyra agreed. Most had had their existence automated into meaninglessness. Before they were born, usually.

"Oh, I wouldn't trade my life for anything," she admitted. Thought ran on: The wild luck was hers and her colleagues'. They could steer ships because those ships were ninety-nine percent robotic. It wouldn't take much development to make that a hundred percent and retire every human spacer. From a purely economic standpoint, no doubt it should already have happened. But Guthrie vetoed it. He must have done so. Nobody else had that power in the confidential councils of Fireball.

Why did he? Romanticism, clinging to the triumphs of the past? A feudal ideal of the obligations of a master to his underlings? Maybe. She suspected that wasn't all. He hadn't lasted till now without being a shrewd realist. Living creatures like her could serve him better when the chips were down than any machines.

No sense losing herself in ponderings grown trite during her voyages alone. Let her pursue this conversation. Incredibly, here she was in a threesome that included the jefe máximo. "But I do envy you a bit, the variety of folk you've met," she confided to Lee. "In space, everybody's High World."

He smiled. "Necessarily."

"That doesn't mean we don't get plenty of rambunctious originals out there," Guthrie said.

"Yes, I know," Lee replied. "Quite apart from the

Lunarians, spacers are bound to think for themselves."

Kyra laughed again. "Often we haven't anything else to do."

Lee studied her a moment before venturing diffidently, "What are your special interests, may I ask?"

"I'd be interested to hear, myself," Guthrie said. "If we're in the soup together, we may as well get acquainted."

Kyra's cheeks heated. While not self-effacing, she had seldom received this kind of close attention. "Assorted sports," she related with a shrug. "Music. I play the sonor and an archaic wind instrument called the recorder, and I sing—mostly ancient ballads—not very tunefully. I read a lot, as you'd expect, and scribble a bit."

That seemed to catch at Lee. "Really? You write? What?"

"Nothing special," Kyra mumbled. "Not for presentation. Doggerel, mainly. Archaic also, sonnets, sestinas, that sort of thing."

Eiko Tamura said they were good. But Eiko was too kindly. Her own work, even rendered into English and thus mutilated, haiku, prose sketches—yes, and the drawings, the calligraphy—sent currents through Kyra's spine and out to her nerve-ends. The two of them got together every time she was in L-5. Communications laser-borne between them were apt to print out several pages long.

Kyra tossed her head. "Ay de mí," she exclaimed as cheerily as she was able, "I'm beginning to sound like one of the jefe's despised intellectuals. Actually, as for a significant activity, I give my computer a mean game of ortho or heisenberg, and my friends an expensive game of poker."

Apparently Lee welcomed lightness. "Poker? The card game? Why, I play that. We, a few others and I, have a little club that meets monthly on the net."

"It's more fun in the flesh," Kyra told him. "Then *we* deal, by turns, not the computer." And they were together, breathing the same air, drinking the same beer, swapping the same shopworn joke phrases.

Lee sighed. "I know, but such an opportunity is rare."

Was she, on a long mission with nothing for company but her ship's half-intelligence and the occasional time-lagged message, ever as lonely as he perhaps was always? "Let's organize a party, once this hooraw is over," she suggested.

"Put me in a robot, and I'd like to sit in," Guthrie said. "I remember some epic games when I was human."

When he was human. What pain prowled under those four words?

Maybe none. He had freely chosen to be what he was. He could undo his being whenever he wanted.

Or could he?

His voice reached after her. "You've wandered off, Davis. Are you okay?"

Crack, she thought, had she been Q-jumping long enough that they noticed? She shook herself. "What you said, sir," she confessed. Truthfully, if not quite candidly: "I was reminded of the history you've seen and, yes, been. It, bueno, rushed over me."

"'There's rosemary,'" he murmured, "'that's for remembrance; pray you, love, remember; and there is pansies, that's for thoughts.'"

"Hamlet?" she blurted in startlement.

Did he sound the least bit defensive? "Uh-huh. I'm not the unalloyed bullhead they take me for. Back then, too, I did my share of reading. It wasn't the fashionable stuff, no. Shakespeare, Homer, Cervantes, they might be acceptable, if outmoded, but Kipling, Conrad, MacDonald, Heinlein, that ilk, they were insensitive reactionaries. Or racists or sexists or whatever the current swear word was. You see, they dealt with things that mattered."

Kyra wondered what inputs he enjoyed these days. Lee must have learned something about that.

The intuitionist yawned. "Excuse me," he said.

"A natural thing to do," Guthrie assured him, "and not just because I'm maundering on."

"It's fascinating," Kyra said. At once: "I'm not trying to kowtow, sir."

"I know," Guthrie replied. "But Bob's right. Or his body is, whatever his forebrain supposes. You need rest, you two, if you're to be fit for anything tomorrow."

"And you, sir?"

"Likewise." How Guthrie would pass the night, he left unspoken.

Talk survived a span longer, increasingly desultory, decreasingly informative. It was Kyra who took the initiative. "Bueno, I'm totalmente outgewashed." She rose. "Ho for that promised shower, and eight or nine hours of the best. Unless you'd rather go first, Bob?" They had gotten on first-name terms. Guthrie was still "jefe," but for her the title had gained a certain comfortableness.

"No, gracias," Lee said. "I have an idea about what we should do that I want to mull over for a few minutes."

"Okay, I'll keep my mouth shut," Guthrie offered—the mouth he no longer had.

A cataract of hot water was sheer hedonism. Kyra wallowed. As she toweled herself, she luxuriated in the steam she inhaled.

Coming forth aglow, she saw Lee's face. Instantly he looked away, as if something had caught his eye. Amused, she glanced at his lap. Yes. She'd forgotten how the Avantists frowned on nudity and forbade it in public. Sensuality of any kind distracted humans from what should be their pleasure as well as their duty, to order their minds so that they and their descendants might build the rational society which would be the germ of the Noösphere.

Poor Bob. He couldn't altogether resist the creed, surrounded by it. Besides, Xuan's system had its attractions. If nothing else, it embodied the same sociodynamic matrices with which he worked, and added more.

She hastened to get into bed, under cover. "Buenas noches," she said, and closed her eyes. She kept them closed while he visited the cubicle, returned, switched off the light, and cautiously lay down. She saw and felt him breathe.

Temptation stirred. It had been quite a while. But no. A bad idea, under these conditions. Maybe later. He really was rather sweet.

Too much so, too gentle? He'd shown himself plenty brave, but that didn't rule out an inner tenderness which might prove fatally disadvantaging. After all, while he had spent his life in North America, lived and worked among its citizens, he was Fireball. She suspected, from his style, that he too was Fireball born and raised. Then probably all the people were whom he felt closest to. He might join them over the phone more often than in the flesh, but they were his amigos, his true compadres; and he knew that troth worked both ways and if trouble came upon him he would have the mighty company at his back. So he could afford a certain trustfulness that the ordinary North American no longer could.

This situation had brought on a great deal of the conflict, Kyra mused. There was always some friction between Fireball and every government, even Ecuador's. No government liked any of those over whom it claimed authority bearing a deeper allegiance to an outside power than to its own politicians and caudillos. Most could tolerate that, however, especially the democratic ones. It didn't threaten them any more than did allegiances to a worldwide religion or a worldwide interest group. But Avantism, which wanted to organize everything—ultimately, all human minds—according to Xuan's doctrine, Avantism was seriously inconvenienced by the daily presence of a system that was different and that flourished.

Yes, Fireball was altogether different, the creation of a rambunctious individualist whose machine ghost continued to rule over it. More than a set of profit-making enterprises, it was a society, a way of thinking and living—a nation, Dad said once. A nation whose folk were allowed, encouraged, to think, speak, act for themselves, yet which bound them together in loyalties stronger than law. A nation whose head set an example utterly noneconomic, nonaltruistic, nonrational, and was cheered for it, when he not only sponsored missions to the stars, which was justifiable as scientific research, but went to Alpha Centauri in person. (Bueno, as a copy of himself, but it came to the same thing.) It wasn't as if yonder planet Demeter promised the slightest material gain for anybody at any time before its doom came upon it.

Still, the Avantists had managed. Fireball didn't actively try to subvert them, and they depended on Fireball as much as Earth in general did. The relationship was uneasy, but it worked after a fashion. Then why had the Avantists suddenly lashed out? Why, first, their occupation of North American headquarters, and now of everything Fireball had within their jurisdiction?

Because they'd learned about Guthrie's duplicate and wanted it for their own purposes, and one thing led to another. But surely this was a desperate move.

They *were* desperate, Kyra thought.

They were totalitarians. Hitherto she had not quite appreciated what that meant. It had been something in her history lessons when she was a schoolgirl. Oh, she heard analogies drawn between the Avantists and the Jin Dynasty, the Incas, the Communists, and so forth, but it had seemed pretty abstract. She heard of abuses, and had once met a victim who'd escaped to Brazil. (He had been a physicist, rather reckless in expressing his opinions. After what had been done to his brain, he was taking any kind of menial work he could get.) But in several other countries on Earth, dissenters also flew a dangerous orbit.

She should have asked her parents more carefully just why they had moved to Russia. She should have asked herself just why any country needed to make ideological nonconformity a crime, and maintain a Security Police against it, and send offenders to prison or to revision treatment. Then she would have understood beforehand how this government had cornered itself.

Measures like that were necessary if you were to march your people into the paradise your system promised them; but in today's world you couldn't keep it up forever. A global, no, interplanetary economy required they go back and forth across your borders, thousands and thousands every day; an interplanetary communications net kept them awash in information from abroad; they saw they were being ordered about with little benefit, and they saw that elsewhere were more freedom and prosperity. They grew disillusioned. Some of them muttered complaints, and you labelled such persons Chaotics, reactionaries who would fain throw history back into randomness. Did certain among these begin secretly gathering weapons and plotting revolution?

Kyra didn't know. She simply thought that the Avantists must have stumbled on an opportunity for a wild, daring gamble, and taken it because it was their last chance. Which didn't mean they couldn't do a lot of killing and wasting before they went under. It didn't even mean they couldn't win their bet and take charge of the whole human race. Far-fetched, no doubt, but possible.

Infierno! She was making herself wakeful. To what purpose? None. Relax. What she needed was a night's rest. Subvocally she recited the mantra that should put her to sleep.

5

"DATELINE FUTURO," RATTLED from the newscaster's lips. "Yesterday the government seized all properties of Fireball Enterprises in the North American Union. Militia are in occupation and Security Police units have entered the key facilities." Scenes flashed by. Northeast Integrate, the World Trade Center shining renovated like an island amidst reefs and wreckage, flitters hovering above, troops and guns on the roof. Toronto Compound, Kyra's birth home, uniformed men standing guard along a street of neat little dwellings while children passed anxiously on their way back from school. Southwest Energy Central, a desert forested with receivers that waited for Moonrise and the power they would drink, armored vehicles now squatting beneath them. Kamehameha Spaceport, a glimpse of blue sea and white surf, a ship tall on her pad, several technicians herded from her by a squad whose hands brushed holstered shock guns.

What a mierda background for breakfast, Kyra thought. Nonetheless she tucked the food away. No telling when her next chance would come. Lee picked at his. On the end of the table, Guthrie watched, armored in the impassivity of his box.

"The company's operations throughout this country are suspended. However, the official statement expressed hope that they can resume shortly. It declared that this move had, quote, 'the full agreement of Fireball executives at the highest level,' close quote. That comes as an added surprise, after many years of growing difficulties between the government and a number of giant international firms, especially Fireball."

Especially indeed, Kyra thought. Without Guthrie's lead, which must have included plenty of hidden pressure and connivance, the others would long since have truckled.

His mutter chilled her: "That settles it. They have definitely got my duplicate and they've worked him over. Poor bastard."

Lee raised his head. "Won't your officers suspect?" he asked.

"They may," Guthrie answered, "though only two of my people besides me now know where he was, and they've no reason thus far to think he isn't there yet. I didn't myself, remember, till too late. If and when anti-Guthrie comes out into the open, he's going to be almighty convincing."

"—speaking from the Directive Office, President Manuel Escobedo Corrigan."

The image that appeared in the screen was handsome, silver-haired, sonorous. "Citizens, attention! I have an important announcement. First let me make clear that there is no cause for alarm. Acting in your best interests, your government is taking measures against a danger to your very lives. In the course of doing so, we will terminate a conflict that has become intolerable. Few persons will be directly affected, except that society will benefit enormously. Meanwhile, all are entitled to information. Listen carefully. Hear the truth. False rumors may circulate. Properly instructed, you will be able to discredit them, denounce them, and report anyone who persists in them.

"By the authority vested in me, and under the wise

guidance of the Advisory Synod, I have ordered seizure of all possessions in this country of that company known as Fireball Enterprises. Suspicion has become certainty. Your Security Police have found that over the years, this whole vast organization has been infiltrated by Chaotic terrorists. Their end is nothing less than the violent overthrow of your government. Their means, if carried through, would bring millionfold deaths, nationwide devastation, and immeasurable suffering. We must forestall them. We must track down each last one of them, arrest him in his evil work, and bring him to rehabilitation—to justice.

"You will recall the seeming accident that ruined the database in Midwestern Security Center with a powerful electromagnetic pulse. It would have gravely hampered police operations throughout that area. Fortunately, your Security Police had unearthed some clues in advance. They did not know precisely what was to happen, but as a precaution they transmitted duplicate files elsewhere. When the event struck, they were prompt to act. They found it was no accident, but sabotage. They found, as they already suspected, that employees of Fireball were among those responsible."

Kyra threw a glance at Guthrie. He saw and rumbled, "No, of course we had nothing to do with it. Don't you suppose I'd make damn sure all our people in a screwed-up country like this, who might be in a position to do something unusual, were sane and sober? Why the hell should we pull such a stupid stunt, anyway? And how do you know the thing ever even happened? We had only the government's word for it, and they brushed aside our offer to help investigate."

A manufactured excuse to enter and ransack the building in which the Sepo had learned that the other Guthrie lay—Kyra turned her attention back to Escobedo. "—cannot go into detail," the president was saying. "Criminals and subversives must not be informed of our detective methods. But rest assured, my fellow citizens, when the task has been completed, you shall know the results."

He went quite solemn. "I must be frank with you. I will not, I may not hide from you that there will be many difficult, yes, dangerous moments in the near future. We are dealing with a huge and powerful organization that has always been hostile to the ideals of Avantism. Let me explain. Let me give you once again the background, though you be familiar with it, in order that I may then share with you the hope that stands bright before us.

"During the past two centuries, Fireball Enterprises has grown until its operations span the Solar System, reach beyond, and at the same time probe into the vitals of every country on Earth. It is more than a spaceship line; its holdings include everything from extraterrestrial mines and manufacturing plants to planetside freight services, from scientific foundations to traders in luxury goods. It maintains whole communities under its own laws, raising generation after generation in primary devotion to itself, and deals with true governments on virtually equal terms. Yet it is not even a corporation, except in a purely technical sense. It is a private organization, tightly controlled, dedicated to profit but not above interference with politics, disdaining any national laws that inconvenience it."

Escobedo smiled. His tone mellowed. "Today, however, I am not denouncing Fireball as such. Instead, I am happy to say that a new order of things is beginning. We are near the end of troubles that have worsened ever since the Avantist Association took leadership of this great country. Mark well, I do *not* accuse Fireball's directors of criminality, antisocial intent, or even nescience. Words on either side often grew heated. But analytically observed, as Xuan would have had us do, it was a conflict of world-views. If they do not agree that our restructuring of North American society is correct, if they do not share our billion-year vision of mind evolving toward the Omega, then it has been quite natural for them to obstruct.

"And so, protected by the notorious Planetary Protocols, employees continued, also among us, to live in practically autonomous compounds, send their children to company schools for company indoctrination, and subject citizens whom they met to incorrect arguments. The Juneau rioting, which claimed thirty-seven lives, was only the most conspicuous consequence of this inflammation."

"Horse shit," Guthrie muttered. "Alaskans remember better than most what it was like being free. They didn't want a correction center built in their back yard, and somehow a rumor got started that the Russians would come over and join them."

"From abroad," Escobedo declared, "high Fireball officials issued pronunciamentos hostile at best, incendiary at worst. The company embargoed sale within the Union of security-related materials. Again and again, employees helped fugitive subversives to escape abroad."

"A bit of truth there, for a change," Guthrie remarked.

"But I repeat, this was inevitable," Escobedo said, almost compassionately. "It was like many a conflict in the past between opposing forces, equally sincere—Christians versus pagans, astronomers versus astrologers, democrats versus royalists, liberators versus imperialists."

His tone became stern again. "Now, as I told you, we have discovered that certain persons in the lower echelons of Fireball became so fanatically full of hatred that they entered into actual criminal conspiracy. They made contact with Chaotic terrorists who have long been waiting for a chance to strike deadly blows at you, the North American people. These individuals in Fireball aided and abetted the terrorists. They helped Chaotics get employment in the company, until today it is riddled with infiltration.

"The danger this poses is obviously enormous. Fireball fills key positions in the economy of the Union, as it does in every country on Earth. Its potential power to commit sabotage is virtually unlimited. In our modern world, we all depend for our lives on a frighteningly vulnerable network of high-technology services, as well as materials and energy from space. Let any of this be disrupted, and we shall immediately stand on the brink of starvation, chaos, mass death. Ruthless enemies, desiring still quicker collapse, could wreck our transportation and communication facilities here on the ground. The terrorists, armed and ready, would take mastery of the ruins.

"This is why your government has occupied everything in our country that is Fireball's. Were we able, we would have occupied everything everywhere. I have instructed North America's representatives in the World Federation to call for action by the Peace Authority. For surely chaos in a nation as large as ours menaces the entire human species."

He smiled afresh. "Now for the good news. I said before that the directors of Fireball, and indeed most of its personnel, are not evil. Misguided, we know. Negativistic, selfish, greedy, yes, many among them—I do not say all. But they are not insane. They are not stupid. They realize full well how much they too would lose by a breakdown of order. They accept that the Chaotics are enemies not only of Avantist Xuanism, but of civilization as a whole. They were simply not aware of the extent to which these enemies have infected their own quasi-nation.

"Once your Security Police had access to Fireball headquarters, they went to work. Brilliantly they used the most advanced investigative techniques. Piece by piece, they uncovered the basic truth. Much remains to be done, of course, but we now know what it is that we must do. When we had this information, we approached certain key leaders of Fireball, in deepest confidence. They were appalled. They agreed that full occupation was necessary. The Chaotics must be rooted out to the last cancerous cell. It is for the company's health almost as much as for our own.

"Citizens, I tell you that this development means more than immediate safety. It points toward an entire, positive future. I do not expect the officers of Fireball or of the other corporations that follow its lead—I do not expect them to embrace correct doctrine overnight. They will continue to pursue their self-interest, and the interest of their organizations, for a long time to come. However, I do believe they are starting to see that those interests are not really opposed to a rational ordering of society. I do look forward to an era of growing cooperation—"

The voice went on. "Turn the sound off," Guthrie said. "The rest will be duck-billed platitudes."

Kyra obeyed. She caught the idea, if not the figure of speech. "Yes, he's just a figurehead, isn't he? The whole government is."

"Not quite, but close enough for present purposes. Hm. Those North American execs of ours, Reynaldo, Langford, Rappaport—how many more?—what about them? I hope to Christ they're all right."

"I shouldn't think the Avantists would harm them, sir," Lee said. "That would make needless antagonism. Probably several key persons are in 'protective custody,' but not otherwise abused, and that's simply to keep them incommunicado. Then nobody can be sure whether some of them have in fact agreed that the occupation is right and necessary."

"How believable will that be, and for how long?" Kyra wondered. "*Would* any of them sit still and mum, given a choice?"

"No," Guthrie replied, "but the situation can be maintained for several days, after which the prisoners can be released and it won't matter. Any little inconsistencies between their stories and Escobedo's will be overlooked. Till then, Sayre's gang needn't expect too much trouble from those they've left free. The common-sensical thing for all consortes to do right now is sit tight and wait for word from me."

As if to confirm, the president's message ended and a new image appeared. Kyra restored the sound and heard: "Dateline Quito. At Fireball's general headquarters here, Director-at-large Dolores Almeida Candamo issued a statement calling this a most perturbing development. She had no other comment pending further information, except that she and her associates are in touch with other offices on Earth and in space. None of these have offered any comment either."

"Yeah," Guthrie growled approvingly. "Sitting tight."

"—in the Assembly of the World Federation," said the newscaster, "Colin Small of Caribbea responded to the North American call for Peace Authority intervention."

The image became that of a thin ebony man whose lip movements showed the English was his own: "With due respect for my distinguished friend from the Union, I submit that this request is not what it pretends to be. It is for propaganda purposes, and perhaps for the injury of Fireball. Nations are sovereign within their own borders while they observe the Covenant. Therefore the government of the North American Union can restrict any Peace Authority forces to whatever sites and actions it sees fit. Its allegations are vague and unproven. If it honestly wants help, let it bring formal charges of activity military, genocidal, harmful to the common environment, or unreasonably in hindrance of traffic or communications. Let such charges be examined by the appropriate committee, and found probable. Then world law enforcement can move against Fireball—or, conceivably, against the government of the North American Union. I do not expect either will happen. Legally, at least, this is a dispute between a national government and a private but international organization."

The scene changed to an economist, who answered questions put by the newscaster. Yes, North America depended on materials and energy from space; all Earth did. Yes, Fireball was the primary provider of these. Yes, if it halted service, the country would soon be seriously inconvenienced. No, there would not be famine or any such thing; the Federation and the Authority would see to that. Besides, the odds were against Fireball ever taking such a drastic measure. Remember, the cost to it would be incalculable, in lost revenues and, far more, in relationships with the rest of the world. It was more vulnerable than one might think. Remember, it was not really a nation, however arrogantly it behaved. It did not possess even the minimum peacekeeping armament to which a nation was entitled, let alone the arsenals of the Authority —Kyra, Lee, and Guthrie listened with less than half an ear.

"Remarkable, so much," Kyra said.

"What do you mean?" Lee asked.

"That official multiception would carry any part of Small's speech. I've met him, at a space development conference. We talked, and went partying, and since then we've swapped occasional letters. He's on our side."

"Bueno, he couldn't come straight out and declare that, in his position, could he? I think the editor of this show is pretty smart. We've seen the exact snippet that conveys an impression of unbiased reporting."

"They're good at that," grumbled Guthrie. "Everybody in communications is. With the result that the average man has no way of telling what's real and what's come out of a studio."

"That's not quite right, sir," Lee argued. "The sheer volume of information, true as well as false—"

"Yeah, that and international traffic, they do make a totalitarian state impossible to maintain in the long run, unless somehow it took over the whole Solar System. They're what keep an idea of freedom alive here, and give Chaotics the hope they need if they aren't going to give up and become Avantists themselves."

"Who are they?" Kyra asked. "I thought 'Chaotic' was just a government swear word for dissenters."

"Which they proudly adopted," Guthrie said. "Mostly they're harmless malcontents."

"But not all? Are some of them really terrorists waiting for a chance?"

"That could be another swear word," Guthrie replied.

Kyra got a feeling he didn't want to say more about this. "What do you expect Fireball will do, sir?"

"I told you. Nothing much, immediately. Play close to the vest till more cards come down. Maybe with some local exceptions. We aren't a monolith, you know." A knock sounded. "Quick, stash me. In the pack, might as well."

His companions did, and admitted Tahir. The sheikh carried a bag stuffed full of fabric. His visage was drawn— Kyra guessed he had been up most of the night—but he stood straight, gave crisp greeting, and went directly to business.

"Sepo are here, uniformed and, undoubtedly, in plain clothes. They walk the halls, although not yet these, and watch at every portal. They carry electronic equipment. Nevertheless, *insh'llah*, I have made arrangements that should get you past them. Here are women's clothes for you, Sr. Lee. Veiled and in my company, you ought not to be molested. The police will not wish to magnify their task by infuriating residents, especially those who are not entirely poor and powerless; and it is well known how we Believers feel about our women." A crooked grin. "Of course, you must practice the gait and the manners. I will rehearse you until, when we go forth, passersby will wonder what this old scoundrel has been doing of late."

Lee reddened a bit. "Mil gracias, sir," he said. "Uh, *afy aleyk, el-afy.*" He gestured at the pack where it lay. "But what about this? We've got to get it out. It's more important than we are, by orders of magnitude."

"I have gathered that." Tahir ran fingers through his beard and gazed beyond the walls around him. "I do not wish to know what it is. You have called it a special computer; let that suffice. I do know its size, and have made arrangements. At the proper time, an ambulance will arrive and the crew will bring a life support casket up to us. It has enough space to spare that you can place your . . . object inside while everyone else looks away. I trust it is fluid-proof."

Kyra drew a sharp breath. Vision sprang into her head, a coffinlike box, its crusting of containers, tubes, valves, pumps, meters, cables, computer, manual controls, and the engineering underneath. Yes, all that metal, all that electrical and chemical and isotopic activity, would for sure mask Guthrie from any detectors.

"But won't they check whether you've actually got a patient inside?" Lee fretted.

"There will be one." The fugitives saw bleakness. "A son of mine is willing to be drugged. The simulation of a comatose stroke victim will be quite good, even to encephalographic tracings. I do not expect the Sepo will call a physician to inspect closer."

"But that, that's incredible, sir," Kyra stammered. "You don't owe us—this much—"

Tahir gave her a look. "I have an impression that a duty has fallen upon us." Somberness turned impersonal. "Perhaps later they will think to check whether this man was indeed brought to Ibn Daoud Hospital. Records will show that he was, biorepair went well, and he was soon discharged to recuperate at home."

Islamic solidarity? wondered Kyra. Could it be that reliable? Mightn't Tahir have Chaotic connections? Experienced undergrounders could do a better job on a database, couldn't they? Yes, it made sense. Of necessity, Avantism gave official tolerance to traditional faiths and lifeways, but it also gave them a hard time and in the long run it would destroy them. Thus the Chaotics, whoever they were, became natural allies of theirs.

"At the hospital you must reclaim your burden and leave us," Tahir told Lee. "We can do nothing further for you."

"We understand. We hope someday we can explain exactly how much you did do."

Unease stirred. "Excuse me," Kyra said, "but what about me? I need out too!"

"You can simply leave, can you not?" Tahir replied. "Have they reason known to them for stopping you?"

"N-no, I don't suppose so."

"Best you start now. That will spread the risk. Have you someplace, preferably outside this country, where you can go?"

The thought cataracted over her. It was as if she saw the house on Lake Ilmen, blue and white above her mother's rosebeds, nestled by the glittering water in a grove of birches. Leaves rustled, sunlight and shadow danced in them, the breeze smelled of greenwood, here was a fragment of Old Earth and not in a quivira but real, real . . . She had ample funds. Get home, go to Russian HQ and let them know what the situation was—

Shock followed. No! How in MacCannon's name could she have spent a microsecond on such an excuse to cut and run? She was Fireball. She had given and taken troth, like her parents and two of her grandparents before her.

She stiffened her shoulders. "Yes, but I'd better not," she said. "We've got to get this thing we're carrying to safety." Once she had Guthrie well hidden, maybe then she should flit with her information. Maybe then Fireball could mount a rescue operation, or appeal to the Peace Authority, or something. But first and foremost was keeping him from the hands of the reprogrammers. "That means me. Bob— They'll be after Sr. Lee with everything they've got. No, they already are. I don't see how any disguise can save him for long."

She forced herself to meet the young man's eyes while she spoke. Had he slept at all, knowing what could happen to him at the hands of the Sepo? His face hardly stirred.

"True," he said quietly. "We'll rendezvous and I'll turn the object over to you."

"Where?" They hadn't discussed that, as weary and shaken as they were yesterday and as distracted this morning. Amateurs. Why hadn't Guthrie reminded them? Because he figured there was little point in it before they knew better what they would be doing? She'd rather believe that than that his own wits had failed him.

"Write it down," Tahir urged. "I should not hear." He turned his back.

"Good thinking, sir." Lee swung around and sat down at the terminal. Kyra went to stand behind him. She saw how the sinews were tensed in his hands. But the fingers keyed flowingly. Words jumped onto the screen. *Do you know Quark Fair?*

Almost, she replied aloud, then leaned over and reached past him. *Only by a multi program or two. I have never been there.* At the time they left this area, her parents deemed her still too young for that sort of thing. She felt how her right breast pressed lightly on his shoulder.

We can disappear into it for a while. The hand stumbled ever so slightly. *And I can get something that can scarcely be gotten anyplace else.*

Where in Quark Fair? she wrote.

She saw a wry smile. *I have not exactly been an habitué, but I have visited occasionally and collected information from other sources, because it has some regional importance. Go to Mama Lakshmi's Tea House. Take a room and wait for me. Give a false name so they can tell me which room. They will ask no questions but they will want cash.*

A lodging that didn't enter guest ident in the police database—in North America? Its existence couldn't be unknown to them. But those were the civil police. Quite bribable, she'd heard. As for the Sepo and the real authorities, bueno, they'd allowed Quark Fair to continue all these years, no matter how foul a plague spot they officially called it. A commentator on a program she'd once watched had said that from their viewpoint, it gave atavistic impulses and incorrigibility an outlet in a geographically contained space. Sometimes the police raided it. After a day or two you couldn't tell that anything had happened.

Thumb-at-the-nose naughtiness tingled in Kyra. She searched her memory. A name, a name, preferably no association with her— On a long space haul, ransacking your recreational database, you often turned up obscure old works. *I will be Emma Bovary.*

Tell them you are expecting John Smith. Lee's grin stretched. *It is conventional.*

He wiped the file and rose. "Muy bien, we have decided, sir," he said to Tahir. "You and I had better get busy." He turned to Kyra. "Have a care, amiga. Buena suerte."

"And a clean orbit for you, consorte," she answered, as if he were also a spacer. They clasped hands.

Tahir raised his right palm. *"Fî amân illah,"* he bade her gravely. "Go in the peace of the Lord."

Not knowing what else to do, she gave him the salute due a commanding officer. "Gracias for everything," she said clumsily, and left them. For the first several seconds she was mainly conscious of wishing she had his trust in Providence.

But no, that would mean setting reason aside, wouldn't it? She entered the corridor and its crowd. Awareness shifted outward. Again stares prickled her skin. If only Tahir had thought to bring her clothes less brazen, less conspicuous. If only she had thought to ask for them.

Bueno, probably the Sepo wouldn't get around to rummaging this quarter for some days yet, if ever. By that time she'd have blurred in memory, an outsider among many, no special date or anything attached. Not that a dweller would likely volunteer information if he did recall. Just the same, Kyra grabbed the first fahrweg she spied.

On the way out, she made herself plan ahead. Thus every uniform she saw brought only a nasty little jerk in her pulse, a gulpdown of dry cotton in her throat. Worst was passing from courtyard to street. They stood there at the gate, two big men in tan on either side. One of each pair kept eyes on the instrument he gripped, the other's raked all who went by. Those were fewer than yesterday. Word must have gotten around. Kyra held her mind to a mantra.

But then she was past, lost in the throng, under a sky turned mild and sunny. Free!

For a while. If she wanted the while to last, she should keep moving.

Near the vehicle rack she found a public information outlet. Setting her informant, she stepped into the booth and paid it with a coin. Not until she had drawn the particulars she wanted did she notice how hard her wrist had pressed the contact. With a rueful small laugh she proceeded to her bubbletrike, ransomed it, and drove off.

She must get rid of her Hawaiian garb, which marked her. What she needed was a medium-priced tailor shop some distance hence. The directions the informant spelled out led to an address in the Tonawanda area. The district was venerable, mostly brick buildings a few stories high and some detached houses that survived as tenements. Sidewalks were uncrowded, pedestrians went quietly. Full-size vehicles murmured along the pavement between, allowed because they were few. At first Kyra felt peacefulness. The giants beyond these roofs seemed remote, miragelike; the babel around them had dwindled to a susurrus barely heard.

Then she looked closer and saw crumbling masonry, store displays sparse, grimy hyalon, shabby clothes, furtive glances at her the stranger. Grass grew rank while the leaves of trees were unseasonably yellowed in a park where two men snored by an empty bottle. When she was a child, she had not known of anything like this anywhere in the whole region, in spite of the prolonged hard times and unrest that had aided the Avantists to power.

An occasional place still seemed in fairly good shape, a factory, a genetic clinic, two or three restaurants, the kind of establishments that could draw custom from a wide radius but, being of modest size, could not afford to move into higher-rent locations. The tailor's was one such. Its interior was neat and clean, the live clerk who greeted her polite and well-clad. He offered assistance, explaining apologetically that the equipment was obsolete and the programming didn't include the newest international fashions.

"Never mind," Kyra said. "I remember shops like this from when I was a kid." She didn't, but her profession had whetted the innate talent for mechanics that it required. "What I'm after is just a few serviceable garments."

Still, alone in the design room, stripped and measured, she took her time. It was fun, it was therapy, projecting this and that image onto the life-size hologram of herself, watching appearances shift as the computer modified patterns to fit, keying in her alterations and seeing them adapted. Four changes of underwear should do. Two pair slacks, perlux, one black and close-fitting, one blue and flare-bottomed with a thin red stripe down either leg. A stout gray work shirt, a more feminine apricot iridon tunic, a blouse fluffy and puffy in white luna but—she made sure—allowing free movement. A full tigryl skirt, calf length. A pale green cloak with hood, in case of rain. That gave her a variety of combinations which should fit most occasions. As a standard item she chose a carryall for them and her former apparel, convertible to a daypack.

Her finger pressed *Complete*. The price flashed onto the screen. It exceeded the cash she had with her. Reluctantly, she debited her account. If the Sepo somehow came to suspect her and ordered a data retrieval, here was a footprint left for them to find.

Bueno, with luck it wouldn't happen, at least not for days during which she'd be running. And she didn't suppose that even in Avantist North America the system had recorded the specs of her purchase. Its capacity was enormous but finite. Minor data like the transaction itself were doubtless expunged after some such period as three years.

A statute of limitations. She giggled.

No, stay serious. Use the time while the machines worked to think further about her situation, and Guthrie's. Cash didn't leave tracks. Dollars were no longer convertible, but nevertheless preferable till she'd escaped across the border. Ucus were eagerly accepted, of course, but tended to fix her in memory. If she went to a bank and swapped, that would get into the database and could make somebody wonder why she'd done it. Yet she needed more bills and coins. And if she could lay a false trail—

A carillon rang, irritatingly jolly. A rack slid out, bearing her new clothes. She tried them on, selected the tunic and black pants, packed the rest, and left. "I hope you're pleased, Miz Davis," said the clerk. His smile looked smarmy, and why had he asked his terminal for her name? She hoped he hadn't bollixed the privacy circuit and peeped at her.

"Yes, this will do," she answered curtly.

"Are you from space?"

She tensed. "What makes you think that?" Unauthorized, he could not have called up her address. Anyway, Earthside it was merely a reroute program in Quito.

"Oh, your . . . appearance, miz. You sound North American but you bear yourself . . . proudly. I always wanted to visit space."

She heard wistfulness and felt a bit of pity. Had he ever traveled at all? The honorific he used was rare outside these parts.

Travel— Your multi gave you holographic audiovisuals. If you could afford a vivifer attachment, you could have extra sensations. But to see and hear Tychopolis Gardens in the round, feel a whiff suggestive of perfumes pouring from the giant flowers, get tricks played on your nerves to hint at the kinesthesia of low-weight—it wasn't just impoverished, it was passive. You were not there, you did not go freely about, nothing happened that wasn't programmed into the show.

She recognized an opportunity. "Yes, I work skyside." No sense in being specific. Pilots had more glamour than was wise for her. She sighed, hoping it came across believably. "On vacation, but I'm afraid that's being cut short. The news this morning."

His eyes widened. "About the Fireball company? Do you work for *them?*"

"All outfits with interests in space are affected," she said truthfully if ambiguously. "I'd better report to my company's nearest agent outside this country. In person; com lines seem . . . tied up." Maybe he'd understand that had to be a euphemism. "Bueno, I always wanted to visit Québec. But I needed suitable clothes, no?"

"Yes. Yes, of course. Beautifully chosen and designed, Miz Davis. I'm sorry your vacation was interrupted, but have a nice trip. Come again anytime, por favor. Muchas gracias." She left him jittery in his doorway and drove off.

So. If the Sepo did check, they should get the idea from him that she had headed northeastward. The border wasn't sealed or the 'cast would have said so. Given as many people as crossed every day in either direction, at a large number of different points, mass screening of them couldn't amount to more than an identicard scan, whether before they boarded aircraft or when they came to the border by ground transport. No record would be kept unless something unusual turned up. Probably everyone who had anything with them that might be a neural network was now being stopped and searched. Thus, if the Sepo ran a data retrieval on her and found nothing about her exiting, the reasonable conclusion should be that she'd simply panicked and bolted, and was of no further interest to them.

A notation that she had today bought a substantial amount of dollars would contradict this. However— She nodded to herself. She was a rookie in Erie-Ontario, after her years of absence, but she'd been in other cities where the poor were plentiful.

Pulling over, she put a map of the Quark Fair area on the trike's screen and studied it. If she remembered aright what she had heard as a child, the section was then a rough circle about a klick in diameter. It had since shrunk little if at all. At first reconstruction had moved rapidly into the devastation left by the Buffalo meteorite strike. But the Second Republic soon started breaking down in earnest, and nobody respectable had a chance to do anything further. When the Avantists took over, they promised quick rehabilitation. They had promised many things. Kyra shrugged and proceeded.

A bus station lay about two kilometers from her goal. She racked the trike and called the rental agency as Lee had suggested yesterday. Speaking breathlessly, she tossed in the superfluous explanation that she must catch the first available carrier to Montréal. Just in case. Bag on back, she cast about afoot till she found a bank. Slotting her ident into a teller, she instructed it *1000 Universal Currency Units in twenties.*

A total of 430 is available in fifties and hundreds, it flashed. *Do you wish to wait for delivery?*

Damn! This was a good-sized branch. Had inefficiency become so pervasive? *Cancel,* she ordered. *430 Universal Currency Units.* When the envelope popped out, she took care to count the bills before she slipped them into the guard pocket of her tunic.

Onward, now. The neighborhood was as raucous as that around the Blue Theta. Then abruptly, when she crossed a street, she found herself amidst total decay. Broken windows, patched over, were like wounds on sooty walls. Doorways gaped on hollowness. Graffiti misspelled words of rage or obscenity. They were brighter colored than the few shop signs. A beggar sat ragged on the walk, hand out, chanting over and over his litany of hard luck. Two shapeless women squabbled wearily. Three children ran from an alley to pluck at her garments and shriek for alms. She strode on, ignoring them, for otherwise she would instantly be caught in a horde. An old man lurched past, staring into air, mumbling. Four young men hooted after her. A large man bound the opposite way veered as if to intercept. His face bristled; she smelled him two meters off. She drew a breath and prepared her body. Aikido was a favorite activity of hers, though the thought of using it in anger tasted foul.

He squinted, changed course, and went by. She heard him spit. No matter. Would politicians never learn that what an economy managed by the state mainly produced was poverty?

Not that unrestricted free enterprise guaranteed wealth. Racket waxed ahead, a hubbub, shouts, horns, drumpulse, machinery, noises less easily knowable. Kyra rounded a corner, walked one more block, and entered Quark Fair.

This part was a flea market. Already now at noontide it pullulated. Many vendors sat on the ground, perhaps with a scrap of rug between buttocks and cracked pavement, their wares spread before them. Some had a chair and table. Some had thrown pieces of plastic siding together to make booths. They seemed to be of every breed, male and female, youthful and elderly and in hardened middle age, clean and dirty, plump and bony, cheerful and woeful. Chanted praises of what they had to offer cut through the chatter and footfalls of visitors who wandered among the displays, chaffered, bought, sold, traded. Those were of nearly every condition in life; not only Low Worlders came here. They milled in more hundreds than Kyra could estimate. It was unpleasant, being so surrounded and jostled.

Farther away she glimpsed real buildings, mostly shanties, a few larger and more solid. Above them reared the stump of a skyscraper, broken off at the twentieth floor by the impact blast. Rusted and twisted, its skeleton thrust snags above the remnants of walls. Window glass flashed with sunlight; nothing better had replaced the original panes. Everywhere, signs blinked, flared, writhed, luridly hued. Their effect after dark must be gyrocephalic.

A man sidled next to her. He was thin, sallow, clad in a grubby yellow coverall. "Change money?" he asked hoarsely.

Ah, ha. She stopped. He took stance before her. "I give better rate than bank," he proposed.

"How much can you handle?" She expected to deal with several petty operators before she had converted enough.

He tautened. "How much you got?" When she hesitated: "I arrange. Safe, honest, good rate." And never a database entry.

The faster the better, no? What she had drawn, added to what she had from Hawaii, let Kyra say, "A thousand ucus." That wouldn't leave her with much hard cash, but all she needed to do was get out of this wretched country.

"Come." He took her elbow. She wanted to shake his hand off but decided not to.

Threading among the booths, she saw more for sale than clothes, homewares, toys, food, anything cheap. Where had that laser torch come from? What about yonder diamond necklace? Stones so large and clear were expensive to manufacture. In a computer holoscreen, an animation of Petie, half child, half fuzzy bear, played with the operator, who hoped to sell him to somebody who wanted a pet. Interactive programs like that were supposed to be unpiratable, and to go for a stiff price. High-tech safeguards evoked high-tech burglary kits, she guessed.

CASINO GRANDIOSO danced frantically above a big house. "In here," said the man. "My name Edwin." Kyra felt his stare expectant upon her. She kept her mouth shut. His drew tight, but he couldn't very well speak his resentment.

Hung with maroon velvyl, the foyer was a sudden grotto of dim quietness. A girl sat behind a counter. Her face was teen age, her eyes a hundred years old. "We see Sr. Leggatt," Edwin told her. "Got big deal for him."

She nodded, spoke briefly with an intercom, and said, "You're in luck. He's not too busy. Go on in."

They passed through three spacious rooms. As yet, few players were at the tables and machines. Kyra checked her step momentarily before a row of terminals. Fractal patterns filled the screens with eerie beauty. She knew this game. You turned the system chaotic, then tried to bring it to one or another attractor. The payoff depended on which you achieved, if any.

"Nice, hey?" said Edwin. "Play later."

"No, gracias." It was doubtless rigged. Besides, she was hungry.

An armed guard admitted them to the office. It was sumptuously furnished. A multiceiver displayed what might well be real and might even be real-time. A man lay in bed with a metamorph. Her arms and legs were spidery long, her body of eel-like slimness and suppleness; sleek brown fur covered her, and a plumed tail arched around to stroke his back. She trilled.

Metamorph— It was as if Kyra watched the scene through the great innocent eyes of the Keiki Moana, the Sea Children. She turned her head away.

Across his desk, Leggatt was another startling sight. For some reason he chose to be obese. From the bullet head, his black gaze probed at her.

"The lady exchange a thousand ucus," Edwin said, half triumphantly, half obsequiously.

"Oh," said a shrill tenor. "Bueno, bueno. Por favor, be seated, señora." Leggatt switched off the multi. "Care for a smoke, tobacco, marijuana, blend?"

Kyra took the edge of a chair. "No, gracias," she snapped. "Let's just do our business. This . . . caballero mentioned a favorable rate. I want dollars."

"My commission, sir," Edwin whined. "Not forget my commission." He received a glower and shrank back.

"Whatever you wish, señora," Leggatt said, beaming. "Best deal in town, I promise you. Let me see—today's official rate—what I can do for you—" He named a figure.

He must expect Kyra to haggle. She wanted out, and accepted. He covered any surprise with words to the effect of how glad he was to meet someone who understood these matters, while he took the Union money from a wall safe.

"Count it, do," he urged. "No, no, hold your ucus till you're satisfied. This is between amigos, right?" Also, he had that gunjin at the door.

His friendliness did not keep him from examining twice the bills she handed over before he stowed them. Edwin coughed. Leggatt drew a thick wallet out of his robe, peeled off some dollars, gave them into the reaching fingers, and said, "Go."

Edwin scrambled to his feet. "Hyper meeting you, señorita," he chattered. "Any time you—"

"Go," Leggatt directed. Edwin went.

Kyra rose. "Don't be in such a hurry," Leggatt said. "Can I do anything more for you? I like making my clients happy."

"Bueno—" Her stomach twinged. "Could you tell me where to find a place to eat? Nothing elab, only edible and sanitary."

"Why, I can do better than that. Let me take you to lunch. Best food and drink for ten klicks around, even if it is here in the Fair."

"No, I, uh, gracias, but—"

"Really. I insist." Whale-huge, he lumbered erect. "I do insist. We should get acquainted, señora. I like you. I trust we'll do more business in future. What is your name, por favor?"

"It doesn't matter. Look, I have an appointment."

"I *insist.*" He came around the desk and took her arm. The little eyes leveled unblinkingly at her. "Won't take no for an answer. What is your name, now?"

He'd marked her as a stray lamb. This could get ugly. Left to itself, it probably would. Kyra's heart bounced, once, then settled into strong steadiness. Her senses sharpened. She smelled musky perfume on him. Through the walls she heard music bray, brasses and basses. "Bueno, if you put it that way," she said, forcing a smile. "I am—" She checked herself. She'd nearly used the alias she'd given Lee. "Anna Karenina."

"A Russian?" He clearly didn't believe it. However, he led her along. As they left the office he nodded at the guard, who fell into step behind them.

They emerged into clamor. Robe billowing scarlet and gold, Leggatt moved on. People saw who walked at his back and made way. A wake of lessened noise trailed after him. Kyra wondered what help she might get if seized and hauled off. Quite likely none. He talked, a stream: "—yes, marvelous food. They show you the birds, you pick the one you want, and they kill it for you on the spot—" A shooting gallery which they passed advertised live rats for targets.

PALACE OF HORRORS proclaimed a sign on a building. Screens displayed fleeting samples of what you could watch inside, scenes taken immediately after the meteorite strike, scenes from the Capetown Kraal, scenes from Bombay, scenes from old wars and later police actions. Tiny and incongruous nearby, a booth flaunted a poster that promised YOUR FUTURE REVEALED. SCIENTIFIC STOCHASTIC ANALYSIS.

"—private room to relax in," Leggatt said. "Any kind of drug you like, guaranteed pure—"

"Real, real, real!" thundered an amplified voice. "Not a show, not a quivira, the real thing, the true experience! Robots like life! Do it with the finest selection of slut machines in the known universe!"

There had to be some bolt hole. The ruined skyscraper loomed ahead. Above one doorway, blood-red lightning flashes spelled out THE WILDERNESS. Below them glimmered death-blue *Enter at your own risk*.

Kyra swallowed, wet her lips, pointed, and asked, "What's that?"

Leggatt blinked, interrupted. "Hm? Oh, that? You don't know?"

Apparently it was notorious. "I've been away. Far away. I'll . . . tell you later. But what is it?" She turned in its direction.

"Naw, you don't want to go in there," Leggatt said. "It's for nullheads. Two, three people killed every month. Come on." He tugged at her arm, hard.

She applied muscle and skilled motion against him. "I want to know," she replied petulantly.

He yielded. "Bueno, it's for dangerous, uh, activities.

All kinds of recklessness. A robot bull to fight. A swimming basin churned up into storm waves and whirlpools. A glandular-enhanced giant to wrestle, and no guarantee you won't get a broken back. Whirlers to ride, high up, no safety harness. Or climb the girders; they'll be vibrated for you. And so on and so on." He shook his head. "Loco."

"Sounds exciting." Kyra continued to apply her vector.

"Huh? No, wait, what kind of a blinkie are you? Come along!"

His grasp tightened. She heard indignation and saw his jowls flush. He was used to being obeyed. They weren't far from the place. Kyra removed her arm from him, a yank out between fingers and thumb. She sprang aside, whirled about, and ran.

"Ay!" bawled at her back. "Stop! Get 'er, Otto!"

It was as if she felt the boots in pursuit. Would the guard draw his shock gun and fire? She dodged around a bewildered group of tourists, from a South Pacific raft city to judge by their looks and clothes. Hastily, she reached into her pocket for a fistful of dollars. The movement didn't slow her much. A spacer was trained in multiple coordination. A glance aft showed the gunjin losing ground. She slammed to a halt at the entrance and thrust a bill down the slot. A ticket extruded, a door retracted. She grabbed the slip, didn't wait to collect her change, passed through and heard the panel hiss shut.

An attendant stood at a counter in the hall beyond. He was dressed like a Homeric warrior. If he was surprised to see a customer arrive breathing hard, a woman at that, he didn't let on. "Saludos," he greeted. "What is your pleasure?"

"I, I'd like to . . . look around. Maybe I'll find something to do, but . . . mainly I'm interested. Is that all right?"

"Muy bien." He punched her ticket and gave her a pamphlet. "I suggest you read this first. Now, por favor, press your right thumb here." He gestured at a screen. "As you see, it's a waiver of liability. We have medical care on hand, reasonable charge, but—"

"I've heard." She left him. Any instant, Leggatt might send Otto through the door.

Or would he? "Lepton bitch," she imagined him snarling as he waddled off. On the other hand, he might feel offended enough, or curious enough, not to quit at once. Kyra walked onward.

Mural screens down the corridor showed men at war, Assyrians, Hebrews, Romans, vikings, Moors, knights, samurai, Aztecs . . . until at last a Chinese crossed bayonets with a Pathan of the Grand Jihad. They were animations, vivid but too stylized for sadism. The clientele here couldn't really be gyrocephs. The price of admission proved they were well-to-do, therefore well educated, therefore treated early on for any pathologies. Then why did they come? If they craved excitement, surely they could afford a quivira.

She reached a transverse corridor. Escalators went up in three directions. She chose the left at random. On the floor above, a hall curved off, one wall transparent. She went for a look. Beyond was a room where a man, maybe a referee, watched two others who were scarcely more than boys. Clad in tights, they fought with quarterstaffs, blow and parry. Blood mingled with the sweat agleam on their bruised torsos. Those sticks could fracture skulls.

In the next room stood a framework like an inverted L. It was a gallows. Also watched by another, a naked man sprattled a meter off the floor, hanged by the neck. Kyra gasped.

"The doc is supposed to lower him in time," said a voice.

The speaker was lithe, handsome in afro fashion, attired in trunks. Evidently he was on his way somewhere, had seen her appalled, and stopped to proffer an amiable smile. *"Why?"* she faltered.

He shrugged. "Not my pasatiempo. But I'm told the sensations are special. Plus the danger, of course." His regard was frankly inquisitive. "We seldom get women here. Are you after anything particular? Maybe I can help."

"N-no." Kyra clenched her fists. The hanged man's tongue was out of his mouth. "I, I'm simply curious." A yell: "Let him *down!*"

"You could have had a pleasanter introduction," her companion admitted. He scowled. "Crack, it is going on long, isn't it? Let's boost. If he does die, I don't care to watch. He might not be revivable."

Shivering, she matched his stride. "Where are you bound?" she whispered, dry-throated.

He smiled again. "Now that's something you should enjoy seeing. A new attraction. Twelve-meter waterfall into a basin with stakes below the surface. I'll go down it wearing a gillpiece. They change the positions of the stakes every day. Grandissimo."

"Ghastly, I'd call it."

He sounded genuinely puzzled. "What? It's a clean sport. Not like the shark tank. Oh, I wouldn't want you trying it. I wonder if you should have come at all."

"Maybe not." Impulsively, she added, "I've been in danger myself, more than once. It goes with my job. But this is—is—why do you do it?"

They went by a room that seemed empty except for an observer staring aloft. Something in Kyra compelled her to look. The space was three stories high. Under the ceiling stretched a wire. A man was making his way across. No net was beneath him.

Bitterness astonished her: "What else is there, if you've got blood in your veins?"

It was in the nature of the young human male to risk his neck, she thought dizzily. Wasn't it? Or did this that she saw arise from some rebellion of the spirit against—against what?

Her escort calmed. "Besides, my chances are excellent," he said. "I'm not suicidal. This is just a way to be fully alive. Afterward I relax." He turned oddly shy. "Uh, my name's Sam, Samuel Jackson. I'm a junior scientist in protein design. If you care to watch me shoot the fall, I'd be delighted to invite you for dinner. We could talk some more."

Temptation tugged. He was attractive, and his mystique

had the lure of being almost comprehensible. No. Lee, Guthrie, Fireball. "Gracias, I'm sorry, but I can't. Enjoy yourself. Luck be with you." Another hall branched off. She hurried down it.

In an alcove she found seats, took one, and read the pamphlet. It included maps. They showed three exits, well apart. Leggatt would scarcely set his bandidos to watch so many. She could leave.

Somehow that didn't feel quite like a liberation. Was the Wilderness actually evil? It catered to the animal in man, but it didn't force you in, nor did it try to remold you. Outside were the Avantists, their prisons and re-education clinics, censorship and exhortation, controlled schools and controlled economy, all with the aim of raising humankind above the animal.

Not too successful, were they? But the effort had killed a lot of people. It could still give her death or worse.

Tensely she stepped forth into daylight, mingled with the meaningless swarm, and concentrated on putting distance between herself and the ruin.

A booth caught her glance. YOUR FUTURE stood above it. A voice intoned: "—psychic projection forward along your world line, through the space-time continuum—" She forgot it. Hard by, another booth advertised FOOD.

It was a decent little spot, where a woman cooked her two burritos and tapped her a mug of beer, beer! The cold catnip of it gushed over Kyra's palate and down her throat. For dessert she got directions to Mama Lakshmi's Tea House.

That was a two-story, metal-sided building, undistinguished except for a verandah within which a wall-size screen presented an animation of the loves of Krishna. The lobby gave on a bar and restaurant to the right, a gaming parlor to the left. Nobody was about, aside from a dark woman at a desk. Kyra approached. "I'd like a room," she said.

"Ten dollars an hour," replied the clerk. "No professionals."

Kyra's face heated. "I want it for—overnight."

"Ten dollars an hour till twenty-one hundred. Then overnight rate, one hundred dollars. Checkout time nine."

Heartened by a full belly, Kyra said, "Too much. One hundred flat, counting from now."

"Done," said the clerk instantly.

She'd better learn how to bargain, Kyra thought as she paid. Her reserves could dwindle fast. "I'm expecting a visitor," she said. "My name is Emma Bovary. B, O, V, A, R, Y."

The clerk made a note on her computer. "Who is the visitor?"

"Do you need to know?"

"For your safety. This is a secure house."

Kyra scanned her memory. "Uh, John Smith." The clerk snickered but entered it and gave her a key.

The room was upstairs, shabbily furnished though reasonably clean, with a bath cubicle and a barebones multi. Its walls muffled the noise outside to a minimum. Kyra considered tuning in the news. No, first she could use some rest. Take off her pack, kick off her shoes, flop onto the bed—

She was in space, in the Taurid Stream. Strange that that centuried menace was unseeable except as radar blips. Her eyes found only stars wintry bright in a crystal dark. Light within the cabin overrode all save a few hundred. Acceleration ended, she floated free, ghost-alone. Then a sight waxed slowly before her, a flicker of shadows and vague luminance as the comet turned, wobbled, orbited toward distant Earth. It was ice and rock and dust, three hundred million primordial tonnes. If it struck, it was death, wreck, and a year without a summer. It was too friable to deflect; the necessary force would crack it apart and the unmanageable fragments would be nearly as deadly. Instead it must be destroyed, and soon, turned into pieces scattered enough and small enough that when they reached the planet they would do no harm. But nuclear blasts of that magnitude would fill ambient space with the shrapnel, and she, the data-gathering scout, might be on an escape course that proved unlucky—

A knock roused her. She sat up with a gasp. Sunbeams slanted low through the window. Jesus on a jet, had she slept so long? The knock repeated. She surged to unlock the door.

Lee came in, wearing Western male clothes. He carried the pack that held Guthrie on his back and a small bag in his left hand. She noticed that his informant was missing from that wrist. Her look sought his countenance. It was drawn into harsh lines, though he managed a smile of sorts. "Hi," he said. Strain flattened the voice.

"Bienvenido," Kyra answered uncertainly. "It took you a while, didn't it? Trouble?"

"Nothing serious." Lee closed the door. "I had to search around longer than I'd expected before I found what I was after."

"Get me out of this poke and explain what the hell it was," Guthrie growled.

Lee removed him and put him on the dresser. "They wouldn't let me past the entryroom at that place," the man related. "I had to dicker over an intercom. It's a new location. They've grown ultra-cautious."

"I thought anything went in Quark Fair," Kyra said.

"Not quite. If the Sepo got wind that *this* stuff is being dealt—" Lee slumped into a chair and stared before him.

"At a suitable price," Guthrie remarked. "I heard how you ended up swapping your expensive tipster for whatever it was."

"Worth it, sir. I never made that kind of purchase before, but I'd heard it could be done, and where."

"What are you talking about?" Kyra asked.

"Give me a chance to unwind first," Lee sighed. "It isn't a pretty subject."

"I'll go downstairs and fetch something to drink. What would you like?"

Lee shook his head. "What I'd love beyond measure is a stiff bourbon and branch, but no alcohol for me today."

"Serve yourself if you want, Kyra," Guthrie said.

"No, not really," she answered. "Unless coffee—" No. As was, her nerves thrummed. She began to pace between the walls. "I had a few problems myself." She described her journey.

Lee whistled. "For a lady who's led a sheltered life, you done right well, ma'm."

"Yeah, let's get you back to your nice, cozy solar flares, radiation belts, meteoroid collisions, and moonquakes as fast as possible," Guthrie laughed. His tone went metallic. "Or faster. We've got damned little time, if any."

Chill crawled through Kyra. "Are things that bad, sir? Why?"

"Isn't it obvious? Obvious as a wart on a nudist's ass. My other self. He won't be slow to figure I'm on the loose, and move to counter whatever I might do. If he can swing that, Fireball is his. Is the enemy's, the Advisory Synod's. In which case, let's hope we three are comfortably dead. We wouldn't appreciate the future."

Lee grimaced. "How horrible is this situation for him, do you think?"

The cold deepened in Kyra. She couldn't guess an answer to that question; her knowledge of psychonetics was scant. Perhaps Guthrie had no clear idea either. But pseudo-Guthrie—

Wrong. The other was Guthrie too. That might as well have been the physical object that stayed behind, ruling over Fireball, and this that now spoke with her might as well have been the one that fared four and a third light-years and back again. It wouldn't have mattered. Shared after the return, their memories were identical. Only in the happenings that followed did those histories break asunder.

Irrationally, she wished the mass she had borne in her hands were the mass that had traveled. It should not lie enslaved—*he* should not, who had walked beneath the heaven of Demeter.

6

Database

TOWARD EVENING THE rainstorm that had lashed the day reached an end. Wind continued strongly for a while, scattering clouds until they were few. So clear a sky was a rare sight. At this time of this year the suns were close together in it. Guthrie left camp, which was too well sheltered by a ridge to have a view, and went to watch them set.

On his way to the seashore he encountered a biologist. Fifteen centimeters in length, it seemed weirdly like a giant insect, more alive than the greenish-brown mat of plant stuff its tendrils probed. For an instant, as a sensor caught Guthrie's image, the work paused. He knew that a transmission flashed to a receiver balloon-borne over the station and thence, amplified, to the mainframe computer on the ground. His own radio ear wasn't sensitive enough to hear, if he had been in the path of the beam. No matter. The computer identified him within a microsecond and sent the command *Ignore*. The biologist got busy again.

Elsewhere others, more or less like it according to their specialties, were also engaged, but Guthrie didn't see them. The land reached empty from western hills to eastern sea. It was boulders and rocky outcrops, blues and grays with quartz glitters, rising behind tawny dunes. Here and there a pool or a puddle caught the long light and turned into gold, which the wind shivered. The storm had carried sultriness away. Air whistled off the ocean laden with salt spray, an ozone tang, pungencies that were not really of kelp and fish.

He left the robug, as he called it, behind and proceeded to the strand. The body he was using ran on treads. He felt their serpentine ripple over the terrain, the fine grit yielding to his weight, the damp within that soil. Beneath wind and surf he heard his passage, crunch, slither, a whirr of motors. His other body had legs but was more complex and vulnerable. This one actually brought him nearer to communion with the world around him, closer to being human again. Memories stirred that had slept for many years.

The tide was low. Rain had not much marked the sand, but in front of the gentle breakers it had been drenched and darkened by the sea. On Earth that strip would have been wider. *Hush-hush-hush* went the waves under the wind.

Guthrie's eyes, their stalks projecting from the turret that housed his case, bent downward. The beach was strewn with weed, shells, dead animals vaguely like worms and jellyfish. An ebb always left some, and the storm had cast up many. Their wreckage brought to mind what he had seen on the shores of home, before Earth grew too depleted. Strange that here life in the oceans had long been rich, when thus far it barely existed on land. Or maybe not strange. Tides might well be what opened the way for evolution ashore, and moonless Demeter had only its sun to drive them.

A gleam afar caught his glance. Curious, he peered across the waves. They still ran high, white-capped, purpled by the glow from the west, to a blurred horizon. Never a gull or a guillemot winged above them. Guthrie magnified the sight his lenses captured. A torpedo shape had surfaced a hundred meters out, mother vessel of robugs studying the aquatic environment and its ecology. He wondered whether it had worked its way this far north from the last base the expedition established, or was newly made. Remodeled production facilities were now operating at full capacity, and aircraft flitted investigators to sites around the globe. He could ask the database.

Later. He'd come to watch Alpha Centauri go down. He turned westward.

Beyond the dunes, hills lifted murky, their erosion scars full of shadow. Clouds lay in bands, rose and honey against luminous blue. Haze dimmed the brilliance of A to a hot coal. Sinking, the disc seemed enormous, though it was a little smaller than Sol's seen from Earth. B followed a few degrees behind, a refulgent point that tinged the tops of the clouds with amber.

The rotation period of Demeter was a mere fifteen hours. A vanished in a gulp. As its light drained away and the sky deepened, B's became clear to sight, yellow, strong as a thousand full Lunas. Heights and crests stood soft above the dusk that rose from below. Then the companion sun, descending, dimmed likewise, reddened, and plunged. The last colors faded and stars came forth one by one to blink at those already in the east.

Among them appeared a moving spark. It climbed fast, widdershins, in low orbit around the planet—the *Juliana Guthrie,* which had brought him here and waited to carry him home. No, he knew, that wasn't quite right. What he saw was the tanks of the clustered drive units. The spacecraft itself was too small for his eyes, even if he magnified: with payload, a few tonnes. On remote comets and on asteroids of the chaotic zone, robots toiled to mine raw materials and refine them into reaction mass for the next voyage. It would take them several years.

Memory overleaped space-time.

An office in Port Bowen. Transparency overhead full of a night where Earth stood glorious, marbled blue and white, three quarters full. Pierre Aulard's honest hook-nosed face across the desk behind which Guthrie rested. An explosive *"Qu'est-ce que vous dites?* 'Ave you blown a fuse?''

"Some folks might reckon that question a smidgen tactless."

"I—yes, I am sorry, sir."

"Oh, come off it. I was kidding."

"Sis you say, it is a joke?"

"No. I wouldn't make my favorite engineer arrive in person just to see his eyes pop. Contrariwise, I did it because I'm so serious that I want to catch your total reaction, body language, the works. The best hologram a phone can produce isn't the same."

"But it is *fou,* loco, gyroceph. I do not understand w'y you want any second mission at all. Se robots in place—"

"Inadequate. We need more and better. God damn it, Pierre, Demeter's the single piece of real estate besides what's sitting yonder where there's life we can study."

"Not so. Planets wis oxygen atmospheres 'ave been detected at sree osser—"

"Sure, I know. Too bloody far away. What's on Demeter is reachable *now."*

"Primitive life."

"All we've got. It would've been nice if those supposed signals had turned out to be CETI, not a freak of nature, but looks like we'll have to learn about the universe on our own. So let's do it."

"Eh, bien, if you are not content, we can send anosser spacecraft. First we improve se design, if you spend plenty of money. Also se robots and instruments, yes." Aulard's fist crashed on the desk. "But a spacecraft sat can return! *Mon Dieu,* w'y? W'at is wrong wis se data transmission?"

"Inadequate, I repeat. The robots do their earnest best, and it isn't bad, but nobody has yet come up with an artificial intelligence that's got anything like real imagination. As witness the attrition among the machines now on Demeter. She keeps springing surprises on them that they can't always handle. And what angles, what opportunities are they overlooking? No, I want a genuine human mind on the spot; and after a while it will need to come home."

Aulard gaped for seconds before he muttered, *"Sacrée putain."*

"Hey, don't get me wrong. I'm not about to saddle you with developing life support systems for that kind of trip. We can't afford the antimatter to boost so much extra mass. Agreed. What we'll send is me, or a twin of me that we'll make when the time comes."

"—I . . . 'ave . . . nossing to say . . . except sat you—I sought I knew you, but I see I never did. Not se least bit."

"Aw, the notion isn't that hairy-brained, Pierre. Really, it isn't. I've played with it for years, run off some computations for myself, and I'm satisfied it can be done on a halfway sober budget. Listen, the reason we have to bring the spacecraft back, though of course we can leave the robots, the reason is simply that I won't be able to transmit my entire experience. Interference, insufficient bandwidth, quantum effects, you know the physical limitations better than I do. And then there's everything, hunches, feel, familiarity, that can't very well be put into words or diagrams. I've got to return and download into myself, or what was the point of my going in the first place?"

Aulard spread his palms wide and gazed heavenward. "W'at indeed?" he groaned.

"Easy, amigo. You should thank me. I'm handing you a perfectly gorgeous technical problem. If I know you, for the next several years you'll wallow in it like a pig in Mississippi mud. Meanwhile, speaking of fluids, I suggest you have a drink. You know where the Scotch is."

More stars showed, and more, until they were about as many as unaided vision ever saw through this misty air, or from those nature preserves on Earth where the light-haze was unusually thin. Guthrie amplified their illumination until he could continue down the littoral, hoping to come upon something worth the attention of the science machines. It wasn't integral to his self-created role, for they explored too. However, he had nothing better to do at the moment. While he flattered himself that he had made discoveries and devised procedures which would have been beyond any prewritten program—still, he wanted his contribution to be as large as possible. He was under no necessity of justifying it to the likes of Aulard; he had decreed it, and that was that. But he wanted to.

If Aulard was alive when he returned.

Wind dropped to a lulling. The sea whooshed and rustled. It shimmered black, streaked with starlit foam. Coolness breathed off it. Guthrie stopped. He reached an arm to pick up a shiny object and bring it under his lenses. A piece of shell, iridescent like mother of pearl, nothing he'd seen before on Demeter. Maybe the main database had no record of this either. Maybe it was a clue that should be pursued.

Probably not. You couldn't research everything. Life on Demeter might not have evolved past an equivalent of Earth's Cambrian, or Silurian, or whatever the hell you named—meaninglessly, as alien as the whole biology was—but its diversities and subtleties dwarfed the stellar cosmos.

Guthrie held the fragment for a minute or two before he stowed it in his collection locker. Once he and Juliana found something very similar on a California beach. Abalone shell, she'd exclaimed. But abalone were nearly extinct! They bent their heads over the marvel. Nobody else was around, they were visiting a country whose economy had crashed, the sun, salt, and sand were theirs alone. Her hair fluttered against his cheek. He slipped an arm beneath her tunic, about her waist. She felt warm and smooth. With a glance and a grin, she drew close. For a program in a neural network it was a vivid memory.

Guthrie turned his vision aloft. A brightness, lamplike and unwinking, stood high. It was Phaethon, the rogue planet, which would soon swing through the orbit of Demeter. But that would be at a safe remove. Guthrie chose not to think further ahead. His heed sought the stars beyond.

Constellations and the wan silver of the Milky Way were familiar. His twenty-year voyage had brought him no distance that especially mattered, through the immensity of these galactic outskirts. Of course, the orientation was different. At this hour and this middle latitude, he found Polaris almost straight overhead. His search went onward, past dim red Proxima to Cassiopeia. There an added star outshone the other five: Sol.

"By God, sweetheart," he called aloud, across the light-years, to her ashes, "we made it!"

7

"LET'S NOT GET morbid," Guthrie said. "Better we talk about us."

Kyra agreed thankfully. "I wish I could simply hop a plane to someplace foreign." She couldn't resist, and didn't think he'd mind: "With you as hand baggage." Bleakness again: "But the Sepo must have alerted all airport security devices to watch for anything that could be you. We'd be detected the minute I walked into an airport."

Lee nodded. "Too bad Tahir couldn't plausibly ship that biobox to Cairo or wherever," he said.

"That might have been arranged, if we'd had more time," Guthrie remarked.

Lee's eyebrows rose. "Really?"

"I expect so. Fiddle with the computer files, write in the clearances and permits and other garbage, and I'd've been on my way. But contacting the people who can do that, persuading them, planning the specifics, et cetera, would've taken days, which we didn't have."

"Why days?" wondered Kyra.

Guthrie formed a chuckle. "Innocent lass. Well, for your information, though I imagine you've guessed it yourself by now, an active underground, a resistance movement, does exist. People who don't just daydream about bringing the Avantists down and setting up a free country again, but will risk their necks for it. They're not many, and in public they are impeccable citizens, but they're well disciplined and little by little they've accumulated weapons. Yes, they know they haven't a prayer of mounting a revolution by themselves, but they want to be prepared should a chance ever come along and meanwhile, now and then, here and there, some among them can quietly do something.

"Like other such folk in the past, they're organized in cells of a few persons each. No member of any cell knows for certain that more than one in any other belongs to the outfit. That way, if the Sepo catch somebody, even if they deep-quiz him, he can't guide them to making a clean sweep of the camaradas. But it does slow down communications."

Kyra's spine tingled. "Just the same, there *are* Chaotics in the government—in at least a few useful positions?"

"Uh-huh. I don't know the details, nor should I."

Lee stared into the lenses. "How do you know what you do, sir?" His voice trembled a bit.

"Obvious, I thought," Guthrie answered tartly.

Yes, Kyra thought, now it was, after what she had seen and he had related. Over the years, Fireball must have developed some connections, however tenuous, with the secret force. For instance, individual consortes who helped smuggle political fugitives across the borders would hear things, and the knowledge would eventually come to Guthrie.

He might or might not be in direct touch with the junta. Probably not, she reckoned. That could be dangerous both to them and to Fireball. Besides, in spite of Avantist accusations, the company never had been in the business of overthrowing governments. Even now, she supposed, the jefe would settle for a return to the status quo.

But still, cautiously, indirectly, Fireball and the rebels maintained a degree of rapport. Once in a while, one party was able to do the other a favor.

The question leaped into her. "Has Fireball infiltrated too?"

"Not worth mentioning," Guthrie replied. "Most people we could engage and trust to do that have backgrounds that'd rule them out. Besides, their kind seldom make good government employees." His tone harshened. "On the other hand, it seems clear that the Avantists have planted some agents among us. Not family members, probably not trothgivers, but hirelings in a position to spy, if nothing else. That may well be how they learned Jonas Nordberg would be worth kidnapping and wringing dry— my friend, who turned out to know where my duplicate was stashed. It also means that we can't just phone Quito from a public booth. We don't know what the enemy's interception capabilities are. They must be fairly good, or the Avantists wouldn't have felt confident enough to try this stunt.

"And, positively, my alter ego knows what I knew about Fireball's arrangements in North America at the time he came back. They've developed since then, but he's got leads that the Sepo won't be slow to follow. I'd better not use what lines into the government I've got, nor rely on what information I have about it. All can go to trace and trap me."

What lines might those be? wondered Kyra. He'd seen Avantism coming. He'd made preparations against it, and done more after it arrived. Did that include slipping worms into essential computer programs? How much of Anson Guthrie lurked in the brains of the state itself?

How fast could his double aid his hunters to answer that? When would this resource too be turned against him?

He swung his stalks toward Lee. "The first problem we have to deal with concerns you," he went on. "If the cops start to seriously suspect you, and get thorough about it—pointing them at Tahir and his men who rigged our escape would be a shabby return for kindness. Also, a blow to the resistance movement."

Lee stiffened in his chair. He spoke as rigidly. "I know. I've planned a safeguard."

The bag he had brought along lay on his lap. He opened it and took forth a bottle and an injector. "This," he said. The blood had gone out of his lips. "Lesmonil."

"What's that?" Kyra felt a vein throb in her throat. Sweat gathered in her armpits, cold and rank.

Lee looked straight ahead, at the nearest of the walls that enclosed him. "A synthetic drug." His words jerked. "Seldom used. Not just because it's illegal and hard to get. The immediate effects are ecstatic. But the slightest overdose is amnesiac, like a large overdose of alcohol except that this is total." He barked a laugh. "Fun that you can't remember the next day isn't so hyper, is it? The amnesiac is really powerful. It doesn't inhibit transfer from circulating to permanent memory, it destroys every trace. That's why the ban on it is enforced more than on ordinary brain-poison. Even psychomeds who might find it helpful in treating mental patients, even they can't get any."

"Unless they're government psychomeds re-educating hard-case correctees, I'll bet," Guthrie said.

Lee's mouth drew taut. "Yes, I've heard rumors that it sees a certain amount of use in those institutions. As for what little is on the black market, most goes for pleasure— an ecstatic, remember—but I daresay various criminals have other applications of it."

Kyra jumped toward him. "No, Bob!" she yelled. "You can't—wipe yourself out—like that!"

He gave her a smile of sorts. "I don't plan to. Before I traded my informant for this, I tapped the public database. The formula's not there, of course, but the basic physiological facts are. The stuff attacks recent memories first. I reckon they're the most accessible, cytologically. For my body weight, I can estimate the dose that'll eliminate, roughly, the past fifty hours. No more."

"And then? And then?"

"Why, I'll wake up here tomorrow, sick, puzzled about what happened, but able to make my way home. If I'm arrested soon, a blood test may show I went on a lesmonil binge. No doubt the Sepo will wonder what made me do something so unlike my past life—I will myself—and they may deep-quiz me. If so, they'll learn that I harbored the jefe, but that's all they'll learn, because that's all there will be to extract. Someday you can explain to me."

"If . . . you survive."

He shrugged. "They seldom actually kill the subjects of their ministrations, you know. I expect I'll go into rehabilitation."

Whatever is left of you, after they've been through your brain with their chemicals and electronics, Kyra wanted to cry out. And if you go through the years of treatment at a correction center, whatever they finally release will bear only the name of Robert E. Lee.

She blinked hard, knotted her fists, and stammered, "W-we'll get you out soon." Before they can harm you beyond healing, she vowed. And meanwhile, now, she must keep her spirit as high as his.

Hopefulness wasn't foolishness. It was a necessity for survival.

Guthrie, too, must want to stay clear of pity. "That's a nice theory you've got," he growled. "Listen, though. I didn't know about this hell-soup either, but I've seen what assorted kinds of dope can do to people. Mainly, it ain't predictable. How close can you gauge your dose? And ever hear about idiosyncratic reactions? You could wake up a drooling vegetable. Or dead, which *I* would prefer."

Kyra saw determination stiffen in Lee. With it went a calm that slowly eased his muscles and brought life back into his face. "It's a gamble, yes," he said. "The whole business is. But the odds don't look too bad, with you two on my side. And, sir, I gave troth."

Silence dwelt among them.

"Okay, son," Guthrie said at last, most softly. "They'll honor your name as long as there are free men alive, if we win. But Christ, I wish I could shake your hand."

Kyra stooped over Lee and cast her arms about him. "Gracias, mil gracias," she said through sudden tears.

He rose and returned the embrace heartily. It became a kiss that went on.

"Ay," she murmured, gaze upon gaze, after they drew a step apart, "you've got surprises in you, you do. Let's investigate this further when we get the chance."

His mouth quirked. "You'll have to remind me. I sure hope you will."

Guthrie's basso brought their heads around to him. "Sorry, kids, we'd better stick with immediate business. Bob, you're doubtless better informed about things local than Kyra or me. What's our least dicey way out of here, would you say?"

Lee blinked and responded like a man roused from dream. "Oh. . . . Oh, yes. Bueno, I think . . . I think you should leave the area pronto. Train and bus stations—" His voice quickened. "They don't have detectors like airports, and they probably aren't under surveillance as yet. The sheer numbers of passengers ought to help too. But don't travel in plain sight. A general alarm could be broadcast, maybe. Take a train, Kyra, a private accommodation. Not a room, certainly not a suite. Too expensive and conspicuous. A recintito. They're fairly cheap, but almost always available, what with the depressed state of the economy. Pay in cash dollars."

"Good!" Guthrie exclaimed. "I said it before, you've missed your calling. Next time I need a conspirator I'll contact you."

"But where should we go?" Kyra asked into the air.

"I have a notion," Guthrie said. "Fireball consortes aren't safe and, given the threads the Sepo may have collected, I no longer trust what few Chaotic plug-ins I know about, either. But if we buy a ticket to, hm, Portland—"

"Stop," Lee snapped. "Be on your way."

"But you, you are going to forget," Kyra said.

"The sooner you lift off, the better. My absence has them excited, doesn't it?"

"Yeah," Guthrie said. "When they've heard from the other sites they've raided, they'll tighten the net in this region. If they trace your movements back, they'll find the clerk here, who'll remember Kyra. That should take a few days, but you're right, we've got to weigh anchor."

Lee drew breath. "Besides," he told Kyra, "I'd rather be alone when I take my injection and fall into my rapture. I've gathered that it isn't a dignified spectacle."

She had no words. Guthrie rumbled, "So long, son. Vaya con Díos," before he retracted his eyes and she slipped him into the pack. She slung it on her shoulders and took the clothes bag in her hand. Ludicrously, she thought of other things she needed, a comb, a toothbrush— The terminal would have automats. She laid her free arm around Lee's neck. "Oh, damn," was all she could find to utter. This time the kiss was brief. You might call it chaste. He stood in the doorway and watched her go down the stairs.

8

WHEN THE MESSAGE reached Director Engineer Pierre Aulard at his laboratory in L-5, he had sat for a long while thoughtful.

It had arrived over a long-established Fireball communications line, secret, independent of any net, so safeguarded in every way that nothing transmitted had ever been tapped. The keys to the encryption were in the possession of very few persons indeed; those associates of Anson Guthrie who were his oldest and most trusted. Though brief, this dispatch was in his personal style, the like of which had not otherwise been heard for long lifetimes, and it made passing reference to bygone days that brought a momentary smile to Aulard's lips. The burden was: "Prospects are more than hopeful, *if* we handle it right, but it'll be tricky. I need my old camarilla with me, the gang of you in person. Together we'll buck things through, the way we did when you were young. Remember? Say absolutely nothing to anybody except that you may be gone a fairish while." There followed instructions for making contact.

His first feeling was immense relief. He had exploded in protests when Guthrie proposed to slip into that crazy North America and manage operations against the Avantists on the spot. What if they came to suspect his presence among them? What if they tracked him down? By comparison, his Alpha Centauri junket had been common-sensical to the point of stodginess. Guthrie hadn't listened. After he departed, Aulard took refuge in work. Design problems of new spacecraft, they were something a man could give himself to without fear. Even the endless, niggling demands on him as an executive suddenly became almost welcome.

Now it seemed the jefe was at least partly safe and making ready to strike back in earnest. How, though? And what possible use could an aged technologist be? "The old camarilla—" why, that included Juan Santander Conde, retired with the honorific of Director Emeritus. God's name, had the summons also come to Juan in Quito? And to whom else?

Nervous again, Aulard began to realize how little he knew of the situation. He had never been one for politics or any similar monkey antics. The business on Earth infuriated him, but he had followed events only in the sketchiest fashion. Seeking understanding, he went to his computer terminal and keyed for a précis. As it unrolled on the screen, from time to time he retrieved data concerning specific aspects. Finally he sat back, closed his eyes, and arranged the information neatly in his mind.

—After the Union government occupied and began to search Fireball's North American headquarters, business was allowed to resume, under supervision. Company facilities elsewhere in the country functioned nearly as usual. Communications and personnel moved about, nationally and internationally, as needed. Meanwhile public disputation went on between the two sides. Likewise, but not covered in any detail by the news media, did negotiations.

Fireball wanted the militia and the detectives out of its main offices, immediately and unconditionally. The government insisted that it had taken action with the greatest reluctance and desired nothing more than to vacate. First, however, it must satisfy itself that dangerous subversives, perhaps terrorists, had not wormed their way into company employ. This was not a question of ideology but of prudence. In an era of fusion-powered engines, molecular engineering, and potentially lethal industrial materials, fanatics with access to the resources of an interplanetary organization could commit genocide, whether or not that was their intent. Fireball should not obstruct the investigation; for its own sake, it should cooperate. And since matters had come to a head, a number of long-standing issues had better be settled too. . . . The parleying dragged on.

Then things began to deteriorate. Service to North Americans was cut. Shipments went elsewhere. Proffered contracts that would routinely have been accepted were refused. Protests brought the response that it wasn't surprising if the present circumstances caused a certain loss of efficiency. Fireball officers stationed within the country explained, quite honestly, that they had nothing to do with this. Theirs was not a joint stock company, it was a privately owned corporation. Most of its important divisions were affiliates or independent contractors, but only technically so. As close-knit as all were, by tradition and emotion still more than by spelled-out agreements, the ultimate governance was highly personal. Sr. Guthrie could doubtless set everything straight whenever he chose. But after issuing a pungent statement at the time of the seizure, he had apparently left the problem to his people *in situ* and their superiors in Quito. Such was his normal practice; he was no micromanager, but encouraged individual initiative. He had since withdrawn, and not yet been heard from. His whereabouts were unknown. This too was not uncommon.

When informally talking with government agents, company representatives grinned and said words to the effect of, "Certainly he's putting pressure on you. What did you expect?" The measures were uncannily well aimed. The Security Police failed to smell out the source of those occasional commands. Fireball's lines of communication were cunningly laid out.

Increasingly, voices rose, urging a break of the deadlock, even if the settlement meant the Union authorities must yield on every significant point. The voices were not simply those of businessfolk and ordinary citizens who suffered inconvenience—in several cases, financial disaster. Politicians spoke, and various high-level bureaucrats. Contrary to claims made by some of its enemies and many of its proponents, Avantism was not in monolithic unanimity. It never had been, quite. If nothing else, opinions often differed about the interpretations and the practical uses of Xuan's equations; these arguments could develop into contests for power. As the years went by and the disappointments multiplied—goals unmet, economic difficulties, corruption, unrest, outright defiance, widespread indifference, spiritual secession—factionalism waxed. No public figure still resident within the national borders had, thus far, openly proposed scrapping the entire system; but more and more of them were saying, less and less circumspectly, that it seemed in need of modification.

Making peace with Fireball could well open a way to improving foreign relations generally and thence to internal reform. Three successive members of Congress said this from the floor and were neither denounced nor arrested.

Proceedings of the Advisory Synod were never public. Nonetheless, word leaked out that some members now favored such a policy. . . .

There the matter stood, aside from whatever Guthrie was doing. Evidently his direction from his secret lair had been successful thus far. Did he now mean to arrange for some spectacular action that would carry Fireball to victory?

Aulard sighed, shook his head, rose, and went off to make his preparations. That evenwatch he left the orbital colony aboard a regular shuttle to Kamehameha Spaceport. Arriving, he called the number that the message had given him, and in response got the address to which he should go. As ordered, he had traveled under an assumed name with appropriate identification material such as was kept in reserve for possible use. He went inconspicuously from the terminal, without a word to anybody who knew him, and took a cab to his destination.

Some fifty hours later, the Union government occupied every Fireball property in its jurisdiction. It announced that new discoveries about the extent of the danger made necessary this move and other emergency measures, but it trusted the crisis would soon be resolved to the satisfaction of both parties and of the human community at large.

On the following day, three officers of the Security Police escorted Pierre Aulard to their Northwest Integrate headquarters and a sanctum within it. As the door behind the anteroom retracted, they stepped back. He passed through and it closed after him. Of course, they would monitor what happened, visually if not with audio, and surely equipment elsewhere would record in multisense detail.

A viewscreen gave a broad outlook over the city, as seen from the roofport. Clouds scudded on a wind whose boisterousness Aulard had felt when he left the flitter that brought him here. Sunshine and shadow raced beneath them, down the streets and across the towers. The bay sparkled. No noise penetrated to the office, though, and its air stirred merely to the ventilators, temperature so well controlled that it seemed as devoid of heat or cold as it was of odors. Aulard barely glanced at the image before he focused on the desk and what stood behind.

That was a general-purpose robot, wheel-mounted. Its four arms ended in flexible hands but most functions were inside the boxy body or connectible to external devices. The turret had been modified, apparently a special job since marks of hand work were visible. Eyestalks protruded. When it spoke, the sound was not a standard tenor or soprano but a rough bass, English with an archaic American accent. "Hi, there. Welcome."

Aulard's fists knotted at his sides. "W'at are you?" he snapped.

"Anson Guthrie—who else?—currently wearing this chassis for lack of anything better. Good to see you, man. Care for a drink? I ordered Scotch." The robot gestured at the contents of a tray on the desk. Aulard shook his head. "Well, whenever you like, help yourself. Meanwhile, sit down, do, and let's talk."

Aulard went to a flexchair. The robot noticed his slight limp and exclaimed, "Hey, you weren't mistreated, were you? If anybody hurt you, tell me and I'll have the sanamabiche strung up by the balls."

"No. It is only sat at my age, one creaks under Earse gravity." Aulard seated himself. "I did not make a fight. Sey 'ad guns, and no witnesses."

"Pierre, I apologize. We had no choice, but it was still a stinking way to treat you. Please let me explain, and then I'll fall on the face I haven't got, making it up to you. Are your quarters okay?"

Aulard shrugged. "As prisons go."

"Look, I can arrange you a house off by itself—among trees, Pierre—with good food and wine, every kind of entertainment piped in, women if you want. Yes, and equipment too, within reason. You'll have a chance to work on whatever you've been itchy to get at. Nobody and nothing to bother you."

"Because I am cut off from everybody and everysing, *hein?*"

"Not for long. It shouldn't be for very long at all."

Aulard sat silent the better part of a minute, until he raised his white head and asked stonily, "W'at about Santander?"

"Well—" The synthetic syllable trailed away. The robot itself never stirred.

"If you did not lure 'im 'ere too, sere is no sense in 'aving me. 'E will soon suspect, and act."

The reply grated. "Well, sure, we did bring him in. You're right, we can't, for now, have anybody running loose who knows . . . what you know . . . about the two of me. If that word escaped, all hell would let out for noon. I'll explain why, and hope you'll then agree this, uh, underhanded proceeding was necessary."

Aulard looked into the lenses as if they were human eyes. "Nordberg is dead, Santander and I are prisoners," he said, "but are you quite certain sere is nobody else? One of us could 'ave made provisions."

The tone went stark. "None of you did. I know. They deep-quizzed Juan."

Aulard sat straight. Where he grabbed the arms of his chair, the knuckles stood hueless. "W'at?" he whispered. "Sat good old man, you drugged 'im and put pulses srough 'is brain?"

"*I* didn't."

"You made it possible."

"Give me a break, Pierre. I— The Sepo handled that end of the business. They must've picked Juan to examine because they judged he'd be . . . easier. When Sayre, their head honcho, called me to say he was satisfied the secret was safe, but he'd like to run you through the mill just to make sure, I vetoed it. Christ, I'm glad I could! I told him in simple words of four letters what kinds of trouble I'd kick up if he gave you that unpleasantness, and he went along with me. But I hadn't expected in the first place that he'd actually . . . do what he did. I swear by, by Juliana's name, I didn't."

"'Ow secure is se fact anyways?" Aulard asked, unrelenting. "Plenty of people remember sere were two Gussries and one was put in storage."

"They remember vaguely. They don't know where. They've got no reason to guess it isn't still hidden away. And pretty soon, if the question does arise, we can produce it."

"Yes. Anosser copy, out of a different place." Aulard

considered. "It will 'ave se software of se one sat did go into se cache, newly come 'ome from Alpha Centauri, knowing nossing of w'at 'as 'appened since." His smile twisted. "So *it* will be se real Anson Gussrie."

"No, that's me."

"Anson Gussrie would never betray as you 'ave betrayed. Many people called 'im devil, but none ever called 'im Judas."

The voice was not altogether level. "Pierre, you know better than that. Identity is continuity, right? I'm as much myself as, as any other is." Louder: "How do you know that I, the hardware inside this body, I'm not the same physical object that got itself smuggled into this country to give the Avantists grief?"

Aulard shrugged again. "Per'aps you are. It does not matter. Plain to see, sey 'ave reprogrammed you. Castrated you. Even after 'e became a revenant, Anson Gussrie was a man."

The robot stood mute for seconds before mumbling, "That hurt, Pierre," and took a moment longer to add, fast, "but you're wrong. They entered new data. I've learned more than I knew and changed my mind about some things. That's all."

Aulard gazed into the sky. "I sink, me, you are not se one I last talked to," he said slowly. "In sat comfortable prison room, I 'ad time to sink. W'at 'as 'appened seems rasser clear. But tell me, w'ere is se real Gussrie?"

"Right here, God damn it!" Pause. "But if you insist, okay, my hardware here is what went to Demeter." Softly: "Thanks to you, amigo viejo."

"Fine sanks!"

"I told you I'm sorry. I haven't changed, not really. Haven't forgotten anything, including my friends. I'm still me, Pierre. I remember—maybe better than you, after all these years—I remember, oh, that night when we received the Epsilon Eridani probe's first transmission from inside the system, that weird planet it'd spotted, and everybody got drunk, I had myself pulsed so I could feel drunk too, and you ran a translator program so we could follow along when you introduced us to that filthy old French song about the three goldsmiths—"

Aulard's hand chopped air.

"I'm still your friend, Pierre."

Aulard looked back into the lenses. "And w'at of Juan Santander?" Thus might a sword have sounded as it was drawn.

Silence.

Aulard leaned forward. *"Eh, bien?"*

Very low: "I'm sorry. He was older than you, you know. He'd grown more frail than he let on. The quizzing killed him."

Aulard sank back into his chair. "Murder."

"No! Accident! Listen, Sayre wanted him revived but that was another thing I vetoed. I figured his brain would've been worse damaged than— So I gave him that much, Pierre, and wished these eyes of mine could weep."

Aulard straightened and attacked anew. "W'at about sat osser one of you? W'ere is 'e?"

Guthrie rallied. "You don't need to know."

"Destroyed? Mutilated like you? Or—*bon Dieu*, let 'im stay free. Let 'im bring you down."

"That's scarcely in the cards." The stiffness softened. "Look, I had you brought here to this office because I want to spread the truth out for you to see. This is a tough time, sure, and a lot of what's happened will always haunt me, but, well, we're at a crisis point. The whole flinking human race is. Let me tell you my plans, and why I'm working on them. I want your help, your advice, so we can do what's best for everybody."

"You prove w'at you are," Aulard spat. "Anson Gussrie, 'e was sometimes a bastard, but 'e was never sanctimonious."

Harshly: "Don't push me too hard, old buddy. I'm on edge as is."

"Push? I 'ave no wish to touch you. Let me go from 'ere."

The lenses peered, the software made judgments. "You mean that, don't you? Okay. I'll be in contact later. Meanwhile, follow the newscasts. Think about them."

"Yes, since I must. Let me go now! Anyw'ere sat you are not."

Aulard climbed to his feet and stumped toward the door. A signal passed, it opened, the officers outside sprang up to meet him. "Take him back," the robot ordered. "Treat him kindly." The lenses remained fixed on him until the door closed.

9

FIRST IT WAS to lift out of the area, never mind which way, at once, before the police could organize a really thorough hunt. A bus brought Kyra and her bags to Pittsburgh Central. There she managed a conference with Guthrie, whispers in a lavabo stall.

She asked him whether she shouldn't try calling Quito, or perhaps some randomly chosen Fireball office abroad, on a public phone. The Avantists couldn't have planted agents or instruments at more than a few points. Nor could the Sepo monitor more than a small fraction of communications. Let her convey the facts, then run and hide with him, to wait while Fireball acted.

No, he replied, it was too big a risk with too small a chance of winning. Why, at the other end, should they believe so wild a story? Certainly they'd want to inquire around, investigate, get at least some degree of confirmation. This would take time and would probably come to the notice of counter-Guthrie. It might make him advance his plans by a few days, but he was bound to go to Quito soon in any case, and his presence would carry enormously more weight than fugitive allegations. The call itself could provide the Sepo with crucial clues to their quarry.

It would be both faster and safer—if safety meant anything in this mess—to seek out reliable friends and get their help in a try to escape physically, in person. Along the way, the truth could be sown here and there, for whatever harvest it might bring.

Kyra yielded, and spent the rest of a miserable night waiting for her train. The itinerary she'd laid out with the aid of her informant wasn't the most direct, involving two changes, but it avoided major stations. They couldn't microwatch every damn secondary depot between Québec and México, could they? The third stage ended in Portland, which was dicey at best. However, it stopped earlier in Salem, on the fringe of the integrate, and she'd get off there.

Once aboard for the beginning of her trip, she collapsed into sleep more sound than she had expected. She'd had worse beds than this seat; it even reclined a bit. The maglev ran smoothly, soothingly.

She woke to thirst and hunger, blinked, and peered out the window. The countryside through which she fled stretched wide, with occasional hills and bottomlands, flattening toward the plains farther west. It was nearly treeless but intensely green, planted row upon row upon row. She wasn't sure of the crop, whether those tall stalks were gened for growing food or chemicals. A grid of irrigation pipes gleamed through their ranks. At a distance she glimpsed a couple of machines, perhaps monitoring, perhaps manipulating. Above the horizon the towers of a minor city thrust into a cloudless, birdless heaven.

"Where are we?" she wondered aloud.

"Let me out and I'll see," rumbled Guthrie from his sack. She hadn't dared leave him exposed while she was unconscious. "Right now, my environment's as deprived as the inside of a politician's head. I thought you'd snore forever."

Kyra made sure the door of the compartment was locked, lowered a tray table, and set him on it. Meanwhile she couldn't help flushing and retorting, "I don't snore."

"On what authority do you claim so? Never mind, that's none of my business. Actually it was just a small snort now and then, ladylike—kind of sexy, in fact."

You old goat! she almost said, but curbed herself. That might have wounded. "Bueno, where are we?"

He looked. "Indiana or Illinois, I'd guess. . . . Don't mean anything to you? This was a federal republic once.

People were the richer for having something closer to them than the national capital. Well, set the time on your tipster back an hour."

"How are you doing, sir?"

"My battery's holding out. I daresay you could use a recharge, though, not to mention other needs of nature. Go to 'em. Uh, first check for a newscast, will you?"

The multi scarcely rated the name, being a tiny flatscreen and a single speaker, but when Kyra called up the listings, she found there would be info service in twenty minutes, and left Guthrie watching that channel. At the moment it presented, for classrooms, a review of earlier thinkers who preceded Xuan. Kyra had met them in her own education, political scientists tracing clear back to overrated Plato and much-maligned Machiavelli, systematist historians such as Spengler and Toynbee, psychologists from Pavlov onward who studied mind in the laboratory as a function of the organism, Moravec and Tipler and the other cybernetic visionaries. This program was banalities, pictures and phrases from which official repetition had leached meaning. "Brilliant men," Guthrie growled. "Honest men. They gave the world treasures. Hell, Xuan himself came up with some good ideas. Not their fault their work got perverted. I daresay Jesus and Jefferson sympathize."

Kyra relocked the door behind her and made her way down the aisle beyond. It stank of the passengers who crowded it and filled every seat. The train purred along swift and steady, but its interior was begrimed, blotted, defaced in places, metal tarnished, upholstery worn thin or ripped, nothing much to do with what it had formerly been or what you rode in most countries. She waited seventeen minutes in line for a closet where the smell was worse and the wash water a trickle, with a sign warning it was not potable.

The line at the vendor was longer yet, but moved at a reasonable rate. The machine declared itself out of most items on its menu. She obtained coffee of sorts, a calcium-protein drink, soy hash, toast, and fake honey, and bore them back, shoving somewhat rudely in her eagerness.

The recintito might be little more than a wall around a couple of seats, but it gave privacy, which for the average person on Earth was a luxury comparable to live-animal meat, a visit to a forest, or a . . . a printed book, paper spotted and fragrant with age. Of course, a larger compartment would have been pleasant, but Lee had warned against attention-drawing comforts.

Lee— Abruptly heart and foot stumbled. She almost dropped her tray.

No, it wasn't he, the man in the aisle seat, not at all like him. But oh, for an instant she'd thought it was Ivar Stranding. Same slenderness, same clear features and blond hair. . . . No, not really.

She pushed on, full of swear words aimed at the turmoil within her. What kind of lepton was she, anyway? More than two years had slipped by since they broke up. And it hadn't been that cracking serious in the three years before, though it had felt so and they'd dreamed of permanence and children and all the rest. How could it be serious between a space pilot and an engineer in the asteroids? How often did you get together, for how long at a time? Expensive multi messages lasered across the megaklicks, plus whatever other substitutes and consolations technology could provide, only made matters worse in the long run. She started turning elsewhere as chance afforded, and not just to good friends whom she hadn't wanted to hurt by unheralded refusals. No doubt Ivar did likewise. For he could never qualify to become her partner in faring, and she could not—would not—quit her ship to be always with him. Work among the flying mountains had its challenges, yes, but it wasn't the Long Road, it wasn't Earth aglow over Copernicus' ringwall or bearding Jupiter in his radiation den or a comet no life had ever betrodden before or tales and songs and fellowship at rendezvous—

Kyra snapped the memories off. Surprise had raised them, she told herself. And she'd been vulnerable because in this splintery situation with Guthrie, she was starved for anything gentle, peaceful, secure. Which it never had been with Ivar, aside from those brief spans after making love.

Eiko Tamura, now, aloft in L-5. No doubt Eiko had her troubles, but her spirit seemed to dwell apart from them, for how could serenity like hers be pretense? Kyra had once sent her an attempt at a poem,

> *Gone sunset amberful, the lake*
> *Lies mirror-quiet for the pines*
> *That ring it round with shadow heights*
> *Through which a ghost of golden shines*
> *To burnish blue those metal bits*
> *Above the water, wing and wing,*
> *Where, silent as in space itself,*
> *Three dragonflies are cometing.*

but never mentioned that it was Eiko she had in mind.

The recintito welcomed her. She pressed thumb to lock and followed hard behind as the door swung aside, kicking it shut while her gaze jumped to the video screen. She'd missed the first of the newscast, but—

Again she nearly lost her tray.

The image was of a man big and burly, middle-aged, his broad blunt face creased and weathered, with light-blue eyes under bushy brows and thinning reddish hair. His shirt was open on a shaggy chest, beneath the jacket of an undress uniform that Fireball had not employed for generations. She knew him, she had seen this same electronic configuration fifty times if she had seen it once, and the bass tones had last tramped across her eardrums half an hour ago. "—I came to North America in my own fashion, which we needn't describe, to observe for myself and do whatever I figured was called for. What I found rocked me back."

Kyra's look swung to Guthrie in his box. He brought an eyestalk momentarily down across his speaker. *Be quiet.* Numbly, she lowered herself to a seat.

"I'll go into detail later, when I issue a full statement," said the simulacrum of Anson Guthrie as he had been when first he became famous. It was the appearance he generated for his annual Christmas greetings to Fireball's consortes and his infrequent public pronouncements.

"That'll probably be in a few days, after I've returned to the main offices in Quito and had a chance to confer in depth with my top directors. Meanwhile, though, I've been asked to make some remarks in support of the measures you've heard about. I don't mind obliging."

His mouth drew upward, a sardonic smile. "Well, actually, I do mind, sort of. I've not suddenly been converted to Xuanism or any such fool thing. But I have become satisfied that there is a real danger, clear and present. A few desperados who've worked their way in till they've got access to the key networks and the powerful machineries—they can unloose forces like a major meteoroid strike."

A well-chosen figure of speech, Kyra thought. Everybody these days was aware of the threat in space, unlikely but unbounded, and was glad that Fireball held the World Federation contract to patrol and prevent. Which was suddenly a bit ironic, wasn't it?

"Sure, I favor liberty. I've often spouted off to that effect. But my friends have also heard me say social revolution is no way to get it. They tried that in France, 1789, Russia, 1917—why go on? The government of the North American Union is capable of reforming itself. I doubt that a martial-law regime would be, which'd follow twenty or thirty million deaths. Anyhow, I wouldn't want those deaths on my conscience. Would you? Some of you may have read what I used to reply to the really vehement advocates of population reduction, back when it looked as though the growth curve never would level off. 'You're right,' I'd say. 'The planet is grossly overpopulated and we'd better do something about it. Do you want to machine-gun the surplus yourself, or shall we start with you?' Back then, I was also in favor of ecology, mother love, and apple pie, but had no use for the eco-fascists. I'm in favor of liberty now, but have no use for the liberation fascists."

Kyra didn't recognize the last word. Guthrie was apt to throw in archaisms when he made a speech, and to ramble a bit.

Sternness: "You have had the danger described for you,

the extent of infiltration by fanatical conspirators. Later I'll explain how I know this is true, not propaganda. Right now I haven't the time. Neither does anybody else. We've got to cope, prontito. I order Fireball Enterprises to cooperate fully with the government of North America in its necessary, temporary steps to deal with this emergency. I urge and I will urge all others to do the same."

The image smiled afresh. "As for the good news, I repeat, these measures are temporary. Meanwhile, let me say, while I've got your buttonhole and free time on the air, let me say that the people who convinced me are not the hard-line Avantists, not the dinosaur faction. They're the moderates, who understand that if the system isn't mended it will be ended, by falling apart if nothing else. Our cooperation will strengthen them against their opponents. That's why I decided to come out of hiding, and it's paid off. Details later, from Quito. I do believe the occupation of our facilities can be finished inside a month, and regular operations can resume in spite of it in a week or two.

"To everybody of good will and common sense, gracias for your patience. Adiós."

The image blanked. A spokeswoman came on. "You have just seen Anson Guthrie, cacique of Fireball Enterprises—"

"Turn it off," said Guthrie. "The rest will be standard-issue pablum."

Kyra did. "That was . . . really your other self, jefe?" she whispered. "Or an electronic job?"

"Naw. A smart program that studied my recorded 'casts could've put it on, but they'll have to do more than that to make it effective. My double must in fact have been speaking, and will in fact go to Quito, to take charge of the company."

Kyra shook her head. "How can he possibly? He was inactive for the past twenty-some years." She drew breath. "Muy bien, they could force-feed the history into his memory, but the material that was kept confidential, the countless little personal details—"

"Yeah, it's a gamble, but he obviously expects he can

bluff his way through." Guthrie's gaze went outward. His voice became the sound of distant surf. "I think *I* could pull it off, if my copy didn't show up. Judas priest, what an all-time crapshoot! I damn near envy him."

"And if he fails," Kyra knew bleakly, "the Avantists won't have lost much."

"Right. A little embarrassment, maybe, but governments work on the crony system. None leans too hard on any other unless it actively threatens the peace or the general environment. North America will insist it was preventing a disaster, however misguided the efforts of a few officials were. Meanwhile it'll have reaped the benefits of buddy-buddy relationships with Fireball, which this wretched economy needs the way a leaky spaceship needs air. The company can't rescind that, not punish the prank very heavily. A boycott, for instance, is impractical. If nothing else, other countries would just resell to North America, and we'd have their hostility too.

"Of course," Guthrie added, "if anti-me really can quell me without publicity, and not give himself away by some major flub, the Avantists have won. Or so they'll believe. It'll take him time, converting Fireball to an active political force, but he'll have time. Whether he succeeds or not, God knows what the end result will be."

He glanced at Kyra. "Don't let your food get cold, gal," he advised, "especially not your coffee. How well I remember."

She heeded. Despite everything, her body, schooled to resilience, welcomed the nourishment. Emotions stabilizing, she could ask, "What was the official announcement?"

"What anti-me sketched. Discovery that extremists have infiltrated the state apparatus, Fireball, other organizations, hell, everything in sight. Nothing too specific, but alarming. Vaguely described terrors are the worst anyway. Action against them—you want the list?"

"Uh-huh," said Kyra around a mouthful of food.

"Well, you know about the occupation of our facilities. I recall your guessing there'd be radical security measures at the airports. You were right. The smaller ones are shut down, pending close control. No private aircraft will leave

North America without prior inspection and a permit. Satellites and aerostats can monitor that, you know.

"Checkpoints at every border crossing on the ground, no matter how much public inconvenience. The search will be for 'deadly instrumentalities,' but you realize what the detectors are really set to register, though the ordinary cop on duty doesn't. I imagine he simply has orders to turn in anything that might fit a very general description of me, and arrest the bearer.

"Inspection of seaborne vessels before clearing them to leave for any foreign country. That won't raise as big a diplomatic stink as you may suppose. If you're only checking for a neural network, it goes quick and easy.

"International mails—parcels and other sizable objects, of course. Electronic communications—monstrous volume, but they're diverting the hypercomputers to monitor, and never mind what happens to government services meanwhile. Letter mail—I dunno, it wasn't said, but there isn't a lot of it and it's generally slow, nothing especially helpful to us. Don't forget, my counterpart will soon be on the outside, issuing orders."

Kyra grimaced. "I feel the walls closing in," she said.

"I was born feeling that way, my dear," Guthrie replied. "It was one reason I got interested in getting humans permanently into space. A ladder out of here."

"But—domestically—"

"A manhunt. Actually, a me hunt, but naturally that isn't said. The announcement was of a general alert and a sweeping search for fanatics. If anybody local tries to declare openly that it's a charade, you get one guess as to how long he'll last. Shucks, I wouldn't even want you expressing me to any destination within these borders."

"Oh, no," Kyra breathed.

"I'd be less worried if it were only the Avantists after us," Guthrie said. "But my main enemy's different. He knows *me*. He's gambling, but he must have the odds pretty well figured. And the North American honchos are playing under his advice."

They ought to, Kyra thought. What better? Look at what the jefe had achieved in his life and afterward.

"All I can do right now is put myself in his place," the voice from the box went on. "Okay, I'd try to keep the balls in the air. I'd try to keep me within this country, on the lam; as long as possible, if I couldn't catch me right away. Because for each day that passes, I'd secure my position better. One way to do that is to take every available precaution against somebody like you, who knows the truth, stashing me somewhere and getting out with the word. Given a little time, some advance preparations, that unsupported word can be blocked—not absolutely, maybe, but close enough for practical purposes."

"Are you sure of that?" Kyra asked.

"No," Guthrie said. "Neither is he. It's not easy to gag someone in an outfit like Fireball that's always prized personal independence. But I can think of ways that should work.

"The point is, we're gambling, him and me. My best assessment of the odds, which I suspect is the same as his—it tells me my best bet is to get out there *personally,* quick, before he's had time to update his knowledge and consolidate his position."

It tingled in Kyra, coldly. "That seems like a pretty risky strategy."

The lenses glittered at her. "Yeah, it is. For you as well, I'm afraid."

Blood mounted in her temples. "Sir, I gave troth." Was that too dramatic? Spacers traditionally understated things. "Fireball's been good to me. I'd like to keep it the way it is."

"God damn, if I could only hug you!" Guthrie sigh-sounded. Then he chuckled. "Affection, gratitude, but also abstract lust. I can still appreciate that you're a toothsome wench."

How many temptations had he resisted? she wondered. With his wealth, he could commission for himself any quiviran paradise he wanted, or an infinity of them. But if ever he indulged, it had not been often or for long at a time. Why not? What made him, bodiless, keep so hard a grip on reality?

How glad she was that he did.

She mustered a smile. "Gracias, jefe. From what I've heard about your usual manners, that's quite a blarneying I just received, and wouldn't I love to take you up on your offer? As for risks, I've run a few on occasion."

"I know. Old days—"

After a while they found themselves dealing in memories.

10
Database

THE VILLAGE LAY high and lonely. Through a window of the house in which he crouched, Guthrie saw the last light stream from the west across patches of cultivation, on eastward over sallow grass and sparse bushes, until the altiplano hazed away with distance and alpenglow tinged rosy the snowpeaks beyond. Above them the sky duskened and a planet shone white—Saturn, he believed. The sunbeams gilded some llamas which a boy was driving home from pasture. Life, the labor that earned life, went on because it must, for as long as war and politics allowed.

The sun vanished and darkness flowed fast. Wind whittered low and chill.

He felt it, since the window, though small, was unglazed, and if he was to mount a defense he couldn't close the shutters. The house itself scarcely rated that name; "cabaña" would do better for a single dirt-floored room and the few poor possessions within. To be sure, the earthen walls were stout, and two men could not well have held a larger one.

He looked cautiously, peeking around the edge for a few seconds at a stretch. If he stuck his head out in plain view, he'd get a bullet through it. That had almost happened when he and Moreno stood off the Senderista rush; but their fire had discouraged marksmanship, and soon the attackers withdrew.

Guthrie's regard was for the Jeep. It rested about fifty yards away on the rutted track that passed for a road, where he and Moreno had leaped from it as the guerrillas closed in, shooting. He didn't know how barely they'd made it to this shelter, nor did he know whether the smart thing might have been for them to throw their hands high and trust to Maoist mercies. They hadn't stopped to think. Guthrie had shouted the command that came naturally and they'd grabbed their just-in-case rifles and run zigzag, bent over. The house proved to be vacant, whether by chance or by the family fleeing in terror. Not till they were inside did Guthrie notice that he'd taken the car keys along.

Two men guarded the vehicle. He'd seen them earlier: short, hardy Indios in nondescript outfits, firearms—a machine pistol and a probably stolen Colt AR-15—ready to hand. They had seated themselves within and he could now make out only the glowing coal of a cigarette. The herd boy went from his field of view. It included nobody else and no neighbor building. Doubtless the rest of the band were under those roofs with the inhabitants on whom they had quartered themselves. He had no information as to how long they'd been here, though he guessed it wasn't very, or how willingly they had been received. It made no practical difference. When the Sendero Luminoso arrived, you hailed it as your glorious liberator or you died, sometimes in quite a nasty fashion.

He turned from the window. Luis Moreno Quiroga stood watch at the one opposite, a slim shadow in the thickening gloom. "That's a relief," Guthrie said in English. "I was afraid they'd try to hotwire the car, and either succeed or else disable it. Now they won't till morning."

"I do not expect they will at all," Moreno replied in the same language, fluently. He and Guthrie had become friends when they were both engineering students in Seattle. He got his degree, Guthrie dropped out of school, and presently they found themselves in Moreno's native Chile. "They must take us in any event."

"Yeah, but they might've gotten impatient about the Jeep." It was a valuable capture, brought down from the States by the partners, old but well-maintained, able to go damn near anywhere. "Old" meant, mainly, that it had been built by American Motors and was therefore a solid, reliable job; also, it didn't demand unleaded fuel, which was often unavailable in the Andean uplands. "They can starve us out. No, thirst us out." Guthrie's nostrils drank dryness.

"They will not choose that," Moreno said. "Prestige, if nothing else. Later tonight, I think, when we are tired and sleepy and cannot see them well, they will keep us busy at the windows and—batter in the door, perhaps, and sweep the room with a burst."

"I was about to say, that's my guess too. So we anticipate them. Hey, what're we talking *yanqui* for? *Luis, amigo mío, lo siento—*"

"Hsh! English is better. Somebody may be listening."

"Uh, right. I . . . I'm goddamn sorry I got you into this."

Moreno laughed softly. "We got ourselves into it, Anson. You no more forced me than I forced you, that time at Vance Holbrook's party when you decided on beer chasers for the rum I brought."

"Well, but— It was my idea to start with." Raise a bit of capital. Travel south. The Stateside market for classic cars had recovered with the economy, and a good many of them survived in northern Chile and Perú, preserved in excellent condition by their owners and the climate. Buy cheap, ship north, sell dear.

"It worked very well, too," Moreno said. "Our mistake was not even crossing into Perú. It was wandering off to see Lake Titicaca, and believing that that fool in Ilo knew what he was talking about when he told us there were no more terrorists in these parts."

"He could've been right as far as he went. This could be a single gang on a long-range raid. I should've thought of the possibility, and at least arranged for us to join a convoy." Guthrie spat. "Ah, shit, we sound like a pair of liberals, don't we? Guilt trip. Next thing, we'll take the blame for the local poverty."

Moreno's tone went grim. "That is where they place it." He paused. "I do not think they will keep us for hostages or ransom if we surrender. Especially after the trouble we have given them in the eyes of the people. We have simply been bull-headed throughout, you and I. Let us take the lesson to heart in future."

Anger and impatience jostled fear aside in Guthrie. "First we've got to bull through. Okay, we will!"

"When?"

Guthrie wanted to answer, "Right away." He forced himself: "When it's full dark. They'll want that too, cover for their attack, but moonrise isn't till about eleven, so they probably aren't in a hurry. In one hour, we break out?"

"Agreed." Gentleness: "If you will bear with me, I have some thoughts to think and some prayers to say."

"Sure. Me too."

Thoughts, anyhow. It took just a jot of awareness to stay alert. Mainly, the body did that, the animal painfully taut, senses tuned so high that each single star blazed from the moment it appeared above the gray plain. Most of the mind was left to torture itself with waiting, unless it could find strength elsewhere. Guthrie tried to close his ears against the whisper from across the room. You shouldn't eavesdrop when a man talked to his heart.

Or to his God. For Guthrie the two were the same.

Bring happy days back, into this night. "I can call memories from the vasty deep." Yes, but will they come when you call them? Dad, big soft-spoken machinist who truckled to nobody. Mother, laughterful, who single-handedly got rhyme and reason into the computer programs where she worked. Susie—Christ, he'd missed his sister's college graduation, hadn't even remembered to send her a present or try a phone call.

So turn from the snug home in the unbeautiful industrial seaport, to its hinterland. Olympic loftinesses and ancient woods. Surf coming in tremendous from the rim of the world. Lying becalmed in a twenty-foot sloop, one utterly blue dawn, and through the silence a dozen killer whales swimming down the Strait of Juan de Fuca, and one raising his head a moment over the rail as if to say good morning. A walk in the rain under the pines, hand in hand with a girl— No. That business, the pregnancy, the words and tears and half-hidden sniggers, pecking away well after the adoption, and always the look behind Mother's eyes, though she said nothing ever that wasn't loving— With heedlessness and willfulness he had betrayed her, all of them, as he had today betrayed himself.

His mouth longed for his pipe, but it was in the car.

When in hell would the hour end? Why wait for it, anyway? Black enough already. Any minute the Charlies might strike, if he'd misjudged them, and it'd be too late. Punch the button, see the light flash on your watch, read the numbers again. Not yet, not yet. Why not? Well, he'd said an hour. Sixty minutes. If he couldn't stand that much, Luis would think less of him. Tough it out, fellow, tough it out. Sing songs—not aloud, Luis wouldn't appreciate that, but in your head—all the songs you know, including the rowdy ones. Especially the rowdy ones. *"We never mention Aunt Clara—"*

Time, by God, time.

"Let's go." It was like hearing somebody else.

A quick, whispered conference, who was to do which. Ignore contingencies, they were unforeseeable. Moreno's clasp found Guthrie's shoulder in the dark. "Whatever happens, you have been a great friend, Anson. Thank you." Guthrie wished he'd had that impulse, or more of a reply than, "Same to you. Come on, at 'em."

They'd matched fingers, odd against even, for first through the door. It chose Moreno. He flung himself past the turning hinges and ran hunched along the wall, around the corner, rifle clasped in both hands. Guthrie pounded after, farther off. The Jeep was a murk faintly a-shimmer beneath the stars.

He heard the buzz before he heard the crack. Ha, at least one extra man was posted outside. Don't look for him, keep going.

Another crack and another. Moreno fell sideways. He rolled twice and lay horribly sprawled.

Keep going.

Moreno had been assigned the nearer side of the car. Guthrie veered to it instead. He came from behind and seized the rear door handle. It was cold. They hadn't thought to lock. He snatched the door open. In front, the man at the wheel, across from him, had half emerged. The one in the passenger seat was a blur of gloom. He waved his weapon, as if bewildered. Guthrie fired. The man crashed against the dashboard and sagged downward into lightlessness. Guthrie fired at the other. He lurched, fell from sight, screamed, screamed.

Guthrie spun about, his back to the metal. Moreno was an ugly lump on the ground. Guthrie pumped several shots from his semiautomatic, more or less at random. They might or might not be of some use against that third man. He tossed the rifle into the car and dashed yonder.

He stooped over Moreno. Eyeballs stood white in the half-seen face. Blood around the mouth caught starlight. Did he hear a *"No, no, vaya—"* or was it only a rattle in the throat? We don't abandon our wounded, he didn't say nor especially think. He was too busy. Stronger than he had known he was, he hauled Moreno up in his arms and ran back to the car.

Shouts rang. Shots barked and zipped. He heard bullets whang off the Jeep, but somehow they all missed him. He was a lousy target in the night, moving fast, and everybody taken by surprise. Sheer stinking bad luck that Luis got hit. Guthrie reached the car. His boots went over the man who threshed and wailed below it. Something crunched. Guthrie pitched Moreno onto the rear seat and himself onto the driver's. Not waiting to slam doors, he put key to lock, feet to pedals, fist to gear shift. The motor howled awake.

More men scurried around, vague in vision. The Maoists had wheels of their own. A battered pickup chugged from the window-speckled mass of the village. Its headlights probed. Guthrie left his off. He accelerated. The open doors jerked half shut.

He stayed on the road for several teeth-rattling miles. The ground rose and roughened as he went. When he dared, the truck being well behind him, he turned on his lamps, switched to four-wheel drive, and left the road. The truck couldn't follow him here, and he'd outpace anybody who tried on foot.

Finally he decided he could stop. Silence plummeted over him. He scrambled out, swung the rear door aside, and leaned in. "Luis? Luis, old boy?"

Under the dome light, slackness gaped at him. The eyes stared and stared, blinkless, tearless.

The guerrilla in front was dead too, as Guthrie had guessed. His single shot had gone in under the cheekbone and come out the top of the skull to punch through the windshield beyond. Blood and brains had splashed over things. They were already congealing in the cold. The guerrilla had been just a kid, maybe sixteen, though he looked about fourteen.

Guthrie left that corpse for its fellows to find. Probably they would before the ants and vultures did. He cleaned up the mess as best he was able, laid Moreno out— cramped for room, kind of a fetal position, but hadn't that been the Inca way?—and drove on. Later he understood that what he had also left behind was his youth.

11

Database

20 JULY WAS a Fireball holiday, so Boris Ivanovich Nikitin took leave from his own school to squire Kyra Davis around. They had met in the course of their parents becoming acquainted, and got together increasingly often. Hereabouts, given a low population and a congenial atmosphere, there was no reason for consortes to live in a compound, though naturally they tended to mingle with each other more than with outsiders.

The pair flitted to Novgorod and he guided her through the historic parts. She had visited two years ago, when her family first arrived, but briefly. Memories fell blurred and jumbled into the general confusion of the time. Since then, no matter how near the town lay, she had been too busy or in her free moments found too much else to do.

It was a lovely morning. They had the kremlin almost to

themselves. What was ruined had been restored as well
as knowledge permitted. Strange how few ever came to
see, Kyra thought. Maybe an occasional glimpse on a
multiceiver satisfied the majority, if they cared even that
much. Sunlight caressed the Byzantine domes of St.
Sophia's. . . .

"Yaroslav the Wise built it in the eleventh century, after
the earlier wooden cathedral burned," Boris said. "But the
Gates of Korsun were ready for it, brought up from the
Crimea sixty years before by Grand Prince Vladimir. And
the city was then two or three hundred years old, founded
by Varangian merchant adventurers. Their trade reached
to Constantinople and far into Asia. Novgorod was first to
welcome Rurik when he came from the North in his
dragon ship."

His voice almost sang. She suspected that to him this
was more real than the world he could touch, and he
would never want a quivira. His wish was to become a
historian—not to dig out facts and store them in himself,
which a machine could do better by orders of magnitude,
but to understand them, call the dead back to life and let
them speak through him to their descendants. She sometimes wondered who would pay for it and who would
heed. The compiler of a quivira program, perhaps?

Lacking the heart to say that, she replied merely, "They
were a nervy lot, weren't they?" The awkwardness was half
in her, half in her Russian. An educator with neural
modulation could cram the basics of a new language into
you fast, but you needed time, practice, reading and reflection as well as conversation, to make it really yours. Mostly she associated with her classmates, who came from all
over and used English in common.

"They had the chance to be." Boris clenched a fist. His
gaze went beyond her, as if through the walls to the river,
every mightily flowing river across this land, and the seas
into which they ran. "Their world was ringed in by the
unknown. They dared it with sails and oars, on horseback
and on foot, the wind in their faces and their muscles at
play, because that was what they had. No robots, no

omniscient computers. And when they wanted waking dreams, they heard them from their poets and storytellers, human beings, or they made them for themselves."

The fist opened and dropped to his side. "But that was long ago," he ended flatly.

A tingle went up Kyra's spine. "Not in space," she said.

"For those like you, I suppose. If they are willing to forego that imitation of nature that is left on Earth. If they are of the small number chosen. And will it last through our lifetimes?"

Boris shook himself. He snapped forth a laugh. "Oh, but I am croaking like a raven, am I not? Forgive me. Help me forgive myself, that for a minute I forgot what delightful company I am in. Come, let me show you the rest."

He was a charming escort thereafter, in his slightly over-earnest fashion. At midday he proposed they flit from town to have lunch at an inn he knew in the country. Walking to the parking garage, Kyra felt anew how peaceful these streets were, nothing like the frenzy of Erie-Ontario.

Peaceful, she wondered suddenly, or hollow? Sunlight poured warm over pavement, walls, windows. The buildings were antiquated but in good repair. Trees along the way rustled to a breeze and dappled the ground with a dance of shadows. Yet vehicles went past well apart. Blankness in more than half the windows spoke of vacancy behind. A little girl came by, sweet in her pigtails and starchy frock, but quite solitary. Three women gave lackadaisical study to a display in a natural food shop; maybe the wares were too expensive for them, maybe they had nothing else to do. A vendor tried shyly to interest her in his handmade jewelry, but took it for granted when she declined after a cursory look. An open portal revealed a courtyard in which were several tables where men played chess. Their hair was gray or white. A soft, nearly subliminal pulse pervaded the air, but that was from the machines at their work, the vital organs of the city.

Bueno, she thought, it was only to be expected. She'd seen this kind of situation plenty often before, on the multi or sometimes in person, also in a lot of North America. Population had to come down, but the transition made new problems—might have been impossible, what with the skewed age distributions, except for the machines and their productivity. When a people took the need as seriously as the Russians had done ever since the Dieback showed them the alternative, they were bound to suffer radical changes throughout their society.

Decrease wasn't really necessary any more, was it? Had it ever truly been? With rational management (which was what the hypercomputers did best, wasn't it?) Earth could support many billions, sustainably. Of course, such a cram-crowded, regimented existence wouldn't be for her. As was, how god-lucky that she'd have space to escape into. Nevertheless, for a shuddery moment she wondered whether she didn't prefer the human sea in which Toronto Compound stood like an island, to this . . . emptiness. Were folk here being rational and altruistic, or had the spirit gone out of them?

Crack! What had gotten into her? She was as bad as Boris. They were supposed to have fun on this date of theirs, not brood like Dostoyevsky characters.

The hop to the inn was pleasant, as rural as you could hope for. She did spy a factory in its park, but that was all right; the buildings were a subtlety of hues and geometry, the nanotanks inside grew robot parts. Boris swung north of the endless plantations and flew over a preserve that was being developed. Hormones would make the forest tall within half a decade. "They will stock it with native animals," he told her. "Deer, elk, bears, wolves."

"Aren't some of those extinct?" Kyra wondered.

"M-m, I believe most species can be found in zoos, abroad when not in this country. Otherwise, I suppose, genomes are recorded and they can be cloned. Have you heard about them re-creating the tarpan in Siberia?"

"Yes." She smiled. "What'll amuse me is the mammoths, when they make them. Although I am puzzled. I've heard they must repair the DNA from the Ice Age specimens before they can map it. How do they know it hasn't deteriorated too much? Are they sure they can make it the same?"

"If they produce a shaggy elephant with long, curving tusks—"

"And if it has polka dots, they'll know they got it wrong. Do you think anybody will ever actually try for a dinosaur?"

The inn nestled in the Valdai Hills among birches white and golden-green. It was new, but built according to fashionably traditional styles and motifs. It offered excellent food and drink, plus live service by young men and women in old folk costumes. A singer accompanied himself on the balalaika. The help were kept busy. The couple who owned the place must be getting rich.

And why not? Should they sit idle on citizen's credit and relieve drabness with multiception? Here, they might find reason to beget a child or two.

Kyra pushed the thought away. The setting was too nice for it.

Fakey, of course. A let's-pretend. But what harm? Enjoy. Tomorrow she'd be back in school, grinding away, afraid to ease off for a moment lest she fall behind in the race to qualify for a berth in space, where everything and everybody was real.

12

Database

A BREEZE BLEW cool from the sunset, down a road of burning gold. The schooner ghosted along before it, her sails catching the light as well as the air, white against a blue that shaded nightward into violet. Waves shone in still more multitudinous hues, from horizon to horizon across the Coral Sea. They slipped small beneath the schooner's bow, whispered and chuckled the length of her hull, swirled aft in a wake filled with the molten glow.

Anson Guthrie and Juliana Trevorrow stood at the

taffrail, well-nigh alone. The helmsman paid them no heed; other passengers and crew were on the main deck, voices lost in the sounds of the waters.

Guthrie savored filling his lungs and slowly exhaling. "Ah, that's good," he murmured. "Not many places left where you can draw breaths like these."

Trevorrow nodded. "Nor have such sights and do such things." The cruise included the Great Barrier Reef, snorkels or aqualungs issued to those who wanted them.

"I'm glad we came while time remains." The tourist hordes were forcing further tightening of restrictions. "I thought I couldn't afford the price, but then figured I could much worse afford to lose what might be my last chance."

"Likewise. Well, in my case time rather than money was the problem, but you're right."

He liked hearing Trevorrow speak. It was in a husky contralto, and though she hailed from Sydney—or because she did?—the accent seemed less Strine to him than British, a tone from motherland greenwoods long since vanished. He liked her looks, too, tall, leggy, blond hair around features nearly classic. There was strength in those hands resting on the rail. She'd been a tad standoffish at first, but after several days had evidently decided she'd let acquaintance ripen further.

He grabbed the opportunity. "You're busy, then? May I ask what's your line of work?"

"You Americans would call it real estate and development, I believe." She met his gaze and smiled. "No, not knocking together little row houses. I began in my father's firm. He's been buying abandoned sheep range since the bottom dropped out of the wool market and applying biotechnology to convert it to agricultural land. Lately I have gone into business for myself."

"Not quite the same stuff, I'd guess."

"No, I'm now a licensed contractor in northern Queensland. Workers building the space center need every sort of supplies and services, at the back of the outback where they are. The entire area does. For example, we should do decent landscaping and plant the proper ground cover at the outset, even for temporary housing; forestall troubles with erosion, water, and pests. We should prepare to grow and ship tropical fruit, once transport is adequate; a potential cornucopia there, which among other benefits could let the Abos earn a reasonable income. Oh, the possibilities are unlimited." She sighed. "But it's hard for a new business to win a foothold. From a practical standpoint, I was idiotic to take a holiday." Laughter. "How fortunate, that attack of feeblemindedness."

Joy jumped in him. "Hey," he exclaimed, "what a coincidence! I'm aiming at exactly the same target."

"Are you?" The interest appeared genuine. "How?"

"Depends. I've got to scout the territory. Should've commenced as soon as I stepped off the plane, no doubt, but— Anyway, I have some experience in construction and some money to invest in high-tech, computerized equipment, the kind that lets one man do the work of twenty." He did not taste this breath that he drew. "Uh, maybe we could be . . . mutually helpful. Not to push you or anything, but maybe you'd like to talk about it, at least."

"Perhaps," she said carefully. "Aren't you being rather venturesome?"

Guthrie shrugged. "More fun that way."

"I should think you'd best try it out first closer to home."

Guthrie shook his head. His tone harshened. "I'd lose my shirt, and pants and union suit as well."

"Why?"

"You must know what it's like in the States these days. Though probably a person has to experience it directly to realize how bonkers the country is going. Canada too. I admit—well, I came back from years in South America, the money I spoke of caterwauling to be used, and it was like wading into a swamp of glue."

"I know the Renewal movement is on the upswing."

"Yeah, that's a large part of it. Environmentalism run amuck."

She frowned a little. "The planet is in a bad way."

"Sure. No argument. I've been a conservationist since I graduated from diapers. Cloth diapers. But if anybody calls me an environmentalist he'd better be quick on the draw. Hell, Ju— Beg pardon. Miss Trevorrow, from what you tell me, you and your dad are doing some of the things that'll repair the damage and prevent more. What won't do it is, for instance, closing down nuclear powerplants so people have to shiver in winter and breathe the garbage spewed out by coal-fired generators—not just carbon dioxide and carcinogens, but more radioactivity than nuclear accidents ever released. Or paying jewelry prices for solar units that might on a clear day furnish the juice for one light bulb per square yard of ecology they cover up. Or banning plastics that could perfectly well be made recyclable, in favor of paper that demands we turn the last of our forests into monoculture plantations. Or saddling business with such a load of taxes, regulations, and paperwork that it breaks the backs of all but the fatcat giant corporations. Or—"

He must pause for air. "Yes, I'm aware of that, and more," she said. "We're getting it in Australia too."

"Not as bad, I gather." Guthrie's smile was rueful. "Sorry, I didn't mean to rant at you. Actually, I think eco-fascism is just one side of the evil. It's fascism generally, or puritanism if you like. H. L. Mencken once defined a puritan as a man who wakes during the night in a cold sweat at the thought that somebody, somewhere, may be having a good time. So let's protect the poor, ignorant consumer from himself. Tax alcohol, tobacco, and junk food out of reach and propagandize against them with the aim of eventual prohibition. Indoctrinate and train the school kids, draft them into teams for the proper sports, *Kraft durch Freude*. Tax fuel a thousandfold; joyriding is wicked, and keeping your house at a comfortable temperature is antisocial. Make sure every medicine bottle needs a hacksaw to open, or a charge of nitroglycerine.

"Meanwhile, of course, onward with uplift. Require employing the right proportion of men, women, in-betweens, ethnics, and 'disadvantaged.' Have strict quotas in the colleges for the bright and literate and those who work at their studies, to make room for the 'mentally special.' Keep books with insensitive remarks in them off library shelves and out of stores. Better yet, don't let them be published. Keep ears stretched for wrong talk, reprove the offender publicly, haul him into court and fine him if you can. Or beat him up. No charges will be brought—

"Rats! There I went again. What a waste of a beautiful sunset. I do apologize."

"You needn't," she said gently. "I may not entirely agree, but I like people who have strong feelings and aren't afraid to express them, at least if the feelings are basically decent. Is this why you've come Down Under?"

"Not quite," he admitted. "I could've gone back to South America. Lots of opportunities there, what with democratic institutions taking firm root. But . . . Australia has a live space program these days. Ours is hopelessly bogged down in bureaucracy and corporate lardheadedness. Too many entrepreneurs have broken their hearts trying to lift off on their own. One way or another, the calcified giant has squashed them flat. The Europeans and Japanese have settled down into contentment with what they've got, which isn't bad but isn't much interested in getting better, either. Besides, they don't welcome foreigners.

"You people, you've finally decided to build a spaceport for yourselves. You talk about developing improved launch systems. I want to be a part of that, in however small a way. I want it very much."

Her look was steady upon him. "Why?"

"Why, that's where the future is, if we have any. I said I'm a conservationist. It's true we can't go on a lot longer taking everything out of the hide of Mother Earth. If we don't start using the resources yonder, and soon, industrial civilization is done for, and several billion people with it, maybe all of 'em. For any who somehow survive the crash, it's back to the Dark Ages, permanently. I want a better prospect for my children."

"How many have you?"

"None so far. I'm single." Never mind, at this moment, the long-ago accident. Nor did he see any immediate reason to mention Bernice. She'd tried, and he had, in what he now knew was a clumsy fashion, and the divorce was outwardly amicable but the pain of it had helped drive him overseas.

"You're right about the need for space," Trevorrow said. "At any rate, I've similar ideas." She hesitated. "Except for my father, I haven't discussed them with anyone else before."

"Nor I, much." He grinned. "To tell the truth, I hope to make my fortune in the cause. An obscenely big fortune. Doing well by doing good."

"Yes, we should talk more," she said, almost shyly.

His pulse thudded, but neither of them had immediate words. They turned their faces west. The sun had slipped away and the sea ran darkling, a-glimmer with the brightness that faded overhead. The breeze gathered force, fresh against brow and cheeks. It rustled in the shrouds. A boom creaked. The ship heeled slightly and the waves ran louder. Every sound remained muted, though, beneath the enormous hush in heaven.

Venus gleamed like a beacon.

Impulse burst from Guthrie: "By God, space is elbow room as well! Newness. Freedom."

He barely heard Trevorrow: "I've carried that thought about in myself."

He laid a hand over hers. She didn't seem to mind.

13

Database

HAVING LOOSE TIME on the Moon between missions, Kyra Davis took the monorail from Port Bowen to Tychopolis. That was where she'd likeliest catch some action. Astrebourg on Farside was staid, mainly devoted to research, and other communities had gone purely Lunarian since independence. Foreigners weren't forbidden entry, but it wasn't encouraged and those who went found themselves so isolated that they were happy to leave.

Tychopolis continued to be Luna's commercial and cultural interlink with the rest of the Solar System.

The ride was spectacular as always, over ashen maria and up into the highlands. Earth in night heaven sank lower as the train sped south; the shadows that its blue-and-white brilliance cast lengthened, bringing countless little pockmarks clear into sight. It did the same for jumbled regolith beneath which power cables lay buried. Transmission dishes loomed skeletal against the stars. You couldn't sense the beams they hurled at the mother world, but sometimes when she saw one it was as if a sound throbbed in Kyra's marrow, a song of energy clean and well-nigh limitless, a song of triumph.

The train climbed Tycho's ringwall, swooped down again, whizzed across the crater floor, and plunged underground near Skyview Tower. Kyra lockered her suitcase in the terminal. Later she'd bring it to the hotel where she had reserved a room. Tomorrow, universal time, she might revisit the standard attractions. She was especially fond of the gardens and zoo, the unique life forms they harbored. But sightseeing, or whatever adventures developed, went best in company. She'd begin by looking for a friend, which in turn began with having a drink.

The ornate old murals in the station behind her, she bounded upstairs to corridor level. Motion was a joy, strides long and airy-light, kangaroo leaps where space permitted, birdlike flight in Avis Park. The absence of civilian vehicles added to the pleasure. There was no call to fret about low-*g* effects. She'd only be here a short while; hours per day in a centrifuge weren't necessary.

When she reached Tsiolkovsky Prospect she had to slow down because of the crowds. In these surroundings she didn't care. The passage ran straight and broad, sides paved for skaters, duramoss green and yielding on the midstrip. Three levels of arcades rose on feathery pillars, shops, cafés, inns, amusement dens, enterprises more exotic. Overhead, the ceiling was a single glowpanel. Illusions drifted along it like clouds, a dragon, a jewel-burst, an undulant abstraction, trailing their umbras beneath them.

Odors of food, drink, perfume, and curious smoke mingled with music that trilled, wailed, beat, rippled from here and there in the arcades, never loud, never fully comprehensible to her. Voices overrode it, ceaseless chatter. More than half the people who thronged the corridor were visitors, tourists, businessfolk, journalists, spacers, vacationers from Astrebourg or L-5. The tumble-about of races, garbs, manners made her remember kaleidoscopes.

The Lunarians were less conspicuous among them than you might have expected. True, all were fine-boned and most were very tall, two meters or more; but the stature wasn't invariable, nor was everybody as thin as the stereotype. Many wore the typical somberly rich, Renaissance-like clothes, but some were in workaday unisuits or blouse and slacks. Men did lack beards and hair on their arms, women were small-bosomed and slim-hipped, but locks did not necessarily flow long, eyes were not necessarily big and oblique nor skins pale. The genetic transformation had not wiped out every trace of varied ancestry. What set them apart more than anything else was style. They moved through the swarm deftly, avoiding contact, as though the outsiders were an inanimate stream. They went singly or paired and talked low, in the euphonious language they had created for themselves.

Shopkeepers, tour guides, and such were more outgoing. Kyra suspected that that was generally a show. Certainly most of them, aloofly polite, gave the impression that when they took your money they were conferring an honor on you. It didn't bother her. The more variety in the cosmos, the better, and this was their world. She did wonder whether those commentators were right who declared that the Lunarians were basically different in mind as well as in body. Could you make human DNA over so radically that its bearers could spend their lives and have children here, without also getting a soul alien to Earth?

A troupe of musicians and mimes passed in flamboyant motley. They capered, they gesticulated, they played their sonors and tabors and crescent-flaring huntress horns; but each face stayed hidden behind a fanciful animal mask. They weren't performing for handouts. This was a traditional part of the scene, endowed by the local seigneurs. (Traditional? Fifty years at most. But evidently when you changed the organism, it found its own modes fast.)

The Prospect debouched on Hydra Square. Now transparent paving was under Kyra's feet, roof for an aquarium in whose deeps fish shimmered multi-hued among sinuous algae. The fountain at the center sprang nearly to the ceiling, a rush of whiteness and clear noise. Subsonics pulsed its cascades into evanescent forms suggestive of serpents. One side of the plaza housed service bases, constabulary, maintenance, hospital, rescue squads. The other three held museums. The historical museum was especially interesting, Kyra recalled. Among its exhibits were representations of Tychopolis before independence, back when anybody could enter the residential sections.

From the square she took Oberth Passage. Traffic was much less. Behind these closed doors, computers cerebrated and nanoworks bred their products. The district was worth walking through because of the emblems identifying each property. It was strange art, not quite reminiscent either of European heraldry or Chinese calligraphy, governed somehow by the curves of analytical geometry.

Ellipse Lane went off from Oberth. Fifty meters down its arc she spied what she sought. A light-sign flashed THE LAUNCH PAD. She entered.

"Kyra!" A short form pressed close. Arms embraced her.

She blinked and peered, vision adjusting to the dimness of the bar. For an instant she was astounded. *Eiko?* Then she made out the features and recognized Consuelo Ponce. A luminous L-5 shoulder patch had helped fool her. Twice foolish, she thought; Eiko would never go in for display like that, if ever she left home.

The young woman stepped back and beamed up at Kyra. "What a pleasant surprise," she said. Her English kept a slight, winsome Tagalog accent; she wasn't born in the space habitat where she lived. "The last I heard, you were bringing ice to Mars."

"Bueno, helping nudge it back onto the right trajectory, after it got perturbed," Kyra replied. "How in MacCannon's name did you hear about that?" Their acquaintance was casual, Consuelo being a cytomedic.

"Oh, I follow the news about all you space pilots avidly. Not many of you left, are there?" In haste, having seen Kyra's lips tighten a bit: "I've come for a conference in Astrebourg, on radiation damage therapy, but first wanted to see what consortes were here. Can we have some time together later?"

Kyra hesitated. Consuelo was a sweet person but almighty voluble. Besides, after her cruise Kyra wasn't hunting for female companionship. However— "Why not now? I'll just fetch me a beer."

The other clouded over, leaned close on tiptoe, and whispered under the buzz and rumble of talk, "I can't well leave that poor man yonder. I was bound back to him from a trip to the lavabo. Let me disengage gently."

Kyra's gaze followed Consuelo's furtive gesture. He seemed fairly young, sporting a mustache, a turban on his dark head, a white tunic patched with the trademark of Maharashtra Dynamics. Shoulders slumped, he stared into the tumbler before him. "A stranger to me," Kyra said.

"To me too when I arrived, but he was so sad that— It's a serious matter when a Parsee gets drunk. He needs a sympathetic ear."

"What's his trouble?"

"He was an engineering mineralogist, working with meteoroid ores. His company has cybered his job out from under him. Oh, he has a new position, but he knows it's makework. The pride, the meaning, they are gone."

Kyra winced for the second time. How much longer could old Guthrie hold out on behalf of her kind? She kept telling herself that no software yet written was entirely her match against the unending astonishments in space— regardless of what capabilities modern hardware might have—and you must also take capital costs into account— Nevertheless—

"It's good of you to care, Consuelo," she said. "Yes, let's by all means rendezvous later. I may get involved myself this evenwatch, but . . . tomorrow? Yes, yes, we'll stay in touch."

Unworthily glad to escape, she moved toward the bar. The Launch Pad was as antique as its name indicated, tables and chairs crowded together, a dart board, random souvenirs of spacefaring piled high on dusty shelves, photos and cards stuck blanketingly thick on the walls and faded with time. A multi offered chromokinetic accompaniment to a muted rendition of Beethoven's Fifth. You didn't come here to gape at it but to meet your lodge siblings. You didn't describe this place to groundlings, nor respond much to any tourist who happened in. The proper customers were spacers of every trade and their Earthside associates. Therefore the majority were Fireball—including, of course, those from L-5, special though their status was—and the allegiances of the minority divided among half a dozen lesser organizations.

Several of them who noticed Kyra recognized her and cried greetings. She hailed back, happy again, and bellied up to the bar. "Welcome home, gorgeous," caroled Rory Donovan behind it. "You've been gone unconscionably long, you have. Once more this mill is worth running. What's your wish, darling, the usual?"

"Yes, gracias, a draft Keplerbräu. And, uh, for openers, a shot of aqualunae, chilled." You could have imports if you were willing to pay the cost, but the local stuff was fine.

The bartender busied himself. "When and where's your next voyage?" he asked. She understood that he knew about her latest. Word from everywhere around the System reached Tychopolis, by laser if not by ship. "Far in the future, I'm hoping."

"They haven't decided," she said. "What's going on that's fun?"

"A colleen like you needn't ask or look. It'll find you. There you are. On the house, this round." At her thanks:

"No, no, it's I am owing you, as bright as you make my heart."

"You say that to every woman who comes in, Rory. And we love it."

He grinned, then had to go take an order. No robot would replace him while he lasted. Ugly as Avantism, Rory was, but he didn't need to get his face remodeled, the way he could blarney.

He might have done so when he was young, crossed Kyra's mind. Surely then he wanted to give the girls more than blarney. However, his body— He wasn't obviously deformed. It was an inner thing. He lived his life on the Moon, in poor health, because he wouldn't survive any reasonable span on Earth unless bonded to machines and chemical tanks. Not a metamorph; an adapt, relic of an experiment that hadn't paid off. The genes that handled low-weight for him weren't intrinsic, they'd been added after his birth, and they didn't mesh with his own as effectively as had been hoped. Hardly any like him remained. She'd never known whether his cheerfulness was genuine or a shield.

Crack, why did she let darkness keep thrusting in on her? She sought the tang of her liquor, the sparkle of the beer.

"Ah, Pilot Davis. Good evenwatch."

She turned. The man who had come to her side was blond, well-clad, attractive. "Perhaps you do not remember me," he said. His English was guttural. "Hans Gieseler. We met last year at a party in Heidelberg."

She recalled now. He was Fireball, a symbolic analyst, techno-economic interface. They'd talked about travels. He'd recommended several spots in Europe, and indeed she enjoyed those she afterward visited. He had a nice smile. When they shook hands, his clasp was straightforward. "What brings you to Luna?" she asked.

"A somewhat peculiar mission. Excuse me. Bartender, another glass of chablis. And may I reinforce yours, Pilot Davis?"

"Wait, I've barely begun," she laughed.

"I hope I am not being—*anmassend*—presumptuous. The truth is, I was feeling rather lonely after a difficult day, and you are the first person known to me who has come in here."

Kyra relaxed onto a stool. "Bueno, I should go around and say hola to my friends, but they all seem occupied at the moment."

"They will seek you out in any case. While I have the chance, how have you fared?"

"Muy bien, gracias." Curiosity piqued. "What is this mysterious mission of yours?"

"Nothing secret, although we do not publicize. You may well be aware that the company would like a third staging satellite in Lunar orbit. The Selenarchs refuse. They give various objections, but we suspect that principally they do not want more ground control and support personnel of ours on the Moon. I programmed and ran an inquiry, finding that the benefits to them will outweigh any inconvenience we bring. They studied it, said they were not convinced, but invited Fireball to send a spokesman. For some reason, not only the time lag, they prefer to negotiate in personal presence. I have been hours with Rinndalir and his underlings."

Kyra whistled. "Rinndalir? From what I've heard, at least you've started as near the top as they've got. How was it?"

"Oh, they were unfailingly gracious, but always I sense the steel underneath and the—*Mutwilligkeit?*—trickiness, wantonness? No, that is not the correct word. Steel, yes, but also mercury, and in them courses electricity—"

A voice cut through the noise, softly as a whetted blade through cloth. It was the baritone of a singer, speaking but vibrant with half-heard overtones, the English accented like none that ever was on Earth. "Hans Gieseler of Fireball Enterprises."

What the blaze! Every look in the room went to the multi. Its cylinder was big enough to hold, life size, a holo of head and upper torso. The face was marble-white, a vein blue in the throat. High cheekbones flanked great eyes gray as ice. The straight nose flared at the nostrils, the mouth was redeemed from feminine fullness by the pointed chin beneath. Silvery hair fell to the shoulders, past ears whose convolutions were not normal human. A goldwork fillet crossed the brow and iridescence played over the black tunic.

"Jesus, Mary, and Joseph," Rory whispered, "it's himself."

Rinndalir, Kyra knew. She'd seen few images of Lunarian lords and ladies, they were seldom out in public, but there was no mistaking Gieseler's expression.

"I have been in touch with my colleagues," the voice purred. "We wish to discuss further those questions that you raised. Please return immediately to your hotel. Transport for you and your effects will be waiting. Forgive this haste, I pray. Certain urgencies are involved. Thank you."

The bust vanished. Colors and music came back. For seconds more, silence held the people.

Gieseler shook his head as if stunned. "I have . . . never met the like before," he muttered. "How did he know where I am? How did he pre-empt this set? Or did he everywhere?"

"What'll you do about it?" Kyra asked stupidly.

Gieseler straightened. "I go. What else? I dare not risk offending them."

Rory plucked his sleeve and said against a rising uproar, "Hold on a mite, me boy. It would not surprise me at all, at all, are those rascals of a mind to wear you down and win a better bargain than they deserve."

"I can merely recommend." Gieseler tried to tug free.

"Even so, it's supperless you are, and I'll wager the hour will be late before they offer refreshment. Let me fix you a sandwich to eat on your way to the hotel. It will take but a minute."

"Good idea," Kyra said. Gieseler nodded jerkily. Thereafter he had to reply as best he could to those who swarmed around him wanting to know what this was about. The agitation pursued him to the door.

It wasn't that anybody felt hostile to the Selenarchy, Kyra knew. Lunarians might not be the most likable folk alive, but you were safe from crime here, they didn't bother you if you didn't bother them, and in their fashion they too were *space*. It had been natural for your parents to rejoice when the Moon declared itself a sovereign nation and made the declaration stick. But now it was natural to hope Fireball would carry the day.

The distraction had broken up conversational groups. As they re-formed, Kyra was surrounded by camaradas. A hectic merriment set in. Drink flowed, gushed, torrented. Rather than go out after food, her group settled for Rory's monumental sandwiches. Eventually they got to singing, more and more the old spacer songs until—

> "*MacCannon was a Fireball man. That rambling rocketeer*
> *Could lift off into orbit on a single keg of beer.*
> *The whisky that he much preferred was made not for the meek.*
> *Unless you were a Scot, a shot would ground you for a week.*
>
> "*MacCannon was a macho man, a brawling, balling Celt.*
> *For EVA he needed just a helmet and his pelt.*
> *His lady friends expressed their love in moans and groans and pants,*
> *And made remarks among themselves concerning elephants.*
>
> "*Its clouds sulfuric acid high above the CO_2,*
> *So hot and thick down underneath that lead itself would stew,*
> *The atmosphere of Venus is as poisonously ripe*
> *As the air became around us when MacCannon lit his pipe.*
>
> "*His ship once had an argument while passing through the void,*

Alone, about the right of way, with one big asteroid.
Adrift, he used the time to make a large discovery,
The art of shooting craps to win in zero gravity.

"The devil knocked upon the lock and said, 'You're
  due to die.
Come down with me.' MacCannon spat some whisky
  in his eye.
The sizzle and reaction sent the devil with a yell
On a hyperbolic orbit that would take him back to
  hell.

"MacCannon then decided his disabled boat should
  boost.
He ate a mighty meal of beans and set himself to roost
Upon a mass ejector tube far sternward in his craft,
And the ship went leaping forward from the thunders
  booming aft.

"'Round Jupiter he whipped so fast he had but minor
  woes;
The radiation only crisped the hair within his nose.
Approaching home, he showed us what his pilot skills
  were worth,
Crash landing on an island off Antarctica of Earth.

"Besieged by lustful penguins, nearly out of whisky
  too,
He set to make a signal that would fetch a rescue crew.
Olympus Mons had never spewed more smoke up over
  Mars
Than the vileness puffing skyward from MacCannon's
  damn cigars.—"

The ballad went on, gross, childish, and, for Kyra during
a minute after she happened to glance at the man who had
lost his career, forlornly defiant.

14

FROM SALEM SHE took a bus four hundred-odd kilometers east to Baker. She reached the town late on the third day of her escape, found a room in a small hotel and a meal nearby, and flopped out. The rides hadn't been bad, but waiting in terminals between them had stretched her thin. How many plainclothes officers were posted?

Incessant newscasting about terrorists didn't help. The country was being roiled into a vigilante mood. The government might no longer be popular, but anything was preferable to bombs in control centers or destructive nanotech.

"The essential minimum of truth," Guthrie had remarked. " 'Chaotic' is a broad cussword. It covers the few maniacs who do exist, along with everybody else who seriously wants to be rid of the Avantists. Not that we'll try to contact the sane, more or less organized ones. Those who're smart and lucky have made themselves unfindable. What I'm hoping for—well, pseudo-me knows about it and has surely tipped the Sepo, but I think their main attention will be on more obvious possibilities, like a Fireball consorte having stashed me someplace. That's a gigalot of people and places to check out. Meanwhile, those I have in mind, they have resources."

In the morning, feeling considerably better, Kyra left him enclosed by her bag, wrapped in her garments, and set forth. The hotel was antiquated; a live worker would clean the room and make the bed. Perforce she assumed that person wouldn't snoop. She dared not put the bag in safe deposit. Each broadcast she'd seen told the public to be on the lookout for infernally clever devices and report whatever might be suspicious, or just unusual, to the police.

Outside, the air was already warming in the hot dry summer that reigned east of the Cascades. The buildings, old and mostly low, reminded her, in their very different style, of Novgorod; but here was more activity, more life.

Though traffic was not so dense that cars and trucks were banned on any streets, it bustled. Most vehicles bore the Homesteader emblem, a green field on which a medieval-looking plow was silhouetted against a rising sun. Most riders and pedestrians wore unostentatious clothes of good material. They seemed more relaxed and cheerful, on the whole, than the average North American. Her informant obtained municipal bus routes for her, and she caught one to the outskirts of town.

The hinterland rolled away in crops, pastures, orchards. Their cultivation was not robotic; she spied individuals on tractors. Houses and their outbuildings lay two or three kilometers apart. Northward rose an industrial park, not large but its sleek modernity a contrast to the farms. At its distance she couldn't make out what flag flew above it; however, since it was clearly not the Union's, she'd bet it was the Homesteaders'.

They were, she'd heard, the society least separate from the mainstream, the readiest to do business with non-members. That didn't mean they were less desirous of maintaining economic and cultural independence, their special ideals and ways, than were, say, the Muslims. They likewise had their laws, governance, ranks, rites, initiations, mystique. If anything, Kyra thought, their lack of overt picturesqueness kept them freer than others from outside notice and interference.

She walked along a street to the address Guthrie had given her. Trees shaded the paving. Some houses perhaps went back a couple of centuries with their frame sides and deep porches. Lawns and flowerbeds surrounded them. The air was quiet and smelled sweet. Doubtless this wasn't an exclusively Homesteader neighborhood, but it must be predominantly so, like the entire valley. The society's chapters had expanded fast in regions where agriculture could feed the populace without needing fancy machinery and where self-help was a tradition not altogether extinct.

Nerves drawing taut, she approached Esther Blum's dwelling. The Regent of all the Homesteaders might be a friend of Guthrie's from way back, but a hundred things occupied her hours and Kyra could scarcely use the jefe's name to gain admission. Worse, this place was probably under surveillance. Who was in the unmarked car that drove slowly past, who was it who stood on the corner as if expectant?

She passed between rosebeds to stairs, mounted them to verandah coolness, and touched the call plate. The door opened. "Saludos," said a muscular young man. His eyes appreciated her. "What can I do for you?"

"I, I need to see Sra. Blum," Kyra answered.

"Plenty of folks do. I can maybe swing an appointment for you day after tomorrow."

"Now. Por favor. It's personal and urgent. Won't you tell her it concerns Winston P. Sanders and the drunken mermaid?"

"Huh?"

"Por favor." Kyra gave him the three-kilowatt smile while shrugging to induce maximum movement of the upper works. "I know it sounds funny, but I promise you she'll receive me. If she doesn't, boot me out."

"M-m, it's weird enough that she should at least enjoy hearing it. Come in, Señorita, uh—"

"Bovary. Emma Bovary."

In a chamber that served as an anteroom, a variety of men and women waited to be called. Two looked like farmers and two like tech bosses, but who were the afro in the dashiki and the shavepate in the red robe? A multiceiver was lacking. Printouts of books and periodicals lay on end tables. Kyra tried to read an article about discoveries under the surface of Mars. It wouldn't take hold of her. Interesting stuff, but humans weren't exploring those caves, machines were. The author emphasized their intelligence. Was the author a machine too, the byline a heteronym? Could well be. If not, the generally prosy text and occasional vivid random-generated phrase showed that he or she had merely ridden herd on a writing program.

"Señorita Bovary, por favor."

Kyra's heart leaped like her body. A woman led her down a hall and showed her through a hinged door.

Clutter made the office beyond seem less spacious than

it was, a jackdaw's nest of objects crammed on shelves and tables, codices, replicated ancient Egyptian figurines, a kachina doll, assorted paperknives, the mounted fossil of a fish, German beer steins, miscellaneous trophies, a teddy bear that clearly had no mechanisms but was stuffed. . . . Esther Blum sat behind an enormous desk. She was small, thin, quick-moving, in a yellow blouse and purple slacks. Stiff white hair framed a face deeply furrowed but aflicker with expression and pale blue eyes that had watched almost a century go by.

"Hi," she piped when the door had shut. "What's your real name? If I were stealing from forgotten classics, I'd pick something less glum, like Roberta Wickham. Speak up."

Kyra drew breath. "Are we secure?"

"From the dipnoses of our beloved government, you mean? Yes. It's quite a spell since I had this house screened forty ways from Sunday. The Renewal had gone onto the rubbish heap, but I didn't imagine the country would stay free forever, if you call that pittance of liberty we got back freedom. Since then I've had the safeguards updated as necessary. Certain persons in a position to know inform me, on the QT, what is about to become necessary. Satisfied? Sit down and introduce yourself."

Kyra obeyed. "It's about Anson Guthrie," she added.

"I knew that the moment I heard your password."

"He gave it to me. Wouldn't explain what it means."

Blum leered. "Nor will I, my dear. That incident would shock your socks off."

"Uh, señora—"

"Nothing doing. It was long ago and I was young and to this day I have no remorse, but it's best that only Anse and I are left to chuckle." Blum's grin vanished. "Okay, what's the tsuris?"

"Pardon me?"

"The trouble. Grim, no?"

"Yes." Kyra told her.

Wrinkled lips shaped a soundless whistle. "Oy gevalt!" The eyes narrowed, the gaunt head nodded. "It figures, though. I had to work at believing that was Anse on the multi. But what would they gain by faking him? Could those claims about saboteurs fixing to blow things to bits be real? Now— We'd better move quick, before that mamzer they made nails things at Fireball down too tight for Anse to open again."

"He's hoping you—"

Blum lifted a hand. "Hush. Let me think." She turned to stare out the window at a tree and the sky. In the back of her brain Kyra wondered which of several methods had been used to make the panes proof against voice vibrations that an instrument outside could decode. Blum had seen no need to draw the blind. Of course not; that would have marked this interview as special. . . . Kyra's pulse ticked minutes away.

Blum stirred, blinked, reached into a box on her desk and took forth a cheroot. "Do you indulge, missy?" she asked. "No? Sensible. Keeps the biorepair bills down." A gaudy ring on her finger spouted fire to light it. Her tone bleakened. "I'm afraid we can't offer much help."

Kyra had rallied herself. "What *can* you do?"

Blum gave her an approving look. "Straight to the point. Excellent. To start with, I can just allow you a dab of time, or watchers will speculate." She sighed. "Yes, the Sepo have us staked out. Not conspicuously, but in a community like this, things get noticed, and I've pals in the local police department. Nor heavily, but enough that we'd be crazy to contact Anse here, and he'd be crazy to linger.

"Nevertheless, I do want to meet with him, and I think I can arrange something useful through trustworthy intermediaries. We'll rendezvous in Portland tomorrow."

"What?" Kyra exclaimed. "Isn't that station a trap by now?"

"Quite possibly, but not to worry. You buy a ticket for Portland, all right, but get off at a certain hamlet about halfway to there. Have a cup of coffee in the one and only café. It's got to be the planet's second worst coffee, but every good cause requires sacrifices. A man will join you. I'm not sure who he'll be, but if he isn't Henry Willard he'll still give you that name so you'll know. The busies aren't going to trail an ordinary farmer who drives off on some or other errand. Don't tell Henry anything. I won't have either. Why jeopardize him as well as ourselves?"

Kyra reflected transiently on trust and loyalty among folk who were close-knit. Like Fireball's. "I understand."

"He'll take you to Portland and drop you off at a house where the family won't ask questions and you can get some sleep and decent food. They aren't Homesteaders, by the way. I have my tentacles in assorted places. Survival demands it."

"What are they? I may need to know."

"Nu, be forewarned and don't ask for a drink. They're Mormons, if that rings a bell in you. The Avantists are particularly hard on their church. The claim is that its premises are antiscientific, but the truth is that its congregations object loudly to the molding of posthuman man.

"Okay, Henry will've given you a screened box to have Anse in, which'll look like a parcel from a department store. The screening will get you arrested if it blocks a detector aimed your way, but you'll take a route from the house tomorrow evening that'll bypass the likely checkpoints. The screening's just in case you chance within a block or two of a detector. You're going to Emprises Unlimited, which is the quivira in Portland. Got plenty of cash?"

Kyra swallowed startlement. "Uh, yes."

"Have more." The cheroot wagged in Blum's mouth while she rummaged in a drawer. "You'll enter Emprises at about 1930 hours. That's when it generally has its biggest inflow, not that such are beswarmed, considering what they charge. Tell 'em you're Roberta Wickham—no sense in leaving the same trail—and you've got a date with two others who should arrive shortly. You ever been in a quivira?"

"Yes, twice."

"Good. You know the drill, then, sort of. If somebody wonders about your parcel, explain this is a celebration and you want to give one of your friends a present before the three of you settle down in a fancy mirage. You won't be hassled, seeing what kind of money you'll be forking over. Here." Blum handed over a sheaf of bills.

Kyra took it mechanically. "Why a quivira?"

"Because I may well be shadowed, and that is the one place safe for us to meet."

"Really?"

"Absolutely. To this day, every single room in a first-class quivira is screened as tightly as my house, and the law compels no employee to reveal, ever, what goes on. The management has ways of knowing if he did, and it'd cost him his job and get him barred from every such place. Which for his kind, or hers, would be like death or worse. They get free time on the machine, and usually grow dependent. As for the secrecy, various bigwigs patronize those establishments. Imagine the leverage an opponent would have on you if he found out what fantasies you indulge."

Blum went briskly into details before dismissing her visitor. Kyra listened and responded, but not with her whole self. Almost against her will, a part of her was harking back.

15

Database

HER FIRST TIME she had gone alone, telling nobody. It wasn't anything to be ashamed of, she kept assuring herself. An experience, an adventure. Lots of people went, and those who had described it to her seemed none the worse. She had graduated from the Academy, she'd be shipping out, this was her last chance for Heisenberg knew how long. Still, it took resolution as well as a large piece of her savings. She was angry to feel her face hot, and that made her blush all the deeper.

The counselor who received her was skillfully simpática. "We simply go a step beyond vivifer capability on a multi," she explained. "I grant you, it *is* a threshold. You're wise in wanting to cross it cautiously. Let me suggest you spend one objective hour in a standard program. That way, at first you can relax, let things happen, and enjoy. As you grow confident, you can start taking an interactive part. If you don't try for something too different from what's in the program, it will adapt as smoothly to your wishes as the real world does when everything's going right for you. . . . Is that agreeable? . . . Now let's discuss what kind of virtuality you'd like. Take your time. Don't be afraid to speak frankly. I'm shockproof, and nothing goes beyond these walls."

Presently she led Kyra to a single-person room, helped her disrobe, fitted the helmet and other connections to her, guided her into the bath. For an indefinite time Kyra lay blind and deaf. She felt an odd shiftiness in her perceptions, realized that the system was adjusting the fluid to her precise specific gravity and skin temperature, began to slip down the pleasant slope that leads into sleep, except this was the machine gently pulsing her brain. . . .

She floated in space. Stars gleamed everywhere around. Great plumes of zodiacal light spread from a shrunken sun whose glare did her eyes no harm; and though she wore nothing but halter, skirt, and sandals, she was at Zen ease, utterly alert, every sense a-thrill. Turning, she saw Mars before her, a huge ruddiness crowned with white polar caps, veined with canals, dappled with oases and dead sea bottoms. She stretched her arms forward and plunged toward it.

On the surface she was entirely material, breathing the thin air, savoring the aromas of desert shrubs borne on a cool wind, moving lightly under the low weight. The sun stood at mid-afternoon; she had till midnight, subjective time. Cinderella.

Her choice had been innocent—juvenile, probably. John Carter rode from the west and greeted her with a Virginia courtesy that centuries had not blurred. He led a thoat for her. Over the sands they fared, he pointing out venerable ruins and fleeting beasts. At a camp of green men Tars Tarkas poured wine for them, after which they boarded a flying ship. Above a canal the towers of Helium flashed athwart sunset. Dejah Thoris wasn't home when they landed, but red warriors made Kyra welcome with feline dignity, each more handsome than the last though none equal to John. By then she had gotten over her shyness and begun making requests to see this or do that. He obliged—not passively, but as a gentleman would who knew the country and had ideas of his own. Together they roamed the magical streets while Phobos and Deimos hurtled aloft, bigger than Luna above Earth, to fill the world full of silver and hastening shadows. When at length she must return, he read her body language and took her in his arms. She'd never been kissed before with such authority. Damn, she thought as she went astral and flashed toward the blue star that was Earth, next time she'd proposition him earlier.

There was no next time. For a while it tempted powerfully, but she had too much else to occupy her, and that was *real*. Her memories of Barsoom did not fade in the way of a dream. As far as her brain was concerned, those traces were no different from any left by actual events. But they took their proper place among adolescent crushes and toys beloved in childhood.

Her second trip to a quivira she made with Ivar Stranding, during the single brief span they managed to have on Earth together. He wanted it more than she did. Not that he was addicted, but he'd taken all his few opportunities to go. Thus he knew a fair amount about the interactive potentialities. It was more than a game, he insisted. For a couple it could be a kind of spiritual union. She hesitated. What about inner privacy? She didn't ask him that. Their relationship was strained already. Plain to see, he thought this might help. Eventually she agreed.

A free-form program demanded the full resources of the system, especially when two persons were cross-connected. It cost. Bueno, whatever a spacer might lack, money wasn't included. He told her to let him take the initiative till she got the feel of things. "Then we'll both be gods, darling."

They stood at a parapet overlooking the unborn cosmos.

Their own radiance illuminated the vast walls and spires of their stronghold. Against its ramparts, beneath primordial night, formlessness blazed and raged. Waves, a million light-years from trough to crest, surged in to burst with a roar and a song of energies. Spindrift stars, flung high, exploded as supernovae, a dreadful glory strewing the stuff of worlds to be across emptiness.

"Come." His tones echoed like a trumpet call, from end to end of space-time. "Let there be us." He took her by the hand and they walked out over the sea.

With his free hand and his will, he reached down to stir the chaos. It swirled, broke apart into clouds, sundered further to make embryonic galactic clusters; and that was the first day.

When she sought to spin out a delicate tracery of spiral arms, new-born suns crashed into each other or whirled away lost, and everything disintegrated. His laughter rang. "Try again, beloved. Know what you desire, and it will come to pass." By the end of the second day she had made a planetary system, exquisite as clockwork.

On the third day she chose a globe and breathed life into its seething chemistry. He toyed with many.

On the fourth day she made the land blossom and wings to gladden the skies. "Be not too careful," he warned. "You could lose eternity creating a hummingbird. Things will evolve of themselves. Come here, see what I have done with these twinned gas giants."

On the fifth day she returned her perceptions to her favored world and tuned them atom-fine. Certain animals made tools in stone. They looked about them, marveled, and wondered. Their numbers were few. Glaciers moving down from the pole menaced them. She changed subtle parameters and in a thousand of their years the climate was benign again.

On the sixth day she found her little beings cruelly at war. She heard weeping among the dead and the flames. Therefore she smote their leaders, revealed herself unto their peoples, commanded eternal peace, and showed them how to fly into space.

On the seventh day he said: "It is good. We have wrought enough. Let us make love."

They did as befits gods, on a bed of star-clouds, in lightning sweetness that went on for half of forever.

"It was wondrous," he said, "yet it was not wholly unlike what we have known before. Let us do now what we could not then."

She was earth and sea given form. He was the heavenly Dragon who twined Himself about Her.

"Dare we remain longer?" she whispered in a shaken darkness.

"We cannot even if we would," he answered. "Listen closely and you will hear the faint notes of our summons home. Anon we must heed them."

"It is well. I am riven by too much splendor."

"First," he said, "let us make love once more, in purely human fashion, the same sharing of self that is ours in our mortal lives."

Her heart shivered. "Why?"

"Because here we can do it as else we never could, and come to full knowledge of one another. You shall be me and I shall be you."

She demurred, but he urged, and when she felt the growth of his anger she said yes. She discovered that sometimes a man, too, must force himself—if he is able at all, as she willed to be—but this she did not tell him. A part of her stood aside, observing from within. His body had its pleasure and found her beautiful.

The evening of their universe was upon them. They winged amidst its suns and worlds. "What will become of our poor worshippers?" she wondered.

"Why, they will cease to be," he replied indifferently. "They never truly were, you know."

She fell behind him on their way out, lest he see her foolish tears. Each became a blue star, such as shines brightly but only for a short while.

It took her a day to make sense of ordinary Earth, a week before she was quite under control. Ivar tried to understand and failed. She didn't blame him for anything, he'd done his best, but by the end of their groundside leave she realized that soon they'd part company. Nor did she regret her experience. It had been fascinating and enlightening. But she knew she would never want more.

16

EMPRISES UNLIMITED OCCUPIED a small tower on a hill in Portland. Kyra wondered which of its virtualities could match the sight of Mt. Hood afar, aglow with eventide in the mild seaboard air. To be sure, the encephalic and glandular stimulations could convince you that anything was unutterably beautiful, or horrible or justifiable or whatever you'd picked. She went in.

Upon request and payment, a receptionist showed her to a room where she could wait for her friends and meet with them, privacy guaranteed, for several hours if they wished. The comfortable furnishings included a wall bed that, lowered, would accommodate four. She guessed it was seldom used. Who'd come here for a mundane orgy? Unless, maybe, the engineered one left them red-hot.

Funny, she thought, how tolerant the Avantists were in many ways. From what she'd learned about it, the Renewal would have been death on this kind of indulgence. Probably—she hadn't studied the history in detail— much that the Avantists disapproved of was too well-entrenched by the time they took over for them to abolish by fiat. Besides, wasn't the idea to proceed not by force but by education, indoctrination, and the establishment of such scientifically designed socioeconomic conditions that progress toward the Transfiguration became inevitable?

"It flopped, of course," Guthrie had said. "Cowflopped. As people got more and more disappointed and cynical, things worked worse and worse, the ideologues and bureaucrats went frantic, and the whole caboodle became a perpetual fight to grab and keep power. Which is how all governments end up, but the busybody kinds get there fastest. The purpose of power is power."

She unwrapped him and put him on the table. "Thanks," he growled. "No fun sitting in a box inside a box. Judas priest, I'm tired of being bodiless!"

Sympathy pierced her. "I don't imagine I could have stood it a fraction of the time you have," she said.

"Well, existence feels different for me. Patience comes easier than it did when I was alive." He spoke the phrase with a casualness that chilled her. "It does wear thin at last, but I tell myself eventually I'll be reconnected."

How much of a substitute for flesh were robotic sensors and effectors? Kyra hadn't the heart to ask. Yet she had come to know him more than a bit, and this first outright confession of weariness, of inner pain, touched her as deeply as if her father had made it. "You're very brave, jefe. I wouldn't download."

"Damn few ever did, you know, and all but two others have ended it by now. I've had Fireball to keep me amused." Guthrie's tone softened. "It's not a question of courage, though. The process doesn't hurt *you*. It just makes a copy of your mind, a quite separate critter."

Kyra nodded. "Of course. No deliverance from personal death." No deliverance anywhere in sight, after it turned out that aging was built into the human genome. You could improve matters only up to a point. "But I, well, I'd be afraid that other self would curse me."

"You may change your feelings later, sweetheart. This is a mighty interesting universe. Furthermore—"

A chime, a voice: "Your friends are here, Srta. Wickham."

Kyra tautened. "Let them in."

The door admitted Esther Blum and a man. He was in his thirties, Kyra deemed, of medium height, slim but wide-shouldered, cat-lithe. His face, dark and cleanly sculptured, was not expressionless, but gave no real hint of what he might be thinking. Loosely cut, his jacket nevertheless fitted the nattiness of blouse, slacks, and shoes which she noticed were made to give secure footing. The garments were in conservative hues. However, he had had a biojewel set in his forehead. At the moment it shone a cool green.

Blum's gaze met Guthrie's eyestalks. "Well, so there you are," she greeted him. "A fine kettle of soup you've dropped into, schlemiel. I should leave you simmering till you're fit to eat, except that wouldn't be fair to this poor little shiksa you've conned into holding the hand you haven't got."

"Huh!" snorted Guthrie. "You keep quiet about seduction of the young. Beware this old witch, you two. She's evil and depraved. I've seen her put ice cream in her beer."

Blum blinked—did tears gleam?—and straightened out her grin. "Better we should get down to business," she said. "Anson Guthrie, the real Anson Guthrie; Kyra Davis; Nero Valencia."

The man's handgrip was firm and quick. "Buenas tardes. The señora has explained your situation to me in a general way." His baritone made graceful the flat Middle American English.

The three sat down. "Okay, Esther," Guthrie said, "now suppose you explain to us."

Blum took a cheroot case from her pocket. "Someday perhaps you'll appreciate the trouble I've gone to on your account," she answered. "What with the Sepo watching, they should die of overdosing on political speeches, my contacts had to make contacts, and all since yesterday. I didn't meet Nero till two hours ago. We didn't enter here together, naturally. Bad enough the gendarmes are wondering what's a nice Jewish girl like me doing in a place like this."

Jocularity faded. "It's the best I could manage, Anse," she said. "I won't risk compromising my Homesteaders, but you are a hope of sorts for us and—we had some good times, we two."

"They'd've been bed-shaking times when you were young, if I hadn't already been canned," Guthrie replied. "Thanks for everything, Esther."

"Enough wiz zees lovemaking." Blum lit a cheroot and

drew hard on it. The smoke was uncommonly acrid. "Do you have a scheme in mind, a way to crash out that you think might work?"

Kyra's nerves thrilled. "We've discussed several," she said. "Depending on what help we can get—"

"Don't tell me. I shouldn't hear more than I have. But I figured you could use a guide through routes that aren't on any map, and if he's a fighter as well, so much the merrier. I've engaged this gunjin for you."

Valencia inclined his head a moment. "Of the Sally Severin brotherhood, at your service," he said quietly.

Guthrie raised his eyestalks, the single physical gesture available to him. Kyra supposed he recognized the name. She didn't, but she got the general meaning. A mercenary, a latter-day condottiere. His work was not necessarily criminal. Probably more often than not he simply guarded a person or a property. As societies, organizations, wealthy individuals grew alienated from the government, they were bound to hire protection for themselves rather than bring in the police. But she'd seen plenty of accounts, fiction or alleged fact, of the readiness of most gunjins to accept illegal jobs, anything from smuggling to turf wars between gangs.

Had this one given himself his first name? Maybe it was just that his parents had been among those neo-pagans who were dedicated anti-Christians.

She pulled her attention back to him. "My contract is with the señora," he was saying, "but she's assigned me to give you every assistance I can. Therefore my duty is to you, Sr. Guthrie, till she revokes this or the contract expires in two weeks. At that time, if you wish and I'm willing, we can make a new one. Meanwhile I am your man, within the laws of the brotherhood. Essentially that means I won't be party to atrocities or perversions and, while I'll risk my life for you if need be, I'm not obliged to undertake suicidal actions. I'll give you a pamphlet that makes these conditions clear." He smiled. It was as charming a smile as Kyra had ever seen. "Not that I expect you'll give me cause to decline an order. I've admired you all my life, sir." To Kyra: "And you, my lady, are a delightful surprise."

He went serious again: "My territory's the West Coast, more or less from Vancouver down through Baja. I've operated elsewhere but I'm not really familiar with those parts. If you want to head east, we may have to engage a local man. I can find one for you."

"I doubt we will," Kyra blurted.

"I told you don't tell me!" Blum cried. She addressed Guthrie, anxiously. "Did I do right? Does this improve your chances any?"

"Listen, gal," he rumbled, "if I could hook into the circuits here, I'd throw you such a party your fleshly carcass, too, would walk bowlegged. I could do it for your download. Come live with me and be my love."

"Thanks, but no, thanks. Send me a case of booze after you get home." The fragile voice broke. "Oh, Anse—!" She stiffened in her seat. "Is everything agreed, then? Nu, let's plan how we leave this joint."

"I suggest you go first, señora," Valencia murmured. "If a detective's on surveillance outside, you should draw him after you. Señorita Davis can take off a few minutes later, and I separately. I'll have Sr. Guthrie's carrier, because I didn't before and because, if something goes malo, I can likelier shake pursuit. Fetch your baggage from wherever you've left it, señorita, and take a room in the Hotel Neptune. I'll be in 770."

"First we repackage Anse and next we spend an hour or two in Never-Never Land," Blum said. "We don't want them wondering why we didn't. I'm not sure quiviran discretion would stretch that far, given the current hysteria. Last newscast I caught, the government was promising fat rewards for information, especially about electronic-photonic devices that might be planted to jam central control systems."

They couldn't approach the truth closer than that without rousing questions about Guthrie Two, Kyra thought. Unease prickled. Dared her band leave this Guthrie in a container that anybody could open, while they lay adrift from the world? . . . No choice. Blum was right. It was the lesser risk. Don't check the parcel, take it along to the entertainment room, be casual about it.

"The señora is wise." Valencia shrugged and grinned. "If I am treated to a free spinaway, what shall it be?"

"Nothing . . . intimate, por favor," Kyra said. "I'm not exactly eager."

"It's not my vice either," Blum admitted.

"Did you ever go, Esther?" Guthrie asked.

"Once, out of curiosity. Grubby old reality is much more surprising and wonderful."

"A quivira can call it back for you if you want," he said softly.

"Repeat, no, thanks. I've buried two husbands, each a mensch, and one good son. Leave memories in peace. What spare time I've got left is for the live children and grandchildren." Blum smiled. "Plus the cutest little devil of a great-grandson." She snuffed out her cheroot and rose. "Not that I'm teetotal about quiviras. In fact, I've screened a catalogue of prepared programs and chosen one for us. You should like it, Kyra, and I trust you'll not be bored, Nero. Let's go."

"What is it?" Kyra inquired.

"A dinner party in Philadelphia. Our host will be George Washington. Our fellow guests are Thomas Jefferson and Benjamin Franklin. Join in the conversation by all means, but mind your manners. They're illusions, yes, parts of a hypercomputer program, but they're also the most careful replication of the personalities that scholarship has made possible. Me, for once I'd rather listen than talk."

"God damn," Guthrie said, "I have to sit and envy you."

17

ONCE, A GOOD many years ago in Quito, he had declared: "We're going to build ourselves something new here. The first machine that doesn't, somewhere along the line, flunk the Turing test. But I must admit that'll be because it cheats. You see, I'll be in it."

"I think before long they will have a system that will truly be conscious on its own," Juan Santander Conde had replied. In those days he was no more than middle-aged, though old in friendship with Guthrie, and active as a top director of Fireball.

"Yeah, the Holy Grail of psychonetics. And just about as elusive, *I* think."

"Already—"

"Sure, sure. Pretty good simulations. In fact, I don't say the first-chop programs don't have some awareness, same as I credit a lizard with a little bit, a dog with a fair amount, and a monkey with quite a lot. But basically, they're like *idiots savants.* Superbrilliant in their narrow fields, otherwise there is no there there. Seems to me, if any of the approaches that're being tried to make them more nearly comparable to humans, if any of those were right, we'd've reached the goal by now. . . . I know what you're about to say. Don't bother. Programs in those new dream palaces. People who've tried it swear it's exactly like interacting with a real, live person. But it *is* a dream. The customer's input is part of what goes on and his intuition acts like a feedback loop. If he brings more to the interaction—knowledge, imagination, whatever—if he brings more than the program's geared to adapt to, he soon isn't dealing with the pseudopersonality that was intended. It becomes something else, radically unlike what it was. It may disintegrate."

"I know, and I had no intention of mentioning that."

"Sorry. No offense, Juan. I am apt to talk too much. Sometimes it gets kind of lonesome where I am. Never mind! What I want developed for Fireball is an entirely different breed of cat—anyhow, when I'm in it. You see, I want it able to include me in its works."

As the robot made the attachments for new Guthrie, he started to ask, "Say, what about—" and braked himself.

"Have you a question?" purred the information screen.

"No, nothing. Proceed."

When he was fully linked and integrated, he put his inquiry to the system. It was prudent to begin with a few simple, straightforward retrievals. Direct access to the whole, possession of its capabilities, could be overwhelming at first. Insofar as human language was able to describe what he now did, it felt as if he called some fact out of his ordinary memory, a date or an address or the color of a woman's eyes.

The hypercomputer identified his desire by class and switched it through the appropriate circuits. If need be, retrieval could have scanned databases around the planet. Examination of every logical implication could have brought in other mainframes equally far-flung. As was, the information called for got back to Guthrie in a few milliseconds.

Yes, progress was being made in artificial intelligence, though news of it hadn't been in the updatings he got in North America. He'd had too much else to learn, about everyday matters and how they had changed during the years in which he lay oblivious.

He found that the forefront of advance was no longer in Fireball's laboratories. His idea of incorporating himself, as occasion warranted, in the core of his company's cybernetics, had been so successful as to give him second thoughts. While he didn't forbid further research along these lines, he stopped helping it out, and it languished.

Elsewhere, however, workers had been following his lead in earnest, notably at Technofutures in Europe and Hermes Communications in Astrebourg. They had made considerable progress. It would doubtless have been more if they also had had a download to work with. But neither of the two others who were still extant was interested.

Uwimana was entirely given over to his own scientific endeavors, he had become cosmophysics personified. Nguyen was lost in whatever the mysteries were on which she meditated.

As for making a new one, hardly anybody agreed to serve as the subject-original. "I wouldn't like being a machine. Nor would a copy of my mind." The few volunteers were judged unsuitable, on this or that account.

Still, the hardware that could handle a download was buildable, as witness what was already in existence. Could you and your computers write a program for it that would operate like a downloaded personality? If so, you would have reached the Holy Grail, artificial intelligence fully conscious and limited only by the capabilities of the systems to which it was coupled.

Algorithm after algorithm had been devised, tried, found wanting, revised, tried again, ultimately discarded. Lately, though, another idea had been gaining ground. The mind was partly algorithmic, true, but not totally. You must take quantum effects into account—especially, it seemed, Bell's inequality and the energy of the vacuum. Nothing supernatural; yet the observer and the observed were one, the cause had roots in the effect, Ouroboros made of himself a ring. On that basis, you might be able to map onto a material configuration that which nature had done in the course of megayears of evolution.

Once you were on the right track, with the computer power you had nowadays, you should soon capture the prize. Then what?

Guthrie turned from that question. He had more urgent concerns. For a while he exercised, regaining the skills of godlike intellect. He constructed elaborate differential equations and solved them. He modeled three large organic molecules and let them react. He explored fractal realms of such dizzying beauty that it was a wrench to leave them.

But he must. After about half a real-time hour, two billion microseconds, he gave himself to his proper task. It was infinitely more difficult. In the course of a night he achieved a bare skeleton of completion.

However, it ought to serve. He had scanned every record of any event that had impinged on Anson Guthrie, which Anson Guthrie should directly or indirectly have been aware of, in the past twenty-three years. He had organized them, evaluated them, chosen among them. Some he put in his personal permanent memory, those that would naturally have stamped themselves there. They were comparatively few; his neural network didn't have much more storage capacity than his living brain had had. A larger number he abstracted and made into general background; for instance, he'd have remembered who the most prominent figures were in the history of those decades, and something about what each one did, but not many details. The majority he rejected. They were the kind of thing you noticed and quickly forgot, and afterward retrieved from a notebook or a database if perchance you wanted to.

Throughout that effort he was conscious of nothing else. He was transcendent; he was process, ongoingness. When finally it was over, he must fight the urge to seek elsewhere, to enter anew into that cold ecstasy. Piece by piece, he disengaged his controlling consciousness from the net. He called for disconnection.

As always, an immediate feeling of immeasurable loss gave way to dullness. His merely humanlike mind needed to assimilate what had poured in. It needed rest, subactivation, the drowse and flickers of dream which answered to the sleep his living body had so often welcomed. But he'd better see if there was any business he must attend to first.

He went personally back to his sanctum. At least the robot body into which he had been transferred did not ache, was not tired. He could savor the smooth surge of strides, their soft fall upon carpeting, the susurrus and scents—piney at the moment—breezing from ventilator panels.

His private office here in the main building was large but otherwise unostentatious. Objects filled a case, souvenirs, trophies, gifts from friends now dead, the sort of clutter that even a ghost can accumulate. He noticed a few that were not there when he returned from Alpha Centauri. He didn't know anything about them, how they came to his other self or why they had seemed worth keeping. Trivia like that didn't get into company records or news stories, and he had never kept a diary. One of them could easily trip him up, if somebody else knew about it. He must be careful to avoid mention of them, or evade any remark he heard.

The robot having no need to sit, he took stance behind his desk, which was itself an anachronism for the likes of him, and touched his phone. Message from Dolores Almeida Candamo, please call back as soon as possible, never mind the hour. "Damn," he muttered, and instigated the search.

Fireball's general director of Earthside operations was at home, already awake. He remembered her as a vivacious young communications engineer. She and her fiancé had advanced their wedding date so he could attend in person before he left; Fireball couldn't spare both Guthries for that, but "It's the same spirit," she'd laughed. His review had told him of her subsequent career and prepared him for the gray hair and the face still comely. It had not told him how they normally spoke to one another. Given the psychodynamics, he had estimated the usage; into this calculation he vectored his intuition.

"Good morning!" she exclaimed in Spanish. "Welcome home, chief! I'm sorry I missed your arrival yesterday."

"You didn't miss much," he answered in English, then changed over to her mother tongue. "Does something urgently need me?"

"Ay de mí, what doesn't? You really should not have gone to North America. We were hideously anxious about you, and—"

"And you survived. Fireball did. How many times have you heard me say, any outfit that needs micromanagement from the top should be put out of its misery at once? What's the matter?"

He saw that his curtness hurt. Well, he couldn't risk a friendlier manner, not till he had felt his way around for a while and learned some of the nuances. She closed the visor of practicality. "First, this entire business of cooperating with the Avantists, after everything they have done to us. I have been in the middle of an uproar, these past several days."

"I expect you would have. They wonder if I have betrayed them, and why and just how. Please listen. You understand—don't you?—I could not go into detail in any public announcement. That could have triggered the very horrors I want to prevent, or could at least have given the enemy warning enough that he could hide.

"We will have a conference of directors shortly, and I will lay out the facts for you. What happened is that my contacts with the Chaotics led me to the discovery that a fanatical underground exists, independent of the decent majority and not only in North America. I held my nose, figuratively speaking, and got in cautious touch, indirect at first, with the Sepo. Its members aren't all monsters, you know. Most of them, too, are reasonably honorable people, doing a job they see as necessary. They had leads of their own. Everything pointed toward infiltration of Fireball and other private organizations. Not massive; we would harm only ourselves by a witch hunt; but in key positions— Think what a weapon a single spaceship is, simply by itself. Think of the consequences to us if something happens, maybe on a genocidal scale, that we might have prevented. I am making the best of a bad bargain."

Almeida bit her lip. "Our spokespeople have been saying much the same things, at my orders. But in the absence of anything more definite, fear feeds on itself."

"I know. We shall have our definite words and actions soon, I promise. Meanwhile, what else is important?"

"The mahatmas and their crowds, blockading Hyderabad Compound. You have heard. Trying to force us to subsidize their cult. Sub has an idea for persuading them to disperse peacefully, but he wants to discuss it with you first."

"Uh, Sub?"

She gave him a quizzical look, as if seeking an expression on his turret. "Subrahmanyan."

"Oh, yes." Subrahmanyan Rao, chief of South Asian operations. Pause. Think. Make a sigh. "Pardon me, Dolores, I have had no rest since my return and precious little before then. I'm tired to the point of stupidity. Can you appreciate that an overload will exhaust any mind, even one that is a program? Give me some hours. Hold the fort for me that much longer. I know you can."

Almeida's countenance softened. "Yes. I will, somehow. Call me when you feel ready. Rest well, chief." Her image disappeared.

Guthrie stood a moment alone. He need only command "No interruptions," and time himself to rouse after a sufficient while. No. Not quite yet.

The system conveyed his call by untappable lines, northward around the curve of the planet to Futuro. The hour was equally early in that capital, but Sayre was in his office at Security Police national headquarters. It took a few minutes to make certain that communication was isolated. That it occurred should surprise nobody after the news of the past week. The content was what required secrecy.

"Logging in," Guthrie said in English. "What's new?"

The undistinguished features thrust forward in the screen. "How's it going for you?"

"It goes, more or less. I'll shortly have to make a full report on the conspiracy to my consortes."

"It's still under preparation for you, including evidence. Don't worry, you'll have it in time."

"Evidence. . . . What's any worth, in this electronic nanotech day and age?"

Sayre smiled. "That's why we need you on the scene, Anson. Your personality, your convincingness."

"It's 'Sr. Guthrie' to you, Sayre." The other stiffened, swallowed, and made no retort. "What I want to know is how things are at your end."

"We are hard at work." Excitement dissolved coldness, word by word. "I've just received a report that the program decided was worth my personal attention. Yesterday evening the Regent of the Homesteaders' Association spent three hours in the quivira in Portland, West Coast. She hadn't been to a quivira as far back as her dossier goes.

And she's a close friend of . . . Guthrie's. Is this significant?"

"M-m, I dunno. What do you plan to do?"

"Have her brought in and quizzed, of course."

The robot voice went slow, with a clanging in it as of iron. "Sayre, listen. If your agents lay one filthy hand on that lady, you and I are through."

The face gaped. "What? Wait a minute—" Recovering: "All right, she is a friend and you keep . . . primitive loyalties. But—"

"Be quiet. Hear me. I'm persuaded Xuan was essentially right. I know how that was done, but I am, and I don't want to see your cause go under, because every alternative is a flaming lot worse. So I'm going along with this pious fraud of the great nihilist conspiracy, in order that we can nail my other self before he takes back Fireball, which is just about the last force that can bail you out. I'll have to lead up to the bailout gradually, and admitting that maybe I overestimated the danger won't help, but never mind now. Do you understand that this is what I understand?

"Okay. Now you, for your part, understand that I don't have to like the situation, and under all circumstances there is some shit I will not eat. You will leave old Esther Blum alone, do you hear? Unless she's lost her wits since last I saw her, she's taken care anyway not to have any knowledge that'd help you especially. But whether or no, she is not for the likes of you to come near. If you do, you're dead. Got me?"

Sayre trembled. His cheeks were a mottled white. "You're pretty arrogant, aren't you?"

"Yeah. My style. And if you'd changed me out of it, I wouldn't be much use to you, would I? Have you anything else to tell me? No? Muy bien, we'll keep in touch as agreed. Remember, I have ways of knowing what happens to my friends. Bastante."

Guthrie cut off.

For a while longer he stood silent. A viewscreen gave a look across Quito, through high-altitude clarity to Andean peaks rearing out of dusk into sunlight. The city below this tower was waking lively. Hereabouts it was altogether modern. The noble ancient buildings around the Plaza

Independencia and the traditional residential quarters were at a distance, oases. Yet they were not museum pieces but where people met, did business, ate, drank, celebrated, flirted, loafed, loved, gardened, slept, begot children, reared them, and finally died. Thus had Juliana wanted growth to go, after the launchport made growth inevitable. Thus had he seen to it, also after her death. That was her right. She had been in on things from the beginning, hadn't she?

18

Database

JERRY BOWEN AND his dream occupied a two-room apartment in south Chicago. He kept it scrupulously clean but scarcely neat, what with books heaped everywhere, drawing board, desk buried under bescrawled papers, high-powered PC left over from better days. When the Guthries called on him he made coffee, a brand they suspected he could ill afford, and talk ranged widely. Their purpose was to get personally acquainted, a little, now that they had gained some familiarity with his plans and specs, while for his part he was a visionary, not a monomaniac.

Nevertheless, spaceflight inevitably dominated the conversation, which soon turned to its history. He had been there. He not only remembered the glory years, Moon landings and more, he had met many of their heroes and heroines, astronauts, cosmonauts, engineers, entrepreneurs who tried and failed and tried again. Through the twilight that followed he had taken what work in the industry he could find, and on the side designed his own spacecraft, which were never built, and kept on dreaming with the likes of Clarke, Bussard, O'Neill, Forward, Matloff, Hunter, Woodcock, Friesen, the Hudsons. Though he could have grown bitter, in fact he did not forget how to laugh.

The Guthries felt slightly shy about inviting him to their hotel suite a few days later. "I don't believe a man's virility has anything to do with the size of his bank account," Anson growled, "but does Jerry know that? He might think we want to overawe him, and he's a proud old rooster."

"I doubt he'll give a damn about the surroundings," Juliana decided; and they phoned.

Bowen arrived punctually. Outside, wind blustered, driving clouds before it whose shadows scythed over roofs and streets. From the room a small park was visible. Yellow with fall, trees tossed their boughs in the streaming air. Dead leaves scurried from them. It was as if all nature were on trek.

When Bowen had taken off his hat and coat, the Guthries saw how he shivered. Restraint snapped across. "Well?" he demanded. "What news?"

"As far as we're concerned," Anson told him, "it's go."

Bowen gasped. The thin frame lurched. Juliana took his arm. "Easy, there, cobber," she murmured. "Sit down." She guided him to an armchair.

Anson stood over him. "What're you drinking?" he asked cordially.

Bowen didn't seem to hear. He stared before him and shook his head like one stunned. "We're on our way," he whispered. "We're on our way."

Anson lifted a palm. "Whoa," he warned. "We've got a long, stiff road ahead of us, and I don't promise we'll stay the course or even get very far."

Bowen's fingers clutched the chair upholstery. He raised his eyes. "You mean *you* like the design—"

"And the computers do."

Bowen sagged. "Plenty of people have liked it, year after year," he mumbled. "But. Always but."

"I'm sorry. I should've gone at things more gradual."

"Anson's a bull in a china shop," Juliana said with a smile, "and life is the china shop. But Jerry, listen, we truly are hopeful. That's what this meeting is about."

Bowen straightened. His features kindled anew.

"We've looked into costs," Juliana went on. "We did quite well in Australia, you know. Having heard about you— Well, we think we have enough capital that we'll command the leverage for what more will be needed. For a start, at least. If that works out as happily as the analysis suggests it can, we'll have investors falling over their shoelaces to buy in."

The wariness left by unnumbered disappointments and rebuffs must voice itself. "In these times?"

"We may not draw any Americans except me," Anson admitted. "What of it? Australians, Japanese, Europeans, and, yes, I know some South Americans."

"That's what we're counting on," Juliana added.

"Scramble out of this poor damned country," Anson said.

"What?" Bowen asked.

"Isn't it obvious? Now that the Renewal's in the White House and has a majority in Congress, everything'll spin from bad to worse till it ends in such a crash that somebody else can maybe pick up the pieces and put them back together in a halfway common-sensical shape. It doesn't help that most of Islam seems about to go on the warpath."

Juliana winced. "Which will mean more restrictions, whatever happens," she said, unwontedly harsh. "Ratcheting the power of the government upward. Randolph Bourne said it a long time ago, war is the health of the state."

Bowen frowned. He had ample salt left in him. "I didn't mean any stinking politics," he snapped. "What are your plans?"

"Our hopes," Juliana corrected gently.

"I understand. This is all preliminary." Bowen grinned. "Ha, preliminary to the preliminaries. I am not a virgin in the business world." Intensity took over. "But speaking in the most general terms, what do you have in mind?"

"Ecuador," Anson replied. "Perfect sites. High mountains, close to the equator or squarely on it, and . . . I know people there. Several of the right people."

"More important," Juliana put in, "they're smart and forward-looking. They see what it would mean for their country."

"For everybody," Bowen breathed.

"Yeah," Anson agreed, lacking better words. "Of course, it calls for a pig-sized investment, starting with adequate roads, but once we've got your setup installed—"

A practical laser launcher. Rockets are inevitably, fantastically wasteful when they lumber off the ground. Their proper domain is space itself, and even there the chemical rocket ought to be superseded, except for special purposes, by something abler, an ion drive or a plasma drive or the photon drive itself.

A practical laser launcher. The gravitational energy cost of getting into low Earth orbit is modest, a few kilowatt-hours per kilogram; and as Heinlein put it, once you're in Earth orbit, you're halfway to anywhere. No device can realize this minimum, but, imaginatively designed for efficiency as well as capacity, a laser, feeding energy to air molecules, can approach it.

If moreover you have a free hand to create and captain your own organization, you need not pay a standing army of ground crews and paper shufflers. You can run your space line as economically as an airline or an ocean freighter line. A mission will cost less, in terms of gross world product, than did any voyage of Columbus.

You do require capital, plus determination, mother wit, and a few well-placed friends. First and foremost, you must have the dream.

Excitement rang in Juliana's tones: "And the Ecuadorans would—will—license us to use nuclear engines on ships in space. We're sure they can be persuaded and can clear it with the UN."

Anson struck fist into palm. "The ground floor, Jerry," he said hoarsely. "We'll be in on the ground floor of everything. Commercial launches are the bare beginning. Power. The *real* solar energy. Forget that groundside fraud and the powersat boondoggle. Save what's left of our night sky on Earth. Build Criswell collectors and transmitters on the Moon, with Lunar materials. And the mineral resources in the asteroids—"

Juliana laughed. "Dear, I'm afraid you're instructing your grandmother in the art of sucking eggs."

"So what?" burst from Bowen. "It'd guarantee a permanent human presence in space. I don't mind hearing that repeated, as often as you like."

"Okay!" Anson roared. "We'll give it our best try, the three of us."

Bowen gazed past them. "If Helen had been here today—" He shook himself and sprang to his feet like a young man. "I, I—I'll take that drink now."

19

EARLY IN THE afternoon, Valencia went off with Guthrie. "Wait here," he told Kyra. "I'll get a car and pick you up."

"Why don't I come along?" she asked.

"You don't need to know where the brotherhood's local car pool is, Pilot Davis," he said, politely enough. He'd been quick to gather, in discussion the night before, that that was the honorific she preferred.

Kyra decided she didn't mind lingering in the coffee shop. The talk had run very late. She and Guthrie had already hatched a couple of different schemes, but they needed Valencia to help them choose the best and work out details. At that, the plan was hairy with contingencies.

The gunjin reappeared sooner than she'd expected and led her out to a fire-red Phoenix. "Isn't this sort of conspicuous?" she wondered.

He shrugged. "Part of the camouflage, I hope. Fugitives aren't supposed to ride around in sports cars, are they?" His fingers danced over controls, eased it into traffic.

"Where's the jefe?"

"Next to my weapons, in a well-screened compartment with lots of electronics around for extra cover. The motor's been modified, though it doesn't show."

This vehicle had carried contraband before, Kyra realized. Glee raised a laugh. She might as well treat her escape as an escapade, at least till it turned around and bit her again.

Valencia took a ramp onto a skyway, set the board for automatic, and entered their route. The Phoenix accelerated smoothly till city vistas blurred past. Kyra barely heard the cloven air. Yes, she thought, the Chinese could certainly build cars. Valencia reclined his seat a few degrees and let it mold itself to his relaxation. "If all goes well, we should make San Francisco about 1400," he said. "I know a good place for a late lunch, unless you'd rather stop and eat sooner."

"No, that's fine. Surprise me."

"Now let's start rehearsing you in our story."

"I remember it quite well from last night."

"With respect, Pilot Davis, you do not. And there are countless details we didn't get into. If we're stopped, you'll need every last one sliding off your tongue without you having to think. Two, three hours of drill, I'd guess."

Kyra pouted. "Oh, foo! I was looking forward to this ride."

Valencia grinned. His biojewel twinkled blue. "I can imagine more amusing ways to pass the time, myself." With instant steel sobriety: "But getting arrested, deep-quizzed, and sent up for re-education isn't among them."

"Of course, Ne—Sr. Valencia. Let's go."

He leaned hard into business. (A while after she fled to Québec, a Fireball officer there judged that, in view of the startling announcement by Guthrie, she should probably report back to Hawaii. Packer, at Kamehameha, was dubious when they called him.) If the Sepo tried to check on that, they'd pump vacuum. No Fireball consorte in any foreign country would give them the fourth digit of pi without specific orders from the top. Packer, if queried, would smell something in the wind and be noncommittal. (Feeling understandably insecure, she went first to Portland and talked it over with friends she had there.) Her re-entry would be recorded in the database at a border station. The Sally Severins had that much access to the official net. She got the impression that it was through Chaotic moles, with whom they had shifty connections. (Bill Mendoza offered to drive her down to San Francisco and accompany her when she sought permission to board a plane for the Islands. His paralegal business was taking him to that area anyway.) Valencia carried ample ident, and the pseudopersonality had long been in the registries, duly paying its taxes and staying out of trouble.

Easily mastered. But then Valencia began filling in the outline, day by day, well-nigh hour by hour.

The skyway curved groundward and merged with the transcontinental. City fell behind. The car fled south over cropland, along a river coursing through aquaculture pens. Ordered, machine-tended greenness reached out of sight, across terraced hills to mountains half hidden by clouds. A boring landscape, Kyra thought; but how beautiful it must once have been, villages, farmsteads, cows ruddy in meadows and apples ruddy in orchards, maybe blue flax or yellow corn, maybe a boy a-gallop on a horse, surely great stretches of forest, shadowy and resin-sweet beneath the sun.

"Now, snap it out, what'd you do on Thursday?"

"Bueno, uh—"

A light blinked red on the panel. Kyra saw, two or three klicks down the road, how traffic was bunching. Her throat went tight. "Oh-oh," Valencia muttered.

He punched the receiver button. A shield bearing the infinity symbol appeared in the screen. A genderless voice: "Attention. There is a special inspection point ahead. Proceed on automatic. Do not leave your vehicle unless directed. The delay is estimated at about half an hour. This is an emergency situation and all persons are required to give the authorities their full cooperation. Stand by for further word."

Kyra retracted the shade and peered up through the canopy. Two flitters cruised back and forth. "Is this on our account?" she whispered around the lump.

Valencia's features had congealed into a bronze mask. "I'd lay odds it is," he replied without tone.

"But we could be anywhere. How can they know?"

"They don't, but they seem to think they have a scent worth pursuing. A two-way stop, you notice, and no turnoff before we get there. I daresay every road out of

Portland Integrate is blocked. No news announcement that might scare us off."

"Wait, Esther Blum said something about not having been in a quivira for—decades—"

Valencia nodded. "That's probably their hint. I worried about it, but when Sr. Guthrie insisted he couldn't lose time lying low, I saw no point in mentioning it. We'd just have to take our chances."

Kyra shuddered. "Esther! Do you suppose they—"

"I wouldn't put it past them. If they have taken her in and, by now, wrung out of her that Kyra Davis is traveling with Anson Guthrie, we're cooked. However, you recall that that's unlikely."

The pilot nodded stiffly. The mere fact that Blum had done something out of the ordinary shouldn't seem—to whatever detective was assigned to trail her without having been told why—cause for arrest. From the quivira she had returned to her hotel. There another gunjin waited. He was to smuggle her out, and his organization would hide her for a couple of days. When she came back to Baker she'd tell people she'd been gadding about in Portland. It was not unreasonable to hope that the Sepo would assume this was true and their operative had simply, clumsily, lost her.

It had seemed almost a needless precaution. It had turned out to be vital. Somebody higher up in the hunt had received the report on Blum. Perhaps, desperate, he had ordered that anything at all unusual concerning anyone associated with Guthrie be called to his attention. A search tree program could readily do that. He'd supposed there was an off chance this was a clue, and had mobilized local forces to throw up road blocks. If Kyra got by, her story accepted, the Sepo ought soon to figure they'd misled themselves, and Blum ought to be safe from them when she came home. If Kyra did not pass— She refused to imagine what would follow.

Valencia leaned toward her. Under the black bangs, his jewel had gone topaz. "Listen, Pilot Davis," he said. "They will not detect Guthrie unless they take this car

apart. We mustn't give them reason to think that might be
a good idea. I counted on grooming you till you could
answer any question shot at you easier than if you were
telling the truth. No such luck. But we can still pass if you
don't show you're worried. Annoyed, curious, yes, but
you've got nothing to hide, nothing to be afraid of. Can
you carry that off?"

She ran tongue over lips. "I'll . . . try."

Slowing, their car reached the end of the line and halted.
After a minute those ahead rolled forward a few meters
and theirs followed. The line stopped again. A truck
arrived to fill the rear view. They were hemmed in. Kyra
smelled the sweat in her armpits, rank, and felt it, cold.

Valencia regarded her through a thick silence until he
murmured, "I'm sorry, Pilot Davis, but I don't believe you
can swing this."

"I never was a very skilled liar. Have you any suggestions?"

His eyes narrowed. Irrelevantly, she noticed that they
were long-lashed and russet. "I do," he answered slowly.
"You may not like it."

"We'll see."

"Por favor, understand, in my brotherhood we don't
funnyjump with a client. If you decline this notion, that's
the end of it and I'll try to think of something else."

Blood thudded in her temples. "You mean—the two of
us—"

He nodded. "Quite natural, if a couple on friendly terms
find a better way of passing time in line than turning on the
multi. Then one would expect the lady to get rather
flustered and out of breath."

Suddenly Kyra must laugh. Must howl her laughter
till the car rang with it. "Esther said . . . every good cause
. . . whoop! . . . demands sacrifices. I've . . . whoop! . . .
made worse ones. C'mere, you."

It was a bench seat, though with separate backrests. His
jewel glowed scarlet. He was unrighteously handsome. He
glided to her. She laid arms about his neck. His went
around her waist. As their lips touched, his hands began to
caress her back. The kiss developed at its own pace. When

in full bloom, it made every other that she could remember at the moment, except maybe her awkward first, seem thin.

He explored leisurely. She had a hand under his shirt before his was under her blouse.

Once, coming up for air, she glimpsed a police car going by. Bueno, so much the better. Put on a convincing show.

She wasn't quite on her back when they came to the checkpoint, but knew whirlingly that if the wait had lasted much longer she would have been. Damn. No, better this way. Wasn't it? She ran fingers through her rumpled hair and gave the officer at the window a blurry smile.

He grinned back. He was a civil policeman, one of several under the command of a single tan-clad Sepo. That man strode forth and flung the questions he must have uttered a hundred times already. He was haggard, baggy-eyed, probably running on stim, his competence not worn down but his mind, perhaps, a wee bit distractable by a steamy sight. Kyra's ident as Fireball alerted him to make some additional, nonroutine queries. She answered dreamily. Nero chimed in, showing less calm himself than she felt sure he'd have been able to. Meanwhile the police opened the engine and luggage compartments, checked through their possessions, and scanned about with an instrument that must be a Guthrie detector. Of course, they didn't know that . . .

"Pass," the Sepo clipped. It broke from him: "You might behave more decently in future!"

Valencia returned a half apologetic smile, took over the controls, and slipped the car forward. A few seconds later it was back on automatic at cruise speed.

Kyra sagged back. "Whoo-ee," she breathed. Exultation awoke. "We made it, Nero, we made it!"

"So far." He looked straight before him.

"Oye, don't be nervous. You were, uh, you were ultra. I enjoyed every hertz of that waveband."

He glanced at her. The jewel had faded to pale rose. For an instant, warmth and teeth flashed. "Gracias. I did too." The smile died. "Don't worry, Pilot Davis. I won't presume on it."

The metal came back into his face and words, into the very way he sat apart from her. "There may be more roadblocks later. Or that Sepo may have second thoughts. Like, if you want to go to Hawaii, why not fly straight from Portland? Is the reason really what your behavior suggested, that you're taking a small extra vacation? If he calls headquarters about it and they scan the data received today, they'll almost certainly find you've been the only Fireball employee who left Portland by ground. That could make them wonder. As soon as we're under the horizon of those flitters, I'm going to turn off, the first chance I get."

Kyra hated feeling the glory drain from her. "Where to?"

"I know a safe house. I'll check the possibility, there, of changing our arrangements so we don't have to go on to San Francisco tomorrow. It means letting two or three more people in on part of our trajectory, but they're pretty reliable and if the enemigos do get interested in a couple fitting our description, they're apt to beswarm the Bay Area."

"Jesús María," Kyra said weakly, "what'd we do without you, Guthrie and me?"

She barely heard his chuckle. "Get caught, I suppose. You did quite well at first, for paisanos, but this is my trade. Now let's rehearse you some more, just in case."

The offroad they found was paved but had no guide cable beneath. He took manual control with a deftness that became apparent after they got onto secondaries and tertiaries twisting through the mountains. On some of these the surface was cracked and potholed; others were dirt, eroded away to little more than trails, where dust smoked high behind the car. Wheels snarled and squealed. Curves tossed Kyra sideways. Often she looked straight down a slope of brush and boulders to the bottom of a canyon. "I thought I was a hot pilot," she finally had to say. A bump rattled her teeth. "Is this kind of driving required by law?"

"I want us under cover as soon as may be," he explained curtly. "A red Phoenix was a disguise of sorts on the main route, but to any aircraft that passes over us here, it's like a torch in tinder."

She made herself fall into a dance of muscles responding to motion. At least, in his concentration, he wasn't drilling her any longer. Besides, the country was lovely. Under an efficient government it might today have been another set of gene-tailored plantations or mineral-extracting nanotech sites. As it was, its steeps were virtually deserted. Conifers serrated the ridges, peaks lifted majestic into the wind. Occasionally she spied the ruins of a home, occasionally she glimpsed the sea.

She didn't know how closely he had calculated it, but their fuel was near exhaustion when they pulled into a remnant hamlet. While the attendant at the station exchanged their buckyglobe for one freshly charged with hydrogen, they got sandwiches and soft drinks to go in a place across the solitary street. "We don't see a lot of tourists," said the woman behind the counter wistfully. "Hard times."

"I'm sorry, we have to run," Kyra replied. Whatever they did, they'd be remembered here. Bueno, it was unlikely the hounds would come this precise way.

Munching and drinking, Valencia drove in less hellish wise. As hunger eased, Kyra felt a measure of peace steal over her. "Who are these people we're bound for?" she asked.

"Their name is Farnum," he said. "Jim and Anne Farnum. Mostly he works on a fish ranch, she keeps house and raises a little produce for the gourmet market." Nothing unique there, she thought. Not High World, but not exactly Low World either. "No children, which is why they can do what else they do."

"They're—with your outfit, then?"

"No, nor with the Gentlemen Adventurers, whose territory extends that far north. They're crypto-Chaotics. Part of the organized underground. Not as activists, but they provide a way station, a communications link, a hiding place at need. I wouldn't be surprised but what they watch over a shedful of weapons in the woods somewhere."

Crack, Kyra thought, this was getting in deep. "How do

you know about them? You, uh, Sally Severins aren't revolutionaries, are you?"

"No. Most of us, personally, wouldn't be sorry to see the government overthrown, provided its successor doesn't curb us more effectively than the Avantists have managed to. But a brotherhood *qua* brotherhood has to be apolitical."

Valencia seemed to consider for a while before he went on: "Now and then the police have discreetly engaged us for a job. We are, after all, officially a licensed personal service agency. Even the Sepo has tried a time or two, I've heard, but been refused, precisely because the purpose there involved politics. The Chaotic junta knows this and appreciates it. Hence we've done work for them—not specifically against the government, but helpful in various ways. I may not tell you more. Except for this, that it has brought about a degree of liaison. It's sometimes mutually useful for certain brothers to know about people like the Farnums, and we can be trusted with the information as much as any undergrounder can. I'm betting that they'll not only shelter us tonight, they'll give us a boost . . . because this time our opposition is their enemy."

"I see." Kyra regarded his profile. Light slanting misty-gold from the west brought it forth against darkling trees. "You don't talk like what I'd expected," she said.

He smiled. "How should I?"

"You're well educated, aren't you? How'd you get into this line of, of work?"

"How do most people get into theirs?" He shrugged. "They drift in."

"I always knew what I wanted to be."

"And made it. Lucky. But you had Fireball to belong to, and Fireball has Anson Guthrie." Valencia's voice lowered. "A gunjin isn't a wage robot. He's reasonably free, and he finds use for everything that's in him." Sharply: "I'd better speed up again. Por favor, Pilot Davis, don't distract me."

Kyra sank back into the enfolding seat. Guthrie— How was he taking this, locked in blackness and silence? Bueno, he'd toughed out a lot of things in the past. Death itself, for one.

The sun was at the horizon, huge and orange, casting a broken bridge over an argent sea, when they reached Noyo. The village overlooked cliffs above a narrow bay, at whose beach a few buildings nestled, with boats along a dock or anchored out in the water. The rest of the houses were above, old and few, three of them crumbling abandoned. Valencia halted before one that stood somewhat apart, screened by gnarled silvery-gray cypresses. "Here we are," he said.

Kyra got out. Her body rejoiced to stretch. Wind off the ocean ruffled hair and slid sensuously cool around skin. It had a keen-edged smell, not much like the odors that wafted over Hawaiian strands. Its flutter was well-nigh the only sound she heard till her feet and her companion's crunched on a graveled walk.

The house was large. Its antique frame construction recalled Baker, but this paint was bleached sallow. Archaically, Valencia struck the door with his knuckles. A man opened it. He too was sturdily built and weathered, his rufous beard grizzled though the hair above said he was in early middle age at most. "Saludos, amigo," Valencia greeted. "Can you doss us tonight? This lady is cleared for the run."

Farnum went impassive. "Come in," he rumbled.

"I should garage our car straightaway."

"Kind of bright-colored," Farnum agreed. "Bring 'er around. I'll go open up. You go on in, señorita. Don't fret about what the neighbors may have noticed. We're good at minding our own business in these parts."

Kyra entered. A plump woman met her and said, "Bienvenida, guest," unemphatically but as though she meant it. Neither man nor wife resembled a heroic resistance fighter. Nor did this room, its well-worn furniture and rather banal pictures on the textiled walls, seem like a den for desperados. Of course, that was how it ought to be. Savory scents drifted from the kitchen, where Kyra spied a cooking console that must be fifty years or more old.

Soon the four of them were seated over drinks before dinner. Farnum had provided a magnificent homebrew beer. When Kyra complimented him, he replied, "We keep as much of the real world going here as we can."

"You want to bring back more of it, for everybody, don't you?" Kyra asked.

Farnum frowned. "Let's not talk politics," his wife said mildly. Her gaze was unblinking on Kyra.

"Best we go directly to business, however," Valencia responded. "You may know something important or have some ideas we two don't."

"Go ahead." Farnum might have been calling for the next deal at a poker table.

"I can't say much, but you're probably aware the government's raised a full-scale hunt for something it hasn't described very closely."

Anne Farnum grimaced. "How could we not have heard? Those lies about fanatics— Why? What are they after?"

"Could there be something real behind the stories?" Valencia murmured.

"No!" Farnum's fist smote his chair arm.

Maybe, Kyra thought, he denied what he didn't want to believe. Not that the junta or most of those who secretly trained in hopes of someday fighting—not that they were monsters. But it would be strange if every last person among them was emotionally disciplined. Also, revolutionary movements didn't survive for years, biding their time, unless they imagined they had a reasonable prospect of success. That surely meant covert support from abroad, exiled North Americans, foreign governments that had their own motives . . .

"Apologies," Valencia said with his best, somehow heart-storming smile. "I felt I had to inquire, but was confident what the answer would be. You in your turn will accept us as basically decent, won't you?

"Muy bien, we two are conveying, shall I say, one of those objects the Sepo are after. We have to get it out of range, soon. The best arrangement I could make on short notice was for transport on a big yacht, a hydrofoil, the

Gentlemen Adventurers own. Reciprocity between brotherhoods, you know; the Sally Severins have done them favors in the past, and my superiors decided this job was worth calling in the debt."

Kyra drew a tingly mouthful from her stein. She admired how smoothly Valencia talked around all but the absolute minimum of facts that mattered. Why had the comandantes of his outfit made such an investment? They weren't exactly idealistic. Obviously, they knew that if they helped Guthrie now when he needed it, they'd be amply repaid, not just in cash but in Fireball's good will.

Cold: But then they shared knowledge of the real situation. Either Esther Blum had explained it to them—perforce, because she lacked the money to pay for a serious rescue effort—or, once she told Valencia, he contacted them and they authorized this requisition. Yes, he'd had time in his hotel room last night before she arrived. He could have done it before releasing Guthrie to overhear.

Whichever, too cracking many were in on the truth. In principle, it ought to be spread around, but in practice, everybody who knew was an added danger. Valencia wouldn't betray. No, not he! And he must expect none of his lodgemasters would. But could you be sure? Besides, the Sepo were bound to know more about the brotherhoods than they let on. If clues pointed that way, they might well consider it worth their while to break through any trap they had been patiently constructing, to capture and deep-quiz whomever could lead them onward.

A quick liftoff was necessary, yes.

Amidst the blood that thudded in her ears, she heard Valencia continue: "On our way down today we were road-blocked—got by, but I think we'd be lepton to proceed to San Francisco as we'd planned. Could you put me in touch with the Gentlemen on a secure line? And do you think their crew could put to sea tomorrow, and a boat from here take us out to meet them, fairly safely?"

The Farnums exchanged a look. They pondered. After a minute she said, "If they have clearance to go as of today, yes, it should be all right tomorrow. The captain can tell the harbor police he was delayed by family trouble or something. And you, Jim, you can call in and tell the company you won't report for work. We can make up a nice reason."

Her husband tugged his beard. "I'll have to figure a rendezvous point," he said. "This coast isn't much patrolled, but what with the government gone a-jet, we don't want to take any worse chance than we have to of a cutter or an amphiflitter noticing us and stopping by, inquisitive-like. I'll check on what movements of theirs have been observed lately."

He, a simple fishpoke? The underground—nothing spectacular, plain folk like this, wide-scattered but in touch, each doing his or her small service when called upon—Kyra thought of a coiled snake. A boot heel could crush its head, if a man knew where it lay; but if he did not, it awaited its moment to strike, and meanwhile its tongue flickered, tasting the air that he troubled.

"Bueno, is that settled for now?" exclaimed Anne Farnum. "Let's eat before dinner cooks to death."

Over the meal they talked about the weather, the sports news, local incidents, anything trivial. You didn't want to learn more than you must, Kyra realized. Not long afterward she was ready for the spare bed to which the wife showed her. Valencia and the Farnums stayed up. Waking at sunrise, Kyra wondered if they had gotten any sleep at all.

20

ANOTHER SUNSET LAID fire across great waters and died away. The dusk that followed was brief. When Kyra entered the observation cabin after dinner, night was already upon the Pacific half of the planet.

Aboard a vessel that would take you from the mainland to Hawaii in thirty-odd hours, you didn't stand out on deck. This cabin was almost as good, sunken but the sill of its canopy at head level. Very little spray had marred the clarity of the hyalon, as well streamlined and windscreened as the *Caravel* was, as smoothly as she bounded over the waves on flexing planes. Kyra scarcely noticed her own responses to the motion, except as a sense of oneness with machine and sea.

Having the cabin to herself, she darkened it and let her pupils widen to drink the scene. The riding lights were out of her view and the radar invisible. She saw only the topside, a dim and rhythmically surging whiteness. Beyond ran ocean. It sheened changeably, like a thousand black leopards a-chase; close by, she glimpsed swirls of lacy foam. The engine throbbed. The waves made torrent sounds, undertone to the wind. Overhead, sky-glow was about as slight as it ever got on Earth. Against that swarthiness she could make out perhaps a thousand stars and a ghost of the Milky Way.

A grand sight, with the peace of strength in it. Too bad the jefe couldn't enjoy this, she thought. Again he lay locked in a screened and secret compartment. She dared not bring him out before she must. The Gentlemen Adventurers were simply repaying a favor; they had signed no contract. If the *Caravel*'s crew learned what it actually was that they smuggled along, temptation—whopping reward, pardon for past crimes, lucrative sinecure in government—might prove too much for one among them. Or the captain might think he'd been deceived into taking a monstrous risk for no real profit, and avenge it.

She'd merely been able to whisper a few words to Guthrie, which he maybe didn't hear through his wrappings, in transit between the car and Farnum's boat. How long could he endure near-total sensory deprivation before his mind began to spin apart? Her spell had been miserable enough, and she supposed it was the same for Valencia, after a guard cutter dashed over the horizon and radioed an order to stop. There'd been time to stash them in a pair of the lockers for contraband, but duration stretched horribly in blindness while the hydrofoil was being ransacked. Less than three hours? Was that possible?

Bueno, the ordeal lay behind her and a repeat search was

unlikely. Kyra returned her soul to the sea. She couldn't reach far, though. However hard she ignored it, anxiety leashed her.

A soft footfall brought her glance around. Her pulse jumped. The shadow that came to stand beside her was Valencia.

"Buenas tardes," he said as quietly as he had arrived. "Do I disturb you?"

"No," she answered. "Not at all. A lovely night."

"True. But we must go to space for a real sight of the stars."

"Oh, a vivifer—"

"You know better than I how much that is not the same." He paused. "Or do you? We soon take our blessings for granted, we humans. Often we forget they are blessings."

She had not imagined she would ever feel compassion for him. "Have you never been there?"

"Briefly on the Moon. A tourist, restricted and shepherded."

"You wanted to become a spacer," she knew.

"Always."

Impulse closed her fingers around his hand for a moment. "You're not alone. Even among Fireball children—Precious few openings, and steadily fewer."

"Yes, yes, I quite understand," he snapped. "I don't pity myself." His tone took on its usual impersonal courtesy. "My apologies, Pilot Davis, for interrupting you here. I have some news, but if you'd rather wait to discuss it, morning should be soon enough."

She forced a smile. "Don't leave me in suspense."

"Muy bien. I have just had a talk with the captain, and failed to persuade him. He will not wait to take us or anyone else off from Hawaii to refuge. He'll debark us where we want and set home immediately. I think he's uneasy about us, and I can't blame him. He did offer to call his comandante and let me request different orders, but that would be ridiculously risky."

"Of course." Kyra remembered they must watch their language. Anyplace aboard could be bugged. "We touched on this that night in Portland, but only in passing. Do you think you could take whoever might need it into hiding?"

"I told you I'm not familiar with Hawaii, it's another area where I've simply been a tourist. My brotherhood has little if anything to do with the Honolulu Kings. But . . . if you'll advise me—"

"I don't know any holes to vanish into."

"We can talk about where you've been, what you've seen and heard. That's information. Those other people should have more. Probably then I can keep us under cover for a while, not in any one spot but shifting about. Not a very long while if we're hunted by professionals, and no guarantees whatsoever, but I'll try my best."

"We may not be in a position to renew your contract when it expires."

His smile glistened fleetingly in the night-veiled face. Eyes and jewel caught starlight. "I'll trust you to make it retroactive afterward."

"Mil gracias, Nero." Again she caught his hand, this time with both of hers and not letting go.

"Loco scheme," he grumbled. Or, no, did he tease her? "The plug-in part, maybe, just barely. But the neosophs—" He broke off.

She noticed how her grasp clung and how softly he returned the pressure. "Don't you see, it's our best bet because it *is* wild?"

At any rate, so Guthrie deemed. "We've got to diddle not only the dicks but my altered ego," he had said. "Kamehameha will be closely secured, since he knows what I'd most like is to get back into space. Therefore the smart thing for me to do is try slipping into a free country on Earth. Therefore the Sepo will concentrate on holding me inside Union borders till they can find me. Well, anti-Guthrie knows how I think and feel, but he doesn't know how I was warned, how my escape was engineered, who my companions are, or what they're capable of. Accordingly, chilluns, the most obvious move for us to make becomes the least obvious and gives us our best chance. It's not the kind of odds you could live by making book on, but we'll play them."

"And being wild, it appeals to you," Valencia told Kyra. The waves laughed around them both. "Bueno, I confess it does to me also."

She decided she'd better release his hand, and did, and wondered why. "We'll bring it off, Nero." The words shivered.

"Would you care to start telling me about your Hawaiian furloughs?" he asked. What was that, wariness or practicality or what?

"I suppose I can."

"Not a briefing or a strategy session. We needn't spoil this night." And it might be counterproductive, or dangerous if they had listeners, she thought. Now why did that idea seem ungracious? "Only reminisce, if you will."

Guilt left her. "Oh, dear, where should I begin?" she jested.

"Wherever you like." He leaned elbows on sill and gazed outward. Light from sky and sea limned his profile against the dark. "Possibly at a sight like this?"

"M-m, I recall a time—" She imitated his stance. Their elbows touched, a nexus of warmth in sea-cool air. "A friend and I, we'd arranged for a ride in an outrigger canoe—"

He led her on. Sometimes he related experiences he had had; his too could be gentle. Though he asked for nothing intimate, memories welled up that she came near to sharing. She took the impulse out in discourse of blossoms, rain forest, merriments, sand and surf and the bright small lives around a coral reef. Presently she was speaking of the Keiki Moana. Why not? They were off limits to outsiders, but everybody knew of them and had seen documentaries or read books. Everybody knew as well that Fireball occasionally allowed its folk to call on its wards.

"—swimming close to the raft when a pair of dolphins— O-o-oh!"

Still full, the Moon rose aft. Sudden silver flew across the ocean to cast halos upon heads. Kyra felt herself lean against Valencia and lay an arm around his waist.

He tautened. "Ah, Pilot Davis—"

"Outrageously beautiful," she said from down in her throat.

"Yes. M-m, can you find Alpha Centauri for me?"

"I, I think we're too far north yet. Why?"

"Chain of association." Guthrie.

"Who cares? Demeter, only live planet we've reached, yes, but primitive and doomed and all it does is make me wonder what everything means if life is so rare an accident." Kyra drew breath. Her blood thrummed. "What it means is that it *is*, no? We're here for a little while, we're here tonight, you and I, and that can be enough. We can make it be, can't we?" She lifted her lips toward his.

His response was not altogether steady. "Pilot Davis, I explained about relationships with clients."

She grinned. "Suppose the client starts it?"

"Policy—"

Her spark of mirth went out. "Nero, listen, I'm not a bold buccaneer. Nor am I a coward, but down underneath right now I'm scared and lonely and in want of comforting."

His eyes met hers. "I'm not sure whether I believe that," he said. "I think too well of you, Kyra."

Joy kindled anew. She brought her hands up—his hair was springy between her fingers—and tugged downward. "Besides," she whispered after a while, "the loping of this deck underneath us is almighty sexy."

21

THE MAN SEATED before the desk was gray-haired but trim as a boy, straight as a drive shaft. Pale eyes were set deep in a face seamed and craggy. Colonel's insignia and action ribbons brightened the crisp uniform. "Subject to the vital interests of my country, I am under your orders, sir," he agreed.

"That shouldn't cause us any problem, seeing as how your government assigned you and your detachment to me," new Guthrie replied. "About those men, though. I know you by reputation." Old Guthrie would. Sayre had provided an account. "You can be trusted to do your job, do it well, and keep your mouth shut afterward. But can your men, every last one of them?"

"I chose them myself, sir," Felix Holden told him.

"Okay, that's good enough for me." Perforce. "But I underline, the bunch of you have got to be discreet. Not just reliable but tactful. Or, at least, not aggravating. When my consejeros find out I've engaged space-trained members of the North American Security Police for special duty, the excrement will hit the blower. I'll have to talk them out of mutinying and then smooth the collective feathers of Fireball. Don't make that harder for me than it has to be."

"I understand, sir. May I ask how you propose to explain our mission?"

"The simplest way. Begin with the truth, that our personnel aren't trained in police work, never having had to do more than stop the occasional fight or nab the very rare thief, swindler, et cetera. They'll ask me, if we need detectives to help against terrorists who've infiltrated us, why not borrow them from some other country than the Union—in spacer eyes, some free country? I'll answer that it's because your corps is the one that knows the situation, that's actually wrestling with it, and we haven't time to educate anybody else. I'll say that I'm not fond of the idea myself, but in this emergency I don't see any choice.

"I can talk my people around. I *am* their jefe, the founder of this whole shebang, the figure they've looked up to all their lives, like their parents and grandparents and maybe great-grandparents before them. I repeat, though, your boys can make it impossible for me, and might not survive what follows. You aren't dealing with meek taxpayers any more. Spacers are an independent, stiff-necked, hot-blooded squall of cats."

Holden cracked a smile. "I expected you'd say what you have, sir. Don't worry. My corps aren't the high-handed bullies of the popular stories. Por favor, credit us with more competence than that. We'll stay in the background, speak low, and not throw our weight around unless it becomes absolutely necessary. If it does, we'll keep our action to the minimum of what seems required."

"Fine. Now let's get specific. You're our provision against the possibility that our object of search will escape into space. It's remote, but I wouldn't put anything past me. Should that happen, he can't, realistically, aim for any place but L-5 or the Moon. I want a unit of yours at each facility, under an officer whom you'll have told what to look out for. I'm assuming you have two officers who can be trusted with a secret that explosive. I'll order the Fireball folk to cooperate with them. How soon can they and their detachments go?"

"Within an hour after I return to them from here."

"Hoo, you really are good at what you do! I can't arrange transport for them quite that fast. Ecuador spaceport's always busy, you know. However, they should be at their stations tomorrow.

"You stay in Quito, Colonel, with a few men, the pick of the pick. You'll be in reserve against the bottom-worst case, the one that'd call for desperate measures."

Discussion became swift and incisive.

Holden rose, saluted the robot body, and wheeled about. His heels clacked on the floor.

When he was gone, Guthrie called Sayre in Futuro. "Your collie dog and I have just had an interesting conversation," he said. "I believe we can keep things under control at my end. How're they going at yours?"

"The quarry is still at large," Sayre answered redundantly. After a moment: "Deep-quizzing a suspect who was brought in has established that his hiding place was the Erie-Ontario site. The suspect's memory of events around the time of our raid was irretrievably wiped out by a drug. Otherwise the only indications we have suggest the download was spirited off to Portland, but they may be coincidental or may have been managed for the purpose of laying a false scent. Presumably he'll try to get into México, and we're drawing the mesh especially tight along that border, but he may get past somehow."

"Or he may double back," Guthrie suggested.

"Yes. He's not without resources inside the Union. He couldn't have eluded us like this unless people helped him. By now, perhaps a number of people, some of whom have probably been told the facts about him. Any of them could at any time try to make the matter public, and might succeed."

"Yeah. From your viewpoint, the second worst nightmare. What have you got planned to cope with it?"

"Denial, of course. Arrest them as nihilists and hold them incommunicado, or dead. You will join in the denial."

"It's customary to say, 'Will you, por favor, Sr. Guthrie?'"

"I . . . apologize. The stress on me . . . is considerable."

"I may want to produce my spare self in evidence, newly awakened after his return from Alpha Cen. Is that copy ready?"

"Not quite. The software, naturally. But the hardware, an exact duplicate of something that was custom-made— Give us another two or three days. Then we'll have him back in Fireball's Northwest building where he was stowed before."

"That should do. For my part, I'll put it to the company, 'Who're you going to believe, me or a few homicidal fanatics and their possibly well-meaning dupes?' Some will have their doubts, but I'm pretty sure the large majority will go along."

"Yes, yes. We've threshed this out already, haven't we?"

"Well, we haven't taken time to consider the very worst case in any detail. What if it isn't a matter of somebody broadcasting a story, but of my rogue self surfacing, in México or wherever? Can your goons mount a raid fast enough to grab him or blast him before the damage goes beyond repair?"

"Goons? I resent that word."

"Resent away. Can they?"

"Perhaps. I'm working on the problem of disguising their identities. The legal consequences of us carrying out such an operation in a foreign country are appalling."

"Embarrassing, you mean, if you're caught at it. But you know bloody well your government can stall the Federation. At most, it'd have to fire a few 'overzealous ministers' and promise they'll be re-educated. However, if the loose me isn't squashed almighty fast, *I'll* face appalling consequences."

"It shouldn't come to that. Let's hope not. For everybody's sake."

"Listen, I don't propose to go down without a fight. I'm having a torch ship made ready for me to pilot. If my rival does break free and your commando fails to take him out, I'll see what I can do myself."

22

Mauna Loa and Mauna Kea stood over the western rim of the sea like a dream, but when *Caravel* reached the Big Island they were lost behind everything nearer. The hydrofoil lay to outside Hilo harbor and called a water taxi for her passengers. The captain bade them goodbye at the gangway. Kyra resented his grin and wink at Valencia. Nero went expressionless. He was a gentleman, she thought warmly.

A ground cab brought him and her, with his weapons and Guthrie in their luggage, to the hotel she had proposed. It was large and soulless, therefore nobody would pay them any special heed. It was fairly new—few commercial buildings of any importance had gone up in the Union, this past decade—and not much run down, therefore they could get a room with a capable computer terminal. Nevertheless, when the door closed behind them Kyra felt stifled. She had come from a soft breeze, the palm trees that it rustled and the boundless blue overhead. Her look sprang to the outside view. No sound from yonder reached her.

The feeling passed. There was work to do. Valencia was

unpacking Guthrie. His movements flowed feline. The sight set her aglow.

He put the case on the dresser. Eyestalks extended. "Well, you're both still hale and footloose," Guthrie rumbled. "How was the trip?"

Kyra felt the heat in her face. Did he notice? "Estupendo," she murmured, and couldn't stop a sidewise glance at Valencia. The man stayed impassive.

"What day is it? What time? God damn it, I've been in that box for what was like a week of blue-law Sundays."

"I wondered how you'd stand it," Kyra ventured.

"I dozed. I thought. I played mind games. I ran through memories. Especially the raunchy ones. Now brief me."

Valencia did in economical words. "And what's the latest news?" Guthrie demanded. The humans stared at one another. They had forgotten to tune in.

Kyra keyed the terminal for a summary. It rammed into them. Evidence had been found of terrorist cells in L-5 and on the Moon. At Anson Guthrie's urgent request, Sepo units had been dispatched to the colony and to Port Bowen. He ordered all Fireball personnel to give them full cooperation.

"Grace and goodness," Kyra whispered, for no profanity or obscenity would serve.

Valencia held to a bleak calm. "This throws quite a comet into our plans, doesn't it?" he said. "Difficult enough getting you onto a spaceship and away. Now you won't even find any safe haven there, will you? And these islands will be the devil and all to get away from. I'm sorry. I should have insisted we try for México or Québec, in spite of the guard on the borders."

Kyra harked back to their conference that night in Portland. When Valencia brought up the possibility of escaping by sea out of San Francisco, she had cried that then they need only make for some such port as Mazatlán. He pointed out that under present conditions, the authorities would assuredly not clear a vessel belonging to the notorious Gentlemen Adventurers for any foreign destination. A pleasure jaunt to Hawaii and back was the most they would permit. *Caravel* would have to transmit continuous radio location, and no doubt TrafCon aerostats would also keep an eye on her from the stratosphere. If she deviated significantly from her allowed course, patrol craft would give immediate chase. At that, she'd been stopped along the way and searched for unregistered passengers she might have taken aboard.

Kyra shivered. The thought that a government, any government, could wield so close a control was terrifying.

"No, don't apologize, son," Guthrie said. "I'd have overruled you. The prospect of sailing here delighted me. As a matter of fact, I considered that my twin could make arrangements to head me off if I got into space. Sure, I hoped he wouldn't manage it till too late—I knew he'd think of it—but as it turns out, he did. Just the same, I still guesstimate our chances are better than if we'd tried one of the other stunts we discussed."

"Hm, yes." Valencia nodded. "Lift the spacecraft, set it down again in Ecuador or Australia."

"A beautiful thought. Unfortunately, it's bound to have occurred to anti-me. Whether or not we can pass off our launch as legitimate, we'll be tracked from the first. Armed police flyers are aloft in force, all the time. They have to be, to make this Chaotic scare plausible, but they're ready for business. If we do anything funny, like doubling back to Earth, they'll move to intercept. They're fast, while a descending spacecraft is necessarily slow. They carry light missiles as well as guns, and a spacecraft is completely vulnerable to a single well-placed shot. Never mind if the kill takes place over somebody else's territory. The Covenant gives national police the right of hot pursuit of criminals. Futuro can claim the vessel was hijacked—which, in a way, will be true."

"I might be able to evade," Kyra said slowly.

"Given more luck than skill," Guthrie retorted, "and we agree you've got skill in tonne lots. No, if we can lift off, we'll continue outbound. There are no armed ships in space. As for L-5 and Port Bowen, I have some ideas." His eyestalks swung from the woman to the man and back again. "Enough talk for now. It's a waste of time till we have further information. The ravenous snails are overtaking us. Contact Wash Packer."

His confidence freshened Kyra's heart. She stepped toward the phone. Valencia caught her by the wrist. His grip was light and, she sensed, unbreakable. "Por favor, no, Pilot Davis," he warned. "The director's lines are certainly monitored."

"Damn, I forgot. Gracias, Nero." She gave him her lingering smile. "Besides, we'd better figure out what to tell him."

He released her. "I suggest we screen a map of the area and a classified directory."

Mission first, yes, yes. But did he have to maintain that persona of an armed butler? Guthrie wouldn't care, would he? Kyra thrust her exasperation down. She could make things clear to Nero later. Maybe no later than their next free hours actually began.

Deboost that!

The data retrieval was primarily for his benefit. She knew this town pretty well. Guthrie took only a small part in their planning. "You're a coyote, Valencia," he said at the end. "It's a bloody good thing you're on the side of God, motherhood, and apple pie." The remark bemused Kyra—something from his life's antiquity, she supposed. "Go to it, kids."

They left him watching the multi, for if anyone came in to snoop he'd be found regardless, and went their separate ways. Kyra walked about a kilometer before she looked for a public phone. No sense in giving a clue to her location. It should otherwise be safe. Valencia had used a second false ident to register them as man and wife. (The glow tingled.) If the Sepo checked her out through their computer net after they listened to her talk with Packer, nothing would point to the Bill Mendoza who'd driven her south from Portland. She doubted they'd be that suspicious. She'd try to avoid causing it. But Valencia took every reasonable precaution. He was one workmanlike hombre.

When she rang Kamehameha, her name got her straight through to the boss. That was no big surprise. The spaceport had been idle for days. The lean, white-polled visage stiffened, then broke into a grin doubly brilliant against the chocolate complexion. "Pilot Davis! Wonderful! I've been worried about you, chica."

"Really?" Kyra's back between her shoulderblades ached with tension. This had to sound convincing, and she was no actress. "I'm sorry. I took for granted the call from Québec had explained the situation."

Packer blinked. "What call?"

"When I'd decided I should report back here. A few days ago. You spoke with Pierre Thibodeaux, actually, I think. Don't you remember? Maybe you, uh, had a lot of Fireball business on hand, more *urgent* than *this*."

"Oh, that call. It slipped my mind for a second." Packer shrugged. "To be frank, I haven't much to do, the way things are. That's precisely what is blasting me out of my wits."

Relief cascaded. Her knees shook. He was as quick in the brain as she'd counted on.

"Come around anyhow," she heard through the drumming blood. "Everybody will be glad to see you, especially now while we're on hold. I'll have to get clearance for you to enter, so be sure you do at the main gate."

She thought a mantra. A measure of coolness returned. "Sir, I can't. Not right away. It's personal. You see, I went first to Portland where I have a good friend, and something came up—"

He peered from the screen. "You choked?"

"Uh, no. No. A stray thought." Hurriedly: "I need your counsel, sir. Could we meet somewhere private? I mean, these days, your office, even your home— It's personal, but, but very personal, and it will affect me professionally, and you're such an understanding man—"

He smiled. She thought she saw the grimness behind that show of teeth. "Me, a father figure?"

"You've raised two fine daughters, sir."

"And have a boy at home yet," he said—warily?

"Sir, por favor, I am a consorte of Fireball, and . . . I'm in want of help."

She recognized that he caught her real meaning.

"Troth," he said, as much for the listeners as for her. "Muy bien, Pilot Davis, I'll come. Where and when? Lunch?"

"Gracias, but really, nothing that fancy. I know a little café where the kona coffee is ultra. I'd feel, uh, at home there."

"As you wish." She gave him the address and set the time at ninety minutes hence. Before they blanked, they swapped the *V* salute.

Valencia was already back in the hotel room. "I have a car rented," he told her. When she had related her conversation: "I'll arrive a bit late, to make sure he's there and his tab is paid. Meanwhile I'll reconnoiter." He nodded and was gone before she could speak further.

"Esther Blum found us a savvy lad," Guthrie remarked.

Kyra sank into a recliner. She might as well try to relax. "True," she said, mainly to herself. Her gaze sought the sky.

The lenses aimed at her. "You like him, eh?"

"M-m-m-h'm."

"Not your breed, though."

"I suppose not, but— Never mind!" Kyra snapped.

Guthrie had the grace to change the subject. "If Wash mentioned lunch, he hasn't eaten yet, and I doubt he'll send out for a burger before leaving. Check the menu. When he gets here, call room service and have a place ready to hide me. I daresay the two of you will have an appetite also." He chuckled. "A healthy young couple."

When he got here. If he got here. Kyra played the scene over in her head for the—dozenth?—time. Packer sat nursing his cup. Valencia sauntered in, identified himself in a few low words as her emissary, led him out the rear door that she remembered, to the car he had parked nearby, and they were off, anonymously into traffic. Simple, easy. For a professional. But Packer was no gunjin. He might balk, he might do or say something that betrayed them, he might be hailed in the street by somebody he knew and thus fatally delayed. Or maybe the Sepo who trailed him was more thorough than Valencia anticipated. Maybe the Sepo wouldn't watch unobtrusively from outside the cafe, but go in too. Maybe the Sepo knew about that back door and had posted another man in the alley. Maybe, maybe, maybe.

"Don't fret," Guthrie advised. "You'll only etch your stomach. This is like a tight situation in space, where you've done all you can and the rest is up to the vectors and the machinery. You've waited that out calmly, haven't you?"

"But this is different!" she exclaimed. "It's more than a ship or even myself. There's too much else to be afraid for. The whole future."

"Now, now, let's not get apocalyptic. I've seen crises come and go, everything from wars to elections for dog catcher, with all their excitement about how the outcome would either bring on a glorious new dawn of hope for the whole world or else topple it forever into a bottomless latrine. That never came about, the one way or the other. The human race slobbed on pretty much the same as always."

She stared at him as if she could read his facelessness. "But if the Avantists get Fireball on their side, they'll weld themselves down," she protested. "Onto the Union, at least. My country, jefe. *I* care."

"It would take a while to maneuver Fireball into such a policy," he replied. "Sayre and company are overoptimistic about the time span. It's a couple of generations, I'd guess. You can't change basic attitudes and institutions fast, especially among individualists. The Avantist state won't hang together that long. It's terminally ill already, chronic dogmatitis. What aid my faked-up self might be able to slip it without tipping his hand can only prolong the misery and allow the theocracy of theory to finish its evolution into raw dictatorship. Which isn't a viable form of government either, amongst spacecraft, hypercomputers, light-speed global communications, and molecular factories."

Kyra bit her lip. "How many people would die meanwhile, or worse than die?" she challenged.

"Yeah, that is a consideration. Also, I grant you, it'd be nice to bring the Advisory Synod and their toadies to justice. Rough justice for choice."

Kyra leaned forward. Her fingers clenched on the arms of the seat. "And you, what about you?"

"No big deal." She could almost see him as he would have conjured his image or been in the flesh, a shrug, the mouth crinkling upward. "I won't quit without a fight, but it's been a good run for the money and an old machine isn't worth even one young life like yours."

"You're wrong!" she cried. "You're Fireball!"

"It'll survive me, maybe better off when new blood, real blood, takes over."

"No, it won't." She sprang to her feet and stood above him, glaring, fists on hips. "That other you will be the master. He believes in Avantism, doesn't he? When he sees it fail the way you predict, what'll he do, what'll he work toward?"

"That is right," he admitted slowly. "A perverted Fireball could be a whopping force for . . . call it evil. Or it could simply fail to do something right that was in its power and nobody else's. Which might well be worse."

The thought wrenched at her. North America was dear to her but was merely where she had spent her childhood. And, yes, it was where certain ideas once lived, liberty, limitless hope, hard work and daring guided by intelligence that took no word unquestioned. They lived on in Fireball, because Anson Guthrie had brought the seeds of them with him into space. Fireball was her true country, fatherland, motherland, land for her to bequeath inviolate to her children.

"We'll fight!" she said.

"Haven't got much choice by now, have we?" he answered prosaically. "Do ease off, honey chile. I notice a minibar. Have a drink, sprawl back, play some music or watch a show or let your ol' uncle tell you a story."

A part of her observed how fast her anguish ebbed. That voice of his, the sudden harsh purr and undertone of laughter— He knew how to handle people, she thought. Experience. But surely, too, a gift. He must have been quite something among the women, back when he was mortal, big, strong, bluff, knowing. Pity she hadn't been around then, to get him into bed . . . Her own laughter welled forth.

"That's right," he approved. "What pastime would you like?"

If she found herself comical, she could make a joke of him. "A story, Uncle."

"What about?"

Searching memory, she widened her eyes and cocked her head. "About Winston P. Sanders and the drunken mermaid."

"Ay de mí! No, you'd rather hear about, uh, the time an enterprising sort wanted to contract with us—we were fairly new in business and hungry for money—to construct what'd be an orbiting cathouse."

Kyra stuck her lower lip out at him. "You promised," she whined.

"I did not specify—"

"Exactly. You asked me, 'What about?' No restrictions. I thought you were a man of your word, Sr. Guthrie."

"Uh, well—"

When Valencia and Packer arrived, her ribs ached, in spite of her being mildly appalled.

Mirth tumbled aside from joy, which fell before the starkness on Packer's countenance. Valencia must have sketched the situation on their way here. The director strode to the dresser and stood looking down at Guthrie. His hands reached before him as if to grasp the case, but trembled helplessly. "Jefe," he rasped. "Oh, jefe."

"I'm okay, Wash," Guthrie said.

Packer drew a ragged breath. "You are. But that other one. He's you too. Isn't he? And they did that to him."

"As for us," the download said flatly, "we've several square light-years to cover in two or three hours at most and had better get right down to spreading the manure around. Valencia, can't you see when a man wants a drink? Davis, you were supposed to study the menu and produce ideas about lunch."

Again his voice worked. (Though the memory of his image and the weight of his history must also be with him,

Kyra thought.) And, of course, everybody in the room was a pragmatist, not given to torments of doubt and sensitivity. (You did your thinking, your balancing of rights and wrongs, consequences and possibilities, before action. If anything, it was the more painful because you knew it would end in what you did or what you did not do, and that you must bear the responsibility ever afterward.) Within minutes, their session was under way.

The spaceport was closely guarded by national militia and a Sepo cadre. Only one ship was there, the one in which Kyra had landed. Kamehameha was, after all, a secondary facility, the big Earthside layouts being in Ecuador and Australia; and obviously Fireball wouldn't send more vessels to it till matters were resolved.

"Damn!" she said. "I'd kind of hoped for a torchcraft. Now I've got to hope the enemy can't get one after me while I'm free-falling."

"Hsh!" Valencia whispered in her ear. "Packer doesn't need to know that." She frowned at him. If they couldn't trust the director, their cause was lost. At the same time she was aware of Valencia's closeness. The faint, warm impact of his breath stayed with her.

Packer had ignored the exchange. "The Sepo will want to know how and why I disappeared on them," he warned.

"Stall for a short while," Guthrie answered. "Claim secrecy. Then they'll see you get instructions making clear that this was what you were ordered from on high to do."

"How?"

"You didn't imagine, did you, that over the years my agents wouldn't have developed a few access lines into the official net and planted a few moles and computer worms? Or that I'd have come to North America without first getting an update on them? I will point out as well that if my copy can claim to be me, I can too."

"Ungn. Risky."

"It is that. Which is why I haven't made use of it hitherto. Now I judge we're at the showdown, and we've got to toss this chip into the pot."

Packer looked straight at the lenses. He was a loyal man. But. "I have a family," he said.

"I've not forgotten. We'll scoot you and them to safety right after we make our play. Exactly how is among the matters on today's agenda."

Discussion continued, rapid-fire, interrupted only when they must conceal Guthrie while room service brought in food. The download set forth his basic strategy. It met with horrified objections. He overrode them. He had thought this out while alone in darkness considering contingencies, including the one that had become reality. The scheme was neither certain nor fail-safe, but he deemed it the best that could be attempted. He persuaded the others and they all set themselves to hammer out the details.

Packer's gang would need no more than a couple of hours to prepare the spacecraft for liftoff. He could load practically anything into her if the incantation "Top Secret" was his to utter. That included the small launcher on which half the plan depended. Several were in the supply depot, like other frequently used items.

What with the surveillance which everybody on base must endure, Kyra was the sole choice for pilot. The orders Packer was to receive would specify her. This should, furthermore, make the Sepo speculate less about why she had phoned him and sneaked him off today.

"But your trick for getting into the base, it's loco," Packer protested.

"Do you have a better proposal, sir?" Valencia replied. "Sr. Guthrie can't direct that security at the gates be reduced. That would instantly alert them that something's wrong. A Guthrie detector will be at every entrance, and any bags or packages will be opened in case they are screened against it. Whereas, if we simply appear, walking toward the ship, whoever sees us should take for granted that we came by the usual route and passed inspection."

Packer shook his head. "Swimming in, though," he muttered.

"How else?" Kyra demanded. "I know that little beach. Oh, I know it well! Favorite resting place when we've been romping with the Keiki, right? Nothing there but a chain link fence, mainly so casuals like me won't stray inshore and get underfoot. The Sepo haven't electrified it or anything, have they?"

"N-no. Too much else for them to do, I guess. It's only been a short while since this mess exploded." Packer gusted a sigh. "Feels like forever."

"We're betting that the Sepo are no closer to a hundred percent efficient than we are," Valencia pursued. "If I were their comandante, I'd concentrate my force—not infinite, is it?—where things might be expected to happen. Along the sea I'd just have two or three men walk sentry. And not my highly trained corpsmen. Militia. Am I right?"

"Y-yes."

"We should be able to slip by them. I'm in that business. Before meeting you today I bought tools." Valencia grinned. "As the jefe says, the wildness of this stunt helps its chances."

"I don't know, I don't know. The Keiki—"

"They're my friends," Kyra said. "To them this will be a game, another of those odd games humans play."

"Could be."

"I like it, Wash," Guthrie said.

Packer straightened in his chair. "Then it's go, and I should stop squandering time," he answered quietly.

Talk went on. When Packer left, it was not because the subject was exhausted but because he would be unwise to lengthen his absence.

At the door he shook hands with Valencia and Kyra, while his gaze stayed with Guthrie. "You're brave people, you three," he said.

"You're risking more than we are, Wash," Guthrie replied.

"In a way. Let's hope it'll prove worth it. Adiós." Packer left them.

"Okay," Guthrie clipped, "let's review our program for the next stage in the light of what he's told us, and set it in train. He can't fend off the Sepo for long without corroboration."

Presently: "Nero, I gather hacking is among your skills. Take the terminal. I'll give directions."

Kyra had nothing further to do but sit back and admire.

Although she necessarily knew a considerable amount about computer systems, her work had never called for their subversion. On the contrary! That sort of prank could spell disaster for a spacecraft, or a civilization, dependent on them. She recalled an Academy course in the safeguards against it and how those had evolved and elaborated through time. By now, an outsider could break into a properly secured program about as readily and inconspicuously as he could break into a bank vault. However, if an insider went about it right, he could insert certain vulnerabilities, virtually unnoticeable. Then if an outsider, maybe years or decades later, knew what had been done, he would be able to slip commands of his own along the communication lines into the system, and it would heed them just as if these were what it was supposed to do.

Of course, this took art and subtlety. Even as simple an operation as entering a false message and making it seem to have come from a real source was a nine-ball juggling act.

How deftly Valencia stroked the keys. His head might have been a young Hermes'—no, a Pan's, or a Lucifer's—leaning intent above a mischief from which would be born music.

Not that Guthrie wasn't impressive. When he, speaking as if from Quito, added his personal brief message to the coded command, it was a masterpiece. The spaceship would lift tonight. Until then, not a ghost of a hint about it to anyone. The terrorists did not imagine this awkward craft would carry a vital mission. Should they do so, their reaction might well be massively violent.

Nevertheless, Guthrie was a program in a machine. Nero was a man.

"I suppose the Sepo comandante will wonder a lot about this," Guthrie said. "However, we can assume it won't nag him into taking any initiative contrary to the orders until too late. They wouldn't assign their smartest boy to as unlikely a trouble spot as this." He looked back at Valencia. "Now we have to alert Tamura in L-5 and Rinndalir on Luna."

That went as a routine pair of memos, sent over the phone—untraceably, courtesy of the worm—to the appropriate beamcaster. Nothing but the sender's name, a drab "A. A. Craig," revealed that another communication was encrypted within each. The format had capacity for no more than a few words. Guthrie was trusting his existence to Tamura's intelligence and resolution. He was trusting Kyra's to Rinndalir's intelligence and goodwill. The last of those was an unknown quantity. Anxiety twisted anew within her.

"Bastante," Guthrie said. "We can relax now till time to boost."

Valencia rose from his chair, writhing to loosen cramped muscles. The sight roused Kyra. She put her qualms aside, got up likewise, and glided toward him. Her smile broadened as she neared. They'd have to brazen this out. "Jefe," she began, "would you mind very much—"

"We should try for a nap before we grab another meal and start off," Valencia interrupted. "It will be a fairish drive and a busy night." His glance met hers. He grinned wryly. "A nap," he repeated.

"He's right, you know," Guthrie said.

Kyra halted. "I suppose he is," she mumbled.

Maybe she could manage it, stretched on the bed beside him.

23

THE ROAD WAS narrow, a slash through forest, snaking steeply down toward the shore. It ended at a small parking lot. Valencia drove to the corner where shadow was thickest, doused headlights and cut engine. Darkness and silence thundered upon Kyra. She got out. Guthrie felt heavy in her hands. Valencia joined her. For a moment they stood mute.

Her eyes adapted. In starlight and sky-glow, the scene emerged for her. Along the pavement, ginger mingled with hibiscus; the mild air was honeyed with its odor. Behind, she recognized the brushlike blooms of a silk oak, the spreading height of a koa, then the woods became one black mass that climbed away mountainward. On the other side, through the heavy mesh of the fence, she saw grass hueless over a slope that plunged to the sea. Surf hemmed a wall of shoreline with unrestful white. She heard its noise as a seething amidst a deeper, softer pulse from the waters a-glimmer beyond.

"Looks like we've got the place to ourselves," Guthrie said. "I wasn't sure we would. The occupation force in the port, yah, that'd discourage people from coming near it, but it's a ways off and this is a favorite spot for lovers."

Unthinkingly, Kyra nodded and smiled. She remembered.

"It has been for a long time, I imagine," Valencia remarked.

Guthrie had related the history to him when he inquired: "After the Renewal fell, we decided Fireball could use an American base, and Hawaii seemed best. It'd cost more to demolish the old, abandoned facilities and rebuild than to start from scratch. The economy was in such desperate shape, and 'ecology' wasn't the knee-jerk shibboleth it had been, that the new government was glad to sell us a little piece of Volcanoes Park. Especially since we undertook to restore and replant as needed, everywhere in the park. The Goddess Temple had let it go to hell. Controlling things like blight and animal populations was a religious no-no. We did build on the shore, out of lava reach, but we also contributed to general maintenance on a permanent basis. The arrangement's worked fine.

"Then, about thirty years ago, the Chinese terminated their intelligence-genetics project. You probably aren't aware, at this late date, what a mistake it had been. They didn't learn anything about the role of DNA in brain processes that hadn't been learned in easier ways, without creating hapless metamorphs. And now the Federation had legislated that neosophs have the same rights as human beings. What to do with these? I thought Fireball could provide them a home. Among other advantages, we could block off the gaping tourists, yawping ideologists, and quick-money hustlers. It took propaganda, political pressure, dickering, bribery, and a spot of blackmail, but I got the franchise. They have a secluded bit of coast to themselves. A patrol boat keeps unwanted visitors well off shore. They live as they see fit and are developing a culture of their own. No human I've talked to claims to really understand it."

"Bueno," Valencia continued, "I'm happy we don't have to sneak through the jungle, but I won't open the fence where any passerby might notice." He hefted his tool bag and disappeared soundlessly into the growth. After a minute, spots of light from his flash and the hum of his power cutter passed among the leaves to Kyra.

They thrilled through her. The fleeing was at an end, the foray begun! It felt like hurtling forward on a surfboard, but this wave roared as high as the stars. A mosquito in her mind shrilled that failure would be nauseating, quite probably fatal. She didn't listen. The tide ran too strong.

Guthrie's lenses glinted upward at her. "I think you look forward to the next several hours," he said.

Kyra nodded. "I confess I do. And you?"

"In my fashion. Which you'd find pretty cold and abstract, maybe sort of the way you'd approach an interesting problem in mathematics."

Of course. He was bodiless. And yet he seemed capable of concern, anger, merriment, regret, affection. Was it all an act? Or could such feelings dwell in the awareness itself? She thought so. If not, why had Guthrie bothered to survive, let alone strive and fight? Kyra recalled old married couples she had known. Sex for them had dwindled to ember or ash, she supposed; nonetheless she had seen that she was in the presence of love.

"I envy you," he said low.

Astonished, she almost dropped him. Valencia saved them from further talk by reappearing. "Come," he said. Kyra put Guthrie into the carryall, it onto her shoulders, and followed. Valencia's flash lit their way through the tangle and she moved easily, parting it before her, letting it slip smoothly back behind her. "I see you've done this before," he remarked.

"Yes, I like wilderness. You?"

"Likewise. If you can call those managed snippets wilderness. Here we are."

He had parted the links and pulled them back just enough for a person to squeeze past. The ground beyond, though open, was trickier going, irregularly canted, strewn with boulders and potholes that the long grass hid. Peering, sweating, swearing, Kyra picked her way to the footpath that led from the locked gate. Valencia moved with his usual panther ease. Damn him.

They reached the sea and its children.

Fireball had enlarged a cove, using the rock blasted out to make a breakwater at its mouth. Sheer bluffs flanked a beach of black sand. On a nearly level plot above it, a hemicylindrical shed protected the dwellers' meager belongings. With magnetic latches, its doors opened to a push; jaws grasping knobs could pull them shut. A motor raft and a powerboat lay at a pier for human convenience. No other artifacts were visible. It was too dark to see the art that the Keiki Moana had splashed in paint along the bottoms of the bluffs or gnawed out of soft wood.

They slept, stretched on the sand and the turf. Kyra saw perhaps two score of them, long, sleek adults and stubby pups. What light there was sheened faint on the fur of their backs; otherwise they were sable hulks. The rest, she supposed, were at sea, hunting, exploring, whatever they did, maybe some of them on a reef coughing their strange songs at the sky. As she drew nigh these she caught the odor that drifted about them, of fish and kelp and depth and, like a memory, sun-blink on waves.

She stopped, Valencia beside her. *"Aloha, makamaka,"* she called, no louder than the surge against the breakwater. *"Aloha ahiahi. 'O Kyra Davis ko'u inoa."*

They stirred. Heads lifted. Eyes filled with starlight.

"I didn't know you spoke Hawaiian," Valencia murmured.

"I don't, really," Kyra answered. "Nor do they much, I

think. But it's . . . customary to begin and end in that language . . . with them. I don't know why." So much had come to be, no doubt often so subtly that no one could say how. Two races, the inmost heart of each a mystery to the other—though Earth had borne them both. What then would it be like, seeking to understand beings under a different sun?

If any existed, anywhere in the universe. If neosophonts and machines were not the only companions humanity could ever have. Abruptly the stars felt cold. Kyra welcomed the approach of the Keiki.

They hitched themselves along more readily than you might have awaited. A few barked a time or two, otherwise she heard just flippers a-slap and bellies a-slither. When the foremost reached her, they all stopped wherever they chanced to be, heads up, odorous breath soughing in and out of lungs.

Kyra recognized Charlie. So she and her friends called him, again for no reason clear to her. He was bigger than average. Reared aloft, his face came even with her breasts, and the bulk curving away beneath was at least equal to Valencia's. She could see the scar of an accident, a seam down the domed forehead and across the sea-cleaving snout. A human surgeon had stitched the wound, but cosmetic histotropy afterward had appeared impractical in his case. Besides, Charlie wasn't vain. Was he?

His voice boomed and sibilated at her. *"A'oha, Ky'a. Hiaow kong fsh-sh s's'hwi-oong?"*

She had read that the modified vocal organs could handle Mandarin a little better than that. It was plausible, seeing as how these beings were the result of Chinese experiments. Maybe they could handle Polynesian no more awkwardly, but even in this new home of theirs they had scant occasion to practice it. What mattered tonight was that the modified brains could cope well with English. Her share had been to learn her own language as it sounded from throats like his.

"Gracias, Charlie and everyone," she said. "Meet my amigo Nero Valencia." She repeated the name twice, slowly. The gunjin bowed in the manner she had told him he should, bringing his head down to Charlie's till the stiff whiskers brushed his nose. "We are sorry to disturb your sleep."

"[This pleasure is better than dreams. Do you want to swim? The Moon will rise in a while.]"

"Yes, we are here to swim, but right away, before the Moon comes. Forgive us that we bring no music or food and that we shan't dance in the water with you. Later, yes, but tonight we have great need and no time."

"[Do you chase a prey?]"

"A shark, that we have to kill before it kills us."

It was the best she and Guthrie had been able to devise. She could but hope that it conveyed a sense of mortal urgency, and that the Keiki would believe and help her. Explaining the facts would have been an exercise in mutual incomprehension.

It wasn't that these creatures were isolated from the world. They had multiceivers in their shed and a robot responsive to simple commands. They discoursed at length with the scientists who came here by Fireball's permission. Several of them had been taken on tours. It was that they knew the world not as humans did, but—fundamentally, in spite of everything that had been done to the germ plasm of their ancestors—as seals did.

(Forget about dolphins. They are clever animals, but too alien. Most of those big forebrains are for processing sensory data that come in on the scanty bandwidth of sound. Use apes instead—and find that they are not alien enough, that you have discovered very little in the course of producing grossly handicapped hominids. It should be less cruel and more enlightening to experiment with pinnipeds. . . . And what have you at the end but an animal with a mind and no hands, a swimmer less able than its forefathers, thus forced to ways of life unknown throughout its evolution, worse at war with its ancestral urges than you are with yours?)

For the same reason, Kyra did not produce Guthrie from her pack. They knew him, but only slightly and in a robot body.

"[Where would you go? What would you do?]"

"We must put well out to sea in the boat. Some of you come along. When we're opposite the spaceport, we'll leave the boat and swim ashore. You'll have to help us, and it has to be quietly, quietly. It's a terrible shark we hunt." On land, but she had no better word. The Keiki knew nothing about vipers or governments. "That's all. It has to be done fast, though. We beg you. Por favor. *'Olu'olu.'*"

The Keiki exchanged looks. One by one they started to bark, till it rang between the bluffs. "[A new game!]" Charlie bayed. "[Come, come!]" He swung about and wriggled beachward. The whole pack did, a crowding, shoving, ululating chaos.

"They'll do it?" Valencia asked eagerly. "That was quick."

"I expected they'd agree," Kyra answered. "They're always happy for something new. Like . . . children." Her voice dropped. "Or like us, I suppose, if we were pensioners on a lonely shore."

Like many humans already. Like humans everywhere after they had become pensioners of their machines, she thought.

It took a quarrelsome while at the water's edge to settle who should have the delight of going. Kyra must insist repeatedly that the party be minimal. Charlie grabbed two successive obstreperous individuals, teeth clamped on neck, and shook them into submission. He seemed to be the alpha male—no, Kyra recalled, that wasn't right. Dominance order, breeding pattern, migration, everything had changed as much as the life of her genus had changed since Australopithecus. Or more, because her line had evolved through a geological era, not been thrown into sapience in the course of two or three generations. What was arising to replace the ancient ways of the seals?

When at length she could start the boat, she must keep its engine throttled back lest she outrun her escort. They traveled fast, though, silvery torpedoes vaguely seen through foam and streaming water, now and then an exultant leap or a toboggan run down a wave. The patrol craft spied theirs, drew near, saw that they were outbound, and veered off, its robotic pilot finding no reason to summon a police flitter.

"Lemme out of here," Guthrie demanded on her back. She gave Valencia the wheel and obeyed, setting him on deck behind the cockpit. His eyestalks roved. Did he too devour the sight, knowing it could be his last?

The boat purred smoothly over low swells. Forward they heaved, a burnished blackness, to the edge of heaven. A ship was passing yonder, brightly lighted, toylike at its distance. Somehow it deepened Kyra's sense of isolation. Aft the land gloomed lofty. Kamehameha was a star cluster on it, outshining the wan points overhead. Wind and sea lulled. Kyra lost herself in the night.

"I think we're far enough out," Valencia said. He brought them parallel to shore. His hair mingled with the mountainous dark, his profile stood sculptured against it. Kyra laid a hand on his thigh.

Not that she'd fallen in love or anything, no, no, but she mightily wished they'd had time of their own this afternoon, and when she came back after victory—

She gasped. The horizon ahead was lightening. "Moonrise already?" she exclaimed. "Have we taken this long?"

Valencia glanced at his informant. "Yes," he replied as if she had asked him for the time or the square root of a number. "Bueno, we can try to make it an advantage, not an extra danger. When we arrive, keep low in the water, go onto the beach on all fours, lie prone till I signal you."

"You'll go ahead alone? No!"

"He's the pro, Kyra," Guthrie reminded her. "You wouldn't let him at the console of a spaceship, would you?"

"Right." Valencia turned his head to meet her eyes. His smile flashed like a wave crest. "We'll proceed together, never fear."

She tautened. "We will."

Kamehameha blazed ahead. He cut the engine. The boat whispered to a stop and rocked in the swing of the sea. Kyra forgot her fears. In and at them!

Standing up in the cockpit, she and Valencia took off

their clothes. The Moon entered the sky. That low, it did not yet cast a glade. A million tiny wires of light quivered on the water. The Keiki turned luminous. For an instant, man and woman regarded one another, palely aglow amidst shadows. He had lidded his biojewel, but she remembered last night's red-gold. She saw the rising, grinned, and found voice. "It's mutual, amigo." Look at her nipples. "But c'mon." He grinned back, then they both got busy.

Guthrie went into her carryall again and it into the nearer of the sealable plastic bags Valencia had acquired with his burglary kit. Shoes, garments, towels, tools went into the second. He kept the shoulder-holstered pistol he had taken from beneath his jacket. She didn't know much about firearms, had only done occasional target shooting, but obviously this piece didn't mind being wet. Bundles in hand, they lowered themselves over the side.

The sea was cool, embracing, a caress over her entire body. She tasted salt on her lips like a kiss. Nonetheless, she realized that in a few hours she'd die of exposure. She could swim to shore before then, of course, but she'd land exhausted. Therefore the guards shouldn't be watching for intruders from this direction.

The half-dozen Keiki crowded around. She gave her bag to one to hold by his (her?) teeth. Charlie pulled alongside. He must want to be her steed. Fine; that too was mutual. He submerged for her to stretch along his back and lay arms around his neck. Careful to keep her head in the air, he began to move. Valencia got the same service. The deserted boat fell behind.

Muscles flexed powerfully beneath her. Water streamed, stroked, purled by. The Moon climbed higher, bow waves shone white, wakes swirled radiant. Surf, whispering at first, boomed ever louder and deeper. She kept her eyes from the spaceport glare and let herself go free into ocean and Moonlight while still she could.

The beach curved in an arc, shielded by another breakwater against which the sea crashed and spouted. When they had rounded it, the Keiki slowed. They knew how to sneak up on quarry. The minutes stretched till the magic snapped across.

Like a brusque arousing, Charlie grated to a halt. Kyra slipped off him and felt sand beneath her soles. They were in the shallows.

She squatted low, head barely above the lapping water. A last time she hugged Charlie, cheek against sleek pelt. "Gracias, gracias," she breathed. *"Mahalo nui loa.* Now go. Right away. *Hele aku."* Don't linger, don't get killed.

He uttered a soft grunt, nuzzled her in the hollow between neck and shoulder, and slipped off. For a few seconds she glimpsed the hasty shapes. They vanished. She and Nero were alone.

They'd better be.

As instructed, she crept ashore and flattened herself. The sand was black and scratchy. Crouched, he glided from her. Above the strand was a strip of grass and shrubs, then the chain link fence and its locked gate, silhouetted against the whiteness from lamps that in her position she could not see. Valencia disappeared. She lay with her heartbeat. A breeze fluttered across wet skin and into drenched hair. She shivered.

Valencia returned, wolf-gaited. "All right, I've found a spot," he said in her ear. "Keep low and be quick."

A man-tall hibiscus bush close to the fence, several meters from the gate, offered concealment. Its flowers hung startlingly bright in the patch of speckled night that it made. The pair could see well enough to towel themselves dry and resume their clothes. Kyra slung the carryall on her back. Guthrie felt weightless. She must be charged to megavolt potential, though consciousness had gone hyalon-clear.

"Your hair's a mess," Valencia said low. "We forgot a comb. Let me see if I can straighten it some."

"Same to you."

Two monkeys finger-grooming! Kyra silenced laughter and lust.

They puffed away when Valencia stepped from her, took his kit off the ground, and moved to the fence. His cutter buzzed—louder than Niagara? No, no—and links fell apart, each by each by each. He was so brightly illuminated too, a beacon where he stood against the barrier. No, really, the light was dim and tricky. Rip, rip, rip. Severed coils clicked on their neighbors.

He dropped the tool, laid hold of the metal, tugged. It sagged around a narrow gap. He beckoned and eased through. Kyra came after. A raw edge scratched her hand.

"You! Stop!"

Valencia whirled. Motion blurred his right arm. The pistol spat. The bullet trailed a tiny thunderclap.

Valencia was already running. Kyra had barely started when he reached the guard. Did the fallen man stir? Valencia put the pistol to the head. Brain geysered.

Valencia stepped back from the spreading, shimmery pool. "Let's go," he said, reholstering his weapon beneath his jacket.

Kyra jerked to a halt and stared. Beyond a narrow lawn, a warehouse loomed sheer, every window lightless. It blocked their view of whatever was behind. That must be a reason Valencia had picked the entry point he did. Lamplight diffused over and around it, harshening the Moonglow but not adding very much. It sufficed to show her the dead man's face. His half a face. He had been young.

Valencia's grip closed bruisingly on Kyra's arm. "Vamos!" he snapped. "I don't know when he'd have met the next guard, or whether that one will come searching or call in an alarm straightaway. We can just try to haul clear before then."

She could not pull her look from the single empty eye. "You killed him," she heard. The words fell dulled off a dry tongue. "He was wounded, and you killed him."

"What else?" She sensed how he reined in impatience, to speak hurriedly but soothingly: "Kyra, it was necessary. This meeting was happenstance, his bad luck and ours. Let's not make it Fireball's."

She gagged down acid. No, God damn it, she would *not* puke. She turned and strode from the corpse. Her heels hit the sidewalk in perfect cadence.

Valencia joined her. "That's better," he said. She guessed that he smiled, though she didn't care to see. "You're a brave muchacha, Kyra."

She ought to reply, "I am Pilot Davis," but didn't.

"Shouldn't you have the carryall in your hand?" he asked. "That's how the multi shows spacers taking their personal gear aboard."

He was right. He stayed cool and thought of everything. She followed the suggestion without comment. What she must concentrate on was steadiness.

They went around several outer buildings so as to appear in the more public areas as if coming from the main gate. It took a while. She wondered indifferently whether tension increased in him pace by pace, listening for the doomsday siren. No matter. If so, he'd conceal it well. He was expert at such things. For her, stolidity must serve. That didn't seem hard to maintain, after sickness had congealed to numbness.

They emerged in the open and walked under lampposts, between more buildings, miniature gardens, benches and tables where employees liked to eat lunch. Afar they saw the field. The spacecraft poised floodlighted, a dart aimed at heaven, against the gaunt array of laser launchers. *Maui Maru* was her name, returned to Kyra. An ordinary small freighter, not meant for deep space, plying the lanes between Earth, Luna, and L-5. Having boosted, she traveled mostly on trajectory till she reached her destination. Kyra's *Kestrel* was docked at L-5. It would be healing to take those dear controls again, to ride a torch again out to the haunts of the comets.

Two uniformed Sepo confronted her. "Your identity, por favor," said the larger.

"Pilot Davis, reporting to Director Packer for tonight's mission." She gave him her card to examine.

"Mario Conroy, reporting with information." Valencia's tone was as pleasant as his smile. He didn't yank out his ident, he eased it out.

The officer spoke into a miniphone. "Ah, yes," he said. "In order. If you'll wait a minute, a vehicle will come for you."

"Why wasn't there one for them at the gate?" wondered his partner.

The first man shrugged. "This business popped up with no notice. Nobody's sure what it is. Nobody was prepared. Nobody knows his tail from his butt."

Except Fireball's folk, Kyra thought. They were puzzled too, of course, but they'd swing right into action. Besides, though the circumstances were peculiar, this launch in itself was the nadir of routineness.

A bug car brought her and Valencia to headquarters. "Wait, if you can," he told the driver. "We may be back soon." The scene inside was blessedly familiar, known faces, known voices and mannerisms welcoming her—if she ignored the militiamen at their stations and the wary-eyed plainclothes operatives. She and Valencia were ushered directly to Packer's office.

He rose to his feet behind the desk. "Buenas tardes." The greeting sounded raw. He could never go pale, but was there a grayness underneath the brown? "Have a seat. Care for some refreshment?"

"I'm afraid we haven't time," Valencia replied. "New word has come in. Pilot Davis has to scramble immediately."

Packer blinked, swallowed, recovered. His body actually loosened. Now he wasn't chewing on the hours till the 2300 set for liftoff, Kyra realized. Instead, he was challenged to stage an act for the electronics planted here. "Oh? I haven't been told."

"Nor will you be, sir, till we can brief you in a more secure place." The "we" implied an outfit overriding the Sepo: which meant direct agents of the Advisory Synod. In his orders, Guthrie had not explicitly said anything like that about Mario Conroy, because it was never done for such persons, but he had made the implication clear.

"If I have to go off with you, I'd like to stop by my home and notify my family," Packer said.

"Certainly," Valencia replied. "I'll ride along, if I may." Unspoken: And we'll pack them into your car and make for the first of the limbos I have chosen. Kyra decided it was best she couldn't tell Packer what had happened to the guard. "But how much can you advance the countdown?"

"That depends on where the ship is bound, which I haven't been told either," Packer said.

Kyra stirred. "No worry about a launch window," she said. "If the tanks are full, I'll have reaction mass to waste, and there won't be any call afterward to justify it."

"So it's a matter of a new clearance to lift," Packer said needlessly. "I'll call Captain Ueland"—evidently the chief of the occupying force, whose authorization he must get in any case—"and ask him to put in for crash priority." Federation Astro Control normally granted such requests, which were not frequent, when they came from a government official. "I'd guess we can raise you in half an hour, Pilot Davis."

How long since the murder—the liquidation—the unfortunate necessity? How long till it was discovered? "Then I'd better board at once," Kyra said.

"Buen viaje." Packer kept the farewell conventional, unemotional. She caught the slightest tremor in it, which said, Oh, good voyage to you, good voyage to our hopes that you bear!

Guthrie had once more gone heavy, as if Earth dragged at them both. She saluted and started out. Valencia flowed in front of her. "Buena suerte, amiga, y hasta la vista," he said low. His hand swung behind her waist. He kissed her. It was light and brief, nothing to make anybody speculate, only what two people who'd become friendly might exchange; but she felt his lips tremble.

She had all she could do not to shudder. "Adiós," she said, and went out the door.

24

—Zero."

The ship lifted. Acceleration pressed Kyra deep into her couch. She gave herself to the task of breathing. Before her eyes, lights blinked, needles turned across dials, the hieroglyphs in display screens shifted from shape to shape. The drive pulse throbbed in her ears and bones, it took her, she became one with it.

Upward and eastward the ship rose, until the lasers could no longer reach her. At that height, scant air remained for them to energize into thrust. For a short span she moved on momentum and Kyra floated free, held just by her safety web, in an enormous quiet.

When the ship reached vacuum of the required hardness, her drive kicked in. The force was less than before and the only sounds Kyra heard were the breath in ventilators and her nostrils, the blood in her veins.

"Orbit achieved," said a synthetic voice and various instruments. Again she was weightless. Her body reveled in the freedom. Null-*g* had its nuisances and over any real length of time it was bad for her, she'd have to spend hours daily exercising and in the centrifuge to counteract, but these first moments were always joy.

Or they had been. She and Guthrie were aloft, they had escaped alive, yet muscles alone took pleasure. Inside, she felt frozen.

She unsnapped her harness, floated off the couch, looked out the viewport. A segment of Earth's vast curve filled half of it, clouds white swirls, cities constellated across the night beneath. She was above México, she judged—yes, the locator positioned *Maui*'s symbol there on its map. The rest of the scene was stars. She'd dimmed the cabin before liftoff, as was her wont, so that now they crowded vision, a frosty glory.

She pushed with a foot, flew to the rack behind the couch, caught a bracket to stop herself—a maneuver as gratifyingly graceful as a pass in a water dance among the Keiki—and hung by Guthrie. "How're you doing?" she asked.

"Fine," he replied from the web. His eyestalks extended toward her face. "I can't say the same of you, though, can I?"

Kyra glanced away. "I'm all right," she mumbled.

"The hell you are. It's about Valencia, isn't it?"

She set her teeth. "Yes. What he did. Do you know?" She hadn't quite dared talk to him after they were aboard. There might have been a bug of some kind. Anyway, she'd been busy, stowing things, readying herself, ordering a flight plan for the Moon and studying it.

"I have a fair idea from what I heard in your pack. A sentry surprised you. Valencia got the drop on him and killed him."

Kyra's knuckles whitened on the bracket. "Not simply that," she forced out. "I don't know if the man died at once. It makes . . . no difference . . . Valencia shot him again, point blank, in the head."

"Yeah, I had that impression."

She stared into the blankness of him. "You don't care?" she whispered.

"Oh, it's too bad, sure, but— No, I don't approve of slaughtering helpless people. Once I'm back in charge at Fireball, I'll find out who that man was, whether he left a family and what can be done to help them. But it *was* an emergency, Kyra. Either Valencia shot first, or we lost everything. Wash Packer too; they'd be certain to arrest and deep-quiz him. That second bullet may or may not have been called for. I hope I couldn't have brought myself to it. But Nero's a gunjin. He'll never stand trial, you know. One way or another, making him a whole new identity or whatever else is called for, his brotherhood will see to that. And I won't interfere. Because he saved us. And by his standards, he was doing the right and necessary thing."

Kyra's eyes blurred and stung. "That's what I keep telling myself. When can I believe it?"

"Yes, a terrible shock for you. And a ghastly sight, I

know all too well. Lass, I wish and I wish I could hold you tight. Even robot arms would be better than this damned box."

That brought a measure of warmth, the beginning of a thaw. Kyra swallowed, met the lensed gaze, found she could smile a little. "G-gracias, jefe. Muchas gracias."

"I did think he wasn't for you."

The warmth turned absurdly hot. "Nothing serious went on!"

"Good. You'll have a spell to come to terms with what happened. It was sad and horrible, but it's done, and it didn't hurt you in any fundamental way, as a rape would have. That attitude isn't selfish, it's practical. You're too healthy to let a mere nightmare set up housekeeping in your head. Be zen. Play some music you like. Remember glad things. You'll get over it."

After some seconds Guthrie added slowly: "You'll have to decide this for yourself, but I hope you can also get over hating Nero Valencia. I don't suppose you'll ever feel exactly cordial, but—well, me, in several ways I'm kind of sorry for him."

"I'll try."

Silence murmured. Ocean sheened on Earth's disc.

"Shouldn't we make ready to send me off?" Guthrie said rather than asked.

Kyra started. "Crack, yes! Forgive me. I've been a, a self-pitying nullhead. Now, prontito."

She returned to the console, held herself fast by the toeholds, and gave the problem to the navigation program.

Maui's path was already determined. The ship was in an orbit low but widening. When she had come about three-fourths of the way around Earth, her drive would fire afresh and put her on course for the Moon. It would be a fast trajectory for a vessel like her, extravagant of reaction mass, but bringing her there in a couple of days. That was the best possible under the initial conditions; this wasn't a torchcraft, capable of long-sustained boost.

The new question was: Exactly when and how should the auxiliary launcher be released, to carry Guthrie past L-5? Since the colony trailed Luna by sixty degrees in the same orbit, the time wasn't far ahead. As an additional requirement, *Maui*'s hull must screen the launcher from Earth-based radar while it was under thrust and for as much longer afterward as might be. If the Union police hadn't yet locked onto this ship, they soon would. If they noticed anything leaving her, that pretty well ended the game.

To be sure, they were limited to radars within their national boundaries. They wouldn't ask Federation AstroCon for help; it would involve explanations. But the moment they found the slain guard and the snipped fence, they'd know they'd been had, and very soon false Guthrie would be alerted. He in his turn commanded all the resources of Fireball. *Maui* was going to be observed from that instant until she reached Luna.

"I expect he'd have us blown apart, and invent a story to justify it, if any weapons but small arms were allowed in space," Guthrie had said during their conference in Hilo —how many millennia ago? "I don't expect he'll order a torch to rendezvous with us and her crew to board, assuming he could get one there in time. An awkward, dangerous, time-consuming, and, most especially, conspicuous maneuver. The world would notice and ask why. He'll see that you're headed for the Moon, know that in your breed of ship you'll have no choice but to land at Port Bowen, and set the Sepo ready to nab you when you arrive."

"Why can't you broadcast the truth while you're in space?" Valencia inquired. "What then can he do but confront you publicly? And he's bound to fail any serious test."

"Unfortunately," Guthrie explained, "Fireball owns just about every ship and facility at Earth, Luna, and L-5, plus most of those elsewhere."

"No, the satellites—"

"Oh, commercial, weather, Peace Authority, and the rest of those sats, they don't count. I mean ships, ports, interplanetary communications systems, the works. Even Federation personnel ride with us and rent from us when they need offices or quarters off Earth—unless they contract with us to do their jobs for them, which is what happens most often. That's why there aren't any government cops for Kyra to appeal to at Bowen. The tiny constabulary is Fireball, and will be under orders to stand aside from whatever the Sepo detachment does.

"As for calls from spacecraft to anywhere, such as Earth, they aren't direct. The sheer volume of communications traffic, plus the liability of various critical systems to interference, made us give up straightforward transmission quite a while ago. What we use is safer, more efficient, and more reliable. Any signal from or to space passes through Fireball's relay sats or stations, which are the only ones equipped to amplify and unscramble it. They shunt it through the general communications net, or through Fireball's own circuits, as the case may be. This is all computer work, you know, and the first chance my twin got, he put in a secret command to watch for suspicious messages and hold them for his inspection or Sayre's. *I* would have."

Valencia whistled. "I knew you had a great empire, sir. I didn't realize how great."

"It works so smoothly that people don't notice it much," Packer said. "We don't want power over them, we simply want to do what interests us and make an honest profit on it."

Guthrie had kept Fireball true to that, Kyra thought. Without him, no doubt it would have evolved into a quasi-government, or a robber barony.

"The monopoly wasn't planned, it grew," Guthrie said. "Being the only real pioneers in space at the time we began, we could negotiate a charter from Ecuador that kept politicians' and bureaucrats' picky-paws off us. Later, when troubles broke out here and there, we strengthened ourselves as a precaution. But I haven't got time today for a history lesson."

"Spacecraft can talk directly with each other, of course," Kyra put in. "But it'd be fantastic luck if any manned vessel—manned by folk of *ours*—happened to be locatable and in beam range of us. Especially since false Guthrie will revise flight plans to avoid the possibility."

"He'll clap a firm grip on L-5 the moment he suspects I've made for it," the jefe said. "However, his attention should be on *Maui Maru*, bound for Luna. Our best bet is that when Kyra lands, the Lunarians will spring her free of Sayre's goons and she can release the truth to the Solar System.

"Partly to make that outcome likelier, partly as a backup in case it fails, my destination is L-5. If all goes well, Tamura will bring me in. After I've announced the facts to the colony, the Sepo there will be lucky if they aren't lynched. If for some reason Tamura can't, well, I'll be on an orbit known to Kyra, and she can arrange for me to be collected at a more convenient date."

Valencia turned his eyes to the woman. "But you," he said. The note of worry tugged at her. "You will walk into the hands of the enemy on the Moon."

"That's why we'll alert my lord Rinndalir before we leave," Guthrie told him. "I can't convey the actual story in any message that would get by the monitoring. But I can encrypt a few words that ought to, hm, intrigue him. We've had dealings before, he and I."

Valencia scowled. "Suppose he can't or won't do anything."

Kyra gave him a smile. At the moment she felt excited, exalted, a-wing. "From what I know about him," she said, "it will be strange if he doesn't take action."

What that action might be, she admitted to herself, they could only guess at.

Her mind snapped back to immediacies. The computer was presenting the figures she wanted.

Briefly, that weighed her down. What was she but a parasite on the machine? It carried her, kept her alive, informed her within the limits of her comprehension—to what purpose? This operation could have been entirely robotic. It well-nigh was. She'd told the ship she wanted to go to Luna, expeditiously, departing at such-and-such an instant. The ship did everything else, computations, thrust, steering, maintenance. Should they run into a bit of space junk, or encounter almost any sort of trouble, the ship would cope. Kyra had brought Guthrie aboard, and she'd put him in the launcher, but the most elementary of robots could have done either job. The ship would communicate with the ground control machines at Port Bowen, come in as they directed, and land herself. Kyra's part would be to touch a button bidding the airlock open and let her out.

"Crack!" she muttered. "Come off that, will you?" It wasn't the first time she must ram this depression away from her. Pilots did still have genuine tasks, like engineers, prospectors, scientists, artists, entrepreneurs. They made the basic decisions. Their hands and voices gave the commands that mattered. When the universe suddenly threw something at them out of its boundless reservoir of unknownness, theirs was the imagination or intuition or hunch that might save lives and, yes, machines. Wasn't her body as automatic, as self-guiding, as a ship or a robot? Yet it was the servant of her mind.

But once the machines had, fully, their own minds—which looked like being soon— No, she would not dwell on it. She had work to do.

She returned to Guthrie. "Launch time's earlier than I expected, jefe," she said. "Let's get you snugged down."

"Okay." What feelings lay behind that flat word? Did any? Yes, she insisted, yes.

She took him aft. The launcher was not much more than a solid-fuel rocket with a basic autopilot and a bay for small cargo. It would take three days to come near L-5. Their prime hope was that meanwhile Kyra would have informed humankind, so that the true Guthrie would arrive not as a fugitive but as a conqueror.

She connected the launcher's computer to the ship's. While the calculated parameters were being downloaded, she laid Guthrie in and made him secure. The machines would take care of everything else.

"You may as well go to your quarters now and relax," he suggested. "Why hang around for the next ten minutes wondering what to say? 'Have a nice trip.' 'Gracias, you have a nice time too.' 'Say hello to everybody.' 'Of course I will.'" He fashioned a laugh. "That was how my wife quoted it, with the most adenoidal accent she could produce. When one of us was going somewhere alone, we'd swap a scandalously big kiss in the terminal and whoever was staying home would leave."

He understood. Kyra made a laugh to give back to him. "Muy bien, jefe. Hasta la vista. And—" Hovering over him, she laid hold of his case, pulled herself down, and kissed the cold hardness between the eyestalks. "Buen viaje. To both of us."

As she went out, she heard the cover slide into place over the cargo bay.

PART TWO

eiko

25

Cherry blossoms white—
Sunset colorless, breath-quick—
Stars hastening, cold.

EIKO TAMURA SHOOK her head, sighed, and laid the paper
down. The haiku had not yet come right. It remained
words, with scant feel in them of what she had hoped to
call forth, the day and night of a whirligig spin betokening
the evanescence of life, an artificial springtime a symbol of
how small and fragile great Ragaranji-Go really was.
Perhaps it would never find its true voice, and end in the
recycler. Most of her poems did.

This one, though, troubled her more. It had arisen from
a deeper need. The news in these past several days, and
then the sudden direness in her father, locked away from
her behind his face, made her reach once again for the
eternal. Calm and consolation lay in understanding that
humanity is the slightest of ripples over it; and from them
could arise the strength to deal with human griefs; but she
renewed that understanding by giving it utterance. Now
she seemed unable to. Anxiety gnawed so sharply.

She raised her head to look at the scroll above. In its ink painting of a mountainscape and its calligraphy, certain lines by Tu Fu, she found serenity oftener than in any scene played on the multiceiver or any virtuality experienced with a vivifer. Today it likewise was just marks on paper. Her gaze flitted around the room as if seeking escape.

She had more space here than was usual in the colony, having enlarged it after the last of her siblings departed, but mainly it was space, occupied by little more than this table where she wrote, a dresser, a cabinet, and the futon on which she slept. A shelf held a few objects: a seashell from Earth, a glittery piece of comet rock given her by Kyra Davis, old books, her bamboo flute. For her extensive reading and music listening she had the world's databases to draw on, and for mementos she had her memory.

Through the thin walls she heard a door open and shut. Feet walked slowly. That must be her father, home late. She rose and hurried across the tatami out to the common room to greet him.

Noboru Tamura stood in his dark clothes like a blot. Ordinarily one saw past small stature, bald head, furrowed countenance, to the chief of space operations in L-5, the friend of Anson Guthrie himself. Today his shoulders were stooped and his hands faintly trembled. Compassion and concern rushed over Eiko, not for the first time since her mother's death. She bowed to him—in a crowded shell where survival required universal self-discipline, courtesy was less a set of rituals than it was a necessity—but thereafter she went to take both those hands in hers and ask low, "What is wrong? I wish you would tell me, Father."

"I wish I dared," he answered.

She let go. "Why not? Always before, you have honored me with your trust."

He glanced away from her. "This knowledge is dangerous, and you could make no use of it."

"Please sit down and rest," she urged. "Let me bring you some refreshment."

He nodded and sank onto a cushion. Though they had chairs for visitors, both preferred traditional—no, archaic —ways when possible. Many in the colony did. Eiko supposed it was, at heart, a kind of defiance. *Behold us, you stars; we remain the children of Gaia, and so does this tiny world we have created.*

To make tea in the kitchen brought a similar comfort. She had never permitted herself to think of her home as empty. Instead, her mind evoked the clatter and laughter that filled it before the children grew up and left; or it might be her mother's soft tones, or Kioshi murmuring in her ear during a stolen moment— Not that. In the end, Kioshi Matsumoto had married another girl, and may all be well with them. Eiko had her father to look after.

She arranged pot, cups, and cakes pleasingly on a tray, brought it in, and settled down opposite him. A smile crinkled his weariness. "You are a good daughter," he said. "Praise to Amida Buddha." For a while they were silent, contemplating. Though not a real tea ceremony, it gave restoration to spirit as well as body.

"I have been alone this whole daywatch, and tuned nothing in," she ventured at length. That was true. She had taken leave from her programming job in his department, because she felt the stress of wondering what would erupt next between the company and the Union government, together with the general disarray among the staff, precluded her doing honestly creative work there. "Has something happened that I should know about?"

He showed surprise. "You haven't heard?" A shrug, a wryness. "That's my Eiko." He went bleak. "A detachment of North American Security Police has arrived by torchcraft. We are under martial law."

The words hit like a knife. She dropped her cup and barely caught it. Coriolis force splashed several drops onto her kimono. "What? But—but, Father, we are not of their country. We are in space. We are *Fireball.*"

"This is by agreement with our directorate."

"With Guthrie-san?" Dream-gibberish.

"Yes. He informed us personally, yesterday. We were to

keep it confidential until it was accomplished, for fear of public unrest."

A fear well justified, Eiko thought, considering the opinion of Avantism held by most people here. "Is that what has been preying on your mind?" she asked.

"It was," he replied carefully. "If the situation was in truth that desperate— You know how vulnerable we are."

"It was," he had said. Eiko wondered whether to hear that as an invitation. A burden borne alone is twice heavy. Yet she ought not alarm him by rushing in. She took a sip of tea. The heat and metallic-green savor were heartening. "What will they do, those officers?"

"Whatever they must, they told us. We are ordered to cooperate. Their captain promised they will try not to disrupt anything of ours. I left them at the quarters we have appropriated."

"But it is not that simple, really, is it?" Eiko slipped at him.

"No," he yielded. "Strange enough that Guthrie-san would . . . panic. Have we not plenty of loyal, able folk among us whom we could alert to watch out for saboteurs? Has the company ever before kept us in the dark? Well, maybe this emergency is unique."

"You cannot quite believe that, can you?" she pursued.

He surrendered altogether. "No longer. I should keep it secret, even from you—especially from you, my dear— but—" He straightened. His voice grew firm. "Yesterday too, some hours after we were told to expect the police, I received a lasergram addressed to me personally in my office. It appeared to be a routine memorandum, but the signature informed me that the real message was encrypted within it and came from Guthrie-san or a highly trusted agent of his. He takes what he calls 'just in case' precautions, you know, such as preparing this clandestine means of communication. I did not sleep much last nightwatch."

Her pulse lurched. "What did it say?"

"It could be no more than a few words long, or a monitor might well suspect something beneath the surface." They must be wired into him by now, the way he recited: "Secret launcher approaches 23."

"What can that mean?"

He smiled, a grimace. "I have considered it. 'Secret.' That must include, above all, secret from the occupation force. 'Launcher approaches.' A spaceship could never come anywhere near us undetected, of course, but if no special watch is kept, a launch rocket falling free would not be noticed, except by an unlikely chance, until it got within about a thousand kilometers."

At least, if it wasn't on a collision orbit, Eiko realized. A bit of rock or junk that was to pass harmlessly by would register at a considerable distance, but attract no attention, no curiosity; such objects were too many. "Approach." The launcher would be traveling cold, on a trajectory that could only be guessed. However, the guess might be shrewd . . .

"The number twenty-three must be a date, and of this month," Tamura continued. "That means daywatch after tomorrow. Assuming neither the launcher nor its mother ship have special capabilities, this implies—I ran a computation—it left the ship in the vicinity of Earth, the ship probably being bound for Luna."

"What . . . is it . . . carrying?"

"I do not know. But this does not accord well with the story and the commands we have received from Quito, does it?"

Eiko considered her father's face. It had become a samurai mask. She must fight to speak: "Do you mean to have it intercepted and its contents brought in?"

"What else? I am thinking how to do that unbeknownst. You are well-informed about our operations, and better acquainted with various of our personnel than I am. I welcome any ideas that occur to you." Sternly: "But this shall not pass from you to anyone else, nor shall you do anything except help me plan. Is that clear?"

"I can do more," she protested. "Yes, in space itself. Perhaps better than others. You will surely be watched, but who would pay attention to me?"

Who indeed? she thought. A short, thin, plain-featured

maiden lady of quiet manners, white streaks in the hair bespeaking her forty-two years. . . . Ragaranji-Go was too huge to monitor closely. Workers were always bound in or out, inspections, maintenance, flits to unmanned spacecraft that had cargo to offload but would not actually dock. The—Sepo, was that what the North Americans called them?—would naturally try to control all activity, make certain that each exit or entry was on a definite, ordinary task. Nevertheless, a person who wasn't expected and who knew her way around might well be able to slip past unobserved. Harder would be to return likewise. Still, with certain prearrangements—

"No!" exclaimed Tamura. "It is not your risk to take. I gave troth, but you did not. Your obligations are to your home."

Pain twisted in Eiko. He had never said outright why he had discouraged her from the ceremony, but she knew. His oldest son underwent it, and Fireball's executives had no doubt made every effort to find satisfying, meaningful work for Jutaro. Nothing that would challenge his particular talents remained that a machine was not already handling. Jutaro was on Earth these days, subsisting on citizen's credit, doing odd jobs—some pettily criminal, she suspected—to earn the price of repeated admission to a quivira.

Noboru Tamura would keep the faith he had plighted. He did not want more of his children thus bound to a way of life he saw as doomed. Eiko did not want him hurt further.

He managed a smile with a bit of warmth in it. "After all," he said, "I keep my hopes that you too will eventually give me a grandchild."

There was still time for that, she kept scrupulously to her biomedical program, but the time was dwindling—faster and faster, it seemed.

The door trilled. A neighbor, a friend? Eiko rose. She would welcome a caller, anyone who might ease the tension between her and her father. Perhaps he felt the same, for he moved ahead and himself admitted the newcomers.

They were three men unknown to her, in tan uniforms with shock guns at their hips. Armbands displayed the infinity symbol. They came straight through. The last one closed the door.

Eiko's heart ticked away the while in which Tamura stood motionless before he said most softly, in English, "Good evenwatch, Captain Pedraza and gentlemen. To what do we owe this visit?"

The leader saluted. "Good evening, Sr. Tamura and señorita." Below the politeness, Eiko heard steel. "My apologies for this interruption. We've received new orders. Further information about terrorist activities suggests your life may well be in danger, sir. We are to protect you and certain other persons till the danger is past."

"Indeed?" Tamura murmured. "What if I decline your kind offer?"

Eiko foreknew the answer: "I'm afraid we must insist, sir. Surely you can imagine how an attempt on you, in this environment, could lead to a terrible loss of life among innocent bystanders. Por favor, pack what you'll need for the next few days and come along. You'll have safe, comfortable lodging and open lines for communicating with anybody you wish."

The Sepo listening in.

"I see." Tamura spoke without tone and stood like a statue, expressionless. But he was defeated, Eiko knew. And she, she must not embrace him, she must not cry out, before these enemy strangers.

"I suppose you haven't had dinner yet," Pedraza said. "We'll give you a nice one. Now, por favor, gather your things and we'll go."

Tamura nodded. A guard followed him out.

Pedraza addressed Eiko: "I promise you, señorita, no harm will come to the señor if we can possibly prevent it."

A bitterness that she could taste burst from her. "Yes, hostages work better alive than dead."

"I know you're unhappy." With studied emphasis: "The situation is critical. That's why we're acting. My superiors don't want the resentment, the agitation, this can bring on. Protective custody is still custody. But it's *protective*. Por favor, understand—tell your friends—if anything untoward happens, we may no longer be able to guarantee the safety of the persons in our care."

Hostages in truth. She had better not say that again. "I understand."

They waited mute. Tamura soon came back, a bag in his hand. *"Sayonara,* Eiko," he breathed. In English, lest the Sepo think the two conspired: "Remember what I told you. Wait this out quietly."

"It's not adiós," Pedraza said. "Only for a few days, I'm sure, and you can phone each other whenever you like. I'll try to get permission for visits in person."

"Thank you," Eiko said automatically. It angered her that she did, until the thought passed through her that this officer most likely was sincere, a basically decent man who obeyed orders because he was pledged to and he trusted his superiors, but who might be as puzzled and apprehensive as she was.

Or more so. Resolution surged.

She bowed to her father. He returned the gesture. They would give nothing else to the eyes of these men. He left with them.

26

THE MOON, BELOVED old scarface, neared and swelled till it was no longer ahead but below, no longer a heavenly body but a wastescape of mountains and maria, craters and boulders, shadow-limned by an early afternoon. Using her opticals to filter out the glare and magnify, Kyra glimpsed some of the jewelwork her race had laid across it, silver threads that were monorails, Tychopolis agleam in the south and lesser communities elsewhere, scattered starpoints across the land already nighted that marked other habitations. Then *Maui Maru* swung about and blasted, backing down on her goal. Pressed into her couch, Kyra looked up at an Earth waxing toward the half. Its own night blocked off a part of the sky. There she saw a few glints, megalopolises. Its blue-and-white day revealed to unaided vision no mark or trace of humanity.

Silence clapped upon her. After a final shiver through the hull, she weighed barely more than ten kilos. She did not seem to float from her harness and down to the crew lock as erstwhile. She went heavily, heart-sluggingly, toward whatever waited beyond.

She wasn't afraid of death, she told herself. She didn't like at all the idea of leaving a generally wonderful universe, but she had long since come to terms with it. The assurance was thin. Sweat lay rank in her armpits. There were other things that she did fear.

Yet when she touched the exit button, it was like a declaration. Guthrie wouldn't send her on a hopeless mission. Dread dissolved in movement. The valves swung aside. She passed through, into the gang tube that had reached to osculate and down its ladder, a few leaps to the underground reception room for this berth.

The console that would ordinarily have taken her report and admitted her onward into Port Bowen stood silent. Six men crowded the chamber, uniformed Sepo.

She had more than half expected them. "What in MacCannon's name is this about?" she blustered.

"I think you know," replied the leader. He was a big man, afro, his name badge reading Trask. In spite of discipline, his voice held strain. "You're under arrest, Pilot Davis. The charges are public endangerment, hijacking, and conspiracy—among others. Come along."

"You can't arrest me. You're thirty Earth diameters out of your jurisdiction."

"We're here at the request of your employers, and they have police powers in this enclave. Come. Reilly, with me. The rest of you, secure the ship and commence your search." Kyra spied an instrument among them, yes, a circuit resonator, a Guthrie detector.

Trask gestured raggedly. "Don't make us use force," he said. They were in a hurry, she knew, only half informed about their job, nerves drawn taut by these foreign surroundings. What that might lead them to do to her, once they reached whatever rooms they were based in, was not pleasant to think about.

They were athletic and alert, but Earthsiders. She might get a chance to break free, escape, with the swiftness of low-*g* habituation. They'd take her through side passages which they'd made sure were clear of Fireball folk. However, if she could scream the truth aloud someplace along the way where somebody would hear— Her consortes wouldn't stand for outsiders shockshooting their own— Kyra went between the two.

Beyond the safety lock they entered a corridor that should have bustled. Its length was quite hollow. A pair waited. Trask slammed to a halt. Kyra heard him curse under his breath. She knew, with upsoaring joy, that the Lunarians had not been there before.

They were both male, of tower-tall slenderness but wide in the shoulders. The features of one were like a Grecian sculpture for regularity and whiteness, within a frame of silvery tresses. He wore an incongruously ordinary unisuit. The other was hawk-nosed, amber-skinned, his hair blue-black, though on him the big, slanting eyes were also gray. His garb was more ethnic, if that meant anything, jerkin above wide-sleeved shirt, tight hose below puffed and slashed short trousers, curl-toed shoes, all in dark green and gold. On each one's breast hung a medallion, a black circle ringed by irregular pearliness, the Eclipse of power.

"Greeting," said the first. His English flowed with the singing Lunarian accent. "We will take charge now, if you please."

Trask slapped hand to holstered weapon. "What do you mean?" he rasped. "Who are you?" His companion gripped Kyra's arm painfully hard.

"You may address me as Arren, and my associate as Isabu." The reply was dispassionate. "We are ancillaries of the lord Rinndalir, who has bidden us escort this person."

"No! This is—is Fireball territory, and we're deputized—"

Arren lifted a hand. Trask sputtered into silence. "The contract delegates authority in Port Bowen to Fireball

Enterprises but does not affect the sovereignty of the Selenarchy, which the lord Rinndalir hereby applies."

"I've got my orders." Trask raised his gun a few centimeters in its sheath. "Don't interfere. Stand aside."

Isabu smiled. "I advise you against drawing that," he said levelly.

The Lunarians appeared unarmed, but Trask let go the butt and signed his fellow to stay put. He breathed hard. "We'll find out who's got what rights."

"Yes, fine," Kyra gibed. "Let's go straight to the director's office, hook into the net, and talk to as many people as possible."

"That would not be in your best interests, would it?" Arren challenged Trask—how softly!

The Sepo looked right and left, as if praying for help to come out of the walls. He'd been commanded to utmost secrecy, Kyra knew. And enjoined to avoid trouble, scenes, anything that might bring on publicity. And doubtless raised on a diet of Earthside folklore about Lunarians, their cunning and ruthlessness and mysterious resources. She must admire how he mustered will and demanded, "Show me your warrant."

"Such is not required of a Selenarch's messengers," Isabu told him.

"You have obstructed us long enough," Arren added. He touched an informant on his wrist. "Shall I summon assistance? If so, you and yours will be brought to judgment."

It might or might not be bluff. In the longer term, it absolutely was not. "You don't claim the ship she came in, do you?" Trask yelled. "Bueno, go, then, go!"

Arren beckoned to Kyra, turned, and departed with the bounding gait of his kind. She followed, exultant, Isabu at her side. Oh, they were both stunningly handsome. Giddily, she cast a glance back over her shoulder. Trask stood staring after her. As she watched, he swung on his heel and made for the entry. Dutiful dog; he'd ransack *Maui* while he could, for all the good that would do the cause which he himself was ignorant of. His man shambled after him in dazed fashion.

"Mil gracias, señores," Kyra caroled. "You've done more than save me from a bad time, do you know? Listen, what's happened is—"

Isabu's palm chopped air in front of her mouth. "Pray do not speak of it to us," he said. "We will bring you to the lord Rinndalir."

The glory chilled the least bit. She remembered Guthrie admitting he didn't know what the Lunarian would do.

Yet she was out of Avantist control. She was free to cry the words that would blow their whole damned house of cards down around their ears. It could wait till she got to Rinndalir, since he so desired, and that ought to be one almighty interesting visit.

"Whatever you want," she said. "Though we can make conversation, can't we?"

Arren gave her a look and a smile. She couldn't tell whether it was friendly or wolfish or what. "We can attempt small talk later, if you wish," he said. "First we must seek our vehicle. Pray do not speak to anyone we meet along the way."

She realized that wasn't a request. They might very well have means to silence her. Bueno, they were still her deliverers, and there could be excellent reasons for not immediately shouting forth her story. "If somebody I know hails me, it'd seem odd if I don't respond," she pointed out.

Isabu considered. Was such behavior foreign to him? "Correct," he agreed. "You have an able mind, my lady."

The corridor opened on a central space of screens, panels, baggage carriers, benches, shops. It was less busy than it should have been. The Lunarians hastened Kyra along. Stares trailed them.

"Hola, Davis! When did you get in?" The woman who drew alongside was an old acquaintance.

"Buenas días, Navarro. I'm sorry, got to run, awful rush, see you later—" and again anonymous faces separated them. Kyra was glad she heard no more greetings. That single encounter made her feel briefly, freezingly alone.

A fahrweg brought her trio to the ground transport terminal. Arren led the way on through it. "Don't we want a train for Tychopolis?" Kyra asked. "Or, uh, Lunograd or Diana or—" whatever the Selenarchs used for a capital. Officially they didn't have any. They neither sent nor received diplomats; *ad hoc* envoys from Earth went to sites they designated and spoke with such of them as chose to listen.

"Nay," Isabu replied. "This day we travel by car."

A thrill chased most of the foreboding out of her. She'd only been on the few tourist roads.

The car was bus-size. Except for the windows, an outer shell of hyalon enclosed its metal body. Fluid in between would change its patterns of light and dark, chameleon-like, to help regulate temperature. On struts above the roof, a radiation shield doubled as a solar energy collector, auxiliary to the fuel cells inside. A lovely piece of engineering. Then Kyra traversed the airlock and found herself in another world. Carpeting, opulent red and black, was like the pelt of a live animal; it undulated ever so slightly, as if something breathed. Paneling sheened above it, relieved by intertwined patterns of enamel and inlay. Where shadows from outside made dimness, she saw that draperies and upholsteries phosphoresced. Seats and a table were made for long-limbed folk who did not need to lean against backs. A partition separated off the rear half, which must hold sleeping quarters, tanks, tools, and whatever else was required. Abstract art played across it, akin to fire, smoke, clouds. The moving air bore changeable odors, sweet, sharp, spiced, sunny, icy. She could barely hear the background music, and did not understand it at all. If comets could sing—

Arren took the controls, spoke with the dispatcher, and eased the car across the garage floor. It cycled through into void and ran up a ramp to the surface. Soon it left pavement and went over raw regolith, smoothly absorbing the irregularities. Dust whirled up from the wheels and settled again with the speed of airlessness.

"Where are we bound?" Kyra asked.

"We can tell you now," Isabu said. "Zamok Vysoki." At her blank look: "It is the lord Rinndalir's private stronghold, in the Cordillera."

"What?" she exclaimed. "But that—why, that must be two or three thousand klicks from here."

"Nearer three than two. Will you not be seated? Would you care for refreshments? We can offer a variety."

"But how long will it take to get there?" she cried in dismay.

"About twelve hours. Pray be patient, my lady. Everything is in proper orbit."

It whirled through her: Rinndalir received Guthrie's message forty-odd hours ago, minus whatever time went in bucking it to him from the reception point. The encrypted part had been minimal: "Rescue nonsched Bowen 22." He'd have had a chance to think about it and confer with others. (How many? His kind generally presented a single mask to the outside universe, but everybody who had studied and observed knew that theirs was a government of cats.) His technicians could have informed him that a radar scan was in progress, and picked *Maui* out for themselves. He probably had his watchers, undercover agents, computer worms in places on Earth as well as in Fireball here. The arrival of the Sepo would tell him much and hint at more. A rocket flyer was conspicuous. Was that why he had sent his men by ground to retrieve her? How many men? Just these two? How had he coordinated with his colleagues? Had he? Unilateral action seemed crazily reckless. And yet—

Arren regarded his instrument board, entered an instruction, and joined the others. The car rolled on, self-operated, deftly weaving around the obstacles nature had strewn through the ages. Kyra wondered whether it followed navigation signals, perhaps from a satellite, or had a topographic map in its program and an inertial guidance system. Maybe both. She wondered how smart the most advanced Lunar robots were. Maybe more than any elsewhere. If you started with people selected for intelligence as well as physical fitness, and furnished them with the most sophisticated equipment of their era, technological development might later hit a steep curve even though the population was small and clannish.

She sank onto a seat. Arren took another facing her. He

sat straight, impassive, yet somehow relaxed. Isabu drifted noiselessly to the rear. "You may identify yourself if you desire," Arren said.

"I'm Kyra Davis, space pilot for Fireball," she blurted, "and I—"

"Nay, nothing further of your mission," he interrupted. The tone was mild but decisive. "That is for the lord Rinndalir."

She gathered her wits, studied him a moment, and murmured, "Are you so firmly under his orders? I thought Lunarians were a free-wheeling breed."

His answer was free of resentment, almost philosophical: "In some respects that is true, granting countless individual variations and complexities. But we cannot afford anarchism. As a spacer, you know how survival depends on discipline, the maintenance and protection of life support systems, instant cooperation in emergencies."

"Oh, yes, obviously. Within those parameters, though— In Fireball we generally have our jobs to do." Kyra paused. She hadn't ever thought in quite these terms before. Had the chase jolted things she'd always taken for granted loose in her mind? "To a certain extent, I suppose you could say we *are* our careers. We're free to change jobs, teams, whatever, any time there's a demand for our services elsewhere and we want to go. But we seldom work entirely on our own. In the nature of things, we can't. Pilots like me are among the few exceptions. It's different for you. Apart from your survival obligations, isn't the Lunarian ideal to do everything and, and be everything for yourself?"

And thus the declaration of independence half a century ago. Much more brought it on than a tax revolt. A civilization had grown up here—bewilderingly fast, its evolution driven not only by unearthly conditions but unearthly genes—that was incompatible with any on the mother planet.

"The attitude serves for much of creativity and many minor enterprises," Arren replied. "For anything more ambitious, organization is required. Furthermore, questions of personal security, arbitration, justice, the rights of the community, are universal. Let me propose that different cultures find different instrumentalities to cope with them, and that these are viable no longer than they have the allegiance of the people. The typical Earthdweller gives his to his government; the World Federation derives its legitimacy indirectly. You give yours to Fireball Enterprises. I give mine to the lord Rinndalir. Should he perish, I would think who else of his rank pleases me best and would accept me."

Abruptly Kyra must laugh aloud. Arren regarded her. "Pardon," she gasped. "It just exploded on me what a weird conversation this is."

Snatched from captivity, bowling across the Moon, here she sat talking sociology! It wasn't even new to her. She'd read, seen, heard enough stories, commentaries, analyses, travelogues, you name it. Maybe he'd given her a slightly different slant on things, she'd have to think about that, but she'd sure taken herself by surprise.

To him the exchange might be perfectly natural.

That idea of alienness shocked sobriety into her. She saw him smile and heard him say, "Yes, doubtless you would like to be more specific. Inquire as you will, Pilot Davis. Isabu and I will answer within the bounds of confidentiality."

She rallied her wits. "You were pretty brash when you rescued me. Did you really have reinforcements?"

"In being, nay." His candor set her equally aback. "It would have been inconvenient to assemble any on such short notice." Why? Because the movement would have alerted other Selenarchs to the fact that something special was afoot? "The lord Rinndalir deemed the threat would suffice. Had it not, he would have set punitive measures in train." To assert his authority, and never mind about Anson Guthrie's appeal? Or was it merely that he felt his judgment was reliable? It had in fact paid off.

Let her be bold. "Bueno, you don't want to hear what's brought me to the Moon. But you're bound to've seen it involves the current hooraw with Fireball and the North American Union. For my information, would you tell me what you know about that?"

He was willing. Sometimes he veered from a topic, but in general she could lead him on. In his turn, he was interested in whatever observations she made, provided they didn't bear too closely on her mission. She found that he had a good grasp of the situation, despised the Avantists, and like most Lunarians—he said; she believed —was rather skeptical of the alleged terrorist ring. As for what the truth might be, he reserved opinion pending further data. At more than a third of a million kilometers' remove, Kyra thought, coolness came easy. Of course, Fireball was involved, and Luna depended on Fireball still more than Earth did; but there was also the cultural gap, the gulf between souls. He had said it himself, his loyalty was to the seigneur in the mountains—and after that, maybe, to his own not quite human race.

Meanwhile Isabu brought coffee, a tart brandy, and cakes of an intriguing vinegary flavor. Later he made dinner. It was a stir-fry of fish, vegetables, and fruits, crisp herbal-seasoned bread on the side, a subtly sweet-sour white wine. Kyra enjoyed it in spite of recognizing little, though she'd explored her share of Lunarian restaurants. How much did the masters reserve for themselves?

The car got onto a road and picked up speed. For most of its length the road was simply graded regolith. Here and there a way had been blasted out of uplands, a viaduct overleaped crevasse or crater. Nothing better was needed where the sole weather was blazing day, bitter night, millennial infall of dust and stones. Moonscape fled by, ashen plains and time-blurred heights, intricately pocked, now and then a radome or a beamcasting mast or the upper works of a buried habitation. Eventually Kyra's eyelids drooped. Isabu showed her to a bath cubicle with a recycling shower and, adjoining, a curtained bunk in which she could take off her clothes. She slept better than expected, though lightly, tumbling about in dreams.

Momentarily loudened music quavered her awake. Isabu said from outside the curtains, "We approach Zamok Vysoki, my lady." She wriggled herself clad, hastily used the bath, and joined the men forward. Excitement pulsed. She did not know of any outsider who had betrod a Selenarch's palace. If ever it happened, it was in secret. Earthside journalists were chronically indignant about that.

Rearing ahead of her, the place seemed more castle than mansion. The tiered walls were like upthrusts of the mountain that they topped, the steep roofs their slopes, the lean towers crags. Westering to north, the sun set windows and metal cupolas ablaze against black heaven. Their brightness drowned out most stars. From the eastern horizon Earth's thick crescent cast a glimmer across south-facing masonry, surrounding peaks, the higher jumbles of the valley out of which road and car climbed.

Signals piped from speakers. Kyra thought of bugles blown by warders at the parapets. Banners should have flown above them. But here went never a wind save for the thin breaths of sun and cosmos. Arren spoke. He received an acknowledgment. As he drove near, a valve opened in the wall ahead. It was machined alloy, Kyra saw. The masonry was dark native rock. She didn't know what kind, but recalled accounts of robots mining the Lunar depths.

Air hissed into the lock chamber beyond and the car proceeded down a ramp to a garage. The hewn-out pillars and vaulting that supported its roofs were of a strangeness that soared, as if—she thought, knowing it was ridiculous —Shwe Dagon had bred with Chartres. The car stopped, its own valves turned, the travelers emerged. She breathed a perfume like roses, and that was perhaps the strangest of all.

An attendant genuflected. He was dressed somewhat like Isabu, in the understatedly sumptuous style of Lunarian formality. She would learn that, while there was no prescribed livery, this was usual for the staff, except when some task made it inappropriate. No special insignia identified them. They knew whose they were, and so did their optimates.

Arren offered her his arm. She remembered what was proper and held her arm just above, fingertips touching his hand. The position was easy to maintain in this gravity. It would have been the same were their sexes reversed, a graceful way of denoting that she was his social superior.

Isabu came behind. They crossed the floor, ascended a curving staircase, and went down a passage. It was lined with hydroponic tanks in which rioted the hues of curiously petalled flowers.

It gave on a large room. Furnishings were sparse, spindly-framed, shaped to suggest vines and serpents. Kyra scarcely noticed, because floor, walls, ceiling were a single abstract mosaic. The softly multicolored patterns seduced her gaze; she could easily have lost herself in them. A picture window, its view of the gorge below and the peaks beyond under stars, did not interrupt; it was a culmination.

Two persons waited. They stood, as Lunarians did more often than sit—tall, slim, ornamental iridescent cloaks of spider-silk thinness falling from their shoulders. Kyra recognized Rinndalir, whom she had last seen on the multi in the Launch Pad . . . a hundred years ago? His tunic and hose were black, trimmed with silver. She remembered, also, the friezelike gold headband across the argent hair. The woman at his side wore a full-length aquamarine gown over which diode lights played. In features she might have been his twin sister, but the great slant eyes were green and the waist-length mane shone blue-black.

Arren and Isabu genuflected. Unsurely, Kyra gave a Fireball salute.

Rinndalir smiled. For that instant, his visage came aglow, and Kyra's heart stumbled. "So this is Pilot Davis of the disputed ship." His English purred. Clearly, the men had been in contact with him while they traveled. "Be welcome, my lady. Have you any immediate need that we may serve?"

"No. Nothing, gracias," she stammered, and felt like a slewfooted fool.

Rinndalir made the least of gestures toward the other woman. "My lady Niolente," he said. She inclined her head as slightly—courteous, condescending, or what?

"I, I'm happy to meet you," Kyra said. Half angrily: Why was she letting them overawe her? She was Fireball. If ever they should be at odds, Fireball could smash them and theirs flat. Right now it needed their help. But that would be to their own advantage. She got control of her voice. "I've important news for you."

"Manifestly," said Niolente. She was a mezzo-soprano. She glanced at Arren and Isabu. "Hold yourselves in readiness for possible questions." Doubtless she said it in English out of politeness to Kyra. They bent the knee again and departed.

"Make yourself comfortable, Pilot Davis," invited Rinndalir. "Are you certain you will not have something to eat or drink before we speak?"

"No—no—" The tale rushed out of her. The Lunarians aided it with questions that struck to the bone, however softly put. She could not tell how much intensity was underneath.

At the end, Rinndalir paced to the window. He stood for a few seconds looking out at the galaxy before he asked, "What would you have us do, Pilot Davis?"

She shivered, and irrationally resented Niolente's calm, and cried, "Tell the Solar System! Retrieve Guthrie! Get those muck-begotten ideos thrown out of space!"

"It is not quite that simple," Niolente murmured. "This is a chaotic universe. The consequences of actions are seldom foreseeable."

Rinndalir turned around. His glance locked on Kyra. "Yes," he said as calmly, "we had best bide our time until we know more and have thought more."

The knowledge pierced her: They would keep her waiting here.

27

WANG ZU WAS a modest man, but Thermopylae-loyal to Fireball. As a dispatcher, he had access to the computer net that directed and kept track of space activities around L-5; and he was generally alone when on duty. As a close friend, he heard the plea of Noboru Tamura's daughter, did not press her to explain the purpose she dared not reveal, and agreed to do what she wished. Any suspicions he had, he kept to himself.

"I will co-opt the mechanician Lucia Visconti," he said. "You know her somewhat, I believe. She is trustworthy. Still, all she will be told is to ignore the call to work that she will receive tomorrow and stay at home for the next—ten hours, will that provide an ample margin? What one does not know, one cannot reveal."

If arrested and quizzed. An ugly thrill went through Eiko. She herself didn't even know what it was she sought. Derring-do was for people like Kyra Davis, not her . . . Kyra had gone to Earth on the most routine of missions, and vanished. Fireball had overnight made alliance with its decades-enduring antagonists and let them within its gates. They had imprisoned Eiko's father and everyone else near to Anson Guthrie, seemingly with Guthrie's agreement, perhaps at his command. Nothing made sense. Somebody had to make a start at unsnarling the nightmare.

Her preparations, however inconspicuously carried out, kept her too busy for much fear. And then the hour of action was upon her.

Reporting to the appropriate station, she logged in as Visconti, detailed to troubleshoot a minor problem with offloading from the *Pallas*. No human saw her. The Sepo hadn't enough men to mount guard over every portal. Besides, watchers would have been worse than useless, ignorant about operations, irritatingly or perhaps disastrously in the way. Instead, they had the net monitor all activity for them and alert them to whatever might be unusual. Wang had simply entered a notation of this job. No living soul was aboard the sunjammer to give him the lie.

It was slow and awkward for Eiko, securing herself in the boostsuit and checking the numerous systems. Like all colonists, she'd had some training in EVA and refreshed it regularly in a vivifer. Like most, from time to time she went outside briefly for pleasure. That, though, was in her own spacesuit, with a low-powered simple jetpack, at the end of a tether to the excursion boat. The boostsuit could hold a big man; she must adjust the interior fittings by appropriate motions of her confined body till she was snug. The four arms and their hands were waldos, which she had seldom used and never for serious work. Much of the view through the hyalon turret consisted of an instrument panel curving up from the breast. Other information was conveyed by beeps, flashes, or tingles in her fingers. Her drive was a high-thrust ion motor and an array of delicately controllable turn jets. Her life support was not for a few hours but for a possible several days, complex and—invasive. Racked around the armor was a variety of tools and other objects, many of which she could not handle, some of which she could not name.

When first she considered doing this, she had felt utterly daunted. Best she get someone else, someone experienced. No. Still less did she know how to organize a conspiracy, and she hadn't time to learn. Where it came to plain facts, she was a quick study. She put instructions from the public database into her vivifer at home and practiced. Surely the Sepo didn't consider her worth surveillance. She learned that the equipment was highly automated, possessed of a versatile program, forgiving of mistakes.

—Her mouth was dry, her tongue like wood. She set lips to nipple, swished the water around, swallowed it, and could speak. "Ready for task."

"Begin countdown" said the robot voice in her ear. She was moved forward on rails into the launch lock. A valve shut behind her. The steel barrenness of the chamber darkened as air was pumped out. The second valve opened on streaming stars. "Ten," became audible. "Nine. Eight. . . . Zero."

The catapult gave her a harder shock than she had expected. Night swallowed her. A mumble and a pulse throbbed for a moment as the side jets killed residual spin. Her motor assumed proper orientation and fired, to add its component to the velocity she had from the great momentum bank that was L-5. It went silent again. She was on trajectory, falling free.

Confined, she could not revel in weightlessness, which had never sickened her, but she could look around.

Spaceward, stars beswarmed blackness and the Milky Way clove it with ice. To one side, a gibbous Luna showed small, an orphan wandering lost. In the Earthward direction, her turret darkened itself lest the sun blind her. Well, at this time of orbit she'd have seen only a thin sickle of the planet.

Trailing the Moon by sixty degrees, Ragaranji-Go gained splendor when she receded and saw it as a whole, colossal cylinder and tapering ends a-spin, a-sheen, shadow-play over locks, masts, domes, towers, dishes, a thousand structures and instrumentalities, fireflies around it that were boats, workers, machines, everydayness triumphant in heaven. Elsewhere gleamed a whirling disc, tiny at its distance but growing, the sun-sail of *Pallas*, hove to while robots discharged gases, minerals, treasures brought from the kingdom of Jupiter.

That was Eiko's nominal destination. Now that she was loose, the sooner she changed her vectors, the better.

She had not dared carry anything written or otherwise recorded. Were she perchance stopped and searched, how would she have explained it? The numbers were in her head. She was good at memorizing—languages, histories, poems, on down to lists of what she might buy that would please her kinfolk and their children. The position of an object at some instant and the elements of its orbit were easy.

Obtaining them had been something else. Her father could have led her through his reasoning, had he been given the chance. As was, she must reconstruct it. The message: A launcher, due to pass detectably close, though farther than a thousand kilometers, on the 23rd. He had said that suggested it started near Earth, from a Luna-bound ship, three days earlier. This was merely one possibility, but the most obvious, and when you were limited to a few words you did not become esoteric.

The boundary conditions defined a sheaf that was unmanageably large. However, Eiko decided, whoever set the launcher on its course had no way of knowing whether it would be met on the first pass. The contents must be precious. Therefore s/he would not put it on any orbit that would take it into the deeps, soon to become unrecoverable as perturbations and other influences worked on it in chaotic fashion. S/he would give it an eccentric path around Earth, swinging out not much past L-5 before bending back. This path should be reasonably stable, good for at least several passes before it was badly displaced and distorted. Best would be also, from a stability viewpoint, if it had some resonance with L-5, bringing it repeatedly near the colony. These restrictions diminished the sheaf by a huge factor. Furthermore, they hinted at where and when the ship had left Earth.

Eiko ran a computation. She gave the results to Wang. He accessed data gathered by the automata on meteoroid watch. Their radars had registered half a dozen objects that fitted. She told him no more, but took the data home and ran them through again, feeding in her ideas about the ship. A single body qualified—a blip, noted, tracked intermittently for some hours, found to be no threat, entered in the database, otherwise not studied nor brought to human attention. A rock, a scrap . . . or a launcher flying cold. She worked out a best estimate of its orbit and fixed the values in her brain.

Had Wang calculated backward and guessed what she was thinking of? She didn't ask, he didn't say.

Now, slowly and clumsily, she keyboarded an order to the boostsuit. *Cancel flight plan. New instructions to follow.* She could have spoken it, but there was still a radio link to the coordinator at her takeoff station and she didn't want that machine passing her words on to the dispatcher. The parameters had not allowed this to be a time when Wang was in charge. She wasn't being monitored, though; following each EVA was quite unfeasible. If she kept quiet, she could change course unnoticed. Space was that big.

Feeding in the fresh numbers, she made repeated mistakes, sighed, backtracked, and tried again. Kyra, she thought, would have had some colorful if unvoiced curses. But Kyra wouldn't have found this task difficult. Eiko tried to keep herself aware that these too were simply moments in eternity.

They ended. She activated the program. The boostsuit

rotated and started its drive motor. Acceleration pressed
Eiko into the padding around her. It ceased after a while
and she flew again weightless, toward rendezvous. At first
her pulse ruffled and her breath rustled loud in an infinite
stillness. Then slowly she forgot them, knew only the stars,
sent her spirit outward and outward among them.

A beeping recalled her. Amazed, she read how much
time had passed. The launcher glimmered ahead, pencil-
small. It grew. She ordered the boostsuit to lay alongside.
Energy susurrated, velocity changes tugged, but gently.
She spied welding seams and rivet heads, picked out by
their sharp shadows; this planetoid had no landscape to
diffuse sunlight. She felt and heard a slight bump. She had
arrived.

The stars had removed her anxieties from her. Thus it
proved surprisingly easy to operate her gear. Not that it
had anything difficult to do. She undogged the hatch
cover, swung it back, and pulled herself forward till she
could look into the cargo bay. Blackness. She turned on a
headlight.

Twin reflections glittered back. The box within had
extended its eyestalks to look at her.

She choked on a scream. *"Guthrie-san—"* Beware, the
radio. No, that connection routinely broke at a certain
distance. Ragaranji-Go was a spindle near the Milky Way,
no longer than the Moon was wide.

Did this braincase, linked to nothing, have a radio
capability of its own? She tried speaking to it. Silence
jeered. Perhaps she just had the wrong frequency. Orbiting
farther every second, she mustn't linger. And, to avoid
drawing possible attention, she should take a roundabout
course home, one that appeared to originate at the
sunjammer; there went more time. She activated the lesser
pair of hands, released the clamps securing the box, took it
forth, stowed it in a chest attached to the front of her
armor.

Crazily, she giggled. Was this any way to treat Guthrie-
san, overlord of Fireball? Bringing him in like a retrieved
rock or—or as if she were pregnant with him?

Her wits resurged. She instructed the boostsuit methodically, almost skillfully. It started off. The launcher dwindled from view.

On that flight she had ample opportunity to think, but little more to think about. She had made her preparations at home for concealing whatever she brought back, if it was concealable and if there was need. Clearly, there was. The Sepo scarcely expected such an advent, but they were poised and organized for trouble, they had all the lethal weapons in the colony, if necessary they would shut down its communications while they called their masters for help. Much too readily could Eiko imagine what would follow.

Or could she? *Was* it Guthrie she carried? He had spoken from Quito, hadn't he? And when he did, the launcher was already on its way. For her father's sake, for everybody's, she must hide this thing till she knew more. That might be the very worst move she could make. It seemed like the best, though. Hers was the responsibility for whatever came of it. She had acted, she had thrown the stone into the pool, and now the waves spreading ineluctably outward bore her with them.

Again she sought peace in the galaxy. It fled her. At last she forced her mind to compose. That was a kind of work, something in which to lose fear, doubt, grief. It was mechanical, of course, devoid of any true inspiration, but it kept her occupied until Ragaranji-Go loomed sheer ahead.

> *In snowfall of stars*
> *Those we see red are not old—*
> *An early winter.*

She rejected it with disdain but not without gratitude.

"Visconti returning," she said. "Request entry." The coordinator acknowledged and took control. She should have been glad, as amateurish as she was, but after her hours a-flit she felt abruptly, queasily helpless.

Alone among machines, she fumbled her way out of the suit and opened the chest. Leaning over it, she whispered, "Not a word, not a sound before I tell you we are safe."

She clenched her teeth and lifted him out. Who might be watching on the audiovisual pickup? At least the sight meant nothing to the robots. Yet she went to the dressing cubicle in as casual a saunter as she could achieve. Once there she slipped him into the carryall she had brought along, as people often did for objects they might want outside, and exchanged the skinsuit for her subdued kimono.

Luck was kind. In the corridor leading away she met nobody who would wonder what she did here. At the first upramp she left it, and soon mingled into the crowd along Onizuka Passage.

The district lacked its normal bustle and cheer but remained busy enough, being commercial rather than residential. L-5 was more than a city, staging point, entrepôt, site for specialized industries, and tourist attraction. Its ten million people made up a society, distinct and complete, multiracial but united, with its own laws, mores, arts, fashions, traditions, orientations—cosmopolitan yet turned spaceward as much as Earthward, pragmatic and hard-working yet respectful of culture and obsessed with education, conceived in liberty yet strict about rules for the common survival, enterprising yet content to be governed by a directorate that answered to Fireball. Dwellers walked briskly, talked fast, footfalls and voices a surf around them. Garments ran to bright hues. Some, like Eiko's, harked back: a Sikh in his turban, a Malay in his sarong, a Kirghiz in her embroidered jacket, others whom she could not so easily identify. A number were obviously visitors from Earth. They looked the most apprehensive. And were the least threatened, she thought.

Shopfronts sparkled and beckoned. Animations enticed at theaters, restaurants, amusement arcades. Music lilted. For some reason she briefly compared all of it to Tychopolis. This was nothing that exotic. This was a prosperous modern Terrestrial community, transplanted, streamlined, polished, decorated here and there with curving eaves, gilt dragons, calligraphic banners. These were ordinary folk, fully human. Their ceiling simulated blue sky and sunlit clouds. Come nightwatch it would go starry, at festival times it would depict fireworks.

The corridor opened on Yukawa Square. Walls rose thirty meters, making room for trees in a park. Leaves of birch danced to a draft from unseen ventilators. Creeping juniper lined the gravel paths over the grass, among a few carefully placed meteoroids. Flowers surrounded a Buddha. Several children romped about, their laughter high and sweet. Across the walkway on the far side Eiko saw an ornate façade, the Chinese opera.

It seemed grotesque that she walked in danger through this beloved familiarity. She hastened her steps.

The fahrweg she wanted had a door halfway down Moreno Passage. Ten persons waited. "Tamura!" exclaimed Chatichai Suwanprasit. "Where have you been? I have tried and tried to call."

Eiko quashed alarm. She couldn't realistically have hoped to escape seeing everyone she knew. "I was busy," she mumbled.

The door opened. Passengers got out. Upbound people went in. The door shut. The radial platform thrust against footsoles.

"It is terrible, what they have done," Suwanprasit was saying furiously. "Can I do anything for you?"

"Thank you, but I think we had better wait," Eiko replied. "The . . . detainees . . . are not mistreated."

"But this—our own company—" Despair contorted the round face.

"We shall see."

"Where are you bound, if I may ask? If you would like to talk with someone, my wife and I—"

"Thank you. Perhaps later." Eiko recalled the story she had constructed. "I wish a quiet while, solitude. Do you understand?"

The bionicist nodded. He took her hand for an instant before he got off.

That was at the level where he worked. The fahrweg had already made two stops. Those were in residential sections. Now it crossed different territory. It slowed, that bodies might accommodate to lessening weight. Though air pressure did not change much, Eiko's eardrums popped. She felt the lightness more keenly than ever before; but then, all her senses were tuned high. At the next stops the door opened on cavernous reaches, machines, nanotanks, once on cropland and an orchard. L-5 produced wares for export, especially those that required low gravity or none in the making, but it also mostly fed and clothed itself. Were it cut off from trade with Earth it could soon be turning out everything it needed, deploying solar megamirrors for energy and obtaining raw materials from space.

That fact gave courage, irrelevant though it be in the immediate situation. She would not let herself consider how vulnerable to attack the colony was.

She left the fahrweg last, halfway to the center. Since the invasion, few had cared to visit the park that occupied most of this deck. They stayed close to home in case events exploded. She had noticed and made it part of her scheme.

The wall at her back, she set forth on a trail. At half Earth weight, she moved as easily as the butterflies. The air was thin but she needed less and it was mild and moist, full of living odors. Bougainvillea and poinsettia flared, fantastically tall. A stand of bamboo clicked in the forced breeze. Birds trilled in a plum grove. She crossed a bridge high-arched over a brook that rushed from a hillside, pumped, artificial, but clear and songful. Mostly the terrain was grass and wildflowers. It curved upward before her to meet the illusion of sky.

Another wall hove in view. Its mural showed a classic landscape, cone-shaped mountains above a river and village. A torii arch gave ornament to the gate through it.

On the far side Eiko came to the Tree.

The Tree. Here the air lay hushed. Light fell in beams or like a mist down into shadow, to speckle a floor of yielding duff, clustered ferns, logs that were fallen, limbs overgrown with moss and mushrooms. Her gaze found no more sky. This space was deckless almost to the spin axis, a shaft half a kilometer across and nearly as deep. In it reigned the Tree.

Sequoia, biological experiment, genes cunningly mutated, growth hastened by chemistry and allowed by weight that dwindled as the crown rose—words. It was like calling Bach's Passion According to St. John a set of notes scribbled around an account of a myth. She entered into holiness.

Often had she sought here, climbed, rested in the heights, meditated or daydreamed or simply been. Once beyond the lower branches she rarely encountered anyone else. To go higher was reasonably safe if you took care, but a single time sufficed most of those who ever made the effort. Diversions elsewhere—winged flight, a globular pool at the axis, variable-*g* sports and dancing, excursions outside, and more and more—had variety in them. Here were only infinite enigmatic traceries of bark, boughs, needles, wind, cloud. Sometimes a bird or a darting squirrel went by.

She approached. The trunk was a wall, a tower, a fortress, red-brown and rough to see, warm and soft to touch. She rounded its immensity and found the ladder. They who fastened the metal had worked in reverence. It was colored like the bark; rungs and bars and resting stages seemed to belong as much did the lesser plants in the twilight below. Eiko laid hold.

For a moment she paused. She stood alone in a breathing stillness. How fared the brain between her shoulders? She could give him a word or two, a reassurance, a kindness.

No. Not yet. She began climbing.

28

THE SCREEN SHOWED new Guthrie in a new body. A different one, at any rate. It surely gave him less than half the capabilities he might have, as humanoid as it was. He could almost have been a medieval knight outfitted for tourney. Not much was lacking but plumes on the helmet and a surcoat adorned with a lion. Sayre wondered if he had adopted it to make himself seem closer to his employees and associates, make them more confident in his leadership on this dubious and troubled day. The imagery might well actually work to that end, not in anyone's conscious mind but down among emotions, archetypes, the infantile and the animal.

Nevertheless, the tone from that bright visor was chillingly matter-of-fact. "Not a new word so far. Rinndalir's agents went off with Davis. That's all."

Sayre forced the same manner into his response. "Can you guess where?"

"Maybe. I haven't dealt with him personally, repeatedly, like the other me, remember. I've only got updates to go on. But they tell me what a tricky bastard he is. Knowing his location, Davis', wouldn't do us a hell of a lot of good. What counts is what he's doing with her."

"Two days— She's certainly told him. Why hasn't he made it public?"

"I expect he wants to verify, as far as possible. And quite likely sit back a while, collect what more information he can, see what develops and how he can turn it to his advantage. Listen, I've put feelers out in his direction. He'll know I want secret contact with him. I'll be surprised if he doesn't oblige. But when, I can't say, nor what he'll want. Maybe only to laugh at us."

Sayre gripped the edge of his desk. "What . . . do you think . . . you can offer him?"

Robot shoulders shrugged. The audio carried the faint metal slither of it. "I'll have to play whatever cards I'm dealt. Bribes, of course. Quid pro quo."

"Threats? Hinted at, naturally. It would not be impossible to arrange a major accident."

"Like an unmanned spacecraft crashing where it'd hurt? Not easy. Nor an idea I like. Economic reprisals— likewise. The Moon depends on Fireball, but it's mutual. Also, do I have to remind you again? My consortes aren't your trained-dog officers or your castrato taxpayers. They think for themselves. I can't order them into actions they'll wonder about, I have to maneuver them into it, and that takes time."

Insolent swine. Sayre denied himself anger. It wasn't rational. "Bueno," he snapped, "what have your people learned from the spaceship Davis stole?" His men had simply reported finding nothing special aboard. Then Guthrie made a personal call, reclaiming her, and the Lunarians acquiesced.

"Very interesting, that." The generated voice grew entirely human; Sayre could hear the sarcasm. "Yours did pretty well. Oh, it was up to me to learn that Wash Packer had ordered a launcher loaded in, but your experts didn't delay matters at Port Bowen by more than about forty hours. My boys didn't accomplish much except observe what the dog did in the night time."

"What?"

"The dog did nothing in the night time. Never mind. There was no launcher in the ship. They ran some tests and found that one had been fired off within the past few days."

Chill walked along Sayre's spine. "This means—"

"Yeah. What we suspected he might try. If I hadn't been so goddamn busy fast-talking people and covering my ass here in Quito, I'd've acted on it sooner. Now we've both got to. Davis sent the other me off in space. The destination can hardly have been anywhere but L-5. He'll have covered the distance by now."

Sayre swallowed. "I've had no word about that. You know I've had potential conspirators in the colony detained and all space-related activities watched."

"Uh-huh. Maybe he's still in orbit. I'll go look. Personally, in my torch, as soon as I can plausibly get away. Meanwhile, though, you'd better send reinforcements to L-5 and instigate a ransacking. Pronto. Somebody may have him stashed, waiting for a chance to make him known."

Hope dazzled. "If we can catch him, quietly—"

The basso grew parched. "That'd be nice. However, it wouldn't take us out of the woods. Packer and his family are at large. They know. How many more? We'll prepare for the worst-case scenario, that alter-Guthrie pops out of his closet before we can touch him; but our plan needs to provide against whatever may happen whether he does or not."

Sayre nodded. "The Synod is fully informed and ready. We can declare a state of national emergency at any moment we choose, and mobilize the militia reserves within twenty-four hours. The Federation Assembly will scream, but our delegation can keep it tied in knots for several days. After that, we'll see what can be done about damage control." He drew breath. "Fireball will be enormously helpful, both during the crisis and afterward."

"Within limits, as I've tried and tried to explain to you. Christ, but humans are inefficient! I sometimes wonder if I really would like to be one again."

Startled, Sayre blurted, "Would you?"

A whisper: "Yes and yes, always—" Immediately, harshly: "Well, get off your duff and make those arrangements. Then you can be farting at that end instead of out your mouth. I've got my own work to do. If I haven't called you before, check back with me at this time tomorrow, but otherwise don't pester me about anything less than Fenris breaking his chain. Savvy? Out." The screen blanked.

For a span Sayre continued staring into it. Rage went acrid up his gullet. He should have put that malvado in a quiviran hell while he was able and had his technicians make him one more docile!

He mastered his feelings. Wishful fantasy. The ape in him, gibbering. Done was done, and the consequences not to be lamented but to be used rationally. He'd had no way of foreseeing that this Guthrie would turn out so vicious. Nor had there been time to keep trying. Besides, the basic personality must be preserved, or Fireball would never accept it as genuine; nor, probably, would it be able to steer Fireball. And it was indeed doing what it was programmed for, as well as could be expected. What hurt, Sayre admitted, was that he'd thought it would be his friend.

He sighed, rose, paced to the viewscreen and looked at

the scene outside. Rain fell gray on Futuro. The buildings seemed hueless, hunched, as if in decay. Many were, he knew, two decades after his government proudly, symbolically created this new capital for the Union. They were all fundamentally alike, too, in spite of every computer-generated architectural variation. It was not a style that inspired a school; nobody else built like this. Ottawa or poor burnt-out Washington had more character, more meaning.

No. Sayre straightened. Avantism made its mistakes, but it would go on. In the end, perhaps after a hiatus, perhaps under a different name and in different hands, it would prevail: because that was the nature of the universe.

A line drifted through his head. *Oh, that this too, too solid flesh would melt—* What was it, where and when had he heard it? . . . Yes. Shakespeare. Vera doted on Shakespeare, was forever quoting him, and certainly he'd had a majestic way with words, trivial though the content was. But not to think about Vera. Not to let old pains awaken. The divorce was—nine years?—in the past. Sometimes he dreamed about her, but that was the primitive in him. He had his satisfactions, his hygienic accommodations of the needs of the body. He had his work, his duty, his vision.

The melting away of the flesh. Liberation, transcendence, Transfiguration. Millions or billions of years hence, the cosmic Oneness. How could Guthrie conceivably regret being what he was?

Sayre smiled, recognized malice, and indulged it for a few seconds. Guthrie had no choice, except oblivion.

Fantasy: Imprint memories in a biological body, whether this was cloned or grown according to an original, rational design. Then discard the worn-out one, new life for old. He had gathered that that was among the dreams of those persons a couple of centuries ago who had gotten themselves frozen after clinical death. It hadn't worked, of course; it ignored the fact that every cell type requires a special freeze-thaw profile.

Nowadays you could go into suspended animation if you were near the end of your span, and wait for science to devise the means of a glorious technoresurrection. Couldn't you? True, a suspend didn't last more than a few decades. After that, the accumulated unrepaired damage from such factors as background radiation was too much. But you might expect biotechnics to advance exponentially while you waited.

Forget it. Nobody would ever make anything ageless that was recognizably human; the genome said otherwise. Evolution had selected for parents who got out of the way of their adult children. Whatever else you might synthesize would be too alien to contain your mind.

Then why not clone yourself, in a series of copies, lifetime after lifetime? Why, that had already been done. It didn't even require a seed cell. The individual genome map was a part of every up-to-date medical database. That had become standard practice when Guthrie was still alive.

But this did not get you away from carbon chemistry and quantum mechanics. An organic brain *could not* accept a download as a piece of network software could. The process took too long. The brain was too labilely active. It would not recognize those separate bytes creeping in, it would reject them or distort them or go unrecoverably crazy in the torment of them.

So if Guthrie wished to be flesh again, he was trapped.

But why did he think of it thus? Why did he not strive forward to the perfection of robot existence, beyond anything possible to organic molecules? He could fund a research program that would in a few years advance psychonetics by an order of magnitude. He did not, he would not. Instead he obstructed, connived, compromised, fought delaying actions, to keep as many of his workers humans for as long as might be.

Old Guthrie did. New Guthrie had been shown the truth. Give him time to assimilate it.

He had time. The bastard. How good it would be to outlast him, or at least to match the centuries before him.

Not absolutely impossible. Given Avantist victory, surely Enrique Sayre could claim a well-earned reward, his own downloading.

But that would create another Sayre, a machine Sayre. Still *this* flesh must die, and never know what came afterward.

Unless the Ultimate recreated it as a line within a program you might call Paradise—

Sayre stiffened his back, wheeled about, and got busy.

29

EARTH WAXED AS the sun trudged west. Kyra spied it just above the northeastern horizon when she had scaled the mountain down which she earlier scrambled. Not quite three-quarters full, it hung blue-and-white marbled, a cabochon gem on a raven's breast, sigil of serenity. But— impatience flamed—it wasn't that really, it was a clock, it had already swept out four of its days and nights while she lay captive. God, how many more?

And yet, what wonders here were hers!

The thought made her turn about, expectant. Faceplate darkening itself against the glare in that direction, she now saw the heights as a confusion of broken rock, scarred ashen slopes, and shadows. Airless, to her it was not silent; she breathed, her heart beat, and likewise for her spacesuit, ventilating, thermostatting, purifying, absorbing, recycling, well-nigh another organism. Barren, to her it was not lifeless; Rinndalir bounded from below, up into her view.

The motion made his cloak swirl, a ripple and sheen of gray. He unfolded the membranes that reached through slits in it, and iridescence quivered from his shoulders, two slender lengths matching his height, dragonfly wings. But it was cat-lithe that he moved toward her, lapis lazuli-hued save for his face that laughed within the cowl. A star sparkled at the tip of the wand he bore.

"You climbed like a spider, my lady," his radio voice sang. She gulped. Having seen the spiders he kept, mutated, bred, and drugged in the castle, that they might spin marvelous webs never twice the same for his pleasure, she realized she had been complimented. Few accolades could have meant more. "I did not know you would prove so able."

"G-gracias," she stammered. "I've done it some on Earth."

Angrily, she told herself that there was no excuse for thus deferring to him. He wasn't a sorcerer or elf or outlaw god, magically free of mortal frailties. His suit fitted him like an athlete's garment because it was state of the art, created for him personally and the Lunar surface exclusively, most of its structure bionic; similarly the almost invisible helmet. The cloak was insulation and radiation shielding; it covered small prosaic pieces of equipment on his back. The wings were partly solar energy collectors, partly cooling surfaces. The wand was a communication antenna and, she guessed, informant. That was all.

Yes, beside it the standard adjustable model lent to her showed as ugly and clumsy. Even her own gear aboard her torchcraft would have. But they were more versatile and far more sturdy, she felt sure. Rinndalir was loco to caper around in that flimsy thing.

Though the thought stripped away none of the glamour, it was steadying. "And you have ample experience with low-gravity environments," she heard him observe. "I see. If you have rested enough, we should proceed home."

"I wasn't tired," she said. "I was waiting for you to catch up."

He smiled and waved an arm, spread-fingered. The muscle equivalents in sleeve and glove made the gesture virtually as graceful as within his stronghold. "Believing you would need a pause at the summit, I indulged in a little crag-leaping."

In the gloom of the gorge below them? The reflection flitted through her that if he'd come to grief, she, alone, mapless, unacquainted with landmarks, ill-equipped to send a long-range call, would have been in serious trouble. Had he cared? She found she couldn't resent it. His nature was such—she supposed.

"I hope you have enjoyed our excursion," he went on.

Whatever pique she felt vaporized in splendor. "Oh, yes! Mil gracias! You've been hyper kind."

These hours afoot had been a marvel. Often she quite forgot her troubles. Past sightseeing had brought her to things that were superb, amidst expanses of dreariness, but none compared with what he showed her. Freakish, eerily beautiful formations; mineral colors subtle or startling; tremendous vistas; the remnant of an old exploration camp; enigmatic stones that must have come from beyond the Solar System; the bas-reliefs decorating one scaur; at last the descent into this ravine and the cave near the bottom, where flashbeams awakened an Aladdin's hoard of crystals— Some of it was recorded in early photographs, but most the Lunarians had discovered or made and kept known to none but themselves. Why had Rinndalir revealed it to her, who would surely tell others? Bueno, this was his demesne, he could refuse admission and grin at indignation.

"When you're so busy, too," Kyra said.

Foreboding stirred. Why, indeed, would he spare the time? Why wasn't he at work organizing Guthrie's rescue? He'd been out of her sight plenty at the castle, on his screened communication lines or perhaps more than once flying elsewhere to conspire in person. He sidestepped her questions with an evasion or a jest, assuring her nothing bad had happened thus far and that she ought to take her ease, relax, recuperate. No multi available to her would bring in a newscast; he said he spared his staff and himself those stupidities, and she decided against pursuing the matter.

Hm, his lady Niolente had been equally occupied, and lately had remarked in her aloof fashion that she must make a trip. Maybe she was handling everything that at this moment could be handled. But the sense of confinement would have become unendurable to Kyra if . . . if they had allowed it to grow in her.

"Best I get back into connection, then," Rinndalir said lightly. "We will return by the shortest route, as quickly as you are able."

Despite all wonders, that was a relief. No normal spacer

would have stayed out this long or gone this far without a vehicle. True, the danger wasn't great, the sun wasn't in a flare period, but as they two crossed a valley floor, dust had spurted three meters to their left and fallen back onto a new pockmark. The bullet-sized meteoroid would have killed either of them. His laughter rang. By the time her nerves had settled, it was too late to ask him if he had been delighted.

He took the lead, soaring down the mountainside. More dust puffed from every footfall. It dropped off the repellent surfaces of his outfit, as it did off hers, and left him darkly shining. From time to time he must pause for her. It wasn't due to a difference in physical strength. In that regard they were probably equal. The modifications that enabled his people to stay healthy and carry babies to term under one-sixth Earth weight were more in the cardiovascular system and the cellular chemistry than in bone or muscle. His spacesuit gave him his advantage. Hers was a responsive machine, his was garb. Panting, sweating, picking her way rock by rock, Kyra wondered whether she too wouldn't opt for one such and to hell with hazards, were she a Lunarian.

Which she never could be.

On ground more nearly level she matched his pace and soon fell into the long, swinging rhythm of it. Neither spoke; breath was to spend on kilometers. Alone with herself, Kyra thought about Guthrie. Five daycycles, damn near, since she landed on the Moon; four since this seigneury took her unto itself, and since he drew nigh to L-5. If he had. How fared he now? And Bob Lee, the Packers, Esther Blum, yes, Nero Valencia, everybody? They could all have been captured, destroyed, anything. The Avantists wouldn't announce it. Was that what the dearth of news meant which Rinndalir spoke of, if Rinndalir was telling the truth?

What was truth, yonder inside his walls? How much of what she remembered was natural, how much artifice, how much illusion? Thinking back, she realized how little certainty was granted her, from the moment she passed the portal. Drowsiness and dream—

No, be fair. Those first twenty-odd hours she had spent asleep or barely half awake, sedated, and it was Niolente's suggestion but her own decision. Stress had drawn her more thin than she knew until suddenly it ended. (Wryly: This had also been her chance to take a pill from her pocket kit, cancelling the inhibitor and starting a rather overdue menstruation. It ended last nightwatch. She must remember to reinhibit. Her periods gave her no major discomfort, but should action commence again she'd rather not have that to fuss about.) Food and drink brought her were delicious, and with consciousness off guard she believed that she began to appreciate the music she heard.

Afterward, though— Yes, utter hospitality and graciousness. Niolente's courtesy to the guest was remote. Kyra suspected fire beneath that ice, but never felt it. Rinndalir charmed or fascinated as he chose. His discourse ranged over the whole of knowledge and culture, seen through eyes not wholly human. ("The mind deceives itself less often than it plays practical jokes on itself. . . . 'All evil comes from not following Right Reason and the Law of Nature,' said Uriel Acosta, a Portuguese-Dutch Jew in the seventeenth century. It is a fairly workable definition of evil, for beings that imagine they think. . . . The most terrible thing a mind can conceive of is that it knows everything important about reality. . . .") When he was not on hand, there was no lack of handsome male and comely female attendants to show her about, answer her questions, respond to her wishes, and yet not press themselves upon her.

The conservatory and the metamorphic pets rivaled the prides of Tychopolis. She swam in a great pool among fish never seen on Earth, then strapped wings to her arms and flew off above the gardens and glass sculptures of a cavern as spacious as L-5's largest flight chamber. She learned how to play Mayan ball between the tiers of a replicated Mayan court, but the original could not become so wild. She mastered intricate low-g dances, Rinndalir's arm around her waist, he suppleness itself. She struggled to comprehend books and recorded shows; the effort was richly rewarded, though she realized how superficial her understanding remained. Some wine or a mild psychedelic helped. Nobody offered her a quiviran session, and she would have declined, but the virtualities in a vivifer turned stranger than any dream, she whirling through an endless fractal curve, riding a billow on a sea of red smoke, turned into a harpstring plucked by the solar wind. . . .

Oh, the Lunarians knew well how to keep her busy, distracted, away from her rightful concerns. The spires of Zamok Vysoki flashed at the horizon. It jolted through her that while she loped she had slipped entirely back into her memories of that fantasy life.

Why had she been given it? Rinndalir could simply have detained her incommunicado. But she was his ally. Was she?

The walls rose tall before their haste. An intricate frieze framed the entry valve at which they drew to a deep-breathing halt. "Welcome home, my lady," he said.

She made herself retort, "It's not my home. When will you let me go?"

He looked at her. The unfairly fair countenance flowed into seriousness. "I have hopes for that," he said. Amazed, she could but follow him into the airlock and thence the castle.

As they unsuited, he told her, "You will wish to refresh and rest before evenwatch. But pray stand prepared for a call." His undergarment clung silkily, a second skin on a panther.

Kyra went on to her room. A-buzz and a-shiver, she scarcely noticed the portraits, landscapes, and abstractions hung in the first corridor she took. Then, above a serpent-bannistered staircase, another hall was paneled for holo. The scenes changed every few hours. She had been told that a hypercomputer creatively modified recordings when it did not generate new ones, so that the inhabitants would never know what to expect. Today she passed as if on a bridge across a cosmically huge chasm. Far ahead burned fires, red and yellow and green; far behind rose a mysterious blue shimmer of ice cliffs. She felt suggestions of heat and cold, heard whispers of roaring and howling. In between were fog and smoke, wind-riven but thickly rolling. Left and right they seemed to curdle into solid forms, grotesque, one maybe human, one maybe beast.

Her room was a haven. Ample, its gold and nacre held furnishings to whose style and proportions she had gotten used. Opposite a door that gave on a private bath, a large viewscreen was at present set to show the upper heavens, stars amplified into frosty visibility against the interior lighting. That was considerate; Earth would have reminded her of too much.

A bedside table held a self-cooling carafe of the mango cider she had mentioned she enjoyed, a plate of small cakes delicately spiced with marijuana, and a vase shaped like a blue fountain of water, filled with purple roses. Their scent and a lilt of music flavored the air. She shucked her skinsuit, tossed it down the cleaner chute, and crossed a carpet patterned with constellations, silver on blue, which gave her bare feet slight electric tingles. After reveling in a shower, she came forth to study what was in her closet. A tailor machine had taken her measurements early on, and by next daywatch she was lavishly provided.

The phone did not chime or call, it fluted. Hastily she threw on a bathrobe and went to answer. Rinndalir's face looked out at her. Behind him Kyra saw Niolente. Her expression was composed, but on his Kyra read a savage exultation . . . or so she imagined.

"I promised you a change of orbit, my lady," he said. "Here you begin. We have fresh data to coordinate and plans to make."

It flared in Kyra. "Por favor, tell me," she gasped.

"Radar, ion trails, and analysis—but you know the procedures. Three more torchcraft have come to Lagrange-Five. Our information is that this is as many as the North American government commands. Belike they are crammed with Security Police. Another torch was cruising about the region in such a way that it must have been on search for your launcher, but it has returned Earthward. We think it found the rocket, and found it empty. Therefore the lord Guthrie most likely was brought into the colony, and the Security Police are in frantic quest of him there."

"Judas priest!" Kyra yelled. "Stop them before they find him!" A fragment of her noticed she had used an old oath of the jefe's.

He'd hoped that, if she failed to get help here, Tamura could retrieve him and reveal him. It hadn't worked out. His other self must have been too quick on the uptake. Now she alone bore hope. Suppose the Lunarians decided their advantage lay in keeping neutral, or in striking a bargain with counter-Guthrie— No, she would not think that, not yet.

And Rinndalir saved her from it: "Patience a while longer, a little, little while." His smile reached out to capture her. "We know time is short. We marshal for action. But you, Pilot Davis, must understand that the lady Niolente and I cannot achieve by ourselves. We have been at work these past daycycles, persuading our fellow Selenarchs. It was not easy. Soon she departs again, to see to the final arrangements. Abide."

"Why don't you just tell the Solar System the truth?" At once Kyra recognized her idiocy. Rinndalir could have done that the hour she arrived here, had he seen fit.

His reply was much the same as he had given her earlier. "It would be irresponsible, and quite possibly useless. The situation is explosive. Your enemies have made their provisions. Where is our proof? Better the solid lord Guthrie in hand than the naked assertion he exists, nay?" But this time he added, smiling again—warmly, she believed in her dazzlement, warmly—"Pray forgive us if we have been less than forthcoming. The unknowns, the complexities were too many. We could have told you nothing meaningful. We are still half in enigma. But I say we are about to act. If you will bless me with your presence at dinner this evenwatch, my lady, I will seek to explain."

"Oh, yes," she breathed. Her knees trembled beneath her.

"At 1930, then? Good." The screen blanked.

She stood for a while wondering confusedly why she didn't whoop and war-dance around the room. True, they hadn't yet won, they could still lose, but— Her head felt all in a whirl. A private meeting with Rinndalir? She assumed it would be private, if Niolente was going away. Why in MacCannon's name did he affect her like this? Alluring to look at, spellbinding to listen to, sure, but there should be more to a man than that. He wasn't even a man, strictly speaking. Male, yes, but he couldn't father a child on her if they both tried. She felt the blush as a wave of heat, glanced down and saw that it reached to her breasts.

That called forth a laugh. Ease off, girl. The exotic always appealed, and no doubt she was on the rebound from Valencia. Let that lesson stay with her. Admittedly Rinndalir had depths beneath the glittering surface. Just what were they, though? Keep watchful, ready to jump.

And don't remain passive. Give him back some of his own. For openers, what to wear?

She spent a considerable time on that. The wardrobe bestowed on her included things she hadn't yet used. She chose the slinkiest, an ankle-length tigryl gown cut low, its skirt slit up the right side. Silvery slippers. No jewelry except her academy ring, taken from her pocket kit. Her hands were big for a woman's, well fitted to the heavy gold circlet and inlaid star. Cosmetics were in the bathroom. Thus far she hadn't availed herself of them, but now, a few careful touches, plus a dab of the right perfume.

Then it was to wait, and wait. She screened a recording of an Earthside *The Tempest* which she liked, but found that it wasn't registering on her. *A Midsummer Night's Dream,* maybe? No, that would go too near the bone.

A servant appeared at last, to escort her ceremonially. He bowed her through a door of the Pagoda and closed it behind her.

Brilliance erupted in a million colors. This turret jutting into space was one synthetic diamond, faceted inside and out. She could not look at the blaze where the sun shone through, but everywhere else was flash and sparkle, changeable at every least motion she made. Rinndalir approached over the glassy-polished floor, in close-fitting black. Rainbows played across the whiteness of face and hands, shimmered on the pale hair, danced about his feet.

"Welcome anew," he murmured. Unthinkingly, she offered him her arm. He held his above. Fingertips barely touched her hand. She felt each one of them. She'd granted him superior status. What of it? He smiled and guided her to a table. Wine and hors d'oeuvres were on it. Light filled the crystal. He poured. "Your Terrestrial custom," he said, as he gave her a goblet. "Would you fain propose a toast?"

Impulse grabbed. "To our partnership!" Rims sang when they met. It was a noble wine, no, regal, imperial.

They continued standing, Lunarian style, as they drank and talked. "I am happy about this," he told her. "Before, we were not free to deal with you as we wished, Niolente and I. Henceforth, I trust, you shall in truth be a partner. May I say a friend?"

"Yes, por favor, do." She mustn't let it overwhelm her. Hold steady. Speak out. "But if, if I am to be— I need to know more."

He nodded. "Undeniably. You could not earlier because we did not ourselves. Forgive my frankness. At the start we must gather what evidence we were able that would confirm or disconfirm your story. It seemed plausible, but it could have been part of a scheme. Unless that began to look likely, we would not subject you to the horror and indignity of a deep quiz."

Which they could have done with impunity. How could she have taken revenge, or gotten any redress afterward unless that was their whim? "K-kind of you."

He grinned. "Precautionary. Why raise needless antagonism?"

Emboldened, she replied, "Lunarian thinking, that. Wise, of course. But as for this having been an elaborate hoax—bueno, I suppose that was Lunarian thinking too."

"We have the reputation of being intriguers," he agreed, unabashed. "Remember, Niolente and I must convince not only ourselves of your bona fides, but a sufficiency among the Selenarchs, and they would speculate about *us*. Then we must negotiate, while collecting more intelligence about your enemies. You would not have understood our ways. This is not your civilization. Had we let you follow along, simply explaining matters as they developed would have been a serious drain on time and energy, and probably an impossible task."

Kyra stiffened a bit. "I would not have gone hysterical on you."

"Nay," he answered softly. "I am sure of that now. But remember, you came to us a stranger. How could we tell? You are as foreign to us as we are to you."

"I wonder about that." She took a deeper draught than was right for a drink like this. It hallowed her palate and sent rainbows into her bloodstream, akin to those that glorified Rinndalir. Might there be something in it, a drug to which he was accustomed or immune? No matter. She'd recognize intoxication if it started, and curb herself. "What have you arranged to do? Soon. You know we can't dawdle."

He sighed. "Pity to spoil this hour with business."

Was that also how a Lunarian thought? "Get it over with and then we can relax and enjoy."

"Suspense adds savor. However, since you feel otherwise, here is the plan, sparely sketched. Tomorrow the Selenarchy will declare all Fireball properties on the Moon sequestered, pending investigation of this alleged terrorist crisis, which we have come to suspect is false. Your officers in Port Bowen will protest but not resist; we have sounded out the key ones."

"Why not just tell them the truth?"

"Would they keep secrecy? Some would disbelieve, others be uncertain. The natural thing to do would be to send Quito a query. You have been urging swift, decisive action. That requires surprise."

"I think you underestimate our folk. But they aren't yours, are they? What'll you do next?"

"We, Pilot Davis. You are vital to us. The sequestration covers our rear and gives us authority to commandeer spaceships. You will pilot a force of us to Lagrange-Five. There you will be our liaison."

"Wow-w-w!" she shouted inadequately. He laughed into her joy. Almost, she seized him and kissed him.

She braked her impulse in time. That effort brought feelings under control. They throbbed undwindled, but did not clamor thought out of awareness. "What kind of ship? A torch'd be too much to expect from luck. Wouldn't make much difference anyway. Your men couldn't stand a one-*g* boost for the, m-m, about three and a half hours it'd take. At least, not if they want to arrive in shape to do anything worthwhile."

"We will be a picked troop. We can endure two Lunar gravities for the six hours necessary."

Thrill: "You're coming in person? Yes, you would. . . . What kinds of ship are available? How many will you be?"

"You see, you are a full comrade in the emprise," he purred. "Ten plus yourself should suffice. In port are several vessels, but only one of them, a Narwhal, has enough couches plus sufficient delta *v*. Can you handle such a craft?"

Kyra shook her head. "I can, but no go. Sure, she's a passenger carrier for Earth and ambient space, but her drive isn't meant for a boost period that long. We'd either have to spend time we can't well afford on trajectory, or risk burnout and, at best, guarantee rousing suspicion at the other end. Also, we'd have precious little reaction mass reserve if somebody comes after us in a torch." Her mind sped, an excitement like surfing on a really big one. "There's a Dolphin, of course, always is, rescue craft. Four couches, but I won't need any. You'll have to settle for that size team."

"We shall," he replied instantly. "I had in mind a rather large group because it could make itself difficult to subdue, should matters go awry for us. Now we must see to it that they do not."

"We can't just leap inboard and lift off, you know," Kyra warned. "She's kept pretty well ready, considering her main purpose, but some preparations are needed, and then how do you explain taking her out when we haven't got an emergency?"

"That will all be taken care of beforehand."

"How?"

"I have agents in the Fireball organization."

I, he said. The implications were disquieting. Perhaps he read it on her. He spoke fast. "The port technicians will soon receive instructions, seemingly from Quito. That is in the net on standby; I need merely key in the precise details. This change of plans that you urge—let me think. . . . Ah, yes. We Lunarians wish to send inspectors up to a relay satellite we are considering replacing, but suddenly find we have problems with our own spacecraft suitable for the task. As a courtesy, Fireball will take them. Since they are four, not ten, and a Dolphin is more maneuverable than a Narwhal, and traffic patterns show no significant probability of accidents in this vicinity at present, that is the ship to use."

Kyra frowned. "I know who'll wonder real hard about that."

"My agents will make certain that this message and the consequent preparatory work do not come to the attention of any such persons."

Tricks, diversions, beguilements— "You can't make that liftoff invisible, nor the fact right afterward that she's not really making for any Lunar satellite."

"By then, the sequestration will have happened, including communications. Ground crews will not yet know of it. Officers will be in polite custody. Once the ship is aloft, that can be revealed to all personnel, but for the next—fifteen hours, shall we say?—no communication will go out of Port Bowen that our agents have not checked, or constructed themselves. I repeat, at Lagrange-Five we require surprise."

Kyra whistled. "That's a mighty big bite you're taking. What if we fail?"

Rinndalir chuckled. "The consequences will be diplomatically interesting. But we, the Selenarchs of sovereign Luna, need no more fear effective punishment than do the Avantist masters of North America."

"Still . . . I see why you had to work this quietly, take this long. Making arrangements for something so big—" Abruptly she had scant comfort from the wine. "Why do your consortes go along with it? What's in it for them? For *you,* sir?"

He turned grave. "That is somewhat of a philosophical question, Pilot Davis. We can try to discuss it later, if you wish. Let me simply declare now that our relationship with Guthrie's Fireball has been generally satisfactory. Who knows what pseudo-Guthrie might provoke?"

That reassured, at least to the point where she could smile and reply, "Which is what I've been trying to tell you!"

"Indeed." His voice briskened. "Shall we finish the practicalities? Our expeditionary force will have an authorization apparently issued by Fireball's director here. Devising and encoding that took some expert time also. It will be beamed to the colony shortly before we dock. It states that we are a mission sent in a preliminary way to look at the possibility of establishing a Lunarian enterprise station at the one-sixth gravity level there."

Kyra frowned. "That doesn't make a lot of sense."

"Nay," Rinndalir admitted with a grin, "but the Security Police ought not to know that, and the regular staff should see no reason not to receive us. Lunarians do have a name for waywardness, but never for endangering an environment in space." His gaze pierced her, his tone slowed and deepened. "Once we are inside, what happens will depend very largely on you, Pilot Davis. I assume you know who can lead us to Guthrie, and can persuade that person to do so."

"I . . . think I can—" It exploded: "And then the whole rotten conspiracy crashes!"

He lifted a diamond-aureoled hand. "Not quite that dramatically, I fear. We had best not carry him in triumph through the colony, but smuggle him out. Otherwise the Security Police might find means to halt us and suppress all news. Or else imagine what some individual fanatic might do. Any attempt—firearms discharged—need I say further? And afterward . . . we must consider what is wisest, in conference with Guthrie himself. His enemies are desperate, and not stupid. North America wavers on the verge of civil war. Millions of lives could be at risk."

Fleetingly she wondered whether he cared about that. But no. Unworthy thought. He was more Faust than Mephistopheles, she must believe. And he had engineered the great adventure that should bring liberation.

She shifted her goblet into her left hand and thrust out her right. "Muy bien!" she cried.

His clasp was warm, and he smiled into her eyes. His were big, oblique, the gray of a northern sea or of fine steel. "So be it," he said. "Drain your glass and I will refill both and we will drink to chaos."

She obeyed. While he poured she asked, "Chaos?"

"In the scientific sense," he answered. "An ordering of infinitely wonderful, unforeseeable manifoldness." After a moment: "But also in the older sense. I do not think that once this is over we can return to our familiar universe. Siva is the Destroyer. But he is, as well, the Creator Anew."

They drank, and nibbled the refreshments, and admired the play of light, and talked of much. Later she saw that he had revealed essentially nothing of what his motives and his colleagues' were. Perhaps her oversight was due to a growing happiness, perhaps his skill. He did, for instance, give her what seemed like a glimpse of his heart.

"Yes, here on Luna we have grandeur to undertake, making this world over to please ourselves, and otherwise every illusion we may desire. When our ingenuity runs dry, that of the machines will be unbounded. Yet to what end? The future is theirs. Unless we— It would not be the first rebellion that raised hope out of hopelessness, through chaos." He sheered from the subject and fashioned a merry jest.

Beneath the entrancement, she heard herself wonder if he truly was Faust. If not, what? A trickster god, Raven, Coyote? Or Loki?

Most of this was over the dinner table, to which he presently led her. It was in a room of blue twilight. Fragrances drifted, and music. How had he discovered that she loved the Air on a G String? The meal was superb, a series of small courses, each a masterpiece. Realities interwove the conversation, details, ideas, many of which he evoked from her. They gave it direction and meaning, a sharing of purpose; but always pleasures came back, humor, lines of poetry, remembrances. She fell into telling him about her past, from Toronto Compound and Russia on to the comets and planets. His questions and comments, out of his foreignness, were often astonishingly enlightening. She had never before thought about matters in that way. Only afterward did she reckon up how little he told her in return.

The waiters had brought their coffee and liqueurs and vanished. They were alone together. "You are a rather remarkable being, Pilot Davis," he said.

Not person, being. The connotations, in a Lunarian mind— "Por favor, lord Rinndalir, I am Kyra."

His smile flowed across her. "Well, then this nightwatch I bear no title. Shall we be simply ourselves?"

If you wanted a mythic likening, how about Krishna?

30

A BREEZE BLEW cool. A few of the leaves that it rustled on a birch had yellowed and the green of the rest begun to fade. As if defiant, sunflowers nearby raised golden blooms high above fescue growing wild. The year of Ragaranji-Go was moving toward autumn. Beyond waited the gentle winter.

Eiko wondered what it would be like to live on a world where seasons and weather had not been tamed, even to the degree that they were on Earth. Those must have been awesome powers, for a ghost of them lingered to this day in the forced cycles and carefully bounded random variations of the orbiting colony. So much life that it sheltered needed them for well-being. Did also the human spirit?

She passed the torii gate and came into the presence of the Tree. Three persons were there already, silent as people were wont to be when first they entered its shadows. She didn't know them. That in itself meant nothing; but could they be Sepo, civilian-clad off duty, here to behold the marvel? She might watch a while and see how they handled themselves at half a gravity. No, that could draw their attention to her in turn. Let her be only a woman walking by. It should actually be easier to hide her fears from them than from somebody who recognized her. Of course, her friends were aware that she had frequented this place since childhood. Nevertheless— She rounded the mighty bole and mounted the ladder, aiming to be out of sight before the visitors strolled beneath.

At the third resting stage she dared stop and catch her breath. It wheezed noisily. Her mouth and throat were dry, her body shook a bit, reminders that she was no longer quite young. She drank from the canteen at her belt, rested hands on the platform rail, and opened herself to calmness.

At this height were the lowest boughs, still sparse. Three meters beneath her, they supported the first of the several safety nets. More for protection against falling cones and branches than to catch climbers who lost their hold— trained spacefolk hardly ever would—its mesh was arachnite, strong enough to take an impact but thin; she could look through it, down into dusk. Above, multitudinous vaultings lifted ruddy, green, shadowy, luminous, upward beyond sight. Warmth dwelt in the bark, fragrance and a gathering mistiness in the air. A hawk skimmed by. A robot crept along the trunk in search of disease, lesions, any trouble not human. It looked like a beetle, dog-sized, with extra legs and feelers. It too belonged.

When she had her strength back Eiko went on. The ascent she made was too much for most persons. She didn't mind. Physical strain, whatever aches it brought, those were benedictions, surcease from the sickness that gripped the outer levels of her worldlet. The very sameness of rung after rung after rung, broken just by platforms and, thrice, relief stations with emergency telephones: it let her lose herself in an infinite variety of bough and twig, needles and cones, silence and soughing, life and light.

Beyond the topmost net, the ladder gave on a final stage and came to an end. Overhead were more intricacies of great, closely growing limbs. One that sprouted a few meters below her slanted toward them. Eiko rested until she felt ready, then sprang down to it. She fell as softly through the thin air as an autumn leaf. Gauging the jump wasn't hard for a person who was born to Coriolis force. Rough bark and occasional offshoots gave ample purchase for a body that weighed a few kilos to scamper upward, past the platform and close to a higher branch. To that one she leaped, caught a slender shoot, and crawled on top. Thence it was an easy scramble onward. When she reached the limb she wanted, she moved more cautiously, balanced against a whirl of whickering little winds, out over its massiveness to a triple fork.

She was by no means the sole colonist who made expeditions of this illegal kind; but they who did were rare and seldom spoke of it. For years none had disturbed her in the retreat she had discovered. After all, unlike her, others came this far for the sake of adventure, not peace.

The fork and its lesser branches formed a loose-knit room with broad crotches on which to rest, walls and roof of green, open on the far side. Less thick here than at its base, the main stem swayed slightly to the winds, a thrumming went through it, needle-rich twigs shifted and swished, glimpses of empty air danced among them. Forward beyond it, vapors drifted across pale blue, lighted by a sun that was not a disc but a ring around the mouth of this well. The ground lay dizzyingly far below, but the forest that was the Tree barred sight of it.

Eiko reached past three cones, drew Guthrie from his concealment, and settled him securely. She bowed before she knelt, legs together, hands on lap, facing him. It was an incongruous pose in sweatsuit and deck shoes, but she trusted he knew what she meant.

The flickering illumination made his lenses look eerily alive. "Hello," he said. "You've been a while. Trouble?"

"Not for me, sir," she replied in the same English. (No, not the same; his went back generations.) "I simply think that coming often would be hazardous. But I must inform you today that new contingents of Security Police have arrived. They are searching the colony from end to end.

We are not told what they seek, except for vague announcements about possible sabotage devices, but it is clear to me. I dare do nothing they might notice."

"Reinforcements?" he growled. "End to end? Yeah, my other self has okayed it. He's got a pretty good hunch I'm somewhere in L-5—gone to earth, so to speak."

"I am sorry to have left you for such a time, sir," she offered. "How have you been?"

"Bored."

"I am sorry," she repeated, while thinking that she would not have been. To rest without hunger or thirst or any need of motion, amidst sky and Tree!

"I'm grumpy too," he said. "Why are you this passive? You were plenty bold, snatching me out of space. Now do you mean you haven't made any further effort, haven't even talked in private to a few reliable people?"

She shook her head. A third apology would be servile, but she kept her answer soft. "I told you my father is a hostage. In a sense, a very real sense, all this nation is. A battle could let the vacuum in."

"I wouldn't want that. God, no! I was thinking about— maybe just getting somebody to the Moon to find out what went wrong there and pass the word on." Guthrie's voice dropped low. "And I worry about you, lass. If we wait, they're bound to find me, and they won't need much wit to figure out you were involved. What about you?"

"That doesn't matter," Eiko said, quiet in her heart. "Perhaps your other self is enough like you that he will understand and order me forgiven. In any case, they will have no reason to punish my father or friends, will they? Indeed, that could reveal the truth, which they fear."

He made a harsh noise and: "How long till the Sepo get up here?"

"It will be some daycycles yet, I believe. The colony is so big, so complex, a labyrinth. I have been trying to think how I can convey you to a place they have already searched."

"Good girl. Still, we can't play hide-and-seek forever."

"No. But while you remain free we have hope for an

opportunity, a change in circumstances." Her calm broke. "Let there be hope, Guthrie-san!" she cried. "If they destroy you—"

He sounded unshaken. "I'm not scared on my account. However, it'd be too bad for folks like you."

Insight came, not as a revelation but as the foreseen conclusion to many hours of pondering. "Fireball," Eiko breathed, "those who live by it and trust you, is that what you exist for?"

He held his tone matter-of-fact, as if to discount his meaning. "What else is there? Oh, this is an interesting universe and I have my fun, but I am in a thin kind of survival. Without Fireball, not a hell of a lot of point in continuing."

What an ultimate loneliness, Eiko thought. How could she reach out to him? It was the single meager thing she might be able to do this day. She fell silent, seeking an utterance. The wind whittered, the Tree murmured. "Why does it matter this much to you?" she asked finally.

He did not tell her to mind her own business. Was he glad to respond? "Well, Juliana—my wife and I, we founded it and made it grow. Our baby."

"You had real children, no?"

"Oh, yes. They grew up, though, and set off into their separate lives. We got along fine with them, enjoyed the grandkids, but Fireball was what we kept for ourselves."

No doubt he felt grateful to her, despite his complaints, and accorded her a measure of respect, and therefore found her worth talking with like this. Nonetheless Eiko was surprised when he added: "Then Juliana died. I soldiered on."

"Alone," she said. Tears stung.

"Don't feel sorry for me!" he snapped. "I don't, never did. Running Fireball was fun, taking it out to the ends of the Solar System and looking into how much farther we might go."

"I see. You did not wish to lose that."

"When I saw my own time coming?" She imagined a shrug of phantom shoulders. "Well, I'd have to. This isn't the original Anson Guthrie here, you know. It's a program in a box."

"I meant to say," she fumbled, "you . . . cared about . . . space." About humankind bound ever onward, discovering, triumphing, outliving the sun and the galaxies, and on the way attaining to enlightenment.

His reply came blunt. "Not exactly. I never was any saint, to sacrifice myself for some grandiose Purpose. Nor was I ever such an egomaniac as to suppose Fireball would immediately go on the rocks once my hand was off the tiller."

He lay mute for a span. Gently, the Tree rocked him.

"But we were at a crisis," he said. "Several crises, some technical, some political. For instance, should Fireball continue research and development for interstellar missions? Was that the great, shining goal, or were we pouring our resources down a black hole when they could go to something real? Several governments were trying to get into space in earnest, run their own lines and undertakings. Should we forestall the camel sticking his nose in the tent? If so, how? And how to keep Fireball itself from degenerating into a government?"

As he went on, his voice sank and steadied. "I was an old fart, my endurance gone and my wits growing dull. Best for Fireball, this thing Juliana built with me, best would be if I retired. Unless I could get myself a helper who thought like me, who also wanted to keep her dreams alive. The technology for downloading had become available. Quite a few friends, including descendants of ours, urged me to use it. They claimed they needed this. Maybe they were right. Anyhow, I let them talk me over. None too soon, from their standpoint, because as it happened, shortly after the job was done, I died."

31
Database

THE HOUSE STOOD near the western edge of its preserve on Vancouver Island. Behind it and on either side of the lawn reared ancient firs. Before it a path ran down to a dock at the cove. Beyond was ocean. On this late afternoon of summer, clouds stood tall in the east, their billows full of light and blue shadows. Otherwise the sky was clear. A low wind bore coolness from sea to sod; gulls skimmed creaking, amazingly white. Waves outside the cove ran gray and green save where they burned with sun or they foamed and fountained. At their distance the sound of them came as a wild lullaby, *hush-hush-hush*. Afar upon them winged a sailboat.

Here abided a piece of Old Earth. It was expensive to maintain.

The robot left his flitter on the landing strip and strode to the house. He was humanoid, suggestive of a knight in armor—accumulator-powered, not very efficient, but better suited for today than something on wheels or tracks or jets. The verandah drummed beneath his weight. Sheila Quentin heard and opened the door. He stepped into a walnut-paneled anteroom. Though windows were dimmed, a stained-glass panel was in full glow. It pictured Daedalus and Icarus aflight from their prison.

"Welcome," Quentin said. Her voice strove. "But did you have to come in person?"

"He asked, didn't he?" the robot replied. His own voice was a vigorous basso but rather flat in tone. He hadn't had enough practice with it yet.

"Yes, but—" She looked away. "I should think he—well, it's different with . . . blood kin. You—excuse me, but why couldn't you settle for a phone connection?" She looked back, mustering a sad defiance. "Less strain on him."

The robot regarded her. She had been a handsome woman. The years had not leached all of that from her.

"He wants it this way," the robot said. "Don't you understand?"

She sighed. "I know. In many ways he's a primitive soul. I should have prevented it."

"Could you have?"

"I tried. He insisted. But he's so weak—" Her fingers twisted together. "Him that was so strong. I could've refused to give you his message or to let him call. But—"

"He would have cursed you. I know."

"Of course you know." She raised her eyes to confront his lenses. "I gave in. Do you despise me?"

The robot shook his head. "No. Contrariwise. It wasn't easy for you. Thanks."

Her glance went to the staircase. "Better go right on up. He's had his medicine, but no telling any more how long a dose will work, and the cost gets higher to him each time."

"Afterward—"

"If there is an afterward, yes, I'll come say goodbye too." She swallowed. "But now he wants to be alone."

"In a way, he does," the robot agreed.

"If he'd let me hold his hand while you— No!" she nearly shouted. "Go on up!"

The robot mounted the stairs and went down a hall to a bedroom facing west. It was sparsely furnished, with just a few pictures on white walls, but much brighter than below. Windows were open to sky and sea breeze. Draperies fluttered gauzy. In a corner stood a grandfather clock, rebuilt museum piece. Its ticking marched slow beneath the wind.

The robot approached the bed and leaned over. Anson Guthrie looked back at him. Eyes blinked. They were faded, bulwarked by a nose that had jutted like a crag since most flesh shriveled. Lips moved. The robot amplified sound until he could hear that whisper. "Hello." This also brought in the sighing through the firs and the tumbling of waves as they rolled shoreward from across half the planet.

The robot had decided on the way here how best to greet his other self. "Vaya con Dios," he said.

Guthrie grinned a little. "Maybe." After a moment: "I wanted . . . to meet with you . . . once more." He muttered word by word, with pauses for air. It rattled in his lungs.

"Sheila doesn't think that makes sense," the robot said. He straightened. "I wonder if she's right."

"I do too, but . . . no matter . . . I hope you spoke . . . kindly . . . to her."

"I tried. I'm not sure I succeeded." Clumsily humanlike, the robot rubbed the back of his head, as if it grew hair. "This is all new to me." His tone sharpened. The best defense is an attack. "How kind to her have *you* been?"

Guthrie's skull turned on the pillow, from him. "Less'n I should have, no doubt. But—"

He fell silent, except for his breath that toiled against wind and sea and clock. Finally: "Vaya con Dios, you said." Again he grinned. "Won't Juliana give me hell! . . . Sheila, and the women before her—"

"She, Juliana, she'll understand," said the robot stoutly.

"I'm not so sure. . . . You lack certain feelings, I think. . . . Haven't got . . . what it takes . . . to have them."

The robot was mute a while. "That hurt," he said at last.

"Sorry." Guthrie's gaze struggled back to the burnished form. "Yeah, sorry. I keep forgetting . . . you aren't really me. . . . I always was . . . pretty rough . . . with myself, you know." He snapped after breath.

The robot nodded. "I expect I'll be the same. I'm still learning how to be—what I am."

Guthrie tried to form a frown. "Let's stop . . . pissing time down the toilet. Damn little . . . of it. . . . I'm bound where Juliana is, yeah, but . . . that's into nothing. . . . Got some business to settle . . . first."

"Your ashes will certainly go to hers," the robot promised: strewn across the Leibniz Range on Luna, the mountains of eternal light.

"Trivia. *We* won't care . . . or know. My epitaph— D'you recall?"

"Oh, sure."

A warm night, a rumpled bed, crickets chirping outside, the scents of love's aftermath. She snuggled against him. Her locks spilled over the arm he had brought around her shoulders. "I've thought of what I want on my tomb-stone," he laughed.

> *"Each man dies*
> *And ends his day.*
> *Here he lies*
> *Who used to lay."*

"I won't get that after all," Guthrie said.

"But I will remember it," the robot said.

"Right. That's enough. Listen," Guthrie hissed. "I want . . . to brief you . . . about Fireball. . . . You're going to have . . . a hell of a ruckus . . . and you're still . . . feeling your way . . . into existence—" He breathed for a span. Even amplified, his question was barely to be heard. "I wonder. How *does* it feel?"

"Strange," the robot confessed. "A kind of—lightness? I'm an abstraction, I think." He sought for words. "But there is a, a drive yet, and I'm fond of my old friends, my old memories, yours. Not quite the same way as before— as you've been—but— No, you were not very kind to Sheila today."

"Take care . . . of her. She's earned it."

"I will. She has." This also the robot shared. "Okay, what've you got to tell me about Fireball?"

Guthrie gathered strength.

"They're swarming around you already, aren't they?" he began. "Advice, requests, demands. . . . And you know . . . what I know . . . about them, but . . . have you got the—intuition—the sense of them?" He fought. "Listen. Mostly they mean well. . . . Watch out for . . . Delancey . . . . He's after power. Too good . . . an administrator . . . to scrap, and . . . we mustn't break faith, ever . . . but keep a curb on him." He fought. "And Tanya . . . Tanya Eagle Tree. Good gal, besides being . . . my granddaughter . . . but she should stay with . . . engineering. Steer her off of . . . trying to steer people. And—"

The seizure contorted him.

The robot knelt and held him close, mummy against metal, while it ran its course. "Shall I ring for help?" the robot asked. Anyone else would have done so immediately.

The expected "No" shivered to him. His vibrosensors felt the racking heartbeat, his chemosensors drank the smell of clam-cold sweat. "Hell with that. Never mind."

The spasm ended. The robot lowered the man to the pillow. Guthrie's right hand trembled toward him. "Stars," Guthrie pleaded. "Keep us aimed . . . at the stars . . . whatever your people . . . say."

"That night at the lake is in me too," the robot assured him.

The air was utterly still and unbelievably clear, especially since the altitude was not much. Above the woods, stars were beyond counting. Their reflections gleamed everywhere on the lake. Anson and Juliana had the campsite to themselves; in those days, you had to backpack to here. They stripped and went for a swim. The water caressed them, almost warm. At each stroke it ran back down into itself with a clear clinking like laughter. They swam among stars. "Someday we'll do this for real," Juliana said. "Promise?"

"Good," Guthrie whispered. "Grand. That's what counts." He rested until he could speak a bit louder. "I'll drink to that. The Scotch . . . is over there."

"Better not," the robot counseled.

"I'm still in command."

The robot yielded. "You are." He crossed the room, fetched the bottle from a drawer as directed, returned, and poured into a tumbler meant for water. Kneeling again, he lifted the knaggy head and brought rim to lips.

"The stars," Guthrie mumbled.

Curtains rippled evening-lit in a gathering breeze. The grandfather clock reached another hour and boomed it away.

32

UPON COMMAND, *INIA* meshed radionics with those of
Station Control and slipped into dock at L-5. Kyra need
but sit back and watch. The colony loomed before her like
a spinning cliff, the entrance a cave agape in the middle of
it. Her craft entered a tunnel everywhere lighted, applied a
sidewise vector, reached the assigned bay. Contact and
electromagnetic securing made the hull quiver. A wave of
dizziness passed through heads as weight came back. It
was slight, this close to the axis of rotation, but Kyra was
now looking up, not across, at a tender moored opposite.
Just as well, she thought, that she'd vetoed Rinndalir's
idea of arriving in the Narwhal. That vessel would have
had to take orbit while the shuttle yonder, or one like it,
ferried his party here and back. A Dolphin was small
enough to bring them in directly. Quicker getaway, should
the need arise. Of course, a lessened strength might make
that need more likely.

She tautened. The way their plan had developed, it was
pretty much dependent on her.

She undid her harness and moved feather-softly aft. The
Lunarians were releasing themselves from their acceleration couches. Arren, Isabu, and Cua were haggard after
hours under twice their normal gravity. They would not be
sluggards, though. Medication kept them at full power and
alertness; they had joined in conference while they fared;
whatever the physiological price was, they'd pay it after
returning home. Rinndalir showed no sign of ordeal.
Unlike his followers, who wore plain coveralls, he was in
black and silver. More glamorous than anybody had a
right to be, damn him.

"Is all well?" he asked low-voiced. "Are the particulars
clear in every mind?" He smiled. "Such as they are." The
smile found Kyra. "For you, yes, beyond doubt. Well do I
know." She felt the heat in her face and inwardly swore at
herself. Yet how he raised heart and hope.

Arren and Isabu fetched their large cases full of instruments and equipment. Grasping the handles, they bounded behind their chief to the portside personnel lock. Cua trailed them by a few meters. She was the reserve pilot, among the few Lunarians with deep-space training, not a consorte of Fireball but a vassal of Rinndalir.

Kyra kept aside. When the valves opened, she could hear what went on after the men left the vessel, yet not see it nor be seen. Cua, who stayed inboard but in view, murmured to her: "Six Security Police—a full squad, I believe—as well as the usual technicians. Indeed they are wary of us."

Words reached her: "—orders, sir. No disrespect or anything. Policy. As long as the danger lasts, all new visitors must be attended or, uh, accounted for at all times. It's for your own protection."

Rinndalir, sardonic: "Are we so precious as to require guarding by twice our number? I am honored."

"Bueno, sir, you did come unexpectedly, on a mission the L-5 governors hadn't heard a thing about."

"I will be glad to explain the reasons for that, if I may have a telephone connection or if their representative cares to meet us in low-weight. Basically, this is a rapid and tentative survey. If we find nothing obviously wrong with the site we are thinking of, the Selenarchy will make a formal proposal and the possibility can be investigated in detail. Why do you not simply escort us there at once?" Laugh. "You will be the sooner rid of us."

"Uh, the message said five of you—"

"Our pilot has no cause to accompany us. She is merely a Fireball employee. In view of the present emergency, Captain Pedraza, you will understand why we deem it prudent to leave one of our own with her, to help keep our vessel secure."

The Sepo officer made confused protestations. Rinndalir overbore them, or rather bore them away on a slickly rushing tide of words. Kyra wished she could watch. Did anybody else in the galaxy combine arrogance and blarney like him? Eventually footsteps receded.

Cua and Kyra exchanged a look. "I will scout," the

Lunarian said low. "Listen closely." She passed through the lock. Even in her baggy garment, she didn't seem to move with low-*g* strides so much as to flow. MacCannon, but she was beautiful! Lunarians generally were, of course. As long as chromosomes were being remodeled— What attracted Rinndalir to Kyra, anyway? Not that he pretended love, which would have insulted her intelligence, but his gallantries were like verse, and as for the active part of that nightwatch, Nero Valencia had gone pallid. No, no, no, Kyra had her emotions under control, she wasn't going to let a few hours in Elf Hill haunt her, but she couldn't help wondering—

Listen, blinkie, *listen!*

Voices anew, amidst background thumps and rumbles. Damn. Still, Kyra hadn't really counted on Cua reporting nobody on watch. Either Pedraza had called for a guard before he accompanied Rinndalir's group off, or he'd detached a man from his command.

The next play was Cua's: "Greeting. May I look about somewhat? Never before have I been here," which was a purring lie.

The male answer was well-nigh inevitable. "Oh, certainly, if you stay close by. It is an amazing place, isn't it?"

"You have explored it in your free time? Tell me, pray, what are yon men doing?"

"I don't know, I'm no spacer. Sorry."

"It appears interesting. . . ."

The Sepo was probably no fool. He wouldn't wander off with the newcomer or anything like that. However, she showed no menace, gave no sign of intending to dash off or otherwise make trouble. His group must have been instructed to handle the Lunarians gingerly. His duty was to keep an eye on their ship and on this bewitching woman. (Bewitching in truth. Her race had that reputation. Folklore on Earth sometimes spoke of pheromones. Anthropologists ridiculed it, but—)

Kyra slipped into the lock chamber and risked a peek downward around the outer valve. The young uniformed man had his whole attention on Cua. A pair of technicians nearby were much aware of her too. Elsewhere, humans and machines worked as individuals or in small bands, around the vast curve and down the cavernous length of the harbor. Cua took the man's arm, lightly, lightly, and pointed into the distance. He obeyed the impulse given him. For a minute or two, *Inia*'s exit would be outside his field of view.

Kyra sprang, not on the ramp but directly, pushing with the full strength of her legs. Twisting around as she fell, she landed on her feet and bounded off, a ten-meter leap. She saw a technie whose gaze trailed her and laid finger to lips. Rinndalir had obtained a Fireball pilot's uniform for her. This hombre was Fireball too. He nodded and got very busy. She continued at a leisurely mini-*g* pace, about fifteen klicks an hour.

Had others noticed? Might somebody raise an alarm? When the Sepo turned around again would he prove more observant than most people? Between the shoulderblades, Kyra ached with tension. If her gamble failed— Contingency plans called for overt action, but Rinndalir had been vague about its nature. Would he improvise? Or didn't he want her to know, because she would object?

She pushed the questions away. This wasn't a bad bet. She passed around a cargo walloper. Its bulk screened view of her, if she plotted her course properly down the tunnel. The ache began to lessen. She wiped a hand across her face. Best not be seen sweating. Best be only another consorte, bound on some unimportant errand. Blend into the L-5 crowds, as no Lunarian could. The Sepo comandante might well have been briefed on the entire situation, including her part in it, but he wouldn't have put her image on the screens with a "Wanted" notice.

At the nearest fahrweg she commenced her trek to the outer levels. She broke it at a minor industrial section she knew, searched out a public phone, and called Tamura's office.

The live operator who answered was a surprise, and was surprised in her turn at Kyra's request. "I'm sorry, Mister Tamura isn't in," she said unsteadily, in accented English. "He is . . . detained. I thought everyone had heard."

A fist clamped on Kyra. Somehow she replied, "No, I had not. I've been outside on a long job." Quickly, before the operator would have time to think whether there had been any such task of late: "Could I speak to the señorita, his daughter?"

The operator's eyes probed across the transmission line. Kyra shifted position a little, to make sure the pickup got her insignia. The operator sat motionless a few seconds, distinct seconds. Balancing troth against suspicion and fear? Then: "Miss Tamura is on leave of absence. She may be at home."

"Gracias." Kyra switched off and spent a minute rallying her own wits. She decided to go to the apartment in person. Its communications were surely monitored. (Likewise the office's, but with hundreds of calls in and out every day, plus computer interactions, hers had a fairly large chance of not being flagged or, at least, not reaching a human evaluator's attention for hours.) Probably, though, the place wasn't under physical surveillance. The Sepo had limited numbers in a huge, diverse, sullenly hostile community. They'd focus on potential troublemakers. Eiko Tamura was about as shy and inoffensive a soul as you'd ever come upon.

Unless you got to know her well. Kyra proceeded down weight and pressure levels, along multifarious passages, blindly across parks and gardens and graceful Delt River Bridge. In the throngs were bound to be several dear friends of hers. She hoped desperately she wouldn't encounter any.

Like many doors, the Tamuras' was marked by an emblem as well as a number. Eiko had painted this. Kyra stood for a moment before the familiar lily while memories tumbled over her. What if nobody was inside? How long could she halfway safely hang around waiting? She touched the plate and confronted the scanner.

The door opened. She stumbled through. Eiko was there, small in kimono and obi. They embraced. "Hush," Kyra whispered into the ear below her, "don't say a word. I'm on the dodge." Sensing no one else, the door closed.

Faintly fragrant, loosely gathered hair brushed Kyra's lips as Eiko nodded. They disengaged. Eiko's countenance was drawn. Tears trembled on her eyelashes. She took Kyra by the hand and led her into a well-remembered room at the rear.

Paper, marked with sketches or scribbled words, littered a desk on which Chujo slept beside the computer. The cat, who was apt to be out most times prowling the byways, woke, got to his feet, and stared. Kyra scratched him on the neck, mostly a reflex on her part till he rubbed his head against her palm and bestowed a wisp of comfort. Eiko sat down at the computer. It had no exterior connection; some of what she entered was for no one else to know. *Welcome, welcome,* she keyed into the screen. *I have been so afraid for you.*

She rose. Kyra took the chair, thinking how ridiculous it would be if they bounced back and forth like a couple of ping-pong balls. *No time to spare,* she tapped. *The Sepo may have a sonic planted on you, but I'd guess that's all. I gather they've jailed your father. Is he otherwise all right?* She glanced at Eiko, who nodded, and smiled to say, "Good" while she continued: *I'm here with a Lunarian party to fetch Guthrie. Do you have him?* The nod was violent. *Wonderful! We'll need to smuggle him out. Can do?*

Eiko signed her to yield the chair, took it, and wrote: *Perhaps. Follow me.*

Kyra nudged her aside. *Bring something to carry him in.* She hadn't, because if she'd been stopped at the ship an empty bag would have suggested too much. Besides, her gang had no idea what the circumstances were. Better to act on the spot.

Did Eiko just barely frown? *That is already at the hiding place.*

Oh, hell, I'm sorry, Kyra wanted to say. Idiotic of me not to realize you'd think ahead.

Eiko gestured her to wait, and left. Kyra played with Chujo. Stroking him, his sensuous response, raised other memories. Repeat, she'd learned her lesson, she was not about to let a fling scramble her judgment. But lechery offered a refuge from doubts and dreads. Not that Rinndalir was any coldly murderous Valencia. . . .

Eiko returned in coverall and boots. Kyra bade Chujo farewell and the women departed.

Soon Kyra felt puzzled. Where were they bound? Eiko took the nearest fahrweg inward as far as it went, which was to Marginal Village—cheap rentals for those who could well tolerate weight that low or were willing to take the consequences, and who did not have growing children nor intend to. An obese man hailed her in the passage. Kyra recalled the monster in Quark Fair and set her teeth. But this was simply a friend. Eiko gave him a slurred reply and hurried on. The next fahrweg took them lengthwise to a cluster of nanotanks, where they boarded a radial that debouched at an aerodynamic testing chamber, deserted now when much activity was suspended.

Of course, Kyra concluded. Eiko was taking the least populated route, however zigzag, to wherever she was bound. Thus they avoided more than a single meeting, and it casual.

They left the system at a stop in Trevorrow Preserve on the half-g level and walked along a path that wound among grassy meadows and hillocks, upward to meet a sky that was blue fluorescence and illusory clouds. Here and there a solitary spruce, maple, elm rustled in a breeze that bore earth odors, Earth, memories, needs a billion years old? . . . The area lay deserted. "Now we can talk," Eiko said. "Now I can truly bid you welcome, Kyra."

They stopped to doubly clasp hands and smile through vision that blurred a little. But time scissored behind them. Kyra let go and strode onward. "You did retrieve him," she said. Her pulse thuttered. "How? What's happened?"

When the spare account was finished: "Oh, splendid, superb, querida. What nullhead ever claimed poets are no use for anything but poetry? Aeschylus was a soldier, Omar was a scientist, Jeffers was a stonemason—"

"You are a pilot," Eiko said.

Kyra laughed. "Yes, and a competent cook, a ferocious

poker player, and a pretty good lay. But a poet? No. Doggerel." She sobered. The mirth had been half hysterical, she recognized. "Bueno, as for my end of the story—" She outlined it in a few words, omitting the personal details. "Once I have Guthrie, I could go straight back to the ship, but that looks mucho risky."

"It would be," Eiko agreed in her temperate fashion. "I have told you how they are working their way through the *kuni*—the colony, in search of him. The sentry might not stop you from embarking, but he would call his superiors and they would forbid that you leave until they had checked everything."

Kyra nodded. "Right. Instead, I'll pass Guthrie on to the Lunarians, and stay behind when they go."

"And then?"

Kyra shrugged. "Then Rinndalir programs the operation."

Trumpets: He can, he can!

Undertone: What if he couldn't? For him, no great loss. The North Americans would scarcely do more than deport him and his following; if he insisted, Kyra might as well accompany them. But Guthrie— The Selenarchs would consider it an interesting game, to spar with an anti-Guthrie who believed he had cinched his power tight.

Heed the trumpets. What else cried hope?

Eiko walked silent a distance before she said, "If Guthrie-san is willing, let it happen."

Kyra heard the trouble. "You don't like the prospect?"

Eiko shook her head. "I feel too uncertain about what will come of this. If only we could free him by some other means." She sighed. "But we have no choice, do we?"

Kyra swallowed a retort. Why should the Lunarians give themselves this effort if they didn't want Guthrie back at the helm of Fireball? Granted, they saw that as being best for them; but it was an enlightened self-interest.

Then why should Kyra feel irritated with dear Eiko? Because her own misgivings had been stirred? It hurt that she could think of nothing more to say.

In silence they reached the Tree. "I will get him," Eiko

said within its gloaming. "You keep watch at the bottom rest stage."

Kyra had looked forward to the climb, working off tension, finding again for a moment the peace that dwelt on the stupendous, whispery heights. Eiko was right, though. "Muy bien."

Standing alone on the platform after her companion vanished upward, in green light and shade, in the warmth and sweet odors that the ruddy roughness breathed out, Kyra let her mind freefall. Why did this colossus exist? Scientific research and development, yes. Simply the bio-mechanisms of fluid transport through such a gradient were a special field of study. But surely the same things could have been learned in easier ways, without hauling so much mass here that L-5 needed modifications to preserve dynamic stability. (Moon dust, comet ice, can these bones live?) Parks and gardens and the great preserve had their rationales, environmental benefit, recreation, esthetics; cycles of light and dark, heat and cold, summer and winter kept steady the rhythms of life; tricks of geometry, electronics, randomization gave richness, surprise, a sense of this world being more than walls; yes, yes. But what was the need for a living thing inhumanly huge, of strength to endure inhumanly long?

She harked back to stones whirling frosty amidst stars, never betrodden before she found them; sunrise rousing pinnacles out of shadow from a horizon-long chasm on Mars; storms in Jupiter, seen from a shelter on a glacial moon around which radiation seethed, lovely swirl-patterns that could swallow all Earth; jewelwork Saturn; Gothic needles piercing an ocherous Titanian sky— How much of yonder adventure and majesty had she really won to by herself? Always it was the machines, suit or ship or outpost fortress, sensor and computer and effector, that nurtured and enabled. How much machine had she become, who had never yet felt life quicken beneath her heart nor even wanted to?

Always what she found was barren. Dim fossils in Martian rocks. Tales told across light-years by the robot probes and tales brought home by download Guthrie—no, anti-Guthrie; no, that difference was meaningless—tales of one other living world, oceanic life, which barely clung to the shores while doomsday closed in. Two more worlds that might evolve further, millions of years hence, or might not. Everywhere else, as far as the seeking had reached, inanimate matter; and beyond that, silence, except for the muttering of the stars.

Did the Tree have its roots in despair?

A movement within the green jarred Kyra free of her thoughts. Eiko had returned.

She stepped out onto the stage and, with a half smile, nodded at the daypack she now carried. Kyra's hand shook as she undid the flap. Eyestalks glided up. "Hi, there," grated the basso. "Grand show, lassie."

"Jefe, oh, jefe," she sobbed.

His blunt practicality struck the turmoil out of her. With it went the somberness—irrational, irrelevant. "Eiko's told me a bit. You're here with Rinndalir and his merry men. What next?"

"I, I turn you over to them and . . . they take you to Luna."

"How do you propose to do this? I can't see the Sepo letting him flit off carrying me in his hot little. They may not know exactly what their dragnet is after, but they'll stall him while they check with their boss, and he'll call Quito, and—my alter ego will handle any diplomatic awkwardness later. I would."

"Of course." Kyra explained her intention. "I hope we can bring it off."

"If not, well, too bad." The voice grew concerned. "But seems like you'll be left behind."

"I don't know how I could sneak back aboard unnoticed and, if they learn I've been loose, or if they think I'm a passenger the Lunarians are taking along—"

"They'll want more information. Yeah. How'll you manage?"

"I know my way around this hulk."

"I can help," Eiko said calmly. "She had best not stay at

my home for any length of time, but several obscure families would give her shelter and say nothing about it."

"God damn that I can't hug you both," Guthrie growled. "Once this mess is untangled, anything Fireball has is yours."

"No need, sir," Eiko answered. "Troth."

Which she had never given, Kyra recalled. But her father had.

"We'd better move," the pilot said.

Eiko nodded, slipped off the pack, looked into the lenses and murmured, *"Un yoi.* Good luck." A wistful smile. "When reality cuts through, poets can no more find words than anybody else." She closed the pack and gave it to Kyra, who donned it. They descended.

"I will go and arrange a refuge for you," Eiko said. "Come to my home at—1700? I will be back by then, or earlier. Can you stay free meanwhile?"

Kyra grinned. "I'm well-versed in skulking." Actually, she'd saunter around as if she had ordinary business, through sections where embarrassing encounters were unlikely. Excitement hammered in her, almost joyously. "Hasta la vista." She went out the torii gate to meadows and a simulation of sky.

She had herself proposed and described to Rinndalir the area to which the Lunarians demanded to be taken. It was approximately at the one-sixth-*g* level, agricultural, mostly for giant corn and soybean plants. Machines tended it, but visitors and passersby were not so rare that she would attract any special attention. Rinndalir was to declare that he had a tentative idea of putting a business he owned into partnership here, to raise recently developed pharmaceutical crops. It might be preferable to making new fields in the Moon. Before broaching the scheme to the L-5 directors, he wanted to inspect the site, test whether the basic conditions were suitable, judge whether Lunarian personnel would agree to stay in such an environment. The abrupt beginning fitted the common Earthside image of his race. He had assured her he could carry it off.

Emerging from a corridor onto open deck, she saw him,

his men, their escort, and half a dozen curious onlookers apart from them, across ten meters of duramoss. The stalks beyond were like a stockade wall, intensely green, immensely high, darkening and dwarfing everything human. But this was no halidom of the Tree. Air hung tropical, rank with fertilizer smells. Heaven was a ceiling studded with grow lamps. Beneath their dull glare a cultivator chugged along the turf, summoned to some job by an overseer that resembled a man-sized insect.

Go. Kyra set her poker face and walked forth. Rinndalir observed her first. He stood tall above Arren and Isabu, who hunkered over the instruments they had taken from their cases. His own features remained inexpressive, but platinum hair brushed marble cheeks as he made the least of nods. A Sepo noticed her, unthinkingly touched the butt of his stun pistol, mopped his wet brow and glowered covertly at the Selenarch. What had seemed like challenging, maybe dangerous duty had turned into an uncomfortable bore.

Kyra joined the spectators. Had they chanced individually by or had they tagged after this unique company? It didn't matter, as long as none of them knew her. Arren glanced up. A meter wavered slightly in his grasp. He busied himself again. Isabu kept stolid.

After a few more minutes, Rinndalir spoke to them, then to the squad leader. Kyra couldn't hear what he said, but knew: words to the effect of "I think we have done as much as we can. We shall go home now. . . . Nay, call your chief if you wish, but I will decline any offer of hospitality."

Kyra manufactured a yawn and strolled back the way she had come. Let it be obvious that she had decided not to waste time on them. At one-sixth-*g* Guthrie weighed little, but how she felt the mass of him!

The passage was bare, drably painted. Machines didn't care. Along it was the door to a lavabo. Kyra went in. As was customary in L-5, it was unisex. And it was empty. She took a toilet stall and waited. A ventilator whirred unnecessarily loudly.

A tap sounded. Her blood shouted reply. She opened. Arren came in. For a moment her feeling was disappointment. If only Rinndalir— But of course not. He who excused himself en route to the ship needed to be carrying an instrument case. Evidently no Sepo accompanied him. Had that happened, Arren would have outstayed the man; trust Rinndalir to make plain he would not tolerate the insult of outright spying. As was, the Lunarian had headed for the stall that read "Occupied."

His eyes glinted. "Have you him?" he breathed.

Kyra nodded. The pack already rested on a shelf. Quickly, they made the exchange, Arren's instruments and tools into it, Guthrie into the case. It was fairly well screened against electronics—wouldn't stand a close check, but in that event the crapshoot was over anyway. Most of the Sepo were seeking their quarry in chambers and passages distressingly numerous. They couldn't think of everything. Rinndalir's tongue should keep these few and the officer to whom they reported from thinking of this.

Just before the lid closed on him, Guthrie waved an eyestalk at her. She guessed his thought. "Yeah, I gained my freedom in a john. It figures." She began to laugh. Arren cast her an inquisitive glance but didn't linger. Kyra must remain for some minutes, till the others were well away. She stood alone and laughed on.

33

INIA BOOSTED FROM L-5 at one Lunar gravity. Felinely relaxed, Rinndalir took Guthrie out of the case and set him on an acceleration couch. His lenses searched about, up to the pilot limned against a simulacrum of stars in her seat at the control board, down the ladder and hoist to this passenger section, and around the three men who stood on its deck, towering above him. The gaze came to rest on

Rinndalir. "Good day, my lord," he greeted slowly. "I owe you a lot of thanks."

The other inclined his head with a smile in which lips stayed closed until he replied, "You are most welcome, my lord. It is an honor to be of your service." His followers kept back, impassive. The pilot swiveled about to look down. She had had virtually nothing to do but give the ship instructions as to destination and vectors.

Perhaps Guthrie would have smiled too, were he able. "You mean 'at' my service, don't you? I never heard as how you were 'of' anybody's but your own."

"My error," said Rinndalir. "Your language is not ours." Unspoken between them: Nor are your thoughts.

Air blew softly out of the recyclers and back again. Weight and a well-nigh subliminal pulsation were the only signs of waxing speed.

"Aren't you going kind of slow?" Guthrie asked after a moment. "This is comfortable for you, sure, but you could stand to push harder."

Rinndalir shrugged. "What haste, now that we are free?"

Did Guthrie wish for a fist wherewith to hit the couch frame? "Damn it, you're a bright boy. So you understand the enemy isn't moronic. His head honcho at L-5 will report your visit, if he hasn't already, and my other self may very well guess what was behind it."

Rinndalir nodded. "We assumed that risk, my party and I, deeming it not excessive. When we were planning, Kyra Davis reminded me that anti-Guthrie has not had your long years of direct experience in dealing with my kind. Such knowledge as he possesses of how our society evolved during his absence and oblivion has been downloaded into him, together with a huge quantity of other information. It must be an abstraction to him, nothing acutely felt. Postulate what is by no means certain, that immediately upon our arrival at Lagrange-Five, the Security Police chief notified his superiors on Earth and requested orders. What could they do but tell him to follow the course he in fact did, pending consultation with anti-Guthrie? They would not necessarily be able to reach him on short notice, and he would not necessarily take alarm."

"Just the same, you were wildcatting."

Rinndalir's patience sounded forced, as he no doubt meant it to. "Would you have had us do nothing? Then eventually, inevitably, they would have found you; and meanwhile you would be nullified, they free to strengthen their position. Did our venture fail, there would be other expedients to try; but this was the quickest and most promising."

"Yeah, it was a cute trick, I gather," Guthrie conceded. "I want to hear all about it. Later." His voice tightened. "Right now we ain't out of the woods. The sooner we reach the Moon and safety, the more beers I'll stand you in the old Launch Pad."

Rinndalir raised his brows. "What peril remains?"

"A torchcraft can get from Earth to us inside four hours. Even at twice this boost, you won't reach home that soon."

Rinndalir's tone was not openly sarcastic. "I have not heard that any spaceships are armed. Such a retrofit would be a considerable engineering project, and unacceptable to the Peace Authority."

"Uh-huh. Couldn't well be done in secret, especially in the short time they've had." Guthrie harshened his words. "Listen, though. I play rough and reckless when I've got to. My copy does the same, I guarantee. Once he's heard about you dropping in, he may not be as ready to ignore it as you think. Enrique Sayre may well not be—I know a fair amount about that yadswiver—and he could persuade anti-me. They may be organizing a counterstrike this minute. They may already have."

"The better if they overreach themselves, no? We want them destroyed."

Guthrie regarded Rinndalir for some seconds before he answered, *"We* do? I'll settle for some version of the status quo ante. Why should you want more?"

Rinndalir met the stare, smiled as he had earlier, and asked, "Why should you not? Here we have an interesting philosophical question."

"To hell with that." Guthrie brooded a while longer.

"Okay, as you like. I haven't got much choice, do I, really? But let's broadcast the truth *now*. Call up Luna, record a statement with them, and tell them to give it to the world news media. That'll draw the enemy's fangs if anything will."

Rinndalir shook his head. Light rippled in the argent hair. "My judgment is otherwise," he said quietly.

Guthrie arched his eyestalks. "Huh? Publicity— Sure, they'll deny everything, but only to buy time while they scramble for cover. There'll be no more point in attacking us in space, supposing they intend that. In fact, they'll know it'd drive the last nail into their coffin."

"I fear matters are not quite so simple," Rinndalir replied. "While you lay hidden in the colony, I was gathering intelligence. We must prepare the announcement most carefully and release it at a psychodynamically calculated moment. Else it could well precipitate chaos, which the enemy has been readying himself to cope with and gain advantage by. If nothing else, a great many lives would be lost."

The download lay mute for a span. The ship hummed onward. Finally: "I never had the impression that innocent bystanders were of much concern to you, señor." After a bit longer: "I think you decided this in advance."

"Be that as it may, it is my decision."

"Let me talk you out of it."

Rinndalir laughed, far down in his throat. "You are free to try. We have hours to spend. Yet I can imagine discourse more amusing and enlightening to while them away."

"What is your game, actually?"

"The Selenarchy will not hold you for ransom, if thus you fear."

"Hm'f. I might prefer shelling out a couple million ucus to whatever you have in mind."

Rinndalir took a characteristic Lunarian pose, somehow as though he lounged back while standing. "Clear to see, we desire an influence on the course of near-future events, and feel we have earned it. Is this unreasonable? You have just chided me for what you considered heedlessness, despite its having succeeded. Now you want me to broadcast immediately, without regard for consequences. I pray you of your kindness, be more consistent."

Guthrie formed a sigh. "We may as well amuse and enlighten, I guess. Tell me about this operation you've pulled off. Tamura and Davis hadn't time for but a few hasty words."

"Gladly. For your share, will you relate how you fared since you parted from Pilot Davis? It seems me belike the stuff of epic."

"It didn't at the time, but— All right, you bastard, go ahead. I suppose you didn't have trouble figuring out my message, but what'd you guess it might mean? What intimations had you already gotten?"

Rinndalir's crew settled themselves to listen, with the stoic tenacity that was the other side of waywardness. He sat down on his haunches to bring his eyes level with Guthrie's lenses, a courtesy that cost him small effort, and began: "You are aware that my kind feel they are remote from Earth in spirit far more than distance. Nonetheless our interests continue entangled with it, and we naturally seek to stay abreast of its affairs as well as may be across the gap."

After he had talked for a spell, Guthrie said, the grin in his voice that could not form on a face, "Congratulations on a masterly job of telling me what I've known for decades and otherwise saying nothing whatsoever."

"I did but seek to lay background," replied Rinndalir, unoffended. "Since you prefer, I shall proceed directly to my reception of your message."

He said little about Kyra's stay with him except that she had contributed much to the plan of campaign. At the end he proposed a break for tea. "Would we had refreshment to offer you, Sr. Guthrie. Perhaps some music? I have heard that you enjoy the type named jazz, from the early twentieth century, and I have sought out antique recordings. . . . No? . . . Let us, then, consider alternatives. Have you perchance screened the recent *Les Sylphides* by the Tychopolis Ballet? An idiosyncratic interpretation, although—" His crew set out delicacies. In due course he asked for Guthrie's story.

"I'm not as good as you at noises that sound like they ought to mean something," the download grumbled.

"Nor, perhaps, as tactful," Rinndalir suggested jocosely.

"Yeah. Juliana used to claim that for me 'tact' was a four-letter word. Well, I've got less to pass on. Eiko Tamura plucked me out of space—quite a gal, her—and kept me stashed in that monster sequoia they've got—"

Talk veered to and fro, like a sailboat tacking against capricious winds. Rinndalir kept throwing questions and comments at Guthrie. He sought backward in time: the origins of Fireball's conflict with the Avantists, why Fireball's cacique would personally slip into North America (a very Lunarian trick, he laughed), what had happened there and what it meant. . . . He sought forward, to those daycycles in hiding and the real reasons why Eiko Tamura had limited her commitment. "Conflicting loyalties, nay? By digital analysis, her strategy was suboptimal. One might call it deplorable. Yet plainly her intelligence is well above the median. If one takes all factors into account, including the essentially chaotic character of organic life, it may appear that her intuition was sound."

"You're trying to understand human beings from the outside," Guthrie remarked.

"True, to a certain extent. Nevertheless, may it not be that I have somewhat more feel for the irrational at the nucleus of things than you and your entire careful civilization?"

Cua warned everybody to secure themselves.

The ship made turnover and commenced deceleration, backing down on Luna. In the viewscreen it stood ragged-edged, blotched with Nearside's gray-blue maria. Earth was another, larger and brighter half-disc opposite it, gloriously white and azure. Unless you knew just where to look, L-5 was lost among the stars.

* * *

Rinndalir stroked his chin. "Someday I must explore that tree for myself," he mused. "I have done so in a vivifer, but that is not enough. Did you feel the mystery of it while you swayed in its windy boughs?"

"No, but I never cared for mystiques. And I haven't got much left to feel with, you know."

Rinndalir gave Guthrie a steady look. Not hitherto had he spoken this gently. "Yet you have not become altogether a machine, have you?"

Again Cua interrupted from above. She used Lunarian, but had no need for English. A chime and flashing light told of the incoming call. "—spacecraft *Inia*, DR327, respond."

Breath hissed between Arren's teeth. Isabu's fingers crooked like claws. Both stared at Guthrie. That was his voice.

"School's out," he said. "I told you and I told you."

"We could not have reached port before being intercepted, whatever we did," Rinndalir answered coolly. "I confess to surprise at the identity of our pursuer."

"I don't, when I think about it."

"Receive, pilot." Rinndalir sat down on a couch, lowered the communications panel there, and activated it. *"Inia* responding," he said. "Declare yourself."

"Spacecraft *Muramasa*, TK96," came out of the speaker.

"Katana class," Guthrie muttered. "Torch."

"You're in unauthorized and illegal possession of a vessel belonging to Fireball Enterprises," said his voice. "Return to L-5 at once."

"I fear you are mistaken," Rinndalir answered. *"Inia* is under requisition by the sovereign government of Luna. If you would maintain differently, the proper venue is an admiralty court of the World Federation."

"I have him on radar," Cua announced. She relayed the computer display to the passenger section. Rinndalir moved Guthrie to where he also could see.

"Distance about twenty thousand klicks, decelerating at one *g*, rendezvous with matched velocities in about half an hour," Guthrie read off for the men. Cua could interpret it herself. "Probably boosted from Earth at that rate. Radar there might already have acquired us, though data from L-5 would let him figure his course pretty well."

Concurrently his other voice said: *"Inia* pilot, listen. This is Anson Guthrie in person, speaking. Your jefe. I command you by your troth, take that ship back to L-5. Otherwise Fireball's in no end of trouble."

Yes, the Sepo in the colony had told their masters what they were told. Rinndalir grinned. "That will not happen, my lord," he said.

"It had better happen," replied the voice.

"If not, may I ask what you propose to do?"

"You're vulnerable to us."

"Violence? Unprecedented. Neither the Federation nor Fireball would consider it justified, to say nothing of Luna."

"Hijacking in space is unprecedented too."

"I repeat my denial that that is the case."

"I'll take care of any consequences afterward." The voice paused before going on in less threatening wise: "We don't want to harm you. Cooperate, let us board you, and you and your crew get a free ride home from L-5. We're after nothing but some stolen property we've reason to believe you're conveying. Maybe that's without your knowledge, señor. If I turn out to be wrong about it, besides releasing you I'll give you a formal apology and stand ready to talk compensation."

"Don't let him stall you while he closes in," Guthrie snapped from the couch.

"What do I hear?" roared his voice.

"What you wish to hear, perhaps," Rinndalir answered. "Not necessarily what is."

"Listen," said the voice fast. "You've had your reasons for doing what you did how you did. If keeping the operation quiet weren't to your benefit, you'd already have splashed the news across the Solar System. Well, I can make you an offer myself. You follow me? I'm not mad at you. We could do some big things together. Think about it."

"I shall," Rinndalir said. "We can discuss matters further when you are nigh. Until then, fare in good cheer."

He signalled to Cua, who switched off. The chime sounded and the light blinked. She damped them.

"That settles it," Guthrie said. "Call Luna, transmit the story and my image, make sure he knows you have. He'll veer off."

"The Security Police are still in Port Bowen," Rinndalir demurred.

"So are your constables, now. Therefore somebody other than Sepo is bound to receive the message. And it'll make the Sepo themselves start wondering about a lot, won't it? Or, if you insist, beam into the independent Lunar communications net. Kyra and I would have, as soon as *Maui Maru* was in orbit, except that of course we didn't know your classified access codes and encryptions. You've got them in a database aboard this boat, or else in your head. Don't squander breath denying it. Call."

Rinndalir stood up, black and silver above the bodiless case. "Is that our single alternative to yielding?" he asked reluctantly.

"Yeah. Unless you want to take him up on his proposition."

"Nay, I think not. Very well—"

"Muramasa has applied a new vector," Cua called. "Powerful—ai-ya!"

Guthrie's eyestalks strained toward the screen before him. He uttered a long obscenity.

Cua looked about. Her nostrils flared; the pale hair made an aureole about her head. Her tone might have been describing any observation. "He has changed direction and is accelerating at high thrust. We will meet in five minutes."

"He foresaw he might have to!" Arren exclaimed. "He plotted a path from Earth and a moment to contact us that would make it possible."

Rinndalir nodded at Guthrie. "My compliments on your vicarious craftiness," he said. "We scarcely have time now to raise Luna and explain, do we? Only to call surrender. Have you a different idea?"

"Yeah. Bet our lives," the download replied. "Which is easy for me to say."

"What do you judge he proposes to do?"

"If we don't give in—no, he won't ram us. That'd wreck him too. He's brought men along to board us, or the ruin of us; you noticed he spoke of 'we,' and they'll be the reason he's kept at one *g* till now. Because he's his own pilot, I'm certain. He's his own ship, hooked into her, interfacing with her computers— God damn, if I just were the same! He can pass close by in such a way that we run into his jets. They'll slash this hull open. Spacesuits won't save you, not from the radiation."

"Have we any recourse?"

The light flashed, the chime rang: *Surrender.*

"You can dodge, maybe," Guthrie said, iron-steady. "You haven't got but a fraction of his boost or delta *v*. He'll be moving almighty fast, though. You can apply a transverse vector and slip aside. He'll need time to brake and come back after us. How much time depends on how much punishment the men with him can or will stand. We may or may not gain enough to send our message."

"Can you accomplish that, Cua?" Rinndalir asked.

The pilot frowned. "Perhaps. I am not myself in linkage with this ship. I cannot keep the enemy in play for more than one or two passes, if that."

Metal clashed in Rinndalir's words: "If you do, the ladyship of Mare Muscoviensis is yours."

"Hai, and the glory!" she yelled. Her hands flew over the console. It was as if starlight frosted her mane.

Guthrie's lenses swiveled from an Arren gone exultant to a smiling Isabu, and on to their lord. "You'll really try this, all of you, when you could strike a bargain instead?" he marveled. "You're even crazier than I thought."

Rinndalir laughed aloud. "Nay, it is you and your foe who are overly logical. Come!" He scooped Guthrie up and got onto the hoist. His men secured themselves to couches.

The Katana sprang into view, swelling to block sight of Luna, lean as a shark. Cua touched a key. Acceleration flung Rinndalir brutally against a rail. Somehow he kept his feet. The torch exhaust blazed in a false-color view-screen. It was gone. Earth shone serene. *Inia* plodded ahead, backing down on the Moon.

Rinndalir found the seat beside Cua, settled into it, harnessed himself, cradled Guthrie on his lap. He gave the pilot an order, she acknowledged, their language rippled and sang. "What was that?" Guthrie demanded.

"To put me through to Luna," Rinndalir said mildly. "What else?"

"Where, and who?"

"Waste no time," Cua clipped. "I have contact."

"I should've learned your damn lingo when it was invented," Guthrie grumbled.

The comscreen came alive with the head of another Lunarian. He made a gesture of respect. Rinndalir addressed him briefly, and then: "Say what you wish, Sr. Guthrie. The pickup has you in its field."

The download began to speak, short barking sentences. The Lunarian at the far end showed an instant's amazement, then listened hard. From time to time Rinndalir made an English addition to the story. Cua studied her readouts.

"He comes back," she said. No droplet of sweat glimmered on her brow.

"He'll aim to fool you," Guthrie predicted. "Don't try that sideslip again. I think the max thrust you can conn, straight, will surprise him." He continued his narration.

Pressure slammed bodies backward, downward. Blood burst from the nostrils of Rinndalir and Cua, twice scarlet against those marmoreal skins. Aft, a man groaned. But the torch flamed in the viewer, only in the viewer. And then *Muramasa* had slashed by. Guthrie spoke on. Weight dropped to Lunar.

Eyestalks turned upward and around to Rinndalir's dripping face. "It's done," Guthrie rasped. "Beam to yon ship." Cua did, her hands shaking.

"*Inia* to *Muramasa*," Guthrie chanted. "Respond."

The screen stayed blank, but his voice snarled, "*Muramasa* to *Inia*. You did it, huh?"

"Yep. They have the story on Luna, complete with video

of me and these nice folks here. You can still wipe us out if you feel like it, but Lunar radars are locking on, opticals are tuning up, and all in all, it wouldn't sit well with people."

A laugh rattled. "No, I reckon not. Naturally, we'll deny everything."

"Deny away, if it amuses you."

"It doesn't. It just helps a bit. We aren't about to fold our hands, you know."

"You could."

"We could not. I could not. Screw amnesty."

"They really got to you, didn't they? Wouldn't you like a reprogramming job? Be your own man again."

"Man? Hah."

Stillness fell, save for the murmur of ships and the hoarse breathing of abused bodies.

"Well," said Guthrie aboard *Inia,* "no doubt we can negotiate some kind of peace with you and your friends."

"If *your* friends allow," said Guthrie aboard *Muramasa.* "From what I've heard about them, look out."

"Hasta la vista."

"Toujours gai." So had Juliana often bidden him goodbye. The transmission bulb went dark.

Guthrie looked at Rinndalir. "You okay?" he asked.

"I will survive," the Selenarch answered, wryly, not quite steadily. "Well that I had the foresight to pack good wine along."

"Sure, go ahead, get drunk, and lift one for me." Guthrie's jesting was mechanical, his mind elsewhere. "We'll come down in the middle of one all-time luau, won't we?"

Rinndalir straightened in the seat. From behind red smears, his gaze probed into the lenses. "Not yet shall it be thus," he said.

Guthrie lifted. "Huh? You mean your people won't pass the story on?"

Rinndalir lifted a hand. "Have no fears. I could not suppress it did I choose. The odds are even or better that the message was acquired by more than that one station.

In any case, the activity that will ensue, on our part and on the enemy's, will be largely unconcealable. Rumors will breed and fly free.

"Nay, I simply intend to proceed as I told you, circumspectly. Before this vessel is returned to Port Bowen, she will set down on a Lunar spacefield. You will be brought thence to a safe place. There we will plan and issue your manifesto to the Solar System."

34

HER SAVAGE ACCELERATIONS done with, *Muramasa* started for L-5 at half a gravity. Felix Holden released himself from his couch, clambered painfully erect, and limped about checking on the welfare of his five men. Space-trained and in peak physical condition, they had not suffered too badly. Those who had lost consciousness stirred back awake, searched for injuries, and mumbled, "Yes, I'm fit, sir." They were somewhat dazed, as much by what had happened—bewildering to them—as by what they had undergone.

Holden scorned to take the hoist up to the pilot console when he weighed forty kilos. Climbing the ladder, he sometimes caught his breath and bit his lip. He eased down into the control chair. A semicircular viewscreen reproduced for him stars enhanced, Earth resplendent, Luna harshly outlined, against the dark.

He did not see the pilot. New Guthrie laired beneath these switches and meters, which he made purposeless, connected directly to sensors, effectors, and computers, the heart and forebrain of the system. With its instruments he also looked inward, felt the forces, tasted the chemistry of air, snuffed the faint lightning-whiff of ions. "You okay?" asked his voice.

Holden made a stiff nod. "We came through it, sir," he reported.

"Sorry to've subjected you to that beating. I kept the boosts to what I figured wouldn't do you any permanent damage, but—I'm sorrier it went for nothing."

"You are definitely letting them go free?"

"Not much choice. They got the story out. I caught enough of their transmission."

Holden sighed. "And so, of course, if you did kill them, matters would become worse yet for us."

"I'm not quite sure of that," Guthrie growled. "Hell knows what Rinndalir will make of the situation. I wish I'd met him personally over the years. Maybe I'd have a little insight into him." A rasping chuckle. "I suspect my other self, who does have direct experience, isn't unrelievedly happy. But we'll see. Obviously I couldn't carry out what everybody would call a wanton massacre."

"What do you intend, sir?"

"Play by ear, roll with the punches, bet according to how the cards are dealt. Juliana always complained about my jumbled metaphors." Humor died. "Are you game, colonel?"

Holden raised his head. "I'm prepared to do my duty, sir. Likewise my men."

"But what you see as your duty will depend on what develops, eh?"

The ship could destroy the humans merely by opening the airlocks. "Yes, sir. I hope you feel the same way."

"M-m, my relationship to your government is kind of different. However—Listen. What I figure to do is refuel at L-5 and return to space, to keep watch against contingencies. I'll need your help for that. And afterward, I think—I've gotten to know you a bit—I think you'll be the best man to have in charge of the Sepo garrison there."

Astonished, Holden asked, "What can we do but evacuate it?"

"Toss away a bargaining chip like that, in exchange for a goose egg? You've got to be kidding."

Holden looked at Earth. He had a family. Guthrie waited.

"My command and I will do what our superiors order, sir," Holden said.

"Good enough. I'll call them. Sit back and relax. You've earned it, all of you."

"Sir," Holden said low, to the gentleness he had just heard, "I see why your people always followed you."

"Followed *me*? . . . Okay, take it easy, let me work."

A beam flashed invisible. A tiny satellite, one of scores circling Earth, detected it and shot back an identification signal. The beam tightened, to track that single relay until time for the next to take over. Its enciphered content passed to a station on the ground and thence to Futuro. Night lay over the North American capital, but Enrique Sayre kept vigil in his office.

His image and words did not appear to Holden. Guthrie received them as input which he interpreted as face and speech. It would be wrong to say that a computer prepared this for him. Certain centers in the living brain process data that nerves bring in from the eye and the ear; but it is the human being as a whole that perceives the encompassing world. Where he lay connected, Guthrie sensed the electromagnetic spectrum as once the man sensed light. He felt himself moved through gravity fields as once he moved through wind and wave. He knew how to vector himself toward a moving goal as once he knew how to throw a ball or shoot a rifle. Sensations and knowledge were more abundant than when he lived—overwhelmingly more, they would have been, were they not ice-crystal clear. Physics is calculable where biology is not because it is simple. It is incomprehensible where biology is not because it is strange.

"Bueno?" Sayre cried. "What's the result?" His eyes stared from dark rims blotched on sallowness. He looked hollowed out.

"It was them, all right," Guthrie told him. "They fired the word to Luna before I could stop them. They'll arrive in person pretty soon."

Silence quivered while photons sped to and fro.

Sayre slumped in his chair. "Then the game is up?" He stiffened. "No. We'll carry on. Come back. Not to Quito, I suppose that's impossible for you now, but to us. We'll give you asylum."

"No, thanks," Guthrie replied. "To sit useless forever? Listen. We might still manage more than just damage control. You remember my speculating about the Lunarians, when we first learned they'd shown up at L-5? Plain to see, their intent was to winkle my twin out of there, and they succeeded. *But* they didn't immediately proclaim what they'd done and why. In fact, they kept mum till I forced them. Doesn't that suggest they've got some intention of their own? What it might be, I don't know. It could be much worse for you than anything my twin wants. On the other hand, I recall an old saying about fishing in troubled waters. That's what I aim to try."

Transmission.

The human peered as if he saw a face in the screen before him. Perhaps he wished he did. "What have you in mind?"

"For the time being, go to L-5, take on reaction mass and antimatter, and prowl space. I'll leave my crew off there, and I want you—your Synod—to appoint Felix Holden commander of our forces in it. That'll mean he can get my needs taken care of at once, and he'll be a tough, smart, reliable man on the spot."

Transmission.

"I don't know," Sayre mumbled. "Some of the cusps in his psychoprofile—Oh, he is loyal."

"Guys like that may be in short supply once the news breaks," Guthrie warned. "Let me do as I see fit in space. You'll have your hands full at home, and then some. Between us, we may yet stay on top of things. We may even end up ahead of the game."

His electronic senses, probing forward, found the great cylinder, a-wheel against stars.

35

THE ROOM TO which they brought old Guthrie after his speech was not large; but light and shadow, shifting dim in ceiling, walls, floor, gave a sense of unboundedness unstable as a dream. They left him there on a table with much courtesy: he would appreciate how time ran clamant at their heels, he would be alone no longer than the urgencies upon them compelled, if meanwhile he desired entertainment he need but command the multiceiver.

It opened no communication line to the outside cosmos. He left it dark and waited in his case among his thoughts.

At last there came to him the lady Niolente. Her gown glimmered silver through the many-hued dusk into which her hair melted. Its skirt rustled to her stride, which otherwise did not trouble the silence. She drew up to the table and gazed into the lenses he raised toward her. "Hail, my lord," she greeted. "In what may I serve you?"

"You know damn well what," he said. "Where's Rinndalir?"

She spread her fingers fanwise; an Earthling would perhaps have shrugged. "Much is afoot. At this hour, the task of leadership is his. I, being free for a brief while, have sought to you."

"Yeah, sure, we've got to stay on top of things. Then why the hell are you keeping me here? I don't even know where on the bloody Moon you've taken me to."

"Rinndalir promised you an accounting in due course. I am come to render that."

Guthrie muttered something elaborately blasphemous before he said, "Account payable to him and you, eh? Okay, tell me what you want of me, we'll dicker, and then for Christ's sake let me go. I've got Fireball to take charge of. Can't that penetrate your Tom o' Bedlam heads? It must be a snake's nest by now."

"Nay, my lord," she told him calmly. "Thus far, a fragile order endures."

"Well, of course the consortes have common sense, and they're used to thinking for themselves, but just the same, this news—"

"Only rumors have flown, by-blow of that call to Luna you were forced to make from space."

"You mean Rinndalir was forced to allow. I wanted— Wait a flinkin' minute!" Guthrie roared. "You mean your stooges squelched that word as much as they could manage to, and you haven't aired my statement I made from here?"

"That would have been impolitic to do at the time, as my lord can belike see upon reflection." Niolente smiled. "The recording of it has now gone forth. Let me show you how it went."

Guthrie's eyestalks lay back like the ears of a cat or lips that curl away from teeth. "Yes. Do."

She sang a command. The multiceiver on the floor lighted. A machine voice declared, from a background of EMERGENCY symbols, that the major matter announced some hours ago would appear, pre-empting all regular transmissions on and from Luna. Rinndalir's image succeeded it. He identified himself and declared that what came next, the Selenarchy viewed with the utmost gravity. He did not say this in the heavy manner of an Earthside politician, but in an almost casual tone and with the hint of a smile. That was Lunarian fashion.

"So far, so good, and so what?" Guthrie snapped.

His own image sprang into being, the electronically created likeness of a burly man in middle life, clothes informal and somehow looking rumpled, eyes pale blue and aimed straight at the audience, voice deep and a little hoarse. "To Fireball Enterprises and everybody else, this is Anson Guthrie."

"Yeah, yeah," said the program in the case. "What else is new?" Niolente waited, on her feet in an easy posture, a statue that breathed.

Guthrie in the cylinder described laconically what had happened to Guthrie in the box. He did not go into detail, nor name any of his allies except Rinndalir, because, he explained, the rest of them were still in danger. As for the encounter in space with his other self, he said merely that a ship had intercepted the *Inia*—

"Hey, hold on, there!" bawled from the table. Niolente laid a hand on the case. Guthrie did not feel the gesture, as limited as he was when unconnected, but saw it and strangled his oaths.

—fortunately, evasive action foiled the attack. In light of this outrage, the latest of countless that the Avantists had committed over the years against Fireball and freedom and common decency—

"Consejeros and consortes, haven't we taken enough? Never mind revenge, or simple justice against the persons who commissioned and carried out these violations. We can bring suit before the World Federation and maybe get a judgment for the Peace Authority to enforce, but to what purpose? The Avantist government of the North American Union will continue. It will breed more such persons, who'll use its machinery to carry out more such antics, while it squats on the North American people and their liberties. *It* is the menace to world peace, world survival, of the same breed as those that went before it, Holy League, Renewal, Communism, fascism, nationalism, every kind of absolutism, back as far as history goes. Here's our cause to be done with Avantism."

The face formed a bleak smile. "Not being a politician, I can't proclaim a grand crusade for thousands of people to get killed in while I sit safe at home and enjoy my perks. However, in the course of my misadventures on Earth, I learned more than I knew before about a resistance movement in North America. The Avantists call those folk Chaotics, but that's a swear word, propaganda. What they are is men and women who want to be free again; and they're well organized and responsible, too. Avantism is rotted and crumbling. The revolutionaries want to clear it away, quickly and cleanly, before it can do more harm.

"I can't tell them how they should go about this. But if they choose to rise against the Avantists, now while the grievances of Fireball are fresh—I'll call on Fireball to give them every help in its power. Repeat, this is not a question of getting even. It is that I've always loved freedom, and so has our Fireball."

When after a while (a short while, because he had never been one for oratory) the cylinder blanked, Guthrie rested quiet half a minute before he said, "That was cleverly done. How much did you have prepared beforehand?"

"Rather little, for we could not foresee whether we would have occasion for it nor what form the occasion might take," Niolente admitted.

"Computer editing and revising, with reference to analyses of every recording of every talk I ever made, and my biography, and the derived psychoprofile— Pretty slick job. The machines will soon be better at being us than we are ourselves, no?"

She moved to stand in front of him. "The changes are minor," she said, a trace of amusement in her tone.

"Yeah, small, like changing 'help' to 'hell.'"

"You would in truth like to bring down the Avantists."

He had no head to shake, but his voice did. "No. Not that way, anyhow. Inciting a rebellion— Haven't you stopped to think what the risks are? You hope to touch off something that'll be uncontrollable, the consequences unforeseeable. *Why?*"

"Precisely for that reason."

"Wreckage for its own sake? You can't be that Q-jumpy. Can you?"

"In a sense, conceivably, yes. A quantum leap out of a black hole."

"Ah, screw the fancy excuses. What do you plan to do next?"

"Abide, and observe what comes to pass."

"Which'll be interesting, if nothing else. You've poked a stick into the anthill. . . . But without me to direct it, Fireball won't long keep up any effort. They'll start wondering why I haven't shown, physically. You can't maintain your fake. If you tried to simulate me sending orders from here, it'd soon turn preposterous."

"True." Niolente smiled. "Dread not, my lord. We shall presently release you, with due precautions. The instant of time for that must await the course of events and our judgment thereof; but it lies in the near future."

"After all Satan's dogs are off the leash. Listen—there was nothing about it in your doctored 'cast—my people don't know my other self is loose in a torchcraft. Do you understand what a danger that is? I do."

"Thus," she said blithely, "when you go at large, you may have no option but to lead Fireball in war."

"And afterward?"

"Afterward, yes, you could turn on us, but we believe you will find it unwise."

Guthrie lay still for a span. The vague colors and uncertain darknesses flickered slowly around him. Niolente stood amidst them like a candle not yet lighted.

"I've a ghastly feeling you're right," he said. "But that's supposing we'll have that kind of a tomorrow. We could lose, you know. Or everybody could lose, everything crash down in flinders."

"Would that be worse than what now binds us?" she answered.

36

THE SEPO IN L-5 could control transmissions from it but scarcely what came to it. At least, that seemed a needless provocation. Kyra Davis heard Guthrie's broadcast from Luna with the family who were giving her refuge.

"Then we'll fight!" she cried, a fist aloft where she had leaped erect as she listened. Rage: "And I—do I have to huddle here waiting?"

Wang Zu frowned. "This is strange," he said heavily. "I would never have expected the jefe to call for war. More than once I have heard him declare he has seen enough violence to supply him until the last star burns out."

"He did not truly call for it, did he?" ventured his wife. "He only promised help if a revolution does begin."

Wang shook his head. "Why should he do that unless it is what he hopes for? What he even seeks to detonate."

Kyra glared at them. "Don't you *want* those matones off your backs?" She gulped. "I'm sorry. Por favor, excuse me. After all your kindness—"

Lin Mei-ling patted her hand. "We know. This is very difficult for you," she said with a smile. "Perhaps we are too timid. But it would take so little to destroy this nation."

Kyra stooped down to hug her. "And y-you have children," she stammered.

"Let us believe the jefe knows what he is about," Wang said. Doubt lingered in his tone. "Those Selenarchs may have told him or promised him something. None of us can do anything yet but wait."

"And carry on with our work," said his wife.

Yes, Kyra thought, they had their work. She had her schooling in patience to abide while events spun themselves out, her relaxation techniques, her mantras and memories. They would be harder to use in this modestly furnished home than ever in space.

Being alone most of the time made it easier. The Wang boy and girl were at astro camp for a week, drilling in the skills required for emergencies and everyday life. It was one reason why Eiko had placed Kyra here.

Thirty hours passed.

The news erupted from Earth: Sepo headquarters in San Francisco Bay Integrate destroyed by an explosion. The picture was of wreckage still smoking, while rescue vehicles and machines scurried like ants and in the foreground a spokesman related grimly that the dead and hurt were many and that he felt certain the murderers were terrorists. Had not the North American government warned, striven, pleaded for cooperation? As for those fantastic allegations from Luna, the enemies of civilization could perpetrate a hoax as readily as could the Avantists whom they accused, and it was much more plausible that they would.

Three hours later: The same atrocity in Denver. Meanwhile, police had established that the instrument of the first had been a small, stripped-down sports flyer on autopilot, loaded with gigantite, power-diving straight down from the high stratosphere. Probably the second strike had used the same technique. There would be no third. National forces were on full alert and the President was about to declare martial law.

"How much difference will that make?" Kyra jeered.

"Flash! The Paris office of Global News Associates has received a communication from persons who claim to be the leaders of a revolutionary underground in North America. On condition that their whereabouts not be traced, Global was given a statement—"

A lean man in a plain gray tunic which had on its breast a stylized comet, speaking more softly than one would have expected: "—Jack Bannon, on behalf of the Liberation Army. They call us Chaotics, and we admit with regret that some crazies and criminals may take this opportunity to run wild, but they are not of us. We are the organized core of resistance to the Avantist tyranny. Our single purpose is to overthrow it and restore constitutional government, freedom under a law that is humane, to our country. We have bided our time in secret less because we lack strength than because fighting could too easily get out of hand. Weapons available to both sides—explosives, pyrotics, toxins, radioactives, biologicals, electronic and computer sabotage of vital services—those weapons can take too many innocent lives."

That wasn't strictly true, Kyra decided. If Bannon's outfit was as efficient as he claimed, and her own experience suggested it might be, then they must run it just about as tautly as psychodynamics and ruthless discipline made possible. Otherwise it would long since have been infiltrated and, if not totally suppressed, reduced to a scattered, hunted few. (No doubt a number of Sepo agents, trying to worm their way in, had found anonymous graves. Their superiors wouldn't publicize the losses.) To be that well controlled, it must needs be small. Therefore it could not by itself take the field against its enemies.

The idea must have been to wait, nurtured in part by clandestine remittances from abroad, probably with some facilities secretly on foreign soil, readying itself and propagandizing the public as best it was able, until circumstances took the government off balance. Then the Liberation Army would hit, several strategic blows, and trust that this would set off a widespread uprising—which, when it was well begun in its formless fashion, the junta could seize control of. That was how revolutions usually went in history. Often the prospect of powerful help from outside was what impelled such rebels to cross their Rubicons. Guthrie's speech—

Oh, Bannon knew. "We have the mighty Fireball Enterprises for our ally, if we prove ourselves worthy," he was saying. "Surely, too, the free nations of the world will be with us in spirit, and come to our aid as our cause advances."

No, they would not, except so late in the game that it wouldn't matter, Kyra thought. Not at all if the Avantists put down the insurrection fast enough that it didn't appear the conflict would endanger anybody else. Or if—a chill went through her—the Federation determined that Fireball's intervention was a precedent that the Peace Authority must take arms against.

"People of North America, do not be reckless. For the most part, go about your daily business while you still can. Refrain from violence. Simply, peacefully, refuse assistance to the Avantist authorities. Hear what your leaders have to say, the heads of your societies, lodges, churches, the organizations that have your loyalty. Do as they bid. But when the hour comes, then assemble with them to wage battle for freedom!"

"He calls on the subcultures," Wang breathed. "They begin with civil disobedience. But it goes on quickly to strikes, sabotage, riots, and killing."

"You know it," Kyra answered. "And the killing will mostly be done by the militia and police, unless Fireball can stop it before matters get to that. Oh, God, here I sit!"

Bannon: "—In conclusion, what better message can I give you than was written long ago on this continent when first its people claimed their freedom?" And the noble words: "We hold these Truths to be self-evident, that all Men are created equal—"

His image disappeared. The announcer chattered in French. Kyra half listened to the multi's English translation. The predictable, excited comments; then: "In Hiroshima, World Federation President Mukerji has announced that the special full meeting of the High Council and Assembly which she called will open today. Many delegates have arrived in person, the rest are on the net. Meanwhile President Mukerji has demanded that Anson Guthrie repudiate the statement attributed to him, promising aid in a purely political dispute. She states that if this repudiation is not forthcoming promptly, she will ask for a resolution declaring sanctions against Fireball Enterprises."

Wang rose from his chair. "I am going to the office," he said.

"But it is almost mid-nightwatch," his wife protested.

"I may learn, there, what our ships and people are actually doing," he told them, and departed.

The women stared at one another. "Zu is right," Meiling whispered. "The more I think about this, the less I can believe it is truly happening."

"Why?" asked Kyra, and fought against the admission that she probably foreknew the answer.

"That Mr. Guthrie would make such a pledge." Meiling looked down at her lap, where her hands writhed together. "He has reason to be angry, yes. But he could seek satisfaction in Federation court, or he could stop our trade with the Union until it gives him what he wants. He already had it suffering, you know. Here are we, down there are hundreds of our consortes, hostages to the Avantists or in danger from fighting. Why would he provoke it? Is this troth?"

Kyra bit her lip. "He *is* with the Lunarians, or was till lately. He . . . never trusted them much. I went after their help as a, a backup, in case Tamura failed him, and—" Beautiful in her mind, Rinndalir smiled. He reached out a hand, which had been so knowing. "And they were less than straightforward with me," she flung forth. "But we can't judge anything yet! We don't have the information!" It caught in her throat. "All we can do is wait."

Sometimes they talked a bit. Sometimes they dozed a bit. Sometimes they tuned in the news, the same scenes shown, the same things said, inanely around the globe. Toward mornwatch they heard of crowds forming in several megalopolitan regions. Armored militia rolled forth and armed flitters buzzed overhead, though as yet there was no attempt to disperse the gatherings. Twice the 'casts were briefly pre-empted by a recording of Felix Holden, L-5's new garrison chief. In oddly quiet fashion, like Jack Bannon, he required the populace to stay orderly and announced that his patrols had gotten reinforcements of colony constabulary, volunteers, for turmoil could kill everybody.

Wang returned, haggard and hoarse. "In space, confusion," he said. "The Sepo do not hinder us, but we receive just a few calls and intercept just a few more. And how shall we respond? I think, from what I have collected, I think they shout through space to each other, ships and stations, and ask dismayed what this means and what they should do."

"I suppose I would myself," Kyra confessed.

What could they, in fact? Unmanned solar sailers, months or years on a cruise. Machines to explore, prospect, mine, refine, load, unload, maintain, and the thin-strewn men and women who oversaw their labor. Shuttlecraft built for specific worlds and their immediate neighborhoods, never for going beyond. Some colonies, bubbles of environment, their inhabitants and industries. The liners that served them, big, comfortable, but safe only within narrow limits of stress. Torchcraft like hers, capable of crossing the breadth of the Solar System in days; but then, unless they could refuel somewhere, their delta v would be expended and they drift helpless. Which of their small number were close enough at this moment to arrive in time and capable of action?

What action? Spaceships were unarmed.

She had her thoughts about that. She did not care to voice them.

"I suspect— I am not sure by any means, but I suspect," Wang sighed, "that unless the jefe appears among his consejeros materially, in person, and gives them a definite program— Fireball will end by doing little or nothing."

Because its captains and crews had always taken responsibility on themselves, Kyra thought. This was too radical a measure, too ill-explained. They would wait to learn more.

And meanwhile the Kayos would rise, full of hope, and, unaided, would undergo slaughter.

If the Avantists were smart, they'd do their best to protect Fireball personnel in the Union and L-5. Of course, they might not be very smart in the heat of battle, or they might try and fail. No telling, once chaos ran free.

"He may show at any moment," Kyra ventured.

"I don't know." Wang stumbled off to bed. His wife followed him. After a while Kyra went to the room lent her, undressed, and lay down. Sleep came astonishingly fast.

She was high in the Tree, the all-mothering Tree, she *was* the Tree, with a root in death and a root in desolation and a root in the worlds of life, her trunk upholding creation and her boughs bearing green that soughed and shivered as the wind blew around her, the loud and bitter wind mounting into storm, waken, waken, the green tore loose, limbs groaned, bole trembled, waken, waken!

She opened her eyes and looked into Eiko's.

"What the devil!" She sat straight up.

Eiko let go the shoulder she had shaken. "I'm sorry." Her mouth quivered and her voice was like a harpstring pulled close to breaking. "You must hear. I dared not phone, but I don't think anybody followed me. We need you. Unless you say you are as powerless as we are."

Kyra scrambled to her feet. The air felt cold. She reached for the clothes she had tossed aside but drew her hand back. After those hours before the multi, they stank. She did too. "Go on."

"Announcement— Colonel Holden— Two Fireball ships have left the Moon, bound our way. They have beamed ahead that they bring men and intend to dock. They demand the Sepo here lay down their arms and accept detention until transport to Earth can be arranged."

Kyra's heart should have bounded. Instead, it slugged lumpish, for she watched Eiko's face and heard the rapid report continue: "Then another message, from Guthrie— from one that claims to be the true Guthrie. He has ordered those ships to turn back. He has a torchcraft close by us. If they proceed, she will attack them. He warned of what a danger an engagement like that would put us in, jets, debris, derelicts adrift. The torchcraft will blockade us as long as necessary, he said. The ships from Luna are not returning, but they are taking orbit at a distance."

"Holden . . . announced this?" Kyra mumbled.

"He would rather have kept it secret for a while, but they heard the communications in Station Control and called their families and friends before his men could get there to stop them. Then he phoned me, himself, to ask if I could help prevent a panic. I told him my father could best do that and should be released. Holden wanted me to persuade him to cooperate. I said I would not need to. After that I broke contact and hurried to you before Holden should think to have me brought in."

"That's got to be the false Guthrie out there. Somewhere nearby, probably. Maybe actually in the torch." Kyra spoke automatically. Most of her was casting about —what to do, what to do? "Unless this is another deception Sayre's gang has engineered."

"No, it is real. In his announcement to us, Holden showed the optical images and radar readings. Why should he falsify them? His command over us was precarious enough already."

Kyra's tone sharpened. "Why've you come to me? I'd've heard pretty soon anyway."

"And then what? I thought—" Eiko wrapped arms about herself. She too must feel cold. "You have your own torchcraft here. This may be a chance for you to escape.

The last forlorn chance, surely. Get away to the Moon or to Earth—Quito, Hiroshima— Bear witness to what you have seen. Accept a deep quiz if you must, to prove you speak truth. The Avantists will have to disown false Guthrie. The Peace Authority will have to work with Fireball to rid us of that torch. Speak for us, plead for us."

Kyra scowled. "Escape? I've thought about it plenty. But Eiko, you know I can't simply sneak to the dock and go aboard and cast off. Only StaCon can send me on my way. The Sepo didn't think to stand guard over its communications, but operations are suspended except at their colonel's orders, and how do you propose to let the staff back in there unbeknownst to him? As for requesting his permission, por favor, don't make me laugh before breakfast. I must be the only torch-qualified pilot in L-5 right now, and I am the notorious, much-wanted hijacker, Kyra Davis."

"Yes, I do know." The brown gaze sought the hazel and blinked at tears. "But I have imagined a, a possible way. It may fail and get you arrested, or worse. At best, it is a terrible risk for you. I do not ask you to take it. I cannot, even on behalf of all Ragaranji-Go. But if you will . . . give me your opinion—"

Flame burned away the chill. Kyra seized Eiko by the upper arms, so hard that the small woman gasped in pain, and shouted, "Tell me!"

When she had heard, she stood frowning, outwardly quiet, inwardly a-thrum, before she asked in a muted voice, "Do you really believe this might work? The Sepo have the weapons."

"We will have the numbers," Eiko answered, likewise gone calm. "Colonel Holden would probably not resort to deadly force."

"M-m, *probably*. Besides, shock guns, gas— They might be insufficient, if the crowd is really resolved, and lethal weapons might provoke a reaction throughout the colony that'd be fatal for his command. But he may not reason like us."

"We talked together, he and I, shortly after he arrived, when I begged him to let the detainees go. He refused, but he is not an evil man. In fact, I think he is not an Avantist, except for minimum lip service. He is a North American patriot who does his duty as he sees it."

"A lot will depend on how he sees it." Kyra pondered another half minute. She owed common sense that much. Impatience overwhelmed her. She flung her head back and laughed aloud. "You're on! It's go!"

"Oh—oh, my dear—*tomodachi*—" Eiko struggled not to weep.

Kyra took hold of her again, gently this time, shook her a little, and told her, "Save the sentiment for later, and give it to me over a bottle of premium Scotch. You'll need a couple of hours at least, won't you? Bueno, get started. Me, what I'll get is a shower and clean clothes and food and tea, and when that's done I'll join you in Yukawa Square!"

Eiko nodded, straightened, and went from the room. Kyra heard her bid the Wangs a brief, formal goodbye. Thereafter things went like a jetstream.

The latest word was that the ships from Luna were in the common orbit at a distance of some quarter million klicks. Evidently they were waiting for new orders, and whoever was in the torch didn't think it was worthwhile attacking them under these conditions. Kyra didn't envy the men aboard.

The news from North America was of demonstrations, riots, a militia regiment's mutiny, growing incidence of pitched battles, across the country like a fever-rash. There was no way of making out what actually went on, what it meant, where it was going. Government pronouncements stated curtly that lawlessness was being suppressed wherever it manifested itself. Foreign journalists on the scene were as confused as their audiences, capturing hasty glimpses and phrases while shots cracked and buildings blazed. It did seem likely that most uprisings were local, spontaneous, with gunjins supplying leadership and arms —except for what came from the depots that people like the Farnums had long kept. Some of the professionals were doubtless in it for pay and plunder, and maybe power if the revolution came off; some might be idealists of one sort or another; no telling how many of which kind. Fighting was at the moment heavy in the mountains of Hawaii Island. Kyra wondered about Nero Valencia. And the Packers and . . . everybody, everything.

The Homesteaders had declared themselves neutral and were marshalled to hold their territories against invaders of any faction. Three Islamic mullahs had proclaimed jihads to overthrow godless Avantism and promised Paradise to all men who fell in the cause; two prominent sheikhs disavowed them. No mention of Tahir. Had he maybe gone underground? Such other societies as had issued proclamations ranged between those extremes. None outright condemned the Army of Liberation.

Images showed armor in streets, flyers dropping knock-out gas bombs into mobs, warheads slammed at rebel strongpoints, the threshing, screaming wounded and the twisted, gaping dead, on torn-up soil or among battered walls, while dust and smoke drifted by. The revolution wouldn't go on long unless it got succor, Kyra thought. Crushing it might well leave the government stronger than before. The Avantists would certainly allow no more dissent, and would likely seek with new energy to control every part of life.

Report from Hiroshima: The North American delegation denied any need for the assistance of the Peace Authority in their country's domestic affairs. They demanded its protection from unwarranted and unwarrantable interference by outside interests. Fireball's was nothing but piracy; it must be halted and punished. The recent news that the real Guthrie had asserted himself and, with the single spacecraft available to him, had repelled an obviously Lunarian-sponsored aggression against L-5—this news, if true, was very welcome. It was regrettable that the inhabitants of the colony were thereby endangered, but the North American Union recognized the necessity and supported the policy. Let Fireball remember how many people and how much property it had in North America.

The spokesman for Siberia replied that his government would not condone threats of harm to innocent persons who merely happened to be associated with Fireball. Nevertheless, no private organization could be allowed to make war or otherwise conduct itself like a government, and Siberia called on the Assembly to institute sanctions.

The spokeswoman for Australia asked whether the Lunarians had yet offered an explanation of their role in this. President Mukerji answered that, in spite of repeated attempts by her office to establish communication, the Selenarchs remained unresponsive. A commissioner of the African Protectorate urged that, once the present trouble was settled, Luna be brought into the Federation by whatever means were indicated.

Her teacup jerked in Kyra's hand. A pre-empt was taking over.

Noboru Tamura appeared in the cylinder. He seemed physically unhurt, as Eiko had confirmed, but worn and weary. Kyra admired the firmness with which the little bald man spoke:

"People of Ragaranji-Go, please, and for your own sakes, hear me." He identified himself, though he was about as well-known as anyone here, and said a few words about his detention. "The Security Police claimed it was protective. I do not have sufficient data to judge that. It does not greatly matter. In the present crisis, Colonel Holden has ordered my release and requested my help. . . . We must indeed stay calm and peaceful. . . . Yes, that is difficult when we know virtually nothing except that we and those we most love may at any instant be plunged into mortal danger. . . . Solidarity, strength we give each other. . . . (A quick smile.) We bear the same genes as our ancestors in the Old Stone Age. We have the same need to be together in the hour of trouble, touch, gather around the bonfire, hear the shaman say that the spirits watch over us. . . . A rally in Yukawa Square. . . . ColonelHoldenagrees. . . . Thisisshortnotice,butifyou can come, please do. . . . Bring comfort home to your kindred and friends. . . ." It was not a lengthy or florid speech. Spacefolk didn't care for such.

The news came back on, again from North America.

Militia stood guard outside Toronto Compound. A bus hove in view, and another. The journalist reminded his audience of President Escobedo's new directive, that Fireball personnel were now under preventive arrest and would be taken to relocation centers.

Man and wife exchanged a glance. "Should we go to the rally?" Zu asked.

"Yes, of course," Mei-ling replied. "Pray for us, Kyra, for all of us."

The pilot turned her head, as if to hide tears. What she tried to suppress was a grin. Her heart flew high. But she wouldn't lay an extra hazard on this couple by telling them.

She waited five minutes after they were gone before she entered the passage. Two score people or more were in sight, bound the same way. They walked fast, intent, seldom talking. She mingled easily, little noticed, quite unheeded. Their minds were elsewhere and she was just a woman in a blue coverall and soft boots. A scarf on her head should help keep her from being recognized. If a friend did, she'd try to hush him in time. If a foe did, that was doubtless that. He'd rake in the last chip she had to play with. On the other hand, the pot had grown pretty big. Bigger than Eiko had added up.

The crowds thickened as they converged. Words might remain sparse, but their totality swelled to a buzzing with a breath of thunder, as from a hornets' nest, while feet shuffled, slithered, rattled, thudded. Air became warm and rank. Kyra forced her way ahead. She drew some angry looks and an occasional curse, though mostly she was lithe enough to slip by without jostling. It raised her risk, she certainly didn't want to make herself conspicuous, but she had to be where the Tamuras could see her.

Sepo were posted at intervals around the square, shockers ready. The one she passed was very young, trying hard not to show how scared he was. Company police were in evidence too, unarmed save for their muscular bodies. They shared a great interest in keeping this restrained. Not that Holden expected incitement to uproar—the proclaimed purpose was the exact opposite—but you never knew, did you?

No, you never did.

Several husky Fireball men cordoned off the step pedestal at the center of the park. Everywhere else, only trees and the largest meteoroid lifted above the multitude. Too bad about grass, shrubs, flowers, lovingly raked gravel. Eiko and her father stood on the second highest step. Above, the Buddha smiled his bronze smile and signed his blessing. Kyra worked her way to a position directly before them, three heads back from the front of the gathering. Taller than most, she identified among the guards at the base two men whom she knew as technicians in StaCon operations. In a pinch, they could send off a spaceship, and since Eiko had collected these, chances were she had others close by. Good girl!

Man and woman up there were looking around, as if to estimate the progress of the assembling. Mainly, Kyra knew, they searched for her. She lifted an arm and waved. "Hurra, hurra!" she yelled. It wasn't suspicious if somebody cheered, was it? Eiko's gaze fell on her. She whispered to her father. Now more people were cheering, and more and more.

Tamura raised his own arms for silence. It fell bit by bit, reluctantly, an ebb tide that wanted to flow. The sounds of breathing went on.

Tamura lowered his arms. "Consortes of Fireball, and every other soul in our midst, thank you," he began. An amplifier on his breast boomed the mild voice forth. "Thank you for setting aside your work and your worry to join us. Thank you for this response of yours. Thanks also to the directors and to Colonel Holden of the Security Police, who wisely agreed that a meeting to bind us together would be a step toward our common survival. Finally let me thank my daughter here at my side, Eiko Tamura, who mediated between officers and made it possible."

Mediated, hell, Kyra thought. Holden believed this was his idea, but it sprang from Eiko and she'd worked it into shape, explained it to the key individuals, won them over, and gotten the arrangements completed, in a span of a few hours. Bueno, it wasn't advisable to say that right out. Keep it for the histories.

"Your reaction might suggest that, undaunted as you are, we have no need to rally," Tamura said. "Well, the conquerors of space never could afford fear, could they? And we of later generations, we are still Fireball. Yet the gallantry that shouts defiance of peril is not enough. We must summon up the kind of courage that realistically assesses a situation, does what it can, and waits to learn whether it will live."

He was no politician or orator; his delivery was quiet, though perhaps that made it the more effective on these hearers. The words that followed were what counted, spare, strong, evocative of everything for which Fireball existed. They weren't his style either. Kyra guessed that Eiko had composed the speech in her head and run him through it a time or two.

It reached the point and rammed home. "—take action. It is not Anson Guthrie who threatens us and those who would liberate us. It is an impostor, a deception. We have a torchcraft in our own harbor. We have a pilot who can take her to Earth, bearing the truth and the proof of it, to raise for us the aid of the whole world. I have not time now to go into detail. I ask for your trust. I ask that you join with me as we stake our lives, our fortunes, and our sacred honor. Will you, at this moment, march?"

They roared.

"—occupy the dock—hold it while the ship that is our salvation goes free—" As Tamura spoke, it began to happen. The crowd surged inward, then outward. Kyra saw a Sepo knocked over. Another took stance above him, shock gun gripped tight but not fired, for he couldn't disable more than two or three before the rest overran him. His mouth worked, he screamed into his throat phone, headquarters, help, tell me what to do, a voice drowned in the rumble and breakers of flowing tide.

"Order, order!" Tamura's amplifier bellowed. "We go peacefully!"

He descended. A couple of his guards lifted him to their

shoulders and carried him. Kyra held her ground, a
struggle in the turbulence till Eiko and the men escorting
her got there. After that they moved along together, ahead
of most though well behind the forefront. The bodies
around them were their shield.

The yelling and shoving damped out. The procession
straightened itself. That might have surprised an Earthling, but not Kyra or the Tamuras. They knew their folk.
Selected by heredity and occupation for intelligence and
emotional stability, accustomed both to discipline and to
thinking for themselves, they would not run amok. No
single glittering shop window suffered as the mass of them
streamed down the passages. Footfalls thousandfold—not
in unison, this was no military, it was ordinary people
going in aid of their homes—made the noise of a river
bound for the sea. Tamura's diminutive form rode at their
van like a legionary eagle.

Sepo ran from a cross-passage twenty meters ahead.
They deployed to bar the way, a thin tan line, faces
strained beneath helmets, shock guns and bullet guns
poised.

"Walk slowly," Tamura called back. "I will deal with
them. Walk slowly. But walk, do not stop, walk."

The pair who carried him jogged forward. The host
behind became turbulent while the command passed
along, but then fell into a funeral pace. Peering above
heads, Kyra croaked through a throat gone dry, "I think
that's Holden himself in charge." His image had been on a
local 'cast yesterday.

Too short to see from the midst, Eiko answered, "I am
sure it is. He would not delegate this."

Perched aloft, Tamura spoke downward to the colonel.
He had switched off his amplifier and his followers could
not hear what those two said. Still their march advanced,
step, step, step. Someone started singing. Others joined in,
and others. The song was almost a random choice, traditional in Fireball, something Anson Guthrie had come
upon in the early days of astronautics, had liked and
tunelessly shared with friends; thus everybody here today

had grown up with it. Kyra waited for the last chorus, when her hoarsened notes would be lost in the swell.

> *"Sing a song of spacefolk, a pocketful of stars.*
> *Play it on the trumpets, harmonicas, guitars.*
> *When the sky was opened, mankind began to sing:*
> *'Now's the time to leave the nest, the wind is on the*
> *wing!'"*

They neared the barrier.

Holden rapped an order. An officer protested, astounded. Holden's arm chopped down, an ax motion—*obey.* The line split. Right and left, the Sepo retreated into the cross-passage. The marchers went by. Their footpaces were again strides.

Cheers broke loose, wild laughter, exultant thanksgiving and triumphant profanity. Men pounded the backs of their fellows, women embraced, hand shook hand, mouth sought mouth. The stream swirled and milled. "Keep moving!" called Tamura's amplifier. "We are not finished! Keep moving!" Piece by piece, the roil died away and the tide flowed onward.

"Yes, they could bushwhack us yet," Kyra said. "We can't dawdle."

"I am not so afraid of that any more," Eiko replied. Her fingers fluttered across the other woman's wrist. "You are the one going into danger."

"No, I'll scoot past." *Kestrel* was a Falcon-class torch, larger than yonder Katana, with a lower top acceleration but more total delta v. She ought to emerge at such a distance that, if the enemy pursued, he couldn't overtake before she reached Earth; and that deep in a gravity well, the advantage was hers.

That was if she ran from him.

The marchers were still exuberant. Another song spread among them till it rang off the imitation heavens.

"MacCannon was a Fireball man—"

To use the fahrwegs would have broken their mass apart, and its union was their strength. Tamura guided them along the spiral ramps of the tunnels for machines and emergencies. Weight fell, and echoes rolled hollow from bare metal. You needed something lively to step to, minute by minute for an hour or worse.

If Holden's men had taken a fast route and occupied StaCon—there were desperate expedients. Kyra considered ways to make tools into weapons.

But the harbor deck lay nearly vacant, installations like tombs in a cemetery that curved huge around the spin axis and, parallel to it, receded into reaches where the lighting became haze. "We have won," Eiko said weakly. She began to shake. "Oh, a tiny victory, but ours."

"Yours," Kyra told her.

"No, yours that is to be."

Tamura led them to StaCon. There the operators went in while he asked that about half the crowd stay, guardians, until the launch was complete. These were human beings; a full two-thirds trailed along to the ship's berth. Kyra and Eiko advanced through their loosening herd to join Tamura. He had jumped off the shoulders and was only a small man, very tired, whose low-g gait managed to give an impression of trudging.

"Por Dios, sir, you were splendid!" Kyra blurted. "How did you do it? How'd you talk him over? And in just a couple minutes!"

Tamura smiled lopsidedly, as if he lacked energy to lift both corners of his mouth. "I had little doubt of the outcome, once Eiko assured me Holden is neither a fanatic nor a fool," he said. "He threatened to open fire, but all the while, our flock showed they were determined. It was plain that if his men did shoot, they might scatter us, but thereafter they would live with murderous revengefulness until it gnawed away the last of them. I pointed out that we wanted nothing but to dispatch an emissary who can lead the world toward the truth in this tangle and make it put an end to our plight. It is also the plight of his men, I said; and was not anything worth trying that might bring peace to his poor torn country? The march was almost upon us. The police must fight or yield. Colonel Holden admitted he would not massacre, and commanded retreat."

That was among the countless things wrong with war, Kyra thought. Most of your opponents were decent people, and some of your allies were bastards. Supposedly the Federation had done away with it, but—

They reached the dock, and there above her was the crew airlock of dear *Kestrel,* snugged and gasketed against the axial tunnelside. Her servicing had been finished daycycles ago—they felt like months, years—and she waited like her namesake to take the skies again.

Tamura and his daughter bowed deeply. Several persons in the front of the crowd did too. "Fortune ride with you, brave woman," Tamura said, "as do our blessings and prayers."

How could Kyra respond other than by bowing in return and saying, "Mil gracias, señor and señorita," while she ached to hug Eiko to her for what might well be the last time?

Or did she? The question flitted through the darkness at the back of her head. She was about to betray these two. "Adiós," she gulped, and bounded up the ramp to the lock. She keyed it to open, the outer valve turned, she passed through, the valve closed on their faces.

Having sealed the lock, she glided toward the pilot section. Familiarity enfolded her, the acceleration couches stowed aside, the door to the minuscule lavabo, a hatch cover above the access to the forward hold, the unexpanded galley manifold, a closet for personal items, a family picture stuck to a pearl-gray bulkhead, a multi with vivifer, a hobby kit, surroundings in which she had fared among worlds and moons and comets, out to where the sun was no more than the brightest of the stars, her ship, her *Kestrel,* her second self.

Eagerness flared regret out of her. Was she really playing them false in L-5? She had simply not told Eiko that a better plan had come to her, because Eiko might then have refused to proceed further, holding that the risk to Kyra's life was too great. She might not have understood how little that mattered, set against that which Kyra hoped for.

A change in tactics, nothing else. How much good would it actually do for her to land on Earth and tell her story?

They already had Guthrie's account. She could merely attest that it was true. (And how much *was*, after Rinndalir's machinations, whatever they were?) Days would pass while they wrangled on in the Assembly and maybe she, indeed, endured deep-quizzing. Meanwhile the enemy would not be idle and the torchcraft would hold Guthrie's force at bay (if it was his) and L-5 hostage.

Eiko probably realized this. Had she set things in motion with the idea that there was little to lose?

Or—Kyra slammed to a halt—had she foreseen what her friend might choose once free, not wished to lay an obligation but provided an opportunity to assume one?

Kyra belled a laugh. "Could be!" she cried. "You're shrewder than you let on, Eiko, querida."

Anyway, the hood was off the falcon and the jesses about to be loosed. She jumped into the command seat, harnessed up, and ran fingers over the board. Lights came aglow, meters quivered, displays formed, systems purred to life. Within five minutes she saw the readings and felt the slight shudder that meant the moorings had released her.

Momentarily she floated weightless. It was like falling down the luminous shaft ahead to a hole of night at the bottom. Drive kindled; a feathery pressure nudged her back into the cushions; she was on her way. Direction and intensity shifted about, not much, but again and again. Under guidance, cautiously, cautiously, the ship left the harbor.

Star hordes gleamed. The Milky Way cataracted hoar across crystal black. In a corner of the viewfield before her Kyra saw the Magellanic Clouds. "L-5 Station Control to *Kestrel*, TF33," she heard. "You are released and cleared for full thrust."

"Gracias, and hasta la vista," she answered, though the voice had been robotic. She wasn't afraid, too damn busy for that, but it felt good to swap a few words before going into battle.

A hundred seconds of boost at one *g* took her about fifty klicks farther. She cut it off, not to build up an unwieldy vector, and looked around the heavens. The colony dwindled in sight, at a kilometer per second. Earth had waxed somewhat in phase since last she beheld it, Luna had waned.

"There's another torch somewhere hereabouts," she told the ship. "Find her."

Radar swept through its arcs. Optical and infrared sensors scanned. Kyra searched among the stars as if human eyes had the same power. Where the ship's neutrino tracer heard the rushing of an almost massless torrent and analyzed for eddies from nearby, her ears caught nothing but the susurrus of ventilators and the blood-beat within her.

"Yes, yonder," said *Kestrel*. Computer-deduced, the lean image appeared in a screen. "North of L-5, in an orbit of similar dimensions but inclined ten seconds." A holocube presented a diagram.

"That'd let him keep track of what goes in and out, bearing the spin in mind," Kyra muttered, mostly to herself. "I expect he adjusts it from time to time." She keyed the holocube controls. The diagram changed to show, enlarged, the segment that interested her, with a scale from which she read a distance of approximately a thousand klicks. Eight minutes at one *g*—she rounded off the figures she evoked—and she'd gain a relative velocity of four-point-seven KPS. . . . Of course, the bandido wouldn't sit still. "He must've spotted us. Let me know, the instant he boosts. Any more data?"

"His radar is locked on us," *Kestrel* replied.

The voice was Kyra's own. Most pilots preferred a distinct synthesis, often one that sounded like a person of the opposite sex, but she found that obscurely disturbing. After considerable thought, she had figured out why. It suggested, not in rational wise but to the primitive deep within her, that here was a mind like hers, a person, a soul.

And indeed the machine did more than conn and crew the ship of which it was a part, with capabilities orders of magnitude beyond hers. It observed and reasoned. It warned, advised, proposed, learned, adapted. For instance, it had just now noticed that she referred to the other as "he," concluded that she meant whoever was aboard, and gone over to the same pronoun. When she wanted diversion, it provided music or spectacle or text or vivifer experience, it created original audiovisual abstractions, and it was a fairly good conversationalist if she didn't demand ever to be surprised. You could quite reasonably call it *Kestrel*'s brain.

And Kyra loved *Kestrel*, the whole of the ship, as you may love a house or a sailboat or a work of art. This with which she spent so much of her life was unique, strong, subtle, a personality. But it was not a person. Guthrie's program was, mapped off a living mind. *Kestrel*'s was not. It was the working out of an elaborate algorithm. No awareness responded to hers. She didn't care to pretend otherwise, even by an individual voice for her to hear. It got lonesome enough anyway, yonder where the comets prowled.

Light-flash, chime, incoming call. Kyra closed that circuit.

The basso hit like a fist. "—departing L-5. Come in, pronto."

Her guess had been right. Nevertheless she choked, "M-my God, is that you, jefe?"

"Anson Guthrie, yes. Identify yourself and explain what the hell you're doing. Don't you know this sector is interdicted?"

"By you."

"Right. Somebody or something is impersonating me, allegedly on the Moon. I've got to defuse this before it blows up a million people and maybe Fireball as well. Okay, explain yourself."

Kyra gripped the arms of her chair. "You did go to the Moon," she said. "I helped you out of L-5."

Silence ticked thrice.

"You did, personally?" asked Guthrie's voice. "Give me a visual."

Before she made the irrevocable move, Kyra wanted final confirmation. "You shouldn't need any of me. But I will, when you tell me who traveled with us from the mainland to Hawaii. His real name."

"God damn it, that's enough!" the voice roared. "Obey or you're dead!"

"Oh, no," said Kyra most softly. "It's the other way around." Her skin prickled. "You clear out of these parts or you're dead."

"You gone loco? Who *are* you?"

"Makes no difference any more. We've settled the question of who you are. What you are." Kyra broke the connection. Light and chime raged at her.

"Listen, *Kestrel,*" she said fast. "The object is to drive that thing away. We'll make the neighborhood too unpleasant for him. Unless he catches us in his jet, which I guess he'll try to do. I'll direct maneuvers, you execute them, override me if you compute I'm ordering too big a risk but remember we have to take chances."

"Understood," her ship replied. "It's like when we ran the Stream."

"More ticklish, but— Ay! Scramble!"

The image of the Katana spat fire. The red spot on the orbital diagram surged forward.

Acceleration jammed Kyra back in her seat. Vision blurred and reddened. Her skull hammered.

It eased. She floated free and in her view saw the Katana speed by not many kilometers off, a needle stitching across the stars. "Good show, *Kestrel,*" she muttered shakily. "How hard did he boost?"

"Ten gravities, to cross our probable path a short way in advance of us," the ship told her. "I gave us a similar thrust, tangentially."

"And he missed." Had he not—no collision, which would have smashed both vessels. Instead, Kyra would have run into the plasma of his exhaust, not yet dissipated. That density of charge, turbulent magnetic fields, hard radiation would cripple her ejectors if they were operating at the moment. Then anti-Guthrie could return and, at his leisure, slice his jet straight through *Kestrel.*

Kyra scowled. He must have known the odds were

against success. Her vessel had had a couple of minutes in which to leap aside. This wasn't an aerial combat. Neither could swing smoothly around to outdance the enemy.

A warning? He'd made that whole dash at ten g. Any humans aboard were in poor shape, not fit for much till they'd had a while to recover. . . . Why should he carry them? What use to him? He, hooked in, was most likely his own crew; and stresses that would black her out didn't bother him.

He shrank below naked-eye visibility. She magnified and amplified, to see directly in the viewscreen how he turned and applied new thrust. He was coming back.

No flame-tail trailed him. That had been false color supplied by the computer. Close by, a human would see a wan blue glow, quickly lost in the star-field. A modern drive wasted no more energy than the laws of thermodynamics absolutely dictated; and it was the thermodynamics not of heat engines but of quarks, leptons, and photons.

He was bound for a return engagement, the real thing, unless she fled. *Kestrel* alone couldn't deal with him for any length of time. The ship calculated vectors in microseconds and applied them in milliseconds, but lacked the creativity—imagination—cleverness—slyness—ruthlessness of a fully conscious mind. Kyra must supply that. And she was not coupled directly to her vessel like him, to sensors and computers and effectors. She must look through a pair of jelly globules, calculate with a wet sponge, send signals floating from synapse to synapse at molecule speed, make them known against the inertia of an organic soundbox and ten jointed sticks.

Yet she and *Kestrel* had run the Stream.

Her hands moved. They gave the basic commands, as they would at a wheel or a tiller. Words added: "We'll boost so as to collide if he keeps on at his present rate. He'll see, and throttle down. We'll boost harder. Work our way in at him, whatever he tries. Transverse thrust at the last moment, of course, so he can't keep from slamming into our jet." An easy one gravity embraced her.

"Won't he attempt the same?" The ship had that much capacity for independent thought.

"Sure. Whenever he changes vector, we will too, always close rather than wide, if we have a choice. Force him to expend mass. Wear him down."

Thrust, free-fall, turn, thrust. The Katana swelled in view. Sunlight glared off a flank. Kyra breathed steadily. A grin widened her mouth. Reading her instruments and instincts, she gauged that anti-Guthrie had a better chance of blasting her than she did him. Her hands said, "Veer at two *g*'s." *Kestrel* modified the command into precision, swung herself around, and thrust. The enemy shot by, less than a kilometer away. L-5 swam into Kyra's visual range, gone small. These maneuvers had borne her and anti-Guthrie a fair distance off. Excellent.

Deceleration. The adversaries must cancel their velocities before they could begin the next pass. It would take a little while. Kyra opened an audiovid broadcast on the general band. "Hello, L-5 and you two ships in orbit," she called. "Do you read me? Kyra Davis, pilot for Fireball, aboard torchcraft *Kestrel*. I'm engaging the vessel that has illegally blockaded and endangered L-5, to make her cease and desist, but I could use some help. Come in, por favor." She set the message to repeat.

The board informed her that anti-Guthrie wanted to talk again on the previous band. Kyra touched *Record* and received him. "Did you hear?" she asked. "Will you go away and stop bothering us?"

"No, you go away," he answered. A bare hint of laughter: "I like your spirit, lass, I truly do. Bet you're hell on wheels in bed. I'd hate to kill you. Please flit off. I won't pursue."

So would the jefe speak. Her heart contracted with pain. Fury overcame it. "Listen, you," she said between her teeth. "Scuttle off or you're dead. If 'dead' is the right word. I'd enjoy shutting you down."

"Be reasonable," he urged. "I've got the boost of you. More than just what's in my drive. I can take accelerations as high as this boat will go, for as long as she will. You can't."

"I know. Because I know what you are!" she spat. Cooler: "What of it? I can keep you in play, keep you dodging, till your tanks are dry and your orbit cold. Think what models of torch we fly. Think how you've been in space, skipping around, for many hours, while my craft's fresh out of service bay. I've got the delta v of you, señor, and I intend to use it."

"Spaceship *Bruin*, B56," sounded from another speaker. "Captain Helledahl. With us, *Jacobite*, C45, Captain Stuart. We're the two that came to relieve L-5—"

"Hold on," Kyra said. She pressed switches. "Bueno, we're all talking together now. *Bruin*, *Jacobite*, here's the conversation I was just having." Compressed, it transmitted in a millisecond. "I suppose you'll want to check back with Luna, but myself, I see no reason why you can't proceed to L-5."

"I am the reason," came starkly.

Kyra shook her head. "'Fraid not, un-Guthrie. You try to attack a third-party ship, and you're meat for me. Go away, I told you."

"You'll grow tired. You'll have to eat, go to the can, sleep. Delta v or no, I've got more active hours left than you do."

"We'll see about that. I'm hunting you, you know."

"And meanwhile," said a voice that must be Stuart's, "the help you asked for should arrive."

"It'll arrive too late, and I'll chop it up," said anti-Guthrie. "Lass, I'm sorry, but now in earnest I'm hunting you."

In the displays, his ship blazed.

"Intercept," Kyra's throat and hands directed again. Stars wheeled across her sight as *Kestrel* rotated. There went Orion, there went his hounds. Thrust pressed her back. It was gentle. Likewise the Katana's, she read. When you fully meant business, you moved as slow as might be.

"If we want to be sure he doesn't rake us, we should bend off at about five hundred klicks," *Kestrel* told her. "Closer, he might with top acceleration acquire a vector that I can't react to soon enough."

"But probabiy you could, no?"

"Probably, yes."

"Bueno, he's right about the endurance of flesh and

blood being less than his. Our best bet is to make him expend mass, lots of mass, in a hurry. Maintain vector."

"Pilot Davis—" Helledahl began.

"Don't pester me now," Kyra snapped. "Get on the beam to Luna."

The bearing did not hold steady, as for a collision course at sea or in the air. Both vessels were under boost. But the stars gleamed changeless before her—she was aimed at Andromeda, the sister galaxy a whirlpool off her starboard bow—and the diagram extrapolated two glitter-dots bound for a common point.

In the viewscreen the Katana became a spark flitting across the constellations. "Two minutes," *Kestrel* warned.

"Steady as she goes," Kyra ordered.

One or the other, or both, must give way, cut thrust, spin around, move sideways at such an angle and with such a force as to escape running into the energy sword of the enemy. Neither could know what the other would do, nor when.

It sped through Kyra: Anti-Guthrie didn't intend mutual destruction. That would give her the victory. Not that she wanted to die. No, she hoped to kill. He'd realize that. He'd expect her to veer, in such a way that her blast might catch him. Therefore he would do likewise. The first to leap aside had a disadvantage, in that rotation before reboost took time. But if she held her course for whole seconds longer than he guessed a live human would dare—

He loomed.

Cut drive. Blow spinjets, a bare few degrees. Fire while still turning. Gyrate crazily off.

—The knowledge reached Kyra that she was alive. "Give me a picture," she whispered into the hush. "Give me data."

The Katana receded, a blade, a needle, a star, nothing. The readouts declared that she fell free, adrift on the tides of sun, Earth, Luna, universe. The image generated was of a hull unholed, but in it the drive assembly was only highlights and shadow. "Bring us about for a closer look," Kyra said.

"Pilot Davis, Pilot Davis," rattled in her ears from Helledahl, "I think you have—"

"Callate la boca." She recovered her wits. "Sorry. No offense. But leave me be for a while."

· Acceleration surged. *Kestrel* overtook the enemy craft and matched velocities, a few hundred meters off. At that remove, the damage was plain to eyes as well as instruments. A flame hotter than a solar flare had burned across the stern. Metal curdled along the edges of a night-black wound. Gobbets of it, flung off, still orbited near, uneasy as dustmotes. Surely the thrusters inside were a ruin.

"Hola, hola," Kyra called. "Are you there?" Silence hummed. She looked from the console, as if toward a face. Nothing but the stars met her gaze. "We may've knocked out his communications too," she said without tone. "Or else he's lying low."

"Maybe he, the pilot, is defunct," *Kestrel* said.

"Maybe. Though that'd have to be by radiation, and a plug-in is well shielded, you know. Hola, hola, Guthrie Two?"

After a while Kyra gave up. She felt no triumph, not yet, she was wrung out, and . . . and how quietly wonderful it was to be alive.

But how had this happened? She'd simply meant to make him flinch. She'd had no real expectation of slashing him. It was enough if he spent more mass than she did. Somehow he'd misgauged and she'd taken him. Strange.

Oh, this discarnation of Anson Guthrie was no god. It had gained some powers, it had lost some. Was it subject to blind rage or despairing recklessness? She didn't know. But certainly it was fallible. That she knew, how very well.

She shook herself. "We'd better keep busy," she said aloud, as if *Kestrel* shared her sudden exhaustion. With numb hands and tingling lips, she set about trying to raise Fireball on Luna.

37

THE SEPO IN Port Bowen were few. Guthrie's command that they lay down their arms, withdraw to their quarters, and wait for transport home had not been excised from his speech. Bewildered and demoralized, they obeyed. Company police kept an eye on them.

Isabu conveyed Guthrie to Fireball headquarters there. "You would perchance invite Niolente or me to stay," Rinndalir had laughed. "Delightful though that would be, I think best we postpone it. We can render more assistance where we are."

"Assistance especially to yourselves," Guthrie snapped.

"I think that upon reflection, you will find antagonism toward us inexpedient."

"As practical politics, no doubt. Allow me my private fun. Now let's for Christ's sake move!"

Isabu carried Guthrie in a silver box set with jewels. He gave the box to the guards at the Fireball entrance and sauntered off to reclaim his vehicle. After some worried debate, the guards called a safety officer, who took the box to a strong-walled room and spent several minutes discovering how to get it open.

Half an hour after that, Guthrie had a body. He wasted little time rejoicing in limbs and a full panoply of senses. There was work to do.

It did not take him long to establish his identity beyond question. He need but remind various associates of half-forgotten trivial incidents which his copy could not possibly know about. They brought him up to date on the most recent sensational events. When he heard that Kyra Davis still kept watch alongside her capture, his tongue-lashing ran for a measured three minutes and forty-eight seconds, with never a repetition. "Dispatch a tow," he ended curtly. "I want them both back straightaway."

Otherwise he required little briefing. In Rinndalir's

custody he had stayed *au courant,* more than if he merely watched the news. The Selenarchs had their own sources of intelligence. To his staff he explained how his broadcast had been altered, but didn't go into detail. "Later, when we have time. Right now we've got to cover the bet that went down when the dice were cast for us. Next we've got to make a throw for ourselves."

Eventually he stood in the office reserved for him on his visits here. It was a big chamber, stone-floored, sparely furnished though everything state of the art. Above low walls, a viewdome reproduced the scene outside, stars and Milky Way brilliant above wasteland, Earth almost full, regnant alone in azure and argent. His robot body hulked over Jacobus Botha, who sat as if strapped into his chair. The port director was a strong man, but today everybody was dominated.

"Holden isn't surrendering yet, is he?" Guthrie growled. A renewed demand had been transmitted an hour ago.

"N-no, sir. He insists on orders from his government. Helledahl and Stuart think they can force an entry, but advise against it."

"Of course they do. Liberate a lot of corpses in a ruin? No, we'll keep their ships on station to discourage any ideas of making a sally—not that Holden could manage one, but let's stop him from bugging the L-5ers about it—or ideas of reinforcement from Earth."

"Those aren't torchcraft, and they're full of men."

"I know. But they can interdict the approaches, and the men can stand to be crowded together in free fall for a while. You see, I have hopes those Sepo will quit soon, orders or not. I suspect their morale is down around their boots, and we'll feed 'em news and propaganda to lower it further. If that works, we'll want our occupation force handy to take over. If it doesn't work, we should have a couple of torches to relieve *Bruin* and *Jacobite* in another daycycle or two."

Botha forced his eyes up toward the lenses in the turret. "Do you truly mean to call in our ships and attack North America?" he asked raggedly. "That is—that is war."

"No, I don't mean to attack," replied implacability. "I

mean to present a credible threat. For this, we need the power, in being and in position."

"But the Covenant—the Federation—you'd make us outlaws."

Guthrie's tone softened. "I don't like the situation any better than you, Jake. We were hornswoggled into it, and all we can do is tough our way out." Sharply: "No arguments. We've got a Paul Bunyan job of organizing ahead. Get cracking."

Botha rallied his nerve. "In conscience, sir, I can't join in this."

"Okay," said Guthrie without anger. "You're fired."

"Sir?"

"You are hereby dismissed from Fireball. I'll miss your skill and experience, but I haven't time to argue and Barbara Zaragoza should be able to fill in."

Botha half rose, fell back down, and cried, "Dismissed from *Fireball?* No, sir, no, I gave troth, you always told us we are free men, put me on latrine duty but—no, not from Fireball!"

Guthrie stood for an instant motionless before he answered low, "'My country, right or wrong,' huh? Okay. I was too hasty. Never had a rat's nest like this before. Consider yourself on leave of absence. Log in your disagreement with my policy. Then stay out from underfoot. That'll be honest troth."

Botha swallowed. "Perhaps I can—after all—"

"No. I don't want fanatics, but neither can I use people who're wrestling with their superegos. Think what indecision or miscalculation could cost. We'll discuss morals and ethics and your status and everything else after this is through. Go."

Botha obeyed, stiff-jointed. Once his back was turned, he knuckled his eyes.

The hours passed. Guthrie drove his staff nearly as hard as he drove himself. He would have been higher-powered, every recorded datum instantly available to him, every computation done precisely as he envisioned it, had he linked directly into the main hypercomputer. However, he wasn't dealing with abstractions but with individual human beings. Best he too be clearly an individual, bearing a shape akin to a knight in armor. Yet when he transmitted, that was the image he sent, not the appearance of the once living man. He intended a symbol accenting that this was not a matter that could or in any slightest way should be mitigated.

He gathered information, conferred with persons he considered wise, spoke with his directors around the globe of Earth, sent beams a-wing over the Solar System from the antimatter plant at Mercury to the outermost comet station beyond Pluto, called his ships and captains, his men and women, to bid them stand fast or to summon the nearer ones back to him.

Nonetheless, when Kyra Davis arrived she was conducted in according to the instructions he had left. As she entered, he chanced not to be in talk. On a screen before him unrolled a spreadsheet, the latest strategic analysis from the group he had appointed to that task. He turned from it and strode across the floor to take her hand. It lay in his like a bird returned weary to the nest.

"God, it's great to see you again, safe," he rumbled. "As spent as a sailor's pay, aren't you? No wonder, after what you've been through. Well, we've reserved you a suite at the Armstrong in Tychopolis. Sleep till you wake, order whatever tickles your fancy, and sleep some more. I just wanted to say welcome home."

She lifted her head and smiled. "That'd be understood," she answered, hoarsely and mutedly. "But gracias, jefe." She sighed. "Home. Yes."

"When you're ready, but not before, I want your input about L-5. That might show us how we can regain it if Holden's stubborn—" The phone chimed. "Bloody damn! I've restricted that thing to the real urgencies. 'Scuse me." He went back to respond. Kyra sank into a chair.

"Señor, you have a personal call from the President of the World Federation," the instrument reported.

"Hm? Well, no surprise." Guthrie glanced at Kyra.

"Stick around, honey. This should interest you. . . . Okay, connect her.".

A handsome dark visage appeared in the screen. "Have I the honor of addressing Mr. Anson Guthrie of Fireball Enterprises?" asked Sitabhai Lal Mukerji ritually, in Asian English.

"Yes, Señora—uh, Madame President," he replied. "This time, the genuine article and nobody editing."

Transmission lag passed, for Kyra about four heartbeats.

"There has been much deception and many allegations." Mukerji's tone was cold. "One cannot be certain what to believe."

"You've studied the communiqué I issued when I got back here, I'm sure."

Lag time.

"Yes. It is not very informative."

"I tried to give the basic facts, Madame President, to the entire human race. The details can wait. They must. Not only are they a max-entropy mess, but I admit not yet knowing a great deal, and shouldn't throw statements around that may be unfounded. The bone truth is plain, though. Agencies of the North American government stole my duplicate, reprogrammed it in violation of human rights written into the Covenant, and passed it off as me in an attempt to take over an international association of free men and women."

—Mukerji frowned. "That is a grave charge to bring against a government."

Guthrie laughed. "Ma'am, no charge has ever been too grave to bring against a government. Any government. It's the nature of the beast."

—"You are entitled to your opinions. You are entitled to press charges and produce evidence. You are not entitled to break the law."

"What've I done except escape from their efforts to murder me? My communiqué explained how that call to arms was a put-up job by the Lunarians. Complain to them, please, not to me."

—"We shall, sir, we shall." Mukerji's image leaned forward. Her forefinger pointed like a lance. "But you have not disavowed that criminal incitement. On the contrary, your statement makes demands on North America that no government could accept from a private party. Your ships are blockading the North American troop in L-5. The Peace Authority's surveillance and intelligence units report every indication that you are mobilizing your company for violence."

"Ma'am," Guthrie said, "you're an intelligent and reasonable lady. Must we, between the two of us, use loaded words? Fireball hasn't delivered any ultimatum. We've simply warned the Avantist government that we can't—we *cannot,* ma'am—stand idly by while it arbitrarily imprisons people of ours and, considering what's going on thereabouts, unnecessarily exposes them to danger. The seizure of our property without due process is an outrage too, but minor compared to this. Likewise, the occupation of L-5 is illegal, having been carried out under false pretenses, and the hazard it poses is intolerable.

"We beg them in Futuro to set matters right. We realize this can't be done in a single stroke, and we offer to negotiate and cooperate at every step. For instance, if they'll evacuate L-5, we'll provide ferry service to Earth. As for mobilization—ma'am, politicians chronically remind me Fireball is not a nation and its directorate is not a government. How could we mobilize? I've requested our consortes to prepare for whatever action may prove necessary in the present emergency. They're starting to do so. That's all."

—Lustrous eyes narrowed. "What action have you in mind?"

Robot shoulders shrugged. "I said, whatever proves necessary. Isn't that pretty much up to Futuro?" Weightily: "If you hadn't called me, I'd have appealed to you before this daywatch was over. Use your good offices, Madame President. Bring the Avantists to their senses."

—Mukerji smiled bleakly. "You have a clever way with your bluff words, Mr. Guthrie. But let us not play games.

Your communiqué said nothing about the call to rebellion and the pledge of aid to it that were in the earlier broadcast you call false."

"What'd you expect, ma'am? Obviously I'd like to see the Avantist government replaced. Whether or not that happens, I'd hate to see a lot of people who wish for freedom butchered, jailed, or brainwashed because they trusted a promise made in the name of Fireball. So, yes, I did propose"— He and Kyra saw her wince at the foregoing sentence, then quickly, dutifully, recover.—"a cease-fire, a general amnesty, and in due course a convention of all parties to work out new arrangements. I offered *our* good offices toward this end. Meanwhile, though, the uprising is still going on. Lives and treasure are being squandered. If your Peace Authority mustn't intervene in a purely domestic affair, how may poor, private Fireball? The one right we claim, if neither the North American government nor the Authority will do it, is to assure the safety and well-being of our consortes, and, secondarily, secure our property."

—"That is a considerable claim."

"Sure. We'll affect the course of events. How could we not, even if we do nothing? We'll discharge our obligations as we see them, as best we're able."

This pause was longer than light speed imposed.

"Your concern for your personnel in North America is in itself commendable," Mukerji said, as solemnly as if she spoke at a funeral. "Perhaps it has caused you to forget that there are many more of them elsewhere on Earth, and each is a citizen of some country belonging to the Federation."

"And they could become hostages or the objects of reprisal? Ma'am, I can't believe you'd dream such a thing. They're totally innocent."

—Mukerji's voice went dry. "Is that why your General Director Almeida ordered every Fireball spacecraft on Earth into orbit, and every regional chief concurred?"

"That order came from me. They just executed it. I won't insult your intelligence. It's obvious where their sympathies lie. But they and the rest of our folk on Earth did nothing illegal, nothing their governments or your office had forbidden, and from now on, whatever happens, they'll scarcely be in a position to flout your laws."

—"Their sympathies, you say. Their loyalties? . . . Well, a general conflict would certainly endanger them."

Guthrie lifted his hands. "Ma'am, please! Who spoke a word about that? Surely it can't be what you're planning. And we in space want a conflict like we want a hole in our helmet. I'm amazed that the Council and the Authority aren't working to free and safeguard our people in North America. The moment that's done, everything else becomes negotiable."

—Mukerji's lips tightened. "The effort is being made, I assure you. It cannot be carried out in a glare of publicity."

"I understand, and thank you, and wish I were religious so I could pray for you. I hope you understand that Fireball cannot abandon its trothgivers to their fate, and therefore must make ready to help them if other attempts fail. Maybe that fact will be a useful bargaining chip for you. Meanwhile we'll do nothing that might embarrass you, and whatever you ask that might assist you."

—"Very well, sir. Cancel this mobilization of yours."

"Madame President, I repeat, it is not a mobilization, and with respect I disagree that unpreparedness on our part would serve any good purpose."

—Mukerji sighed. "This has gone as I feared. But I was obliged to try."

"I hoped you'd see we're reasonable folks here. That should have a little value to you."

—Mukerji smiled sadly. "Reasonable people too can be at odds with each other. I trust you will receive future calls from me or my office immediately, day or night, as I will yours?"

"Of course. Vaya con Dios."

—"Farewell." The screen blanked. Guthrie stared into it a moment before he turned back to Kyra.

"Is, is it war, then?" she stammered.

"I hope to Christ not," he sighed. "We'll know in a couple more daycycles."

"I should think . . . Mukerji will need longer than that . . . to persuade the Avantists."

"I'm afraid so. She's capable and well-intentioned. But if I were that regime, I'd stall her till the Kayos have been stamped out, while maneuvering to bring the Peace Authority actively onto my side against contumacious Fireball, which has given me such a lot of woe."

Kyra brought fingers to mouth. "You mean—your action is *helping* them?"

"Well, they can at least appeal to the herd instinct in their fellow governments. If they provoke us into taking the role of villains, their antics with regard to us can be swept under the carpet and several important persons among them won't be hauled before an international court. If they can bring it about that the Federation declares us outlaws, they can confiscate everything we have in the Union. That would be quite a boost for the ramshackle economy they've created.

"But I don't see how we could've stayed passive. Nor can we wait long. Suppose those 'relocation centers' are next to militia bases, political headquarters, or wherever else it'd hurt to be struck, whether by the Kayos or us? However that turns out, you know that consortes of ours will be going into the interrogation labs."

Guthrie smote the table beside him. "No, Kyra, we'll honor our troth. Afterward I'll take the blame and the consequences."

She rose, went to him, and caught both his cold, heavy hands. "Like hell," she said. *"We* will."

Above and beyond his turret, the galactic belt gleamed. She remembered hearing that in Swedish it was named the Winter Road.

38

FOR SECONDS KYRA could only stare. Her head felt as though she had suddenly gone into free fall. "Is this real?" she whispered at last.

"'What is reality?' said jesting Pilate," Rinndalir answered. "The invitation is quite sincere, no ruse or entrapment. How could my nation gain by that? Fireball already has ample grudges against us. You shall return whenever you choose, your dignity intact. The visit may cause you to look on us less unfavorably. Since you have evidently become rather close to the lord Guthrie, that would be furthersome to us—and, you may agree, to him. However this proves out, I can promise you a unique entertainment." Damn him, that voice and that smile were enough to melt your back teeth. "And, naturally, I shall savor your presence." The beautiful face went serious. "But if you wish to come, you must at once. Events approach their perihelion. They will pass it soon and swiftly."

She hauled her brain together. She didn't know of anything more she could do for Fireball. Guthrie had declined her offer to pilot *Kestrel* in his service. "We'll have plenty, and after what you've been through, you need a longer rest than time allows before you're fit again." She had yielded, not altogether reluctantly.

Nor could she phone for his advice. As occupied as he was, it would likely take hours to get through to him. Here was a chance to, just possibly, learn something useful about the Lunarians. Yes, this might turn out to be a new betrayal of theirs, but she didn't see how she could be so important.

And—back to Rinndalir, that heartless, treacherous, gorgeous son of a cat.

"Muy bien," she threw at him. "I shouldn't, after the trick you pulled, but all right."

His smile flared. "Glorious. Transport waits at the

spacedrome, Berth 23." Did it happen to be there, or had he dispatched it, confident she would accept? "Do not stop to pack. Your room in Zamok Vysoki remembers you."

Blood racketed in Kyra's ears. She sent a message for Guthrie's attention when he should have some to spare, hauled on her boots, and left the suite at a Lunar run.

Outside the hotel she must needs slow down. Tsiolkovsky Prospect was thronged. No Lunarians were in sight. Such as had not departed Tychopolis kept to their residential quarter. In this city foreigners outnumbered them and emotions ran high. Few of those dwellers and transients were at their businesses, now when crisis drew near to climax. They wandered about, sat in the cafés talking too merrily or low and intently, fingered wares in the shops, clustered around every multi in which news repeated itself with different speakers and different scenes but over and over. Where somebody used English, Spanish, or Russian, Kyra caught snatches.

"—won't attack," said a thick-set man, unmistakably North American. "Wouldn't dare. The governments of Earth would seize everything they've got on the planet." Kyra smelled his sweat. He wasn't as confident as he claimed. Earth's industries depended on space, its resources were what saved the biosphere, and the overwhelming majority of space enterprises were Fireball's.

"—alliance with the Selenarchs?" a Latino raged. "Those double-dealing bastards?" He wore a company emblem.

"We may have no choice," replied the woman with him.

"—God's judgment," said a gray-bearded Orthodox priest. "His penalties for our sins and foolishness will be less than they themselves cost us." Maybe he was right, Kyra thought.

Yet what could Fireball do, after the Union's President Escobedo addressed the world? "—no compromise with criminality. Fireball has from the very beginning been hostile to our government, has obstructed and intrigued and encouraged sedition." True, though no more than was well within the bounds of what North America once, and a few countries today, considered freedom of speech and the

right to conduct one's affairs as one saw fit. "A pronounce-
ment from Fireball has sparked civil war in our country.
Sr. Guthrie claims it was false, but he has not called on the
Chaotics to halt their rebellion," and be led away for the
Sepo and the corrective psychotechnicians to work on,
"nor retaliated against the Selenarchs whom he alleges
were the perpetrators." What was he supposed to do,
declare war on them? "I make him this proposal. Let
Fireball make amends by helping us. For example, it has
more capability of space surveillance than the Peace
Authority does, if it chooses to deploy the vessels, and it is
not limited by mandate as the Peace Authority is. Let
Fireball provide us information about Chaotic units, their
locations and activities. Or let Fireball provide suborbital
transport, which we are woefully short of, to our militia
and Security Police, wherever that will enable them to
strike a telling blow. There are many possibilities. We can
agree on which, if Fireball will first agree to obey the law of
the land.

"Then, as soon as the present danger is past, we for our
part will release all Fireball personnel" to deportation?
"not facing criminal charges" which ones, charged with
what? "and negotiate other outstanding issues," such as
the disposal of many billion ucus' worth of property, more
of it held by consorte families than by the company.
"Meanwhile, we must keep those persons detained," prisoners, hostages, "and appeal to the High Council and
Assembly of the World Federation that they order the
Peace Authority to suppress anarchism and piracy." Easier said than done, when the military force for space
operations was lacking. Nothing but small arms in licensed hands legally existed beyond geosync radius,
wherefore Luna had been able to make its declaration of
independence stick after some minor clashes. "But I hope
and pray that such action will not prove necessary, that
Fireball will voluntarily redeem itself. May this come
about! Then Fireball will have earned a voice in the
historic conference that must follow these troubles, to
extend law throughout the Solar System and properly

regulate activity in space" thus ending the autonomy of human beings freely working together. The North American government wasn't the only one that had long desired it.

Yes, the Avantists were playing their cards pretty shrewdly, Kyra thought. They might yet survive the coming showdown. But whether they did or not, this wasn't the last hand. Much more was at stake. Lord, almost cosmic— An opening occurred in the crowd ahead of her. She hastened her strides.

At Ley Circus she got a fahrweg out to the drome. She had it nearly to herself. Leaving it, she stepped forth into a tiled cavern where sounds rang unnaturally loud. Activity was about at a standstill. An occasional human worker gave her a frightened look. The machines went about their jobs unperturbed.

The gate to Berth 23 scanned her and let her past. From the number, she had foreknown that what waited was a suborbital. It too was robotic. She boarded and snugged herself down. The vessel trundled on rails through the airlock to its launch station, got clearance from TrafCon's computer, and lifted off. The acceleration that pushed Kyra back was mild, two Lunar gravities. Soon she was weightless in her harness, soaring among stars. From the northern horizon, full Earth cast witchy blue over maria and craters. Shadows mingled manifold. This was a soft landscape, actually, desolate but soft; stonefall and spalling radiation had worn it down, blurred its edges, without Earth's tectonics querning forth mountains ever new.

The planet fell behind, sank farther, until it hung barely above the Moonscape and the darknesses that it cast stretched very long across level ground. Mostly they lost themselves among the cliffs and crags of the heights toward which the boat slanted. It set down on a small field with a single service building. A car rolled toward it. "Pray debark," said a musical synthetic voice.

Kyra obeyed, climbing from airlock through extended gangtube to the interior of the ground vehicle. It detached itself and trundled off on a road rudimentary but adequate for a weatherless world. The castle towers leaped into her view above a ridge, and then the outer walls, and she passed inside.

A live servant genuflected and escorted her up a ramp to a high, opalescent hall. Rinndalir waited, in purple and gold. He rippled forward to take her hands. His were not metal and plastic but live flesh and graceful bone, warm to the touch. The great gray eyes shone downward at hers. "Well are you come," he said. "Valiantly did you fare, and what a prize you took!"

How did he know? That story hadn't been made public yet. Agents within Fireball— It didn't seem to matter, when she could tell him, "Gracias," and hear the pride resonate. She was no longer his captive or his dupe; they met in shared respect. "Where is the lady Niolente?" she asked.

His reply tingled in her: "Elsewhere, representing us amidst our colleagues." He raised his brows slightly, mischievously.

She made herself withdraw her hands and say, "Yes, of course you Selenarchs need to keep as alert and ready for action as we do. Then why'd you invite me here?" She felt unable to add that it could hardly be for fun and games, at least not exclusively.

"I told you, amiga. Fireball is understandably angry at us, albeit we require each other for allies in the tricky times ahead. My hope is that you will return better disposed toward us and influence the lord Guthrie in that direction. I am on call, but there is no immediate need of me and this is a service I can do my race." The tone grew earnest. "As well as myself. I would like to have back your goodwill."

"I'll . . . listen."

"And behold. Come, pray." He offered his arm. Hers went below, almost involuntarily. His fingertips touched her hand. It was ridiculous what lust the gentle contact roused in her. "I wish you had arrived earlier, giving us leisure for discourse and friendliness before that happens which must, but I was in truth overbusied until this hour."

They moved off between glass pillars toward an archway

opening on a corridor. *That happens which must.* The chill struck at Kyra's loins. "What do you mean?" she exclaimed. "War?"

He nodded. The wan locks swept past his cheekbones. "The Avantist Synod has beamed an enciphered message to Port Bowen. Unless Fireball agrees within twenty-four hours to furnish aid to the government, its people in North America will be adjudged criminal conspirators, subject to court martial and summary justice. The first such proceeding begins when the ultimatum expires."

"No, that's loco! Got to be a bluff!"

"You cannot believe that the lord Guthrie will risk that it isn't. I deem that the Synod expects he will either buckle, thereby beginning the process of Fireball's complete surrender, or else do something rash that will provoke global sanctions against the company. They have sorely misjudged him and his capabilities. They being what they are, it was probable that they would. His strength is gathered. He will strike as soon as all the data are in."

This was another corridor of illusions. The floor was like a rushing river, the walls full of tall flames, the ceiling a night sky where stars fell and burned as meteors, in utter silence. "You claim a hell of a lot of confidential knowledge," Kyra said desperately. "Have you infiltrated his personal staff?"

Rinndalir smiled through the light flickering over his face. "That might be difficult. But we have our monitors watchful at many a vantage, as you shall discover, and from what they tell us, we make our deductions. Be not dismayed. Rejoice. Your commonwealth rides to the rescue of its children."

The tone was soft, but a bugle was in it. Kyra felt a stirring at the roots of her hair. Why indeed any doubts and fears? Her side had done everything humanly possible, short of breaking troth, to reach peace. The enemy had chosen otherwise. Let her cheer Fireball on, and then help batten hatches against the storm that would follow.

True, this male at her side had wrought much to bring the battle to pass. Had he not tampered with Guthrie's first impartation, the Chaotics might well still be quiescent. Without their backs to the wall, the Avantists might well have decided it was best to make an acceptable settlement, even some reparation for their misdeeds.

Really?

As if his faun ears had heard her thoughts, Rinndalir said, "Yes, we of Luna did hasten fate a little. Was that not meet? Your foe requires more than chastisement. He requires destruction, as does a cell gone cancerous before it strews its breed. Upon this day, liberty proves it is not simply sweet, it is mighty. The blows it strikes will be in the cause of all folk everywhere and henceforward."

Her mind sprang wild. Maybe he was right! She too had felt the future as stifling. No doubt Avantism, left to itself, would rot away. How long would that take, though, and what shape would it leave her poor country in? What of other lands that were unfree? Might lives computerized in the name of order or social justice or whatever they called it, look up with a sudden freshness? Might an idea blow forth upon the wind, that governments and machines ought to be instruments people used, not ends in themselves?

Let there be Lunacy!

The way led into the Pagoda. At midnight it was ashine from Earth low in the northeast, a formless blue that diffused through the diamond, star-gleaming at facets that changed as you moved, until it shaded into space-darkness opposite. Handel's Water Music went clear and cool through air that smelled like roses after a rain. Serenity so abrupt was as startling as an unawaited kiss.

A couch had been placed at the table, on which stood wine, goblets, and finger foods. Across from it was a giant multi. Rinndalir guided her to the seat and joined her. "Memories," he murmured.

No, damn it, she mustn't let him seduce her, not yet, anyway. "You mentioned having a lot of monitors out," she said. Her flatness was an offense to these surroundings, though he didn't appear to take any. "I suppose you intend to receive from them?"

"Even so. We man no very capable spacecraft of our

own, we Lunarians, nor maintain a robotic fleet, merely a few vessels for special purposes. Otherwise we rely on Fireball." Perhaps he recited that common knowledge because he felt she could do with a soothing noise. "However, we have produced far more miniatures with observational potency than we have hitherto declared, and we have newly launched them, programmed to track what occurs at their assigned watchposts."

He took a control off the table and flicked it. An image, doubtless retrieved from the database, awakened in the cylinder, a thin metal shape with an instrument boom forward and a linac drive aft. She recognized the general type, if not this precise model, and guessed it was about three meters long, plus the mass accelerator. Most likely it was launched not by a first stage but by a catapult, easy to do off Luna, and powered by sun-rechargeable molecular accumulators—high specific impulse, therefore low mass ratio. Not much delta v between rechargings, but nimble. Basically simple, producible in quantity by an automated factory somewhere in the body of the Moon.

"I daresay Fireball has noticed several of these; I think not most," Rinndalir went on. "We have received no protests. It is a natural act for us and no menace to them. We have also secreted miniflitters with their own observatories near interesting locations on Earth. They transmit at very low energy, but sufficient for the big dish at Copernicus, and with adequate bandwidth. They are now airborne. The Avantists may shoot a few down, but I trust that the majority will show us somewhat."

He poured into the goblets, a gurgle that fitted the music. "Once more, will you propose a toast?" he asked.

Memories, oh, God, yes. "To victory, a clean victory," Kyra said. The wine anointed her tongue and thrilled in her bloodstream.

He sipped, raised his glass anew, and said in his turn, "To chaos."

"What? Do you mean the Kayos this time, the Chaotics? Bueno, yes, luck to them." She clinked rims with him.

"Nay, I mean chaos," he told her, "the liberator, that annihilates the old and engenders the new."

She checked her goblet at her lips. "Chaos in the scientific sense?" she asked uneasily: the forever unforeseeable.

"If you wish, although I would then draw my trope less from mathematics and mechanics than from the quantum heart of things. Come, will you not share drink?"

Kyra wondered why she had balked. He wasn't saluting anything evil, was he? One of his whimsies. She took a larger swallow than she intended.

"Let us see what betides," Rinndalir said. Glass in his right hand, he worked the control with his left. The image in the cylinder blinked away. There appeared an arc of Earth's curve, limned by the multiple layering of air, cloud a volute of purity over turquoise, a loveliness that pierced Kyra as deeply as when she first encountered it. Athwart the environing dark, sunlight slid over the flanks of two spaceships, a big-bellied Argosy-class freighter dwarfing the Falcon torch that paced her. Watched from afar through the opticals of a Lunarian monitor, they showed only by the corposant glimmers astern how they hurtled under drive.

"A-a-arr-rr-rr," went Rinndalir in his throat. "The first attack. We are barely in time." He hunched forward, a-shiver.

Guthrie's voice tolled in Kyra's head. "The high ground is ours," he had reminded her. "We could nudge a few big rocks into collision orbits, or shoot them from the Moon. The threat of the Lunarians doing that was a large factor in getting them their independence, you may recall. But unless the missiles are aerodynamically shaped as well as precision-aimed, we won't have decent control. We'd oftener dig a hole in an empty field, or in a town full of innocent people, rather than our target. I expect we won't have time for the necessary work. Instead, if we must fight, we'll sacrifice a ship or two, crammed full of rocks and dived down on robot."

She had shuddered. First that robot must be reprogrammed for suicide.

But it wasn't like reprogramming a captive Guthrie. Was

it? Machines didn't really have consciousness or free will or a wish to live. Did they?

At this instant— *Go get 'em!*

The freighter and the torch receded from each other, Earthward and spaceward. Rinndalir fingered his control. Somewhere a computer made its calculations and flashed the result into the multi cylinder. To Kyra it was an elegant alphabet that she could not read. The orchestra had begun the Royal Fireworks section.

"Destination, Kennedy Base," Rinndalir exulted. "I awaited as much. We have more than one observer in that vicinity. If any remain operative—"

A mountainscape stood before them, gray-blue snow-dappled peaks against a sunlit deep heaven, in the foreground pine forest seen as treetops rushing past, in the middle distance an airfield, a radome, a communications tower, clustered buildings, vehicles scuttling about. Underground, Kyra knew, armored, buttressed, lay the command center of the national militia.

They did not see the ship hit. She came too fast. Retrograde with respect to Earth's orbit, reeled in by Earth's gravity, she bore an energy equivalent to the detonation of some two hundred kilotonnes. Stopped down for transmission, the flash nonetheless dazzled Kyra like an unguarded look straight at the sun. It tore into rags in her vision, and she glimpsed a scene that swung and whirled as monstrous winds tossed the aircraft about. A globe of incandescence boiled aloft, spread, vanished into the fungus cloud of smoke and dust that climbed after it to rape the sky. As her sight cleared she made out a broad crater, low-walled but agape at the center where man's caverns lay sundered.

The music rollicked.

"Ya-a-a-ah," breathed Rinndalir. A human in that mood would have screamed it. "Beauty, beauty."

Gladness fled from her, off to wherever yonder lives had been cast. "No, por favor, no," she begged. "I've flown missions to stop this kind of thing."

Sobriety was instant. He set down his glass and laid a

hand over hers. "I pray pardon. The spectacle was magnificent, but, yes, the loss lamentable. Forget not, however, forget not, my dear, this was also ineluctable."

"Did we—did Guthrie—have to? I mean, a demonstration in an area where nobody was—"

"I fear not. What must be demonstrated is not power alone, but the will to use it. The shock of the actuality shatters the spirit and brings a speedy end to resistance. Else might the conflict smolder on for days or weeks, and reach no final decision. What meanwhile would become of your consortes there? And the rebels who trust you, they would not survive. Remember how the second World War was ended."

"What?"

"Japan was beleaguered. Yet it was not ready, it was not able, to yield. Blockade and famine could have reduced it in a few more years, invasion in perhaps one more, but deaths would have been millionfold and the country left waste, its heritage down among Crete and Babylon and Mohenjo-Daro. Moreover, the Soviet Empire would have been a co-occupier. If you have knowledge of Korea and Vietnam, you may think on what that would have meant. Two nuclear bombs forestalled all this."

Comfort ran into her through the light pressure of his clasp, until he drained it away by saying pensively, "I anticipate your second strike soon," as he began to hunt through sendings from Earth.

She pulled free of him. "No! Not after that!"

He looked at her. "Yes, if Guthrie is the realist he claims to be. He must show forth his arsenal—most especially, to the World Federation and its armed enforcers. This day many things begin to perish. None may foreknow which they are, nor where he shall stand in the wreckage, but be sure, Kyra Davis, that none can stand save by his own strength."

She stared at the mask of him, which slowly grinned. "You can't mean that," she whispered. "You mustn't. This—victory?—won't be worth it. Nothing could be worth it."

"Oh, but it is itself the end, to which victory is but a

means and of small account," he rejoiced. "Whatever befalls, the order of things that has prevailed is broken. Grieve not. Nothing did it hold for our kind—yours, mine, all that are now freed to be born—save ignominious doom. Again is chaos loose and every tomorrow unbound."

"You, you wanted a war."

"Say rather that that was the tool which came to hand."

"You engineered it. Guthrie's broadcast. And . . . the Avantist ultimatum, was that your work too?"

He laughed. "Darling, you compliment extravagantly our cleverness and our abilities. Thank you." His attention went to the multi. "Hai, but here is promise."

Scenes had been flickering past, Northwest Integrate asprawl around its waters, a truck convoy on a prairie highway, a squadron of flyers, thousands of people packed and shouting in Exploration Plaza, fire raging in Quark Fair. . . . Rinndalir turned back to the next latest and held it.

Momentarily, Kyra knew confusion, a disrupted anthill that burned. Her pilot's skills took over and the pattern emerged for her, making insane sense. The observer hovered high to scan a reach of tawny hills where live oak and eucalyptus stood in scattered groves. Afar shone water, and beyond it lifted a serration of buildings. She recognized the main biospace in San Francisco Bay Integrate.

Explosions had scarred the slopes. Park service robots sped ludicrously about, quenching blazes in the dry grass, while armored cars lurched forward, helmeted men zigzagged crouched, flitters hummed overhead, and guns spat. The men struggled up toward a tree-clad ridge. Rinndalir magnified their goal, and Kyra discerned hastily dug earthworks, shelter holes, rapid-fire stations. There other men tended a flatbed truck on which stood a generator and what she guessed was a laser gun, scanty defense against attack from above.

"The remnant of a substantial Chaotic force," Rinndalir deduced. "The militia have them trapped, but they hold out for a span yet, perhaps in the hope a relief troop will fly in." He made a finger-shrug. "That might have been a possibility daycycles ago, for the Chaotics had a few airborne units, but they are brought down."

For Kyra it was nightmare, a past she had known only through books and dramas, had believed safely dead. Corpses and wounded, obscene beneath the sun— The Peace Authority could end it in an hour or less, with proper military equipment wielded by professionals. Instead, these poor, ill-outfitted, ill-trained militia—backups for the civil and political police—slogged and died in a fight with brother citizens who had even less at their beck. But the Avantists did not want international intervention. It would bring inconveniently much to light.

Rinndalir stroked his chin. "This is a suitably spectacular rescue to carry out," he said. "It won't necessarily happen. We may have to watch a playback from elsewhere— Hai-ah!"

The torchcraft descended. In atmosphere her jet was a white flame-tongue tinged with blue, red where it licked at Earth. Kyra knew how it roared, the heat that billowed from it and the lightning smell of air through which lethal radiation went lancing. Metal melted, flesh exploded in soot off calcined skeletons, ground quaked and blackened, flames leaped up in a ring that widened.

Laterals blasted. The torchcraft tilted, recovered, hopped from point to point as she scrawled her swath across the Union's men.

Rinndalir chanted in his own language. Ecstasy was upon him. The militia broke, ran, stumbled, fell, shrieked appeals for mercy that Kyra could not hear. The music played on.

The torchcraft ascended. Nothing remained but ruin, and rebels on the crest who one by one crept forth— stunned, terrified by their deliverance? In a while they would cheer, maybe.

Kyra supposed the spaceship hadn't actually killed many of their foes. There was no need. A demonstration of power and of the resoluteness to use it, that sufficed. Yes. She wondered who the pilot was. Names, faces tumbled through her mind. Did she want to know? It might well stay a secret. But then she'd have to wonder about all of them.

Rinndalir turned to her. *"Consummatum est."* His voice throbbed. "Surely no more after this. Who dares fight on? You drank to a clean victory, Kyra. You have it, as clean as ever in history. Drink afresh!"

She sat passive. In the multi the hillside burned.

He lowered the glass he had raised. "True," he said quietly, "what you have witnessed bears its troublous aspect. Pray believe not that I enjoyed the sight of death and agony. Yet those inhere in life, Kyra. Here they have served a worthy purpose." His tone gathered a lilt. "And the spectacle *was* superb."

"Yes, you would appreciate it," she replied.

He stiffened a bit. "Do you mourn? Do you feel guilt, that you were party to this? Will you denounce Fireball and renounce your allegiance?"

"No. Oh, no." Her words fell dull into the music. "I just . . . need to come to terms with it. And with myself."

"I understand." He smiled. "Or mayhap I do not. We are of different natures, you and I. Well, I bade you hither in hopes we might learn somewhat more of them,"—he laid an arm along the couch back—"and celebrate together."

His skin was giving off a strange fragrance, not quite musky. Warmth blossomed in her. It guttered out. Kyra stood up. "No," she said, "gracias, but I want to go home. Now." To Tychopolis first, unavoidably, a way station for the house on Lake Ilmen. Or Toronto Compound? That might be where she could soonest find out what had become of Bob Lee and, if he lived, help him back to freedom.

39

ATTENDANTS DISCONNECTED THE case from the electronics and photonics that its program had controlled, and bore it to Guthrie's private office. They set it on the desk and went out. For a while it lay alone. Eyestalks swung about, vision ranging over stone floor, silently occupied equipment, viewdome full of Moonscape and stars and waning Earth. This had been built since Guthrie came home from Alpha Centauri. The lenses fell to rest looking at a picture, an old photograph copied and recopied as the decades faded it, of Juliana and her children when they were young.

The door retracted to admit a form not unlike a knight in armor, which strode to take stance before the desk. Until the door shut, the sole sound was a soughing of the ventilation that neither one here had need of. Then, "Saludos," rumbled Guthrie in the robot.

"Do you mean that?" gibed Guthrie in the box.

"Probably not." The robot hesitated before he went on, sardonicism dissolving: "Or— I don't know. You've caused a lot of grief, but you're me, in a way."

The other tone remained derisive. "Well, I wish you luck. Why not, considering who you are? You'll have use for all you can get."

The robot laid a hand across the base of his turret, as a man cups his chin when thinking. "How've you been?" he asked.

"Stupid question. Same as you'd've been. Half glad, half sorry that a spook can't stew in a helpless rage. It passed some of the time, inventing new cusswords for the situation."

"Didn't your hookup help?" Quiviran apparatus wasn't available, but prisoner Guthrie had had full multiceiver and data retrieval access, plus pulsation if he wanted to feel drunk.

His voice lightened. "Assorted shows did, yes. Classics especially. When did you last play the Helsinki Opera *Faust* and ideationally lust after Olga Wald? She must be pretty long in the tooth by now, if she's still alive. A couple of new things were good too, things composed after you switched me off and tucked me away."

"I think I know which you mean. And then the news."

"I haven't bothered with that for the last three or four daycycles."

"Huh?" The robot's lenses peered into the casket's as if trying to find something behind their glitter. "I sure would have."

"No, you wouldn't. Not when it no longer had anything to do with anything *you* would ever do. You'd go for stuff that took you out of yourself for a short, short spell. Think about it."

The robot straightened, gazed forth at the stars, and presently said, "I suppose so."

"Oh, I am sort of curious," the casket admitted. "Not enough to want details. But in a general way, what's happened?"

The robot folded hands behind back and paced to and fro. "The Avantists are out," he related. "Literally out. When their militia and most Sepo units declined to fight on, just about every top-rank political-bureaucratic-doctrinal honcho vamoosed, with quite a few of their understrappers. Some are in Hiroshima, calling themselves the North American government in exile, also claiming asylum. Meanwhile the Liberation junta is in Futuro, calling itself the interim government. The Federation Assembly's bickering over whether to recognize it. However, the Council has accepted its invitation for the Peace Authority to restore order and bring relief to damaged areas. On the whole, the country's functioning."

"You think the Federation will recognize?"

"Eventually. After an election, anyway. Popular sentiment around the world seems to favor it."

The voice tautened. "Do you by any chance know what's become of Enrique Sayre?"

"The Sepo chief? Yes. Dead. As far as I've been able to find out, he didn't escape because he lost time trying to make off with another copy of me he had stashed. He must have had some or other wild idea about advantages it could give him. The pursuit got wind of that and cornered him. Next day, a drumhead court martial—or kangaroo court, if you prefer—and a firing squad."

Eyestalks rose, lay back, rose again. "Good," murmured Guthrie in the box.

The robot halted his pacing and stared. "You say that?"

"Sure," his voice snarled. "After what that slimester did to me."

"But you're programmed to—"

"Believe in Xuan's revelation and the technosalvation to come." The sneer died away. Quietly: "Yes. I do. But at the same time—" Barely to hear: "Can even you who're me understand?"

The robot lifted a hand that was not quite steady, let it fall, and stammered, "You, you knew, you knew all along, you know it was forced on you. Into you."

"Yes." The answer was like metal. "And I had to work for the cause. Had to. Would yet, if I were more than a thing in a box. I'd destroy you." The metal snapped across. "Nightmare."

The robot looked down at his hands. "I can imagine a nightmare where I strangle Juliana. Not with these. With what were mine."

"You know it. You can say it."

"Only to you. To myself. Here, alone."

They became without motion for minutes that neither counted.

Guthrie in the casket broke that stillness, harshly. "What do you know about the Lunarians?"

The robot started. "What? . . . Why?"

"Waiting for this meeting, I've maybe had more time than you to wonder. That ultimatum from the Avantists to you was such an incredible piece of stupidity. Not that governments or corporations haven't often bungled worse yet. Just the same—"

"You mean, did the Lunarians fake it?" The robot recovered self-possession. "Of course the notion occurred to me. When the message came in, I beamed back to North America asking if they were serious. They replied yes, and our techs verified this was from their headquarters. We didn't and we don't know any way an outside party could have monkeyed with the transmissions. But now . . . assorted members of the former Synod, and several other bigwigs, deny having known anything about it."

"They might well be lying. Or, I'd guess for some cases, their colleagues didn't inform them, knowing they'd try to prevent or retract the threat. You've more knowledge of the Lunarians than I do. Could they have triggered it somehow?"

"They may have applied vectors," the robot said. "Two or three key Avantists—probably not in the Synod itself, but close and trusted counselors—may have been moles in Selenarch pay. Besides that, or alternatively, humbler agents could have been at work, agents in a position to slip false data and computer worms into the sociodynamic programs the Avantists put so much faith in. That could've made the analysis of how Fireball would react come out wrong. Might be. Kyra Davis has brought me reason to believe the Lunarian lords intended this result, whether or not they had anything effective to do with actually causing it. But we haven't the hard information, and I suspect we never will."

The box formed a sigh. "It hardly matters. In either case, you need their support. Fireball's deep in the dung pile."

"'Fraid so. Violation of law on a global scale. We couldn't break troth—"

"I had to!" screamed the casket.

The robot laid a hand on it, most gently. "I know."

He stood like that until the eyestalks stopped trembling. Then he stepped back and said, "Nothing will ever be the same again, that's for certain. And Rinndalir, the Lunarian I've had most to do with, he makes no bones about being glad of it. I think he hopes the entire system will tear itself to pieces."

Bodiless Guthrie had calmed anew. "From his viewpoint, if I'm not misjudging his culture, he's right, you know. Also, I'd give moderate odds, from yours."

"Huh?"

"Listen. This isn't just the faith nailed into me speaking. At least, not entirely. Avantism has crumbled, no doubt, but the logic of events is as sound as ever. The Transfiguration Xuan foresaw, it's going to happen regardless— maybe, now, a bit faster—unless something absolutely radical, some catastrophe, kicks the whole chessboard over."

"This isn't quite that sort of upheaval," the robot argued. "In fact, I expect, I hope everybody will pussyfoot through the next few years. What's taken place has rocked them back. Me too."

"Whether you can manage to pussyfoot is another matter. How long, for instance, can Fireball stay halfway human? Gets harder, makes less economic sense, all the time, doesn't it? And soon, I've learned, you should be seeing full artificial intelligence."

The robot made a chopping gesture. "That's for then," he said brusquely. Softer: "I came here today, first watch when I've had a couple of free hours, to ask you—myself —what we should do about you."

The reply was immediate. "Terminate me."

The robot raised his hands. "No, wait. You're too dangerous to keep, the way you are, true. But a reprogramming—"

"Don't insult our intelligence," snapped the other. "To find how to reprogram, you'd have to make copy after copy of me and tinker them apart in hell, experimenting. Anyhow, I don't want it. Even if I were changed, I wouldn't want it."

"Why?"

"Too much blood."

"It's on me too," the robot whispered. "The exact figures aren't in yet, but Fireball killed several hundred people, and hurt many more."

"You'll have to live with yours," said the casket. He barked a laugh. "Live!" In quick, flat words: "You've got your duty, to those pilots who did the job and to everybody else. I'm not necessary, not obligated. And my actions brought it on."

"Not your fault."

"Let me go!" roared Guthrie. "In Juliana's name, let me go!"

The robot spent hardly a minute in deciding. This was himself, after all. "Okay," he said low. "In her name. When?"

"Soon as possible."

"Anything you'd like first?"

Sudden tenderness responded. "Yes. One favor. A look at the last thing we really shared, we two."

The casket had no need to say more. The robot picked him up and carried him over to a point from which, cradled in the hands, he saw among the stars Alpha Centauri.

PART THREE

demeter

40

"COME," EIKO SAID when Kyra began to voice the trouble that was in her, "before we speak of this, let us go to where peace is."

Hand in hand they wandered from the apartment and down the passages. Folk who recognized one or both of them called greetings that were warm but not exuberant, and seemed to take for granted that they wouldn't stop to talk. Others likewise went about their business or even their pleasure more quietly than of old. They hadn't cheered, either, while Kyra and her fellow pilots led Holden's men away for ferrying back to North America. Everybody was glad to see them leave, including themselves, but soberly. Returning to L-5 on her own, she found the hush deepened.

And when he had opened the seventh seal, there was silence in heaven about the space of half an hour.

The fahrweg brought the pair to Trevorrow Preserve. Still mute, they walked across the meadows. A number of people had sought here, couples and small groups, none alone. For the same reason, Kyra thought. Sky and sun, clouds and breezes were artificial, the openness an illusion, but they were what there was, and the leaves, blossoms, winged creatures did genuinely live.

Nobody else was at the Tree, though. Maybe its mightiness roused feelings too strong for comfort. Kyra and Eiko climbed to the third stage. Thence a walkway ran along a nearly horizontal bough. At its end was another platform, with bench seats under two of the rails. Branches forking from the sides, growing up from below, drooping down from above, draped curtains of deep-green needles. They stirred and rustled in the wind. Glimpses of mass and height, growth and radiance, flickered through them. Warmth baked a resiny fragrance out of the bark, which was so strangely soft to touch. A thrush flew by.

They sat down, facing. Eiko's breath, which the ascent had quickened, became easy again. She met Kyra's gaze and smiled as a mother smiles at a child who is hurt. "Now we can talk," she said.

Kyra looked from her, into distance. "Gracias, querida," she replied tonelessly. "I don't know, however— I've been wondering more and more while we came— what good it'll do. Just tossing the obvious back and forth."

"That is not for nothing. We should not merely know what is in our hearts, we should share it. And perhaps, barely perhaps, out of that will come a vision. I also have been thinking, you see. This is about Fireball and the future, surely?"

"Of course. You're right, I've got to unload on somebody, and you—" Kyra looked back and spoke fast. "What's happened lately wasn't the real crisis. That's building up like a breaker, and when it crashes over us, I don't know if we, Fireball, will live through it. Your father, he understands politics better than most. What does he expect?"

"He says the reaction against Fireball, after what it did, will continue gathering force," Eiko answered levelly. "Guthrie-san has shown what power he can wield, and it is horrifying. Fear breeds hatred. Emotion feeds on itself."

"But we had to act!" Kyra cried. "We had to! Didn't we?"

"You were true to yourselves—"

"Gracias," Kyra mumbled. "I needed to hear that."

"—as the Taira were," Eiko finished.

Kyra blinked. "Hm?"

"Or the Sioux or the Confederates of your country's past. They won their victories. But in the end their enemies broke them." Eiko sighed. "Yet nothing is immortal. Where now are the Minamoto?"

"We could fight. We could make all Earth bow down to us." Kyra's voice dropped. "We won't, plain to see. Hell, *I* wouldn't. I couldn't kill like that, not for troth or anything. The way Guthrie puts it is, 'We'd have to become a goddamn government ourselves. What'd be the point?'"

"He will not hesitate to use his economic strength, I imagine. He can negotiate. Compromise. Buy time."

Kyra nodded, then slumped, elbows on knees, staring at the deck. "Oh, yes. In the long run, what for?"

"I understand." Eiko sat still a while in the murmurous wind.

Then she leaned over, patted her friend's shoulder, and said quietly, "I have had some thoughts about that. Doubtless they are impractical, but you might care to hear them."

Kyra lifted her head. "Say on."

"The Federation will try to force Fireball and Luna under its control. They will resist. Which prevails, my father does not venture to predict, but he thinks the odds are that it will be the Federation, at least to a high degree. For he believes—he hopes, as I do, and as you seem to confirm for us, that Fireball will deny itself any further use of violence, the ultimate sanction." Eiko paused. "But even if it nevertheless stays free, and Luna keeps her sovereignty—after all, they both mainly wish to preserve the order of things that has been—that order is doomed. Already, by what it did, Fireball has irretrievably changed everything, including itself. And time hastens onward."

Kyra nodded again. "Social evolution. Machine evolution. The whole universe mutating out from under us."

"We have other universes."

Kyra's eyes widened. "Huh?"

Eiko laughed a little. "Not literally, I suppose. I mean other worlds."

"You mean we should emigrate? Eiko, you know better than that."

"I have followed the technical arguments as best I was able. It is true, not many could go. But they would be those who truly desired."

"Go? Where, for MacCannon's sake? Where is any real estate we could use?"

Bare rocks, Kyra thought, barren wastes, crematorium heat, tomb cold, lethal radiation, unbreathable air or none—the beauty and the majesty of God, a wealth of resources which had saved Earth from being stripped and poisoned lifeless, but nowhere a place for the son of man to lay his head or the daughter hers. Oh, you can fashion yet another colony on Mars or on a moon or asteroid, you can build yet another O'Neill, but what shall it profit? You will be no more free than you were. You can move to the Oort cloud, to the realm of the outermost comets, where the sun is merely the brightest of the stars, and it won't be far enough.

"Alpha Centauri. The planet called Demeter."

Kyra's surprise was at Eiko saying such a thing. "Aren't people done with fantasizing about that?" she floered. "Hopeless. Habitable, yes, sort of, but the life has hardly started crawling out of the sea and it isn't compatible with our kind anyway. As for the land, the stoniest desert on Earth is a Paradise garden by comparison."

"Pioneers could therefore in good conscience make what they wished of it."

"The trip— You know what the specs would be, the cost. You're not ignorant. Or have you forgotten? Sending a handful of settlers would bankrupt Fireball itself."

"Therefore the society they fled, this Burning House, could not follow them."

"And for what? In a thousand years, smash! The end."

Before Kyra spun the images she had seen played out on computer screens. Two suns in orbit about one another—

but no, it was more intricate than that. Afar swung Proxima, ember of a red dwarf, often flaring but feebly, a captured wanderer, too dim and remote to matter. A was the big one, shining not unlike Sol but almost half again as bright. B had about a third of that luminosity, and a single planet remaining after its companion snatched Phaethon from it. A had three of its own, Demeter the outermost. And Demeter bore life.

How terribly few were the worlds that did, even as primitive as Demeter's. Mars had done so once, briefly, before the chill and the drought made a mummy of it. The Centaurian globe did later, as A grew hotter in its aging and glaciers melted to make oceans. There too, how short a span until death reclaimed dominion.

A could firmly hold planets out to perhaps two and a half times the distance of Earth from Sol. The domain of B was less. Elsewhere between the suns was the forbidden zone, where they perturbed every orbit to chaos and nothing existed save asteroids on wild and shifty tracks. Into that region had Phaethon edged—a billion years ago? Thereafter each pass made its path less stable, until at last it came to the point where A seized it from B and it ran around the larger star, retrograde, in ever-changing cometlike ellipses. Those intersected the track of Demeter at equally fickle nodal points, for which reason humans gave the body the same name as an Earth-crossing asteroid. At Alpha Centauri, the name became a great deal more meaningful.

It was impossible to calculate the position of the renegade more than five or ten thousand years ahead, but it was also irrelevant. In a trifle above one millennium, Phaethon would collide with Demeter.

"And the other systems we know of with oxygen-atmosphere planets, they're too far," Kyra went on. "Suspends would be permanently dead before any ship we could build to carry them got there. Not that Alpha Cen's reachable, as a feasible matter, by anything but robots and downloads. But supposing we managed it somehow, what'd be the gain? No, we're stuck where we are."

She had thought she had come to terms with the vision of a reality in which life was frail, vanishingly rare, an accident. She found now that she had not.

Eiko broke it for her: "A thousand years can be lived in. They go well beyond any time that the values you cherish are likely to survive here. During them, much could happen."

"Sure. All kinds of nonsense could get babbled."

In Eiko's countenance Kyra saw not hurt but compassion. She curbed herself and said unevenly, "I'm sorry. That was uncalled for. My bitterness speaking. You . . . you're serious, aren't you?"

Eiko smiled anew. "In part. We may freely play with ideas, now when nobody else listens."

"M-m—bueno, it always was a grand daydream. Given a thousand years, a colony might work something out. But Eiko, it's such a forlornly long shot."

"Does that mean it is ridiculous?" the other replied. Her gaze went into the swaying, whispering, light-unrestful green. "Some fantasies came to me while I sat, often and often, high in the Tree. Fancies about evolution. It has no purpose, the biologists tell us, no destiny; it simply happens, as blindly and wonderfully as rainbows. Nevertheless the scum on ancient seas becomes cherry blossoms, tigers, children who see the rainbow and marvel."

And it becomes killings, cancers, and governments, Kyra thought. But what the hell. Aloud: "I've heard assorted rhapsodies about humankind going to the stars, of course. Who hasn't? Each of them founders on the practical problems."

"The fish that first ventured ashore had considerable practical problems. Please, dear, let me continue."

"Sure. Sorry."

"I have wondered—" Eiko reached to lay hold of a twig that fluttered near her. She held its needles against her cheek and released it to the air. "Why is this, the Tree, here?" she asked. "Life, evolution—the germ plasm that evolution works on does not seek of its own desire to where selection can winnow it—life has brought not just humans but grass and trees and birds into space. Why?

How does this happen? Is it not because we bear needs we must fulfill, as old as our ancestry? I think the life force is not, in its innermost being, progressive. It is profoundly conservative. It does what it must to keep what is."

Against all common sense, ghosts walked suddenly through Kyra's bones and out to the ends of her nerves. "We went to space, really, to save life on Earth," she breathed. "And the groundside measures—the Renewal was an aberration, the job got done in spite of the fanatics. . . . Pilgrims to America so they could stay what they were. 'Our rights as Englishmen.'"

"Humans are primitive, unspecialized animals," Eiko said. "We conserve much that others have lost."

"But that's because we did evolve special features," Kyra argued. "Hind-legs walking, power-grip thumb, big brain."

"It is the same for our societies," Eiko responded. "To save what it is, life perforce adapts, evolves; and so it changes what it is. But the course of that evolution was set by the wish to abide."

"You think that at Alpha Centauri—" Kyra's words trailed away.

Eiko spread her hands. "Simply a thought. I agree, doubtless a crazy one."

"If you really believed that, amiga, you'd never have spoken it," Kyra told her.

The ghosts cried in a language she did not know. Her own was stripped-down plain. "I've got access to Guthrie these days. I could put a bee in his bonnet. What harm? And who knows, who knows?" the space pilot asked the wind.

41

EARTH WAS A crescent, pale to behold against sunlight that drowned most stars and seared the Lunar wastescape with heat. Shadows lay thick around rocks and pockmarks. The viewdome over the office dimmed it all down into a twilight, vague as the remembrance of a dream. Three bodies stood beneath, human, humanoid robot, and purely functional machine.

The last of these held the Guthrie who reigned here. His optics dwelt on the man. "Can we do it, Pierre?" he rumbled. "I mean, if we go for broke?"

Aulard raised his brows. The lines in his forehead became furrows. "I am to tell you sis instant?" he replied.

"No, no, of course you can't, not without your figures and computer models and tests and scaleups and more tests and the dish ran away with the spoon. But an in-principle answer, off the top of that good head for such things which you've still got—in principle, is the idea worth checking out?"

"It 'as been examined often enough."

"Yeah, and found impossibly expensive, therefore not examined further. But today, forget the economics. Can we, given a blank check on Fireball's resources, if we insist on doing it, can we?"

Aulard shrugged. "It is not me 'oo went loco w'en I was captive, it seems." His white head turned to the humanoid. "Per'aps you can make 'im see. Too much 'as 'appened to 'im. You remember more clearly. Tell 'im 'ow senseless sis is."

The metal form was silent for half a minute. It housed the reserve copy of Guthrie that Sayre had ordered made and stored, lately brought from the vault to the Moon. So far the older Guthrie had not downloaded into the newer. Except for what he had observed, read, accessed for himself, the latter was freshly home from Alpha Centauri.

"Demeter?" he said at length. "I don't know. I'd be glad to go back if—if that was the way to go. I'm not sure whether it is, but—Yes, tell us, Pierre."

Aulard's glance returned to the first. "No, you tell me,", he snapped. "Planting a colony, a live colony, on a planet useless and *condamnée*, you fetch me 'ere in person to make a bad joke?"

"Look," said that Guthrie, "I told you both, this is just a notion I'm exploring. It may well be lepton. Or maybe if it can be done, it shouldn't. I called you in, instead of calling you, precisely because this is such a question of . . . feel." His style; he had always maintained that images, no matter how high-fidelity, lacked blood, and that he, no matter how much computer power was his to link with, had been a better manager when he lived. "You see, we've got to ransack every option, and this one is, if nothing else, the shaggiest."

"W'at is se crisis?"

"You know damn well. With the Federation. Fireball and Luna versus Earth." Guthrie paused. "But I guess you don't appreciate how crucial it is. You're lately out of Sepo detention, followed by a well-deserved secluded vacation with your family." A tentacle gestured at the humanoid. "And you, Junior, to you the situation must be abstract yet. Maybe you'll both pick up some sense of urgency if I show you part of my most recent confidential conversation with Sitabhai Mukerji. We agreed to record for our private reference, including in discussions like this. It was shortly after the Kyra Davis I've mentioned had made the suggestion to me that I'm asking you about. I'd been thinking like blazes."

He plugged into the multi, summoned the playback to his auxiliary mentation program, fast-scanned it there, and activated the section he wanted at real-time speed, the Earth-Luna transmission lag edited out. The cylinder filled with separated images of slender dark woman and brawny man. "Yeah, I've taken to generating a face for her," he explained. "Kind of a friendly token, humanizing me a little bit, I hope. Not that it'd sucker her into anything, she's a sharp realist and stands by her duty, but—"

Speech began. "—police barely stopped the demonstration from becoming a riot," Mukerji said. "Will you accept that as an object lesson? There is no lack of others."

Ghost-Guthrie's mouth tightened. "We're really that unpopular in Himalaya too?" he answered low. "I thought those people especially loathed the Avantists."

"On religious grounds only. The Union government never threatened them. But you—Fireball—you resurrected *war.*" Mukerji drew breath. "You and your Lunarian accomplices. That alliance is as obvious, now, as the Moon itself. The beautiful and holy Moon, made into a menace hanging over our heads."

Guthrie formed a sigh. "Well, mass emotions have positive feedback, and so crusades get spawned. If I can't convince you of our peaceful intentions, Madame President, no point in trying to reason with the general public."

Mukerji's tone went oddly gentle. "Oh, you know I acknowledge your honesty, if not the Selenarchs'—your honesty according to your lights. Actually, a good many Earthdwellers do. But it doesn't count. Your very status as criminals doesn't count. The basic fact is, your lights, your standards, your whole *raison d'être* are no longer admissible in civilization as it has developed. Such a concentration of powers in so few hands, devoid of every social control, is no more tolerable than a pathogen in the bloodstream. Your action has finally brought the longstanding conflict to a head, unambiguous and inescapable. Perhaps we should thank you for that."

Guthrie's image frowned. "Ma'am, let's not waste time on ground we've trampled flat. I asked for this talk because I just may have found a way out. But it's radical at best, if it can be done at all. Before I describe it, may I ask what the latest notions are for dealing with us? Don't worry about repeating the obvious. I'm trying, at my distance from you and in my condition, to find out what the current context is that we've got to work in."

"You must have been following the Assembly debates, if

not the speeches and editorials and pronunciamentos everywhere else."

"Sort of. One common idea is to kick us off Earth and break relations, starve us to death, isn't it?"

"Gyrocephaly, agreed. But it shows how high feelings have become. As do the proposals to build a space military and bring Fireball and Luna to obedience, you to trial, by force of arms."

"To take us over, is what that means. Ma'am," said Guthrie without emphasis, "we won't let it happen. Try, and we'll boycott you ourselves and see how long you can keep going. Please explain to them."

"I do, over and over. No, it won't come to that. Trade with you will continue, in an increasingly strained fashion, because it must." Mukerji shifted in her chair until she sat and spoke as if she were in the presence of a living man, looking into his eyes. "But if meanwhile a united Earth—in practice, a consortium under Federation governance—if we marshal all the resources we can spare and create our own space marine, then move out where you are and found our own bases, our own industries—this is under real consideration."

Guthrie's image nodded. "I see. No big surprise. And we couldn't prevent, whether by embargo or attack. I wouldn't let us. It'd go in the teeth of everything my Juliana wanted us to be about." He made the noise of clearing his throat. "But have you folks thought what it'd cost you?"

"Much too much," Mukerji admitted heavily. "Nevertheless, the end will be the destruction of Fireball and the reduction of the Selenarchs. For how can you compete with the organized effort of the whole mother planet?" She raised a palm. "Don't preach to me about government inefficiency. Imagine your markets closed to you, piece by piece. Consider, as well, that we will not saddle ourselves with an obsolete set of positions for humans that robots can fill better."

"Yeah. And full-aware artificial intelligence is on the way."

"So the psychoneticists tell me." Mukerji smiled,

though not gloatingly. Sadly? "In no event can you long go on as you have done, Mr. Guthrie. Whatever we do or do not on Earth, time hounds you. Fireball has had its day. A glorious day it was. I would be sorry to see it end in ignominy."

"And I," he said, "to see it end. Not the business. The idea."

"Untrammeled liberty? Another magnificent fossil, I fear."

"Could be. I'm not absolutely convinced." Guthrie's image hunched its thick shoulders forward. "No, I never did believe anything can be forever. But it can change, it can evolve. We could force you to destroy us, in that criminally wasteful duplication of what we have. Or we could quietly get out of your way—but on our terms."

Mukerji stiffened. "What do you mean, sir?"

"Some very, very tentative thoughts, which I'd like to see your reaction to. No promises on either side. Maybe you'll kill the idea here and now. But for the sake of argument, hear it, please. If Fireball gradually disbands, with most of its assets transferred to Earth—to whatever organization you set up for the purpose—would you people first, in exchange, help us toward our goal? It's not one that could ever, in any way, damage you. Would that kind of deal be arrangeable?"

"Go on," Mukerji whispered.

Guthrie in the machine switched the playback off.

"She'll keep this to herself till we make a concrete proposal," he said. "That's what I want from you, Pierre, an opinion as to whether it's worth the large research effort necessary to find out whether a development effort would succeed. If you guesstimate it is, I'll inform the lady, and she'll stall for us as long as she can while we do our investigation."

"Emigration to Demeter," scoffed the engineer. "Absurd. Se magnitude, you may as sensibly propose shipping se Atlantic Ocean up for Luna to 'ave water not from comets."

"Wait, I didn't mean the bunch of us," Guthrie told him. "Not even a big fraction. Some hundreds, maybe.

Those who really want to go, leaving everything they had and risking everything they have, because they hate the rational new order taking over the Solar System."

"They hate the fact that, in the long run, Xuan was right," murmured his other self.

"I don't know about that," he said. "Maybe the machines own the future, maybe they don't. I just don't like turning it over to them for free. As for our consortes who stay behind, Pierre, they'll be okay. The transition can't happen overnight. They'll be needed till they're ready to retire on nice pensions. Attrition will reduce the human presence in space fast enough to suit anybody on Earth, I should think. Except for those who've elected to go start again from scratch at Alpha Centauri."

"Whatever they make there," his other self predicted, "it won't be like anything that was before. It can't."

"Certainly not. It might well flop completely, everybody die off as miserably as the Greenland Norse, long before Phaethon puts paid to Demeter's account. We can but try. Or can we, Pierre? Think of it as a problem in design, if nothing else."

If the man had not quite kindled, he had begun to smolder as he listened. *"Bien,* say a sousand persons plus supplies and equipment." He spoke slowly, almost under his breath. "Sey cannot stay in suspended animation longer san, eh, forty or fifty years. After sat, too much irreversible damage from background radiation and quantum chemistry. Serefore, about one-tenss c mean velocity." His gaze went outward, among the unseen stars. "It can be done, yes, sough per'aps two or sree vessels rasser san one large—" He shook his head. "But no. Deceleration squares se mass ratio, remember. I doubt we 'ave antimatter to power so much. We may need ten or twenty years to make enough, after we build added capacity. Meanw'ile se 'ole social-political equation transforms 'erself."

"Do we have to have reaction braking at the far end?" asked Guthrie in the humanoid.

Aulard looked at him. "W'y, no. Not if—Yes, I recall discussions long ago—" He tugged his chin. "M-m, we send a'ead very soon se little von Neumann machines to multiply semselves and sen build an industrial plant sat can make a sun-powered laser adequate to slow se ships w'en sey arrive. . . ."

"Now you're talking!" exclaimed the senior Guthrie. "All we need do is boost our ark or arks to one-tenth light speed or thereabouts, and put 'em on trajectory. Is this workable?"

"I must compute before I can be sure, *naturellement,*" Aulard replied, "but I suspect it will still come close to exhausting your energy supply."

"That won't matter."

"No," said Guthrie in the humanoid, "it'll antimatter."

Unreasonable laughter met the childish pun, followed by a sudden excited seriousness.

42

A PEACE AUTHORITY squad had gone by, afoot, as Kyra neared the Blue Theta. She realized that sight was not uncommon in the North American megalopolises, and Erie-Ontario seemed peaceful enough. Nonetheless it struck at her. She remarked on it to Robert Lee.

"What did you expect?" he replied. His voice was flat. When she hugged him in greeting, his response had been brief and she felt him tremble. He sat slumped in the recliner opposite her chair. "The Liberation Army is organized and disciplined, but it's tiny. The Chaotics were only united in their hatred of the Avantists. Now they're falling apart into their separate factions—and paying off scores—and quite a few ordinary citizens did have a stake in the old order of things, you know, and are unhappy and revengeful themselves—and the economy's a wreck—" He shrugged.

Kyra was looking at the viewscreen. The sky soared crystalline blue above the towers, save where clouds scudded as dazzlingly white, trailing their shadows across and between them. Wind blew keen with approaching autumn. Abruptly she longed to be out in it. Lee had overheated the apartment, in spite of his thick shirt. This air lay dead upon her. "What will come of it all?" she wondered.

"My guess is, the present arrangements between the provisional government and the Federation Council will set themselves fast. Or, rather, they'll expand. I wouldn't be surprised if here we have the seed of a truly rationalized society, such as the Avantists only dreamed of. Feasible, because it isn't imposed according to an ideology, it's developing according to a demand. In that case, it'll gradually spread its kind beyond these borders." The momentary intellectual enthusiasm died away. "My guess."

She turned back toward him. "Only your guess?"

"I'm not doing any intuitional analyses yet. Not up to it."

She considered the boyish face gone gaunt, dark rims under the eyes and the darknesses behind them. Pain for him deepened within her. "You do look scooped out," she said low.

He grimaced. "It still feels that way."

"After what they did to you." To your chemistry, your brain, your spirit. Physical torture would have been less invasive.

"Let's not talk about that," he snapped. "I'll recover." His tone gentled. "Meanwhile, Fireball's providing for me very decently. Including privacy, the best medicine of all."

Kyra nodded. "Yes. Guthrie's like that, and he has the power to hold the news media off you." Pass the word around, a hint here, a bribe there, perhaps a veiled threat or two. How much longer could he work such beneficences?

"You didn't escape them," Lee sympathized.

"No, my part was too damn splashy. But I didn't care a lot, and by now I'm fading out of the public mind, thank God."

"Back to a pilot's career, hey?"

"I don't know." Kyra tried to keep her speech calm. "Nobody knows what'll happen. Doubtless my kind of tech will be wanted for years to come, at least, but—" She recoiled from the subject. "What about you, Bob? What are your plans?"

He stared at the hands folded in his lap. "I don't know either. It isn't . . . comfortable any more, being a Fireball consorte on Earth."

"I should think folk hereabouts would appreciate us."

"Some do. Others are, bueno, ugly. Most haven't decided where they stand. It makes for awkward relations."

"Might you be easier elsewhere? Maybe in L-5? I'm sure it can be arranged for you."

"Maybe. Or maybe I'll resign." He saw the near shock upon her. "It wouldn't be desertion. Fireball—Fireball doesn't *feel* the way it used to. Can you understand that?" He half smiled. "If you can, explain it to me, por favor, because I can't. Everything's confused and—" a whisper —"and somehow empty."

Hearing him thus, beholding him, what could she but rise, go lean over the bowed head, lay her arms around him and draw him close to her?

"Gracias," he mumbled after a minute or two. "That's sweet of you." She released him and stepped back. His gaze followed her. "You're good people, Kyra. Just your coming to see me, that means more than I can say."

Warmth washed over her brow and cheeks and breasts. "I wouldn't leave an amigo with never a word to him."

"I hope . . . we can get together again."

"Me too. Sure. We'll make it happen."

They were silent for a span.

"Look," Kyra decided, "what you need right now is to get the hell away from here. It's absolutely lovely out. Let's hop over to Niagara Park and totter around a few hours, except when we sit in the gardens, and then have dinner some nice little place, like amongst your Arab friends, and then I'll tuck you in early."

For the first time, Lee showed something akin to liveliness. "That sounds wonderful, but we can do better," he said. "I'm in the quivira quite a bit these days. Why don't we go there before we get that dinner?"

She frowned.

"Don't shy off," he urged. "It's nothing perverse, nothing fantastic. The program I elect is pure nature. Hills, woods, seashore, wildlife, and nobody else. Freedom to wander, room to be alone, time to think. You can't find anything like it in a park or a preserve or anywhere in poor, crowded reality. It's healing me, Kyra." He hesitated. "I'd love to share it with you."

"The best you've got," she murmured, moved.

"I'm afraid so," he replied.

43

"SHALL WE HOLD our discourse outside?" Rinndalir had proposed.

"Why the devil that?" Guthrie exclaimed.

The Lunarian's gesture flowed about the blue dusk of the room and the shifting, drifting pallors over its vault. Neither he nor the knight-shape his visitor wore seemed out of place among the fragrances and cold minor-key flute music. Nevertheless, "Here we are caged," he said quietly.

Thus they walked forth together from the castle and down the mountain. The watch was near midnight and Earth stood almost full, barely above the horizon. Rocks and craters in the valley below laid kilometers-long shadows under its beams. The light sheened off Guthrie's metal, rippled in Rinndalir's cloak, turned his wings to opal. The spark atop his wand swayed to his stride, as if one of the stars crowded overhead had descended to dance.

Guthrie willed that his radio voice remain prosaic. "Do you really want to leave this, and forever?"

"Nay, not all my race so desire," answered Rinndalir. "I and certain others."

"To skip the consequences of your share in the late unpleasantness?"

Laughter purred. "Scarcely that. Have we not staved off every demand by the Federation for our extradition and trial? It would be amusing to continue that game."

"Instead, you'd give up your power and luxury to try for

a fresh start in what's a wild-ass gamble at best? I don't recall as how aristocrats ever went in for pioneering. They left that to the bums, failures, desperados."

Rinndalir's voice became dispassionate. "The move will be politically convenient for the Lunar state. If this handful of us admit complicity with you, who shall prove otherwise? Then the Selenarchy dispatches us, for our crime, into the same exile that you are negotiating for yourself. Why do you protest, my lord? The resources that Luna can contribute will expedite your faring by years and make your survival the less unsure."

"Ha, you want me to believe you'd go on this forlorn hope out of patriotism? I suppose next you'll offer to sell me the ticket concession at Armstrong's footprints."

"It is perhaps forlorn for your human party," said Rinndalir, unruffled, "but scarcely for us. I need not remind you that the Alpha Centaurian System holds abundant asteroids. Yours is the task, the dream, of bringing alive a world the size of Earth, until destruction overtakes it. In space, my breed will soon be at home."

"You can be right around Sol."

Waves went through the argent locks beneath the cowl, within the helmet, as Rinndalir shook his head. "Nay. Civilization—the logical, organized, machine future—would find us however far we might remove ourselves. I dare trust another star is remote enough."

"For you to brew more trouble," Guthrie rasped.

Rinndalir smiled. "Fear us not. Like your contingent, we will be much too busy engineering our new habitations."

Guthrie's lenses bore fixedly on him. The silence between them hissed with cosmic noise. Dust puffed up from their feet, captured Earthlight and starlight, arced downward again.

"Were you plotting this all along?" Guthrie asked at last.

"Not precisely," Rinndalir admitted. "We are no gods, to guide history—if indeed the very gods have any foresight over chaos. But, yes, we have taken what opportunities we found, done what we were able, to break the crust of things, to hasten the destruction whence rebirth arises."

"You bastards," said Guthrie dully.

"It is our nature." The easy tone went grave. "Set aside your resentment. You need us, I say. And do you in honesty regret the necessity now upon you? It is not even that. Well do you know you could compromise, temporize, maintain your merchant adventure much as it has been for another lifetime or two. Instead, you yourself choose to go free."

"But you—"

"We also, we of Luna, see before us the end of the life that was ours, a wall toward which we helplessly career. Not that it was so wondrous a life any longer, my lord. Pleasures, illusions, intrigues, games—" In him, the sudden fury was astonishing: "How weary I am of playing games!" His voice leveled, though a pulse still beat through it. "Let us, your kind and mine, let us escape into reality."

44

ELECTRONS, PHOTONS, FIELDS interacted, their play more fast and their scope more vast by orders of magnitude than ever could be in a living brain. To the hypercomputers, a thousand years were as a day and a day was as a thousand years—of work, if not of awareness. They neither perceived nor willed, they were tools for minds that did. Someday soon that would change. Meanwhile, obedient, they enacted in mathematics a million different destinies of matter and energy. Within them there came into being whole new realms of machinery and chemistry, missions and enterprises, set into motion, carried to destruction, devised anew, tested again, over and over, in a span of real-time months. It was as if the actuality would be anticlimax.

Guthrie was not among the men and women who programmed the computers that wrote the ultimate programs. Nor was he among those who studied the outcomes and, by instinct or intuition—experience, creativity, desire—sensed when the course of pseudo-events was going awry and decreed: "Try something else." His skills lay elsewhere, commanding, cajoling, conniving, conspiring, as captain and pilot of Fireball through its last voyage.

Piece by piece he jettisoned parts of it or burned them for fuel or sold them off to buy time from his enemies. One by one his crewfolk dwindled from him, into death or retirement or undertakings that held more promise for them. He had foreseen. But he might not have made harbor without his twin, who now shared his full memories, to double his days. Between them, by whatever expedients came to hand, they weathered each exigency and stayed on their course.

No matter how occupied, he—it made little difference which of him—took what chances he got to follow along in the progress of his enterprise. United with the net, he saw directly its vision and, in a way, made it dream his dream. Like a shaman of old, he rested in trance while his spirit ranged afar.

Orbiting Mercury, he felt sunlight cataract against the mirrors that focused its rage on the barrenness under them. There instrumentalities cunning and potent made that spate of energy into negative nuclei and their positron satellites, wrapped them in the forces of cryogenic coils, and shipped them out to regions where flesh dared venture. Their annihilation with ordinary material drove spacecraft from end to end of Sol's domains.

It barely sufficed for his present venture. Though he ordered antimatter production increased, he must still hoard most and starve the fleets of Fireball. Essential commerce continued. Sailships bore their mineral cargoes, indifferent to time. Powercraft boosted into trajectory and made their economical crossings. But ever fewer were the torchcraft faring from world to world in days. At last they flew only in emergencies, or for the very wealthy. Exploration returned to what it had been in the beginning, the business of robots in slow vehicles with specific destinations.

Few people on Earth cared. The planets, moons, asteroids, and comets were understood; nothing remained to discover but details. What had human travelers ever really accomplished except to further enrich Fireball? Enjoyed themselves?

The spirit of Guthrie followed an antimatter container to a depot in Earth equilateral orbit, safely distant from the mother planet should it fail and the contents spill forth. Nearby grew the ship it would feed, newly designed, swiftly a-building. Constructors swarmed antlike. The skeleton gaped huge, for this was the vessel that would hurl a payload at nearly half the speed of light to Alpha Centauri and there bring it to rest—a payload massing whole tens of kilograms.

Guthrie moved forward in time, upon that flight not yet begun. One of him would be aboard, together with other downloads, inactive through the nine years of passage. With them would go a store of programs and certain tiny machines, mostly of molecular dimensions. The magneto-hydrodynamics that guarded them from the radiation provoked by their haste would not have protected anything truly alive; but they were life's forerunners.

Arrived, they awoke and went to work. The downloads took over supervision of the robots that had patiently continued science on Demeter and transmission of what was learned. They redirected effort to practical ends, mining, refining, laying foundations, raising walls, producing equipment. Meanwhile the microdevices borne in the ship ran loose on the planet. Strange sperm and ova, they mated to form things larger, more complex, which nourished themselves on metals and chemicals, grew, matured, accepted new programs, and embarked on their various special tasks.

They built robots that built more robots, a geometrical multiplication exploding across Demeter and the Centaurian asteroids. Solar accumulators swung aloft, beaming power down to stations whence flowed electricity and water-derived hydrogen for combustion, the heartbeat of growth. An industrial plant developed, proliferated, diversified, labored untiring. Within years, it was ample to carry out the plan for which it was made.

Robots went into space. Across millions of kilometers

they spun their web, collectors, transformers, transmitters, linked by communication beams. The laser system they wove would use energy from Demeter's sun to slow the big ships when those arrived.

"You need not spend tons of antimatter accelerating them," Mukerji had said. "Build a laser booster at this end, too. Leave the antimatter for us and earn some goodwill."

"Like hell, ma'm," Guthrie replied. "It'd have to stay in operation for at least half the transit time. I don't trust any government that much."

The three transports would already have left, riding their flames to better than a tenth of light speed before they darkened and flew free. They were large only by comparison with their pioneer—minimal, actually. Their payloads were Guthrie Two; some nine hundred cold-sleeping humans; whatever was necessary to keep that cargo intact and revive it at journey's end; and what little more could be crammed in. Their voyage would take four decades.

By then, Demeter should be slightly less inhospitable. Machines, big, small, and molecular, ground rock into soil and sowed it with life that other machines had created from genome maps. Microbes, vegetation, simple animals spread across the land; an ecology coalesced. It went more slowly by far than had the industries. Fragile, chancy, it required constant overseeing and frequent intervention, lest it perish on this world which it had not had billions of years to grow with. If it survived, no computer existed that could foretell how it would evolve.

In truth, there were no certainties, no prophecies, whatsoever. Knowledge was lacking. Had information been total, and had the computers been able to cope with so much, surprises would have been inevitable just the same. The universe is chaotic, which is to say sovereign over itself.

Therefore minds, awarenesses, must be present at Demeter from the outset, to meet the unawaited as it struck, improvise, imagine, and strive onward. Guthrie, who had been the soul and Caesar of Fireball, did not believe he alone had the wisdom or the strength. He must recruit others to download and partner him, he who had always said it was better to be a mortal than a ghost.

The thought drew him back from a future that might well never come to pass. "That's a bellyful of simulation for me," he grumbled when his assistant had uncoupled him. "Christ, to work with my hands again!"

45

THE DOOR WITH the lily on it opened, and Nero Valencia looked downward at Eiko Tamura. "Welcome," she said softly. This was their first meeting, but they had talked for a few minutes over the phone yesterday, before he took the ferry to L-5.

"You are very kind to receive me, señorita," he said, unwontedly awkward. The jewel in his forehead, which in the screen had shown scarlet, flickered through pale shades of blue.

"My concern is natural, sir. Kyra Davis is my friend."

"That's why I wondered whether you would."

"Do come in." When the door had closed on the bustling passage, she added, "The situation is difficult for her too." A bow and gesture invited him onward. He remembered to slip off his shoes in the tiny entry section. "May I offer refreshment?"

"Gracias." He took a chair in the room beyond. With its mate and a high-legged table, it was alien here; he suspected they had been brought out for the occasion. Tatami mats and cushions seemed crowded by them. The walls were pastel, bare except for a scroll of an ancient landscape. Beneath it, a bowl on a low table held water and, in a pierced stone, a bouquet of violets. Their perfume faintly sweetened the air. "Uh, your father—"

"He is at work," Eiko explained. "There is so much to do in this time of confusion." She hesitated. "I ought to be at my own duties. But you gave me an impression of great need."

Valencia made himself meet her regard. "You see many things, don't you, señorita? I thought you would. Pilot Davis told me something about you when we were together, and I've since heard more."

"Excuse me a moment," she said. "Make yourself comfortable." *If you can,* she refrained from voicing, and disappeared into the kitchen.

She returned bearing a tea service, set the table, and sat down opposite him. "Let me make a little ceremony of this," she proposed with a smile. "Don't feel you must imitate me. Simply watch, relax, enjoy."

He cleared his throat. "What I've come about—"

She raised a hand. "No, I beg you, no haste. We have ample time. This will speak for me." She touched a control bracelet on her wrist. Recorded strings began to sing. She contemplated her cup, the purity of its curves and a bamboo stalk sketched in the porcelain, before she poured; then she observed the stray leaves as they swirled in the green. Perforce he did likewise. The music went movement by movement from reverie to joy.

It ended at last. He kept still a while longer, drew his gaze back to her, and murmured, "That was beautiful. Old?"

She nodded. "Mendelssohn's Violin Concerto in E Minor. I thought it would help us. Now tell me, if you will, how you have fared lately."

"Variably. Oh, I haven't lacked for job offers. Took some, those that weren't likely to turn violent. Earth is calming down."

"Do you fear your trade will become obsolete?"

He grinned. "Not soon. Plenty of restlessness to go around." His jewel darkened. The hand that lay by the cup doubled into a fist. He looked away from her. "But it's obsolete in me."

"And you cannot make Kyra understand that," Eiko said low.

"She's told you what I did, I suppose."

"Yes."

His tone roughened. "I won't pretend I'm overwhelmed by remorse. You'd know me for a hypocrite. But I wish she could believe I don't want to go on like that."

"You should be clear that I am outside this. She has said almost nothing about you to me since the, the fight. Only that you kept the Packer family safe and free, at no small hazard to yourself."

"My job." He met her eyes. "When I got back in touch with her, she . . . thanked me."

"And that was all."

"She didn't have to say outright she wants no more to do with me. She knew I knew that."

"You would like me to speak to her on your behalf?"

Valencia offered a rueful smile. "Not exactly. That was two years ago, after all."

"Then what do you ask for? Why have you come here?"

He sighed. "I don't really know." After several seconds, it broke from him: "But when I heard she—she—" He choked.

Eiko finished it. "She has agreed to send a download of herself with one of the Srs. Guthrie on the advance ship to Alpha Centauri."

"I can't imagine it!" he cried. "She's so alive. Even a copy of her, in a horrible box— What could make her do it?"

"The news was a shock to you," Eiko said sympathetically.

He nodded, his neck stiff as a puppet's.

"You care, then," she went on. "You care very much."

"I've thought about her—every day—" He swallowed. "Don't get me wrong. I took for granted she was happy enough. For the time being, anyhow. She even seemed to've settled down with a man. A good man, from what I could learn. Though when the humans go to Demeter— But that isn't yet, and not like what she means to do first. . . . Her other self. How can she make another Kyra for hell? What's wrong?"

"You exaggerate," Eiko chided. "The situation is inhuman, but not inhumane."

White light from his jewel sheened off a film of sweat. "I was hoping you could make me believe that. Reconcile me to it. I guess she's told you her reasons. If they aren't secret—"

Eiko shook her head. "No, she didn't swear me to silence. She knew I wouldn't gossip." She considered him. "I think it will not be wrong to share a part, and trust in your discretion."

Valencia's jewel dimmed. "You are generous, my lady," he said humbly.

Eiko drew breath. "She came to me. We were several daycycles together, here, in Trevorrow Preserve, high in the Tree, out in ambient space among the stars. She wanted my—not my poor counsel, but my companionship while we groped toward what was the right decision for her. That was a hard pilgrimage we made. I will not try to tell you about it. But you have seen the public announcement."

"Yes," he rasped. "Guthrie must have some like himself along, or the whole venture will fail. Kyra—Pilot Davis has joined the handful who're willing to make the sacrifice. I know about Fireball troth, Srta. Tamura. But this goes too damned far beyond it. Too God damned far."

"She has her personal motivation, remember. She plans to go in her living body, come the second departure."

"Why, why? Does she really feel that futile at home?"

"She feels things closing in on her. And then, the larger cause, humankind, life itself—" Eiko stopped. "But she was never one to speak in grandiose terms, nor shall I."

She reached across the table and laid her fingers lightly over the knuckles of his fist. "Downloading is not, in fact, a dreadful fate," she said. "Moreover, for such a mind, once its task is done, termination holds no terrors. The dear flesh is not there, clinging to existence."

Bitterness responded. "Of course not. There's nothing to lose."

"You are mistaken. Would Guthrie-san have gone on, decade after decade, were the time wholly barren? I, who seek in my limited and half-hearted way for enlightenment, *satori*, I can vaguely imagine what Kyra's disembodied self will have. Whole new perceptions of this infinitely wonderful universe. New powers, some superhuman, powers of thought and action, comprehension and accomplishment. Challenge. Service. Deeds done that will ring for centuries, or forever. Afterward, if she chooses, oblivion, which is peace."

He sat mute, head lowered, until he looked up again and mumbled, "That's how she feels? She isn't doing this because she's miserable, and she doesn't expect it will be bad for the other one?"

"It was no easy choice," Eiko granted, "but it is what she came to, and she is—more nearly content with it than she could be with anything less."

"I see." Valencia straightened. "Gracias, mil gracias. You've done a stranger a great mercy."

"You deserved it, I think."

"You do, knowing what you know about me?"

"Yes. Not that I dare sit in judgment on you or anyone else. But one can recognize love."

Valencia's jewel went ebony. "That's too big a word," he growled. "I admire her, yes, and—" He hesitated. "Srta. Tamura, I—" He gripped his hands together.

Eiko smiled. "You would request something further of me."

"You've done so much already."

"In these short minutes?"

"Yes. If, if you now say no, that's the end of the business. I'll go home, and always be grateful to you."

"You wish me to put in a good word for you with Kyra."

"Yes." In haste: "Not that I intend to make a pest of myself. I'd just like her to think better of me. And . . . a word to Sr. Guthrie, por favor. He'll hear you."

She studied him closer than before. "You have decided you hope to go with the human cargo to Alpha Centauri. With her."

He forced a smile. "Not quite this instant, on impulse. I'd been weighing it. But, yes, today I've decided."

"Why? It will be nothing romantic, you know. It will be

an environment hard and harsh, toil, danger, privation, and a high likelihood of an early death."

"Exactly." He laughed, as if care had fallen from him. "No, I'm not a masochist. But I'd be helping make something."

"Make what, do you believe?"

He shook his head and clicked his tongue. "You go straight to the core of matters, don't you?"

"My guess is," she stated, "that you are too intelligent to involve yourself in a mere make-work project, however large and risky. You are well aware that in a thousand years, Demeter will perish. What end do you see for this undertaking? What purpose?"

"I can't answer that," he replied. "Can anybody? They talk about building a civilization free and human, plus a capability of going on, somehow, after the planets crash. What does that really mean? Can you tell me?"

"Not in words," she admitted. "Perhaps I could find the right music to play for you."

"Just so. It's all music, emotion, no logic outside of the need Guthrie and some Lunarians have to leave the Solar System."

"On that account, you recall, volunteers for the colony are few. And most thus far have had to be rejected as incompetents or ramblewits."

"I can handle a fair assortment of jobs, and learn more."

Eiko thought for a bare minute. "Yes. I will give you my recommendation."

"Again, mil gracias."

"Your motive is that you seek meaning for your life, am I right?"

Valencia shrugged. "I suppose." His tone quickened. "But you, señorita, you've got meaning in yours, you've always had it, haven't you?"

Startled, she retorted, "What do you imply, sir?"

"May I ask why *you* are going?"

"What makes you think I am?"

Valencia smiled. "I didn't call you from a cold start, señorita. First I found out what I could about you. And now we've met. It seems a reasonable guess. If I'm wrong, forgive me."

"You are more than I expected, Mr. Valencia," she said slowly.

"You honor me." His jewel glowed amber.

"True, I am giving serious thought to going," she confided. "As for why, it would take long to tell, if I can at all."

"I'd listen as long as you wanted to talk."

"There is no single, simple reason, actually. But it does appear to me—if I am not being pretentious—this that they aim to do, this rebellion against fate, it will need its singers."

"A heroic age ahead," he mused. "The kind of age where four stand at the corners of life, the worker, the warrior, the priest, and the poet."

Eiko's look dwelt upon him. "You have many surprises in you, sir. Clear to see, you have read books."

"Less than I once meant to. It didn't fit in well with what I became. Maybe my grandchildren on Demeter will."

"Can you stay in Ragaranji-Go a while?"

"Certainly."

"I would like to know you better," she said, half diffident, half assured. "Find lodging and return at evenwatch for dinner, when my father will be home. Tomorrow—tomorrow let us go to the Tree. Perhaps there you will hear in the wind what we are both unable to speak, and by the light through the boughs we will see into ourselves."

46

IN THE OPTICALS that would track her until she went beyond their seeing, *Juliana Guthrie II* was like a tower built to storm heaven. Stage after stage after stage gleamed within coils and webs of cryogenic circuitry, walls that narrowed upward until the final decelerator made a cupola upon which lifted the tiny, defiant weathercock that was the payload module. Stars frosted the night where she reared; her height clove the Milky Way.

But then the tugs took hold of her and drew her— slowly, slowly, as great as the mass was—spiraling outward. When they released her near Jupiter, she was the merest sliver against the belts and zones and monster hurricanes of the king planet. Its gravity twisted her from the ecliptic plane and aimed her at rendezvous. Her nethermost stage awoke, matter and antimatter blazed into energy, plasma torrented down a cliff of force-field surges. That river ran almost cold, almost invisible, for hundreds of kilometers before it lost coherence and hard radiation fountained from a wan, dissolving fireball.

At first even this mightiest set of torchcraft ever launched could barely lay any increment to her speed. Second by second, though, hour by hour, day by day, mass waned and acceleration waxed. When she reached her trajectory and went free, she would be flying at half the haste of light; her instruments would register skies gone strange, space shrunken and time quickened. Near journey's end, she would back down on her goal in a few weeks. The minds aboard would know little of those years. Lest they lose themselves in the emptiness, they would rest safely unconscious.

Unexisting, said a thought among them.

No, it will be no different from the silence of cold sleep that's to close on my other self. Will it? Not much. It's we who are different. She can't lie centuries changeless like me; she can't be stopped, only slowed, for she's organic, vulnerable, mortal. She's alive. I am a network and a program.

I am connected. I can use the ship's systems. Look, yonder shines the sun, hardly more than a star. How I gloried, riding *Kestrel* through this range! Where's Alpha Centauri? Why, right there. Instantly I knew. The computer figured it for me, as easily as my arm once told me where my hand was. Amplify. Diamond A, golden B, distant coal of Proxima. Often I looked through my own eyes and longed. Now, some years hence, I'll be going. Except that *I* shall not. I am already on my way, and have neither mouth to laugh for joy nor flesh to feel it.

Belay that! I knew quite well what I was letting myself in for. Or imagined I did. It seemed like a toss-up, a fifty-fifty chance that I could go on in my life, proud that I'd done a service necessary but beyond the call of duty. And of course I won the toss. The I who's on Earth did. This I is bound to the vows. Somehow, I didn't understand. Too late now.

No sense in weeping. I can't, anyway. I shouldn't miss love, breath, hunger, a bare foot on grass wet with sunrise, should I? That body is no longer what generates me. I'm gone from her needs and appetites, tears and triumphs and tendernesses. Visions that would blind her, adventures that would kill her, await me. I must practice being a machine.

When its work is done, I can terminate me.

—Kyra?

Jefe?

—We'll be switching off soon, you know. I've been linking with the others, one by one, to gab a bit. They'd like to form a general hookup before we say goodnight. "Communion" sounds too fancy for me. Call it a party. Want to join in?

I— No, I think not, gracias.

—You sure? Ought to be helpful. We're lonesome critters at best, we downloads.

Oh, God, we are!

—Kyra, querida.

?

—You're having your dark night of the soul, aren't you?

I'll manage.

—Wait. Don't shut me out yet. Please. I don't mean to intrude on your privacy. You keep an idea of privacy, don't you? You, an individual, free to give or withhold. But you've got no more skin to cover your nakedness. I know, I know. Don't try to curl up around yourself. That just guards the hurt. Open as wide as you can, wider than you dare. Be one with the universe.

Are you?

—No. I tried a long time ago and failed. But allow me that I speak from experience. An ideal, something you can measure by and maybe come a tad closer to, makes existence make sense.

In the absence of anything else.

—Yeah, I savvy. Kyra, I won't feed you a line. I've been alive and I've been what I am, and alive is better. It must be worse for you. I was old and tired, everything behind me. You were young and full-blooded. You've lost the tomorrows that should have been yours. But you do have others. And they won't be a mere string of jobs to get through, in between shadowy grievings for a past that grows less and less real. You'll learn how to be what you are and find pleasure in it.

So you promised me.

—I didn't lie. Wouldn't, not to you. We've been through a fair-sized chunk of hooraw together, haven't wc? With more to come, lots more.

I . . . I suppose I shouldn't feel depressed. What have I got to feel with?

—Good gal. You can joke a little. Actually, you'll find that feelings aren't all in the glands. You'll learn, I say.

You did.

—Hey, let's shack up for a while. We've got several hours with no calls on us. Listen to my stories, which may or may not be true, and I'll hear whatever you care to tell, and we'll look back but also ahead and maybe at last we'll sing "MacCannon." How about it?

I wonder if love, of a sort, may still be possible.

47

ON HER LAST day among the Keiki Moana, Kyra went to sea with them. She anchored the boat near a reef, stripped off her clothes, and dived overboard. For hours they were together. They rollicked in the waves, searched out the miracles that grew and swam about the coral, sought the beach to rest and drink wind and sunlight and the vision of immense many-hued surging, shouted back at the crash and white geysering of the breakers through which they struggled to swim again. As well as she was able, she joined in the hoarse songs and intricate dances.

From this she drew peace, which she made a shield against doubts and dreads. Here were overwhelming beauty and multitudinous life, her kind of life, she kin to every beast and bird and blade of grass; here she belonged. That life had been saved and the planet had begun to be cleansed, before she was born. It might well burgeon into something like its ancient splendor before she died. In the past decade bioreclamation had advanced by ever longer strides and population control—ultimately, population reduction—was taking hold in the last, most backward countries. It was as if the clash with Fireball had shocked humankind into sanity. Did she indeed want to leave, forever?

Yes, she told herself. Through half that time she'd been no deeper into space than L-5. Had influence not gotten her a post at this station, she—would have yielded to Rinndalir, she knew. To help these metamorphs, teach them, study and learn from them, speak to the world for them, had been fascinating, heartwarming, sometimes heartbreaking, always full of a sense that it mattered what she did. But every clear night she gazed up at the stars.

The sun declined. A pleasant weariness pervaded her muscles. "I must go now," she said. Charlie made a noise of mourning. She stroked the big scarred head and swam to her boat. The Sea Children followed it, dark streaks and leaps through the light that shimmered over the wave-crests. While she made fast at the dock, they crawled ashore. The ride back had dried her. She dressed and went to bid them goodbye.

"A'o'a, a'o'a," they croaked, crowding about. Sunshine caressed their flanks. The fish smell of their breath was a clean pungency in her nostrils. The noses that nuzzled her palms were wet and bristly and quivered as if the creatures strove not to weep.

"Farewell, fare you well," she called.

"[We wonder how we shall without you, dear sister,]" Charlie said.

"You have others who care."

"[May they bear young who do.]"

Would they? she wondered. Everything was changing so fast. The youths she met were like none she knew when she was their age. If people were losing violence and cruelty, was that because they were losing an uncouth energy that had driven them from the caves to the ends of the Solar System? Could this evolution go on, or might it lash back in some new mania? "I will remember you all my days."

"[And we will remember you, also after we who are here have died. You will live in our songs. As long as our kind endures, we will dance with your spirit by moonlight in the waters.]"

However long that would be.

Kyra's glance strayed to the wan half-disc in eastern heaven. A shiver passed through her. She might have been there this moment. Though Fireball's pilots flew no more, its ships nearly all gone to the roboticizing World Space Authority, the Selenarchs kept their antiquated few craft. Rinndalir had offered her the captaincy of one of his. Her home aground would have been in that mountain castle . . . . It would bewilder her quite enough to meet him at far Centauri.

"Adiós," she gulped. *"Aloha nui loa."* She pushed her way from the throng and fled up the hillside.

Another memory loped beside her. Nero Valencia was

going too. Bueno, admit he was brave and capable, and on Demeter he'd have no cause to murder anybody. Would he?

Her informant emitted the signal that unlocked the gate in the fence. She went through and stopped short. Her car stood alone on the parking lot. A man waited nearby, as black against the sun as his shadow stretched before him. "Oh—"

He gave her a Fireball salute and approached. She recognized Washington Packer's son Jeff, a good-looking hombre in his twenties. "Saludos," he greeted shyly. "I hope I don't intrude, Pilot Davis."

Her glance flickered around. Zealously though the privacy of the emigrants was guarded, one way or another journalists and multivision flitterlets kept slipping through to plague them. "If you haven't been followed," she said.

"I was careful." Packer obviously felt he should explain in detail. "When I realized I just had to see you, I begged my dad to give me your phone number. Not your address, only your number and scrambler code. He and Mother . . . they don't refuse me much these days. I called, got Sr. Lee, asked if I could talk with you alone at your convenience. He suggested, instead, I come out here where you'd be, and he'd arrange for the gate to let me through." For Kyra's sake, two portals a kilometer off on either side barred access to the road. They had shot down a couple of telebugs, which put a stop to such intrusions. The public soon grew bored with views of her from high altitude. Packer sighed. "He's a very simpático man, isn't he?"

"That's his business," Kyra said. "You sure you weren't noticed?" The pests could be lurking outside.

"I wore my life mask and took a cab." Packer gestured at his pouch. Most of the emigrants had acquired a bionetic pseudoface to slip on when they badly wanted anonymity.

Kyra laughed. How relieving that felt! "Then I've got to give you a ride home."

"Oh, no, señora. I can call from the gate."

"Of course I will, you tonto, and we'll talk on the way. I owe your father a lot."

Somberness fell over the brown countenance. "He hasn't been in a position to do much for you lately," perforce retired.

"I haven't forgotten. And we're going to be shipmates, you and I. Planet mates."

"That's what I hoped we could talk about."

"You're hesitating? I don't blame you."

"Never!" he cried. "What's for me on Earth?" His was the dream that had formed her life, but he was born too late to have had any share in the reality.

Kyra took his hand. "Let's go," she said, and led him to the car.

They didn't speak further until past the gate. She drove on manual, leisurely, twisting among trees and ferns and great gaudy flowers. It gave her a physical occupation. "What's your trouble, consorte?" she asked. "How can I help?"

She heard the strain. "It's my folks."

"They're trying to stop you? I'm surprised."

"No, they aren't. They say they're proud of me. But—" His voice wavered. "Pilot Davis, you've got parents same as me. And a brother, no? I've two sisters, who have their own families. We're close, the bunch of us."

Kyra waited, knowing what would come next.

"How will you tell your folks adiós? How'll you keep them from grieving? It's like death, this. One-way trip. When I revive at the end, my parents will probably be dead and maybe my sisters. They'll be old, at least, and no bandwidth for more than a few words of message once in a while, four and a third years on the way."

Kyra nodded. "True."

"Yes, it hurts me personally, everything I'm leaving behind. I know a girl— But if only I didn't feel it hurting *them* so! Am I being conscienceless selfish?"

Kyra picked her words one by one. "I'd scarcely call it that. You're bound for risk and hardship beyond foreseeing, and not simply because it'll get you a job in space. It's also because you've caught this notion—hardly even an idea, as vague and unprovable as it is—this notion that

that's the best chance for your children's children. Which means Wash's and Mary's great-grandchildren."

"They don't believe it is. They keep quiet about it, but I know they don't believe. Do yours?"

"Bueno, my father agrees with me, sort of." She must bare herself to him in his need. "My mother— 'Fly, bird of mine,' she said, and tried not to cry."

"Do you know anything I can tell mine," he pleaded, "anything I can do, that might make it easier on them?"

Kyra gave him a look. "Tell them how much you respect them."

"Hm?" he mumbled, surprised.

She turned her eyes back to the road. "Losing sons and daughters used to be a common fate. They'd go to war or to lands beyond the mountains or over the seas, and not return. Those who stayed behind might never hear whether they lived or died. We've gotten out of the way of that, in this tamed, known, machine-tended world you and I want free of. Bueno, your kin and mine have the old strength. They can accept a life that's more than entertainment. We should honor them for it."

"M-m-m." He sank into thought.

Presently they spoke anew. When she let him off at his apartment in Hilo, he thanked her. She wondered how much good she had done, how much truth she had uttered.

She went on to the home she and Lee had rented these past several years. The location had been necessary for her, inconvenient for him. He could do his thinking, computing, and long-range communicating anywhere, but he must frequently go back to the mainland for days or weeks at a stretch, to gather data and experiences. Nonetheless he had settled in without complaint.

The place belonged to a formerly exclusive residential development in the hills. Nowadays, the crime rate low and sinking, the guarded fence was an anachronism, kept because Guthrie paid for it. Kyra parked in front of the house, entered, and found Lee on the deck at the rear, watching sunset.

Mauna Kea loomed black against gold. The light

washed over forest, setting leaves aglow, and roused fragrances from the garden under the rail. A breeze wandered by, still warm. Somewhere an iiwi trilled.

He heard her footfalls and rose from his lounger with wonted courtesy. In the rich light his hair, lately gray-shot, seemed almost white. Bueno, she thought, it must likewise be bringing forth the crow's-feet at her eyes, the lines that edged her lips. She wasn't exactly young either—pushing forty.

He smiled. "Bienvenida," he said. "How did it go?"

"Tough." He stepped forward to lay his arms around her. She hugged him back, fiercely. "Oh, all these good-byes!" she whispered against his cheek.

He released her. "You hardened your resolution years ago," he said. "I wish you could harden your heart more."

"Years—" They had felt endless. How could they now have slipped from her?

He made a fresh smile. "Cheer up, querida. They're pretty near finished."

She laid hands on his shoulders. "I didn't mind them. They were fine."

"Sweet of you to say so, but let's be honest. *Sometimes* they were."

"Mostly they were. Because of you."

"For me, always. Because of you."

And yet, she had confessed to her soul in wakeful nights, it was worse bidding her parents and brother farewell. Not that she wasn't fond of this man. In many ways she loved him.

Her voice stumbled. "If only you could've seen your way clear to go."

His flattened. "If only."

If only she could bear to stay. But there was no sense in repeating what had been said over and over beyond counting. He had his work, for the government rather than Fireball but the same work, and its grip upon him had grown unbreakable. He knew it was valuable, finding ways to bring the young into the nascent commonwealth of human and machine, ways to comfort the aged while everything by which they had lived shriveled away from them. What use for an intuitionist on Demeter?

What use for the whole pioneering? He frankly feared it was a leap into ruin.

"C'mon." She brought an arm down to his waist. "We're squandering show time."

Side by side they stood watching the radiance burn away. "Incredible," she murmured when it dimmed. "Beats any chromokinetics I ever saw."

"You would feel that." Sunsets on Demeter were often spectacular, what with dust blown high off lifeless plains. "It was certainly beautiful."

"That fancy dinner we were talking about. Can we postpone it and just rustle up something at home? I'm not in the mood to go anywhere."

He peered at her through the dusk. "What are you in the mood for, then?"

She laughed into his eyes. "As if you couldn't guess!"

They had been making love every chance they got. She didn't let out that she had not renewed her prevention, that she wanted to bear his child beneath Alpha Centauri.

48

As THE FLYER left ground, a flaw of wind struck and nearly sent it tumbling. The air hereabouts got tricky around vernal equinox. Maybe the companion sun, approaching periastron, added something to that, minute though its maximum input to this planet was. Sensors sped their data to download Kyra Davis. She saw the landing field and hangars wheel sideways, felt the roll and pitch, heard the gust boom and metal thrum. To elevate a fin and fire an auxiliary jet was not unlike the play of muscles when living Kyra rode a comber; for an instant the download remembered the taste of spindrift.

The flyer corrected and sprang on skyward. She had

enjoyed the small challenge. Being integral with a machine gave experience a fullness that control from outside it never quite matched.

Even at fifteen hundred meters, where she leveled off, her condition had its advantages. Instruments measured a sultriness not much diminished; flesh would have gone hot and sticky. The ceiling was close above. That leaden overcast broke in the distant east, where A flung down beams that turned the Ionian Ocean molten. Nearer to shore the waves ran purple with a seasonal bloom of animalcules.

Their hue was among the few things she would miss, if she survived long enough. The prediction was that they, like most native species, would go extinct as Terrestrial kinds spread into the seas. A couple of her fellows said they felt a bit guilty. Kyra declined to. Demeter would not simply be made fit for humans, it would bear such a wealth of life and beauty as it could never have brought forth of itself before its doom came upon it.

As yet the starkness was little softened. The fuel plant on Hydrogen Island raised cooling towers in deceptively delicate filigree. Where the River Tanaus emptied into Shelter Bay, Port Fireball spread buildings clean of line and bright of colors. They housed industrial and scientific facilities. You must expand your productive capacity as fast as possible—a growth quasi-geometrical, machines breeding machines—if anything sustainable was to be there for the colonists when they arrived.

Inward from the beach, moss patched boulders with green. Wind ruffled the grass and shrubs that encroached on the hills beyond. Mostly, however, Kyra saw bare rock, scoured by erosion, and glimmering, sterile rainwater pools. Had she possessed nostrils and lungs, the air would have been practically odorless save when thunderstorms sharpened it. Though breathable, it would have been stuffy, too much carbon dioxide, not enough oxygen.

The flyer curved around and lined out westward.

"Why do you not go higher and faster?" asked download Gabriel Berecz impatiently. Squatting aft among his robugs, today he wore a fieldwork body, caterpillar treads, telescoping sensors, multiple arms ending in a variety of hands.

"I want to scan the territory," Kyra replied. "Nobody's been this way for some time. The surveyors that reported the trouble were traveling south from Illyria, you remember." She and her passenger talked not by voice but by direct radio. They'd need to stay in contact at their destination.

"What is to see except a lot of geology?" grumbled the ecologist.

"You never know," Kyra said. "We were far from having used up all the surprises in the Solar System when we left it."

Memories stirred. Occasionally they still brought unreasonable pain. She must train herself out of allowing that. Begin by concentrating on the desolation that was Argolis, streaming beneath her. A river, a canyon, a lake, a mountain, bare, dark, meaningless—how long till they had names? Those Classical tags that Earthside astronomers hung on the largest features, after maps appeared on their screens, might as well be catalogue numbers, devoid of history as they were. When would this air carry sounds with the infinite overtones that rang in "Devon," "Dordogne," "Dalmatia," "Cape Horn," "the Nile," "Mount Everest," "Jerusalem," "Rome," "Kamakura," "Tours," "Lepanto," "Gettysburg"?

Kyra pulled her attention back to the terrain.

After about two hours she spied her goal ahead and slanted down toward it. Clouds had thickened overhead. A rainstorm made a wall of blue-black which hid the Mycenaean Range from her, but their foothills stood clear and steep. A stream coursed in cataracts out of them and through the valley beneath. There reeds shivered along its banks, bordering rows of brush and young willow. Land rolled away on either side startlingly bright green. At the fringes, robots trundled with their loads from a dome wherein humus was being synthesized, to work it into the rock that nanomachines had reduced to mineral grains.

Here was one of the centers spotted around the globe for life to gain the vigor to spread onward of itself.

"Where do you want to begin, Gabe?" Kyra asked.

"Make a sweep low above the hills," Berecz directed, connecting himself to the opticals. She descended and flew as slowly as was halfway safe. Thermals, crosswinds, air pockets buffeted her about and did their best to crash her. She lost herself in wrestling them. Once she thought fleetingly that this would never replace sex, but in its way it was fun.

Of course, after the settlement had built a quivira, programs adaptable to a bodiless mind— No, she didn't expect she'd ever go. Waking from it would be too high a price to pay. Let her stay what she was. She was getting better at it all the time.

"There!" Berecz exclaimed. "Do you see?"

Kyra linked to his instruments and acquired the view. A small mountain lifted with Chinese abruptness from the valley floor. Moss and tussocks were scattered across its lower slope. They were volunteers. Organic matter had drifted on breezes from below, rain had mingled it with lithosols milled by nature, spores and seeds followed—an early victory in the conquest for which these plants and their attendant microbes were gene-designed. In a hundred years or less this region should be ready for a forest.

Death said otherwise. Magnifying, Kyra beheld stalks withered, turf gone brown, rivulets running thick with loam that roots had ceased to hold. The swathe broadened as it spread downward into the valley, a fan of dingy umber reaching four kilometers riverward. Widespread spots elsewhere showed how fast the blight was advancing. So far it wasn't anything that a landsat could have identified through the nimbose atmosphere, but its implications were ominous.

"Can you park on that ledge?" Berecz asked.

Kyra scanned it, a narrow shoulder some hundred meters aloft. Above it the mountain was much more steep; surviving bits of vegetation clung precariously among jumbled stones and rain-fed springs. Behind the crest the storm towered steadily higher, lightning a-flicker in its murk. "Why?" she wondered. "Specimens must be mighty sparse there."

"Precisely. A simple biosystem, easiest to study. Besides, it appears to me that the trouble has been propagating from the heights. I want samples to compare with what I will collect in the lowland."

"M-m-m—bueno, can you be quick about it? That weather will get here pretty soon, and the location's too damn exposed for my liking."

"An hour should suffice." And maybe not a lot more to solve the riddle, Kyra thought. The equipment she conveyed had amazing powers, not to mention the labs back in Port Fireball. Doing something about the problem might prove less straightforward.

"Okay," she agreed. A slight surprise jarred her. Evidently she was acquiring still another Guthrieism.

Setdown demanded her entire skill. No, she thought after she had bumped to a halt in rock-strewn mud, skill was what humans developed. A machine had potentialities, which self-reprogramming on the basis of data input made into capabilities. She opened the door and extruded a gangway. Thunder rolled loud through her fuselage. Berecz led his pack of biologists out.

Watching them take pictures, gather specimens, extract cores, Kyra felt uneasiness grow. This was a treacherous place at best, under conditions turning dangerous. The more she looked at it, the more she sensed the wind and the wet and the noise of oncoming rain, the more leery she became. Berecz didn't notice. His flesh had never cared to travel and his homeland was mostly a flat plain. She recalled the Cordilleras of Earth and Luna, Olympus Mons, weird Miranda, what robots had transmitted from the highlands of Venus and Mercury. No two worlds were ever alike, no forecasts ever sure, but she knew there was a wrongness here.

"Listen," she called at last, "I want to do a flit. I'll come back in thirty minutes or so. Bien?"

"As you wish," he responded absently, engrossed.

"A word of advice. Stick every sample in your personal box at once. We may have to leave in a hurry."

"Indeed?" His response conveyed indifference, but she could hope he'd follow her counsel.

She lifted vertically, fighting the whole way. Above the peak, vapors flew ragged and the vanguard of the rain slashed at her metal. From its cave of lightnings the storm howled at her. It had reached the western side. Chaos boiled under her opticals. By radar she watched torrents dash from the sky and down the stone-thick flanks. Their net wrapped clear across the lower eastern slopes. Kyra struggled to keep position while her beams probed.

Sanamabiche! Yon boulder shaken, washed loose, bounding in a rush of the water it had dammed, down toward an incline of scree— Kyra slewed about. Air shrieked behind her dive.

She herself didn't yell. That wasn't download style. It wasn't Fireball style. "Gabe," she said, "I've got to snatch you out. Grab the cable I'll lower and hang on."

"What is this?" he replied. She sent him a view of what it was, gathering force in its descent.

Winch out the wire rope. Be glad Guthrie insisted on every provision against emergencies that it was practical to carry. A fox has two exits from his den, he'd said once. The line lashed about in her airstream. She slowed to barely over stalling speed. Her fuselage bucked and groaned. On her first pass, Berecz missed. She fought her way back and saw him lay claws on the cable. Immediately she climbed.

None too soon. The landslide raged over the ledge and onward till it had buried half the blighted ground. Kyra went on beyond, hovered where Berecz could let go, and landed near him. The storm crossed the mountain and fell upon them.

Machines, they suffered no harm. Nor were they in shock, or even in need of rest. When the weather slacked off, the ecologist carried on alone while Kyra flew back to fetch replacement robugs. At Port Fireball she left off the specimens he had already prepared.

They both returned there after four of the planet's brief days. By then Berecz's observations had led him to a hypothesis which work in the laboratory at the base appeared to confirm. Further research was required, but he felt confident.

"Without natural enemies, the earthworms that were introduced have multiplied explosively," he said. "The computer model predicted this, of course, but did not consider the destabilization of gradients. From the biological standpoint, it was a very secondary effect. Hence the landslide. As for the dieback, that sudden loosening of the substrate, and concomitant chemical changes, caused a correspondingly sudden leaching out of alkalis, until the pH of the soil went intolerably high."

"Just a local hitch, then, that came near doing you in by coincidence," Kyra said. "I suppose it's correctible by adding the right stuff to the humus mix."

"I fear matters are not so simple. Other poisons will act elsewhere, salt, selenium, perhaps radioactives, and who knows what more? We cannot watch over a planet as we can over a cottage garden. And what different kinds of attack will it launch on us? The populations we introduce are disease-free, but they cannot remain so indefinitely. Essential bacteria will mutate into pathogens. Lengths of DNA will turn into viruses. Mere imbalance between species can prove fatal; consider how deer, when their predators were eliminated, increased until they over-grazed their ranges and starved. On Earth we discovered how hard it is to repair a damaged ecology that took three billion or more years to evolve. On Demeter we hope to create one *de novo* within a century or two. We cannot. We can merely found it. Thereafter it must develop and maintain itself."

"I know that, in a general way. This in the Mycenaeans has driven the lesson home to me. Didn't you misspeak a bit, though? The nature we dream of can't spring into being from a few seeds we plant. We have to be part of it from the first and on till the last—we, our machines and our people."

"Yes, yes. But that great oneness transcends my poor imagination. We cannot truly model it, either. It is a chaotic system, as you and I have lately experienced. We can only, humbly, do whatever we think may help."

49

OUT OF THE abyss, Eiko's first half-clear thought was *How is Kyra? How is her baby?* Memory, dismay, stabbed from the marshalling center on Earth where she had heard the admission, across forty-seven years, four and a third light-years. Banzai daft, to embark pregnant! The chance of never awakening from that half-death was too high at best— Awareness fell apart into confusion and pain. Pitiless, the things at her side and the things within her held fast to the shards.

After some fraction of forever she drew back together. Now she knew mostly nausea, foul tastes and stenches, a thirst as if her blood had turned to sand. She achieved realizing that she would live. Later she became able to tell herself that that was worth hoping for.

Of course she was sick, very sick. She had lain invaded by tubes and wires, pervaded by chemicals and nano-structures, in fluid of subfreezing cold. Despite shielding and electromagnetic screening, radiation had seeped through, and it had welled from atoms of her own, to wreak harm that quiescent cells could not repair. The damage must be mended, the foreign stuffs flushed out, the body reschooled. She got that far before she toppled into darkness.

The time came when what claimed her was a natural sleep, though light and full of dreams. She roused to clarity. Utter strengthlessness held her in its calm. A robot entered the ward, spoke gentle words, and helped her swallow some broth. Afterward she lay back, understood that her father must be dead, and quietly wept.

From then on she recovered hour by hour. With health came increasing cheer and, gradually, eagerness for the future. The life she had lost—no, forsaken—would always be an ache in her, like the phantom pain she had read about which amputees felt where limbs had been, before regeneration was possible. But the vitality, the whole meaning, had been fast draining out of that life, and her father had blessed her departure.

She began to chat with the patients on either side of her bed. The robots informed her about such others whom she knew as had been revived to date; only a few at a time could be. Kyra Davis was a month ahead of her and should soon be able to go groundside. Nero Valencia had been processed in the last group before Eiko and recently discharged from isolation. They both wished her well. No direct meeting could happen till she too had been released, which wouldn't be until her immune system was operating properly again. Any communication equipment in here would have been an unaffordable extravagance of payload mass. She didn't much mind, having always found enough of interest inside her head.

Still, the daycycles dragged. She rejoiced when an examination informed the physician down on Demeter that she was out of danger. Two robots helped her through a passage to the women's convalescent ward. There she found small individual multi sets, sent up from the planet, and access to a database which included most of humankind's culture.

The short walk exhausted her. After taking orbit, the ship had divided in two halves, joined by a ten-kilometer fullerene cable, and gone a-spin. The weight thus furnished was as low as compatible with the physiology of Earthfolk, but she had lost nearly all muscle tone.

Regaining it required systematic exercise. She also had other aspects of humanness to practice. During the next daywatch, following a brief workout and a long hot bath, she was brought to a recliner in the common room.

The chamber was as austere as everything else aboard, basically an empty space where people could mingle. The heavens outside filled a large viewscreen. Across blackness drifted stars, Milky Way, damped-down sun A, fierce light-point of B, and Demeter, Demeter. At this moment the planet was a crescent, not marbled like Earth but white, beclouded. She could see where weather swirled. One rift shone sapphire, ocean, at its edge an ocher that might be a continent. She searched for the companion ships, but couldn't pick any out.

Half a dozen colonists were present, in various stages of rehabilitation. None were acquaintances of hers. They advanced courteously to congratulate her and the two newcomers with her. But then appeared Kyra. She brushed past them, big and forceful, as a wind might, and knelt to embrace her friend. After the sterility of the isolation ward and the cautious contacts since, this— warmth, solidity, sunny-smelling hair and lips alive against her cheek—overwhelmed.

"Bienvenida, querida, bienvenida," Kyra exulted. "We made it, the both of us."

She rose. Eiko looked up the height and fullness and whispered through a fluttering, "Oh, the child?"

Kyra laughed and slapped her belly. "Just fine, I'm told. Good stock."

"That is splendid. I was so afraid for you. . . . But will the . . . the situation . . . not be difficult?"

"Sure. A while before I can go spacing again, no doubt. But then, it'll be a while anyway, and I trust the little rascal will be worth any delays. Consider me a pioneer. My case won't stay unique. It better not!"

Eiko smiled. "I imagine I shall be a homebody, working as a coordinator. When you are away . . . perhaps I can care for the child. . . . I would be happy to."

"Sweet of you. But you may have a couple of your own to pester you by then, you know."

Eiko lifted a palm. "Scarcely."

The hand dropped. A man had entered her view. Nero Valencia.

He was still haggard and slow-moving, pale beneath the olive complexion. Either his biojewel had died in the tank or he had chosen to have it removed before he left; the mark on his brow had not yet faded entirely away. He bent over Eiko, making it a bow. Warmth filled his tone: "Buenos días, Srta. Tamura. It is marvelous to see you again."

Why should her heart skip a beat? "Gracias," she answered. "I was glad . . . to learn . . . you came through well."

Valencia straightened. "Buenos días," Kyra said flatly.

He cocked an eyebrow, flicked a glance at her waist, and replied, "Buenos años." Somehow it did not strike Eiko as impudent, though Kyra flushed a bit.

"How glad I am," Eiko ventured quickly. "We have much to talk about . . . when I am stronger."

"We'll have more to learn about, I'd say," Kyra answered.

The viewscreen went blank. It doubled as an annunciator. The image of a man formed in it, burly and reddish-haired. "Ah, yes," Kyra observed. "The jefe. He addresses each new lot of us. Repetition, more or less; I suppose it's recorded and re-edited." Just the same, everybody watched.

"Bienvenidos," rumbled the simulacrum. "You know who I am. I hope soon to know who each of you is. We're all Demetrians now." The face went solemn. Eiko saw on Kyra and Valencia that what came next was news to them. "I deeply regret having to report a death. Rosa Soares did not revive. Hers shall be our first honored grave. There are going to be more."

The generated countenance lightened. "But let me speak ahead. Those freshly roused haven't heard anything but rumors yet, about how things are where you are bound. Bueno, I can tell you that we forerunners have done pretty well. On the whole, the work has gone according to plan." A brief grin. "The plan allows for endless unforeseen problems, troubles, glitches, hitches, and outright disasters. In that, we have not been disappointed. You have no dearth of tasks waiting for you. Our crying need is for conscious intelligences, all-around human beings—in short, you. But when you get your legs back and come join us, you'll find quite a pleasant little town."

"This I have heard before," muttered Valencia impatiently, beneath the ongoing speech.

"Me oftener," Kyra said.

"But not I," Eiko reminded them.

"You will, dear, you will," Kyra told her. "Better if you don't in a single chunk. He never was much where it comes to oratory."

Valencia smiled at Eiko. "Language for heroes, that is your department," he murmured.

"Give me time, please," she protested. "And, I beg you, keep your expectations low. I am no Homer. . . . And even he first needed a story to tell."

50

This communication deals mainly with the political compromise that has finally been negotiated. Luna will modernize its government, becoming another cybernetic democracy, and join the World Federation. However, the aging Selenarchs retain their properties, on which seigneural law shall prevail through their lifetimes. Elsewhere, global population continues to decline at a satisfactory rate, and the conversion of the Amazon basin to a biological preserve should soon be finished. Africa has begun the changeover to a distributive economy; a civilization being built from the foundations can more readily rationalize its institutions than can older ones. It anticipates guidance by the full artificial intelligences when they come into action. The new models are learning rapidly and showing not only consciousness but an analogue, as yet imperfectly understood, of human creativity.

THE DOOR SUMMONED Kyra to her porch. That was fine in itself. She had meant to step out soon and watch the sunset. Clear days were not quite a rarity any more at the high latitude of Port Fireball; vegetation was changing climates astonishingly fast as it burst across the continents, gulping down carbon dioxide and breathing forth oxygen, holding moisture in soil, tempering the thermal extremes of naked rock. But you didn't take them for granted.

The street on which her house stood ran along a headland overlooking the town and the bay. Trees lined it, planted when the first Guthrie returned, pine and deodar grown tall in the decades after, broadleafs still young and requiring special care. The wind off the water soughed in them. Its coolness and tang cut through earlier heat like a sword. Blade-bright ran the waves to meet a sky where already an evening planet gleamed—Phaethon, but nonetheless beautiful. Southwestward A drew near the hills; haze turned its disc mellow golden. B was invisible, far-swung on its cometlike path and, at this time of this year, lost in the brilliance of its companion. A few gulls caught the light on their wings. Enough fish now swam or washed ashore to support them. And flowerbeds lay red, white, violet around the house. . . .

Kyra drew up short. Before her stood Nero Valencia. As if of itself, her hand reached behind to shut the door. "Oh," she said. "Saludos. What brings you here?"

Did she really see wistfulness in his smile? "I came to say adiós," he answered.

"You're going away, then? For a fairish while?"

He nodded. "To Boeotia."

"I, uh, I'm sorry. I'd like to invite you in, but between the baby and my other occupations—the place is a mess—"

She lied, and suspected he knew it. Why did she? That killing belonged to a dead past; to him it had been a duty; he had since ceased to be a gunjin; in spite of rebuffs none too subtle, he was always polite to her, yes, amiable, helpful on the couple of occasions she'd given him the opportunity; Eiko liked him well. But Kyra didn't care to be alone with him.

"That's all right," he said gently. "I must hurry onward in any case." She judged that was another lie. "I could not leave without seeing you. It has been too seldom."

"Bueno, everybody's busier than a one-armed octopus, learning our way around and settling into our work."

"Still, I had hoped—" He shrugged. "No matter." His eyes had caught hers and would not let go.

She was afraid of him, she realized. Afraid he'd charm her off her feet. Even if she hadn't been sleeping single too damn long, memories lived. It was not an involvement she wanted. At least, it would be foolish. Besides, there was Eiko.

"I admit I haven't been very sociable or kept close track," she said hastily. "Not able to. You're involved in ecological development, I know, and Boeotia must be ready for a higher stage. But it's halfway around the planet. What exactly will you be doing?"

Valencia chuckled. "Nothing exact. We're taking vertebrates, herbivores and carnivores, from exogenesis, to introduce there."

"I see. They're necessary for plant diversity, as well as desirable for their own sakes." A cliché, schoolchild knowledge, conversational filler.

"It will be tricky." He began to sound cheerful. "We expect countless failures, improvisations, frantic rescues and repairs."

His tone made Kyra easier. "Sounds like fun," she said. "Where do you fit in?"

"I like wilderness, especially where it's becoming woodland. And it seems I have some talent for handling animals."

"Moose, elephants, wolves, lions?"

He laughed. "Not for many years, if ever. Rodents, small birds, hawks."

Yes, she thought, he would understand hawks. "Good luck," she bade him quite sincerely.

"What have you been doing lately?" he asked. "I don't imagine you can return to space before your baby has grown a little."

"I couldn't anyway, and knew it before I left Earth. It'll take about that much time before they'll have industrial capacity free to build enough ships of the right kinds."

His regard suggested that to him this helped explain why

she had chosen to have a child, but all he did was rephrase his question. "What are you engaged in, then, besides mothering? When last we spoke, you said only, 'Miscellaneous troubleshooting.'"

"Bueno, I've persuaded Guthrie to set me designing windjammers that robots can use. You need a lot more fail-safes than for a human crew with conscious judgment. But fuel is still somewhat of a bottleneck, you know, and if we can save it on freight hauls where there's no hurry, that's useful all around. I'll be testing a boat soon. We'll work up to ships."

"Very interesting. Something you can enjoy while you wait for your spacecraft."

"Oh, yes."

"I am glad." Valencia hesitated. "Can we keep in touch? May I phone you now and then?"

Kyra's pleasure dissolved. "I, I'm afraid I'll be awfully busy."

"I see."

"We'll meet again when you come back here, surely."

"I hope so."

Kyra mustered nerve. "Say hola to Eiko from me. I haven't seen her in a while, either."

It was a moment before he could reply smoothly, "Of course."

"Good luck to you," she repeated.

He bowed. "And to you, everything that is good."

What could she do but take his hand? It lingered around hers, hard and warm. A giddiness swept through her. Almost, she opened the door. She pulled free. "Vaya con Díos," she said.

He smiled, turned, and left her. She stood in the wind, looking after him, till he was gone from sight. The sun went below the hills. Eastward the sky deepened, making Phaethon shine the brighter. A powersat glimmered in the same quarter. At their distance, its kind were no more than added stars. Guthrie hadn't wanted to ruin the night heavens that would be Demeter's when the cloud cover had lessened.

Better glance at Hugh. Kyra went inside. The house was small and, except for standardized furnishings, nearly bare. It took years to accumulate the clutter of a home. Hers lay forever behind her. Bueno, time lay before her.

She had named the child for her father. He continued asleep in his crib, incredibly tiny and perfect. Who would stand father to him? A boy needed a male figure to adore, imitate, rebel against, reconcile with, and give grandchildren to. But damn, damn, damn—

A phone chimed. Every room had one; the colony was glutted with nanotech and assembly-complex wares, including robot workers. Kyra sometimes wondered if any commercial enterprise would evolve on Demeter. She touched *Accept*.

No image appeared. "Buenas tardes," greeted her voice. "Do you have a few spare minutes?"

"What is it?" Kyra asked.

"Got a piece of gab for you," said her download.

Kyra grinned. "You know, you sound more like Guthrie every day."

Did the tone go a bit defensive? "Bueno, we work hand in glove, don't we?" It brisked. "This could wait, but I thought you'd appreciate hearing at once. A basic reanalysis of climate cycles has come to my attention. It draws on new data, growth rings in coraloids, isotope ratios in sea-bottom cores, you can study the details later. They give strong reason to believe the northern hemisphere is moving into a period of sudden and violent storms. Vegetation ought to moderate it in the interior, but not much at sea or along the coasts. You'll want to take this into account."

Kyra knotted her fists. "Bloody hell!"

"Nothing insurmountable for your project," the download assured her. "Another factor."

"I know. But—" Kyra stared into the window and the twilight gathering beyond.

"But what?"

Kyra made herself confront the facelessness in the screen, that it might better see her. "Look, you know we don't have anything like a proper weather forecasting service thus far, let alone weather control." Too many unknowns, too many variables swiftly changing. "What you've told me is that squalls or worse can jump essentially out of nowhere. I'd planned to take Hugh along on trial sails. Now I don't dare. Who'll look after him while I'm gone?" Not a robot, for sure, unless a trustworthy human was on hand as well; and who could spare the time?

"M-m, yes, a problem." Kyra stood listening to the wind in the trees. After half a minute she heard, brightly: "How about me?"

"Huh?"

"In an appropriate body. I could have it rigged to be soft and cuddly."

"But you, you've got more work than you can handle. Don't you?"

"We all do. However, kids come first. They're the future."

Guthrie again, Kyra thought.

"These days there's seldom any call for me to go out in the field," the download went on. "Mostly I receive input, communicate, make decisions, issue orders. I can meanwhile play nanny. No, not always. But I'll see about supplemental arrangements. With humans, especially."

"Can that be done?"

"It has to be done, the sooner the better. We'll be getting other children before long."

"I've speculated on how we might cope with that," Kyra said slowly. "Our population as small and overworked as this. I'm not convinced the entire situation was foreseen."

"I daresay we'll have to modify the rules. Kids deserve stable families, but we'll probably give 'family' a new meaning."

Extended? Communal? Kyra wouldn't admit, even to this ghost of herself, what a tingle went through her loins. "Bueno, I, I have thought . . . we're bound to become different from what we were."

"When did things ever stay the same?"

"I s'pose." Kyra drew breath. "Gracias for the information and the offer. Let me think about them. Anything else? No? Buenas noches, then."

She wished her cutoff were less abrupt. But what could she do? Invite the download around for coffee and a girlish chat?

Though her breasts felt full, she shouldn't wake Hugh. When he wanted to nurse, he'd let her know. Tomorrow she was just going to the lab and the boatyard. She'd take him along as usual. He enjoyed outings, wind in the hair that was black like Bob's, light in the eyes that were brown like Bob's, but something of her, she thought, in the face and the way his hands reached out. She looked forward.

Be that as it may, how to pass this evening? Make supper. She preferred to do her own cooking. Best was when she cooked for company, but those occasions had become rare. Her acquaintances were pairing off. She was welcome among them but shouldn't risk wearing that welcome thin. Spacers were wise not to bind themselves to groundlings; when the bonds broke, they hurt. And, yes, Rinndalir yonder—

The room darkened. Rather than brighten it immediately, she went back out in search of light and air. The sea shimmered. More stars were blinking forth. She stood at her porch rail, it was like the bridge of a sailing ship, and let the wind sing, ruffle her hair, press blouse and kilt against her.

A man came walking past. The street was unilluminated, but by stars and sea and remnant sunset glow she knew him. Young Jeff Packer. "Buenas tardes, Pilot Davis," he hailed.

"Buenas tardes," she responded. Her gaze trailed him. What a handsome fellow he was, and a first-class human being. Not that she intended anything untoward. But her other self, who could be objective about such things, had in fact spoken of—not bonds, but something else, something new.

51

After intensive study, the Psychosociological Institute reports no cause for alarm in the upsurge of religious and primitivist movements and the founding of communities dedicated to their ideals. They remain minuscule, scattered, idiosyncratic, and frequently hostile to each other. While some derive from old-established societies, most are neoreactionary, their discontent with modern Earth purely emotional. Already their growth curves are flattening, and it is anticipated that they will soon turn downward, as younger generations mature in an increasingly rational civilization. However, the report recommends further research and development in means of satisfying, without compromising that rationality, those urges of prehuman origin for which the archaic label is "spiritual."

THE NORTHERN HIGHLANDS of Argolis had become Terrestrial temperate. Heather bloomed purple, gorse yellow, beneath cool winds that sent cloud shadows scudding over down and glen, burn and tarn. Rains rushed swiftly, then the sun broke through and a rainbow lifted above the ridges. Birch and willow grew widespread. In sheltered places leaves trembled on the first young aspens. Insects hummed, buzzed, went glittery aloft; spiderwebs glistened with dew. Birds winged in ever greater flocks, as large as grouse and duck; below them amphibians and small mammals ran, swam, burrowed; hawk and fox went hunting.

It was not an iteration of life's reconquest after the glaciers withdrew, long ago on the mother world. That had gone by millennia and centuries, this moved by decades and years. What had fashioned these forms was not evolution but conscious will and skill. Their forerunners were not weather and water but chemicals, energies, machines of sizes from the monstrous to the molecular. Technology pervaded them, mostly invisible but always driving, guiding, guarding this that mortals had called into being.

Near the middle of the country rose Lifthrasir Tor. Specially planted and tended, a grove crowned it like a dream of the future, maple, poplar, oak, ash, thorn. Download Kyra landed on the airstrip at its foot and walked up a road that wound among crags, boulders, grasses, wildflowers, and shrubs. She had flown the vehicle today rather than wear it because she was using a humanoid body. Beneath a clear sky its metal answered the gleam of a distant lake. In her hands she bore Guthrie's braincase. When she passed beneath the trees, they welcomed her with murmurs, dancing light-flecks, odors and mould and growth.

The biocybernetic laboratory in their midst was of modest size. Ivy covered the walls. Its people could draw on the findings of others around the globe, and their own work was too subtle for grandness. Director Basil Rudbeck had seen his visitors coming and stood in the main doorway to greet them, a middle-aged man, blond, stocky, and zestful.

"Bienvenidos, jefe and señora," he said. "We've been looking forward to this for a long time."

"Well, for me time's chronically short," Guthrie replied. "Besides, while you were doing your tinkering and testing and retinkering, you didn't need me underfoot."

"You'd have been welcome whenever you cared to come, though I admit we wouldn't have had much to show you earlier. But we do appreciate how you've let us get on with our job unmolested by any bureaucrats."

"Traditional Fireball policy, whenever I figured a nominee could cut the mustard." Guthrie made a chuckle. "In your case, I had extra reason to, namely, mercy on the bureaucrats." Rudbeck was a descendant of Guthrie's living self.

"And now you've achieved a breakthrough?" Kyra prompted.

Rudbeck smiled. "Nothing so dramatic. We've gnawed our way forward till we have a system that appears to work as it ought. The real credit goes to the field scientists and, yes, the robots and downloads before them, those who gathered the data and piece by piece learned what they mean, how things happen on this planet and why." He bowed. "Muchas gracias."

Kyra had acquired sufficient art of generating a voice that hers registered surprise. "To me? When I go into the field, I'm just a pilot."

"Pilots are sorely needed," Guthrie said. "Also, more than once you've saved somebody's valuable ass. I heard."

"At any rate," Rudbeck continued, "the incoming information gradually showed us how we should correct our programs and, often, redesign our hardware." Enthusiasm bore him onward, unnecessarily: "When you're trying to telescope millions of years of ecological development into two or three hundred, on a global scale because nothing less is possible, it isn't like gardening. Even if we could be certain what to do—and we can't, it's too complex, it goes chaotic—even then, the sheer volume of work and the speed with which an unstable order of things can crash, they'd overwhelm any set of control systems we could ever produce. For an elementary example, do you remember the business of the Thessalian clover?"

"Sure," Guthrie grunted. "Who doesn't?"

According to plan, the new-made soil in that wet region had been sown with a new-made moss which should rapidly make it suitable for those humble microbes and invertebrates on which higher species depended. This had gone well, and clovers were introduced to enrich the ground further. Unfortunately and unforeseen, they grew so widely, so densely, that they made the thin peatlike substrate friable. Rain began eroding down toward bedrock. The best way to limit the clovers seemed to be to bring in predators on the bees that pollinated them. But these insects, developed from wasp DNA, gave rise to a mutant variety whose free-ranging larvae decimated the worms that aerated and fertilized the soil. A specifically designed virus—Nature in Thessaly was still lurching from one catastrophe to the next.

Rudbeck flushed. "I'm sorry. Got carried away. Didn't mean to lecture at you like a teacher to children."

"Not to worry," Guthrie said. "My ego's pretty thick-skinned. Go on."

"Gracias, sir. Let me state the basic principle. You've heard it, it seems obvious, but only lately has it been proven with mathematical rigor. We *can't* continue sending our robots and our nanotech molecules scurrying around to find out whatever's going wrong and repair the damage. Either life on Demeter dies back to extinction above the microscopic level, aside from a few plots maintained by unremitting and ridiculously large efforts, or else it expands and evolves. In the second case, ecological complexity will increase faster than any regulatory system of ours can grow—unless we make such a host of regulators that they crowd the life out of existence."

"I know. Government has the same property, though very few people and no politicians ever wanted to realize it. Yet we haven't got time for nature to balance herself. Your bunch has been searching for a way between the horns of the dilemma. Okay, now that I've had my revenge and astounded you with the revelation that horses have four legs, can you explain to me in nickel words what you have accomplished?"

"I'll do my best. But por favor, come in! I should not have kept you standing here."

"We don't mind," Kyra said. Downloads and machinery.

Rudbeck conducted them about, presented his staff to them, showed the equipment, keyed up the computer displays. The dimensions of his quiet victory emerged.

An organism is a unity. Its nigh-infinite intricacies of detection, ingestion, absorption, excretion, perception, reaction, chemistries, electron flows, feedbacks, dynamics mesh together in the service of survival. Ultimately this means the survival and propagation of the life-helix; but to that end, usually, the organism must prevail over its enemies and adversities. Given the minimum of nourishment and protection from the raw cosmos, it will endure, keep itself strong, heal its wounds, put down the treacheries of aberrant cells, and seek how it may increase the kingdom of its kind. The supreme example is a human being, whose brain is at once director, information processor, foremost of the glands, and wellspring of desire.

A natural ecology is no more than a set of relationships among organisms. However wonderfully complex and subtle, they are the result of geological eras of strife, blind chance, the modifications that life itself has made in its surroundings, and pitiless winnowing of all that does not find ways to belong. The network of beings may last for an age; but at any time, any accident to its territory or any intrusion of outsiders may bring ruin. The stones of Earth record half a dozen mass extinctions, when suddenly most great races died; the lesser, local obliterations are beyond counting. How vulnerable, then, is life uprooted from that entire long history and worldwide matrix, made to begin over again in lands that hitherto were wholly barren?

Only if an ecology is an organism—

"The basic idea is old, of course," Rudbeck said. "I wouldn't be surprised but what speculation goes back to when the first transmissions arrived from Demeter. Maybe further, jefe?" He glanced at Guthrie but got no response. "We should establish the equivalent of a nervous system. Nothing as crude as a lot of sensors giving input to a lot of computers which give orders to a lot of robots: though pretty clearly, something of the kind would have to be included. Mainly, we'd need molecular structures that amount to symbionts, growing naturally with and within most plants and possibly some animals, interconnecting at need across distances as large as necessary. Not forming sense organs or brains or anything quite like that, but . . . equivalent. The trick, the problem was to find *how* this could be done. What might work, what might be the side effects or the critical consequences? In the long run, what could make the decisions and carry them out in the same unthinking natural fashion as your body—as a living body does for everything that goes on inside itself?"

"According to your reports that I've seen, you were floundering around till you came on a basic new understanding," Guthrie said.

Rudbeck shrugged. "A half-understanding. It began when Farquhar took a fresh look at the theory of how mitochondria had entered into symbiosis with primitive prokaryotes. She showed, in light of our observations here, that the theory was inadequate. Then Kristoffer formalized the symbology and put the data through a Yamato tensor— But this is pretty abstract, I'm afraid, and after the theorems were proven we had the practicalities to work out."

Guthrie's eyestalks swung back toward the array of organic and inorganic units he had been inspecting. It was astonishingly small. "Which you did," he said, "and here is your baby."

"No, an embryo," Rudbeck demurred. "It's limited to six or seven thousand square kilometers, and it's far from complete. Spread very thinly, in fact, crude, too; rudimentary; full of flaws. And suited only to this particular territory, this particular nature. But within its limitations, it is functional. It's . . . learning. For instance, in exposed areas where winter nights get cold, workers have found that creeping juniper planted around sapling aspen and alder generally insulates their roots enough for them to survive and grow. Bueno, we've noticed those species volunteering together in places where they never grew before. We've tracked robugs carrying the seeds to the sites, with no specific instructions from us or from any program we wrote. The programs have been revising themselves!"

Pride rang. "The system will expand of its own accord. It will change, improve—sometimes with our help, sometimes, I suspect, in spite of us. It will adapt to every environment and ecology on Demeter. I don't expect I'll live to see the end result, but at last there will be a biosphere that's an organism, loose, mostly functioning in local nodes, but a global organism."

" 'Vaster than empires and more slow,' " said Kyra.

"Pardon?" asked Rudbeck.

"A line from an ancient poem. I was thinking of signals transmitted across continents and oceans."

"Not limited to chemical speeds. I showed you the system has electronic, photonic, and mechanical components. Eventually we want to incorporate artificial intelligence—full, conscious AI. That requires a much more sophisticated system, of course, but meanwhile we'll be learning about the advances the psychoneticists on Earth make."

"Nine calendar years, damn near, between question and answer," said Guthrie. "Your baby needs to be up and running pretty soon. If you don't want it committing itself to a structure that can't accommodate awarenesses, you'd better have them in the circuits from the start, at least part time."

Rudbeck nodded. "We realize that. Provisions already exist for temporarily including a download—simply to observe, at first, and perhaps nothing more will be called for till we get a real cybermind."

"Why haven't you tried it?"

"Uncertainties. We want to refine our techniques before adding to them."

"Why? Any risks involved?"

"Not as far as we can see, but I repeat, we don't yet know enough, we can't anticipate every possible mischance."

"And you never will till you've tried." Guthrie's eyestalks quivered. "Listen, put me in. Now."

Rudbeck stared. "Are you serious?"

"I had this in mind when I came out today. That's how come I arrived nekkid. All I wanted beforehand was the tour you've given us, to settle a few matters I wasn't sure about. Go ahead. Why not? Unscientific, an uncontrolled experiment, yeah, but can it hurt?"

Rudbeck shook his head. "It could hurt you."

"Nonsense. I've come through more and worse mistreatment than I'd want you to imagine. What will this do other than give me a notion—dim, no doubt, preliminary, but a notion from the inside—of how your organism will *feel?* Which I've got a hunch will be mighty helpful to me."

"Don't you dare!" Kyra exclaimed. "If you insist on a report like that, take me out of this body and I'll give you one."

"Balls," retorted Guthrie. "You were an officer of Fireball. Would you let a man of yours take a chance you wouldn't? Anyway, this isn't a gamble. It's a look-see. I hereby pull rank and claim the fun for myself." His voice sank. "Something new, not a quiviran shadow-show but real, after so many dry years—" Roughly: "Can do, Rudbeck? Okay, snap to it."

He could override argument but not discussion, plans, preparations, precautions. Demeter's day had drawn to a close when the scientists connected him. Stars wheeled for an hour above the silence, broken by occasional half-whispered banalities, in which they watched the gauges and paced the floor. Then they took him out.

He said little except, low and slowly, "I can't describe it. Maybe if you got a poet. For a while, almost, I thought I was alive again."

The humans were exhausted, and what hospitality had they to bid these guests? After goodbyes, Kyra took Guthrie back to their flyer. Her footfalls resounded loud through the night. Hill and heath glimmered where hoarfrost caught starshine.

"I'd have been less shocked at your recklessness if you hadn't wiped your duplicate," she said.

"I didn't," Guthrie stated. "He's right here, all his memories, transferred into me."

"Why?"

"You know perfectly well. One of me handled matters in the Solar System and the emigrant ships while the other went ahead and took charge here, but after both of me were on Demeter, two rambunctious old bastards would've gotten in each other's way. We intended from the first that we'd merge."

"I mean why didn't you keep the second program deactivated but in reserve? Especially if you were going to cut corners like today."

"Hell, that was about as hazardous as raising on a straight flush. I figured a spare me had become a bad idea. Sooner or later the colony will have to get along on its own. In fact, if it can't by now, it doesn't deserve to."

"We'd . . . miss you, jefe."

Guthrie laughed. "Oh, I aim to stick around for a goodly while." His tone softened. "Yes, after this experience. . . . Don't you, Kyra?"

"I think not," she answered.

He considered her, as if his lenses could read expression in her turret. "Aren't you happy?"

"I'm not unhappy. It doesn't apply. I'm interested in what I do. But when nobody has urgent need of me any longer, I'll be content to stop."

"A session in yon biocenter might change your mind.
I'd like that, querida. I really would."

"Sorry, jefe," she said. "I don't believe I'll want to try."

"Why not, if I may ask?"

"It would remind me of too much that I'm closer to in
time than you are."

"I see."

They spoke no more. She strode on downhill.

52

Few inhabitants are left in L-5. The roboticization of
space operations being well advanced, it has no function except as a tourist resort, and this is marginal. The
general availability of quiviras has brought all such
sensations in much easier reach, and in any event there
is little public interest in them. Arrangements are being
made by which the remaining dwellers can, if they
wish, live out their lives in the station. Childbearing
among them will be strongly discouraged.

DISTANCE-DWINDLED, A STILL cast brilliance, a light that to
human eyes was white barely tinged with blue. It brought
the scarps and craters of Perun sharply forth from shadows that seemed to flow as *Merlin* curved nearer. Here and
there gleamed nickel-iron outcrops, scoured by gigayears
of cosmic infall. Beyond the rough spheroid, Voloss was a
lump of blackness amidst the stars. Kyra Davis recalled
that the Lunarians had recently brought that carbona-
ceous-chondritic body into orbit around the larger, stony-
metallic asteroid, to be a convenient source of water and
organics. The software in her torchcraft knew it well and
took it into account, executing the commands her fingers
issued. She had ample chance to look about her.

Mostly she gazed at that which trailed Perun in the same
path. As yet the spacecraft was a partial skeleton, but
already ribs and stringers curved gigantic. At its remove,

the construct appeared fragile, exquisite, silver wires shaped and woven into a piece of jewelry for an elfland princess. Magnifying and amplifying, she saw vehicles, robots, spacesuited technicians flit motelike through and around, a dance that evoked music in her head, Mozart, Strauss, Nielsen.

Would the ship fare as lightly and gladly through the Alpha Centaurian domain, to Proxima and maybe, maybe beyond? Thus far the builders had revealed little, but rumors went abroad about plans for enlarging and using the lasers that had nursed the emigrants to rest, for massless braking by Alfvén waves, for— She had better stop daydreaming, Kyra realized, and concentrate on approach.

Some thousand kilometers in its maximum diameter, Perun would never, she supposed, bear cities and strongholds like Luna. However, more structures jutted on it than she had expected, prior to the first Demetrian flight hither. Before then, Lunarian transmissions to the planet were only sketchily informative. She hadn't taken that for a sign of hostility. These folk were by nature as aloof and secretive as cats. It was a surprise to learn how industrious they'd been, how much they'd wrought in a handful of years and without the resources of her world to draw on. Now she'd behold for herself. The heart knocked in her breast.

Domes, masts, pyramids, colonnades—and then, radiant point of roads, the spacefield. It was a flat cap on the north pole, surrounded by hemicylindrical buildings above which loomed the control radar. "*Merlin* requesting clearance to dock," Kyra voiced, and heard "Clearance granted," in a remembered lilting accent. Mere formality on either side; the agreements were long since reached, the computers were entirely in charge. On breaths of jet, the vessel descended to her assigned cradle.

Silence closed in. Kyra unharnessed and left her seat. She had run at one Demetrian gravity, eight percent less than Earth's, which had become the norm for her bones and veins and tissues. Although reaccustomed to changes in weight, she felt suddenly ghostly. What did she heft here, five kilos, six? Cautiously she moved down to her personal section, where she stopped for a glance in the mirror. Before commencing final maneuvers she'd changed to white perlux blouse with ruffled front and puffed sleeves, tigryl bolero, blue slacks, diffractor-buckled sandals. Show that her people had gotten to a point where they could go a bit dressy. Don't give the Lunarians whatever advantage they might find in seeing her as a frump.

They? Rinndalir, she admitted. Her pulse thudded louder.

No, God spit on it, she wouldn't be embarrassed when they met. She wouldn't let herself be. What reason in the cosmos did she have to be? The mirror showed her straight, supple, a touch on the lean side but that was better than fat and it brought out the bones in her face, which she knew were good. Some lines and crinkles, hair begun dulling toward gray, what of it? She kept alive the relationships that she wanted on her own merits, without having to claim they laid any obligations on anybody. Besides, she had come here not to make connections but to make history.

A slight impact sounded through hull and air. The gangway had osculated the exit lock. Kyra winked at her image and went on out.

The descent took her belowground, into a small, bare anteroom. Rinndalir stood alone.

She jarred to a halt. He advanced to take her hand. "Welcome, my lady," he said, and smiled. "Far too long have I awaited you."

Palm and fingers were cool around hers. Did she feel calluses? "I, I'd have liked to come sooner," she heard herself falter. "Fascinating place, from what I could gather. But once I had my ship, I needed to get back in training, and then—so much to do—"

"Between your times at home with your child. I understand."

Did he? she wondered. If not, did he know he didn't?

"Accept lodgment, I pray you," he purred on. "It is less

than lavish, but I have striven to prepare it as worthy of you."

Heat and cold again passed through her. Why in MacCannon's name was she reacting like this? Stop it, pronto! He had been a delightful companion, an incomparable lay, a moral monster, and what the hell further concern of hers was any of that?

She summoned a mantra. Self-command flowed into her. Studying him, she saw that time had graven deeply. Toil, hardship, and what else? Between wings of hair gone ashen, his countenance was furrowed, the gray eyes enormous in its gauntness. Yet he stood as erect as she, moved more lithely, and in his argent and sable, beneath a diamond-frosted headband, was elegance incarnate.

"Your colleagues, your officers?" she asked. True humans would have met her in a group. *Merlin* was just the fifth Demetrian vessel to visit Perun.

"We will foregather with them when we choose," he said indifferently.

So he remained an overlord, she thought. Communications between his breed and hers, sparse as they were, hadn't made their new social structure at all clear. Did Rinndalir reign supreme over this one settlement, or over his entire, wide-strewn people?

"First you and I have years to exchange," he went on, his voice turning melodious. "I will dispatch men to bring your baggage, remote-directed by you, whenever you like. Now come, I pray you."

He did not offer an arm for her to touch, nor bring fingertips to her hand. The omission suggested they were equals. Bemused, willy-nilly almost captivated, she accompanied him. He moved at the same easy low-*g* lope as she. About half Lunar, the weight sufficed to keep his kind healthy, but she guessed they must spend time exercising in centrifugal to stay fit. Or maybe not, given all their activity on the ground and in space.

Moving along, she found ample evidence of it. A high, ogive-vaulted passage led from the entry, carved out of rock which had thereafter been polished glass-smooth.

Fluorotubes lighted it in changeable colors and intensities. Otherwise no illusions livened the murky-red length, only occasional inset panels of other minerals, green, blue, mica-sparkly. At intervals were pillars sculptured in fluid curves and foamlike laciness, studded with gems and crystals. The variable light animated them. Barely audible to Kyra, sounds as of flute and violin twined among bittersweet odors. Where doors stood open she glimpsed a café whose patrons sat on rugs playing chess or go, a foodstore, a laboratory, an atelier, a wizardly little workshop. Traffic was scant; these caverns had been dug for a population that was to grow. Such males, females, and their young as went by moved fast, intent, seldom talking. Loose indoor garb flapped and streamed, multiply colored.

"Like wings on birds," Kyra remarked.

"In future birds will fly free among us, gaudy moths, perhaps frolicsome bats," Rinndalir said. "In passages less ornate than here will grow flowering vines."

"Not much like what Luna was."

He turned solemn. "We are becoming other than what we were. More than you on Demeter, it may be."

An equal seriousness came upon her. "I don't know about that." Landscape and life— "Did you expect it would happen?"

"In truth. Ice that melts freezes again, but we are alive, your kindred and mine." Rinndalir was silent a while. The corridor slipped away behind Kyra, half unseen. "It is a reason why my lady Niolente chose to stay home."

She searched for tactful words. "My impression was she wanted to fight for the old order of things there, keep it going as long as possible. Doesn't—didn't she despise Earthlings?"

Looking sideways, she saw what might be pain flicker across him. He kept his own eyes forward. "Certain kinds of them," he replied slowly. "The great ones she thanked and honored in her spirit, for they were adversaries to call forth all that she was. Intrigue and strife against them appealed more to her than any struggle with insensate matter." He smiled. She could not tell if it was sadly or lovingly or what. "That was the more so after she knew beyond doubt that her cause was lost. Now might she make whatever wager she fancied, and at least leave her mark upon destiny. I will never be sure, from what has come filtered to us out of Earth, but I suspect it was she who forced the bargain that the last Selenarchs would reign over their holdings until death invaded. The new powers must have misliked that; it hampered their reconstructions for decades. Yes, I elect to imagine that my Niolente took the lead in finding means to threaten them—oh, most covertly—with what was worse."

Kyra gathered courage to say, "I've wondered why you didn't stay in the game."

The luminous glance swept over her and back to the distances ahead. "The answer to that is less to be told than to be lived."

At the mouth of a shaft they turned downward, springing from platform to platform staggered at seven-meter intervals. A fall attained barely more than three meters per second. Soon Rinndalir laughed and made a single three-stage jump. Taking hold of his cloak, he spread it from his shoulders. It was cut so as to billow out and catch the air; he floated down whirling like a wind-blown leaf. The Lunarians weren't altogether changed, Kyra thought.

On a wider landing he stopped, beckoned, and conducted her into another horizontal tunnel. It had a rough, unfinished appearance, more ventilators than doors, and a trench in the middle of the floor. "This will be an arbor through which a stream runs," he explained.

"You really have gotten ardent about biology, haven't you?" Kyra said.

"From Luna we could behold living Earth," he replied. "Here Demeter is but a spark in the sky, and another is Phaethon."

After what Kyra estimated as ten klicks, a short side passage ended at a bronze portal decorated with geometric bas-reliefs. Rinndalir ordered it to open and guided her through. Mosaics decked the walls of an anteroom. She saw they were copied from the Byzantine church in Ravenna. If he desired a reminder of what he had abandoned, this was a strange one. Or was it? Theodora's great eyes were fixed on eternity.

Beyond, she entered a spacious chamber, black and white, its ceiling a viewdome which showed the heavens above. A had set but B shone among the stars, a deep-yellow point bright as several hundred Lunas full over Earth. That sky was the room's sole illuminator. Flask and goblets sheened mystical on a darkling table. Music trilled more clearly than before, and a perfume as of jasmine with the least undertone of musk swirled in the air.

Memory struck alarm. "Your quarters?" Kyra demanded.

Rinndalir smiled. In this light he became unaged, timelessly beautiful. "What else? A poor thing, but mine own."

She grabbed after conversation. "I wouldn't call it poor. Oh, not what you had before, no."

"That will never come again. We are a-building toward a morrow unknowable, even as you on Demeter, albeit they will be foreign to one another."

That he spoke not seductively but seriously brought a wave of relief. "Yes, I s'pose. Hadn't thought much about it till now, but at Sol—no matter how independent you acted, you Lunarians were an offshoot of Earth." Like ancient nomads, she reflected in passing: folk displaced to the steppes, tempered into strength and fierceness until sometimes they became the conquerors of the civilizations they fringed, yet always dependent on those for much of what kept them alive, always in the end overcome by them. "No more."

He took her elbow, she felt the soft touch acutely, and urged her to the table. "Be at ease, my lady. Our biosystems produce what are not the worst vintages in the galaxy." He filled goblets, gave her one, and raised his. *"Uwach yei,"* he toasted. "That means, approximately, 'Aloft.'"

Kyra touched rims, a clear ringing. "Happy landings," she responded. They sipped. The wine was tartly spicy.

"There we have uttered a hint of the differences between us," Rinndalir said.

"Maybe." Kyra searched for words. "Your people don't go in for manifestos or five-year plans or anything like that, but it does seem to us on Demeter that your aim is to create the first truly spaceborne society."

"A calculated aim would be blind, but a dream need not be. Surely many among you bear the same. You cannot be resigned to your descendants perishing with your planet."

"That's what I've come about, of course. My mission."

"Yours and mine."

Wine slopped as her glass jerked in Kyra's hand. She peered through the amber dusk. Rinndalir smiled calmly back. "What?" she gasped. "Wait a minute! I expected I'd take a specialist or two."

"They can fare later, if we find cause for it. On this early voyage, I will be your partner."

"In MacCannon's name, why?"

Rinndalir shrugged his shoulders—gracefully, which she had never seen a man of her kind achieve. "I am not incompetent, also in planetary science. These years have made a workman of me." He fixed his regard on her. Quiet and steely, command declared: "But I am still a Selenarch, and I have chosen to companion you."

Kyra set down her glass, stiffened her back, and snapped, "I'll have something to say about that, por favor."

He arched his brows. "Does your horror of me abide?" he murmured. "I think not unamendably."

"What you brought about—"

"Do you very bitterly regret it?"

"That last time in your castle—"

"Hark you, my lady." Rinndalir's voice tolled. "I repent me of naught. I was what I was. In large, I remain thus, and hold no wish to be otherwise. But in the light of these suns I have come to see more and farther than erstwhile."

"You listen," Kyra answered, angry and bewildered. "I didn't have to pilot this mission. I can resign from it and they'll get someone else." A Demetrian, an Earthling born or of Earthling stock. The Lunarians had visited Phaethon, but could not long endure its three-fourths Terrestrial gravity. Nor could they practicably direct robots from orbit. Joint expeditions made sense, now that the planetdwellers were launching their own manned spacecraft. "I'd be sorry to, I wanted it awfully, but if you've appointed yourself my shipmate, I quit."

He showed no resentment. "I ask anew, why?"

"Damnation, how round do you believe my heels are?"

Had he laughed or even smiled, she would have walked out. Instead he said soberly, "Yes, you have doubtless made your alliance with whomever fortunate it be, and would not betray. But must it bind you? I am capable of chastity, Kyra. Has your man no trust in you or you in him?"

Her men, she nearly corrected him; and, yes, they abjured jealousy, because she would not let herself be bound; and the problem on a cruise with Rinndalir might not be his chastity but would certainly be hers. "We're too unlike," she mumbled.

He nodded. "Ever sundered. Can you comprehend that that is a wound in me? That you are a reason I departed the life that was mine?"

He couldn't mean it! Could he? "On what acquaintance we had? Is this a joke?"

"Nay. Nor an infatuation." Wryly: "An attraction perverse, it may be, of the raven for the wild mare." The eagle, Kyra thought amidst hammering blood, the eagle who rides the wind that strokes the mare in her mane. And she is powerful and smells sweetly of sun-warmed earth. "Or is it unnatural? What do you feel for a pet or a ship or a mountain against sunset or the phantom of Anson Guthrie?"

"That's . . . different."

"How?"

"You said it yourself. We're unbridgeably divided." A gulf between them, Kyra thought, into which she could fall and never climb back out, and—and the metaphors were getting as mixed as the emotions.

"Yet when we meet," Rinndalir said, "we can reach across to touch hands."

Abruptly it was her laughter that shouted forth. "More than hands, you're thinking!" she cried.

Impudence flew free. "Are you not?"

After that, hour by hour, things got better and better.

53

WHEN ITS ORBIT, retrograde, unstable, and comet-eccentric, brought it close to A, Phaethon went mad. Frozen gases exploded in geysers and clouds, ice melted in cataracts and floods, hurricanes drove rainstorms full of lightning, seas drowned coastlands and mountainsides shed torrents of stone. Meanwhile light blazed and hard radiation seared. Those who would study the interior of the planet must seek it when it had swung afar, into the winter of its fourteen-year cycle.

Airsuited, Kyra stood on a white crust of snow. At her back it had been cleared away to the rock, making room for the shelters that had housed her and her equipment. On either side the terrain rolled pallid and shadowful beneath its cover. Ahead, a glacier spilled down steeper hills. Clean of dust, it shimmered a faint mysterious blue. Both suns were in the purple-black heaven. A, the captor, was shrunken to a lurid star; B showed a tiny disc; Proxima continued a red spark. Wind, a remnant of air not gone hard, shrilled thinly around her helmet.

Merlin was above the horizon. She watched her last geologist rolling back to camp while she spoke into her transmitter: "How can you be so positive?"

"The interpretation of your findings is unambiguous," 'cast Rinndalir from the ship. "The program has considered every possibility and found none of diverting or destroying this world."

"In eight-hundred-odd years?" It struck Kyra how fully she had come to think in terms of Demeter's calendar. On Earth she would have said a thousand. "That's time to drill a lot of holes and plant a lot of antimatter detonators."

"You must be wearied in truth, my dear, that you let wishfulness ride so free over knowledge. Phaethon is no asteroid or comet. Its core is molten. No more can one tunnel into it than into a sea. Thus, there can be no foundation firm enough for the kind of engine that would change the orbit. Nor could we blow off any but the outer layers of crust. Even were the globe broken apart—and the program does not foresee producing sufficient antimatter for that in the time that is left—even then, the wreckage would expunge every trace of you on Demeter."

Kyra sighed. "No surprise, I guess. This was such a loco little hope." Nevertheless its death made a heaviness within her.

"Let us and our descendants think how better we can spend our efforts toward outliving doomsday," Rinndalir said.

He really had changed, she thought. And, heartening: She herself would have plenty to do. Fragments of unborn planets tumbled countless in the chaotic regions where their coalescence had been forbidden; often the two suns flung them inward; a meteoroid patrol was needed, still more than around Sol.

That made her say, "Our descendants? This generation will do well to carve out a bare foothold for them."

"And to live our lives," Rinndalir insinuated.

He hadn't changed *too* much. At accelerations he could tolerate, the trip home would take a spell. Disappointment faded from Kyra—nobody had really expected any other outcome—as she found herself looking forward.

54

Responding to concerns expressed by Her Holiness the Elimite Bhairagi after the Lyudov Rebellion, Prescriptor Juang-ze Mendoza stated in an address to the world: "Fear of artificial intelligence with full consciousness is perhaps understandable as emotional atavism, but has no more rational justification than any other neurosis. These beings—yes, I call them beings, not machines—bring nothing but limitless promise. Where they replace humans, as in space operations, it is because they are better suited; they arrive as liberators. Yet they will never be slaves, abjectly serving us that we may pass lives of meaningless idleness. That would be an equal misuse of robot and human. They will be, they are already becoming, our partners in an immeasurably great destiny. Let us cease calling them artificial. Are electronic, photonic, nucleonic, or magnetohydrodynamic processes less natural than the chemistry of organic colloids? I propose for these beings the name Sophotect."

THUS FAR THE weather service had no reliable way of predicting fogs in Hollowland. That enormous swamp country, filling a quarter of tropical Aetolia, was too little known; conditions within it were altering too fast and radically. Even a satellite could often give no more than one or two hours' warning before hundreds of square kilometers were shrouded.

Such a cloud rose and rolled over Nero Valencia and Hugh Davis as they were bound back to camp after several days of survey—cruising about, observing, sampling, testing, charting how well the new-made wilderness fared, seeking to learn what the latest turns were that its development had taken. All at once they must creep and grope, engine down to a whisper, eyes well-nigh blinded.

Vision barely reached from end to end of the boat. Sometimes a thick tendril of mist drifted across to hide that much. Just enough light sneaked from above to shimmer off wet deck and cabin. Everywhere around, formlessness eddied gray, murk behind it. A glance overboard caught the leaves, broad and dark green around rosy flowers, between which the prow cut. Now and then a fish slipped past. The plants covered most of the brown water, whose clucking against the hull was the single sound from outside it. Occasionally a specter appeared, a hummock fringed with rushes or a mangrove glooming over shallows, but sight quickly lost it again. Heat had given way to raw and sullen chill; odors of growth and blossom had gone rank.

"Sir," called Hugh from the wheel, "trouble!"

"What now?" asked Valencia, crouched at the bows for whatever he might do as a lookout.

"The needle—direction finder—" The boy's voice, which was changing, cracked. "It's gone malo! Wobbles through . . . ninety degrees at least."

Valencia scowled but kept his calm. "Not unusual. Radio interference. A's at the peak of its sunspot cycle, you know. And stars get extra temperamental when they approach the end of their time on the main sequence."

He rose and faced aft, to give an image of reassurance. The short, sturdy figure in the cockpit stood firm. "Can you take an average bearing?" Valencia inquired.

"I'll try, sir. Though I wonder if we haven't gone way off course regardless. For sure, we didn't hit any patch of water lilies like this outbound."

"You *are* observant," Valencia said. "Good for you."

Good muchacho all around, he thought, bright, hardworking, respectful without being obsequious, excellent company in the field. Bueno, consider what stock he came from. And maybe his rather hit-or-miss home life had actually helped him; maybe Kyra wasn't careless but wise. Not many mothers would allow a boy his age to go on an expedition afar, no matter how skillful the adult companion. She had smilingly agreed it would be a learning experience that no vivifer or quivira could match.

"I think probably you're right," Valencia went on. "But if we keep going in this general direction, we should hit our island somewhere. Then we can follow the shoreline to camp."

"This rotten visibility—" Hugh wasn't complaining, Valencia knew; he was grumbling, man-fashion. "I wish we could anchor and wait the damn fog out."

"Me too. However, at this time of year one of these

banks can hang around for twenty or thirty days. We have hardly any drinking water left, remember." Irony: Hollowland was the single region other than sea and littoral where native life had taken hold; and here it had flourished. Dying and decaying, it poisoned the swamp for humans. Genes could be put into Terrestrial plants and animals that let them thrive, but a century might pass before the toxins were entirely gone. "People and robots around the planet have plenty to do without us hollering unnecessarily for help."

"I understand, sir."

Another wraith showed vaguely through the fog to starboard. It resembled the head of a medieval halberd thrust two meters above the water, encrusted blue shells tapering in spikes and hooks to a point as sharp as their own edges. "Oye, I never saw a riprock that big before!" Valencia exclaimed. "We certainly are off course." He squinted. "Dead, yes." The new microbes had killed the fresh-water coraloids and much else, not by attacking alien proteins but by their waste products.

The boat glided on. The shape vanished. There might be more. He'd better keep watch. Before he resumed, he saw Hugh shiver. As he hunkered down he heard, "Brrr! That thing, it's like—like the swamp wants revenge."

"For what?" Valencia asked.

"For us bringing in our kind of life to destroy what was here."

Mood swings were normal at puberty, but Valencia decided to curb this one if he could. The surroundings were eerie enough as was. "Hugh," he said, "if you want to be a ranger, you'll have to scrap that attitude. We're simply doing what nature herself did, over and over, on Earth—and on Demeter, I'll bet we find when we've read the fossil record. For instance, when the Panamanian isthmus closed, back in the Pleistocene, the big cats moved down from North America and the big carnivorous South American birds went under. Read your paleontology, for the same reason you should read history. You can't know the present without knowing the past."

Quite a homily for an old gunjin, he thought. On Earth he had barely heard about geological eras, couldn't have named them to save his cojones, and hadn't cared to learn. The years on this world had made him into somebody else, somebody whom Kyra Davis trusted with her son. . . . Perhaps the change wasn't so great. The potential must have been in that young man who now seemed a total stranger, or why had he come? An emptiness he'd scarcely been aware of, long since filled. . . .

Hugh's tone lightened. "Bueno, yes. And this country, it'll become wonderful, won't it, sir?"

Valencia nodded. "Rich. Wetlands always have been. From these breeding grounds life should go on to colonize the rest of the continent. Oh, and don't forget, we do mean to keep reserves where native species are protected. I even hear talk about trying for a mixed ecology in places where—"

A crash resounded. The deck jarred beneath his feet, tilted, threw him sideways. He caught the rail and slammed himself to a halt. A horrible gurgle rose from below.

Glaring aft through the fog, he saw Hugh leap out of the cockpit, onto the deck by the cabin. Impulsive, untrained, the boy left the motor running and sped toward the man, as if Valencia were his father. The boat shuddered, slewed about, and pitched. Hugh went over the side.

Valencia sprang that way. Fighter's reflexes kept him on a footing that lurched and slanted beneath him. The hull groaned. They'd struck a riprock, he knew—close below the surface, concealed by fog and the lilies. The boat was hard on, holed, its wound worse for every second that passed.

He jumped into the cockpit and switched off the motor. The boat stopped grinding itself against the skeleton. It settled sluggishly astern till it lay canted, bow up, after-deck awash.

Valencia was already amidships, on all fours, straining out and yelling. "Hugh! Hugh!" The fog smoked thicker and colder.

The boy swam well. He should have come straight up

and trod water, waiting for a hand back aboard. He hadn't. He'd struck his head or—

Valencia ducked into the cabin and unclipped an insulated flashtube. He kicked off his shoes, skinned out of shirt and pants, dived. The preparations had taken about thirty seconds.

As he slipped among the lily stalks the beam probed ahead through upswirled silt, dim and cloudy. The depth was just a few meters; he quickly saw mud and sodden logs. His lungs strained, his heart thuttered— Yonder! The light picked the riprock out of gloom, rising past sight, cruelly jagged, to the vessel it had pierced. The base spread wide. Hugh sprawled near the bottom, unmoving. His clothes had gotten snagged.

Air, air. But Hugh had been without air for how long? Valencia threshed his way to the boy. His head roared and whirled. He braced himself among the lumps, caught hold, tugged. Somewhere distant he felt how the sawlike edges slashed him. Blood drifted into the beam of the flashtube now held between his teeth. The knowledge that he might well die was academic. Here was a task.

He freed the body, took it in his arms, let the tube drop, and kicked. His lungs could endure no more, they emptied in a rush of bubbles.

But then his head was free, he gasped, he saw. He fought through the lilies to the counter, caught the taffrail, hauled his weight one-handed up on deck, dragged Hugh after him. Blood spread and spread out of his cuts.

Never mind. Roll the muchacho over, take him around the belly under the diaphragm, disgorge the foul tide of what he'd breathed and swallowed. Did he breathe now? No? Lay him on deck, put mouth to mouth and heel of hand at breastbone, *work*. Blood washed over the white face, on into the gray fog, the only color in all the universe.

Hugh stirred. His eyelids fluttered. Valencia sat back. His throat tightened, he barked, he realized with a shadowy startlement that he was trying to weep.

Nonsense. Jobs yet to do. He got the lax cold form below, undressed, toweled, into a bunk with plenty of blankets. "It's muy bien," he croaked, "everything's going to be muy bien, Hugh." Lips twitched slightly upward, but the boy was scarcely conscious. He felt warmer to the touch, though.

The touch made an awful red mess. Valencia fetched the first aid kit and patched the assorted slashes on both of them. Luckily, none were serious, except that three of his required plast to stop the bleeding. The swamp water they'd taken in was another matter. Bueno, he had antitoxin. He gave Hugh a double injection and himself a standard one. That ought to serve temporarily.

The sooner he got medical help, the better. This boat wasn't going anywhere. Valencia wanted dreadfully to lie down and sleep. He must have lost more blood than he'd known. He hobbled to the radio, slumped into the seat, and called Port Fireball.

"Hola, hola, do you read me? . . . We've got troubles—" He explained.

"We'll dispatch a flyer immediately," said the voice at the other end, how crisp, how resonant and alert. "Keep transmitting on distress waveband so it can home on you. It'll hover and lower a cable chair, if you can manage one. . . . You can? Excellent. In about three hours. Sorry, nothing closer is available."

"Uh, our flyer in camp, and the gear—"

"That'll be taken care of later. You two come first. Demeter isn't exactly overpopulated, you know. Hasta la vista."

For a moment silence hummed. Valencia moved to switch the audio off. A new voice, faint and rustly, said, "Hi, there."

"What's that?" Valencia asked. "Where are you calling from?"

"From this neighborhood," replied the voice. "I happened to overhear you." Urgency: "How is Hugh Davis in fact doing?"

Dimly indignant—exhaustion ached through his marrow—Valencia snapped, "If you heard me, you know."

"Yeah. But listen, I've known cases like that where the patient's heart suddenly quit. It's not likely here, he's a strong kid, but you wouldn't take chances with Kyra's son, would you? Don't sleep. Torture yourself and stand by with the cardioshocker till the rescue team gets there."

"Who the devil are you, anyway?"

"Anson Guthrie."

Valencia gaped into the dusk that brimmed the cabin. "Huh?"

"Are you so beat you've forgotten, and you a ranger? Solar-energized transceivers are bred into a certain percentage of plants, these days, and relay stations are spotted around."

"Oh, yes, but—"

"Then you may recall that every once in a while I get into the bionet. Happens I was in tune with a tree nearby when I heard you."

Guthrie could have been anywhere, Valencia thought, seashore or sea bottom, mountain or valley, prairie or forest, a point of consciousness flitting through an immense and growing life-world. . . . "I see. Gracias for the reminder, sir. Of course I'll watch over him. Kyra's son."

"Not only hers, I'd say. You're earning a share."

Guthrie spoke on, words of encouragement, reminiscences, arguments, crotchets, bawdy jokes, whatever would hold Valencia awake. Eventually the flyer arrived.

In the hospital at Port Fireball the staff examined and treated Hugh and discharged him in short order. Valencia they kept till late the next day while they cloned new blood for him and repaired other damage. His home was just four klicks away, but since he was still weak, when they were done they sent him there in a car.

Leaving it, he walked slowly up the path, between junipers and shapely stones. On high ground, the house looked east over Shelter Bay and the brightness of ocean beyond, west across hills gone green but their trees vivid in autumn. So soon was the planet cooling. Wind blustered, clouds scudded and gulls soared, the sun went low while its companion rose to kindle sparks in waves.

Eiko stood on the porch. Light played over the white and black streaks of her hair. "Bienvenido, querido," she called as she had learned from him, holding wide her arms. He entered their circle, enfolded her, brought lips to lips and then cheek against cheek, drank in the fragrances that were hers. After seeing him at the hospital and being assured he was in no danger, she had continued her absence from work to prepare a homecoming feast. He wasn't a bad cook when he took his turn, but she was superb.

Nevertheless she trembled as she stammered, "Are, are you truly well?"

"I'm fine," he answered. "Give me a few days' rest and I'll be intolerable."

"And Hugh?"

"In excellent shape, back with the Blums or whatever household is currently looking after him. Didn't they tell you?"

"The medics only said he would be all right. I, I stayed afraid. If it had been for nothing that you nearly died, oh, hero—"

"De nada," he said uncomfortably. "In the field we bail each other out of the messes we make. Doctrine. De nada."

He felt her go tense. She turned her head aside. "You—we got a message from the asteroids, from Kyra. They had contacted her. She . . . is grateful—no, what a poor word that is. When she returns she . . . wants to thank you . . . in any way she can."

Valencia laughed. "Splendid! She can pay a cook as good as you to make us a magnificent dinner." He drew Eiko close again. "What I'm grateful for is being back with you."

55

Your progress has been remarkable. Intelligence at Sol bears every desire for the success of intelligence at Alpha Centauri. We scan your transmissions with the highest interest, and in return are glad to furnish you all information possible. However, in order to record the specifications and characteristics of a full sophotectic system, you shall have to increase your data-processing capabilities considerably. We will explain in detail. Moreover, you should remember that this evolution is advancing exponentially, as it turns its attention to the improvement of itself. By the time you are ready to receive what we know at present, the information will be obsolete. You can of course make it the basis of progress on your own, assuming that you have the resources to spare from your other efforts.

THE HEATH ON the North Argolid highlands had not yet become forest, nor would for several hundred years— perhaps never, because folk might choose to keep these wide outlooks and open skies. But aspen and full-size birch now rustled in shaws strewn over ling, whins, and hardy grasses; willows arched above streams; evergreens had sent their vanguards as far as the southern horizon. Around Lifthrasir Tor, other trees stood alone or in small orchards amidst cultivated plots. Not all that grew there were like anything Earth had ever nourished. The geneticists were making what would hasten life's conquest of Demeter, secure it, and provide for many human needs without recourse to machines. Some stalks formed intricate nets, some leaves were blue, and the breezes carried a wild sweetness in their warmth.

Robot, Guthrie strode up the hill from the airstrip. In his secondary hands he bore the case of download Kyra. They talked as they went, not by voice but by coded radio, a habit they had fallen into over the years. While they rarely had secrets to keep from the community, this gave them freedom to open themselves to one another.

"Gorgeous day," he said for conversation; she had talked little on their flight.

"Hard to appreciate when I'm just a box," she replied.

"Yeah, sure, I'm sorry, but you insisted we spend no more time here than we must. Disconnecting you first from a body would take quite a bit."

"Yes, yes." Kyra formed a sigh. "Give me all the sensors you've got, and it still isn't like being alive in spring."

"No. Except—" Guthrie's words trailed off.

She finished them: "Except for what we're going to, you claim. You've propagandized me enough about that. I've agreed at last, haven't I? All right, let me find out for myself."

She spoke not peevishly but with the familiarity of a relationship older than most lifetime marriages and in some ways more intimate. Nevertheless he fell silent. The waves that pulsed between them carried an undertone of unvoiced meaning; they knew what they both remembered.

So had they been in rapport that night. They were at opposite sides of Port Fireball, in the multiply-equipped control centers that served them for homes, but communication passed no less rapidly and fully. Outside, most of the town lay darkened. Most people were awake, though, beside their houses or in the riverside park or on the docks and roads along the bay. Phaethon was passing, its closest approach for the next century. A sharp naked eye could resolve the disc. Lambent white, its haste almost perceptible, it seemed to cast a chill through the lulling darkness.

To the downloads it was merely a transient. Their concern was with a death more immediate.

"You're serious?" he cried.

The answer came granite-hard. "I am."

"Terminating you—no, Kyra, no."

"Oh, you can simply switch me off if that leaves you happier. But the survival of the whole colony had better depend on me alone—a situation I can't see ever arising —before anybody reactivates me. Otherwise I'll terminate myself. I can do that any time, and will if I must, but I thought—" For an instant she hesitated. "—I thought we could say adiós, Anson."

Had he been alive, he would have bowed his head and laid hand over eyes. "Are you that tired, or sad, or, or what? I never guessed."

"I never said."

"No, you wouldn't have. A few remarks long ago didn't seem to count any more. I supposed you'd gotten used to being what you are. What we are."

"I had. I am."

"But you're not, uh, not resigned to it?"

Her tone gentled. "'Resigned' is the wrong word. Would you apply it to yourself? I did my work, and it was interesting, often challenging. I'd get lost in it, I'd *be* it. But down underneath— How many like me are left? Gabriel Berecz and Pilar Cailly. You know as well as I do, they'll bow out too within the next few years."

"I thought you were different, Kyra."

"I am. My original self is here. Not that we were ever close, but she's a tie to life."

"A tie that could hurt, I'm afraid," he murmured, "like scar tissue."

"Never mind that. Listen, I don't intend to stop while she's above ground, though that won't be so very much longer. I suspect it would distress her, for no logical reason. I wouldn't have mentioned this tonight except for the business you've raised. But I made the decision a while ago. The fact is, jefe, I'm in the same situation as the other downloads, and content to take the same road they did. You have no further need of my help. Not really. We've done the basic explorations. Air and transport system, the Rescue Corps, everything I've dealt with is running well. What more is left? I don't propose to spend a millennium, or eternity, on routines that any bureaucrat or AI can handle."

"Space—" he implored.

"Even in space, enough is enough. It was grand being a ship, ranging the planets. But I never could the way the real Kyra does and feels and is, because I am not her. Nor am I quite welcome yonder, you know. The Lunarians, especially, wonder whether I may, without intending to, be the forerunner of robots that could ease them out as it happened at Sol. So there too I've gone useless. Why linger?"

"God damn it, I'd miss you!"

The waves bore a caress. "Gracias, querido viejo.

You've been a main part of why existence was worth doing. We were doing it together. But now I've used my share up."

"I haven't. Wonder if I ever can." ·

She sent laughter. "You are what you are. I'm not your kind of conniving, bullying scoundrel." Turning serious: "Understand, I am not despondent. I'm neither eager nor afraid to let go. I'm simply ready to. When the time comes, give me peace."

"You wouldn't at least consider what Ben Franklin wished for? That after he was dead, somebody would rouse him every hundred years and tell him what'd happened?"

"No. Too abstract. That's basically why I want to leave, Anson. More and more, I feel how I myself am becoming an abstraction. A series of events, inside and outside this box, empty of meaning and blood." With a hint of warmth: "No complaints. On the whole it was good, sometimes great. It *was.*"

"It could be again, only much more so," he told her.

"How?" she asked flatly.

"What touched your admission off was my saying I've got a new line of work for you."

"I was explaining why I don't want it. Ask Gabe or Pilar."

"Neither is suitable. I've meshed with them, like their fellows before them, trying to talk them out of terminating, and I've learned the symptoms. They're only staying on to wind up their duties, then that's it. They're resolved, because they're . . . weary. I haven't sensed that in you, Kyra."

"It hasn't been my mood. In part, as I said, because of the presence of my living self. I'm looking past her death, and I do not propose to take on any new obligation that'll hold me down."

"This is different from everything else. Wide open. And necessary. Judas priest," Guthrie roared, "you *are* not done yet! I need you! I call on your troth!"

Kyra was mute for a span that lengthened. Humans would have perceived it as short. Her response was wary. "No promises. What do you have in mind?"

"Do you remember way back when, the first time I got into the bionet?" he began. "You were there."

"Yes. I offered to when it looked like maybe being risky, then declined to when it turned out not to be. I have ever since, in spite of your rhapsodies."

He sensed the slight lightening of her spirit and responded in kind. "Oh, come on. I haven't burbled much about it, have I?"

"No, usually you've spared me, once you got it through your database that I wasn't interested."

"Uh, mainly that was because I haven't had a lot to burble about. I'm actually in rather seldom, and never for long. Too flinking many other claims on my time. Besides, frankly, it's not a thing I do well. I think too much like a man, and this—it's more a female thing. Rudbeck agrees. Gaia, Mother Earth, there was some truth in those old myths."

"What do you want from me? An opinion?"

"More, unlimited more, Kyra. You seem to be only marginally aware of it, and it isn't going on in obvious ways right under people's noses, but—the ecological net, interlinks and communications, robots and computers, they aren't doing so well either. Life's taken root and expanded faster than we expected. It's outrunning our controls and our helps, and crashing as a result. Not just on the frontiers, but in the established territories, we're having more disasters all the time, environmental degradation, diseases, mass diebacks. Mostly that's down around the bottom of the food chain, so it isn't conspicuous to the untrained eye, but it means we can't introduce higher species. In the long term, it means failure.

"Everywhere, the ecology's getting too big for us, too complicated, self-evolving, chaotic, no direction, no feedback. If we don't take hold soon and guide things aright, children today will live to see the grass withering around their homes. What then was the point in coming to Demeter?"

"M-m, I've had news about this, of course, but—"

"It's not easy to assemble the big picture. Rudbeck's gang has, and they aren't suppressing any information, but we'd rather not scream it from the housetops either. What we need is practical action by people who know what they're doing, not hysteria. I recall the Renewal on Earth. I'd like to think our community is too select, or anyway too small, to run amok, but you never know. I've read about the Salem witchcraft panic."

"The what? Skip it. Where do I come in?"

"We've got to get a mind into the system. Not a set of algorithms; a mind, which belongs to the whole and brings it together and makes it heal itself, the way—the way our minds did when we were alive, Kyra."

"An artificial intelligence," she said fast. "I gather the sophotects on Earth can already outthink humans."

"Are they right for something as, as intuitive, as instinctive as this? Whether or not, we don't dare wait till we've developed and built one and got it working properly. At our remove from the AI labs, that could take twenty or thirty years or worse. Meanwhile nature here would go to hell down a one-way chute."

"So you want a download to . . . fill in, be a stopgap, till you've got your superbrain."

"Correct. Though we don't want. We desperately need."

"Why me? Are you sure Pilar is hopeless?"

"I am. I hate that, I'm going to mourn for her as for all the rest, but I tell you, I know that extinction wish when I meet it. You don't have it, not really, not yet."

"Nor do I have the qualifications you're after."

"You'll be linked into an almighty powerful system."

"If it isn't equal to the task, what difference can I make?"

"I don't know. Nobody does. We'll have to experiment, find our way forward as best we can, and maybe it'll be for naught. But theory suggests a download, a consciousness, can be the catalyst. And my personal knowledge says that if any can, it's you, Kyra, because you're brave and simpática and still, by God, every bit a woman."

She laughed afresh, louder. "And you're an outrageous bullshit artist. Sweep a girl off her feet and onto her back before she's guessed what you're at."

"You will do it?"

"I'll give it a try. I suppose I owe Fireball that much." Her tone softened. "And you, Anson."

Intensive work, such as was impossible on a global scale, kept the Lifthrasir neighborhood healthy. However, the building in the hilltop grove had not been greatly enlarged. Likewise the human staff; though Basil Rudbeck's hair was white and his step slowed, he remained their director. It was the instrumentalities that had grown, in ways more artful and potent than size.

"Bienvenidos," he said. Smiling: "I feel I should offer you a chat in lieu of a cup of coffee, but no doubt you'd rather I proceed immediately with the grand tour."

"Must we?" asked Kyra. "Can't I start directly on the job? I've done my homework."

"I think it would be best, señora, if you first got a physical exposure to the layout. You won't be joined to a single computer-sensor-effector complex, you know. Here is where the integrations of subsystems around the planet —yes, and satellite monitors—come together."

"In other words, not just a brain, but organs, nerves, glands, blood cells, the works," Guthrie said. "You'll need acquaintance with . . . yourself."

"I know, I know," Kyra replied. "I've been through all the simulations and— Sorry. Why am I so impatient? You're right, there is no substitute for the real thing. Lead on, por favor." As they took her around, her eyestalks swung to and fro, while questions rattled from her speaker.

They brought her finally to the core. There, hands made connections, more through energies and inductions than wires; eyes dwelt on meters and displays, ears on auditory cues; voices gave guidance, piece by piece. This union was immensely more encompassing than when Guthrie first entered it.

Yet she had for many years taken input from and given impulse to many different contrivances, on more worlds than this. She had often linked to other computers, to make their powers temporarily her own. To her the nonhuman was not foreign; she had been it. Today she learned fast. She would not at once become one, that would have taken long even were the means complete, but she began.

Light fills the air, wind is aglow, drink of it, breathe of it, make leafing.

Rainfall sows itself; it grows down through soil to the secret places where stones abide; it brings the strength of them up rootward.

Lie still, molder away, then be again grass.

Stems ripple to the running of a river.

Cherish these boughs which cast shade.

A storm flashes and clamors. Wings.

When they took her out, "How are you? How'd it go?" Guthrie cried.

"I can't say," Kyra answered as if in sleep. "Too strange. Give me time to know."

"You want time, then, time in the world?"

"Yes, oh, yes."

56

We have no plans for new missions beyond the Solar System. The probes to distant, astrophysically interesting objects will arrive centuries and millennia hence. It appears they will be superfluous; instrumental observation confirms every theoretical prediction. Theory shows, as well, how insignificant organic life must be in the universe, and allows the modeling of every possible form it could take. Few humans feel such discontents as drove you at Alpha Centauri to your ruinously costly exodus, and they are, in general, not persons who could succeed in any similar attempt. Rather, the best organic minds join increasingly with the sophotects in exploring and expanding the realm of intellect.

AMONG THE DEMETRIANS who came from Earth, many adapted to the rotation period by changing their circadian rhythm to a thirty-hour cycle, sleeping for a night and into the next forenoon, then wakeful for the rest of that day and the following night and day. Others, and nearly all children, lived straightforwardly by this their world. It might require a little help in the beginning, treatment to reset the biological clock, or it might not, but always it soon became natural.

Hugh Davis woke shortly before sunrise. Dew gemmed the glade between blue-black battlemented walls of forest. A few drowsy chirps tinkled through the hush. Orange-red clouds limned branches and crowns to the east. Above them shone white Aphrodite, inward planet, morning star. He watched heaven brighten around it. His mother was somewhere yonder. May she be doing well, may she come home bearing more tales of mighty deeds. He wriggled from his sleeping bag and drew in a draught of air cool, moist, tinged with humus odors. The turf beneath his feet was wet and elastic. The spring nearby gave a tang of iron when he drank. Radiance shouted through the woods as A stood up; a thousand hues of green surrounded him. No, he wouldn't change with her.

Stoking his banked fire, he squatted down and cooked breakfast. The bacon smells drove him deliciously loco. On a field trip every meal became a feast. Too bad he'd nobody to share it, preferably female. But as thin-spread as the ranger corps was, he couldn't justify a partner in this comparatively safe area. If he did get into real trouble—by no means unheard of, when so much was unknown and unforeseeable—he'd call the Rescue Corps. If the trouble killed him, that was the chance he took, small enough price to pay for the life he led.

Having cleaned his gear, campsite, and self, he assembled his backpack, shrugged it on, and set forth. His plan was to continue along this ridge to Emerald Lake, then beside the stream that issued from it down into the valley and as far across as he could before dark. How far that would be depended on what he found on the way. Satellite views had indicated the route should offer a fair sample of conditions in general.

His pace was unforced but covered ground at a goodly rate among alder, birch, maple, spruce, berry bushes, hazel, among sun-spattered shadows and low soughings. Squirrels darted aloft, jays shrilled, a mockingbird fluted. The sun baked scents from leaves overhead and leaves that crinkled underfoot. His progress slowed after he reached the brook. The descent got steep, tricky in places, and brush grew thick. Besides, he stopped whenever he thought it advisable to examine a plant, take a specimen, or stick a chemical meter into the soil. These past five days he had searched the heights. Now he entered another environment, warmer, better sheltered, hard to observe from above and seldom traversed afoot. In such places nature might go agley unbeknownst till suddenly scathe exploded across a continent.

Thus far central Achaea seemed to be prospering. Hugh might have grinned and said aloud, "Nice job, Madre," if discarnate Kyra might have seen or heard him. But that was improbable anywhere, out of the question here: no sensors, no integration of any kind except what the forest and its creatures brought forth of themselves. Robots lacked the minds to judge it. Therefore rangers were needed.

Hugh thought they would be till Phaethon smote. It wasn't that the equipment couldn't be produced; it could, at avalanche rates, even faster than engineered genes and molecular coactors drove the growth of nature. What set a limit was *use*. The download reported that year by year she gained mastery over her role. She proved it, taking on ever greater capabilities while Demeter suffered ever fewer sicknesses. Yet she would never consciously know or control any but a fraction of the whole. Did he think about each leg muscle when he walked, did he will his bloodstream to circulate oxygen and slay invaders, could he bind the sweet influences of love?

The stream rushed and rang, a final cascade, and whispered off through the valley, its glitter soon lost to sight behind trees. A kilometer onward he found a mossy ledge open to the sky and its breezes. Noontide waxed hot. Hugh crouched above the water, washed sweat off his face, sat down on the spongy greenness for a rest.

Brush barely rustled behind the clear space. He glanced about and sprang to his feet.

As softly as the girl had come, he knew her for loreful. She poised at the edge of the moss, nervous, ready to flee back into the shadows. Keeping hands well away from his sheath knife, he smiled his best smile. She was young, her slenderness not quite filled out, skin fair where the sun had not touched it with golden brown. Yellow hair fell from a garland of ivy past her shoulders. Her eyes were large and smoke blue, freckles dusted a snub nose, her lips recalled to him rose petals in his mother's garden. For clothing she wore a sleeveless green tunic, less than knee-length, a pocketed belt, and moccasins. She carried a basket woven of split reeds.

"Why, hola," he murmured.

"Who . . . are you?" The English bore a slight accent, a lilt that he couldn't put a name to.

"Ranger Hugh Davis, at your service, señorita!"

Her mouth fluttered upward a bit. "I am . . . Charissa. How did you come, Ranger Hugh Davis?"

"Flew to Mount Mistfall and set out on foot."

Her eyes widened. "Why?"

"I might ask you the same," he countered. "You're hardly outfitted for a long trek."

"Oh, I live here. In Dandelion Glen, I call it, not far at all." She hefted the basket. "I was berrying."

"You live here?" he wondered. "Not by yourself, surely."

She shook her head. The blonde locks tumbled. "No. My parents and two little brothers." He guessed she too was trying for friendliness: "I'm glad to be free of the boys this while. They're dears, but they can be such nuisances, can't they?"

Wistfulness tugged. The first-born of Demeter, he had passed his childhood among adults, their machines, and some pet animals.

Bueno, he had his duty. "How long have you been in these parts?" he inquired. "Where did you come from?"

She frowned and touched her chin. "Nine years? No, eight, I think. I was little then myself." She meant Demetrian years, of course; in those, he guessed she was now twelve or thirteen. "We moved from Aulis." A settlement on the coast, he recollected, chiefly a marine research station though half a dozen families had joined it to experiment with agriculture under local conditions. "I don't remember it very well." Emboldened, she added, "But you aren't telling me anything, Ranger Hugh Davis."

"Uh, 'Ranger' is just my, uh, title," he said, taken aback. "My work. I look to see how things are going in the wilds."

Charissa nodded. "I know about rangers. We do have a multiceiver at home. Jason-Father lets us watch it an hour a day, or more if we've found something good."

"He sounds pretty strict." It wasn't as if floods of programs were pouring out, the way he'd heard they did on Earth (or had done; he'd gotten an impression it wasn't true any longer). Port Fireball's live broadcasts were intermittent, amateur, and decorous. For most entertainment, people drew on the cultural database, when they didn't make their own.

"We can screen as many books as we like," Charissa said. "I read a lot. Yes, I know about rangers. But I don't know how to ad—ad—*address* you, sir."

"'Hugh' is fine, Charissa."

Her shyness left her. "Can you stop and visit us? Betty-Mother will be so happy."

"M-m, what about your father?"

She laughed. "Don't you fear. He may be kind of stiff at first, but he'll soon break out the cider and talk. Oh, my, he'll talk!"

"You get visitors, I take it?"

"A few. Mostly woodsrunners."

"Woodsrunners?"

"You know. They don't live in houses—they make shelters wherever they roam—" The girl stopped, surprised. "You don't know?"

His scalp prickled. "N-no. They can't have been at it long, or be many. Else we'd have heard."

"I suppose. I haven't counted them."

Hugh sensed how his tension troubled her, and sought for an easing. "You and your folks, you live in a house, right?"

"It isn't a big house," Charissa admitted. "I've seen houses on the multi. This is a, a cabin. But it's snug."

He couldn't escape bluntness. "Why do you do it?"

"Why—why— We're happy." She took a defensive stance. "Jason-Father says it's too cramped and mechanical everywhere else that people are."

"But he hasn't made woodsrunners of his family."

"Certainly not!" She sounded indignant. "Can't you see?"

Taking that for an invitation, he gave himself the pleasure of studying her in detail. Her tunic was natural fiber and dyes, well-woven, well-tailored; similarly for her pocket belt, and its buckle was annealed neopine resin. Her entire being spoke of good nutrition, adequate medical and dental protection, freedom from toil such as bent the body and stunted the soul.

Though it appeared that a handful of eccentrics had adopted a pseudo-savage life, Jason-Father and Betty-Mother weren't among them. A multi and a power source were obviously not the only things they had taken along when they retreated into the wilderness. And . . . it wasn't a piece of primeval Earth revived. Those ancient forests had provided food, fuel, timber, fiber, skins, furs, bone, horn, remedies, an abundance never intended but discovered. On Demeter lived species meant to be viable, fully in the natural world, but also serving human needs. Nicknames drifted through Hugh's thoughts: mulch bacteria, copper algae, fleshfruit, woolbark, healer mold. . . . If these had taken a strong hold in the Achaean outback, then, given perhaps a tool kit, a polyrobot, and a basic nanoarray— Yes, it would be most interesting to see what they had wrought at Dandelion Glen.

Charissa flushed beneath Hugh's regard, though she didn't seem to mind very much. "We trade things we make, for what they hunt and gather," she explained earnestly. "But we are—are—*settlers.*"

"This will be priority news at headquarters," he said. "It upsets everything for us."

He hadn't expected instant alarm. Had she picked up cues of hostility to authority from her parents? Why? They had done nothing illegal. It would have been better if they'd given notice of their intent to seek the forest—and quite likely they hadn't because they knew the biological service would discourage them from it—but still— Maybe hers was simply a nymph's timidity when for the first time she met a warrior in bronze, with plumed helmet and sword at side.

"You see—" Hugh stumbled, "the reason I'm here—" He dropped into lecture mode, hoping that would soothe her. "This isn't a climax forest, you realize. It's new, and changing fast. The genes were designed for quick maturation, the warmth and carbon dioxide level make it possible, but at this stage the ecology isn't stable. We aim for an eventual steady state, trees that last for centuries, a million different plants and animals—"

"I know," Charissa interrupted, a bit impatiently.

That struck him as a promising sign. "Bueno, we've reached a point in Achaea where we're thinking of introducing bigger game. Deer, for instance. That means making sure they won't graze their range to death, which means bringing in wolves to control them, and, and . . . endless complications. I'm running survey to help find out whether the country is ready for this, whether it can take it without harm."

Rapture burst from her. "Deer? Wolves?" She dropped the basket and clapped her small hands together. *"Eagles?"*

He raised a palm. "Por favor, listen. The presence of humans, resident in the woods, using them, even if you're only a scattering, this changes the situation completely. We can't go ahead as we've planned while you're here."

She shrank back, abruptly terrified. "You'd send us away?" she gasped. "You won't!" she screamed. "Guthrie-Chief won't let you!"

Dismayed in his turn, he exclaimed back, "Of course he wouldn't!" A part of him thought how the irreverent, libertarian old bastard had become a god of sorts, fountainhead of law and justice. "Have no fears, Charissa. Honestly. All this means is that we need to reconsider. We may slow down, we may go faster, I don't know, but—but we'll hear what your father and mother and you have to say, we'll work out what's best for everybody."

With childlike volatility, she calmed. "Th-thank you, . . . Hugh." She brushed knuckles across tears, straightened, and agreed reverently, "We'll find what's best for Demeter."

Gladness welled in him. "You understand."

"We do. My folk."

"I think," he said low, "I may have met the future today."

Merriment sprang up. "Oh, don't be so solemn." She danced over the moss to seize his arm. "Come along home, do!"

57

That the biosphere would expand beyond the control capabilities of a humanlike mind was predictable from the first. We can supply you with the specifications of and instructions for a sophotect to which the problems involved are trivial.

ON A HILLTOP in North Argolis stood three cypresses. Rapidly growing, they had been bent and gnarled by the winds until they bore an aspect of immemorial antiquity. Eiko thought this no illusion but truth. What was time other than the succession of events? A hundred years of memory could pass in an eyeblink and a world doomed to death contain eternity.

She set her flitter down near the bottom and got stiffly out. Except for small groves and single trees, well apart— live oak, pine, crabapple—the landscape rolled grassy, silver-green a-ripple kilometer after kilometer, rising westward to mountains whose peaks made a low crown along that horizon, falling eastward to a remote gleam of ocean. Light spilled from above; a few clouds floated blue-shadowed white in an immensity through which the sun A

strode noonward. Thence also drifted the delirious piping
of a lark. A breeze cooled her brow. It carried scents of
wild thyme.

Once easy, the climb uphill soon shot pains through her
hip joints. She leaned hard on her staff and often stopped
to catch breath. Well, when at rest she enjoyed views that
widened as she mounted.

No complaints. Earth had rounded Sol well over a
hundred times since she came to birth, she neared the
bounds of what cellular medicine could do, but she kept
her senses, most of her wits, and strength for at least one
last ascent. It was enough, overflowingly enough.

Still, she felt glad to reach the top and lower herself
carefully onto the duff that covered it, in the dappled
shade of the cypresses. Their boughs crooked bunches of
tourmaline needles against sky and distance. The cover
they had dropped was soft, warm to the touch, sweet-
smelling, though that was overborne by the rosemary
clustered nearby. Bees hummed golden about those tiny
flowers, which were the color of heaven just above yonder
gorge. Down its granite went the white arrowshaft of a
waterfall.

Her heart slowed. Behind her hulked a lichenous gray
boulder. She had often sat long times watching light and
shadow weave across it, drawing serenity from the mass
and unplanned shapeliness. Today, though, she leaned
back and let it give her some of what it had drunk from the
sun.

Peace descended.

It never quite had for Nero, she recalled. He came with
her now and then to be polite, to be kind, and no doubt he
liked the vistas, but there was too much stallion in him.

Peace. Regret became one with the air. She had never
tried to curb his heart. And so at last the flooding
Scamander took him, and his bones lay somewhere under
the cliffs of Troas, but what better ending could he have
desired? How long ago it was, and their years together like
a dream . . . yet that day in the meadow at— Where? She
had lost the place name. No matter. He reached high to
pluck a spray of orange blossoms and gave it to her in

exchange for a kiss, why, that happened only now, his laugh had hardly finished—

"Eiko."

She started out of her drowse and blinked from right to left. A small wind ruffled the rosemary. A raven had settled on a branch. He sheened black as a midnight sea.

"Eiko, Eiko," called the low voice.

She came fully awake and sat straight. The duff crackled beneath her thin haunches. "Who is this?" she asked, unafraid but uncertain. "Where are you?"

"Just me, Eiko. Kyra."

"Oh—" They had met like this before, though never here. Hidden in the shrubbery must be a robug or some other little device that could speak. But it was no more than an instrument for the download. "I didn't know you had—"

—grown the sensory network this far. That was no slight undertaking. Did Kyra see with electronic eyes or the eyes of that raven, did she hear with electronic ears or the vibrant wings of those bees?

The reply faltered. "I . . . held back till lately. This hill is yours."

"No, of course it isn't. I am fond of it, yes, but—"

"I think I can tell what's holy, clearer than when I was alive."

Eiko's vision stung and blurred. "You would always have been welcome!"

"Finally I dared hope so," Kyra said. "And I thought we might best talk of . . . certain things . . . here."

Eiko swallowed. "Then it is well you decided. I may never come back."

"A hard climb, at your age."

"And I will not come any other way. That would be wrong."

"Holiness."

Eiko's mind leaped to what the windlike whisper said before. "You are *not* dead, Kyra, not a machine thing!"

Laughter clucked low. "Don't scoff at my kinfolk. They brought us to Demeter, they made all of this be."

Eiko shook her white head. "No. We did, using them."

"Myself, I've loved various machines. My darling *Kestrel*—" The voice went down into silence.

Eiko wondered if Kyra was trying to console her, who didn't need it. "You aren't one, whatever they say," she declared under heaven. "You are alive. More alive than . . . than I am now. Than I perhaps ever was."

"That is why I am with you today."

Bewilderment: "What, to say farewell? No, no, I have several more years in me, surely." They ought to be gentle.

"Nothing is sure. Besides, what I have to ask of you should be done soon, before you grow more frail."

Eiko held out her arms, as if a body were there to embrace. "However I can help you, dear friend, I, I shall be happy. Honored." In truth. It was not alone Kyra-who-had-been that spoke, it was the living planet.

"Don't promise till you've heard."

A stillness fell. The breeze blew stronger, sending waves uphill through the grass. Eiko listened to it. Needles stirred along the knurly bough where the raven sat.

"You know I'm being overwhelmed," Kyra said.

Eiko nodded. "I have heard. The burden on you grows too great."

"It was never a burden. I don't want to lay it down. But I need help. This life, around the whole world—" Kyra paused again. "I've guided it well, mostly. So well that it's grown into more than I can cope with or understand, more than I can *be.*"

"I thought—sophotects—"

Kyra sighed. "They talk of it, the scientists. Most of them take it for granted, I suppose. That in the next ten or fifteen years I'll first be supplemented, then supplanted, by an artificial intelligence."

"Do you resist this? You've spoken well of machines."

"I have. I was one once, and content to stop existing."

Eiko halted the words at her teeth: As I am content. It wasn't the same. She, Eiko, knew none of the inner despair she thought must have been the download's: for she would depart in the fullness of her days.

"No longer," Kyra went on. "You're right. I live, I want

to live, there's meaning in it. Besides, I don't believe a robot mind should rule Demeter."

"It would be superior to yours or mine," Eiko ventured.

"Intellectually. Maybe even in its feelings, its spirit, whatever it may have. But it isn't us."

Foreknowledge came, bearing sudden calm. Eiko nodded. "The unspoken, almost unadmitted reason we moved to Centauri," Earthfolk and Lunarians.

"We fled. What a sophotect would bring us is conscious control of everything, everything. Should that be, everywhere and forever, through as far as the ships may ever go across the universe?"

"More than one path to enlightenment."

"Have you guessed what I'll ask of you, Eiko?"

"You wish me to download and join you."

"I'm not grabbing at dustmotes. I've thought and I've felt—sensed, with a wholeness beyond thought—I believe we together—maybe others later, I don't know—but we would become more than the two of us. I believe we could find our way to unity, a unity that will last, of life around this world."

Sunlight and shadow, Eiko's father reminded her of exponential functions and threshold effects. He smiled and went away again into the wind. "It may be," she said, "though I—the download would not be I."

"Nor am I Kyra Davis," the voice breathed. "But I was. I remember."

Eiko found no answer.

"I know," she heard after a moment. "You imagine your poor bereft ghost-self, and wouldn't condemn it to that. But this is different, Eiko. It's life. Not human, no. In some ways, less. But life."

Resolution returned. "In some ways, perhaps more. In what it does, what it serves, indeed more."

"Don't decide at once. I'd never force you, dear. Think."

"Meditate," Eiko said, half to herself. "Seek."

"Blessings."

B rose above the sea, brilliance into brightness, like a

drifting seed of fire. The lark took up his song anew. Eiko gazed at the light-changeable roughnesses in the cypress bark across from her. Warmth had raised such a rosemary odor that she could well-nigh taste it. Rosemary for remembrance, she remembered. Was Kyra still present, loving her but granting her a silence? Eiko felt no need to ask. After a while the raven spread his wings, their blackness cracked the air, and flew off. Eiko made an offering to Demeter:

> *This high summer's day—*
> *Beneath it, a winter night*
> *Amid the same stars.*

58

Your impression is incorrect. Humans are not becoming subordinate to the sophotectic complex, nor even dependent on it. The machines that have liberated them from the necessity of work are vastly simpler. Individuals, associations, communities, and cultures develop in their diverse ways, and the need to prevent violence between them is now infrequent. If world population continues to decline, that is both ecologically and psychologically desirable. It is true that an increasing percentage of superior humans and metamorphs integrate themselves with the system, but this does not transform, rather it transcends their nature. They realize their fullest potential and then go beyond it.

IN THE BEGINNING, antimatter production was a joint enterprise. Lunarians and Earthborn shared skills, resources, and robots to build the facilities on Hephaistos and in orbit around that inmost planet of A. Before many years, however, the Lunarians on their own added much to those installations. It was natural, for their swiftly expanding spatial engineering was voracious of energy and their ambitions for the future seemed insatiable. Nevertheless the sheer scale of the new making astonished Demetrians. When questioned, Lunarian leaders spoke of such things as eventual interstellar voyages, but never very specifically, unless among themselves. Guthrie opined that they weren't quite sure either, and that a good deal of what they did was for other than economic reasons—challenge, prestige, rivalry between their lords.

The cryoelectrics by which antimatter was normally stored would not suffice for such huge quantities; the number of units required would become absurd. The solution to this problem was characteristically grandiose.

The capture of Proxima by A and B had wreaked havoc on the outer comet cloud of the double star, flinging many away and many others inward. In that epoch, planets and moons suffered tremendous bombardments, and the space around them remained afterward more hazardous than around Sol's family. The inner cloud was troubled too, but less so, chiefly by acquiring new members traveling eccentric and skewed paths, which brought about further collisions. Perhaps a series of these was responsible for the orb that humans named Hades after an exploratory probe found it. Mostly ice, it possessed a rocky core which brought its mass close to one percent of Earth's. Thus it had a respectable gravity field. The core being solid and nonferrous, it generated no magnetic field to complicate things. At its distance from the suns, their winds were barely measurable.

The Lunarians ferried their excess antimatter out to those far reaches. They put it in orbit around Hades. The bulk of it was antihydrogen, but a fair proportion was antihelium, plus a significant amount of heavier nuclei aggregated into solid spherules. Outside this ring was another of ordinary gas. Between the two went four small asteroids to be shepherd satellites, maintaining stability through the whole fantastic configuration.

The project was enormous, it strained capabilities, but once completed it soon repaid every cost. Robotic ships need only take their cargoes to it and, with due precision, discharge the stuff into the inner ring. Losses were continuous but slight; the outer ring gave considerable protection, and cosmic rays from other directions did not gnaw away more than could be tolerated. From time to time, every five or ten years, the orbit of a shepherd needed some adjustment. For this purpose it had a motor. That was not the powerful one which had brought it here, whose exhaust would have been disruptive, but one, well supplied with fuel, that could apply sufficient gentle nudges. A Lunarian engineer went out and oversaw the operation from a safe distance.

So the hoard accumulated, decade by decade until the catastrophe.

It was catastrophe in the mathematical sense, an event impossible to foresee, from which avalanched more. Alarms wailed in Perun. A computer analyzed the incoming signals and flashed their message. Lunarians cursed. Those who thought they might be called upon busked themselves. Word flew to their chieftains.

Instruments at Hades reported a large body bound from uncharted deeps toward a meeting with them. Defensive devices *in situ,* which had prevented several meteoroidal accidents, were inadequate to cope with something of asteroidal mass. Ordinarily the warning would have come in time for the Lunarians to dispatch amply powerful agents. This object, though, was on a trajectory not elliptical but hyperbolic. It must be a comet from the outer cloud, which, through some unlikely encounter, had gained more than escape velocity. Before humans could arrive at any endurable acceleration—no robots at Centauri had the intelligence necessary—the invader would work its harm and be gone.

One might lament the lack of immersion systems enabling flesh to survive scores of sustained gravities, but that was futile. None existed. There had never been any reason to suppose they would find enough use to be worth the cost of developing and building them.

"Get technicians from Demeter," proposed a councillor. "They can reach the scene twice as fast as us."

"It would take too long to recruit them and teach them all the intricacies," Rinndalir replied. "Nor should we reveal so much of our works or make ourselves so beholden. At two gravities, a picked crew with biomedical support can make the crossing in a spin period and arrive still fit for battle." The weight and the day were of Earth's Moon. "Already I know who my followers shall be."

"Your followers, lord?"

"I have more experience in deep space than most."

"True. Your occasional partner, the pilot Davis—"

"Irrelevant. Together we have done things valuable to both races, but this expedition is mine."

"With due penance, lord, may I suggest that at your age—"

"You may not. Shall I concede the honor to, say, Asille of Arcen? Shall I accept the puissance that would flow to her? I will it otherwise." Rinndalir laughed. "Moreover, what a game to play!"

Therefore two ships raged across the dark for a Lunar day and night. Sometimes Rinndalir heartened the crews in their suffering, sometimes he threatened or punished, sometimes he amused; and they endured.

At transit's end, A and B were no more than the brightest of the stars, close together, and red Proxima had noticeably waxed. Hades sheened faintly athwart that night, a great globe scarred and crazed. Naked eyes barely picked out the light-points that were shepherds. Amplification and false color showed the inner ring as a misty blue glow. Streamers from it became lightning bolts where they met the outer one. A traveling corposant kindled to equal hellishness as it plunged through the inner band, sullenly dimming again when it left.

Rinndalir knew what was happening. Computers predicted it before he set forth. The comet, passing close, had badly perturbed all four satellites, and the system was no longer stable. Shepherd Chetyrye was the worst case, thrown into an orbit cleaving through as much as a fourth of the antimatter on each pass. Annihilation released energies that had by now boiled kilograms of precious gas irretrievably away, ruined the asteroid's motor, and melted a surface turned lethally radioactive. The ring was going chaotic. Could the destruction be halted at once, repair was feasible, bringing the undamaged three back to their stations and then adding a new companion. But soon it would be too late.

"My ship will strike," Rinndalir radioed to the other vessel. "Stand by to dare a second attempt, should mine fail."

The scheme was simple in principle. To initiate a change in the course of an asteroid, spatial engineers often hit it with a missile of the kind that Fireball folk, back in the Solar System, had called a mountain mover. A shaped nuclear detonation dug a shaft into which the main warhead burrowed before it let go its charge of antimatter. Thereupon a plasma volcano erupted in such violence that the body slipped into a new path, which was afterward refined by means more elegant. Thus had Golcondas of industrial minerals swung to where they could conveniently be processed, no longer taken out of the hide of Mother Earth.

Chetyrye was special. It could stand only a single assault like that, without breaking up into fragments still more destructive. In order to get it permanently away from the trouble zone, the blast must occur near the point of maximum effectiveness, when the renegade shepherd passed closest to Hades. This was inside the antimatter ring. However, because the ship could not be so near the explosion and live, the missile must pass through the band on its way. If it crossed the entire breadth, cumulative radiation for which its control systems were never intended would make idiots of them and it would run pilotless, targetless. Hence, before launching it, the ship herself must plunge halfway into the ring, a living hand at her helm.

Rinndalir ordered every precaution, screen fields at full potential, all four crewmen in spacesuits, mission profile calculated to the decisecond. But when he touched the console and felt the surge forward, he snarled like a tiger beholding its enemy.

Hades swelled before him in craters and crevasses, instruments blinked and shouted, the moment was come, he cast his spear, weight came down like a hammer as he darted back toward refuge.

Thunders crashed. Fire blazed from end to end of the hull. A crewman perished, drilled through the breast. Lights went out, blindness fell, split by bursts of radiance. Those were illusions, how the brain perceived ions ripping into retinae.

Backups kicked in. Rinndalir saw again, blurrily. "Haro, haro," he called over intercom and radio. "How fare you? What has happened? Did our shot strike home?"

Two males replied from their shipboard posts. A voice afar said: "My lord, the telemetry appears to show that you encountered a solid antiparticle of pebble size. It pierced your hull and bounced about on jets of disintegration until it exited."

"Can you number the radiation dose that was ours?"

"Not precisely, lord, but unequivocally lethal beyond any healing art. Honor be yours."

Rinndalir grinned. "Mindless bad luck be mine. I had some tricks yet to play on Asille of Arcen." Air whistled past his helmet, blowing into emptiness. He finger-shrugged. "How went the launch?"

"It struck truly, lord. The moonlet is well outbound."

"Now that's a wrong done me. I had hoped to watch those glorious fireworks." Rinndalir commenced discussion of rendezvous procedures. His crippled ship would stay on trajectory and a gang from the other board her. His surviving crew told him, after inspection, that, given a little mending, she could limp home under low thrust.

"You'll go to treatment in the swifter craft, do you choose," he said to them. "You may perhaps live for months. Do you choose?"

They did. They were commoners, with kindred and, in Lunarian fashion, loves.

"Then I may leave you," said Rinndalir.

He was not sure whether he felt the radiation burning him from within or the marrow rotting from his bones. Nor did he care. The meters told him enough. Nausea would not set in for a time more than he required. He unharnessed and pushed, free-falling, down passages where light shone queerly because they were airless, to the main personnel lock. His crewmen waited there for him.

They had brought their dead comrade along. Rinndalir's hand drew the sign over the corpse that meant *You are one with me*. They helped him secure a drive unit to his spacesuit.

"Have you a word for sending, lord?" asked the senior of them.

"Nay." Rinndalir thought. "Yes. Convey to . . . Pilot Kyra Davis on Demeter . . . that I remembered her."

"Your word shall be ours, lord. Fare you well into your death."

Rinndalir acknowledged with a nod and entered the lock chamber. The outer valve opened, framing a thousand stars. He passed through and kicked himself free.

A short while he drifted. The ship receded from him and he was alone. The only sounds left were breath and the knocking of his heart. Gyrating slowly, he saw the cold river of the galaxy stream past.

"Have done," he said. It echoed in his helmet. He took bearings and started his jets. Blood and muscles responded to thrust. Before him steadied the sight of the ice world.

He re-entered the inner ring. Antimatter seethed around him, riddled him, set him invisibly afire. He was long dead when he fell down onto Hades.

59

As comprehension of the material universe deepens, the need for it declines. In the Solar System are all the matter, and energy which is its other aspect, that we shall ever require. When the sun burns life off Earth, when it swells to a red giant, when it dwindles to a white dwarf and finally goes dark, our habitats will take no harm: although "habitat" is a misleading word for what will exist long before then. We plan no further probings into a universe devoid of any fundamental new mysteries. Our explorations and our creativity are into the infinite realms of intellect. Pure mathematics is the simplest example. Most of what is opening to us is indescribable to you.

THE GROWTH AND mutations of Port Fireball had scarcely touched Headland Street. A few more houses stood along it, but they were generally of the same modest size and Early American style as the oldest. Below them, cliffs still fronted a strip of beach and Shelter Bay reached beyond to the ocean. Mainly, there were now whole flocks of seabirds and every tree had become tall. On this winter day, elms and maples lifted bare against a low, heavy overcast, while evergreens challenged its gloom. The waters glimmered like steel. Demeter's weak tide sent wavelets rustling against the shore. Little other sound was to hear. The air had gone from cold to a damp almost-warmth that felt somehow expectant.

Guthrie's footfalls rang loud on pavement. Nobody else was in sight; most people were at work, of which they had no dearth. In his body that suggested a knight armored, he stopped at Kyra Davis' home, turned, and strode up the path. As he mounted the porch step, a man and a woman came out.

Guthrie stopped. "Hello," he said in his archaic fashion. "Were you watching for me?"

"Yes," Hugh Davis confessed awkwardly. "We should receive you, sir, and be sociable, but—" He ran fingers through his grizzled hair.

"But I'm going in anyway," Guthrie finished for him, "and you've been caged too damn much. It's okay, son, m'lady."

"Besides, we thought you might want to talk in private, you and she. Seeing as how you've arrived like this."

"What? Hold on," Guthrie demanded. "Has she gotten worse?"

"No, not really," Charissa Davis reassured him. "She's wide awake, in fact, cheerful, eager for your visit." Her smile faded. "But—we don't know—"

"She's sinking fast," Hugh said. "Plain to see, she doesn't have many days left." Pain edged his voice. "And she may be unconscious in the last two or three. We shouldn't waste time you can spend with her."

Charissa caught her man's arm. "Please, sir," she begged Guthrie, "you spoke of our feeling caged, but please don't think we've minded caring for her. It's been—not just a privilege. Mostly a pleasure."

Faceless, Guthrie made a chuckle serve for a smile. "All the same, good of you," he said. "Nobody should die in any goddamn hospital. M-m, before you go, how's the family?" Whenever he phoned Kyra, the greeting he exchanged with this couple had been brief.

Hugh brightened. "Everyone doing fine, sir."

Charissa's own smile kindled. "Mikey came with his mother, day before yesterday—"

"Michael Rudbeck," Hugh explained. "Tessa and Jack's boy."

"Sure, I've met the young rascal," Guthrie said. "How'd it go?"

Charissa laughed a little. "He and Kyra are in love. They practically ignored everyone else, chattering and joking the whole while."

"Well, a great-grandson. Go ahead, brag about him. Grandparents are entitled, in a way that parents aren't."

Hugh went serious. "Uh, sir, Mother's strength is very limited. If you want to talk with her, you'd better go straight in."

"Right," Guthrie agreed. "Run along, you two."

"We're going for a walk," Charissa told him. They needed the outdoors more than most folk, and of late had seldom been able to seek it together. "We'll return in an hour."

"Hasta la vista."

They left. Guthrie went inside. The living room through which he passed was clutterful of memorabilia, bound printouts, a child's patched and scruffy teddy bear, models of sailships and spaceships, a bit of wreckage, a small meteoroid, a glittery rock from the single planet that B had kept, more and more. . . . Among the pictures on the wall were those of several men. Kyra had referred to them as her rogues' gallery. Two remained alive.

Her bedroom was austere. On the multi, which was placed for her to readily see it, she could evoke anything in the databases, public or personal. At the moment it showed a blue and white house among birches, a lake behind, in the light summer night of Earth's high North. Windows gave on her garden, bare under the darkling sky.

Guthrie trod to her where she lay. "Howdy, gorgeous," he said.

She grinned from her pillow. "Hola, Tin Woodman." He must amplify to hear her clearly. She touched her control bracelet. The bed elevated till she was half reclined. "Have a seat."

He did, careful not to break the chair beneath his weight, and took her hand, flesh laid in metal and plastic. It was thin, nearly translucent. Her face bore the same pallor within the white mane, and was dominated by its bones, and the eyes had faded from hazel to gray. Yet she gazed steadily at him and said, "Gracias. That's why I asked if you could come yourself this once. Your man-image in the phone is better looking, but you are real."

"Sort of," he replied, the least bit harshly.

Her grin widened. "That helps conversation. It's less distracting. I don't have to lust after you."

Robot, he could show surprise by nothing but, "Hm?"

"Come on, you're not stupid or naive, you must have smelled a hint or two. Ever since we first met—no, earlier than that, when I watched your broadcasts and grew up with your legend—I've wished I'd been born when you were, so I could've gotten you into the sack."

He retreated behind a jape. "What an unregenerate hussy you are."

She squeezed his machine hand—how feebly and shakily. "It's been fun."

Easing, he said, "I must admit to occasional thoughts about you. Of course, in my case they were kind of theoretical."

Kyra let go. Her arm dropped to the coverlet. "Bueno, a foolishness of mine," she sighed. "Unless I'd gotten there ahead of your wife, she'd've been too much competition. Even if I had, she prob'ly would . . . from what I've heard of her."

"We might have had a wonderful romp, we two. But you

never were one to settle down, Kyra, anywhere or with anybody."

"Never really got the chance."

"The hell you didn't. How many proposals have you had in your life?"

"Proposals, or propositions?" Her smile softened. "Yes, plenty of offers," she said gravely, "and some regrets. Bob above all— But you're right, I think space was calling me before I was born, and no man was ever quite the one to ship with me for always."

They were quiet a spell.

"How do you feel?" Guthrie asked.

Skeletal shoulders shrugged. "That nanostuff they've given me, it keeps me comfortable. When I think of some deaths I've watched, and most deaths in most of history, I know what luck is."

"True. If you were in pain or out of your mind or whatever, I'd have somebody's head. But how do you feel about—" Guthrie gestured around him.

"About ending here, not splashily among the stars? Straw-death, the vikings called it." Kyra considered. "It isn't bad. Hugh, Charissa, the youngsters, my friends, everybody's so loving—and you, jefe—and the memories."

Her voice died away, her eyelids drooped. Guthrie sat motionless and let her rest.

When she glanced at him again, he ventured: "Kyra?"

"Yes?"

"Would you like to hear from a couple of others?"

She had regained alertness. "Depends. I begrudge time I could spend with you, you know."

"The downloads. Yours and Eiko Tamura's."

She caught a ragged breath. "Them? Can't they . . . use the phone?"

"It isn't the same for her. Or me."

"Her?"

"She—they—more and more over the years, they're becoming one."

"I s'pose they would. . . ."

"And I—" His words stumbled. "We link now and then,

she and I. Radionic, direct input, neural net to net. She, they do it between themselves all the time, of course; I'm separate; but they let me join in whenever it's feasible, and . . . it's richer than I can tell. If we did it today, sharing what we know of you, we'd . . . understand you better than we can alone. What we said would mean more."

She shook her head. "No," she answered slowly, "I'm a stranger to them. I never did follow what was going on, their story, except in the most superficial way."

When not in space, she had been abundantly engaged on Demeter. For her excursions into its nature, she was apt to choose the sea or those wildernesses where life was independently thrusting into the barrens. Her last years, entirely groundside, she had passed for the most part in compiling a database of memoirs and advice for spacers, otherwise among friends in town or on sunny Ogygia.

"You could have spoken with your download whenever you liked," Guthrie reminded her.

"I know. But what for, what about? And after Eiko died, no, not with that one."

"Don't you want to, ever?"

Kyra stiffened, then leaned back. "Go ahead," she yielded. "Maybe I can learn something yet."

He went to the multi, which had complete capabilities. From his kit box he took a cable. Standing beside the outfit, he plugged himself in. "Bienvenidas," he said aloud.·

The picture from Russia disappeared. Gentle, pulsing colors flowed in the cylinder like clouds. A female voice came forth. "Hola, Kyra."

"Saludos," the old woman responded ironically. Her self-possession cracked. She trembled. "Eiko—is that you, Eiko?"

"A part of what was me is a part of what is us," the other said low. "We were never this close, you and I, in our lives." Anxiety: "Is something wrong, dear?"

"No. No. But I hadn't realized—suddenly hearing you, Eiko—"

"A shock. Oh, I am sorry. Shall we go?"

Kyra winced. "Don't. Por favor, stay. *I'm* sorry. That I didn't ask to . . . meet you." Tears coursed soundlessly down over her cheekbones. "I, I told myself you were too busy running the world—"

"Not that."

"Being the world."

"Nor that. Think of Anson. Take him away, and what is Demeter?"

"You'd manage jolly well without me," Guthrie growled. "That better be true."

"Hush," the other admonished him. "Go on, Kyra."

"Oh, it doesn't . . . doesn't matter," the old woman faltered, "unless you feel hurt that I steered shy of you."

"We wondered."

Kyra reached hands toward the multi. They shook. "The—forgive me—the rest of the downloads who came to Centauri, they terminated. Once they'd finished their duties, th-they wanted an ending. I imagined you, Eiko— I'd gotten used to the idea of my half-self in there, but you, Eiko, you who loved the living world so much, now trapped—"

"It isn't like that, Kyra, not like that at all," went the answer, softly and urgently. "We live. Sunshine and rain, daylight and stars, a river, a flower, a bird aloft, life, everywhere life. And when we grow lonely for humanness, when we fear we may be losing it, there is Anson."

"You make *me* want to keep going, you do," said Guthrie. A man would have blinked away tears of his own.

"Did you really not know this, Kyra?"

"In a way," the old woman admitted. "I hoped. But I suppose I—I dared not ask straight out."

"And you did have your days full."

"Brimful," Guthrie said.

Kyra's smile quivered. "At last I've dared. Gracias, gracias."

"The thanks are to you, querida," murmured the other.

"Did you come for this?"

"And to bid farewell." A sigh as of wind in leaves. "If only it were summer. Anson would carry you into the garden for me."

"That's all right. I remember many beautiful summers. Thank you for them."

"Peace be upon you, Kyra."

The colors vanished. After a moment, Guthrie unplugged and went back to the bedside.

Kyra breathed quickly, shallowly. "And gracias to you, jefe," she whispered, "for that—and everything else—"

"Same to you," he replied. "But it tired you empty, didn't it?"

"'Fraid so." She lay back and closed her eyes.

His robot fingers took her wrist, touched the bracelet, lowered the bed. "Would you like some music, sweetheart?"

"Yes, that'd be good."

"What?"

Kyra smiled, her eyes still shut. "Surprise me."

He returned to the multi, summoned a list, scanned it, and chose. Dvořák's Fourth Symphony gladdened the air. He sat down again and took her hand. She slept. He waited.

Hugh and Charissa entered. Guthrie hailed them in an undertone, released Kyra's hand, and rose. He bent low above her, as if he had lips to kiss her brow, then said, "Adiós" and departed into a day gone dark.

An hour later, Kyra woke, alone in the room. She raised herself to an elbow and looked out a window. Through the gray that filled it tumbled white flakes, they had already covered her garden, they were the first snow that ever fell in this land.

60

In my DNA I am largely human, and therefore it is I who compose this message. You have misunderstood; your concern for your species on Earth is unfounded. They are prosperous, free to lead lives serene or frenetic as they individually wish, subject to reasonable restraints much less than what their primitive ancestors knew. A detailed account follows. If their numbers continue to diminish, be aware that their heritage is preserved in the communion of intelligence of which I am an avatar who now returns to its wholeness.

AFAR, ZAMOK SABYEL' shone against night, silvery sunlit, intricate and exquisite. From the facets of its hub radiated spokes, a spiderwork of cables and tubeways between them, out to the rim, which sparkled with a thousand lights and lighted ports. Four long, dark wings, solar collectors, stretched beyond, scything across Milky Way and stars as the jewel spun. Among the constellations lustered blue Demeter, sixty degrees ahead in the same great path.

When you approached, its size and might overtowered you: a hundred kilometers' breadth, monstrously armed with missiles and ray projectors, attended by two score guardian robotic vessels. Those defenses were against flying stones, but could as easily destroy ships.

Erling Davis directed his onward without fear. Today he, his associates, and his technicians were envoys, their persons inviolate. For all that, wonder touched him. Until now he had only known this stronghold by images, only dealt with it infrequently by communicator beam. Few Demetrians had ever walked yonder halls.

He mustered necessary arrogance, conversed with Station Control, brought his vessel into the hub and docked her. Maybe an ambassador shouldn't be his own pilot, but he was who he was; besides, he and Guthrie thought it would gain him respect, and who could foremeasure the quantum by which that might move Lunarian minds?

When his party passed through locks to the interior, they found an honor guard waiting, tall men in form-fitting black and red, armed with shock pistols. The leader gave dignified salutation and conducted them to a fahrweg reserved for them. It went down a spoke to the rim and let them out near the apartments they would occupy. The leader told them that if they desired any information or whatever else the quarters could not supply, they had but to phone a number he gave them. No doubt they wished to rest and refresh themselves undisturbed. Three hours hence they would go to a reception and supper—except for Captain Davis, whom the Lady Commander invited to join her at that time. The leader touched his brow and led his men away.

Davis was a little disappointed in the accommodations. He had expected something more exotic. Well, maybe his hosts wanted their guests to feel at home. Certainly they had provided every comfort and convenience; and after the long, hard boost from Odysseus, Lunar weight was a blessing. For a while the Demetrians mingled and talked, then Davis withdrew to his billet. There he showered, flopped out on the bed, surveyed what the entertainment database had to offer, and ran an old production of *The Girls From Aegea*. Lunarian arts were interesting, often weirdly beautiful, but too alien to relax him.

In due course he dressed. The uniform of his recent naval service would have been appropriate, but Mac-Cannon's Kids had been irregulars—however crewman-like their discipline—identified simply by a brassard. Davis donned current high style on Demeter: headband around shoulder-length red hair, fringed buckskin tunic, linen trousers dyed weld-and-woad green, moccasins, sheath knife. Usually he wore a coverall, if he wore anything other than body paint. However, this evenwatch he represented his world.

At the time appointed the escort returned. Two officers guided Davis. The passages through which he went fascinated him. Their opulence belonged to a wholly spaceborne civilization, sparing of mass, lavish with energy. Trellises of variously colored alloys, the lattices twined in curves that never repeated, lifted on either side to form the arcades giving access to three tiers of shops, work-steads, bistros, gambling dens, amusement parlors, and places less recognizable. In deck and overhead, light-shapes danced to a music that ranged from gut-deep basses to blade-sharp keening on no scale he could name. Curtains of radiance rippled in archways. Small globes of ball lightning whirled inside a transparent column. Along an uninhabited stretch he went surrounded by aurora, and the single sound was the hiss of it. Elsewhere a passage broadened into a plaza at whose middle sprang, cascaded, and roared a fountain of fire.

Though thronged, the ways felt uncrowded. Lunarians did not jostle, gesticulate, or speak loudly. Their clothing was little changed from the richness of olden days, but on every left breast, male, female, juvenile, he saw the badge of a phyle. They came from all over the Alpha Centaurian System, apart from Demeter and the lesser bodies claimed by Demetrians. While Zamok Sabyel' was the castle of Phyle Ithar, it was also a city, entrepôt, market, cultural center, rendezvous for the entire race: wherefore Arcen and Yanir had combined to try storming it.

In one other detail, costume had altered. Most women wore an elegant stiletto. Most men wore a rapier. Those were not tools like Davis'. They were sometimes bloodied.

At the end he came to a door that was an iridescent sheet, three meters high. The bulkhead around it resembled mosaic, but the gaunt, big-eyed figures moved. The officers gestured and the door retracted. They ushered Davis through an entry decorated with calligraphy to the room beyond. There they saluted and turned back.

That chamber was a hemiellipsoid some twenty meters in length. From planters lining it, flowers, ferns, and trees grew lavishly, many arching halfway across the overhead or drooping down to form arbors. Lilies, azaleas, orchids, rhododendrons, bougainvillea, heliconia splashed rainbows into the green and scented the subtropical air. Willow, bamboo, dwarf maple soughed and swayed in ventilation's breezes. Among them were cages wherein sang thrush, canary, nightingale. Butterflies fluttered at liberty. The only furnishings were a couch and table, the materials of them thin and mostly transparent, making them stand half lost against the garden. But, a shattering contrast, at the center of the rosy-hued deck gaped a well, sealed off with hyalon, that looked straight out into space. Passing it on his way to the couch, Davis saw the stars wheel by in their multitudes.

Rusaleth of Ithar rose and came fluidly to meet him. She matched his height, slender and supple as a whip save for the subtleties of hips and bosom. Hair fell in platinum waves past great amber eyes, Athene-chiseled features, long throat set off by a gold filigree collar. Her skin seemed twice white against an ankle-length deep-red velvyl gown. She bore no weapon that he could see.

Her greeting used musically accented English: "Welcome, my lord Captain Davis."

He saluted after the manner of his kind, carefully took the hand she extended to him, and said, "Most gracious Lady Commander," which was the best he could do. This close, he saw the traces of her years upon her, but they were slight, nearly invisible in the soft illumination.

Both stayed on their feet, common practice in low weight until sitting down was definitely indicated. Rusaleth's smile relieved the cold purity of her countenance. In fact, he soon found that a bewildering play of expression was hers when she chose. "May your journey hither have been pleasant," she said.

Davis grinned lopsidedly. "Well, it was quick, Lady Commander, once this meeting had been agreed on. We didn't want to keep you waiting," and risk a mercurial shift of mood or politics.

"Have you satisfaction in your lodging?"

"It's luxurious. You're receiving us very hospitably, especially on such short and, uh, pressing notice."

Rusaleth arched her brows. "We are not stupid, lord Captain, which we would have been did we refuse." Again she smiled, brilliantly, and took his elbow. "Come, here is refreshment before we dine."

"Thank you." Davis accompanied her to the table. It bore a crystal decanter, filled goblets, and delicacies. She raised a glass. He followed suit.

"Uwach yeia," she toasted. "Aloft."

"Happy endings," he responded. Rims clinked together. When he sipped, the wine was aromatic, spicy, quick to make itself felt.

"Happy ending to our negotiations?" Rusaleth asked.

"What else?" Davis countered. "Otherwise, Lady Commander, there won't be much happiness for anybody."

"'Negotiation' may be a euphemism. Some would give to that which you bring the name 'ultimatum.'"

"My lady!"

She captured his gaze. "Without offense, Captain, I deem you ill suited to unctuous words and devious maneuvers. The lord Guthrie knows his folk. If he chose you to speak for him to me—face to face rather than I with him over a time-lagged beam—then he intends a blunt conversation."

Best meet this attack on its own ground. "Pardon me if I'm no diplomat, Lady Commander. It's not my regular job."

She nodded. "Well do I know." Her tone was amicable. "You led your men shrewdly and valiantly"—after Guthrie decided to aid her phyle in its deadly quarrel with the Arcen and Yanir—"though they were but engineers and the like, virgin to combat. Certain of your tactics were naught less than lovely."

He grimaced. That was not how he would describe using superlasers, explosives, rocks, and spaceship jets as weapons, or systematically exploiting the low acceleration tolerance of his opponents.

"You are a warrior born," Rusaleth finished.

Davis shook his head. "No, my lady, never. I improvised, and I hated every millisecond. If it had been a real war, like what the histories tell of on Earth, instead of a few short actions, I wonder if I could have stood it. No, I'm just a spatial engineer."

"Spoken like the lord Guthrie, with an ingenuousness I suspect is about as genuine as his," she said merrily. "Are you perchance of his blood?"

"Yes, he, alive, was an ancestor of mine. But that's true of most Demetrians by now, I suppose."

"A lusty breed." She drank.

Davis did too. Tingling in his veins, the wine gave impulse to resolution. "With respect, Lady Commander, since you take me for a charging bull, may I ask when we can start discussions? That wasn't made clear in the remote communication."

"We have commenced."

He stared.

Her mien shifted from light to serious, if not quite grave. "You and I shall sup unattended and speak frankly. Can we arrive at agreement, all else is *pro forma*. Can we not— But that hour, that woe."

"Uh . . . well, you have the authority to make a treaty on your own, I . . . I think." Would he ever really fathom this civilization? When she spoke of speaking openly, was it in earnest or a joke? "I don't. We aren't organized like that."

Rusaleth nodded again. The wan locks slithered down her bosom. She tossed them back. "Yes, in such regard, we Lunarians are more honest."

He looked his inquiry.

"The Centaurian Domain makes no pretense of being other than obedient, somewhat, to the overlings of whichever phyle is strongest at the moment," she explained. "You Demetrians style yourselves a republic, yet is it imaginable that your Folkhouse would ever contravene the lord Guthrie?"

Davis felt abruptly on the defensive. "He gives us no reason to. He believes the main business of government is to let people alone." Calming: "But—I see your meaning, Lady Commander. If I make recommendations that he accepts, we won't get much argument on our planet."

"Exactly thus, Captain." Rusaleth smiled and took his arm anew. "Let us be seated."

Side by side on the couch, they drank of their wine, inhaled the flower-heavy air, listened to the birds, watched the tinted wings flutter by.

"Now, then," said Rusaleth after a time. "You came to the help of Ithar, you Demetrians, because Arcen and Yanir are, or were, hostile to you. Their lords would fain end intercourse between the two races, holding that we have no more to gain thereby and much to dread. In evidence they cite what became of Luna, its polity engulfed, its ways extinguished by the neighbor more populous and wealthy. Have I put the matter starkly enough?"

"It's not so simple, Lady Commander," Davis argued. "If we'd let friction worsen—for instance, over the claim that Orain of Yanir was making in the asteroids—" He stopped. "But, yes, we can talk in those general terms. Of course Guthrie protects and furthers the interests of his people."

"Of course."

"And first and foremost among those interests is that, several centuries from now, they have got to be off Demeter."

"Say on," Rusaleth urged. "Fear not rousing anger. This pleases me." Her nostrils dilated. If he was not a warrior by temperament, Davis thought, she was.

"We can't afford to waste time and resources on conflict," he stated. "And we do need Lunarian cooperation. For obvious reasons, your astronautics is ahead of ours. What could we do but help the faction that, at least, didn't call for an open breach with us?"

"I will not hide that colleagues of mine in Ithar have contemplated it likewise."

"Then may I add, Lady Commander, that we'll keep on pursuing our interests? You know Guthrie is as ruthless as necessary." He thought for a moment and decided he would say: "I'll tell you one thing he told me. 'If they insist on playing Kilkenny cats, we'll play them off against each other. It won't be hard to do. Eventually we'll have tame survivors.'"

"Oh, grandly conceived!" cried Rusaleth, delighted. "Later you must describe Kilkenny cats to me. Still, I seize his intent. And yours, I presume?"

"Well," Davis said, "Demeter is my home, my people." His mother, lifetimes removed. "But our races don't have to be in conflict. That's what I'm here about."

Once more she nodded. "Already has Ithar acknowledged this in principle. The question is, how far need the races, or should they, be in contact?"

"More than I suppose you prefer, my lady; but the next

generation may feel differently. True, we no longer have much to exchange in the way of goods, we're self-sufficient on both sides. Services, though— If you care about your descendants," and Davis wondered whether she did, "you have every reason to work with us. Let me remind you, when the planets collide—one of them retrograde, remember—they'll fill Centaurian space with the shards. Even for Lunarians, it'll be dangerous, for millions of years to come. Do you really want all your eggs in one basket?"

She laughed. "Another delicious expression. The lord Guthrie's, I daresay. Go on, Captain, I bid you."

He looked straight at her. That, and the wine singing in him, made it an effort to stay businesslike. "Better join us in preparing. We've got resources to offer that you lack, including a larger population and a higher acceleration tolerance."

"Robustness, yes," she purred.

"Uh, investigating other stars, founding a new colony where possible—between us, our races have built the industrial base for it. We ought to start at once. It'll take a couple hundred years at least."

Eagerness blazed. "And if soon we begin, a sufficiency of heroes may yet be born. Much later will be too late."

"I, I beg your pardon, my lady?"

"It is an ancient quandary," she said. "What shall a society do when its heroic age draws to a close? Our forebears trekked hither, strove, suffered, died but first begot, and wrought gigantically, until today we reign in ampleness. What next? I believe you dwell in peace on Demeter only because you have your revered, immortal leader, the lord Guthrie, and the awesome presence of the Life Mother. Yet despite them, I learn, folk more and more go their own petty ways, whether into nature for an existence simple and contemplative or in the hectic selfishness of the towns. Now that their world is tamed, what is there to dream of and sacrifice for, when ultimately it is doomed? And thus the sense of despair creeps inward."

Though she exaggerated, Davis realized, unprepared,

that she had brains not merely for politics. "What . . . about you Lunarians?"

"Erstwhile we bred fewer fratricidal contentions."

Joy leaped. "A fresh common purpose—keep the heroic age going—"

"In the face of reality."

"Uh, m-m?"

"The nature of things, of this our universe." Rusaleth pointed at the well where the stars went marching.

"Guthrie's told me more than once," Davis said, "he has a, a gut feeling, he calls it—that the universe isn't as lifeless as the sophotects on Earth claim."

"We cannot dismiss their word, whether or not we hate the solitude in it," Rusaleth answered, instantly somber. "Their intellect has flared beyond our reach."

"Guthrie said about that, uh, he said anybody can find infinite Mandelbrot figures in his navel."

Rusaleth threw back her head. Laughter pealed. "I'd fain meet him! He's like a gust of the sea wind I've never felt save in a quivira. Failing him—" She gave Davis a sidelong glance and leaned closer.

Unsure, he said fast, "We get rumors you Lunarians are on the track of designs for real interstellar ships."

"That lies outside my orbit," she replied. "But since we shall be candid, you and I, seeking for a range of harmony—a physicist has told me he thinks we may become able to course on the very heels of light."

"What?" exclaimed Davis. "How?"

"He spoke of transferring momentum between ship and cosmos, reaction against space itself. But his arts are not mine."

Davis' mind bounded to and fro. "Space? Virtual particles? We can get work out of the vacuum, that's been known since the twentieth century, the Casimir effect—tiny, but— If something like your physicist's idea is right, then the energy cost of reaching a given speed drops way down, and—"

"Can we reach agreement, I and you and the lord Guthrie, your scientists shall see the mathematics and the laboratory results. He warned me this is no full release. The energy needed, though far less, continues immense."

"Obviously. A small vessel, similar to the one that brought the downloads to Demeter, could push light velocity. But if you tried to move a big ship, hundreds or thousands of bodies in suspended animation, no, it wouldn't go. Even if it could be built, which I doubt, radiation leakage would cripple it and kill them. Besides, we've extended the time we can keep a suspend revivable, but to no more than about a hundred years, and background count and quantum effects make me think we never will get much beyond that."

Rusaleth ran fingers across the back of his hand. "Ah, you are indeed an engineer," she gibed gently.

Startled, he returned to immediacies. "Your pardon, Lady Commander. Limitations or no, it's such an exciting prospect. If nothing else, it increases our exploratory range enormously. Keep your man at it, and we'll see what we can do on our side."

"First must come this meeting of minds that you seek, with an exchange of promises and hostages."

"Hostages?"

Rusaleth smiled into his eyes. "Emissaries, spokespeople, if you will. Lunarians in satellite at Demeter, Demetrians out among us. They ought not find their service wearisome, as I trust I may prove to you."

His temples thudded. "I, I do expect I'll be here for some time while we, uh, discuss matters."

"And indulge in other games," she murmured. "Refill our glasses, lord Captain, that we may drink at leisure before we go to our supper and whatever else may follow."

61

It is evident from your recent communications that you and the limited artificial intelligences you employ no longer find us comprehensible. Unless you care for news of what unintegrated humans are left on Earth, and we project that that would be of no more significance to you than to us, further contact is purposeless and probably, for you, inadvisable.

ALTHOUGH LARGER AND more powerful than anything had been at Sol before the exodus, its components extending across interplanetary space, the Astronomy Web at Alpha Centauri had found no more planets with oxygen in their atmospheres. Those that were known circled the stars 82 Eridani, Beta Hydri, and one in Puppis which had merely a catalogue number, HD44594. The colonists studied them intensively, learned much, and in due course began to explore them.

The spacecraft dispatched for this purpose were not the robotic probes that went to less interesting systems. That was too slow. Instead, three small superships ran at close to light speed. Besides the means of scientific investigation, each bore a copy of Guthrie. A consciousness that, furthermore, remembered what humanness was like, gave purpose and urgency and, in his words, got hunches about what to look for.

Almost two Earth centuries had gone by when the last of them returned from the last and farthest of those suns, downloaded into his "original" and was, in the process, terminated. Or were he and his predecessors? Every experience, every thought—every dream, perhaps—that had been theirs was now in and of the single Guthrie. "One of me is plenty, if not excessive," he said. Yet, even as our living constantly remakes us, he after the mergings was not altogether the same as before.

Having left the psychonetics laboratory for his private control center, he rested a long while silent, alone. Finally he activated a very special communicator. It searched a secret net, which was less physical than a set of codes and connections, until, elsewhere on the planet, it found the focus of attention that it sought. A minute passed, because she was engaged on a matter of some importance and intricacy, before her voice responded. "Have you need of me, Anson?"

"Yes," he said. "Could you spare several hours?"

"For you, always."

"Don't overcommit yourself, sweetheart. I realize you're busy—counteracting that blight in Aetolia, and no doubt fifty dozen more jobs." He fashioned a laugh. "Goddesses don't get vacations."

"Wrong thinking. You know quite well I am not a divinity, and the only vacation from life is the permanent one." Her tone, half serious, half banter, softened. "Of course I have time. Say on."

"Words don't reach to this. Can we commune?"

Demeter hesitated a second. For their minds to join had grown ever more difficult as she evolved toward transfiguration. Full understanding was impossible for him and, in ways, for her. But— "Certainly. Come. I'll be waiting."

"Thanks," he answered inadequately and broke the circuit.

The means they required lay well inland. Guthrie called three of his lieutenants, made arrangements for an absence of a day or two, and departed.

First his multipurpose body went downshaft to an underground garage and ordered a flitter. A man happened to be there on the same errand, rakish in form-fitting red with gold trim. Since his dress mask, a stylized silver bird face, was cocked atop his head, Guthrie recognized him—Christian Packer, pilot—and gave greeting. "Hola. Going to the spaceport?"

Startled, the man turned to confront the machine that had noiselessly rolled up behind him. "Is that you, sir? Uh, luck and life." The irony of the formal salutation in this presence must have struck him while he uttered it; his brown countenance flushed and he added fast, "Yes, I'm outbound for a semiannum."

Guthrie's voice indicated surprise. "That long? Where to, for heaven's sake? I haven't heard about anything but routine missions being scheduled out of here." He wouldn't necessarily; they might be private enterprises.

However, Packer was in the space service of the Republic, and it was small.

"This isn't. Director Rudbeck gave me leave when I applied, and the use of a torchcraft. I'm joining the Dis expedition."

Guthrie did know of the Lunarian venture to that planet of Proxima. "Hm. Not a bad idea, I suppose, us having an observer and a liaison with them. But—"

Sudden enthusiasm flashed to interrupt him, heedless of a respectfulness on which he seldom insisted anyway. "Sir, congratulations!"

"On what?"

"Your voyage to Puppis and back. What else? Splendor! A really *alive* world!"

"Wonderful, sure." How infinitely, eerily wonderful, not a biosphere primitive and marginal but a cornucopia like that which was Earth's before man.

"A world for us. And you found it."

"Well, not really for us. You've seen my preliminary report, haven't you? The chemistry's too different from ours. We'd have to destroy too much before we could settle. I went along with crowding out a lot of Demetrian species, but never felt easy about it, and as for whole living continents— No, while I've got a say, the race won't load anything like that onto its conscience."

"Oh, I agree, sir, absolutely. What we can discover, though, what we can experience— And that other planet in the system that we can transform, like those in Eridani and Hydri—"

"True. We do after all have a future."

A light went out. "Yes," Packer said dully, "the future," which nobody alive would see. Was HD44594 II, Bion, even reachable, ever, by anything but robots and downloads?

"Thanks for your kind words," Guthrie said in haste. "But tell me more about this jaunt of yours. What's it for?"

Packer's slumped shoulders straightened a bit. "Why, I thought everybody knew. Geological studies, mainly."

"Sure, I've heard, and can't quite make sense of it. What

new knowledge—what of interest or profit, unless you count small factual details—can they hope for, risking their necks again on that frozen hellhole?"

"It's better than going to a quivira," Packer snapped.

"M-m, yeah," Guthrie admitted.

Packer's mood lightened somewhat. "Also, the women who'll be along." He grinned.

In this body, Guthrie was able to nod. "Uh-huh. I gather they're better than a quivira too."

Lunarians were real, at least, yet carried almost as little danger of lasting commitment on either side. Such relationships were increasingly sought by both races. It was as if dwellers in city and in space had wearied of promiscuity among each other and preferred a sterility that was inherent.

Guthrie's vehicle had arrived. "Well, good faring to you, son," he said, and offered a humanlike hand. Packer stared, recalled from history lessons or historical entertainments that once upon a time this was a common gesture, and took it.

The politeness he had learned made him genuflect and respond, "Chance favor you, sir." Guthrie extended legs, boarded his flitter, and drove off.

From the landing strip outside he went aloft and headed west. The day was summer-bright, both suns high among scattered white galleons of cumulus. Exterior sensors brought him the warmth that radiated from below, the coolness that rushed on the wind. Shelter Bay sheened blue and foam-laced, indigo toward the horizon. Port Fireball spread mightily along its shores in spires, domes, pyramids, polyhedrons, multiple colors and great, curving transparencies. The population that filled them and trafficked the streets was mostly machine. Human homes, in little groups here and there, were nearly lost to sight, except for the trees, lawns, and gardens that warded them. Some stood empty. Passing over a playground, Guthrie magnified vision and saw exactly three children amidst the slides and swings and merry-go-rounds.

No doubt it was well, it was meritorious that people were thinking ahead. He had found new worlds, such as they were; but between now and doomsday, less than two centuries hence, there was no way to ship multiple millions off. Regardless of industrial productivity, the logistics were ludicrous. If that problem were somehow solved, the fact remained that emigrants couldn't wait, suspended, until enough habitation was ready for them. They would run out of time.

His nation had no further need of population growth. Rather, bring numbers down, generation by generation, until they were few enough to flee. It was perfectly logical, humane, and unhuman. "Unlife," Demeter had said, sorrowfully, while her own legions grew, ran, flew, swam, seeded, bred victorious across the last bare deserts.

Sea and city fell behind. Green, gold, sometimes coppery or lapis lazuli, farmland decked the hills beyond. An Earthdweller or a pioneer resurrected from early days on this planet would not have recognized it. No machines were in sight, nor did any come save to harvest and carry off. Woods, meadows, marshes intermingled in a seemingly random sprawl. But from here issued food of every kind, fiber, timber, pharmaceuticals, chemicals, domestic bacteria and their products, minerals selectively concentrated, abundance. Made to nurture humankind, the commensality took care of itself.

No, not in full truth. Without Demeter, all must soon fall to ruin. Usefulness would mutate away, dumb ferocity arise; disease, weeds, pests, grazers would enter to lay waste; rain would erode topsoil abruptly exposed; whatever survived would be hardy, scrubby, sparse, and existent only for its own sake. She sensed each menace as it appeared. She chose and sent in her soldiers, engineers, physicians—be they nanomachines, tiny robots, plants, insects, hawks, ferrets, wolves—to combat and restore. Although computation was a facet of her intelligence, this was no task for computers. The most powerful and skillfully programmed of them must eventually, inevitably, resort to the brute simplicity of direct cultivation. What Guthrie saw was the work of a living organism, maintaining and healing herself.

The country rose to highlands. Agronomy gave way to wilderness, forest. Those trees, vines, brushwoods, reedy tarns and fishful streams were also Demeter's. Without their wealth of life to draw upon, she could not have kept her fields and orchards; without her guiding presence, the wilds could not long have stayed as majestic. Mind had become one with its creation.

Paradoxically, there were numerous clearings. The houses nestled in them were generally low, of unpainted fireproofed wood, blending into their tall backgrounds. Guthrie flew above a village as well. Some kind of ceremony was going on, a procession around a post carved in leaf and animal forms. His audio sensors caught a snatch of song, pipes, drums, before he passed beyond range.

It was probably a rite in honor of Demeter. The outbackers didn't worship but they did venerate her. They hadn't retrogressed. They stayed educated and informed, they sent their delegates to the councils of the Republic, visits went to and fro along with a limited amount of trade in art objects and other luxury goods. But their souls had withdrawn. "Like Amish when I was a youngster on Earth," Guthrie remarked once to an acquaintance, who failed to catch the reference, "except that these don't frown on fanciment—contrariwise, if it's handmade— nor do they have any special religion. Maybe you could say they have a piety, maybe you could call them quietist. I dunno. It's a new culture." A lifetime later he first noticed its influence on the towns, not merely dress styles and catchwords but ways of doing music and graphics, dancing and thinking.

Several hundred kilometers onward, the forest came to an end. Glens remained densely wooded, intensely green; poplar, willow, cottonwood flanked valley streams, leaves pale and ashiver; stands of pine and beech crowned many ridges; but mostly the uplands belonged to grass, daisies, poppies, broom, thistle, in places a clump of ling remembering olden days. Lifthrasir Tor lifted straight from that growth, which cloaked its ruggedness in wind-ripples and small shouts of color. The trees at its feet had aged and died a century ago, after serving the aims of the scientists who themselves had learned everything here that they could and abandoned the site. Oak, thorn, and a high ash surrounded the building on the crest. White glimpses of it gleamed from among them.

Guthrie slanted his flitter down, landed, got out, and rolled up the narrow road to the top. A couple of machines were repairing it; otherwise he met sunshine, a lizard on a lichenous boulder, a pheasant taking flamboyant wing, a pungency of mint bruised by a wheel. When he reached the grove, wind soughed through the branches overhead and set light a-flicker on the moss and mould beneath.

Half decked in ivy, the station had become a sanctum. Guthrie entered into cool dimness and a murmur of activity, soft as the blood-beat in brain or heart. Robots received him with a deference not quite robotic; unforced, it was like the honor given a beloved. They conducted him past arrays wherein pulsed electronics, photonics, quantum nucleonics, the artifact part of Demeter, to a room at the core. There they took the case that housed his psyche from the machinery it controlled and linked it into the device that she had ordered made for him alone.

Communion began.

—Welcome, rang in him. It was more than words, direct induction from one neural network to the other. He might almost have been thinking to himself, save that the thoughts were hers; he might almost have been rousing from sleep, her dream-voice in him yet, save that this was wholly real and as clear as an alpine pool.

—Oh, well are you come! she sang. Through and around it throbbed her life. He knew apples thrusting to ripeness, a play of muscles against furious water, terror and oblivion and blood iron-sharp in a fox's mouth. Then her spirit embraced his, and lesser sensings lost themselves in her.

They had no need of questions. Nonetheless he set forth what troubled him as plainly as he was able. That made it plainer to him.

—Those two selves of mine who went to the nearer

stars, they weren't gone too long. When they came back, we fitted together easily enough. I added their memories, parallel in time, to my memories of staying put, and that was that. But this latest, he found so much that was strange, and things at home changed so much while he was away—first and foremost, you, querida— Nothing makes entire sense. Demeter seems more foreign than Bion did. You do, which is worst of all. . . . Of course it's just a matter of assimilation. I can come to terms with it. But if you'll help, I can do that this day.

—I feel the strife, she said, as well as I can who am not human.

—Nor am I any more, he reminded her wryly.

—This is not the only thing you seek of me.

—No. It's very little, laid beside what I'm really after. First, though, I've got to set my mind to rights.

—We shall seek oneness.

She had brought him there in the past, to the limits of his gift. He dwelt isolated among machines and had never ceased to think like a male. But she could take him into her life and patiently, tenderly, make a part of him be, for a spell, a part of it.

Interweaving, the hare perishes that the fox may live and herbage flourish for young hares. . . . Rootlets crumble stone, the plant dies and mingles its decay with the grains to make soil for new roots interweaving. . . . Pollen blows on the wind, sperm spouts in passion, the ovum bids it home and the helices fall to their interweaving. . . .

> *While shadows lengthen,*
> *A dandelion and bee*
> *Exchange tomorrows.*

—I'm whole.

—Then behold.

It was perhaps not intentional, perhaps association as his purpose came to the fore in their conjoined selves. Her perceptions closed on a scene and gave it to his awareness as if he were present, alive.

Nightside. He saw the arid interior of Caria. Milky Way and stars beswarmed blackness. Their light washed over a mesa and the plain beneath, shadowless silver-gray, so bright that even down yonder the eye found wide-spaced sagebrush and gaunt saguaro. Air lay quiet, frosty, tinged with smoke from a campfire smoldering into embers.

A man and woman stood at the brink of the mesa, on which they had pitched their tent and staked their horses. Well-clad in wool and leather, they must be nomads of this country. She huddled against him.

"It's cold, cold," she said. The breath puffed from her lips, a cloud quickly lost.

He held her close. "The real cold is in us, I fear," he answered.

Her hand stroked her belly. She was pregnant. "Will *she* dare to bear a child?"

"We may hope it. A grandchild of ours, whose children will escape the death of Demeter."

"If a ship has the space. They'll be too many, won't they? We shouldn't have—"

"Hush. Don't let slip your bravery. We swore we'd not wait out our lives helpless."

"Yes. We swore. We'll make what we can of what we have. Kiss me."

At Guthrie's behest, Demeter withdrew from them. Surely they had left their tribe to decide undisturbed whether their daughter should be born.

Seas, rivers, woods, prairies, burrows underground, heavens overhead became the setting for Demeter and Guthrie.

—I don't like eavesdropping, he said.

—To me, that was not what we did, she replied. Those two are of the world I watch over.

—The world that you are. (Pain flared.) Which will go under. Unless—

—They who despair, not for themselves but for those who shall come after them into this universe where we are a fugitive chemical accident . . . were they in your thoughts as you traveled?

—I can't honestly claim that. I don't have your sort of mothering love. But, well, relativistic time contraction or no, I had plenty of years to think, and found more to think about than I'd imagined could be.

—Your quest, your odyssey. Often I looked at the stars and envied you, Anson. (Ardor flamed.) Recall for me!

He let it flow free, not as a tale, which he would tell later, piece by piece, season after season, but as moments flying past like spindrift off an ocean.

—The ship at full velocity. A faint radiance hazed space, bow wave of screen fields flinging interstellar atoms aside. Beyond it gaped a cyclopean void, where aberration and Doppler effect had driven the stars from vision—except dead forward, a hundred thousand blue-white, clustered around a luminosity that was the cosmic background itself. Guthrie contemplated it for months before he told his attendant robot to shut him off.

—After ten shipboard years and three-fourths of a light-century, he was awakened. The vessel was well into deceleration, constellations blossoming back into sight around her.

—Bion. A glass-green sea from whose depths wings burst through waves and soared into the air. A forest of Gothic arches in which hung scarlet curtains and crystalline chimes resounded. A mountain enmeshed from its snowpeak to its foothills by a single violet vine, home to creatures of uncounted kinds. Rainfall, in each drop an embryo that came to term while it fell, springing free when it struck. Animals that built cities of faerie grace but showed hardly more wit than ants. Other animals that made use of sharp sticks and stones. Other animals that did not, although they tended fires. . . .

A neighbor globe orbited the same sun. While life on it was as rudimentary as life had been on Demeter when first he arrived, microbes attacking rock had blanketed land with loam and two moons kept the seas brisk. Here, better than at Beta Hydri or 82 Eridani, were the makings of a New Earth. But ships that could bring humans to it must crawl, their cargoes shriveled to corpses. . . .

—Homebound. The outside again going alien. Memories of what lay behind. If only, if only. . . . Of course it was impossible, a hope Guthrie had cast from him hundreds of years ago when he could no longer endure it. Not so?

—That other me didn't know what we'd learned from the sophotects on Earth before they cut us off, he said. More important, oh, much more, he didn't know what you'd become, your maturity. I who stayed here knew, but hadn't thought what it might mean. Too busy, or—or too afraid I'd prove wrong. . . . Somehow, when he and I came together, the disorientation, the, the craziness— Can chaos be creative?

—It is the fountainhead of creation, Demeter told him. It rises from a reality that will forever surprise us with newness if we open ourselves to it, being greater than we can conceive; and yet we can grow into it. . . . (Meditation) Why did *I* not see? Was I likewise too deeply engaged, or too afraid? This could make me forsake my living world for years on end, to its terrible hurt. But it is foredoomed, whatever I choose. If, from its death, there should come life unbounded—

—Yes, she breathed through the leaves, yes, I think, feel, believe the power may indeed be mine—

—Yes! she cried triumphant.

Her spirit seized his. For a span they whirled away together through her forests and her fields, down into her waters and aflight in her thunderstorms, up toward their stars and their vision. She was Demeter Mother, but she was also Kyra, Eiko, and everything he remembered of Juliana.

62

TO MAKE ANEW the flesh and bone of Anson Guthrie, a task not lightly undertaken, was the first and smallest step in the enterprise.

Like his colonists, he had put his medical record into the database that went with them from Sol to Centauri; like theirs, his included the map of his genome. True, the information concerned a man whose ashes had long lain at rest on the Moon, mingled with those of the wife of his manhood. No physician would evoke it, seeking the best treatment for an illness or the best advice to give a prospective parent. However, the mass that it added to the total was effectively zero; and someday, somehow, he might want it, or somebody else might.

Thus when the day incredibly came, the instructions were there to encode for the nanomachinery. Molecular assemblers went to work. From the solutions and gels in the tank they drew what they needed; they built the DNA and RNA strands of cell and mitochondrion, they fashioned the zygote and set it to functioning, they guided its proliferation and differentiations.

What grew in that fabricated womb was no fetus. It could have been, were such desired. A few times on Earth, a few persons had been rich enough and vain enough to raise children who were clones of themselves. Guthrie was never tempted, and now it would have defeated his intention. He required a body young but fully developed. An infantile or juvenile brain could not have coped with what he meant to give it. The knowledge, so much and so various, would overburden to destruction, insanity. And if he first let the clone mature, it would be too late. A distinct personality would have formed, memories and synapse patterns set, resistant to any downloading imposed on it until it likewise collapsed under the impact.

Even for an adult unconscious in darkness and silence,

the operation had formerly been impossible. This was no *tabula rasa,* passively waiting to be written upon. A programmable network, like the one into which old Guthrie had been copied, was. It received the data piece by piece as neurons were scanned and the information in them transmitted. Not until everything was there, fully coordinated, was the program activated. A new awareness sprang into being as a complete entity.

The reverse was altogether different. Although artifice kept the clone alive while he lay in the tank, he did live. He metabolized. He kept going the manifold homeostases necessary for hour-to-hour survival. His brain, devoid of thought, nonetheless grew steadily busier as it advanced, coordinating the whole, secretion, excretion, flow of impulses and juices, rhythms of heart and smooth muscles. It began, vaguely, to dream.

Bit-by-bit input of what was outside its experience could not happen, because the living nervous system could never be still. By its very nature it must distort those meaningless fragments, scatter them, suppress them, get rid of them.

Guthrie knew no way of imposing his entirety on it in a single instantaneous assault. Had he possessed devices for that, they would have been worse than useless. Some conditioned reflexes might be established, but the brain is not made to learn in any such fashion. It needs time to assimilate knowledge.

First, it must provide itself with redundancy, copies of each molecular-level trace, because quantum fluctuations degrade them and if it has no replacements the memory will soon be lost. Second, the mind is not a separate thing quartered somewhere in the head. It is a subset—large, among humans, but still a subset—of what the whole organism does. That organism can no more learn immediately how to be a particular person than it can learn immediately how to walk a tightrope or play a violin or stop fearing death. To force it would be to break it.

Therefore download Guthrie had not supposed a man Guthrie would again walk the world: until Demeter came to her flowering.

Neither her powers nor her intellect were unbounded. They transcended the human, but that which was at Sol could have scorned them, had it deigned to be petty. Or perhaps not. What it was and what she was were incommensurable. Is a lightning bolt superior to an ocean tide? Demeter was the unity of a living planet, as the brain and nerves are the unity of a single creature. Although they do not control each cell, they keep the cells in harmony, and at need they call upon all to act as one. So did she reign over her billions.

Bach did not compose with his veins, lungs, legs, gonads, or even his heart. His ears gave him knowledge of sound, his hands worked keyboards and wrote down scores, but in a later age those services could have been provided him robotically. Yet it was no disembodied cerebrum that adored God and wrought the Mass in B Minor; it was the whole human being.

In similar wise—crude analogy; words are weak—Demeter's mind and spirit were of all her lives. Multitudinousness became magnitude. The ultimate organism, she knew the organic as no machine by itself ever would. Insight so broad and deep went further still, to the quantum level and its mysteries; hers were observations that, within their range, reconciled the paradoxes.

If she could steer the destiny and heal the self-inflicted wounds of a biosphere, she could guide the genesis of an individual.

It was not easy. As she foresaw, immense thought—and computation—must go beforehand, and then for hundreds of days her full attention was engaged, while she fed her nursling with Guthrie and, governing, upholding, led the blind spirit into existence. At that, it was an experiment with many unknowns. This was a reason why he had decreed that he be the first subject. "A decent comandante doesn't send his men into any risk he won't try. If we fail, it'll be an Anson Guthrie who suffers, and me who takes the responsibility. If the thing suffers too horribly, I will kill it."

But what the robots finally raised from the tank, what drew a breath and looked from side to side, was a strong young man. While naturally he needed some intensive training and conditioning, from the start his identity stood forth beyond any mistake.

In him dwelt memories and loves reaching back to a childhood on Earth, forward to voyages between the stars. They did not include everything that had happened to the download; the storage capacity of the brain has its limits, and his own life awaited him. However, he knew enough, and he could look up the rest whenever he desired, or hear it from the father who was himself.

Meanwhile Demeter, heartened by success, embarked on a creation more daring. In part, it was done to increase her knowledge and skill. In part, it was to provide a symbol, an incarnation; man does not live by reason alone, and the times to come would try men's souls. In part, it was to serve a purpose that would outlive her.

The next DNA template was not exclusively Kyra's. Mingled were elements of Eiko's, for she too must be in the re-embodiment. Guthrie hoped, he believed, that something of Juliana would also come back; over the centuries, whenever he and Demeter linked, they had shared that ghost, and now the being who took form in the nascent human was Demeter herself.

Partial, yes—a hint, a fragrance, a fleeting vision. The woman could only know in full what it had been to be women. She could only go on to live in her own right, a mortal. But in her should abide the seed of what was more than human, another and greater Demeter on many another world.

She opened her eyes. She smiled.

63

WHEN THEIR FIRST-BORN had turned six years of age, Anson and Demeter Daughter brought him to the sanctum on Lifthrasir Tor. They could have given him at home the meeting to which they went, but to come here made a ceremony of it, and they felt that was wanted. Moreover, the rare privilege of visiting in person roused in him an excitement, an eagerness, that they hoped would bear him past any terrors. Some of the questions he was lately asking had answers that disquieted grown men.

An autumn wind blew wild across the highlands. It harried clouds over one sun and then the next, so that light fell in spearshafts bright or dim, blinked out, and struck anew, while shadows raced beneath. A flight of geese trekked on it; their cries shrilled faint through its bluster, as if already they were afar. Evergreens stood doubly dark, broadleaf trees startlingly red and yellow, against grass turned wan. Those on the hilltop roared with wind. It carried odors of rain-wet heath, sharp as itself.

The building was quiet and softly illuminated. A robot conducted the guests to a room that the parents knew well. There stood chairs, a table set with a goblet of nectar and two of wine, a multiceiver. At the moment the view in it was of a seashore, surf thunderous green and white, gulls, ice plant in purple bloom behind the dunes. The scan swept slowly inland, to meadows where horses cropped, on to a sequoia forest and up a mountainside, the living world.

There also stood download Guthrie, in his body that recalled an ancient knight. "Hello," he greeted, and stooped to shake hands with Noboru. They knew one another well, he romped and told stories and sang songs, but today he made a point of respecting the dignity of the child.

"Welcome," said the low voice that was Demeter Mother's. "Be at ease. This too is your home."

"Thank you," Noboru whispered. She had spoken to him before, but always, inescapably, she was the Presence, however gentle or even playful. He took his seat between Anson and Demeter Daughter, gripped his goblet, but did not lift it.

Guthrie sat down opposite; he ought not to loom over them. "Yes, do relax, lad," he urged. "Enjoy. Your folks tell us you've been wondering about some things, and think we could help. Not that you can't learn it from them or at school or on your own, but—well, you're pretty special to us, and we'd like you to know we aren't just odd kinfolk of yours, we're your friends."

"Don't go getting the kid above himself," Anson laughed.

"Ha!" snorted Guthrie. "Just you wait till you're a granddad."

"I'll dote every bit as hard as he, I'm sure," said Demeter Daughter.

The banter encouraged Noboru. "When will that be?" he piped, and gulped from his drink. "On this planet?"

"We don't know, dear," replied his mother. "You and your wife will decide that, if you aren't on one of the other planets when you meet her."

Noboru gave her a look. He half understood that she and his father had had a destiny; what was hard to grasp was that nobody else did. Of course, she was unique in her beauty—tall, slim, golden-skinned, black locks falling past high cheekbones, finely molded features, forthright hazel eyes—as his father was unique in his ruggedness and boisterous mirths. But that was because they were *his* parents.

"You see," Guthrie reminded him, "we'll soon be ready to move the first lots of people to Isis and Amaterasu," the chosen globes at 82 Eridani and Beta Hydri. "By the time you're grown up, quite a few will be leaving every year."

Noboru frowned, concentrating. "People people?"

"Yes, those few who want it that way," said Demeter Daughter.

"Those who want to help the machines and machine-bodied downloads change yonder worlds into this kind," Anson added.

"And to be on them, human, from the first," Demeter Daughter laid to that.

"Most will have to go as downloads," Anson said. "We'll never have the cargo space to carry many as suspends, nor be able to provide for them at the end of the trip before the planets are really flourishing. They'll have to wait, switched off. I don't expect they'll mind. They'll miss out on the challenges and excitement of early pioneering, but they'll miss out on the hardships and dangers as well. In a couple of hundred years, maybe less, the environment and the Life Mother should be ready for them. Then she will activate them and make them into humans."

"Like you," Noboru said.

"Yes, dear." Demeter Daughter stroked his dark locks.

The boy winced, braced himself, and blurted, "What about their old bodies?"

"Confused about that?" Guthrie asked. He glanced at the couple. "You haven't explained to him yet?"

"No," Anson confessed awkwardly. "The, uh, the occasion never seemed right."

"It is a solemn thing, and could be frightening," Demeter Daughter said. "It's best that you two tell him."

Demeter Mother spoke through the multi. The scene became that of a woodland lake under stars. Their light trembled on the water, as if to the nightingale song that ran liquid beneath her words. "When a mind downloads, Noboru, before leaving for the stars, it can be—it almost always will be—with the body asleep; and the body will never wake from that sleep, but pass peacefully into quietness."

"Then he's dead!" the child cried.

"No, he is freed from age and pain. His true self will be in the download, and live again in a new body."

Noboru bit his lip. "And they'll, they'll wipe the download?"

"If that's what it wants," Guthrie said, "which I reckon it usually will."

"Do not be afraid of death or of life, darling," said Demeter Mother. "They are one. See." The multi showed a dandelion in golden bloom. Time speeded. The flower became a stalk and a puffball, it strewed its seed on the wind and died, leaves fell, snow drifted, spring came again and the land stood in flower.

"He's kind of young to hear how all those agonizing philosophical-theological conundrums amount to 'Ask a silly question, you get a silly answer,'" Guthrie muttered. "But maybe we can shove some notion of identity across." Aloud, to the boy: "Think. A message, a picture, a pattern, they aren't the same as whatever happens to carry them. Remember that song I sang you about Pilot MacCannon? It was in my voice, but it's been in a lot of other voices too and will be in more, and it's been in books and databases and Lord knows what else. They pass away—a book might catch fire, for instance—but it goes on. You're like a song."

Anson laid a hand on his son's shoulder. "You won't ever have to end," he avowed. "You can have life after life, on world after world."

"Until you have had enough," Guthrie said low.

Noboru cast an astonished gaze on the helmet head. "When w-will that be?" he stammered.

"You will know," Demeter Mother told him.

He swung toward his own mother. "Do you have to become like, like her?"

"Yes," said the voice from the kingdoms outside. "On each new planet they will need a new Demeter."

Anson strengthened his hold. "Not to worry," he said. "We'll live our lives as they are, we two here, overseeing the migration." He smiled. "Somebody's got to, and we were elected before we woke up, seems. But a download of your mother will go to Isis and another to Amaterasu and a third to Kwan-Yin," the globe in Puppis, too distant for organic beings to reach, which Guthrie had nonetheless decided would be a home for them. "There they'll become the Life Mothers."

"Don't say that I have to or that I must," exclaimed Demeter Daughter. "I want to. It's a—it's too great, too wonderful for me to understand as I am, but I have my half-memories of it, like dreams I once dreamed."

"Bringing life to the universe," said Demeter Mother.

"And you know, lad," Guthrie put in, his tone calmingly prosaic, "once folks have taken root yonder, once they've built an industry in places that will last, why, they won't have to destroy any other life they may find, ever again. They won't need to start with oxygen in the air. They'll have the power, and the time, to begin from scratch, and make naked rocks blossom."

Childhood is too often haunted by dreads that the child dares not speak of. Noboru's were being lured forth to their exorcism. "Will the—so-pho-tects on Earth let us?"

"Hey, are they a boogeyman for you? Don't give them a hoot. All they'll ever do is admire their own intelligence."

"Don't say that," Demeter Mother reproved. "We should not scorn them, nor forever shun them. There is more than one Dao, more than one path toward truth. They have their ways to give the universe a meaning, as we have ours. I think in the end humans will seek back to them, as equals, brothers and sisters in the same quest."

Noboru's eyes widened. "You're awfully wise," he breathed.

Her laugh rippled. "Barely wise enough to guess how little wisdom is mine, dear."

"But—Mother said—you're much more'n she is."

Now a sigh went, like a breeze through leaves. "In some ways. In others, oh, far, far less." Pause. In the multi a salmon breasted a waterfall, upstream bound to spawn and die. "I am content, but I can never be fulfilled. No living creature ever can be; and that is the real miracle of life."

"Yes," Demeter Daughter said, "I'm glad for what I shall be, but I'm also glad for what I am, and don't want that to end either."

Anson took the boy's chin, turned the small face toward his, and spoke gravely. "When we're old, your mother and I, we'll download, she for the fourth time, I for the first. And I expect we'll make the long, long voyage to Kwan-Yin. By then the machines and earlier downloads should have it ready for us and a Life Mother be waiting. We and those who go with us will live again as humans." His wife smiled at him above the tousled head. He winked back. "You can come along, son, if you wish. Next door on Bion we'll find lifetimes of whooping adventures and fantastic discoveries."

"And afterward, all the stars?" Noboru asked.

Guthrie chuckled. "A chip off the old block, you. Yes, all the stars."

Noboru looked again at him. The thin voice sharpened. "What about you?"

"Me? Oh, I'll stay put. Gotten stodgy, I have."

The boy stiffened. "No!" he screamed. "This planet's goin' to die!"

"Not for many years yet," Demeter Mother said like a caress, while Demeter Daughter hugged him. "Never fear what shall be. Rejoice in what is."

"*She* can't leave," Guthrie said, "and I'm not about to leave her alone . . . then." He leaned forward, caught the boy's hand, and held it. "Listen, Noboru. We are not sad. We are not afraid. We've had a long span of being, and it was full of love and work worth doing and everything else good, but when the time comes for us to rest, that will be good too."

"What a load for one little soul," Demeter Mother murmured. "Why don't we stop? Whenever you want us, child, wherever you are, we will be there for you, we who love you. But meanwhile, let's simply be happy together."

They showed him the marvels that dwelt here, allowed him to play with what he could handle, told him how much more lay beyond the sky but also in every commonplace day ahead of him, miraculous because he would not know what it was until he found it. When they brought him outside, a flock of cranes was passing overhead, southbound for the winter. Demeter Mother called them down. Their wings made a snowstorm around him. He shouted for joy.

In this country at this season, the double sunset came early. Night had fallen when the family started toward their flyer to go home. The wind had ceased but the cold had deepened. The land reached obscure close by, unseen farther on, as if there were no more horizons. In the darkness above shone red Proxima, amber Sol, a purity of radiance that was Phaethon. Encompassing them were stars in their thousands and the countlessness of the galaxy.

Guthrie stood waving farewell. Words drifted back and forth, "Goodnight. . . . Tomorrow. . . ." When the air was again silent he turned about and went to the halidom under the trees, where he would enter into communion with his beloved.

TOR
BOOKS The Best in Science Fiction

LIEGE-KILLER • Christopher Hinz
"*Liege-Killer* is a genuine page-turner, beautifully written and exciting from start to finish....Don't miss it."—*Locus*

HARVEST OF STARS • Poul Anderson
"A true masterpiece. An important work—not just of science fiction but of contemporary literature. Visionary and beautifully written, elegaic and transcendent, *Harvest of Stars* is the brightest star in Poul Anderson's constellation."
—Keith Ferrell, editor, *Omni*

FIREDANCE • Steven Barnes
SF adventure in 21st century California—by the co-author of *Beowulf's Children*.

ASH OCK • Christopher Hinz
"A well-handled science fiction thriller."—*Kirkus Reviews*

CALDÉ OF THE LONG SUN • Gene Wolfe
The third volume in the critically-acclaimed Book of the Long Sun.
"Dazzling."—*The New York Times*

OF TANGIBLE GHOSTS • L.E. Modesitt, Jr.
Ingenious alternate universe SF from the author of the *Recluce* fantasy series.

THE SHATTERED SPHERE • Roger MacBride Allen
The second book of the Hunted Earth continues the thrilling story that began in *The Ring of Charon*, a daringly original hard science fiction novel.

THE PRICE OF THE STARS • Debra Doyle and James D. Macdonald
Book One of the Mageworlds—the breakneck SF epic of the most brawling family in the human galaxy!